THE PEAS AND CARROTS SERIES

Volume One (Inludes books 1, 2 and 3, plus an exclusive short story)

HANNAH LYNN

ALSO BY HANNAH LYNN

Amendments

The Afterlife of Walter Augustus

Fiona and the Whale

Erotic Fiction?

Athena's Child

The Complete Peas and Carrots Series

Peas, Carrots and an Aston Martin

Peas, Carrots and a Red Feather Boa

Peas, Carrots and Six More Feet

Peas, Carrots and Lessons in Life

Peas, Carrots and Panic at the Plot

Peas, Carrots and Happily Ever After

These stories are a work of fiction. All names, characters, organisations, places, events and incidents are products of the author's imagination or are used fictitiously. Any resemblance to any persons, alive or dead, events or locals is *almost* entirely coincidental.

Text copyright © 2018-19 Hannah Lynn

First published 2019

ISBN: 9781090580542

Imprint: Independently published

Edited by Emma Mitchell @ Creating Perfection and Jessica Nelson @ Indie Books Gone Wild

Cover design by Vector Artist

All rights reserved.

No part of this book should be reproduced in any way without the express permission of the author.

PEAS, CARROTS AND AN ASTON MARTIN

Book 1

For Sally,

Wherever you are...

FOREWORD

A brief history of allotments:

With roots spreading all the way back to the Saxons, small parcels of land, known as allotments, have long been a way for people to grow and enjoy their own produce. Varying in size and located throughout the UK, allotments − which can consist of anything from just a single plot, to hundreds of plots gathered together − are leased from local councils or parishes, with tenancies costing anywhere from a few pounds to substantially more.

Allotments became most prominent during the Second World War and the "Dig for Victory," campaign, where their numbers rose to over 1.4 million. Nowadays, numbers are not so high. While it is estimated that less than ten percent of those original plots are left, they are still tended enthusiastically by those 'alloties' that remain.

Often hidden behind housing estates or on the outskirts of towns these are places where a discerning few choose to opt out of the consumerism that arises with vast super markets and convenience stores and instead choose to sow and harvest their own produce. And they do so in the company of quiet, like-minded individuals, all sharing tips on pruning and pest control over cups of tea and homemade cakes and cider. For many it is refuge from the hectic-ness, noise and commotion of the modern world. A place where an Englishman's shed is his castle, hidden full of treasures and capable of providing all the sustenance a person could need.

CHAPTER 1

ERIC SIBLEY SAT across from the solicitor. He was unsure as to what the appropriate or expected response was, given the current situation. He blinked a few times and rubbed the bridge of his nose, then shuffled around on the chair and tried to find a more comfortable seating position.

In Eric's opinion, the entire room, from the Blu-Tacked A3 posters on the window and the laminated desk to the worn blue carpet and instant freeze-dried coffee, reeked of skinny budgets and cutting corners. There was no class, no style. On the other side of the desk, the solicitor looked just as cheap, with his polyester jacket, comic tie and supermarket aftershave.

'Just explain it to me again,' Eric said. 'You're saying I get nothing? None of it? Nothing at all?'

The solicitor removed his glasses and rubbed his eyes.

'No. As I have explained, your father has left you the remaining tenancy on his allotment and his 1962 limited-edition Aston Martin DB4 series four, affectionately known as Sally, on the condition that you fully tend to the allotment on a weekly basis for the next two years.'

Eric shook his head.

'But the house? Everything in the house. The paintings, my mother's jewellery, all of that, it ... it's ...'

'It's been left to the church,' the solicitor finished for him.

'But he didn't even go to church!' Eric thumped the table with his fist. 'He was a bloody atheist!'

The solicitor – who was presumably named Eaves or Doyle, judging from the sign above the door – shuffled the papers in front of him, then returned his glasses to the end of his nose.

'I realise that this is a difficult time for you. But your father was very specific about his wishes. The car will remain in your possession, permanently, provided you adhere to the specified conditions.'

'And if I don't?'

'Then your father has made provisions for that situation too.'

Eric drew in a lungful of air, which he let out with a hiss.

'But Abi? He must have left something to Abi? She's his only grandchild for Christ's sake.'

Eaves-possibly-Doyle massaged his temples with his knuckles.

'I'm very sorry, Mr Sibley, I don't know what to tell you. Perhaps your father felt you'd value these gifts more than the house or money.'

'Like hell he did.'

Eric pushed back the chair, snatched the papers from the table, and strode over to the door. When his hand was on the handle, Eaves-possibly-Doyle coughed. Eric spun around.

'Mr Sibley, before you leave, I have to tell you that it would be considered trespassing if you were to step on your father's property from now on.'

Eric's lungs quivered.

'Exactly how am I supposed to collect the car without going on the property?' he said through clenched teeth.

'Your father has seen to that as well.'

※

The car was being stored in a garage on the outskirts of town. Fortunately, it was a walkable distance as, having travelled from London by train, Eric's only mode of transport was by foot or taxi, and you had as much chance of finding a taxi in Burlam as you did hailing Father Christmas for a lift home from the pub at midnight on Christmas Eve.

The sky was blanketed in dense grey clouds, although for mid-

November it was relatively mild. As he walked, a cool breeze pushed him from behind, carrying the scent of damp grass and river water. Eric's feet skidded on the wet autumn slush. So much for crisp copper leaves and frolicking squirrels. His insides lurched. What was he going to tell Suzy? Only last night they'd been discussing what they would do with the money. Their mortgage would've been paid off for sure, with more than a bit to spare. They talked about buying a holiday house, somewhere in Italy, Tuscany perhaps, maybe a skiing holiday, or the Maldives even. She'd been so excited.

Eric bit back the resentment. He wasn't being callous, he wasn't. Yes, his father had died, and that was all very sad, but he was an old man who'd lived a long life. Far longer than he probably deserved. Old people die, there's no getting around it, Eric told himself, and the fact remained, he deserved the house. Growing up as an only child with his father, he deserved a dozen houses. How many other children began doing spelling tests at three? Or couldn't have dinner before they'd recited all the imperfect and perfect past participles in Latin, French, and Spanish? How many teenagers were made to run three miles every weekend morning to earn ten minutes as a passenger in his father's car? A car that he'd got by swindling a ninety-year-old widow four decades earlier. What kind of normal person did that? There was a traffic cone on the side of the pavement. Eric stopped and kicked it.

'Screw you. I hope you burn,' he yelled.

Then, noticing an old woman walking her Jack Russell on the other side of the street, waved his hand apologetically and carried on walking.

The workshop was littered with tools, reeked of petrol, and was run by men who wiped their hands on their work trousers. It was not the type of place you'd expect to find a half-million-pound vintage sports car, stored away in the corner with only a half-on dust sheet for protection.

Eric's lungs seized with terror as a bald mechanic ran his hand along the bonnet of the car, stroking and caressing the bodywork like it was his own personal prized possession. Eric flinched at each and every movement.

'She runs like a dream,' the mechanic said.

'You've driven her?'

'Aye. Never thought I'd get behind the wheel of one of these in my lifetime. But I'd see 'er goin' up and down them roads. And then when your dad's 'ands went, he came an' asked me one day. Just like that. Wanted to be in her again I guess. Can't blame 'im. Sally, ain't it?' Eric nodded. 'Anyways, we made it pretty regular since then. He had me coming up to the house, taking him out on the bends near every week. I guess that's been what, ten months?'

Eric blushed. He hadn't seen his dad since last Christmas, and he certainly couldn't remember anything wrong with his hands then, although he did remember something vague about letting Abi tear the wrapping paper off his Christmas present.

'Somewhere around then,' Eric said, then straightened his shoulders and asserted himself to the matter in hand. 'If you could just get the keys, I'm in a bit of a rush. I've got rather a lot of things to be getting on with.'

''Course, 'course. I'll get them rightly. I take it you'll be heading up to the allotment?' he said.

'How do you know ...' Eric started, but cut himself short. Of course the mechanic knew about the allotment, everyone knew. This was Burlam.

Eric's parents had moved to Burlam when he was eleven and already at boarding school. As such, the place had never been anything more than an unpleasant vacation home that he was thrust into for three holidays, three half terms, and six exeats a year. He abhorred it. Only an hour from London by train, it was the antithesis of culture and class. In the summer it was full of tourists who wandered along the riverfront, nosing in the quaint shops that sold nothing but tat, while protecting their fish and chips from opportunistic seagulls. In the winter Burlam was a ghost town, other than on the occasional weekend when good weather yielded hordes of bikers to gather at the local greasy spoon and belt around the narrow, twisting lanes, causing havoc to anyone on four wheels. It was not a place Eric liked to be associated with.

Suzy, on the other hand, adored it. She spent her mornings strolling around the marina, taking in the air, and revelling in the grudgingly slow pace. Once or twice she'd suggested they move there, or at least buy a holiday cottage and give Abi the chance to grow up knowing her granddad better. Eric never pandered to the discussion.

He started the engine and closed his eyes. The vibrations buzzed up through the leather work. Tending an allotment for two years? Easy. Eric would tend to a whole farm if he had to. No one was getting their hands on this car. Not in his lifetime.

The car drove exactly as Eric remembered. Loud and stylish and still as argumentative as ever in third gear. The sills looked as though they would need an overhaul in the next twelve months, but apart from that and a little rusting around the inside of the bumper, she was in perfect nick; the way his father had always kept her. Cars had been George Sibley's lifelong love. Gardening, by contrast, was an exceptionally ridiculous dalliance.

※

THIS WAS Eric's first trip to the allotment. Part of the reason was time; visits to George were usually planned in conjunction with a visit to Suzy's sister, Lydia, in nearby Woodham, and thus adhered to a somewhat rigid schedule. Arriving at Lydia's late often resulted in her offering a bed for the night in their tie-dye clad spare room that smelt somewhere between a chiropractor's office and a compost heap. To Eric, spending the night there was only marginally better than spending the night on the toilet floor of a seedy sports bar in Wales the night after a Six Nations rugby match. Better to be in and out quick where his relatives were concerned.

The other reason he'd not visited the allotment was that Eric had no interest in it. He had no interest in feigning enthusiasm over rows and rows of green leaves, each one no different to the next. Nor did he want to hear about what potato blight was. Or how the aphids had ravaged this bean or that bean, or how important it was to get your strawberries covered before the birds came and got them all. And more importantly, he had no interest in spending time alone with his father. After all, it wasn't like he bothered taking an interest in Eric's life.

It had been bearable when Eric's mother was still alive. She'd been the link, the tie, his father's one redeeming feature that allowed Eric to see him as more than merely a dictator who had strived to control every aspect of Eric's life, from his university choice to the houses he lived in, and even the colour that his best man wore at his wedding. After all, if she could love George Sibley, there had to be good in him somewhere, right?

His mother, Josephine, had been the polar opposite of his father. While in public she supported her husband's decisions, privately she'd nourished

Eric's creativity. It was she who convinced George that Eric did not need to attend remedial maths classes after he received his first B grade in a test. It was she who persuaded George to allow Eric to play lead trumpet in the school jazz band as opposed to screeching away at his second-hand violin in the back row of the orchestra. Josephine vocally and controversially supported Eric's choice to study anthropology at university rather than economics or accounting, and had wept with joy, rather than disdain, when he told them that he'd proposed to Suzy, a divorced writer. Josephine was the link, the bond, the elucidation. And when she died, all that was gone.

The allotment was at the far end of town, behind a cul-de-sac of 1970s pebble-dashed semis. The land backed onto marshes and was apparently a hive of activity for the Burlam over-sixties. Although at that moment in time, the only inhabitant of the street Eric encountered was a sour-faced cat with a gammy leg that forced him to lean more on Sally's brakes more than he would have liked so soon after getting back behind the wheel.

With a vision of flying chickens and rampaging goats already bustling around his head, Eric parked the Aston at the far end of the cul-de-sac, where the houses were slightly larger and the number plates on the cars a little newer. He triple-checked the lock, took a photo of the car – in case it was robbed and evidence was needed for the police – and walked the rest of the way.

The path to the allotment was more dirt track than road. Bramble bushes lined the sides of the track and a scent of sodden autumn and manure pervaded his lungs. He glanced down and groaned. Two steps in and his handstitched shoes were already caked in a layer of tar-like mud. Had he known, he would have brought a pair of trainers, or better still hiking boots, but then how could he have known that he would inherit a sixty-square-metre patch of potatoes, as opposed to an eight-hundred-thousand-pound house? Clenching his teeth, Eric tried not to focus on the ear-wrenching squelch of his feet and walked on.

By the time he reached the gate, it was not only his shoes but his socks and bespoke tailored trousers that were black with mud. He bent down, as if to sniff, before he changed his mind, took a deep breath, and kept walking.

A wooden hut, a little longer than a caravan, was situated by the large metal gates. The wood was aged, crumbling, and splintered and emitted a smell of extreme damp and overripe cabbages. A small window was positioned around five feet off the ground, and a glass-covered notice board was nailed to the side of it. Various subject issues were covered on the notices, from Labrador retriever puppies needing homes to information about a beekeeping workshop which was dated three months back.

Eric took a few steps forwards and paused. The area behind the hut was far bigger than he'd expected. Five acres? Ten? He scoured the view. Really, he had no idea. Rows and rows of tended plots disappeared off into the distance. Hundreds of poles stood teepeed with vines coiled up around the outside while dozens of sheds marked out one border from another. There were greenhouses, polytunnels, and scarecrows, along with tarpaulin coverings and oversized planters. Some plots had their own fence while others merged from one to the next. And even in November, when almost all the trees had given up and discarded their leafage in favour of a more skeletal look, there was green everywhere. Eric felt a small gasp of unexpected awe escape from above his Adam's apple.

'So, you've come then?'

Eric spun around.

The man's face was weather-beaten and wrinkled. He sported a ragged shock of white hair, and his vivid green eyes scowled almost to the point of closure. However, the man's most exceptional feature was his beard. Eric estimated, somewhat conservatively, that facial hair of that grandeur would have involved at least two decades of grooming and nurturing. He was unsure whether he was exceptionally impressed by this show of dedication or appalled by the lack of personal hygiene. The man glowered, narrowing his eyes even further.

'About time you got here,' he said.

CHAPTER 2

THE MAN OFFERED no more conversation. Stepping out of the shed, he shut the plywood door, clicked a padlock securely across it, and ambled into the maze of vegetation.

A few steps in he stopped, turned back to Eric, and growled, 'Are you coming, or what?'

Eric hurried to catch up.

Despite the age difference and sluggish speed set by his guide, Eric struggled to keep up. The old man trundled on, oblivious to the quagmire sinking beneath his feet. Eric picked his route on tiptoes. The trodden-down paths were no more solid than they'd been on the track outside, and more than once Eric lost his foot in a concealed mud pit.

On closer inspection, the effects of the cold weather were more apparent than he'd first thought. Most of the bushes had been reduced to spindly-twigged carcasses, and the grass which sprouted from the ground was wilted and yellow as it drooped over the soil. The musty scent of compost caught in his nostrils as the wetness continued to seep through his trousers.

He hugged himself and shivered as he walked. The temperature had dropped, and the lethargic speed was doing nothing to help ward off the cold. In front of him, the old man hunched as he hobbled on. Every now and then he'd stop to cough, giving Eric a few seconds to catch up.

'I didn't catch your name,' Eric said, hoping conversation would distract from the increasing chill and ruined garments.

'I didn't give it,' the man said, then proceeded to erupt into a coughing fit so violent his face glowed magenta.

'Are you okay?' Eric asked after a minute of coughing.

It was more of a lung-wrenching hack than a normal level cough, and Eric was concerned that the old man might drop down there and then. The last thing he wanted to do was perform mouth to mouth when faced with a beard like that. Besides, Eric wasn't exactly sure how to get back to the car without his guide. Fortunately, the man waved away Eric's offer of help.

'I'm old,' he said when the fit finally subsided. 'Bits of you stop working when you're old. You'd know that if you ever spent any time around old people.'

Eric's jaw tightened. He fixed it with the best smile he could muster.

'Is it much farther?' he said 'Only I need to be getting back. I've got lots —'

'Lots to do at the office,' the man finished for him. 'Aye, I know. Don't you worry. I'm not gonna keep you from your precious work. It's just up 'ere.'

Fairly certain he'd been insulted, and unsure as to why this old man grated on him so much, Eric followed him around one last left turn to a point where they could go no farther. They were on the edge of the allotment next to a thick hedge, behind which smoke rose from the chimneys of the pebble-dashed houses. Turning his attention to the plot in front of him, Eric blinked a few times. He took a step closer and blinked again. A small lump swelled in his throat.

Perfectly parallel lines sprang up from the dirt, all evenly separated and equal in size. At one end a dozen beanpoles, decidedly bare but perfectly balanced, waited patiently for spring to test their sturdiness. In the far corner stood a shed, newly painted in rust-red, with a veranda big enough for four and gingham curtains just visible through the glass. Unlike many of the other allotments, which were covered with cheap netting, or else left entirely bare, these bean poles and berry bushes had their own house built impeccably from chicken wire and two by fours. A sliding barn door provided an entrance at one end.

Each row of the allotment was labelled with a small plastic marker, which had the name of the vegetable printed in precise block letters, and even now, in the flurries of autumn, not a single blade of grass was out of place. With his heart in his throat, Eric stepped across one of the beds and placed his fingers against the wooden slats of the shed. A faint smell of paint hugged the air around it. He'd had no idea. All the times his father had spoken about the allotment, Eric had envisioned some grubby plot of land with a patch of potatoes and some green tomato plants wilting in the corner of a greenhouse. This was magnificent. Beautiful. He bent down to the ground and wrapped his hands around one of the plants.

'What the 'eck do you think you're doing?'

Eric jumped back, his moment with the vegetable severed.

'What do you mean?'

'Not this one. That one.'

The old man recommenced his coughing fit and after taking a minute to right himself pointed over Eric's shoulder. Confused and with his heart still racing from surprise, Eric turned to face the plot behind him. His heart sank.

This was everything he'd imagined and worse. Ten times worse, possibly a hundred times. In fact, Eric wasn't even sure that his imagination could've stretched far enough to conjure an image so heinous and abhorrent. Tangles of roots and leaves twisted upwards creating a two-foot blanket of nastiness that covered the entire ground. He could see nettles and thorns and things with jagged leaves that looked like they'd tear at your skin the instant you touched them. Insects, the like of which Eric had not come across since his childhood nightmares, with hairy legs and countless eyes, scurried around in the debris, while flies of various dimensions and wing formations hovered above what Eric could only assume was once a compost heap. There was a greenhouse, or he thought there was, hidden under a mass of browning vines at one end of the plot; and a water butt, tilted at an angle, filled with stagnant, green, and algae-ridden sludge. Rake ends, rusted and clearly tetanus risks, speared out from the undergrowth, and the overall aroma of the place was somewhere between an arboretum, a silage spreader, and a backed-up service station lavatory.

His pulse continued its uncertain staccato rhythm as Eric took a tentative step forward.

'What was that?' he said.

'What?'

'Something moved. In there.'

His guide shrugged. "Spect it's rats. Nestin' in for winter.'

'Rats?' Eric stepped back.

'Probably.'

The man came and stood next to him. And stayed there.

It was a bizarre moment in which the silence rapidly went from contemplative, to slightly awkward, then downright uncomfortable. Had he been on his own, Eric would have probably picked up something near and thrown it into the rat's nest in front of him, or at least kicked something hard and with a substantial dash of profanities. But in the presence of a man who looked as close to joining his dad under the ground as any man he had met, Eric felt the need to withhold any of these possible outbursts. Besides, he was at a loss for words.

He didn't know why he was surprised. He knew his father had been a narrow-minded, egotistical bastard at the best of times, and it wasn't like he didn't have a spiteful side either; Eric had been on the wrong end of it enough times before. But still. Eric hadn't expected this.

'Perhaps if you'd come down last year,' the man said.

Eric raised a sceptical eyebrow and continued to stare at the refuse site in front of him.

'Harder work than people think, keeping an allotment. 'Specially at his age. With no help. And when his hands went —'

'When his hands went, yes I know.'

With a sharp intake of breath, Eric surveyed his legacy one last time before swivelling on his heel.

'Thank you for showing me the place,' he said, stretching out a hand to bid farewell. 'I'm sure I'll see you again,' he added.

'I'm sure you will. And subs are due on the third of January, so don't be late.'

'Subs?' Eric said.

'So technically, he's left me nothing,' Eric said. 'He secured a tenancy. What the hell does that mean, anyway?'

He was back at home, sitting on the sofa with a Thai takeaway on his lap. Even in Sally, the drive home had been a torment. The car had been as flawless as ever – the growl of the engine, the hum of the wheels – but his insides roiled as he swerved around the bends and kept his foot on the accelerator. He wouldn't be surprised if a ticket came through the post in the next couple of days. Wouldn't that be the absolute cherry on the whole damn thing? Eric bit a prawn in two and swallowed it without chewing. What kind of man would do this to his son? What kind of parent would deliberately ensure that his child continued to suffer his miserable wrath even after he was dead and buried? And even if he'd left him a normal allotment, as opposed to the rat-infested, GHO admonished, cesspit of a plot he'd received, where exactly did he think Eric would find the time to go down to Burlam once a week with his work schedule?

Abi was already in bed by the time he got back. He had showered, crept in to kiss her goodnight, then traipsed back downstairs. Suzy had had the takeaway menu ready, along with a large gin and tonic, complete with ice and lemon.

'He left it to the church. The church. The house, the contents. Everything. When did he even go to church?'

'That's not fair. You know they were good to him when your mother died.'

Eric took a large swig of his drink.

'That was years ago. And what about mum's stuff? What about all her jewellery? Her engagement ring? That was meant to go to you. To Abi. Who the heck does he think he is?' He knocked back the rest of the gin then swapped his glass for his chopsticks and scooped up a mouthful of noodles.

Suzy scooched over to his end of the sofa and began to rub his shoulders.

'I'm sure he had his reasons,' she said.

Eric placed his takeaway on the ground and shifted forwards to make room.

'That I don't doubt.'

Suzy dug her thumbs into the top of Eric's spine and began to massage his back and neck. 'God, do I need this,' Eric said.

With her legs wrapped around him, Suzy kneaded her knuckles into his muscles and tried to work out some of the knots. She smelt of lemons, citrusy and fresh, and her hair tickled his skin as she worked. Eric sighed. Even Suzy's magic hands weren't working the way they normally did. He could feel a migraine coming on.

He and Suzy had bought their five-bedroom terraced in Islington nearly eleven years ago to the day, with the sale going through only two months before they'd married. She'd received a sizeable chunk of money as part of her divorce settlement, and Eric – having inherited his father's mindset for thrift and saving – also had a substantial contribution to add to the deposit. It had been in a miserable state back then, with leaking radiators, floorboards that sprang up if you trod on the wrong end, and a smell of cat piss that would disappear in the winter, only to come back even more noxious and pungent than you remembered in the spring.

It had taken three years of hard slog to get it into a liveable condition, and had it not been for the imminent arrival of Abi it would probably have taken even longer. Looking back on it now Eric missed those days. Life was easy as newlyweds. No big decisions except what colour tiles to use in the bathroom and how many plug sockets they needed on the landing.

Despite the occasional recurrence of the cat piss aroma, Eric still loved his house just as much, if not more than back then. He loved the location and the big bay windows and open fireplaces. He liked the low maintenance courtyard garden and the fact that the wide road meant there was almost always room to park the car out front. He loved the proximity to work and nice bars, for the odd occasion he got to go out for an evening. There was also the substantial appreciation in value over the last eleven years. Eric had worked hard to earn this house, and he was proud of it. At least that was one thing his father couldn't take away from him.

CHAPTER 3

A S EXPECTED, MONDAY saw the return of one of Eric's heinous and intolerable migraines. Had he not had two team meetings to run, along with a working lunch with Greg, plus after-work drinks with one of the chief executives of their latest partnering venture, he'd probably have considered working from home until lunch. As it was, he was on the tube at seven and sat in his office by seven twenty-five, trying desperately to evade the dagger-like stabbing behind his eyeballs.

It was a respectable office for someone of his age. Big windows – but not a river view – a solid oak desk, a mini-fridge, and a bookshelf crammed with books on *the art of business* which he had every intention of reading as soon as he got a spare minute. The carpet was vacuumed daily by a cleaner he never saw, and the space possessed an aroma of polished glass with undercurrents of mineral water and freshly pressed shirts. However, none of that helped with his migraine in the slightest.

In an attempt to lessen the pain – that felt like someone was consistently firing a nail gun through his left temple only to have it ricocheted back off the right – Eric had worn his glasses. The narrow-rimmed, square-framed spectacles had the ability to transform him from a successful, attractive thirty-seven-year-old – albeit with a fairly weak chin and slightly receding hairline – to a geeky-looking seventeen-year-old, with an influx of unwanted memories to match.

Eric had worked for Hartley and Nelson since he finished university, and besides the CEOs, one of the senior associate directors, and Margery on the front desk, he'd been there longer than any other employee. For a long time, Eric had worn that fact as a badge of honour. Recently, however, it had become something he tended to withhold as opposed to reveal.

Eric had, throughout the years, looked at other jobs, applied for a few and even been offered a couple, but Hartley and Nelson had always been there with a backup offer, another promotion, one more step on the eternal ladder of leadership. He was comfortable, established, knew what he was doing, and most days could do the job in his sleep. People could rely on him.

His current position was Junior Associate Director, a title vague enough that more senior staff could still dump awkward accounts, clients, and tedious matters on him, but senior enough that he had his own office and spent an awful lot of his time running meetings and disseminating information. For the last two years, the business had been plagued with restructuring rumours. Some suggested abolishing all the Associate Directors in favour of regional ones. Others said they would be going down the sector route; educational works directors, public service works directors, and so on and so forth. Whichever route they picked, Eric wasn't fussed as long as it was a notch higher up the ladder. More money, more power, more respect.

A knock severed his thoughts.

'Come in,' Eric said.

The door swung open. The man who appeared behind it had hair so blonde it was near white, with piercing grey eyes and a watch around his wrist bigger than Eric's fist. He strode, hands on hips, to the centre of the room, before glancing at Eric and emitting a long, high-pitched hiss. 'All right, geezer, you look shit. And rocking the Harry Potter look again I see.'

Eric pushed his glasses down to the end of his nose and rubbed his eyes.

'Migraine,' he said.

'Figured. Seriously mate. You need to take some time off. It's not good you being here. I mean, just looking at you's making me feel queasy. Honestly, I might. Here. In your office. I'm not kidding.'

He grabbed Eric's wastepaper basket from the floor and proceeded to make retching noises into it. Half a minute later, he dropped it back down on the ground, two feet from its original position.

When Greg had first arrived at the firm, Eric had been less than impressed. His constant need for attention, a penchant for saying things exactly as he saw them, and south London accent would put any aspiring soap actor to shame. He wore shirts and socks that Eric deemed more suitable for a night out in Soho than a respectable recruitment firm, and in his first year racked up more complaints with HR over inappropriate comments to the female staff than the rest of the company had in a decade. Two years down the line and Eric still wasn't particularly keen on the guy, but he was the closest thing he had to a work friend. Besides, with a tongue sharper than a sashimi chef's knife and an uncanny ability to slither out of any situation, Eric felt it wise to keep him onside. Still, Eric winced as Greg perched himself on the corner of his desk and began to rattle his pen pot.

'How did the stuff with your dad go? Dinner on you from now on?'

'Not quite that straightforward.'

'Nah, it never is. When my old man died, it was a right mess. Three ex-wives, twelve step-kids. He's the reason I got the snip at seventeen.' Greg pulled a pen out of the pot and lifted it towards his mouth. Eric plucked it back from between his fingers and dropped it down beside his computer.

'Was there something you wanted, Greg?'

'What?' Greg looked at his hand, seemingly confused as to where the pen had gone. 'Nah. Well, just thought I'd give you the 'eds up that the boss is doing his rounds. After next month's projections if you've got them?'

'I'm working on them now.'

'Dandy. Well, I better get on with mine. By the way, have you seen the new girl in HR?'

'No, I don't think so.'

'Oh, you'd know my son, you'd know. I mean, she's got knockers that'd take your eye —'

'Is that Jack heading to your office now?'

Eric did a mock peer over Greg's shoulder.

'Are you sure?'

'I think so, I mean I could be wrong, but ...'

Greg bolted for the door, scattering the pencils all over Eric's desk as he went. Eric sighed. How was it only eight o'clock?

Jack Nelson was a legend in Eric's eyes. Having co-founded the recruitment agency Hartley and Nelson at just twenty-eight, he'd gone on to establish a network of over 400 offices nationwide, owned properties in Europe, Asia, and America, and still ensured that every one of his six and a half thousand employees received a handwritten Christmas and birthday card every year. Rumour had it he spent the entire two weeks of his January vacation writing out all the cards for the upcoming twelve months and that you could tell the ones his wife, Jo, had written by how loopy the *J* was, but Eric had not bothered to investigate this detail. Even after all this time, Eric couldn't help but feel a rush of adrenaline whenever Jack spoke. The man was, after all, his hero.

That morning Jack Nelson glided into Eric's office wearing a royal blue suit offset with an emerald green tie. His hair was silver, but in a way that made it seem like going grey had been his choice. It wasn't just Eric who had a crush on him. 'Swoony' was the word that Suzy would most frequently use in reference to Eric's boss. 'Swoony and dashing.'

He had the airs and appearance of a man from a former generation. The type who knew the difference between a lounge suit and regular suit and undoubtedly owned several of each. His shoes were always polished, but his laces loose, yet they never came undone. He was truly a master of many arts.

Eric stood up as his boss entered the room.

'Jack,' he said.

'Eric.' Jack pushed the door closed in a considered and thoughtful manner, filling the air with tangs of Colombian coffee and genuine leather as he did. 'Got a minute?'

'Of course. Of course. Please, sit down. If it's those projections you want, I was just in the middle of emailing them to you now.'

Jack waved the comment away with his right hand as he pulled out a chair with his left.

'They can wait,' he said. 'Actually, I wanted to have a word with you about something.'

'A word? Sure. Yes. No problem. No problem at all.'

Eric felt the tie tighten around his neck, and a thin film of sweat permeated through the collar of his shirt. Jack didn't have words with people. Jack was a busy man. If you wanted to speak to Jack he had to make time for you; appointments were made weeks in advance. Unless it was something bad, something *really* bad. A lump swelled at the top of Eric's throat as he threw a glance down at his phone. There were no reminders flashing wildly on the screen telling him that he'd missed some important deadline or event. Still, his pulse levelled a notch higher. He had a lunch meeting booked in for this Saturday, and a brunch for the one that followed, but there was nothing he was meant to have attended over the weekend, was there? No, of course not. He'd emailed Jack's PA two weeks ago and told her of the situation. Nonetheless, the lump in his throat persisted.

'Is there something wrong?' he said, trying hard to sound casual despite the ever-increasing constriction around his windpipe.

'Why don't you take a seat?' Jack said.

Bordering on hyperventilation, Eric lowered himself down into his chair. Jack followed suit in the chair opposite. He crossed his legs, then placed his hands on his lap.

An excruciating pause followed. The pummelling in Eric's chest escalated to such a level he believed he was about to vomit. The sweat around his collar had now reached dripping level and his migraine – fearing being upstaged in the pain department – doubled its intensity, causing the whole of Eric's vision to become fringed with a blue-white halo.

'So,' Jack said, nestling his hands deeper into his lap. 'I hear you've been having a bit of a time with it all at the minute?'

'I have?'

'With your father?' Jack said. 'I'm right in thinking he passed away last month, aren't I?'

Eric shook away the neurosis with a relieved sigh. 'Sorry, yes of course. Last month. It was a bit of a surprise. I mean, he was old but still. None of us were expecting it is what I mean.'

Jack nodded slowly as if absorbing every syllable that Eric had blabbered out.

'I was having a look through your file the other day,' he said. 'You know that you're entitled to five days compassionate leave a year?'

'I did know that, yes.'

'But you've not taken a day.'

'No, not yet.'

'Not ever. Well not in the last five years.'

Eric paused. Five years, was it really that long since his mum died? His chest ached. Five years ago, and yet he could still see the casket and smell the lilies as they rose in eddies around her pale skin. Abi had been two at the time, and Suzy had suggested they leave her in London with her godparents for the day. Eric had disagreed, insisting she'd be fine. The truth was he'd wanted them all there together, as if his mother could see one final display of his fatherhood. He'd wanted it to be perfect, that last moment with her, and he needed Abi there for that. Five minutes into the service, and after Abi's four hundredth 'Daddy', Suzy had taken her outside. Eric spent the rest of the service next to his father, trying to decide if he could slip out after reading the eulogy without anyone noticing.

'Look.' Jack's voice brought him back into the room. 'I know these times are never easy,' he said with a mastered look of professional compassion. 'And we all like to deal with things in our own ways, but you've got a lot of time racked up, holidays, sick days. No one would mind if you wanted to take a few weeks, longer even, and get your head around this. Spend some time with your girls.'

He rose from his chair. Eric followed suit.

'No one's saying you have to, of course. But the option's there if you want it.'

'Thank you, sir. I'll think about it.'

'I hope you do.' In two strides, Jack had reached the door and stopped. He twisted the handle, ready to leave, before turning back into the room for one last time. 'And you won't forget those projections, will you?' he said.

Eric did think about the offer for a whole fifteen minutes. That was when his email pinged, and his phone started ringing, and even the migraine had to play second fiddle to the chaos that ensued following the news that one of their clients – one of the largest chains of academy schools in the whole of the UK – was thinking of dropping them as their agency. Even Greg looked slightly panicked by the announcement. The whole office scurried as they rang number after number, trying to arrange meetings to resolve the issue. Eric buzzed through to his receptionist. He would be needing plenty of coffee this morning, could he prepare it for him? And would he ring Suzy when he got a chance? It didn't look like he was going to be home in time to take Abi to her ballet recital after all.

❧

By the time Eric got home, a full body numbness had replaced his migraine. Upstairs, Abi was already in a bed. Her chest rose and fell as she murmured in her sleep, clutching a pair of pink, and slightly grubby, ballet pumps. Eric leaned down and kissed her forehead, absorbing the air around her with a deep inhale. Something about Abi's scent always reminded Eric of blackberries. Blackberries and candyfloss. Wondering if all children smelt that good, he slipped the ballet pumps out from her grip and placed them on the floor before switching off her light.

'Sleep tight, princess,' he said.

Downstairs, Suzy was curled on the sofa with a notepad and pencil in her hand and remnants of her takeaway on the coffee table. Her lips fluttered and wobbled as every inhale and exhale resonated in a snore. For a second, Eric considered taking out his phone and videoing her like this. They'd had more than one bickering match over whether she actually snored, and a video of this would put the matter to bed for good. However, his phone was in the kitchen and even that was too far to move right now. Hooking his elbows underneath her, Eric lifted his wife up, staggered up the staircase, and carried her into the bedroom. Pencil. That was Suzy's scent. Eau de graphite. He breathed it in and brushed an invisible hair behind her ear.

'Your dinner's in the oven,' she mumbled as he tucked her in.

'Don't worry,' he said. 'I'll find it.'

CHAPTER 4

IT HAD BEEN three weeks since Eric had sat in the office of Eaves and Doyle, yet he'd still not had a chance to take Sally out once. For the first two nights, she'd sat on the road in front of the house, hidden under a dust cover, barely an inch of her tyres visible to the world. But Eric had panicked. There had been heavy rain that first night and he wasn't entirely sure he'd wrapped her up properly. Every thirty minutes he found himself jumping out of bed, opening the curtains, and peering down to check if she still looked okay. Sometimes a distant look wasn't enough to quench the fears, and he'd be compelled to don his jacket and brave the freezing cold and gale force winds. Then there was the impossibility of transferring the insurance while she was out on the street. Add to that the fact that Suzy had had to park the Audi a ten-minute walk away in order to find a space. All in all, having Sally at the house was a no-go. Fortunately, he called in a favour with a friend to borrow his garage over in South Woodford until he could think of a more permanent solution.

When they'd been at university together, Ralph had been the playboy of playboys, never sleeping in the same bed twice, never sober long enough to remember where his own bed was. Eric had simultaneously looked up to and down on his comrade for his endless stamina, unlimited supply of chat-up lines, and unscrupulous demeanour. Fast forwards two decades, and Ralph now had three kids, a semi-detached house, and a golden Labrador retriever called Carson in reference to their favourite BBC period drama, a double bill of which was about as exciting as one of his Saturday nights got nowadays. With the youngest of the brood barely a month old, there was no risk of Ralph taking Sally out for a cheeky off-the-books spin without Eric; getting to have a shower was a luxury for him at the moment.

With Sally sorted, life went on as expected. At work, the academies were playing hardball with the company and still hadn't settled on a mutually conducive agreement despite everyone's best efforts. Eric hated dealing with companies like this. Hartley and Nelson were offering them a fair deal, and the company had more than enough money to pay for it, but they still had to take it down to the wire, skimping on every last penny they could. Eric had had to hand over his weekends to paperwork and emails and even had to slip out during Abi's school production of *Mamma Mia* to answer his phone. In fairness, the timing couldn't have been better; in Eric's opinion, a large proportion of children shouldn't be allowed within fifty feet of any raised platform on the off-chance they accidentally misconstrued it as a stage. Still, Suzy hadn't been best pleased by his sudden disappearance, although that was probably because she couldn't think of her own credible excuse to escape.

Apparently, the entire rendition of *Dancing Queen* had been sung a semitone-and-a-half flat and was accompanied by a boy on tambourine who appeared to burst into sporadic grand-mal seizures, and a girl on the recorder who not only gave the front row several burst eardrums but also a solid soaking of saliva to boot. Still, Abi had enjoyed taking part.

After nearly a four weeks of toing and froing, endless emails, and a month's salary in double-shot, skimmed milk, no froth cappuccinos, today was the day they were finally settling on the agreements. The representatives from the academies were arriving at eleven and Eric had everything prepared. He sat in his chair and took a sip of his coffee, followed by a sniff. Something about it wasn't quite right; the milk perhaps? He took another sip. There was a near meltdown last year when one of the new receptionists thought everyone could do with a health kick and swapped the beans in the grinder for decaf. No one would be so stupid as to try that again. Eric took one more sip, decided he wasn't really in the mood for coffee, and parked the cup on the edge of his desk just as his phone began to ring.

He stared at the screen. While the caller was unknown, there was something decidedly familiar about the area code. He watched it ring for another second, trying to place it, and hovered his hand over the red button. Half a second later his thumb swiped down and across and opened the line to the unknown number.

'Eric Sibley here,' he said.

'Hello, Mr Sibley,' a male voice spoke. 'This is Christian Eaves here. I hope you're well.'

Eric blinked. Christian Eaves? Why was that name familiar? He pondered it for a moment. Down the end of the line, a throat cleared.

'Mr Sibley, are you still there? Like I said, It's Christian Eaves here. From Eaves and Doyle. The solicitors.'

Eric was struck by an image of cheap furniture and Blu-Tack, swiftly accompanied by an uncomfortable squirming in the pit of his stomach.

'Of course, Christian. What can I do for you?'

'Well, Mr Sibley. I was just seeing if everything is all right.'

'All right? Yes, well, busy, busy. But other than that —'

'Only I have it on good authority that you haven't visited the allotment since the day of our meeting?' He paused. Eric swallowed. 'I'm sure you remember that in order for the car to stay in your possession, you must ensure that the allotment is maintained on a weekly basis.'

Eric straightened his back and swallowed again, the squirming in his stomach intensified.

'Mr Sibley? Are you still there?'

'Sorry, pardon? Yes, yes I'm still here.'

'Mr Sibley —'

'Eric please.'

'Eric, then. I'm fairly certain I made the conditions of your father's will unambiguous. However, in case you don't remember the conditions, it is stated that if you do not tend to the allotment, the car shall be removed from your possession.'

'It has been a crazy month,' Eric began, then added enthusiastically, 'and I've been very ill. Very ill. Hospitalised in fact. Dengue fever.'

'Oh, well, I'm sorry to hear that. Obviously you're feeling better now?'

'Yes, fortunately, yes, much better,'

'Good. So, we can expect to see you at the allotment this weekend?'

'Well, I, I –'

'Brilliant. Because I would hate this to be anything more than a misunderstanding. And while you're on the line, Mr Sibley, there are a few more questions I need you to answer for me.'

<hr />

'ON GOOD AUTHORITY? ON WHOSE AUTHORITY?' Eric seethed. 'I'll tell you whose authority. It's that damn miserable git with the plot next door. I could go seven days a week and the bastard would still say I hadn't been there once.' Eric was on his second gin and tonic of the evening and had no intention of slowing down. 'Twenty minutes he kept me on the phone. I'm surprised he didn't ask for our bloody wedding date. Bloody good job the academy people were late, or Jack would have had my balls. Thank God that went through.'

'He was only doing his job.'

'He was being bloody nosy. I had to give him Ralph's number too, just to corroborate information. I bet he was straight on the phone to him.' Eric took another large swig. 'You know what he thinks don't you? He thinks I've sold it. I bet that's what he thinks. Well, I bloody well should. It's my damn inheritance. I should sell it. I'm going to sell it.'

'No, you're not. It isn't yours to sell.'

Eric held his malignancy in and sighed heavily. Suzy took his empty glass and swapped it for a full one.

'Maybe I should give it up. Let the church have it. I mean it's just a car. After all, we can always go and buy another vintage DB4.'

Suzy gave him a withering look.

'I mean, we'd have to re-mortgage the house,' Eric said. 'And Abi would have to go to that school down the road where all the kids smell like baked beans and do their homework on used kitchen roll, but we'd get by.'

'You're not going to give it up,' Suzy said. 'We both know that.'

Eric thumbed the rim of his glass until it let out a deep, low hum. 'No,' he said. 'I guess not.'

'So, I guess we're all heading to Burlam this weekend?'

Twenty minutes later, Eric was sitting at his desk with Suzy peering over his shoulder. His laptop was open on the *Burlam Village Website*, specifically the Classifieds. The page contained various lists and headings in colourful blues and greens with a serene picture of the river and sailing boats set as the background.

'I'm not sure this is what he meant,' Suzy said. 'I thought you said *you* had to maintain the allotment?'

Eric continued typing away in the little rectangular box. 'This is just a short-term solution to buy us a little time. Anyway, I'm maintaining it. I'll just be paying someone else to do the digging.'

'I'm not convinced.'

'Trust me. This will see us all a lot happier. Mr Eaves included.'

With a satisfied smile, Eric clicked enter.

'There. All done.'

Half a second later his succinctly worded advert appeared on *Burlam Village Classifieds* page. *"Gardener wanted for allotment plot. Can grow anything. Will pay good money."*

'Now all we have to do is wait for the applicants.'

❦

TO BOTH HIS and Suzy's surprise, there were three messages waiting for them in their inbox when they awoke. One was from a lady named Nancy, who, in her own words, had a special connection to all things floral but a most profound bond with the blooms of the far east; orchids being her particular speciality. She'd also attached a photograph of her window sill, the glass behind entirely obscured by the two dozen potted specimens of all shapes and colours.

'It looks like a funeral home. Or a hospice,' Eric said.

'Be kind,' Suzy replied. 'Besides, you said they could grow anything. Who are the other ones from?'

Eric clicked open. The second message was from a landscape gardening company. Eric considered the option. Expensive, yes, but at least the job would be done. Their website gleamed with displays of ornamental gardens, hand-crafted pergolas, and water features. Although extremely impressive, Eric thought that might be a little way off kilter and so continued to the last message. The final emailer was also a woman, by the name of Janice.

They wrote: 'RE: Allotment; Am an experienced gardener looking to extend my crops. Please contact me should you wish to know more of my credentials.'

'I like her,' Eric said instantly upon finishing. Suzy frowned.

'You don't know anything about her. She doesn't say anything.'

'Exactly. She doesn't ask any questions. She doesn't send creepy photos. She's perfect.'

'She might be old.'

'So?'

'You said the allotment was a state. A health hazard. You can't have an old woman working around in a rat's nest. Especially not now, not over the winter.'

'I'm only asking her to do a bit of weeding. And it's not like I've got her on a time frame. She can have months. She can have years. As long as it's getting better, not worse, then we're all winning. Besides, she doesn't sound old. How many old people use the internet?'

Suzy frowned again. 'I don't feel good about this,' she said.

'You're worrying about nothing,' Eric said, then turned back to the computer and began to type his reply.

CHAPTER 5

FORTUNATELY, JANICE DIDN'T seem the slightest bit put off by the current storms sweeping the UK. After agreeing on an hourly rate over email and arranging for her to start that week, Eric received another message from his newly employed gardener asking to confirm the allotment's site and plot. Until that point, he hadn't realised there was more than one allotment site in Burlam, and he didn't think that writing something along the lines of *vermin-infested cesspit in the corner next to miserable old git* as means of plot identification would greatly enamour her to the position. He decided to wait until lunch and have a rummage around in the files the solicitor had sent him.

Over the weekend, the office had been decorated in an attempt to inject a more Christmassy feel to their working environment. Silver and red decorations hung from the light fittings, tinsel was attached to all the window frames, and some dubiously placed mistletoe hung in large bunches outside the elevator door, in the stairwell up to the rooftop, and above the entrance to the ladies' toilets. Eric would hate to work in HR at any time, he thought, but Christmas must be the pits.

Through the glass windows, he spied Greg cosying up to one of the new graduate interns. She appeared to have a bit more spunk about her than a lot of them, with a nose piercing, a tattoo on her ankle, and a Christmas jumper sporting a knitted image of two fornicating reindeer.

Eric desperately hoped she might give Greg a well-deserved rebuke for whatever misogynistic chat-up line he was currently using, but instead, she flicked her hair, covered her mouth, and let out a coy, little giggle. Eric went back to his work disappointed.

The remainder of the day was spent working through his mountainous to-do list, which – in the prioritisation of the academies contract – had managed to reach the length of a fully grown Burmese python with an overactive pituitary gland. He had an unsatisfyingly dry pastrami sandwich at his desk for lunch, four cups of coffee, three of which were stone cold by the time he got off the phone to drink them, and one bite of an exceedingly crumbly Ginger Nut biscuit. He dared not take a second bite after spewing crumbs everywhere in the first instance during his meeting with Jack. When he finally glanced at the clock on the corner of his computer, Eric did a double take. He quickly fired off a text to Suzy.

'Leaving in an hour,' he wrote, knowing full well he had three times that to go.

It was half-past eight when Eric finally decided to call it a day. The street lights had been glowing yellow for hours, and overly enthusiastic Christmas shoppers hurried about outside. Wrapped up in fur-hooded coats, colourful mittens, and waterproof boots, they scurried in and out of the cold, desperate to secure all the unnecessary bargains they could. Eric gripped the lid of his laptop, went to push it shut, then stopped.

'Bollocks,' he said.

It took him another ten minutes to find the documents from the solicitor. When he scrolled down, he found that not only was the site address and plot number given, there was also an A4 site map attached which gave a Google image of the entire allotment, on which his plot was clearly circled in red.

'It even looks like a shit heap from space,' Eric said to himself.

Omitting any form of formalities or greetings, Eric fired off another email to Janice. Columbia Avenue Allotment. Plot 54, he wrote, then attached the map for good measure.

When Eric arrived home, Suzy was in her study writing. He poked his head around the corner of the door and knocked lightly on the frame. She removed her headphones and swivelled around on her chair.

'You're late,' she said.

'I know, I'm sorry. Time just got away from me.' He ambled over and kissed her on the forehead.

'Have you eaten?' he said.

'I ate with Abi, but there's some quiche left for you in the oven and there's a bag of salad you can have with it in the fridge.' Eric considered the appeal of limp-leafed lettuce and rubbery egg pie.

'I'll get something delivered. Is Abi asleep?'

'Not sure. She should be, but she was still reading when I last went up there. You can go upstairs and check.'

Eric planted another peck on the top of Suzy's head then tiptoed upstairs and into Abi's room.

In daylight, Abi's bedroom was a multitude of pinks, from the princess duvet cover to the sparkly circus tent. A massif of soft toys sat beneath the window ledge. They had bought her toy cars to play with, diggers, and trucks, but she'd veered towards the dolls and tea sets. By the time Abi was five years old, they'd given up. When it came to clothes, she'd chosen her own for years now, and while occasionally she'd pick something a little left of the field – like her superhero dungarees or NYC baseball cap – most of the time it was the dresses that won.

The room was dark, save for a turtle-shaped night light that projected images of stars onto the ceiling above. Eric crept across to the bed and leant over his sleeping daughter. As frequently happened, Abi had fallen asleep with her head on a book, her hair splayed out across the pillow. As gently as he could, Eric reached over, lifted her head from the bed, and slipped the book out from beneath her. She stirred and moaned.

'Daddy?' she mumbled, rubbing her eyes.

'I'm here, pumpkin,' he said. 'Now go back to sleep. *Shh, shh.* Close your eyes.'

'I want to show my drawing. Can I show you the drawing I did?'

'In the morning, baby. Close your eyes and go back to sleep. I promise I'll look in the morning.'

She mumbled something more and then wriggled down deeper into the mattress. Eric swept her hair from across her face, exposing a mouse-like ear.

'Night night, my pumpkin,' he said.

Then he shut the door and headed back downstairs trying to decide whether Lebanese or Chinese was to be his takeaway of choice.

※

ERIC OPENED his eyes only to shut them instantaneously. He winced, squinted, then blinked a few times, slowly allowing them to adjust to the light. It was warmer than he'd anticipated, and the sun shone through the curtains and illuminated the room with a whiteness that made it feel like spring. Eric tried to recall the last time he remembered seeing a morning that bright.

'Fuck,' he said and leapt from the bed. 'Shitty fucking bollocks.'

He scrambled around on the floor, forcing his legs into yesterday's trousers before grabbing the nearest shirt in the wardrobe, and flying down the stairs.

Abi was sitting at the kitchen table creating dubious plaits in her Barbie's hair while Suzy was buttering her toast. Eric bouldered in, red and sweating, fumbling with his shirt buttons.

'What the hell, Suze? What's the time? Why did you let me oversleep?'

Suzy looked up from the butter knife.

'Do you want some breakfast?' she said.

'What? No. Why didn't you wake me?'

Hopping on one foot, Eric struggled with his socks which refused to go on with the heel at the bottom. Suzy set a plate in front of Abi, wafting the scent of the warm granary toast under Eric's nose.

'You said you wanted to sleep,' Suzy said. She glided over and attempted to brush down Eric's wayward bed-hair with her hand. Eric flicked her away.

'When? When did I say that?'

'When your alarm went off. And again, when mine did. I tried to wake you.'

'Well, you should have tried again.'

'I did, and you mumbled something about a half day.'

Eric gritted his teeth. 'When have I ever had a half day?'

'That's what you said,' Suzy insisted.

'Daddy, can I show you my picture now?' Abi said, looking up from her Barbie and ignoring her breakfast. 'You said you'd look at my picture in the morning.'

'I can't right now, pumpkin,' Eric said, squeezing his feet into his shoes. 'Daddy's late. He's got to get to work.'

'But you said —'

'I'll look at it tonight, okay?'

'But, Daddy.'

'It'll only take two seconds, Eric. You can have a look.'

'Please, Daddy.'

'I don't have two seconds. I'm already an hour late.'

He swiped the piece of buttered toast from Abi's plate then bolted to the door, gripping the bread between his teeth as he picked up his keys, phone, and wallet on route.

'Love you,' Suzy and Abi shouted in unison, although Eric was already out the gate and across the road.

The office toilets were the first chance Eric had to check his appearance, and the discovery that he'd paired an orange tie with a pale green shirt was not a pleasant one. His breath tasted of last night's hummus and gin although after a deep dig in one of his desk drawers, he discovered not only a blue pinstripe tie but an unopened pack of Wrigley's mint gum. He hurriedly unwrapped two sticks and folded them into his mouth.

'You ready, big guy?' Greg appeared at his door. Today he was dressed in skinny, dark-purple denims and a shirt covered in tiny embroidered penguins. He had, however, donned a tie.

'Ready?' Eric said.

'For the dynamic duo. Hartley's in today.' He sat on the edge of Eric's desk and picked up a pack of Post-It notes from beside the computer monitor. 'I thought you had hard-ons about the guy? You, Hartley, Nelson. Isn't that where all the fun happens in your head?'

Eric frowned against the barrage of words.

'That's today?' he said, swallowing repeatedly. 'No. It can't be. Crap. Shit. How did I forget that?'

'Dunno, you're the dick who sent about a dozen email reminders last week.'

'Of course. Of course, I did.' Eric tried to regather some composure. He plucked the Post-Its out of Greg's hands. 'Of course it's today. Is he here already?'

'In Nelson's office. Probably wanking off over their bank balances.'

'Okay, great. We'll just give them another five minutes. I'll check everything's sorted, then we'll ask Margery to take them through to the boardroom.'

'Whatever you say.'

'Right. Can you just go and check that it's all set up in there? And remember no flowers in the room. He hates the smell of flowers.'

'Along with garlic, sunlight, and silver bullets apparently.'

Eric ushered Greg out of his office then pulled down the corner blind. With his back against the wall, he closed his eyes, took a few calming deep breaths, and found they made no difference whatsoever. 'Fuck, fuck, fuck.' How could he have overslept? Half day, he hadn't been saying half day at all, it was bloody Hartley day. He kicked the base of his desk, stubbing his toe in the process. How could he have forgotten this was today?

Alistair Hartley was the more silent face of Hartley and Nelson. While he left the day to day running of the firm to Jack, Hartley was still well-known for his tempestuous outbursts or his sudden arrival by private jet from Geneva to cast his wily eye over his domain, demanding info on this account and that account, many of which had been closed for years. It was Hartley who was always threatening to restructure or reconfigure, or just shut up the place entirely. On more than one occasion he'd swept in unannounced, started making ludicrous demands, and fired people on the spot for no discernible reason. Fortunately for those staff, he had no idea who they were or what they did, and after few softening apologies from Jack, they were back at their desks, an amusing story – and probably a small cheque – in their pocket. If Eric were ever to make it to senior associate director, it was all down to getting Alistair Hartley on side during days like today. He took one more long breath which he expelled in a deep hiss. Then he strode out of his office and into the boardroom.

The meeting was the type where everyone, except the person talking, struggled to keep their eyes open. The lights were bright, the windows cracked open to allow a breeze, and an aroma of freshly ground Colombian coffee filled the air, but even that wasn't enough to stifle the yawns. Eric was no exception. Nelson and Hartley took alternate heads at the table while the three senior associate directors and the three junior associate directors – of which Eric and Greg were constituents – filled the seats between. Jack's PA, Graham, was sitting taking minutes while Hartley's entourage of four flitted in and out of the room, disturbing the presenters and completely oblivious to anything other than their lord and master.

One of the senior associate directors was pointing to a coloured bar graph with ambiguous axes and scaling when Eric's phone buzzed in his pocket. His muscles tightened. Fixing his eyes straight ahead and adding an extra nod and a smile, he slipped the phone out onto his lap, glanced to see the caller ID, then tapped the cancel button.

Ralph. Ralph only rang him to whinge. Or to muse and mull over his misspent youth. It was probably a fight with his wife, Sarah, or a hopefully hypothetical question about what to do if you'd got one of the kids trapped in the washing machine. He would call him back this evening; after all, kids were pretty sturdy nowadays. Eric slotted his phone back in his pocket. Thirty seconds later it rang again. Several pairs of eyes rolled in his direction.

'Sorry,' Eric mouthed, a visible heat flushing his cheeks. He cancelled the call again and went to switch the phone off, but as his thumb pressed down, a message pinged up on the screen.

Ring me now.

Eric's chest began beating with an irregular pulse and another two heads shot him unimpressed glares. Smiling widely at his colleagues, he offered a few more constructive nods towards the bar graph. Struggling to ignore what felt like the onset of fatal angina, he attempted to type a reply subtly under the table. Receiving a less than pleasant gesticulation from Greg, Eric reverted to his original plan and switched the phone off. He let out a small sigh of relief as he focused his attention back on the slideshow and the screen that was now showing two differently configured pie charts. One minute later, there was a knock at the door.

'Sorry to interrupt.' It was the intern with the tattoo. 'But there's a telephone call for Mr Sibley. A gentleman called Ralph.'

All eyes went straight to Eric, whose cheeks had transformed from light pink to fire-engine red. His angina progressed to possible heart-attack status. He cleared his throat then offered her his best smile.

'Thank you. If you could tell him I'll call him back when this meeting is over, that would be great.' Eric spoke in as even a tone as he could before turning back to the screen, fake grin firmly in place. The intern, however, did not move.

'What is it?' Hartley barked. 'You heard him, he'll ring the man back.'

The intern squirmed a little, then sucked on her top lip, her gaze still focused on Eric. 'I think it's rather important,' she said.

'It's fine,' Eric insisted, 'I'll ring him back after.'

She hesitated, still unmoving, as she searched for the right words. 'I think you should ring him back now,' she said.

'For God's sake,' Hartley said. 'Is this a goddamn business we're running here or a call centre?'

'I'm sorry, sir,' Eric said. 'Perhaps I should just go and see what this is about.'

Eric looked at Jack, who gave him a small nod of approval. Keeping his head up – but with his insides feeling like a bag of jellyfish that were undergoing electroshock therapy inside his intestines – Eric pushed himself out of his chair and followed the intern out of the boardroom and into the corridor. It was little satisfaction to see that she, too, was fuchsia with embarrassment.

'Sorry,' she said and handed him the phone.

'Ralph?' Eric said down the line. 'What the hell is it?'

'I don't know what you've done,' Ralph said down the phone. 'But they say they're about to call the police. And I'm fairly certain they mean it.'

Eric left a message stressing an urgent family emergency with the intern – whose name turned out to be Emily – to pass to Jack when the meeting ended.

'Make sure he understands that this was an emergency. A real emergency,' Eric reiterated, as he snatched up his keys and wallet off his desk. 'You understand that? It was an emergency.'

'I get it,' Emily said. 'I hope everything's all right. Is there anything I can do to help?'

Eric didn't reply. He dashed for the elevator and slammed the call button repeatedly.

It was a toss-up between the tube or a cab. A tube would be quicker if all lines were running, but then he wouldn't be able to ring Ralph and find out what was going on. A cab would take longer, but then he might be able to placate the situation on the phone. As it was, he decided that time was of the essence and sprinted down the steps into the underground, swiping his Oyster card, and dashing down onto the platform without missing a step. With barely a bar of signal, he texted Ralph. *I'll be twenty minutes*, he typed. Then he got on the train and prayed.

CHAPTER 6

THREE MEN WERE standing outside the front of Ralph's five-bed, mock-Georgian semi when Eric finally arrived. Ralph, looking like a displaced member of the local am-dram society in a velvet smoking jacket and fleece slippers, was holding a mug in one hand and a baby in the other. Had it been another time Eric would have offered some quick-witted jab about fatherhood taking its toll, but at that precise moment his attention was rather preoccupied.

The other two gentlemen in the driveway were – if possible – even less sartorially skilled than Ralph. One, who was leaning against the drystone wall puffing on a cigarette, wore a fleece zip-up jacket – like the type commonly found in garden centres or animal shops – grey jogging bottoms, and a pair of steel-toe DMs. A set of heavy duty bolt-cutters rested on the wall by his knee, and he noted Eric's arrival with a long exhalation of smoke aimed directly towards him.

The final man, who was wearing a grey hoodie and ripped jeans – that Eric felt offered no serious protection from the current winter climate – was busy on the phone. He kept his mouth tight-lipped, occasionally emitting the odd, *umm*, *a-huh*, and *gotcha* until he caught sight of Eric. At which point he turned his back to him, covered the phone, and said something into the mouthpiece.

'What the hell is this?' Eric said to no one in particular.

His lungs were burning from panting in freezing air, and despite texting Greg four times to ask for an update on the morning's meeting, he had received no reply. Only Ralph acknowledged him, and from the manner in which he was bouncing the baby on his hip, he was far from happy.

'If you've got me mixed up in something dodgy, Eric —'

'I haven't. I swear.' Eric lifted his hands pleading innocence. 'This has got to be some misunderstanding.'

'I hope so for your sake. Sarah's only just forgiven you for setting light to her table runner last time you were over.'

'That was an accident,' Eric began, then stopped. People who used flammable table cloths to accent their tea-light centrepiece were never going to be people you could reason with.

'Look, give me two minutes and it'll be sorted. I promise.'

Eric stalked back across the drive to the man on the phone.

'It's for you,' the man said before Eric could speak, and thrust the phone towards him. Eric took the device and held it to his ear.

'Hello?' he said.

'Mr Sibley.' Eric recognised the voice immediately.

'What the hell is this? Who the hell do you think you are?'

'I can tell you're upset, Mr Sibley —'

'Damn right I'm upset.'

'But these people are acting under legal authority. They are *bailiffs*.' Mr Eaves emphasised the word just in case Eric wasn't sure what the gentlemen's roles were.

A rush of heat surged through his chest sending his pulse in an upwards soar.

'Well, you can tell them they've had a wasted morning harassing my friend. I'll see those two in a hearse before I see them in my car.'

His outburst was met by silence down the end of the line.

'Mr Sibley, I'm afraid my hands are tied in this matter. The terms of the agreement laid out in your father's will have been broken. As we discussed, only last week, you had to maintain the allotment —'

'I know. Jesus, it was one week ago. It's been seen to. It's *being* seen to.' Eric clenched the phone in his hand as he spoke.

Ralph had recently gone inside, and the two bailiffs were now standing suspiciously close to the garage. Eric breathed deeply and counted to ten in his head.

'I understand that I need to maintain the allotment,' Eric said, slowing down his words in an attempt to regain a little self-control. 'I have every intention of coming down this weekend.' He paused for yet another composure-maintaining breath. 'I can assure you, I'm doing everything in my power to make this situation work.'

There was another long silence. A light knocking travelled down the line. Eric could see Christian Eaves, cheap BIC biro in his hand, tapping it against his Ikea desk. *Tap tap tap. Tap tap tap.* The more Eric focused on it, the louder it got. *Tap tap tap. Tap tap tap.* Eric could feel his fist clench and unclench as he imagined reaching down the invisible phone line, grabbing the pen, and snapping it in two.

'Mr Sibley.' The silence finally broke. 'If it were merely a case of missing yet another week I could perhaps relent, but a more concerning issue of ... solicitation has come to my attention.'

'Solicitation?' The word exploded out of Eric's mouth. Ralph – who had reappeared in corduroys and with cups of tea for the bailiffs – smirked. Eric's stomach knotted.

'Look —' he began, but the solicitor interrupted him.

'Mr Sibley ... Eric. I feel for you, I do. But I don't have the time for this and neither do you. The conditions have been broken, twice. The car is to be taken out of your possession.'

'No, wait. Please. There must be something. I need that car. I need it. Please.'

A heavy sigh reverberated down the line. Eric could hear his pulse drumming away in his ears. He held his breath.

'Mr Sibley. In case of these events, your father had placed some further documents in my keeping. If you could come down to the office, we could discuss —'

'Yes,' Eric bounced on the spot. 'Yes, when? I'll be there. I'll be down this weekend. Or Friday. I can do Friday.'

'It would have to be today.'

'What?' Eric stopped bouncing.

'You have to come down today. I'm afraid these issues have got to be resolved by the end of the day.'

'But I can't. My boss. The boss,' he stuttered. 'I have to go back to work today. I have to.'

'That's fine. I understand, Mr Sibley. I completely understand.' His voice was relaxed, compassionate. Eric's heart rate relaxed. 'Now if you could just hand the keys over to the two men with the bolt-cutters, we can all be on our way.'

◈

ERIC TOOK SALLY. It had taken another twenty minutes to persuade Eaves that he was going to drive straight to Burlam and have him call off the men with their bolt-cutters. Still, he wasn't going to leave the car unprotected. Eaves had informed Eric that any misdemeanours from this point – such as taking the car to another location – and he'd be forced to call the police and press charges. Despite Eaves' generally pleasant and somewhat wimpish demeanour, Eric was inclined to believe him.

It was gone one, and Sally had adopted a musty scent from the weeks she'd been cooped up. Eric braced against the cold and wound down the windows. A few miles into the journey, the traffic finally cleared. His shoulders sank into the leather seats and Sally's engine ran with a deep purr that swelled to a roar as Eric pushed his foot to the ground. Still, it was impossible to relax.

Even now, as he prepared to take the A12, it took all of Eric's willpower not to turn back towards the office. If he could at least offer his apologies in person, Hartley might be less inclined to remember him as the idiot who disrupted his last meeting of the year. And it would only add half-an-hour to the journey. At the same time, he reasoned, family emergencies – which was most definitely how this situation was classified – did not usually allow for time to pop into the office and offer explanations. He decided it was best to steer clear.

Layer after layer of grey clouds muted the sun's light, while an incessant wind hissed through the windows and scattered leaves across the road. Eric had become adept at ignoring the admiring waves and envious looks that other drivers gave the car at roundabouts and traffic lights. It was a skill he'd inherited from his father. During the old days, when his mother was still alive and he and his father would go out for afternoon trips, they

CHAPTER 7

ERIC GOT A room at the Sailboat Inn. The rooms were chintzy and small and smelt of stale smoke and old people, and the pub downstairs had a menu selection consisting of salt and vinegar, cheese and onion, and prawn cocktail; but it was on High Street, opposite Eaves and Doyle, and it was sixty-pounds for the night. He rang Suzy straight away and ranted at her for twenty minutes before she left to collect Abi from school. For the next ninety minutes, he scanned through his emails, trying to get on top of what he'd missed.

Eric groaned. He had skimmed through twelve different documents, each containing at least a dozen graphs with next to no explanation as to what they supposedly showed. His eyes ached, his back throbbed, this whole thing was a mess. And through it all, his stomach growled. The packet of prawn cocktail crisps left empty on the nightstand had been satisfying, in a dirty and oh-so-wrong type of manner, but in no way warded off the hunger pangs that came from missing both breakfast and lunch. Hunger pangs that weren't helped by the wafts of fish and chips that somehow managed to traverse all the way across the road, rise to the second floor, and drift in through a window that barely opened an inch. Eric gave one last refresh of his emails before he rolled over and shut the lid on the computer. He was halfway to the toilet when there was a knock on the door.

'Who is it?' he said.

There was another knock.

'Hold on.' Eric zipped up his flies and dragged his heels along the two feet of carpet to the door. He cracked it open by an inch.

'Surprise!'

She stood in the hallway, a vision of green against the dirty magnolia walls. Pencil-lead aroma eddied around her, while beside her Abi was still in her school kilt, her white blouse creased under her heavy winter jacket.

'Daddy!' In an impressive display of springiness, Abi attempted to jump into her father's arms, kneeing him squarely in the testicles as she did so. Eric gasped.

'What are you doing here?' he said, dropping Abi on the bed and taking Suzy's bag from her before kissing her on the cheek and trying to ignore the pulsating burning in his nuts.

'We thought we'd surprise you. You sounded so miserable on the phone. So we got the train straight down after school.'

'You didn't have to do that.'

'We wanted to.'

Eric looked around the room and frowned. The majority of space was filled with the bed, but it wasn't that the bed was incredibly big, but rather the room incredibly small. There was a narrow wardrobe and a small chest of drawers with a television perched on top that looked like it had been made in the eighties. Abi was already bouncing on the bed trying to grasp at the cheap plastic chandelier on the ceiling. Eric grabbed his computer and tucked it away in the bottom drawer of the chest.

'Look, it's only for one night,' Suzy said. 'And I thought it would be good. Help end the day on a positive.'

Abi yelped as she hit the chandelier, then landed with a crack that sounded suspiciously like the bed frame giving way.

'Stop that, Abi. Get down off there.'

'Why don't we go out?' Suzy said. 'I thought we could grab some fish and chips and then drive around the houses and look at the Christmas decorations?'

'Fish and chips!' Abi shouted, now masterfully knocking the chandelier with every bounce.

Eric pulled her down onto the bed. 'Why don't you two go? I've still got a few things to see to.'

Suzy frowned. 'You need to eat,' she said. 'And we've come all this way to see you.'

'Well I didn't ask you to.'

The words echoed around in the air between them. Suzy pursed her lips and turned her attention to Abi. When she next spoke, it was in the tone that Eric feared the most.

'Why don't we run you a bath, darling?' she said. 'You're still all stinky from school. Then, when we're done, we're going to get fish and chips, and Daddy's going to drive us around in Granddad's car to see all the pretty Christmas lights. Won't that be lovely?' Eric clenched his fist and forced a smile which he quickly transferred from his wife to his daughter.

'Mum's right. Why don't you go into the bathroom and see how many spiders you can find?' he said. 'I found four when I was in there earlier, and at least one of them looked poisonous. I bet you can't find that one.'

'I bet I can,' said Abi and dashed away into the en suite.

'Look,' Suzy said, annoying Eric further by being the first one to speak. 'I'm sorry if we surprised you. I thought it would be nice. You haven't been home to speak to Abi in a week. She misses you. I figured this way we'd be able to spend a bit of time together somewhere away from home.'

'But she's got school tomorrow. We can't just pull her out whenever we fancy. Do you know how much that place costs?'

'Yes. I do. You seem to have forgotten that I pay half?'

An uncomfortable silence expanded between them. Eric's stomach rumbled audibly. He opened his mouth to speak then shut it again. The good old *Abi misses you* card, naturally she brought that one out. Didn't she think if they could afford for him to work less, he would? Did she think he actually enjoyed staring at a computer screen until his vision blurred?

Suzy had still not dropped her glare. Her hands were on her hips and her chin set forwards in a way that made Eric shudder.

'I need twenty minutes to go through my emails,' he said in a sulk. 'And we're not having fish and chips inside the car. They'll stink her out.'

'Perfect,' Suzy said, trying to conceal the twitch at the corner of her lips.

They ate their fish and chips on a tiny Formica table in the corner of the takeaway, sitting on fixed-position, round stools that Eric could barely slide past. Despite the stench of week-old oil, and the insipidness of their chef, the food was surprisingly good. While Abi and Suzy shared a portion of fish, Eric went for the battered sausage. After all, how much worse could it be than prawn cocktail crisps? And after deciding to embrace whatever damage had been done to his stomach, he ordered a side of mushy peas, curry sauce, a spring roll, and a bag of scraps.

'This is yummy,' Abi said, licking a week's recommended intake of salt off the back of her knuckles. 'Why don't we eat this every day?'

'Because we'd all be suffering from type two diabetes,' Eric said.

They concluded their meal with two Magnums and a strawberry Cornetto from Mick's corner shop before they wiped down their hands with some wet wipes then clambered into the car.

'Do you know, I think this is the first time we've all been in here together,' Suzy said as she checked Abi's makeshift seatbelt.

Eric glanced at the mirror. Abi had her nose pressed to the window.

'I'm sure it's not,' he said.

'It is.'

'Well, we'll try to do it more,' he said, at least half meaning it.

Eric had hated taking Abi for rides in the car when his father had been alive. George had thought nothing of flying down the lanes regardless of the speed limit with Abi, barely out of toddlerhood, screaming, 'Faster! Faster!' in the back. Any voicing of his concerns would brand Eric dull and institutionalised, or else see him accused of trying to suck the fun out of everything. Now, if he'd tried going at those speeds, it would have been another thing altogether. There was never any winning with his father.

'Daddy, Daddy! Look at those. Look at those. Stop! Stop, I want to see them!'

Abi pressed her face against the glass.

'Look! There's Father Christmas and Rudolph and a sleigh and a snowman and a palm tree and everything!' she said in one breath. 'Isn't it beautiful?'

'Why is there a palm tree?' Eric quizzed, pulling up outside the Burlam equivalent to the Vegas strip.

'Well Father Christmas has to go to hot countries too, doesn't he?' Abi reasoned.

'He does indeed, honey,' Suzy said.

While Eric considered the electricity implications of twenty thousand watts worth of fairy-lights, Abi continued to stare in wide-mouthed awe at the voltaic monstrosity.

'Can we do this to our house, Mummy? I want a reindeer on my roof.'

'Not a chance,' Eric said.

'Why not?'

'Because it's horrific —'

'Horrifically expensive.' Suzy cut into his response. 'Because it's horrifically expensive, darling.'

Abi sucked on her bottom lip pensively. For a minute she looked as if she might let the subject go.

'But we can use Granddad's money,' she said.

Eric and Suzy exchanged a look.

'What was that, sweetheart?' Suzy said.

'We can use Granddad's money. When Katie's granddad died, her mum got given all his money, so they could go skiing and to Disneyland, and then Katie's mum left her dad because she didn't need him anymore because she had all her granddad's money. We could use our granddad's money to buy decorations.'

Her big green eyes looked longingly at her parents, but it did nothing to calm Eric's rapidly boiling blood. Suzy reached out and squeezed his hand. He couldn't respond. His mouth had transformed to sandpaper and a writhing tightness corkscrewed through his gut.

'Right,' he said. 'I think we need to be heading back now. It's already well past your bedtime.'

'But we could use Granddad's money, couldn't we?' Abi said again.

'Maybe next year,' Suzy said.

AT SIX FORTY-FIVE Eric was standing outside Eaves and Doyle. Although the water at the Sailboat had been hot, the shower had possessed about the same amount of power as a salivating, expectorating camel. No amount of scrubbing had managed to remove the grimy, unwashed feeling that came from sleeping in cheap, guest-house bed sheets. Having risen early, Abi and Suzy were now taking a wander along the seawall in a vain attempt of seal spotting. The plan was for them to get the first train back, but it was still another hour before that left, so they had plenty of time to kill.

It was one of those crystal-blue days when the sky was so clear you could be misled into believing it was summer. Until, that was, you stepped outside and could no longer blink due to your tears freezing in their ducts. There was no breeze and no clouds, but an icy coldness hung in the air, crystallising everything it touched. With prior warning, Eric would have at least brought some form of jumper with him. As it was, he was open to the elements.

Eric blew on his fingers in an attempt to fight off the cold. Already his toes were numb, his ear lobes burning, and his jaw clattered so furiously he worried that he might crack a crown. Doubting his sense in arriving early, he scanned down the road, spotting Eaves on the other side of the High Street.

The solicitor was wrapped in a thick tweed coat, with a woolly bobble-hat, and scarf around his neck. While the coat appeared of decent quality, Eric noted that the hat and scarf looked like something left behind at the end of a charity table-top sale in aid of underprivileged otters.

'A bit nippy,' Eaves said, stretching out his hand to shake Eric's. Eric accepted, but only after a notable delay. 'I'm ever so sorry, about yesterday,' he continued. 'I hope the Sailboat wasn't too awful for one night.'

'These things happen.'

'Indeed, they do.'

The solicitor, Eric observed, was making no attempt whatsoever to open the door and let them in. His hands were firmly by his side, entirely devoid of keys. Unless the door possessed some form of high-tech biometric lock that was invisible to the untrained eye, Eric decided keys were entirely necessary, if not crucial in the given situation.

'Shall we go inside?' Eric said, wiggling his toes to check for the onset of frostbite. Still, Eaves made no attempt to unlock the door or even make a move towards it.

'I thought you might like to get some breakfast,' he said. 'The Sailboat isn't known for its cuisine.'

'Pardon?'

'Well, it's a bit of an early start and all. And I can never think quite right until I've eaten. I thought we could head to The Shed?'

Eric blinked. All the brownie points Eaves had gained in arriving early disappeared.

'Sorry, you want breakfast?'

'It's the most important meal of the day.'

Eric blinked again. 'Can we just get this over with? I'm rather pressed for time.'

'Oh, of course. Of course you are.' Christian Eaves paused and bit down on his lip. 'Only it will take just as long here as it would there. The only difference being the fried eggs and bacon. And to be honest, it's a fair bit warmer in The Shed than the office. You know what these old buildings are like. Gotta keep tabs on the electricity bills.'

'Well, I —'

'Don't worry, it's a great service. We'll have you fed and on the road in no time.'

Too dumbfounded to object, Eric followed the solicitor down the road and towards a small, wood-clad building on the seawall. Only in Burlam.

CHAPTER 8

IF NOTHING ELSE, Eaves had been right about the temperature. Within a minute of setting foot in the cafe, Eric's previously numbed toes and fingers tingled with pins and needles. He flexed his joints and tried to avert any oncoming thawing pains; the attempt failed miserably, and a burning sensation fired up through his palms. Shaking his hands about, he followed Eaves down a narrow passage and past a service counter.

The Shed was a curious establishment with a multitude of little dining rooms all running off one main corridor. It possessed low ceilings with several well-placed beams that could easily have resulted in a mild concussion for anyone over five-foot ten; it smelt, if possible, even greasier than the previous night's eatery. This time, however, the smell of fats could be categorised into subtler bouquets of bacon, sausage, and black pudding.

'Griff,' said Eaves, greeting a man as he came out from the kitchen. 'The back room free?'

'It is for you. You having the usual?'

'Probably, but I'll take a menu, anyway.'

Griff gave one sheet of laminated paper to Eaves and one to Eric, who held it by the corner and tried to put as little surface area between his skin and the oily plastic as possible.

'It's good coffee too,' Eaves said, leading him down one set of steps into a little room in the corner. 'Proper stuff, none of that instant rubbish.'

The back room came as rather a surprise. With three long windows and a large conference table tucked against one of the long walls, there must have been seats stacked up for at least thirty people. The floor was wooden – laminate but still pleasant – and there were normal sized tables too, currently set out for three of four covers, with doily tablecloths and small vases holding plastic carnations. Eric took a seat on one of the wheel-back chairs and quickly gave the menu a once over. It was all the usual fare; full English, bacon butties, that type of thing, only they were given supposedly amusing names like the Fat Bastard or the Wimpy Git.

'The names were even worse when they first started, but they had to change them due to all the complaints,' Eaves told him.

'That does surprise me.'

After the previous evening's overindulgence, Eric settled on a Whiny Bitch egg white omelette, with a side of fried mushrooms, and an espresso. Eaves went for the Fat Bastard. Had they been friends, Eric would have been inclined to say something, but he managed to hold his tongue. Once their order had been taken and their coffees had arrived, Eaves finally deemed it time to start business. He shuffled around in his seat and placed his palms on the table.

'I really must apologise again for yesterday. And before I forget, I have to give you this.' He reached into his pocket, extracted his wallet, and pulled out three twenty-pound notes. 'For your room,' he said.

Eric hesitated. It wasn't in his nature to take money, but this man had cost him, not least for Sally's petrol to get down there.

'Thank you,' he said and took the money.

Underneath the tweed coat, the solicitor was wearing the same cheap suit as before, only this time he was tieless, and the top button of his shirt was undone.

'I'm going to be honest with you,' he said. 'Your father thought something like this might happen.'

'Of course he did. That's why he did this. So he could make the whole event as painful as possible.'

Eaves shook his head.

'No, I don't think that's the case.'

'You didn't know my father.'

'Well, actually —'

'The hell you did,' Eric stopped him before he could finish.

Eaves pressed his lips together then took a sip of his coffee. It was a long sip. Eric's muscles twinged with irritation at it.

'I'm sorry if I offended you,' Eaves said when he finished his sip.

'You didn't.'

'Good. Then, as I was saying. Your father had expected something like this to happen and in preparation put in a series of contingencies to ensure that you got to keep the car.'

'Except actually leaving me the car?'

'Yes, well I do see how that appears somewhat contradictory. Anyhow, the first condition was that you had to come straight down to Burlam when requested. And that you stay in Burlam when asked to do so.'

Eric took a moment to digest the words.

'You mean that all this hanging around, missing work, coming at the drop of a hat. That was all part of his game?'

'I wouldn't call it a game —'

'And everything yesterday, all the crap with the bailiffs, that was all part of it too?'

'I can assure you that the bailiffs were very real. Had you not come down to Burlam immediately, they would have taken your car.'

'This is ridiculous.' Eric slammed his fists on the table, bouncing the cutlery with a clatter.

'Whiny Bitch?' Griff appeared behind Eric and placed the plate down in front of him. Apparently oblivious to the tension encircling him, Griff continued on. 'Can I get you anything else? Ketchup? Brown sauce?'

'I'm fine, thank you,' Eric said through gritted teeth. Eaves also quickly shook his head, dismissing the restaurateur-cum-chef.

'While your father's methods may seem illogical to you, I'm only doing as I was instructed to do.'

'The fry up? This place. Is this all part of it too?' Eric said.

'No,' Eaves said. 'I just really fancied a cooked breakfast. My wife has me on an oat bran diet and it's about as enjoyable as munching on cardboard. This is all my doing.'

'Then you can pay for it.'

Eaves smiled. 'I was going to anyway,' he said.

The solicitor picked up his fork and speared a piece of sausage. Eric looked on longingly; his egg white omelette looked distinctly insipid by comparison. He took a mouthful and chewed, only to find that it tasted as good as an egg white omelette could. A few more mouthfuls down and Eaves reached around and into his coat.

'Your father wanted me to give you this. I haven't read it, and this is where my instructions end in regard to second chances. From now on, if you fail to abide by the agreement, I will be taking your car. There are no more do-overs.' He slid a small white envelope across the table, then stood up and retrieved his coat. 'I do hope everything turns out all right for you,' he said.

'What about the rest of your breakfast?' Eric said. 'You've barely touched it.'

Eaves shrugged. 'Damn oat bran. Can't eat more than a mouthful of anything now without, well, you know. Anyway. Take care of that car, Mr Sibley. And of yourself.'

With Eaves gone, Eric ordered another espresso. What he really wanted was a large portion of the black pudding and streaky bacon, but Eaves' last remark about the bran had made eating substantially less appealing. The envelope continued to lie flat in the centre of the table, and even when Eric had finished his second coffee, he decided to order himself a sparkling water, and then a portion of toast and jam. Anything to delay the inevitable. When his toast was done, his phone buzzed with a message from Suzy saying she and Abi were safely on the train. He stood up, took the envelope, slipped it into his pocket and left, leaving a tenner on the table to cover the extra food and drink.

Outside, the sun was doing an admirable job at battling the cold. Still, Eric kept out of the shade as he walked and managed to maintain a degree of warmth to his face. It was a shame he didn't like sailing. Days like today he could imagine himself out on the open sea, the sail flapping in the wind, Abi laughing as she joked around in her little orange life vest.

He ambled down as far as the yacht club, his mind focusing on nothing but the breeze and seagulls. When he reached the end of the path where the pavers disappeared into the grass, he turned around and retraced his steps back to the car.

It was only when he was tucked up in the bucket seats, the warm leather moulding to his body, that Eric took out the neatly typed letter and began to read.

TO MY ONLY SON, Eric,

ERIC PAUSED. At least this meant there wasn't about to be some long confession about a life of bigamy and seventeen other children spread between John O'Groats and Land's End. After wasting a moment dwelling on the possibility of endless siblings, he came back to the letter.

TO MY ONLY SON, Eric,
I can only imagine your disappointment. No doubt you have disowned me and cursed my name many times since receiving news of your inheritance, but the fact that you're here, now, reading this letter, proves that there is hope for you and for me.

It may surprise you, but I've tried to express myself to you in person, both before your mother's passing and since, but believe me when I say stubbornness and pride are hard to relinquish after all these years and now, with less time left than I would have hoped for, I've given up trying to teach this old dog new tricks. At my age, more than ever, time is better spent rejoicing in what you can do, not dwelling on what you can't.

Somewhere along the line, I lost sight of what mattered in this life. I put the emphasis on what I could achieve instead of focusing on what I had achieved and as such ignored the most important gifts I already had. Though, worse than my failings as a husband and father is the fact that I've passed these failings on to you, my son. My deluded ideas of success and wealth. My misguided ideas of what life should be like. I've made you place value on things that are worthless and seen you cast aside and neglect those that are most precious.

This is not a lecture. I'm far too old to lecture and you're far too old to listen. And I'm not asking you to do this for me, I'm asking you to do this for your mother, for your wife, for your daughter, but most of all for you. You may not see it now, but what I have left you is worth more than money, more than the house.

. . .

Eric turned the paper over and searched for a conclusion; some final farewell or at least a signature to prove that that sans serif typescript was his father's own composition, but there was none. He flipped the paper back again, read once more through the words, then folded the letter back into the envelope. A heavy weight had descended on his chest.

'Screw you,' he said and threw the letter onto the passenger seat.

CHAPTER 9

ERIC HAD HAD every intention of driving straight back to London. Suzy had messaged to say she'd be getting off at Woodham and going to visit her sister Lydia, which on the plus side meant that the house would be empty for him to have a shower and get himself sorted before going into work; on a less positive note, it meant they were seeing Lydia. Eric deleted the first reply he wrote and instead sent a diplomatic *Have fun*. Now, not only was Abi missing school, she was being indoctrinated into Lydia's *all of life is brilliant which is why we've made you a dreamcatcher out of twigs and cat fur for Christmas* mindset. Perfect.

The day had maintained a powder-blue skyscape, and the salt breeze brought with it a tang of earthiness from the marshlands. Eric focused on the feel of Sally as he tried to block out all the other conversations going on inside his head. It was only when he'd been driving for over a minute that he realised he was heading in completely the wrong direction.

'Sod it,' he said as he passed some familiar pebble-dashed houses. A minute later he was parked up outside Columbia Avenue.

Unlike his previous visit, the ground was rock solid, and a sharp frost gripped the bushes and grasses. Eric pulled his sleeves down over his hands then folded his arms as he tried to protect them from the cold. The pinboard was still in place on the shed, this time with a few extra notices and three sealed envelopes each addressed with a lot number. Eric gave them the once over and moved on.

Full of confidence he marched onward, down the exact path he'd previously taken with his elderly guide. The place felt more familiar than expected; he remembered a couple of the more ornate fences and well-maintained plots, and several of the raised beds jerked his memory too. After a couple of minutes, he reached a large blue water butt that he distinctly recalled from before and turned left by it. Two minutes later he saw another and turned left again.

'Must have done that too soon,' he said to no one in particular.

It took eight blue water butts and triple that in number of turns before Eric admitted what he'd known six butts earlier. He was lost. Every other plot, it appeared, had a tall, blue water butt. Every fourth lot had a yellow shed, and he could have sworn that a particular scarecrow, with a green shell-suit jacket on, was moving around just to wind him up. Eric became decidedly concerned that he might never manage to find his way out again, let alone find his abhorrent excuse for an allotment.

'Can I help you, deary, you look a little lost?'

Eric spun on the spot, muttering to himself as he moved.

The offer of help came from a small woman who appeared to have been plucked straight from the pages of a Beatrix Potter tale. She wore a thick khaki duffle coat with brown trousers, brown ankle boots, and a tartan headscarf that was wrapped around her chin in a manner that made her eyes look larger than a barn owl's. She hunched over slightly as she hobbled forwards while balancing a pair of thin-rimmed spectacles on the end of her nose, enhancing her overall owl-like demeanour.

'I'm looking for plot fifty-two,' Eric said.

'Fifty-two.' Her eyes popped, magnified to preposterous proportions behind her glasses. 'Oh.'

The little woman stayed rooted to the spot. After a minute, Eric considered the possibility that she might have frozen when her throat emitted something between a squeak and a cough.

'Sorry? I didn't quite catch that,' he said.

She squeaked again. Eric leant in closer.

'I'm Janice,' she said.

'Janice?' Eric frowned. He pursed his lips, then inhaled an exceptionally long intake of air.

For the next five minutes, Janice showered Eric in apologies. Apparently, she'd passed her news about the extra allotment to her neighbour Geoffrey, who had then told his wife. She, in turn, had conveyed the information to her sister-in-law, whose neighbour from across the road was friends with one of the committee members and was also the nephew of Christian Eaves.

'I'm terribly sorry for having caused such a problem. I wouldn't have offered to help otherwise.'

'Really, it's fine,' Eric said.

'You see it's such a long waiting time here —'

'Honestly. Please, don't mention it.'

'Unless you inherit one, or you're on the list —'

'I'm rather short on time —'

'If there's anything I can do.'

'Yes. Yes, there is one thing.' Eric's tone stopped her gabble mid-flow. Janice's eyes bugged beneath her spectacles. 'You could show me where plot fifty-two is.'

The apologies continued, even as Eric followed Janice weaving between the rows.

'I'm not as quick as I used to be,' she said over her shoulder. 'Bunions. Damn things. Lucky my hands and knees are still on side. It's just up here though, you were almost there.'

In less than a minute, Eric recognised where he was. In front of him sat the perfectly manicured allotment and rust-red shed with veranda he'd been so keen to claim. Next to it sat his own disgusting septic tank of a plot, complete with festering, algae-filled, blue water butt and dilapidated greenhouse.

'Well, this is you,' she said. 'How lovely for you. No doubt you'll have this spick and span in no time. And lucky you, having the plot next to the Kettlewells. Wonderful couple. Temperamental at times, but wond ... oh look. Speak of the devil.'

Norman Kettlewell glowered at Eric with his cat-green eyes before commencing yet another coughing fit.

'It was all a misunderstanding,' Eric said before the accusations began.

'Aye, you can say that again. Trying to get a pensioner to do your work for you. Bloody big misunderstanding.'

'That wasn't what I was —'

'Well if you've come to say farewell, you can consider it said —'

'That's enough, Norman. The man has said his apologies, now it's time to move on.'

A woman, Eric could only assume was Norman's wife, was doing the talking, after which Norman erupted into a coughing fit. While Eric considered that the fit could indeed have been genuine, it could also have been an opportunity to stop his wife berating him. Half a minute later when he was still going, and his eyes streamed, Eric conceded that it was most probably genuine.

'Cynthia,' she said, stretching her hand to Eric, which he promptly took and shook. Then to her husband, she said, 'Why don't you go and sit in the shed for a minute. Catch your breath?'

Doubled over to the knees, Norman shook his head, but when he went to voice his objection, he could barely breathe.

'Shed. Now,' Cynthia said.

This time, Norman moved.

With Norman and his bronchial malaise shut away in his shed, Eric found himself at the mercy of the two elderly women. The pair were polar opposites to look at. Cynthia, with her mane of dyed burgundy hair and plum colour lipstick, looked like she'd be more at home in a 1950s cocktail bar than an allotment, as opposed to Janice, who Eric wholeheartedly believed lived in a hollowed-out tree with nothing but a log fire and mice dressed in waistcoats for company. Both, however, had the ability to talk nonstop over one another, without a second to digest or breathe. Perhaps it comes with age, Eric thought as they continued to prattle away. Maybe you reach a point where you become worried that your conversations are numbered and therefore try to squeeze as many words as possible into each one, regardless of the situation or how many people are present.

'It was an impressive plot this time last year,' Cynthia said. 'Your father was a very good gardener. Very good. Had an impressive crop of runner beans, from what I remember.'

'And his gooseberries,' Janice overlapped. 'Don't forget his gooseberries.'

'I hadn't forgotten his gooseberries, I was just mentioning his runner beans.'

'Well, anyone can grow runner beans. They don't take any skill at all. If you want to acknowledge someone's gardening skills, you don't praise their runner beans.'

'I'm sure they were equally impressive,' Eric said diplomatically.

Cynthia smiled knowingly. 'He said that about you. Never liked an argument. Always a peacekeeper. How's little Abi doing? I have to say we miss the updates. She was just starting swimming lessons last we heard.'

Something tugged beneath Eric's sternum. Abi had started swimming lessons over a year ago. She'd already got her one-hundred-metre badge and moved up from the tadpole to the turtle group. He was almost certain he'd spoken to his father several times since then but racking his mind, he couldn't think when or what they would have spoken about.

'She's doing well. Spending the day with her mother,' he said.

'Oh, has she not got school?'

'Teacher training day,' Eric lied.

There was a brief pause during which he felt the eyes of the old women scrutinise him at an uncomfortable depth.

'Are you planning on doing any work today?' Cynthia said. 'I only ask because Norman's got a spare pair of gloves and wellies in the shed if you need them. You won't want to be getting those nice shoes of yours covered in mud.'

Eric raised his hands apologetically. 'Unfortunately, I have to be getting back to London to see the girls. I should have already left. I only dropped in to have a quick recce.'

Both women looked notably disappointed.

'Already?' said Janice. 'Such a shame, you've hardly got here.'

'I'm sure he'll be back soon enough,' said Cynthia. 'And then you can bore him with tales of your bunions like you do the rest of us.' She reached out her hand. 'Have a safe journey back. And I'm so sorry about your father.'

'Thank you.'

His phone buzzed with an email, and though he ignored the message he glanced at the time, surprised to find that it was already gone ten.

'Thank you for all your help,' he said, bidding the ladies farewell before he dug his heel into the ground and began to walk away.

'Where do you think you're going?'

Eric stopped. He didn't need to turn around to know Norman's face was going to be sporting a glare and grimace. What he didn't know, was how he'd managed to install such a lingering bee in this old man's bonnet. Slowly he turned around, fastening his teeth into a perfectly aligned smile.

'I'm sorry,' Eric said. 'I didn't want to disturb you. Anyway, I'm off now.'

Norman's torso leant out of his red shed door. A second later his legs caught up, and he limped the few steps across the empty vegetable beds.

'Eric was just going back to London,' Janice said. 'Abi's got a teacher training day.'

'Mid-December?'

'Private school,' he lied.

Norman locked his eyes on him and a cold shudder ran the length of Eric's spine. His eyes were impressively green, Eric thought, although he may have found them more impressive if it didn't feel like they were trying to bore a hole straight through his eye sockets into the centre of his cerebellum in order to render him entirely extinct.

'Aren't you forgetting something?' Norman said, his gaze unmoving.

Eric cleared his throat awkwardly. 'I don't believe so.'

'You don't say? What about that old inheritance of yours? What about that contract?'

'Norman.' Cynthia struck her husband on the arm. 'Don't be so rude.'

'Rude. I ain't the one that's being rude. He's the one who's done nothing. Nearly two months now he's left that patch to go to waste.'

'Norman, this is not the time.'

'It's exactly the time. You know how long the waiting list on one of these plots is? Do you?' He wagged his finger in Eric's direction. Eric stuttered.

'I ... Well, not exactly, but I've heard it's quite substantial.'

'Eight years. Did you hear that? Eight years people have to wait for a plot like this to come around, and you're there letting the whole thing go to spoil. Your father did more work with his zimmer frame than you've done since you got the place. Christ, this is worse than the bloody mole fiasco.'

Eric bit his tongue, hard. Diplomacy, he told himself. Be diplomatic. After all, two years could be a long time if this continued. He took a deep breath in through his nose.

'Mr ... Mr Kettlewell, isn't it? Norman. I really am sorry about the state of things. I am. And I will get around to sorting it. But right now, I have to get home.' Norman harrumphed again. Eric ignored him. 'I'm so grateful for your understanding over all this mess. I can assure you I will be back in the new year to get the whole place sorted. Hopefully, we will be able to start afresh.'

Finishing with his best salesman smile, Eric reached out a hand. Cynthia and Janice were beaming, Janice so much so that her bespectacled face now looked bizarrely reminiscent of an elderly praying mantis. Norman, however, did not move a whisker.

'Well,' Eric said, retrieving his hand, and placing it back beside his leg. 'Ladies, it was lovely to meet you. Norman, nice to see you again.' For the second time, he braced himself and moved to leave.

'Weekly maintenance.'

'Pardon?' Eric turned back.

'Weekly maintenance,' Norman growled, still statuesque on the same spot. 'That's what you've got to do right? That's what your father said. Every week, down here making this place better. That's if you want to keep that car.'

Eric sniffed and raised his chest.

'Mr Kettlewell, the legalities of my father's will are entirely confidential —'

'Bollocks to that. Who do you think typed out all his letters when his hands went?'

'Norman.' Cynthia's voice was different this time, wary, threatening.

'Well, who does he think he is? Confidential my arse. His father was a good man. A good man. But I know men like you. I know what you're about. Your father might have thought there was something worth saving, but you money grabbing types are all the same, and we don't want you here.'

'Norman, that's enough.'

'Tell me then, twice he's trotted down here in his fancy-pants suits and pointy shoes and not lifted a bloody finger. Not once. And d'you know how many times he's mentioned his father? Not once. Not a single bloody word. No sir, you can please and thank you all you want, but your smarmy manners don't mean nowt to me. Either you do the work, or I'll see that you're gone. And that pretty little car you value so much goes too.'

Eric found himself momentarily dumbfounded by a man who was essentially a life-sized garden gnome.

'I ... I ... well I'll have you know ...' he began, but within a second his stuttering astonishment was gone. In its place was something hot and angry that had his back teeth grinding together with more pressure than an industrial Delonghi espresso maker.

'You want me to do some gardening?' he said. 'Now?'

'At last, the boy understands.'

'Oh, I understand. I really do,' Eric said. 'You want me to tidy up. Now. Today.' Eric could feel the adrenaline taking hold. 'Today, when, as it happens, I found out that I drove seventy-five miles and missed what could be one of the most important meetings of my career because my father wanted to ... to what? Save me?' He paced the length of the plot. 'I can assure you, Mr Kettlewell, I do not need saving. Not even a bit. And if I did, my father is the last person I would go to. The very, very last. And here's another thing. You did not know my father. Not the father I had. Because if you did, if you knew even an inch of him, you wouldn't have the gall to stand there in front of me and tell me he was a good man. I knew my father, and I knew exactly what he was.' He stopped pacing and placed one hand on his hip and the other on the swampish water butt. 'But if you want me to do some maintenance, then that I can do. In fact, that would be my pleasure.'

With his glare still locked on Norman, Eric sidestepped along the grass, where he placed both hands firmly against the slime-covered plastic of the water butt. 'This maintenance enough for you?' he said. With one giant shove, he sent the whole thing toppling. Water sloshed over the side, cascading into giant streams of green-smelling gunk that spread across the ground in front of him. It stank as it spread, oozing out in all directions.

'I think it looks better already,' Eric said and with a satisfied smirk marched back to his car without getting lost once.

CHAPTER 10

ERIC COULD SMELL the algae on him all the way to London. He had cleaned off his shoes and washed his hands and was certain he hadn't transferred any of the pungent slime into the car, but the smell remained all the same. *I may smell like this forever*, Eric thought. Once I was Eric; now, Algae Man. He was delirious, he had to be.

After the final incident with the water butt, Eric accepted there was no possibility of him going straight into work now, not even to apologise. The email that buzzed earlier had been from Jack, telling him to take as much time as he needed, which was a nice sentiment, but utterly pointless. What he needed was the time back; a time accumulator to restore the hours wasted on his father's pointless pilgrimage.

The letter had fallen into the footwell of the passenger's seat, where it fluttered about demanding Eric's attention. His father wanted him to fail, Eric thought. He could see it now. The whole thing was merely a fantastic way of alleviating a selfish old man's guilt at wanting to leave his son nothing but miserable memories. This way George died the good one, the one who gave his son a chance. It was Eric who was branded the villain. It was a smart plan. Only it wasn't going to work. Not this time. Eric was determined.

The lunchtime traffic was its usual abomination, and by the time he reached home, Eric regretted his choice of a Whiny Bitch breakfast even more than he had in the morning. Still, he refused to allow himself to eat until he'd fully eradicated the stench of algae and rotten vegetables from his skin. He dropped his shoes on the porch, threw his clothes directly into the washing machine – switching it on to the intensive clean setting – then sprinted up into the shower where he double-scrubbed everything from his ankles to his fingernails. On the second scrub, he chose to use Suzy's expensive pink gel over his more subtly scented man-wash; even jasmine and wild lavender was better than he currently smelt. Properly clean for the first time in two days, Eric sauntered back downstairs and gathered a selection of cold cuts from the fridge to munch on while he tackled his emails.

Nothing stood out as urgent, besides the minutes of yesterday's meeting that – so the email read – would be discussed at another meeting next week. Meetings to discuss meetings. What a fantastic use of time. Eric was still studying the screen in front of him, trying to prioritise his seemingly endless to-do list, when another email, in the middle of the page caught his eye. His throat tightened. After hovering the cursor over the message for a solid fifteen seconds, he clicked open.

'Sorry about today. His bark's much worse than his bite. I hope he didn't upset you too much. Have a long rest over Christmas and we'll all start over in the new year. It was lovely to meet you. Cynthia.'

A softening sensation momentarily floated through his stomach before it instantaneously hardened.

'You think I'm going to fall for that,' Eric said and shut the lid with a sizeable force.

Suzy and Abi were back at three. While Suzy drifted in serenely and delicately pecked her husband on the cheek, Abi was bouncing off the walls.

'They've got nine rabbits. Nine! Can we have one, Daddy? Can we? Uncle Tom thought they were both girls and if they don't find the babies homes, he says they're going to eat them. Can we have one, Daddy, pleeeease? We can't let him eat them.'

'I thought Uncle Tom had an excess of experience in mammalian genitalia,' Eric said. Suzy shot him a glare. 'No, we can't, Abi,' he said. 'Rabbits are vermin. They're not pets. They're tailless rats.'

'That's what you say about hamsters.'

'The same is true.'

'What about gerbils? They've got tails.'

Sensing the need for a distraction from the rabbit topic, Eric nodded to the canvas bag in Suzy's hands. 'What's that?' he said.

'Leftovers. Lyd made a lasagne for lunch.'

'Is it edible?'

'It's yummy!' Abi said, jumping up and once again kneeing Eric in the testicles.

'Abs, honey, can you go put the lasagne in the fridge? Then go check the computer and see if the teachers have emailed you any work.'

'The teachers email you?' Eric said.

Abi raised an eyebrow. 'What do you expect them to do, text me?' Then, shaking her head at the idiocy of the older generation, she disappeared into the kitchen.

'So,' Suzy said, kicking off her shoes and moving into the sitting room. 'What did he say?'

Eric slumped down into the armchair opposite, then reached into his pocket and withdrew the letter.

'See for yourself.'

Once Suzy had finished the letter, she folded it neatly and placed it back in its envelope before leaning back into the sofa, her lower lip disappearing under her teeth.

'And that's not the worst of it,' Eric said.

'No?'

'No, the worst part is that this whole rigmarole was part of his plan. Me missing work, me spending the night down there. It's all some twisted game that he's mapped out for me from beyond the grave. He's probably got years' worth of stuff ready to torment me with. Decades even.'

'What else did the solicitor say?'

Eric shrugged. 'Not much. Apparently, this is the last chance I'll get. Either it's maintain the allotment or give the car back. Oh yes, my day just keeps getting better and better.'

Suzy stayed silent, which was her typical response when she had something she desperately wanted to say but suspected that Eric's views would differ from hers quite substantially. After a couple of minutes, she levered herself out of the chair and left Eric to his laptop. The rest of the evening went in a blur, except for the lasagne which stood out as an unexpected highlight of the day.

'Perhaps you should come across to see them next time,' Suzy said.

'It wasn't that nice,' Eric replied.

With Monday and Tuesday lost, Eric's feet barely touched the ground for the remaining three days of the week. He attempted to gain information from Greg about whether Hartley had given any hints about creating a new senior associate director position, but evidently Greg had lost focus after Eric left the meeting, apparently on account of glimpsing indications of more intimate tattoos on the red-headed intern.

Jack popped his head through the glass door several times. 'Alistair was impressed with the contract you put together for the Fortune account. Very impressed,' he said. Eric gave an internal sigh of relief. At least he hadn't made an entirely horrific impression.

Ralph, on the other hand, hadn't been best pleased to see Eric return with the car.

His arrival at the house had coincided exactly with dinner-time for the three wildlings, and as such all conversations transpired over clatterings of cutlery, flying yoghurt, and dubious lyrics to well-known pop songs.

'It's called *Uptown Funk,*' Ralph said, as his eldest belted out his own, less censored version. 'Funk, son. Funk.'

'Are you sure?'

'Yes, quite sure.'

'So, it's *Up town* —'

'Funk you up. Yes, definitely funk you up.'

'Huh, who knew?'

The child – Joshua? Jonas? – went back to painting eyebrows on his sister with various condiments and desserts, leaving Eric and Ralph to continue their conversation.

'I don't know,' Ralph said. 'Sah went mad over the thing with the bailiffs. I missed the baby's nap time. It put her out for days. You have no idea what it's like with three. They have to nap. They have to.'

'It won't happen again. I swear. It was all a misunderstanding. And I'm trying to sort out something more permanent for the car. I just need another couple of months. Three max.'

'Two max,' Ralph said. Eric agreed and sprinted out the door before

Ralph changed his mind and Eric was roped into helping with bath-time and bedtime. There was only so far his friendship could stretch where Ralph's children were concerned.

<hr />

IT WASN'T until Friday evening that Eric finally managed to find time to have a meal with Suzy. The takeaway was already dished up when he dragged himself through the front door at nine fifteen.

'Abi already in bed?' he said.

'She tried to stay up.' Suzy handed him a plate. 'But she's knackered. You know what the last day of term is like. All Christmas parties and sugar crashes.'

'Today's the last day of term? Shit, how did that happen?'

'I have no idea.'

They carried the plates through to the living room and balanced them on their knees to eat.

'What time do you want to leave tomorrow?' Suzy asked after a mouthful of chow mien.

Eric looked blankly at his wife.

'Tomorrow, Lyds. You do remember it's Christmas next week, don't you?'

'Of course I do.'

'And what do we always do the weekend before Christmas?'

Eric let out a long, drawn-out groan. 'But you saw her on Tuesday? Surely that counts?'

'We saw her, Abs and I. You didn't. Besides, we didn't take gifts. And it's tradition. So yes, we're going.'

'But what about the allotment?'

'What about it?'

'I have to go.'

'You went on Tuesday. And the email from Cynthia said she'd see you in the new year. I don't think anyone's expecting you to go in over Christmas. I know it said every week, but there have to be some reasonable concessions.'

A guttural moan rose from the base of Eric's throat as he bit into a prawn spring roll. He waited until he'd chewed and swallowed before he spoke.

'I know what their plan is, and I'm not falling for it. No, I need to go this weekend. I have to.' He mulled the issue over during another mouthful of spring roll. 'Could we not just go to your sister's in the morning? I can leave after breakfast and pick you and Abi up on the way home? That way I've only lost half-an-hour or so.'

'You have to stay longer than that,' Suzy said. 'Besides, I've told her we're coming for lunch.'

'Well ring her and ask her if we can come earlier. Blame me. She always likes it when you blame things on me.' Suzy didn't look convinced. 'She'll be the hero. She'll love it. We'll just have to say how grateful we are a hundred and fifty times. And there's a foot rub in it for you,' Eric added for good measure.

Suzy exhaled loudly. She was still frowning, but her pout had diminished slightly. Eric sidled up beside her and nuzzled into her shoulder.

'You're my angel,' he said.

'I'll ask, that's all. But if she can't change, then you're still coming.'

'Tell her I'm happy to have turkey for breakfast if that helps.'

Lydia was fine about changing from lunch to brunch, so by eight thirty the next morning the three of them were piled in the Audi, the backseat a menagerie of silver-and-gold-wrapped gifts. The car reeked of plastic and frivolously spent money. Eric hadn't bothered asking Suzy about taking Sally. She wasn't keen on Abi going above thirty miles an hour in her, and Eric was on too much of a mission to have to think about things like speed limits. Besides, as well as the fact it had been pouring with rain all night and showed no signs of stopping, he needed the boot space.

The winter sky was fully in place, and along the street faint remnants of smoke twisted up from the chimney stacks. Had it not been for the cars, electricity pylons, and lampposts, they could have been in Victorian London. Eric breathed in the smell of wood fires and long nights. According to his phone, it was dry in Burlam and had been all week. He'd believe that when he saw it.

Abi was already glued to her iPad as they drove along the A12, and Suzy rambled on about the latest freelance pieces she'd been asked to write. Eric's mind was elsewhere. Time management. That was all this business with the allotment came down to, decent time management. And decent time management was something Eric was exceptionally good at.

They reached Chelmsford in good time, but rather than taking the route down to Woodham, Eric steered the car left towards the town centre.

'Where are you heading?' Suzy asked. 'I said we'd be there at nine thirty, it's already ten to.'

'Don't worry,' Eric said. 'It'll take five minutes. Promise.'

CHAPTER 11

ERIC CONSIDERED POPPING into a town centre the last weekend before Christmas and expecting a quick turnaround about as likely as turning up at a vegan festival in a pair of crocodile skin loafers and sheepskin jacket and expecting to be invited to share a tofu burger. Still, he grinned to himself smugly as he veered away from the dozens of tail-lights, all vying for a handful of empty parking spaces by the town centre, and headed over to the other side of town. They continued through two industrial estates and past a handful of new car showrooms before taking a left at two consecutive mini-roundabouts and drawing up at a prime spot directly in front of Tools4U. He reversed in, cut the engine, and turned to Suzy.

'Do I even want to know?' she said.

'I'll be fifteen minutes, tops,' Eric replied. 'There's a garden centre up the other end of the road. Why don't you take Abi to have a look around? I bet they have animals. They always have animals at garden centres.'

Suzy raised her eyebrows and sucked on her top teeth before turning to Abi and motioning that she could undo her seatbelt.

'Fifteen minutes tops,' she said to Eric, and then back to Abi added, 'come on, let's go look at the guinea pigs.'

'Remember to tell them you want to buy something,' Eric called, as they crossed the road ahead of him. 'They only let you stroke the things if they think you're actually going to buy one.'

Suzy offered him a dismissive wave and headed off towards a large green building. Eric went straight to the bright blue doors.

The chrome-accented foyer of Tools4U smelt of metal and manliness. Having done his research online, Eric had identified four tool hire companies in Chelmsford. Two of them were big chains, and the third was shut until the new year. While the big chains offered all sorts of promotions, like double deals and accidental insurance, free pickup and drop off, Tools4U had come out top in Eric's mind, partly because of its location on the outskirts of town and partly because the website featured only photos of tools. This was opposed to the chain stores' websites, which contained hundreds of images of overly smiley people man-handling machinery in carefully curated poses that ensured a perfectly even mix of gender, ethnicity, and age was gained in every shot.

Eric stepped inside. It was surprising how primal and arousing the petrol and woodchip aromas were. The shelves, stocked twelve feet high, exuded a sense of power with their gleaming metal engines and masculine words like *horsepower* and *throttle* written in bold. Even the roof was manly with its thick metal girders and exposed ventilation systems. After two minutes perusing, he remembered the time constraint and headed to the service desk at the back.

It took three forceful coughs before the freckled youth behind the counter raised his head from the computer screen. Although he met Eric's gaze with a smile, Eric felt it was definitely an enforced customer-service smile as opposed to a genuine, pleased-to-see-him smile. Eric reciprocated nonetheless. The youth in question looked a little over eighteen, with cinnamon red hair, cut into a John Lennon style mop-top, and a blanketing of ginger freckles. Despite the weather, he was wearing a memorabilia T-shirt of a band which Eric thought sounded familiar – if for no other reason than its distinct assonance to a venereal disease – and had a single headphone jammed into one of his ears.

'Hello,' Eric said. 'I need to get a chainsaw.'

The boy plucked the headphone out of his ear and stashed it in his pocket. He leant forwards over the counter, locking eyes with Eric.

'Sure,' he said.

'Excellent.'

'Is there any type of chainsaw you had in mind?'

'Yes,' Eric said, straightening his back, and feeling most authoritative. 'I think I need something with a decent HP. Preferably with low vibration, spark arrest muffler, and decompression valve.'

The corners of the young man's mouth twitched.

'Wow, you do sound like you know what you want.'

'Basically, I want whatever's best. And I don't mean to be rude, but I'm in a bit of a rush.'

The youth's twitching lips pressed tighter together.

'Okay, I get that,' he said.

He stood up and came around to the front of the counter at an infuriatingly leisurely pace. From the shelves beneath, he selected a thin looking brochure, which he placed in front of Eric.

'What kind of work are you doing, exactly? I mean, are you thinking of felling an entire woodland, or just chopping down a few saplings? If you have a look in the catalogue here, you can see there's a range of different models depending on —'

Eric waved him quiet.

'Yes, I read all that online. What I'm after is the 550XP. It did say you had it in stock. If you could grab me one and get the paperwork sorted that would be fantastic.'

The youth took a step back.

'Sir,' he said with a slight hint of trepidation. 'If you don't mind me asking, how often do you use chainsaws?'

'Why, does that affect the price?'

'No, of course —'

'Then why are you asking? I told you want I wanted. I also told you that I'm in rather a rush, and I'd hate to have to waste the weekend before Christmas ringing up your customer service department in order to lodge a complaint.'

The young man's nostrils flared in and out, and a glimmer of something unpleasant squirmed behind Eric's belly button as he puffed his chest out farther still. He hated acting like a prick, but some people were just born time wasters. He met lads like this all the time. Give them the slightest hint of power and they leapt forty metres above their station. He had read up on every specification and chainsaw know-how list the internet had to offer. There was certainly nothing this jumped up little pot-head could tell him that he hadn't already read on Google.

The youth finally dropped his gaze and went back behind his desk.

'Of course, sir, I'll get someone out back to prepare the XP for you now. There are just a few bits of paperwork that need reading and signing. I hope that's okay? Unless you'd like a demonstration on the machine first?'

'That won't be necessary,' Eric said.

'I thought as much,' the redhead said, then he offered Eric an even faker smile than he had when he first arrived.

It was another twenty minutes before Eric left the shop. There had been an unending stream of papers to sign – insurance waivers, credit card details, deposit refund criteria – before he could leave. By the time he'd squeezed the chainsaw bag into the boot and clambered into the driver's seat, they were well behind schedule. Suzy had an extreme version of *the look* on her face. A thick crease had formed between her eyebrows, and her chin set in a position that told Eric his best hope was to drive fast. He kept his mouth shut and at 10.00 AM, thirty minutes late, they pulled into Tom and Lydia's driveway.

The contents of the hanging baskets hung by the porch were dead and decaying, although their rather morbid presence was offset slightly by the oversized wreath that covered the upper half of the front door. There was a family of reindeer – or possibly rhinos – on the ground by the front step, obviously homemade with their jagged, sawn edges, protruding nails, and stuck on googly eyes. It reminded Eric of a family of creatures from a Tim Burton animation, only infinitely more sinister.

'Suze! Abi! Come in, come in.'

At forty-two, Suzy's sister, Lydia was every bit the aging hippy, with braids in her hair, denim skirt, tie-dye leggings, and homemade Christmas pudding jumper.

'Eric,' Tom stretched out a hand. 'Good to see you. Good to see you.'

Tom was one of those unfortunate men who had started going bald before he'd even finished puberty and by twenty-two had had a head smoother than an Olympic swimmer's swim cap. He too was wearing a Christmas jumper, though his exhibited a three-dimensional face of Father Christmas which sported a cascade of white threads for his hair and beard. Poor Tom. Eric couldn't help but think the world was mocking him.

'Come in, come in,' Lydia continued to beckon. 'I was just about to call you and see if you'd got lost.'

'Sorry,' Suzy said. 'Eric had a few errands to run.' Lydia reached out and accepted their coats as they peeled them off their backs. The house was warm with a hot, radiator-fuelled heat and filled with smells of fresh baking and farmyards. Outside, a cockerel crowed multiple times. How no one in the estate complained about the noise was a mystery to Eric.

'Hugo and Ellery are outside, Abi. The chickens got loose again, so it's a bit of mayhem out there. I bet they'd love your help.' Then glancing at Abi's feet, added, 'There are spare wellies in the utility.' Abi looked at her mum for permission.

'Can I?'

'Just make sure you wash your hands properly before you eat.'

'I always do,' she said, then vanished out through the back of the house.

Now inside, Eric realised the outside of the house had got away lightly with only a wreath and demented deer family by way of decoration. From where he stood in the hallway, it appeared as though every inch of the three-bed semi had been plastered in tinsel, fake snow, or else some other homemade Christmas monstrosity. Paper snowflakes – the type he'd briefly tried to make with Abi some years before when she stabbed herself accidentally in the thigh with the scissors – were strung on the bannisters, while salt-dough stars and pipe cleaner angels hung off the lamps. Tissue-paper Father Christmases and six-inch high elves were staggered along the carpets leading the way to a six-foot Christmas tree while half a dozen wilting poinsettias were set along the staircase.

'Well,' Lydia said. 'Food will be another fifteen minutes. It's frittata, I hope that's okay? I'd planned on doing a full roast, but of course, with you coming earlier than expected ...'

'Frittata sounds lovely,' Eric said diplomatically, then to Tom, who was pouring a bright orange, reduced-alcohol Buck's Fizz, added. 'Not too much for me though. I'm afraid I've got to head off after food.'

'Lyds was telling me,' Tom said, handing him a full glass. 'What a mess.'

'You don't know the half of it.'

'But we don't need to talk about any of that right now,' Suzy said. 'Tell me, how did the boys' nativity go yesterday?'

'Oh, it was fantastic,' Lydia gushed.

'Fantastic,' Tom agreed. 'Without a doubt, the best *X-Men* nativity I've ever seen.'

The frittata was palatable, bordering on tasty. It could have been enjoyable were it not for Tom and Lydia's insistence on mentioning their own eggs every twenty seconds. Eric estimated that he could have bought his father's house back off the church had he been offered a menial ten pence for each time they were commented on. Dessert was alcohol-free Christmas pudding, which they ate obligingly, and was followed by present giving which took place around the tree directly afterwards.

The four adults, three children, and their Old English Sheepdog, Broccoli, crammed into the tiny room. The parents took up positions on the sofas, leaving the children scrambling around the coffee table trying to find a patch of carpet not covered in spray-painted pine cones or clumps of matted fur. The room smelt like a dog-friendly arboretum, or rather what an arboretum would smell like if the only trees it contained were pines and the dogs that walked there stank implausibly of sulphur and Pedigree Chum.

The tradition of meeting at Lydia's for Christmas had started over a decade before. Suzy and Lydia's parents had long been part of the cruise ship scene, and only once since Suzy and Eric had met had they visited over the Christmas period. That year Eric had insisted they all go out for lunch.

'We have plenty of room at ours,' Suzy had said.

'I'm well aware,' Eric replied.

Nowadays Eric didn't get involved in Christmas preparations. Especially not gift purchases, even when the direct family were concerned. A few years ago, Suzy had asked him for a bread maker for her birthday. He had had every intention of getting her one, but when he got to the store he was swayed by a self-driving vacuum that scurried around the house sweeping up dust as it went. He thought it was fantastic and comparable in present terms. Apparently not. Since the incident, his credit card had been the only requirement of Eric during festive and holiday seasons.

That afternoon, Suzy, who had done all the shopping weeks in advance, watched as her purchases were opened to an appreciative chorus of *oohs* and *ahhs*; an organic llama wool crocheted scarf for Lydia along with a pair of silver earrings apparently from Abi, a Leatherman multi-tool for Tom, and a set of build-it-yourself motorised dinosaur kits for the boys. By contrast, Eric and Suzy received the standard bottle of homemade elder-flower wine, this year accompanied by a set of psychedelic homemade clay coasters.

'We thought the colour scheme would go perfectly in your house,' Lydia said.

'Definitely,' Suzy said.

Eric wondered where exactly in their house fluorescent pink, vomit green, and turd brown all mingled into one.

Having opened the remainder of the presents, all eyes were on Abi as she tore at a small parcel of crinkled – and blatantly recycled – Christmas paper. She ripped off the Sellotape, cast the rubbish aside, and pulled out what appeared to be a yellow knitted condom with wings.

Eric's jaw hung loose as he attempted to fathom the gift.

'Will you use it?' Lydia said to a wide-eyed, mystified Abi.

The silence was palpable. Even Tom appeared to be having a hard time keeping a straight face at the disturbingly fashioned gift.

'That's lovely!' Suzy said finally, rescuing the situation by the skin of her teeth.

'What is it?' Abi said. Using her fingertips, she pinched the atrocity, stretching the fabric lengthways, then along its girth. Eric wanted to vomit.

'It's an egg cosy,' Lydia said. 'For your boiled eggs. So that they stay warm. Look, it's a little chick, there are its eyes and beak. Ellery made it himself.'

Lydia rotated the condom around, showing that it did indeed have eyes, big scary psychotic eyes that would no doubt appear in Eric's nightmares for years to come. A second silence followed. Lydia and Ellery's smiles stayed frozen on their faces, their foreheads crinkled in expectation. Eric's own pulse took a speedier pace as he stared at Suzy, who in turn had her eyes locked on Abi, willing her to say the right thing. Abi held the object in her fingertips, out at arm's length, and turned it over in her hands.

'I don't think I like eggs,' she said.

Eric decided then would be as good a time as any to leave.

CHAPTER 12

THE INTERNET HAD indeed lied about the lack of rain in Burlam. As Eric approached the town, the puddles grew wider and deeper, and sprayed up and under the wheel arches with a deep, sloshing whirr. The sky had a true winter feel about it, desolately vast and almost violet in colour. The bare-branched trees that lined the winding roads gave the impression that he was driving towards the end of the world, not merely the end of western civilisation and culture as he knew it. The Audi's heater blasted steel-smelling hot air out into the car, keeping his fingers warm and his windscreen clear; another definite advantage with not having brought Sally.

Eric was surprised to find the allotment a veritable hive of activity. Several figures huddled over their little beds or else pottered amongst the bushes. Amidst those brandishing rakes and trowels and other forms of multi-spiked-instruments was the wood-dwelling owlet, Janice, who was crouched close to the ground in a manner that would have left Eric's thirty-seven-year-old knees wincing at the strain. Eric searched for another route to his plot but didn't know the way well enough. He had no choice but to head straight on.

Deliberately avoiding any sideways glances, Eric strode past her as fast as he could, his eyes forwards, and the chainsaw bag – which weighed heavy as it perched on his left shoulder – shielding his face from her view.

There was no way she could spot him; not with the bag covering him and the fact she was facing the other direction. Still, he daren't look in her direction. He was well past the end of her neighbouring patch when a shrill voice cut the through the relative peace.

'Woohoo, Eric?' Eric stopped, then immediately regretted the decision.

'You should have kept walking,' he said to himself. Forcing his lips up into a toothy smile, he inched himself around to face her, the chainsaw wobbling precariously as he did.

'Janice,' he said. 'I didn't notice you there.'

'Oh, I'm so glad you came back,' she said, hobbling across the grass towards him. 'I was a bit worried last time. You know, what with Norman being the way he was.'

'It's all fine.'

'Norman will be Norman. Some days I don't know how she puts up with it, I really don't. But then he has a good heart. A very good heart.' Her eyes lit up. 'You should come and meet everyone else. There's lots of us out today.'

'I've seen.'

'We're all trying to make the most of the mild weather before the frost comes back, you see. You can't do much in frost, not when the ground gets as hard as it does, but that rain last night loosened it all up. I'll tell you what, it's a good time to dig your runner trenches. It's a good time to check your compost heap, too. Now listen, people think compost makes itself, but it doesn't. At least not good compost. Good compost requires —'

'Sorry,' Eric interrupted. 'I don't mean to seem rude, only I haven't got much time today.' He nodded to the chainsaw, now resting against his knee. 'I've only got this for a couple of hours. Perhaps I can meet everyone else the next time I'm down?'

'I'll hold you to that. And I've got the memory of a fox.'

'I'm sure you have,' Eric said, hitching the chainsaw back onto his shoulder and wondering exactly how good a memory the average fox had.

The decision to knock over the water butt had not been a wise one. The branches and debris were now covered in a thick, congealed green slime that, while adding a splash of colour to the vastly brown terrain, filled the surrounding area with a redolent musk not dissimilar to that that you'd find in a hippopotamus' sleeping chamber.

Eric touched a patch of the slime then withdrew his hand rapidly. He wiped the gunk onto the back of his trousers. His eyes travelled across the length and breadth of the plot, a weight building in his stomach. Where the heck did he start?

Rather than deliberating over which end of the patch was more disastrous than the other, Eric decided to unpack the chainsaw on the premise that he'd work out what to attack with it once he'd figured out how to get the thing going. A nervous tingle of adrenaline spread up from somewhere around his bladder as he unzipped the bag. He hadn't appreciated how new it was in the shop. Nor the size. The metal blade glinted in the winter light as Eric brushed his hand across the chain. Sandblasted and perfectly smooth.

Eric whipped his hand away, blushing at the inappropriate tenderness he'd just shared with a 3.7 horsepower piece of hardware. He checked over his shoulder and, after deciding no one was the least bit interested in his mechanophilic tendencies, began to tackle the job at hand.

After unpacking the item in question, Eric skimmed through the instruction booklet. He double read the safety issues, oil filling information, and instructions on how to start the engine. He had already read up on cutting angles and correct grip positions on the internet at home but decided it wouldn't hurt to have another quick read through on those too. Using the labelled image on the back page, he identified all the main features – from the chain sprocket cover to the back-handle guard – on the actual specimen. After twenty minutes, a hesitant petrol fill, and his back already aching from being leant over for so long, Eric was ready to start.

Holding it again resulted in yet another influx of adrenaline. He was going to enjoy this, Eric thought to himself. Really enjoy it. He knelt, checked the chain break, and slipped off the cover, before pressing the decompression valve. Standing upright, he secured the saw with his foot. His pulse rose an extra notch. Was this the right type of ground? Or was it too soft? Would he be better off moving it over to one of the patios to start? Choking back the fears, Eric grabbed the cord for a pull start. Was it far enough away from his body? What about kick back? Chainsaws like this all gave kick back, didn't they? It was no good. Eric let go and stepped away. His hands were quivering, and his legs trembled, his earlier confidence all but gone.

'Man up,' he said out loud.

'You can do it,' a voice called back from somewhere behind him.

Eric spun around and saw a man on crutches, with a very wide grin, waving at him. He hurriedly looked back away.

With a lump still lodged in his throat, Eric secured the chainsaw yet again. This time he didn't wait for any of the doubts to start creeping in. He took one deep breath, held it in, and yanked. There was half a second of silence, in which the air trembled as he held it in his lungs and the taste of iron ran thick under his tongue, before the engine spluttered, then coughed, then roared into life. Eric's heart leapt. It was like being a child again, not that he ever got to play with chainsaws as a child, but still, his whole body felt electrified with energy.

'Throttle, throttle,' he reminded himself and pushed down and out before placing it, still running, on the ground.

Aware of the deadly machinery at his toes, Eric stepped away from the running power tool to resurvey the land in question. With so much to be done, and no one place seeming any better than the another, he picked up the chainsaw and began the assault exactly where he stood.

It was exhilarating. Every slice felt like a weight from his past had been cut from his shoulders. *Thwack*. That branch was the time his father told him he wasn't allowed to audition for the school musical. *Thud*. That one was the time Eric had to cut his honeymoon short because his father thought he was having a heart-attack. *Thump*. That was the time he left him a shitty little patch of weeds as his inheritance.

Eric cut the engine, placed the saw back on the ground, and stepped away to deliberate his next move. Sweat slid down his forehead and into his eyes. He wiped it away with the back of his hand. He liked the chainsaw. He really liked it. He liked the feel of it in his hands, the weight of it in his biceps, and the release as it cut through the debris. He liked the sound, the smell. He liked it all apart from starting the bloody thing; that still terrified him. Still, after a five-minute rest, he stripped off his jumper, tied it around his waist, restarted it, and carried on.

After fifteen minutes, the bushes had been truly decimated. Blueberry, gooseberry, whatever they had been in the previous spring months, they were now nothing more than a broken pile of twigs shrouded in a veil of dust. Eric took another pause and surveyed his handiwork. Predominant aromas of petrol and sawdust knotted the air, and a bubble of pride rose through his gut. It was looking good. Really good. Well, almost all of it was.

With its broken glass and metal framing, Eric had naturally avoided the greenhouse area in his chainsaw-wielding juncture. Unfortunately, now that so much of the rest had been flattened, its obtrusiveness stood out like a Marilyn Manson wannabe at a rendition of Stravinsky's *The Firebird*. Eric kept the engine running as he perused. Its low, growling patter was just loud enough to drown out the ever-increasing chattering from the other allotments. More and more faces peered over the tops of their perennials, having grown interested in his goings-on. He placed the chainsaw on the ground and strode into the rubble, kicking aside the smaller twigs and stones and tossing a long, sawn-off branch, and metal girder to the side. Eric was not a man who left a job half done, and this was no exception. There had to be a way to tackle the greenhouse today. There had to be. He flicked a piece of glass with his foot.

The problem was all the fragments. There were so many little pieces of glass that the only way he'd be able to clear the patch was to pick them all up by hand. There were big bits too though. Huge sheets, the size of a coffee table, jagged and cracked, jutted out of the earth. Even if he did manage to pull those out, Eric wasn't entirely sure he knew what to do with them afterwards. Still, he glanced at his watch. He was meant to pick Suzy up in forty minutes in order to get back to the tool hire place before it closed for its Christmas break. If he drove fast, that still left him with twenty more minutes to work. Crouching down, he began to pick up the glass.

He had done a good job of averting the locals thus far, although he suspected his previous outburst with the water butt, combined with wildly waving a chainsaw, had had something to do with the matter. Now that he was on his hands and knees, however, he appeared to be an easy target.

'Big job you've done there, laddy.'

The man who spoke had crow-like eyes and a long, ratty nose.

'Still got a way to go,' Eric said without lifting his head.

'Aye. You want to be careful. 'S broken glass in there.'

Eric didn't respond. He continued to remove fragments from the mulching soil.

'Big saw you got going there. You know it's –'

'Sorry,' Eric said. 'I don't mean to be rude, only I'm short on time. Is there anything in particular I can help you with?'

The man opened his mouth then shut it again. Without so much as a nod, Eric's head went back down into the weeds. A minute or so later a throat cleared behind him. Eric gritted his teeth and ignored it. He had finally managed to wrap his fingers around two smooth edges of a large sheet of glass and was wiggling it against the binding stems and roots. Letting go of it now would cause the thing to slip back out of his grasp and probably smash into a thousand pieces. The voice coughed again.

'Hey there, laddy —'

'Could you hold on a second?' The sweat was beading on Eric's fingertips. He could feel the glass inching out of his grip. 'I'm kind of occupied.'

'I can see that. It's only —'

'Just one minute, okay? If you can give me one minute?'

'I thought you might —'

'Can you just hold on one bloody second?'

Eric stepped back as he spoke. His fingers squeezed at the sheet, emitting a high-pitched squeak. One inch more, that was all he had to move it, one inch more to free it from all the vines and creepers and finally render this place usable. With the most forceful tug he could manage, his elbows sprang back and for less than a heartbeat, the massive pane balanced in his dampening grasp. Then, as if in slow motion, the whole thing tilted, wobbled, and fell with a sickening crash to the ground.

'Fuck! Fucking bollocks.' Eric kicked the ground, his soft-toed boot landing squarely on the point of a shard of broken glass. 'Argh! Fuck!' he yelled as a searing pain bolted from his big toe all the way up his leg. It was blinding, horrific. Every nerve end from his toe to his calf was on fire. 'Fuck, fuck, fuck!'

'Now, hold on a minute, laddy —'

'Bollocking, buggering —'

'Look here, you might —'

'*What?* What do you want?'

Eric could feel the wetness of blood pooling at the end of his shoe. A smell of ash and burning was muddling in his senses. His head began to swim. He turned to the man with the ratty nose.

'What is it? What do you want?'

The man's jaw momentarily slackened. His gaze lowered onto Eric's bleeding toe before returning to meet his eyes.

'I thought you might want to know that your chainsaw's on fire,' he said.

CHAPTER 13

TO GIVE TOM his due, he managed to keep up the small talk all the way to A&E. Even in the allotment, when Eric was draped over his shoulder, whimpering and wincing with every step as he left a trail of blood from the plot to the car, Tom had managed to maintain a positive demeanour.

'Don't think you've severed an artery,' he said. 'There's lots more blood when you sever an artery.'

Humiliation was an understatement. As Eric limped out, glass shard still protruding from his toe cap, it seemed that every Burlam resident over the age of sixty-five had come out to watch the event. Leading the crowd was, of course, Norman, who had, of course, appeared in time to see the smoke pouring out of the chainsaw. The day was a fail in every way possible. A&E was rammed, full of inebriated adults, children who had swallowed Christmas tree baubles, and doctors and nurses who looked so stressed that they should have been admitted themselves.

He lost the shoe. It could have been a lot worse, but still, seeing the insole ripped mercilessly from the leather upper of his two-hundred-pound outdoor shoes was never going to be a nice event. The doctor on his case wasn't going to pull the glass out without assessing the damage underneath first, so with a delicate hand, he cut around the sole, then the sock. Needless to say, once he'd done that, he pulled the glass straight out anyway.

Later, Eric wondered whether Tom would inform Lydia of her brother-in-law's pitiful screaming, though, at the time, he could barely even think through the pain. Four stitches and a bucket load of shame. It could have been worse, but it really didn't feel like it.

It was dark by the time they left the hospital. Not early evening dark, or just as the moon rises dark, but stars in the sky, all curtains drawn, very close to midnight dark. The tool hire place closed at six and didn't reopen again until the new year. Eric didn't even care. All that mattered was his throbbing toe and battered ego. Besides, Tom had looked over the chainsaw and decided it was most likely just an issue with the oil. An easy fix. Eric would probably only have to pay for the late return, he said. Eric didn't have the energy to respond.

While his foot felt like it had been dunked in a vat of concentrated sulphuric acid and his head was fuzzy, furry, and altogether rather confused from the painkillers, Suzy was beyond half-cut from an exceptionally extended brunch and a teetotal sister who insisted on topping up her glass the entire time. Given that the trains had stopped running, and no one was fit to drive, there was no choice but to stay the night at Tom and Lydia's. Abi camped down in the boys' room, under a makeshift tepee Lydia had fashioned out of bed sheets and old broom handles, while Suzy and Eric got the spare room. The batik patchwork quilt that covered their bed was embroidered with tiny mirrors and golden thread, and smelt of sheep and ayurvedic nonsense.

'Lydia got this when she first went to India,' Suzy said as she hoisted Eric's leg up and onto the bed.

'I don't think she's washed it since,' Eric replied.

He wriggled himself under the sheet, grimacing against the pain of his foot. Through the walls, he could hear the cousins giggling.

'I'm sorry you've had an awful day,' Suzy said. 'I hate seeing you like this. You know it really isn't worth all this stress.'

'Don't say it,' Eric cut her off before she could continue. 'I'm not getting rid of her. Certainly not after today. There is no way that man gets to win.'

'But what is he winning? Your dad is dead, Eric. There are no more competitions.'

'That's what you think.'

'Well if that's the case, what's wrong with you just letting him win? What are you gaining from all this? We hardly see you as it is. The last thing I want is Abi not seeing her father for the next two years because he's too busy at work and down the allotment.'

'That's not going to happen,' he said.

'Hmm,' was all Suzy said in response.

Christmas, and the days that bookend it, were a washout. For six days it rained constantly; hard, vertical pillars of water that turned windows opaque and made travelling anywhere a suicide risk. The sky remained an indolent grey, bleak, dull, and without imagination; Eric reflected the sentiment to a tee. The office shutdown over Christmas made it impossible to get on top of things the way he would have liked. Still, he lay on the sofa, foot propped up with a mountain of cushions, and fired off emails, waiting in vain for responses and silently seething as each half hour passed without so much as an out-of-office reply. Even Jack Nelson took two days to get back to him, and told him not to worry, they would sort out any issues in the new year.

Christmas Day was pleasant enough. Abi was pleased with her presents, which had nothing to do with him. All the same, it made a fuzzy ball of sentiment blossom as he observed the unabashed glee with which she ran into their bedroom, stocking in hand, leapt on their beds, and tore at the paper. From Suzy, Eric got a gin tasting course, twenty types of gin in one afternoon; it sounded ideal. From Abi, he received a mug. The image on said mug resembled something that a goat having an epileptic fit with a paintbrush between its teeth would create if said goat were particularly skilled at painting eyeballs and ears.

'Do you like it, Daddy?' Abi said. 'It's abstract art. We're doing abstract art at school and this is what you look like. See, you're even wearing a tie.'

'It's wonderful, baby,' Eric said, taking the mug in hand. 'Remind me how much we're paying for this school again?' he said to Suzy.

The first day the sun made an appearance was the 28th December. In Eric's mind, the gap between Boxing Day and New Year's Eve was some form of time vortex. The wrapping paper and leftovers had long been discarded and forgotten, yet it was still a sizeable period until the inevitable new year. You could guarantee, during that five-day-long black hole, that nobody you spoke to had any idea what actual day of the week it was, and as soon as the twenty-seventh arrived, no one had any plans either. In Eric's mind the working week would be much better preserved should New Year be shuffled a few days earlier.

Suzy opened the curtains, causing Eric to squint at the sudden onslaught of light. She then redeemed herself slightly by handing him a cup of tea.

'How's the foot?' she asked as she proceeded to remove the duvet and begin prodding at his dressing. 'It looks much better. I don't think it'll even leave much of a scar.'

'I have to be honest, I was worried about that. Big toe scars can be quite stereotyping. People might start to think I belong to a gang or something.'

'Fine. Be like that. So, have you got anything planned for today?'

'Only to catch up on a bit of work —'

'Good. Because we're going out.'

Eric shuffled himself into a more upright position. 'Did you have anywhere in mind?'

'Funny you should ask,' Suzy said.

Eric tried to make her see sense. While Suzy was right from one perspective – if he was going to keep up with this whole escapade then he really couldn't take a weekend off no matter how much he wanted to – she had no real idea what the actual situation entailed.

'It's not safe for Abi,' Eric said for the third time. 'God knows what's lurking about in there. She could catch rabies. For all I know, I already have.'

'You're being dramatic.'

'Besides. I can only just stand. And you expect me to go digging about in six inches of mud?'

'No, I expect you and Abi to sit at the sides and play cards while I dig about in six inches of mud.'

'Wow, that sounds exciting.'

Suzy's *look* followed.

THE THIN RAYS of sun that cast every other plot in the allotment with a narrow glimmer of optimism could do nothing to disguise the dismal landscape that stood before them. A smell of bonfires drifted in from beyond the hedgerows, bringing up memories of crematoriums and ashes. Maybe burning it would be a solution, Eric pondered.

'It looks a lot better than it did,' he insisted. 'I wish I had some photos to show you. It really does look much, much better. Loads better. Heaps and heaps.' But his voice couldn't hide his disappointment.

'See,' he said after another minute's silence. 'I told you it was a stupid idea coming here.'

It did look better than last time. All the bushes and dead plants had been cut back to nothing and one side of the greenhouse had been all but cleared of saw-toothed broken glass. That it looked better was not in question. Whether it would ever look anything more than a health inspector's wet dream, was.

'Just tell me what to do and I'll do it,' Suzy said and pulled on her gardening gloves. 'The sooner we get started, the sooner we'll get it done.'

'I really don't think there's anything you can do,' Eric said, then he stopped talking; he was wise enough to know when he was beaten.

Eric had spied some green gardening bins. They were way back under the notice board at the entrance, so while he and Abi folded out their picnic chairs and divided the cards ready for an epic game of Top Trumps, Suzy headed back to the gate to collect one of the four-feet containers.

'I can help,' Eric said several times as he watched Suzy crouched over what had once been a tomato sack, pulling out another handful of weeds and refuse.

'It's fine,' Suzy said. 'I like it. It's therapeutic.' One by one, she shovelled forkfuls of debris out of the ground and into the bin. Eric sat in his chair, leg extended, admiring his wife gliding between the detritus, attempting to make a little sense out of the chaos.

'Make sure you stick the fork in first,' Eric said. 'Don't just put your hands in. There are rats in there.'

'Can we have one, Daddy?' Abi piped up. 'Harry Nini at school has a pet rat. Can we have a pet rat too?'

'No. Now beat this. Silvertip Shark. Maximum depth, eight hundred metres.'

She went back to studying her cards.

Eric wasn't sure why they'd had a gardening fork hidden in the depths of their utility room cupboards in their London home, but watching Suzy attempt to move the weeds with its skewed prongs and bent handle confirmed his thoughts that they would need to buy better tools. More money being spent without a penny in return.

It was a little under an hour later – when Abi pulled out the Top Trumps Disney Princess cards – that Eric called a halt to the work.

'You should stop,' he said. 'You've done loads.'

'Just another ten minutes.'

'Really, hun, we should head back. Besides, I don't feel right just sitting here watching you and Abi's bored stiff.'

'Rubbish. You're still having fun aren't you, sweetheart?'

'Nuh,' Abi said non-committedly. 'Dad's really rubbish. He only says what's on the cards. It's way more fun playing with you.'

'Fine.' Suzy wiped the sweat from her forehead, leaving a slight smear of dirt in its wake. She stepped back to observe her handiwork. 'To be honest, I'm surprised at how little I've got done. I thought I'd cleared far more.'

'What are you on about? I can see at least thirty centimetres there with no weeds on it at all.'

She swiped for her husband, but Eric caught her hand and kissed it.

'You've done amazingly,' Eric insisted. 'There's always going to be loads to do. We could come down every day for a month and the place would still look like a shit heap.'

'Eric.'

'Sorry.' He hoisted himself up to standing and limped over to the plot. 'I mean it will still look a mosquito breeding-ground cesspool. But you've done an amazing job. Thank you.'

'And it wasn't that bad having us down here with you?'

'I guess not.'

From his newly elevated standing position, Eric gazed past his wife and surveyed the plot behind her. He was reasonably sure he could see where she'd been working.

CHAPTER 14

NEW YEAR'S DAY brought an inevitable headache, aching muscles, and a mouth that tasted of dry slippers and flaccid mushrooms. It was unfortunate that it was the same day of their next planned trip to Burlam.

They had gone to their neighbours, Ben and Belinda, whom they saw on average three times a year: the inaugural summer BBQ, held sometime between May and July; Ben and Belinda's joint birthday, which Eric knew for certain was either in September or October, or perhaps November; and New Year's Eve. His social ties with these long-term friends were in fact so tenuous that when Eric had bumped into Belinda down the Indian takeaway the week before Christmas, it had taken him a solid two minutes to fit a name to the face. She just didn't look right without a sparkly scarf around her neck, white wine spritzer in her hand, and party blower buzzing in an ungainly manner from between her lips. The combination of drink and painkillers resulted in a considerably later start to the day than Eric had anticipated.

It was a damp day, with a hazy drizzle that fogged up the windows and caused frequent, involuntary shivers when he glanced outside and caught sight of the sky. The pain in Eric's foot had lessened to a dull throb which, provided he avoided sudden movements, or particularly trenchant surfaces

– Abi's Lego Princess starship being one of the most recurring offenders – remained moderately pain-free. The leftover alcohol in his system was no doubt helping the situation too.

Suzy had picked up three pairs of gardening gloves in the post-Christmas sales, which she was keen to put to the test. Hers and Eric's were both sturdily made, with thick faux leather grips on the fingers and palms, and a suede cuff which covered a good four-inches above the wrist line. Abi's were much more impressive, with floral linings, fancy stitch work around all the seams, and appliquéd ducks on the top.

Abi had loved them in the shop. Now, however, she'd decided they were too babyish.

'Why can't I have the same as you and Mummy?' she said.

'Mummy and I wanted the same ones as you have,' Eric said. 'Only they didn't do them in our size.'

'I'll look like a kid wearing these,' she said and skulked off to her room, slamming each door in the interim behind her.

Abi's vile mood continued throughout the car journey. The music on every radio station was "crap," the heater was either too hot or too cold or not blowing out enough air or blowing out too much air. Her seat belt was too tight, her iPad didn't have enough battery, and Suzy's driving was making her feel sick.

'I can't spend two hours with her in the allotment being like this,' Eric said to Suzy, not even bothering to hush his voice. 'I want to throttle her already.'

'She's just out of her routine. Why don't we go get some breakfast somewhere first?'

Eric suspected that a large majority of the clientele at The Shed were there with the aim of relieving their hangovers from the previous night, and for a minute he worried they may struggle to get a seat, but when Griff spied him at the door he beckoned him over. They hurried inside, where he found them a table at the back next to a window. Still not feeling brave enough to face a complete Fat Bastard, Eric opted for a Greedy Git, although given that Suzy pilfered half his bacon, black pudding, and one of the sausages, he once again wished he'd ordered up. Abi's meal was, unsurprisingly, wrong.

'I didn't think the beans would be on the bread,' she whined. 'You know I don't like it when the beans touch the bread.'

Steeling himself against the tension building in his muscles, Eric called Griff over for a re-order, this time specifying that the beans be in an entirely separate container placed on the other side of the plate to the toast.

'Why don't you head off?' Suzy said. 'We can walk down when we've finished here.'

'It's quite a walk.'

'It's fine. It'll give missy here a chance to walk off that chip on her shoulder.'

'Are you sure?' Eric wasn't convinced.

'Positive.'

Eric got up from the table and went to settle the bill. He glanced at the scrap of paper, noting that Abi's first breakfast was missing.

'We'll pay for all of it,' Eric said.

'It's fine,' Griff insisted. 'I've got three of my own. Grown up now mind, but little shits they could be when they wanted to. It's no problem.'

'If you're sure?' Eric said, then feeling guilty placed the remaining balance in the little jam jar labelled tips.

Eric was surprised how quickly he forgot about the drizzle. As he entered through the gates, he grabbed one of the green bins and motioned briefly but politely to Janice, indicating the bin as his reason for not being able to stop. The dampness from sweat and the dampness from the rain were soon indistinguishable as he continued from where they'd let off the previous weekend. Perhaps it was the lessened pressure of not having Suzy or Abi with him there, or perhaps the lack of time constraints, but the work seemed easier today. He found a rhythm, fork, swing, dump, fork, swing, dump, and even his foot wasn't hurting enough to distract him.

'Carrot cake?'

Cynthia's flame-red hair was currently hidden beneath the blue hood of her wax jacket. Extended towards Eric was a long tube of crumpled aluminium foil, the insides of which contained a rather orange looking carrot cake.

'I baked it this morning. It's not my best, but it's better than my worst.'

'Oh, well, um. It looks lovely,' Eric said.

'Take a piece,'

'Actually, I've only just had breakfast.'

'Then take a piece for later. Or take some home for the family. I hear you had them up here helping a couple of weeks back?'

As she spoke she was pulling out several slices, sealing them in a ziplock bag which had appeared from her pocket, and handing them to Eric. A quick sniff caused a slight rumble beneath his belly button.

'Thank you.' He took the package of cake, which appeared to be almost three-quarters of the loaf. 'Yes, they just came up to help for an hour or so.'

'And your foot? How's that holding up? You've got to be so careful ...' She stopped mid-flow and frowned. 'I'm sorry. I'm doing that old lady thing, aren't I? Asking you lots of questions and not giving you any time to respond.'

'It's fine.'

'No, I should let you get on. You've got lots to be going on with.' She turned as if to leave, then paused. There was something about the way she stopped, as if suspended mid-animation, that made Eric wait.

'I know you don't really know me,' she said, turning back. 'And I know you and Norman didn't get off on quite the right foot. But I was wondering if perhaps in the next few weeks, if the weather gets a bit better, you might, you might ...'

'Yes?'

'I know it's a lot to ask. I do really. But I was hoping you might be able to take him out in that car of yours?' There was a childlike quiver to her lips when she spoke, and something about her eyes tugged at a place in Eric's chest cavity. 'He used to go out with your dad quite frequently, you see. And I know he misses it. At our age, something like that ... it would mean a lot to him, that's what I'm trying to say. But not if it's any trouble, of course. I don't want to inconvenience you.'

The tug in Eric's chest had built to a point where it now affected his throat as well, and when he spoke the words came out far more hoarse and croaky than he'd expected.

'Well, it's really not very good taking her out in weather like this —'

'Of course, I completely understand. Forget I asked. Forget I asked.'

'But I'm sure in the spring when it's not quite so wet.'

The old woman's face bloomed into a smile, squashing her wrinkles into even deeper crevices.

'Thank you,' she said. 'It would mean the world to him. To us both.'

With a sudden awareness of heat rising to his cheeks, Eric busied himself with the topsoil. He could sense Cynthia still standing there, watching him, but he kept his head down, for fear she might burst into tears or worse still, try to hug him. A few seconds later she spoke again.

'Well enjoy the carrot cake. And I do hope I get to meet the family next time they're around.'

Eric paused, considered his next sentence, and said it anyway.

'If you can hang on a few minutes, you can meet them now,' he said. 'And they can you thank you in person for the carrot cake.'

'I don't want to interfere with your family time,' she said. 'Besides, I ought to dash. I need to be home for when Norman gets back.' With that she scurried away around the back of her potting shed and down the path, stopping to offer a final wave before she disappeared out of view.

IT WAS another forty minutes before Abi and Suzy arrived. The drizzle had subsided into a wet, muggy mist that soaked into the earth and made everything smell like a cheap pub side-salad. Abi looked to be in a better mood, in the sense that she was no longer throwing random screaming fits, but still had a scowl reminiscent of a cat who had just spent three hours with its tail caught in the tube of a vacuum cleaner. Oblivious to the ongoing cold spell and onset of winter, she'd somehow managed to find a strawberry ice lolly, which she repeatedly licked, shuddered, then licked again. Neither the rain nor the brain freeze could deter her from her sub-zero treat.

'You've got a fair bit done,' Suzy said, coming up behind him, and placing her hands on the small of his back. 'It's getting there. It's definitely getting there. Another three or four weeks and you'll have most of it cleared.'

'Yeah, if I can get it all sorted by the beginning of March I'll be pleased.'

'Any idea what you're going to do with the greenhouse?'

Eric cast a disapproving eye over the rusting monstrosity.

'I guess the tip. But I'm not going to think about that now.' He turned his attention over to Abi. 'Right,' he said. 'Time for you to get your hands dirty.' He rolled up his sleeves in a mockery of hard work then kicked up his good heel and dug a line in the dirt. 'I need you to pull up all the plants on this side of the line,' he said. 'But you're not to go over this line. Okay? There's still glass and junk and God knows what other crap in there.'

'Language,' Suzy chided.

'Gotcha. Mustn't go over the line. Lots of crap,' Abi paraphrased, proceeding to lick her ice lolly, and showing no signs of moving. Eric smiled at his wife.

Suzy slipped on her gloves and tied her hair back in a ponytail. A sweet gust of nostalgia swept through Eric. There was something about the way her hands ran through her hair that reminded him of the way she was when they first met. Determined, focused. Not that she wasn't still, he just didn't get to see it so often anymore.

Eric couldn't help but steal glances at his wife. Nothing was ever too much trouble for Suzy, no task too big, no problem unsolvable. She took everything in her stride. Her first husband was a dick, that was for sure, but it was a fact for which Eric would be eternally grateful. If he hadn't been, he and Suzy wouldn't be where they were now.

Aware of the need to refocus on the job in hand, he cast her one more wistful gaze before bending down and attacking his weed problem. Eric was knee high in nettles, grabbing them from as close to the roots as possible when Suzy stopped.

'Oh, I forgot, this was on the notice board for you.' She stood up and pulled a thin white envelope out of her pocket. Eric's name was typed on a sticky label that was stuck on the front. In the top corner, a green stamp consisting of a crossed fork and shovel had been unevenly inked. Eric took it from her.

'Thanks. Where did you say it was?'

'Pinned up on the notice board by the bins.'

Eric shrugged. 'It's probably just something about the tenancy. I forgot I had to pay it this month.' He ran his finger under the seal and ripped the envelope open. Inside was a single sheet of A4 paper, the same stamp on the corner beside some unfamiliar address.

Heat rose up through his belly, accompanied by a definite acceleration in heart rate. It was only a short letter – two and a third lines long, with a couple of extra bullet points beneath – but by the time Eric had reached the final words his fists were balled, his pulse pounding, and his eyes bulged so wide they looked to be making an escape bid from their sockets.

'What is it?' Suzy said.

'They have to be fucking joking.'

CHAPTER 15

ERIC RANG CHRISTIAN Eaves. It took six attempts to get through. Each of the previous tries he stayed on the line – the sawtooth tone cutting through his eardrum – until it went to voicemail. It didn't deter him. While Suzy drove, and Abi slept, Eric kept on ringing.

Finally, he picked up.

'Can they do this?' Eric said when he'd explained the situation in microscopic detail. 'Surely they can't do this, can they?'

Christian Eaves was silent down the end of the phone. The sound of smacking lips echoed several times before he eventually spoke.

'Mr Sibley, I don't mean to sound rude, but firstly, today is New Year's Day which, like most people, I am spending with my family. Secondly, why exactly have you come to me with this problem?'

'Who else am I meant to go to?'

'This sounds like something to be sorted out within the committee. At this point in time, it's not a legal issue.'

'But if they can do this. If they *do* do this, I'll lose the car, won't I? That's what you're saying right? I'll lose the car?'

'If it comes to that. Then yes, but, Mr Sibley, this still might all be some misunderstanding —'

'After all the work I've put in.'

'I'm sorry, Mr Sibley.'

'F-ing bastards.' Eric slammed his fist against the dashboard. Suzy shot him a glare. 'She's asleep,' Eric mouthed, then noticed that Abi was very much awake and staring at her father, her mouth opened in a gawp. Eric took a few deep breaths, mouthed an apology to his daughter, and put the phone back up to his ear.

'Okay, so there has to be some way around this. Something I can do? I've been down at that *flipping* allotment every weekend for the last month and I've got some moderately impressive scars to prove it. Surely that has to count for something?'

Christian Eaves sighed. The vibrations fizzled down the line.

'I really wish that was enough,' he said. 'But unfortunately, you can't maintain the allotment if you no longer possess the tenancy to it.'

'Well thanks for nothing,' Eric said and hung up the phone.

Suzy was staring at the road, pretending to concentrate, with her cheeks sucked in, and hands gripping the steering wheel. Eric considered the fact he should probably apologise for his language but decided against it. He was an adult. If he wanted to swear in front of his daughter, he should be able to do so without being made to feel like he'd personally drowned a dozen day-old Labrador puppies. He sank back into the seat, closed his eyes, and breathed in loudly through his nostrils. Fifteen seconds later his eyes sprang open, he retrieved his phone from his pocket, and with his thumb tapping at a record speed, began to type on the screen.

'What are you doing?' Suzy said in a monotone voice he knew was intended to feign disinterest.

'Looking for something,' he said.

'For what?'

Eric stopped staring at his screen and turned to her. 'Christian Eaves said this was a committee decision. Not a legal one. So, I'm trying to find out who's on the committee. That way I can appeal to their better judgement. Or find out if it's a misunderstanding. Or at least offer them some kind of bribe.' He said the last line with a slightly jovial lilt although truthfully neither he nor Suzy was entirely sure if he was joking.

'Maybe it was meant for your father?' Suzy said. 'Maybe they've been holding onto it since last year?'

Eric shook his head. 'It's addressed to Eric Sibley, not Mr Sibley. And besides, it's dated last week. I mean, Unsatisfactory Cultivation. What does that even mean? What do they expect me to be cultivating? It's bloody winter for crying out loud. And seven days. What kind of notice is that? Surely I can't be the only person with an allotment there who has an actual job. Actual working commitments. They're a bunch of nasty, small-minded, bigoted coffin-dodgers the bloody lot of them.'

'What's a coffin-dodger?' Abi asked from the back.

'Your dad,' Suzy replied. 'If he doesn't start watching his language.'

Eric muttered something quietly under his breath, though judging by Suzy's instantaneous glare he didn't mutter it quietly enough.

The village website wasn't cut out for mobile use, and after ten minutes of trying to find contact details, Eric decided to abandon the task until he was home and on his laptop. In the meanwhile, he checked his work emails. His inbox had filled over the day. Apparently, the academy chain had been so impressed with Eric's handling of their account they'd asked the company to manage another three of their outlets, once again in the education field. Eric's stomach fluttered. Hartley had hinted about restructuring the junior and senior associate directors from regions to focus groups for over a year now. If that were to happen, he'd have to be a definite shoo-in for the education position now. At least that was one bit of good news. Perhaps if he got the position, he could buy another Aston Martin and be rid of the whole fiasco.

AT HOME, Suzy ushered Abi straight into the downstairs shower, rather than allowing her to traipse up the stairs with her mud-covered jeans and ice-cream-sticky fingers. Eric wasn't entirely sure how she'd got so much mud on her, as the closest he saw her get to the actual allotment patch was when she was trying to work out if snails could hang upside down on nettle leaves.

Steam drifted into the room as Eric fired up the computer. He would shower later; now there were more important things at hand.

The allotment committee page was part of the same Burlam website where he'd advertised for help. Eric had initially thought identifying who to contact would be a quick process, but it turned out there were an awful lot of committees going on in Burlam.

There was a carnival committee, a horticultural committee, and the waterways committee. St Andrew's Parish Choir committee and The St Andrew's Recorder Club committee shared a joint page, as did the St Jude's summer, autumn and winter festival committees. There was the Burlam organists committee, the Burlam fisheries committee, the Burlam am-dram committee, not to mention the local vegetarian, vegan, and freegan community pages. There was the school council, the food and clothes banks volunteer pages. The Burlam for buildings, the Burlam against building, the Burlam quilters, twitters, and philatelist pages as well as a whole three extra pages of groups and assemblies that Eric didn't read through because he'd already found what he was looking for. The Burlam Columbia Avenue Allotment Committee. Eric clicked on the link. The page took a second to load. The second it did his throat clamped shut.

The banner across the top of the page was a picture. Eric recognised the setting as outside the town hall although the car parking spaces had been completely overhauled in place of tables and marquees and tents. In the centre, a group of people stood beneath a hand-painted sign that read Burlam Allotments and was decorated with childish drawings of fruit and vegetables. In the centre of the group was a man sitting on a chair. On his lap, a pile of what looked like courgettes and runner beans. Eric almost didn't recognise him, with the flat cap and smile. But there was no mistaking the narrow eyes and sticky-out ears.

'Dad,' Eric said.

Eric was certain that the sudden onset of emotion was caused more by surprise than actual distress, and in less than a minute he'd sniffed back any tears and was once again focused on the task at hand. He scrolled down, paying as little attention as possible to the photos of the harvest festival and autumn fair until he reached the committee members. It appeared a fair glut of people were involved in the running of an allotment. As well as the normal roles you'd expect from any committee – Secretary, Treasurer, Deputy chair, etcetera – there were also more particular roles, such as Trading Manager, Fair Growth Manager, and Pesticide Control Manager. Eric was unsurprised to see both Janice and Cynthia's name on the board of committee members, although at that precise moment there was only one name that mattered.

Eric's fingers flexed then clenched. His nostrils flared. *Chairman*, the page read. *Norman Kettlewell*.

'That miserable old —'

'Eric ...'

'You know why he's doing this don't you? Bitterness. That's why. Spiteful, old-man bitterness. Well if they think they can bully me out, they've got another think coming.'

'Perhaps if you just talk to him.'

'You can't talk to people like that, Suzy, you can't. They don't listen. No, these people need action. And so much for not being a legal case. I've got a legal case. He said he didn't want me having the car. The second time I spoke to him he said that. Probably thinks he's next in line or some stupid crap like that.'

'You need to calm down.'

'And his wife. What a conniving old wench.'

'Eric —'

'No, I mean it. You know what she asked me this morning? She asked me if I would take him out in Sally some time. She actually had the audacity to ask me, when all the time she's plotting this behind my back.'

'Perhaps she didn't know.'

'Of course she knew. And she gave us cake.' Eric stopped. 'Where is it? Where's the cake? You're not eating it. It's probably poisoned. They probably thought they could get rid of me that way.'

Suzy placed her hands firmly on her hips.

'You're being irrational. You know what you sound like, don't you? You sound like an absolute loon.'

'Where's the cake?'

'Abi and I already ate it in the car.'

'When?'

'When you were busy screaming down the phone at the poor solicitor. And look, we're not dead. Not even a little.'

Eric harrumphed.

'Look,' Suzy said. 'Look at yourself.' She took hold of his hands. 'Think of it this way. If what your father really wanted was to drive you mad, like you keep insisting, then it's working. And I thought you said you weren't going to let him win?'

Eric pouted, sucked on his bottom lip, and tried to wriggle out of her grip like a chided toddler.

'As far as I can see, you have two options,' Suzy said. 'You can take a week's holiday, go down to Burlam, and get the place sorted. You said yourself you've got weeks and weeks stacked up. That's option one. Otherwise, you can ring Mr Eaves and tell him that you no longer want to keep the car. I don't care either way. But this,' she moved her hand indicating Eric as a whole. 'These outbursts. They've got to stop. Poor Abi thinks you're having a nervous breakdown. And I'm not entirely sure she's wrong.'

Eric dug his toes into the carpet.

'Fine,' he muttered to his feet.

'Pardon?'

'I said fine. I'll do it. I'll take the holiday. I'll go down to Burlam.'

'Good,' said Suzy. She reached up on tiptoes and kissed the top of his head. From the bathroom, Abi yelled, and Suzy went to her aid.

'If Norman Kettlewell wants my plot acceptably cultivated, he can have it acceptably cultivated,' Eric said. Then he sat at the computer and got to work.

CHAPTER 16

ARRANGEMENTS COULD ONLY be made for the following Thursday. It wasn't ideal, but it was manageable and in turn, meant that Eric could get a lot more real work done than he'd envisioned. He felt slightly bad, lying to Suzy when he left dressed in his jeans and Barbour jacket, his polished black brogues squashed inside his briefcase each morning, but he was doing it for her too. This method meant Eric wouldn't get stressed about missing work, nor would he have to miss out on seeing Abi over the weekend. It was ideal for everyone, really.

He kept a spare suit and a couple of shirts at work, which he changed into in the men's toilets. Although they were from last year and a little snug around the midriff, they looked perfectly suitable for the morning team meetings and staff briefings he had to run. Greg made one or two digs about the tensile strength of buttons, but then Eric refused to take clothing remarks from a man who still wore Velcro fastening shoes. Being at work also meant Eric was able to cover for Jack and take one of the head honcho clients out for lunch, earning him some serious brownie points in the process.

As an excuse for not taking the car each day, Eric concocted a reason about weekday parking charges in Burlam. He also downloaded a birdsong clip to his computer, which he played quietly in the background whenever Suzy rang, and arrived home rubbing his calves and whinging about how much his back ached and knees throbbed. On Tuesday when he had to stay late for an emergency meeting on the restructuring of the Southeast clinics he rang Suzy and told her the trains were delayed – debris on the tracks – which she bought without hesitation. That was the advantage of being a husband that never usually lied; Suzy always assumed he was telling the truth.

On Thursday morning, the alarm buzzed its way into his dream. Eric yawned, stretched a little, then remembering what day it was, bounded from the bed in a similar manner to that which Abi had done on Christmas Day. By the time Suzy had showered and dressed, Eric was on his second cup of coffee and neither his hands nor his feet could make contact with the same surface for more than a nanosecond before finding somewhere else to be.

'What's wrong with you today?'

'Nothing,' Eric said as he bounced from one side of the kitchen to the other. 'Just excited that's all. The allotment's coming on really well. Really, really well.'

'That's brilliant.' She took the cup of coffee from between his shaking hands and kissed him on the lips. 'I'd love to see some photos. Can you remember to take some today please?'

'Definitely.' He glanced at his watch. 'I'd better get going, actually. I was going to take the car down today.'

'Sally?'

'No, the Audi. Sally needs a proper check over before I take her out in this weather. Maybe next weekend though we could all go for a drive? If it's not too cold.'

'That sounds like a wonderful idea. You know, if someone had told me six months ago that you'd be taking a week out of the office to go down and work on your dad's old allotment, I would have thought they'd lost the plot. I'm so proud of you, you know.'

Eric's stomach squirmed as he avoided his wife's gaze.

'Well have a nice day,' he said. 'And tell Abi I love her lots.'

'Will do.'

It was a perfect day for driving, and a few miles onto the A12 Eric regretted his decision not to take Sally after all. It was windy enough that the leaves danced around on the tarmac daring you to chase them, but not windy enough to affect the drive. The sky was cerulean, with white clouds dappling the skyscape. It was only the seventh of January, but it could have been May the air was so mild. *If all the year goes this well,* Eric thought, *I'll be laughing.*

He had rung the company before leaving home. One of their representatives would be at the allotment at ten with a few bits of paper for Eric to sign. Then he'd be good to go. Unfortunately, their representative needed to do several more drop-offs that morning so wouldn't be able to stay and help.

'Would that be a problem?' the man down the phone line asked.

'Not at all,' Eric replied. Everything was going to plan.

He drove into Burlam, down the High Street, and was heading to park in what he now considered his spot, when he encountered a snag in the form of a three axle, semi-articulated, thirty-tonne truck – although none of those features he knew until the ginger-haired, freckle-faced pubescent told him this.

'I thought you worked at Tools 'R' Us?' Eric said.

'*Tools4U*, and I do,' the boy said in response to Eric's question. 'You ordered from one of our third parties. It's all our gear. Just means it costs you more, that's all.'

'Brilliant,' Eric said.

'Actually, you're lucky. We wouldn't have been able to loan you it. Not after the mess you caused with that chainsaw. Have you never heard of bar oil?'

Ignoring his remark, Eric wandered over towards the cab and surveyed the lorry. There was absolutely no way it was going to get any closer to the allotment. Eric was amazed he'd got it that far.

'And you drove this thing? On your own?' Eric said, still searching for the sign of some other member of staff.

'Got my HGV licence four days after my eighteenth birthday.'

'Which was when exactly?'

The boy didn't reply.

'Look,' he said. 'I've backed it up this far. I'll get it down the ramp for you and I'll talk you through the controls, which you may or may not listen to. After that, I've got to go.'

'That's fine.'

The boy frowned. 'I know there's no point in me asking you this. But have you ever used one of these before?'

Eric laughed. It was a deep manly laugh that was meant to give the impression of maturity and knowledge, but on reflection realised it made him sound like one of the villains from a *Scooby Doo* cartoon.

'Of course,' he said.

The boy rolled his eyes. 'Well, let's get this stuff signed and we'll get her unloaded.'

It was a two-and-a-half tonne, zero-tail-swing, mini digger with two tracking speeds, glass-enclosed cab, and a smell of petrol that got the testosterone flowing faster than a *Game of Thrones* mini-marathon. Its miniature caterpillar tracks and pygmy sized bucket reminded Eric of the type of toy you'd have at the seaside as a child, assuming you had the coolest and most irresponsible parents in history.

The boy, whose name Eric had now learnt to be Lewis, gave a brief demonstration, showing Eric where each of the controls were and how small an increment of movement was required.

'It's the opposite of cooking,' Lewis said. 'You can always take more out, but you can't put it back in. Same thing with speed. Just take it slow. Really, really slow.'

'Trust me, I will be going very, very slowly. Snail's pace. Arthritic snail's pace,' Eric said. 'As long as I'm done by nightfall, I'll be happy.'

'Well, I'll be picking it up at four, so you'll need to be done by then.'

'Fine, by four then. Either way. I will be fine.'

The boy pulled out his phone and checked the time. 'Are you sure you're okay? I mean, this flat bit here'll be easy, it's once you get onto those little paths, it gets harder. You've got a full tank of fuel, there's no way you'll use all that. I'd hang on a bit, see you down the lane, only I've got to get this next one delivered for eleven.'

'I'll be fine.'

'I can drive it down to the entrance if you want?'

'Lewis.' Eric stretched out his hand. 'Thank you for all your help. I will see you at four o'clock, and I have your number should any extreme emergencies pop up.'

'I'd rather they didn't.' He gave one more sceptical sigh towards the digger. Eric slapped him on the back.

'Fine,' Lewis said. 'I'll be off. Enjoy.'

Eric had to admit he was more than a little impressed watching Lewis maneuverer the thirty-tonne truck back onto the road and out through the estate.

'And this is where the fun begins,' he said.

Eric had, understandably, watched several YouTube videos on how to control a mini excavator since concocting his plan, and was reassured by the number of hillbillies that managed to manipulate the machinery with careless ease. If they, with their obvious lack of education and limited grasp of grammar, could do it, he most certainly could. Hopping up into the cab and squeezing himself around the controls, a horde of butterflies swarmed behind his belly button. As a stroke of luck, the allotment appeared empty for once, although he suspected it wouldn't stay that way for long. The last thing he wanted was for one particular naysayer to turn up and start interrogating him before he even started.

The engine was quieter than he'd expected, nothing like the high-octane thrum of the chainsaw. More a low, underworld growl. Eric snuggled into his seat, checked behind for any oncoming traffic, then pushed the lever forwards. Slowly and smoothly the excavator followed the route.

With his cheeks aching from grinning, he pushed the lever further forwards and trundled down the track towards the allotments. Of course it was easy; it was driving. Eric was good at driving. He was great in fact. Eric continued to bolster his own ego as he rolled on before glancing at the bare hedges beside him. His stomach fell. Despite his enthusiastic outlook, he was inching forwards slower than a sloth with muscular dystrophy. Still, better to take things slow and steady, he reminded himself. Slow and steady wins the race.

'Sod this,' he said two seconds later, changing his mind.

His thumb twitched towards the two-speed yellow button. How fast was fast, really? After all, if he carried on at this pace he wouldn't even reach the gate by four, let alone do the allotment. And it wasn't like he found it hard. He had perfect control. Eric hit the second speed.

Eric lurched backwards as the tracks clicked into the higher pace. A millisecond later he was back in control. The breeze whipped around the back of his neck as the trees moved past him. His boyish grin returned. This was better. Now he could get some real work done. He angled himself to make the entry to the allotment and glided between the gates like a pro. He would see if he could get a video of this on the way back; maybe Lewis could take one if he had the time. He probably wouldn't show it to Suzy though. No, he wouldn't show it to Suzy, but he may let Abi have a quick peek before bed tonight if she promised not to tell her mother.

Eric was past the entrance and squeezing himself between the first two plots. He had planned his route already, following an in-depth examination of Google Earth along with a few mental calculations. He knew which right and left turns would get him there with the least possible hassle and which paths were too narrow for him to try. The final route he'd decided on may not have been the shortest, but it avoided any nasty turns or bulbous polytunnels. Mentally he recalled his next action.

The excavator was sinking slightly. It was no more than expected, but still enough to churn up what little grass there was beneath the tracks. Eric had studied the allotment's terms and agreements where it was clearly written that this size and type of machinery was allowed. Still, he wanted to do as little damage as possible. Momentarily forgetting about the sinking, he started preparing for his next turn. Turning was always going to be the hardest part. No matter how many YouTube videos he watched, he knew there was no replacement for the real thing. Eric fixated on the T junction and in less than a minute was upon it.

The pulsing in his pressure points deepened and an unfamiliar tension built around his neck as he switched down the speed, held his breath, and turned. Beneath him, the tracks switched course.

It was a perfect turn. Flawless in every manner. Eric fist punched the air. He was the master of all things mini and excavatorous. With a small whoop of delight, he hit back up on the two-speed and continued down the path. That was when he saw it.

It hadn't been on Google Earth, of that he was positive. By the whiteness of the metal and the transparency of the glass, it could have even gone up since Christmas. A generous present, or sale splurge perhaps? Where it had come from didn't matter, what mattered was that it was there. A beautiful, shiny greenhouse jutted out into the path straight in front of him. Eric glanced over his shoulder.

There was no way back. The greenhouse sat parallel to an old blue shed and turning around might cause the arm to hit one of the structures.

Reversing wasn't an option either. He had already churned up the ground so much he could end up getting stuck.

Eric stopped the engine and got out. Using his arms and eyes he assessed the size of the gap. Several times he paced back and forth, arms open at the width of the digger. After his third check, he sighed with relief. He could make it. The excavator could make it. Slow, calm, precise movements, and he'd be completely fine. Eric climbed back into the cab, took a few steadying breaths, then, when he sensed he was as calm as he was going to get given the situation, restarted the engine.

Low speed, that was for sure. The front of the tracks slid between the gap and sandwiched perfectly between the shed and the greenhouse. A second later and the whole digger was enclosed. Sweat trickled down behind his ears. One slight movement of the pedal, or the arm, or the bucket, was all it would take for the greenhouse to come tumbling down. He pushed forwards a millimetre at a time. Every second, a second closer to the end. Soon there was barely a foot to go, before his whole body flooded with relief as the bucket emerged out the other side, then the arm, then the tracks. Eric wiped the sweat from the back of his neck and took a moment. It was only two more turns now to his allotment, this right one, then another left. Only two turns to go.

As he angled the tracks to finish the turn, something beneath him jolted. It was a small jolt, like a piece of earth shifting or a track clicking into place. Eric ignored it and moved forwards. The next jolt was substantially more significant. He glanced over his shoulder. The soil beneath the back of the track was waterlogged and causing the digger to slip. Eric pushed the lever forwards and urged the machine on. It refused to budge. He tried again, thrusting his own weight forwards too in the hope that that would help. It didn't. He could feel his pulse rising, the moisture evaporating from the back of his throat. He needed more power behind him. That was his only option. Closing his eyes and muttering a quick non-denominational prayer, he flicked the two-speed switch up and pushed on the pedal.

CHAPTER 17

IT TOOK A total of nine men, three women, and seven flasks of tea to get the excavator upright and out from of the rubble. It was a mess. Splinters of the blue wooden shed lay spread among the serrated edges of greenhouse glass. Within the destruction were seedlings, twisted tools, gardening gloves, and what only minutes earlier had been an antique radio, but was now nothing more than a bouncing mass of coils and wires.

The noise alone had been enough to generate a crowd. They arrived seconds after the crash; those who could came running; the rest hobbled behind.

'Help me,' Eric called. His head lolled downwards, a trickle of blood running down his forehead. 'My bloody trousers are caught.' People wrenched and tugged, pulling from every direction as they tried to dislodge him from between the levers. For a brief second, Eric believed that this was it, the end. He was going to die there, stuck on his side, trapped in the cabin of a mini excavator, until, with a hard yank, someone tore the seams of his jeans, finally freeing him. With his heart pounding, blood in his mouth, and Mickey Mouse boxers that Abi had bought him on display, Eric crawled out the wreckage.

'Well you've made a right mess there,' someone said. Eric couldn't disagree.

He had had to call Lewis and agree to pay a two-hundred-pound "tip" for the service. Even then they had to call upon the help of the local coast guard volunteers as well as those allotment owners who were able to bend their backs without it taking them forty-five minutes to straighten up – of which Eric was surprised to find quite a few. Still, he didn't think he could have wedged the digger in at a more awkward angle if someone had paid him. Griff had appeared with the flasks of tea and bacon butties, and although Eric wasn't entirely sure who had called him, he was eternally grateful. The sweet liquid flooded through his veins and only when Eric removed the mug from his lips did he see how much he was shaking.

'You're lucky,' Griff said. 'You could have caused some real damage. To yourself I mean.'

It was the bucket that had caused the most damage, coming down squarely through the roof of the shed. The contents had spilt their innards out onto the path, catching in the digger's tracks and twisting into the chain-links. Eric hadn't come out of it unscathed. There were several superficial gashes on his arms and legs and an egg-shaped welt ballooning on his thigh. The whole of his left side radiated as if he'd gone ten rounds in a bullring.

'What a mess,' Janice was shaking her owly head. 'What a mess.'

'I'll pay for the damage,' Eric kept saying. 'I just don't understand what happened.'

'Stupidity is what happened.' Eric turned his head to see Norman standing at the back of the crowd, tight-lipped, and scowling. 'Stupidity and arrogance.'

Eric pretended he didn't hear and carried on trying to piece back together the fragments and wires of the broken radio.

As luck – good or bad he wasn't sure – would have it, the owners of both the shed and the greenhouse happened to be away in Europe. One was visiting his children and grandchildren in Belgium while the other was on an over-sixties singles' event in Amsterdam. Eric left his details with Janice, who promised she'd pass them on. He didn't doubt it for a moment.

It was 4.00 PM by the time he left Burlam, and the sun was already slinking off behind the clouds. Eric's stomach growled. Beside the cup of tea Griff had brought him, he'd had nothing to eat or drink all day, and the effects of low blood-sugar combined with general fatigue and shock were showing. He texted Suzy and suggested they get a takeaway from down by the station and took her lack of reply as agreement. His phone had countless messages and emails, many of which were from the office, but with his head thumping and stomach getting angrier by the second, he decided it would be best to deal with them all later.

He kept to the slow lane as he drove, letting other cars and lorries whip past. The bruises on his leg had started to colour with an impressive blend of purple hues. After the day's events, getting home in one piece was his current priority.

Abi's bedroom light shone down onto the street below. Eric could make out her silhouette, prancing behind the curtains. His chest expanded. At least he was home to see her before she went to bed. That was something. He clicked the key in the door and embraced the rush of warm air. It was like hitting a wall of sheer exhaustion. His jaw clicked loudly into a yawn, his eyelids sagged, millimetres from closing, and everything ached.

'Suze, honey. I'm home,' he said, limping his way down the hall.

'In here,' she said from the kitchen.

Suzy was sitting at the dining room table in half-light. A thin white film had built on her cup of tea. The curtains were drawn, the radio was silent, and the only sounds came from the whirring of the dishwasher and the occasional burst of singing from Abi upstairs.

'What a day,' Eric said, whipping off his jumper and slinging it over the back of the chair. 'I could do with a drink.'

Suzy met his gaze. Her expression was neutral, passive. 'There's tonic in the fridge,' she said and ended her sentence there.

Eric hesitated, partly to see if she was going to make one – somehow a gin and tonic always tasted better when she made it for him – partly because something was nipping at his gut. It was the type of gnawing that occurred when he'd forgotten something important, like an anniversary or to leave money as a proxy for the tooth fairy. Something felt out of place. He glanced around the room. There was nothing different, nothing out of order. No doubt it was his mind playing tricks on him from all the stresses of the day. When Suzy didn't say anything else, Eric went to the fridge and hunted out the limes and tonic water himself. He poured his glass and sat down opposite her.

'Sorry, you didn't want one too, did you?' he said.

Suzy shook her head. 'I'm fine.'

A short silence ensued. Eric took a sip of his drink. It hit the back of the throat in exactly the right place.

'Wow, I needed that,' he said.

With a deliberately exaggerated movement, he brushed his fingers across the cut above his eyebrow and winced. If Suzy saw, she didn't say anything. He did it again to the same effect. A mild heat of indignation bloomed around his midriff. It was unlike Suzy not to question him about his day, particularly when he looked like he'd been in a mud-slinging contest with a sumo wrestler and a cactus. No doubt she'd feel terrible about it later when they went to bed and she saw what a state his legs and side were in.

'So, how's your day been?' he asked.

'What about yours? How did you get on?'

Eric's eyes rolled. 'To be honest. Pretty damn horrific.'

'Oh,' Suzy said impassively. 'That's a shame. You said the last three days had been productive. What happened? Did you not manage to get as much done as you thought?'

Eric observed his wife. She hadn't moved an inch since he had arrived. Her hands were still folded neatly on her lap. Her tea untouched.

'I ran into a few small snags,' Eric said. 'Well. A few huge snags. Took a bit of a tumble too.' He pointed to the cut on his head.

'Looks nasty,' she said, her voice devoid of any form of concern or sympathy.

Eric pursed his lips, unsure of how to respond.

'But the allotment's still looking good?' Suzy said. 'I mean, one bad day's work after three good days. It still must be a huge improvement?'

'Well ...' Eric's sentence drifted off.

'Have you got any photos for me to see today? Abi would like to see them too. She's been telling all her teachers at school how her daddy's given up work to be a gardener for the week.'

Eric's eyes darted around the room. His mouth and throat had become inexplicably dry, and a large lump was forcing its way up his oesophagus.

'So, the unsatisfactory cultivation order, you think that'll be overthrown now? Now that you've done all this work?'

'Well, I don't know. I mean there was an awful lot to —'

He cut himself short as his eyes finally laid claim to his sense of uneasiness. The lump in his throat evaporated to leave a feeling of nausea that spread from the soles of his feet and upwards.

'What's that for?' he said, nodding towards the object by Suzy's feet.

It was only small, but big enough. Big enough to hold a week's clothes, perhaps two.

'I've just packed a few things,' she said. 'Abi and I are going away for a while.'

'What do you mean?' Eric said. 'Where? Why?' A trickle of sweat meandered down his back. He held his wife's gaze, but it was hard. His hands were shaking, his legs were trembling. His whole body quivered where he stood.

'Jack Nelson rang,' she said. 'He couldn't find the folder with the artwork in for the college accounts, I think he said it was?' Eric nodded. Tears brimmed in his eyes. One escaped and slipped down his cheek. 'He wanted to know if you'd taken it with you when you left work yesterday, but he couldn't get through to you on your phone. I said I'd ask you when you got back. He also wanted to thank you for taking that client out to lunch on Tuesday? He said you were quite the star.'

Suzy rose from her chair. Her lips were quivering, but she maintained a poise and posture that cut straight between Eric's ribs. She picked up the suitcase, walked past him, and placed it by the front door. Then she started up the stairs to collect Abi.

'I really thought you were different,' she said.

CHAPTER 18

IT WAS TWO excruciating days before Suzy spoke to him. Eric had spoken to Abi of course – Suzy facilitated a video call to him once in the morning and once before bed – but the phone was handed to and taken from her without so much as a 'Hello, you lying arsehole,' from Suzy herself.

Eric was in pieces. Had she at least called him out on his bullshit, it could have given him something to yell back at. A chance to put his side across. But there was nothing. Complete radio silence. Thursday night, after they left, he ran himself a bath, after which he collapsed on the bed. He was too tired to argue, too tired to explain why his lies weren't that big of a detail, too tired to kick up the fight she deserved and make her stay.

Friday night he convinced himself it was nothing unusual, that it was no different to when Suzy went away on her book tours, as more often than not she took Abi with her then too. He stayed late at work then brought extra papers home, which he spread over the dining room table in an attempt to disguise the gaping vacuum. When he was done looking at them, he put on manly films with unnecessary quantities of blood and guts that Suzy would have never let him watch if she were home too.

But when week melted into the weekend, and the prospect of an unadulterated full day out in Sally was scuppered by ice and salted roads, the lies to himself got harder to maintain.

It was Saturday evening when they finally spoke. The house now smelt of amalgamated takeaways – oil-soaked paper bags, boxes, cartons, and little Tupperware tubs lay strewn across the kitchen worktop – and the stuffiness that occurs from having the heating on for too long without opening any windows.

'We're going crabbing on Tuesday,' Abi said through the little screen on his phone. 'And Uncle Tom says if we catch any really big ones we can take them home and eat them.'

'Tuesday? Are you planning on staying there next week too? What about school?' A burning sensation pricked his eyes.

A pixelated Abi shrugged. 'I've gotta go now, Dad. Aunt Lydia's making meatballs for tea, and they've got cheese in the middle and everything.'

'Cheesy meatballs, you wouldn't want to miss those, would you? Love you.'

'You too.'

'And I miss you. And your mum too. Tell your mum I miss her, won't you?' But Abi was already off screen. He was about to hit the hang-up button when Suzy came into view. Her eyes were off screen, most likely waiting to check when Abi was out of view and earshot. After a minute passed, she faced Eric through the computer and offered a sad half-smile. A flaming great fissure tore open in his chest.

'How are you?' she asked.

Eric sighed. 'Miserable. When are you coming home?'

There was a long pause. A few times Suzy opened her mouth as if to speak, then closed it again. Eric could feel his eyes welling up.

'I know,' he said. 'I know what I did was wrong, and I shouldn't have lied about where I was —'

'You wore different clothes, Eric,' Suzy silenced him as she spoke. 'You left the house, pretending you were going somewhere else. What kind of person goes to that length to cover a lie unless they've got something serious that needs hiding?'

'I told you. I was at work. I was just at work.'

'And when you were late back? On Tuesday when you were late back, you said it was because there was a tree on one of the lines or something? Where were you then?'

'I was at a meeting. I swear.'

'But how do I know you're telling the truth? This could easily just be another lie to cover all the other ones.'

'I'm telling you the truth, Suze, I promise. I wouldn't lie to you about something like this, I wouldn't.'

Suzy sighed and rubbed her temples. Her eyes were red-rimmed; she looked a decade older. As Eric waited for her to speak, she steepled her hands on the desk in front of her and rested her forehead against her thumbs so all Eric could see was the top of her head. He continued to wait. Three minutes passed before she looked up again.

'I don't know what to do,' she said. 'I don't know what I'm supposed to do right now.'

'Come home,' Eric said. 'Please. That's what you're supposed to do. Come home.'

She shook her head. 'I've been through this, Eric. I've done a marriage where all I get is lies. I'm not doing that to myself again. And I'm certainly not doing it to Abi.'

'This is not the same,' Eric was waving his hands at the phone. 'I fucked up. I really fucked up and I get that. I get why you're upset, I really do. And I know it's all my fault. But please, please don't do this. I will never lie to you again. I swear. I swear.'

In an elegant sweep, Suzy wiped away the tears that slid down her cheek. Eric sniffed his back down his throat in a much less demure manner.

'Will you at least keep speaking to me? I can't stand it when we don't speak. Please? Tomorrow night, or whenever. Whenever you want, can we talk again?'

Suzy's bottom lip disappeared under her top teeth.

'We'll see,' she said and Eric's stomach fell. Whenever he said *we'll see* to Abi, they all knew what it meant.

Suzy let him speak to her the next night. It was a somewhat strained conversation to start with. In the background, Eric could hear Abi and the boys shrieking as they ran up and down the stairs. Twice Suzy went off screen to ask them to be quiet. The third time she told them, even Eric was scared.

'So, what are you going to do?' Suzy said.

It had taken thirty minutes of tense small talk but finally, Eric reached a place where he felt he could tell her about the Burlam misdemeanour. By the end of the tale, there was even a small smile on her lips, although Eric was fairly certain it was revelling at his injuries and humiliation as opposed to actual happiness.

'I don't know,' he said. 'The owners were away last week, but apparently, they get back this weekend. I guess I'll end up paying out. Do people have allotment insurance?'

'Even if they do, I suspect digger-wielding maniac attacks aren't covered,' she said. Eric smiled, and for the first time, it was reciprocated. A smaller glimmer of hope flickered.

'So,' he said. 'Any more ideas about when you're coming home?'

Suzy's face immediately hardened. 'Don't push me on this, Eric,' she said, stamping out his little glimmer. 'Right now, I don't even know if I am.'

'But what about Abi, her school? You have to think about Abi.' Then Suzy gave him the glare that told him he definitely should have stopped at the smile.

With his spirits newly dampened, Eric poured himself a gin only to open the fridge and find it entirely devoid of tonic.

'Bollocks,' he said. There was no tonic in the pantry either, although thanks to a spark of inspiration, Eric remembered that they'd shoved a few bottles of spirits and mixers in the cupboard under the stairs before Christmas when the wine racks and surface tops could no longer handle the overspill. He was in luck. He clunked a couple of ice cubes into his glass and took a long indulgent draw.

With nothing on the television, Eric flicked up his laptop and perused the potential new client list Jack had sent around at the beginning of the week. There were some big names on there. A couple of education luminaries to boot. If Eric could land one more of those it would really seal the deal, should the restructure come about. After tidying up a few odds and ends in various documents, he returned to his emails.

His inbox had gained three new additions since he'd last checked, and only one was work-related. He braced himself and clicked the first message, titled *Garden Green House*.

Eric scanned the message. It was short, curt – probably deservedly so – but reasonable in its requests. Allotment insurance was apparently a costly and rather futile experience, and as such the owner, a P. Hamilton, had requested Eric replace the destroyed greenhouse with a similar model. P. Hamilton had also included a link to a webpage showing such a greenhouse on sale for two hundred and nineteen pounds. They had stipulated however, that should Eric be considering any more excavator expeditions, then they would much prefer the toughened glass model, which would set Eric back a further hundred and twelve pounds. Three hundred pounds, give or take. It was a fair enough, Eric reasoned. P. Hamilton had also requested that Eric sort the issue as soon as possible, as they would like to get on with sowing their Bunton's showstoppers in order to gain a good head start on their competitors before competition season began.

'Another weekend in Burlam it is then,' Eric muttered to himself.

With the expectation of another two hundred pounds quickly fleeing his pockets, he clicked on the second email, which was more dramatically titled, *Ravaged Garden Shed*.

Once again, the email began most civilly and stated yet again the problems with getting insurance for allotments and the wish that Eric merely paid the cost of the destroyed items. That was where the good news ended. After quoting Eric an astronomical six hundred and fifty pounds for the replacement shed, the email then included an itemised list of all the objects – once again with web links – that were apparently destroyed at the time of Eric's rampage. The list included: a pair of Japanese secateurs for forty pounds, a digging fork for ninety pounds, eighty pounds for a Bulldog rubber rake and forty-nine pounds for a digging spade. There was also a one hundred and thirty-four-pound wheelbarrow, a forty-pound hedge trimmer, eight pounds fifty for a pressure sprayer and ninety-nine pounds ninety-eight for a Hoselock twenty metre auto-rewind hose, plus accessories. This did not include incidentals, such as seed trays, bulbs, fertiliser, and bug pellets among other things, for which the writer requested an extra two hundred and fifty pounds. Finally, was his vintage Roberts Radio, which was now no longer produced, although a similar model could be picked up, Eric was informed, at any good John Lewis or department store for around a hundred quid.

Eric sat back in his seat and tried to comprehend what he'd just read. A rough estimate brought him to fifteen hundred pounds. Fifteen hundred. Eric downed the rest of his drink and thumped the glass back onto the desk. Who did this person think they were? Fifteen hundred pounds, plus the other greenhouse? This was a month's school fees for Abi and a bit to spare. His tummy muscles tightened, strained, then a minute later flopped out in resignation. There was only one person to blame for the whole fiasco and that was, most irritatingly, himself. After refilling his gin with a double measure, he fired off two responsive emails, both agreeing to pay the stated cost. After which he downed the remainder of his drink and dug out the menu for the Indian around the corner.

❧

It was a pinging email that woke him in the morning. The house was hot, stiflingly so, and condensation ran in streams down the windows and puddled on the sills. Eric had never got the hang of the central heating timer, and adjusting it accordingly was one of Suzy's jobs. As he'd gone to bed the night before, he'd switched up the thermostat in the hope of lessening the chill of an empty bed. It had definitely done that. His skin was clammy, and his hair stuck to the pillow in a way that only usually occurred in summer months or after nights of heavy drinking. He peeled himself out of the duvet and took a sip from the glass of water on his nightstand. 10.00 AM, the clock read. Eric blinked and checked it again. He couldn't remember the last time he'd slept like that. Not that he felt refreshed.

His phone pinged again and coaxed him over from the bed. He flicked on the screen noting the little inbox icon at the bottom. Seventeen new messages had come through since he went to bed. Eric did his second double take of the morning. That number of emails on a Saturday night could only mean an absolute work catastrophe. Or news, important news. He gulped. Perhaps it was about the restructuring. Perhaps Jack had finally caved to Hartley and was giving it the go ahead. With his heart racing, he clicked on the inbox icon.

CHAPTER 19

'IT'S LUDICROUS, THAT'S what it is.'

Eric was on the computer speaking to Suzy. Abi was outside at Lydia's apparently catching newts in the pond, although he strongly suspected the only kind of life present in Tom and Lydia's pond was a particularly virulent strain of E-coli. The kitchen was in a marginally better state, with Eric having collected up all the used takeaway boxes that morning, although the sink was now filled with moulding teacups and a scent of fermenting milk.

'Listen to this one.'

He read off his phone as he spoke. '*Dear Mr Sibley ... blah, blah, blah ...* wait a sec ... oh, here it is. *Your haphazard driving last Thursday caused not only irrevocable damage to my perineal, —*' I'm fairly sure she means perennials here but anyway, '*— it also near obliterated my prize-winning damson tree. I've estimated the cost of replacing this at two thousand pounds.*'

'That sounds a bit steep.'

'A bit steep? I was nowhere near her bloody damson tree. And I was most certainly not near her perineal. Haphazard driving? My driving was perfect.'

'Until you crashed.'

'Yes. But up until that point I didn't hit a thing. Not one.'

'Well, if you're sure ...'

Eric's nostrils flared.

'Sure? Of course, I'm bloody sure. There are messages here saying that I ran over someone's compost heap. They want me to pay for replacement worms. And that I massacred their black currant bushes. One says I deliberately beheaded his scarecrow. I mean, it's obscene. Half of them have threatened to sue me if I don't pay up within a month.'

'Can they do that?'

'Of course not. It's preposterous.'

'Then perhaps you need to get a lawyer involved?'

'And how much is that going to cost us?'

Eric huffed and slumped back onto the bed. Suzy was lying on the sheep-scented batik quilt in her slobby clothes; they consisted of his old tracksuit bottoms and a vest top with a frayed hoody over the top. If only he could hold her, nuzzle down into her shoulder, he might feel just a tiny bit better.

'Please come home,' he said. 'I miss you. I need you. I'm a wreck without you.'

Suzy leant away from the screen.

'We'll talk about it later,' she said. 'I need to go now. I said I'd watch the kids.'

'Have a good day then.'

'You too. And try not to stress about it. And don't respond while you're angry. I'm sure it'll sort itself out.'

'I hope you're right.'

'I usually am.'

Suzy's more forgiving attitude made Eric feel a little more optimistic about the future, and taking her advice, he decided not to respond to any of the emails there and then. Instead, he chose to busy himself tidying. On the slim chance that Suzy decided to come home without warning, a bathroom that smelt of four-day-old underpants and a kitchen fridge that looked like it belonged to a bunch of excessively frivolous students may just be the things to send her away again. After tidying he went upstairs and changed into his running gear. The rest of the day was going to be spent doing useful, productive things, Eric decided. After all, a clear head was what he needed to deal with the situation.

Unfortunately, the next week did not allow him a clear head at all. Abi had apparently got involved in some scouting expedition with the boys, which Eric took as a sign to say they had no intention of returning home anytime soon. At work, Jack had been called away on a family crisis and one of the senior associate directors was stuck in the Maldives due to a volcanic ash cloud somewhere over Indonesia. Eric flitted from one telephone call to another while Greg yo-yoed back and forth to different meetings with various VIPs. Wednesday already felt like Friday, and the thought of another two days like the three just past made Eric's legs heavy with dread. It was Friday night before he finally got to address the issue of the allotments once again, having done an admirable job of ignoring the deluge of emails that had continued to flood his inbox since the beginning of the week.

'I told them I'd see them all tomorrow morning,' Eric said to Suzy as he scooped a chopstick full of noodles into his mouth.

It was gone eleven, and the fact that Suzy had stayed up late so that they could talk, he read as either extremely positive or else terrifyingly negative.

'Are you going to manage that? To speak to them all I mean?' she said. 'I thought there were loads of them?'

'There are, but I'm hoping most of them won't get their messages until it's too late. I only sent it fifteen minutes ago.' Suzy didn't look convinced.

'So what time are you going to meet them? And what are you going to tell them?'

'Well, I've got to sort out this bloody greenhouse too, although I might wait until the rest of the stuff is done. I was going to get there about ten?'

'And you're going to tell them what?'

Eric paused. He had had less time to dwell on the matter than he would have liked, but he had a vague idea. He puffed out his chest as he spoke,

'I'm going to tell them that every incident will need to be verified by my lawyer and should the incidents turn out to be bogus, not only will they be expected to reimburse my costs, but I will take legal action in reference to libel and slander. That should stop them.'

Suzy frowned. 'Is that a good idea?'

'I don't see why not? And I can't think of a better one, can you?'

She tilted her head in a half-shake, half-shrug.

'It just seems very negative, that's all. You've already got this order for unsatisfactory cultivation. Now you want to upset them further by threatening to sue them?'

'They threatened to sue me first.'

Suzy raised an eyebrow. 'Well, that's a great response.'

Eric pondered the thought for a second.

'I'm certain it's the best way. The only way,' he said.

'Well, there you go then.' She smiled. It was only a small one, but it glinted in her eyes and sent Eric's stomach into butterflies.

'What time are you planning on leaving then? Only Abi will want to speak to you in the morning I suspect.' Her nonchalant tone brought the sting of the separation sharply back to the forefront of his mind.

'I don't know. I was planning on leaving about nine.'

'Okay. I'll make sure she calls you before then.'

'I love you,' he said.

'I know,' Suzy replied.

※

ERIC DROVE SALLY TO BURLAM. It wasn't the most sensible idea, with bad weather pestering regions all around the coast, but for all he knew Christian Eaves was at the allotment ready to strip him of his keys and tear from him the last hand-hold to his family life. As such, Eric was determined to get in one last decent drive. Abi had been up at the crack of dawn, so Suzy let her call him at just gone seven. Eric could feel the tears building behind his eyes as she rang off without so much as an *I miss you*. They had only been gone a little over a week, yet it felt like she'd grown up months in that time. His heart ached and burned with the stupidity of it all.

It was while brushing his teeth that Eric decided he'd go and see them the next day. Suzy had said she wanted space, and he'd given her that. But now he wanted to talk. In person. Enough was enough, he wanted his family back. With a substantial amount of force, he spat the toothpaste into the sink, rinsed the bowl, then fetched his driving gloves from the back of his top drawer.

Steering clear of the dual carriageways, Eric took every back road he could. He raced down the narrow, twisting, tree-lined lanes. He soared past the fifteenth-century Church of St Mary the Virgin and drank in the lingering views of the river. His wheels hugged corners time and time again while his lungs bathed in the adrenaline of it all. This was living; this was what it was about.

As he slowed to take a small cobbled bridge, he caught sight of a bevvy of swans circling in the water. The place was idyllic. Three cottages sat on the riverside, one with a *For Sale* sign out in front of it. *Abi would love it here*, Eric thought. She could fish in the river, climb trees. His chest tightened as he tried but failed to swallow the image back down.

He glanced at his watch to distract himself and was surprised to see it was already twenty to ten. If it was to be his last drive, he thought, at least it had been a good one.

Fifteen minutes later, Eric drove through Burlam High Street at less than twenty miles an hour in an attempt to peer into the window of Eaves and Doyle as he passed. It didn't look like anyone was there, which could have been because it was a Saturday and most solicitors were closed on Saturdays, or, it could have been because Christian Eaves was already waiting for him at the allotment.

He had hoped that the drive would relieve some of the tension he was experiencing over today's confrontations. However, as he plodded down the track towards the metal gates – his back and shoulders as rigid as one of Norman's anally aligned beanpoles – he realised that this was not the case. A few metres in front of the allotment entrance he stopped.

His pulse was pounding against his ribs and a film of sweat glazed his palms. As well as the possibility of some very unpleasant conversations and loss of his most beloved possession, this sudden spike in blood pressure – Eric realised to his own astonishment – also came with the realisation he may be losing the allotment too. The infernal patch of dirt had been nothing more than a protruding thorn in his side for two months now and utterly consuming in every way possible. Without the car and the allotment, not only would he have vast amounts of excess time on his hands, but his topics of conversation would be dramatically reduced. Perhaps it was a good thing, he said internally, then corrected himself out loud.

'It would definitely be a good thing.' Eric let out the air from his lungs in one deep sigh.

That was when he heard them. He had just finished his mini self-motivational pep talk when a sudden expulsion of laughter came from somewhere beyond the gates. He bit down. Laughter. Full belly-wobbling laughter. It sounded like a whole group of them, men and women. The nefarious little titters of blue-rinsed grandmas flew through the air like needles to his eardrums.

Eric froze, livid. His pulse took on a new, more violent pacing. They had planned this whole thing together, the lot of them. A plot to rinse him dry. Well, he'd see how well that turned out for them. They weren't going to get a penny from him. Not one. Not even P. Hamilton and his or her obliterated greenhouse and certainly not the damn Roberts Radio.

With his fists clenched and blood pounding, Eric marched through the gates and across the allotment. The mob had their back to him, all tweed coats and wax jackets, and as he approached Eric cleared his throat in a loud and not even slightly polite manner. A man with several piercings in his ears turned around.

'Ahh, look, here he is now,' he said.

The rest of the crowd began to turn. There were nearly twenty of them in total, all of them grinning, teeth on show, ready to devour Eric alongside their Tangtastics and Survivor peas. Eric gulped but held his ground.

'Nice of you to turn up,' one of them said.

'Well, now that I'm here, we can get started.' Eric addressed the crowd with his hands on his hips. He wasn't going to dilly-dally about with niceties.

'So, you are aware,' he said, 'I've read every one of your emails and I've found them to be —'

'Daddy, Daddy!'

Eric stopped. He squinted. Through a gap in the throng, a little figure was squeezing its way through to the front.

'Daddy, look what we made!'

His knees went. Turning it into a deliberate gesture Eric knelt on the floor and stretched out his arms.

'Daddy, guess what we've been doing? Guess what? Guess what?'

Eric failed to suck back the tears as they breached his lower eyelids.

'What is it, pumpkin?' he said, pulling his daughter into his chest and hugging her so hard he thought he might crush her. 'What have you been doing?'

She wriggled out of his grip and back onto the grass where she skipped over to a large box on the ground.

'We've been baking. Mummy and me. We've done loads and loads of baking.'

Suzy stood in the centre of the crowd. Her hair hung loosely about her shoulders and a large tin weighed down her hands. It could have been a decade ago, the way his heart skipped and stalled at the sight of her.

'It's true,' she said, holding Eric's gaze with nothing more than the movement of her lips. 'We have done a lot of baking.'

CHAPTER 20

TO ERIC, IT felt like summer, or how summer would feel if it was so cold it turned the tips of your ears blue and your breath fogged each time you spoke. Suzy glided between the allotment owners, handing out squares of freshly baked brownies and blondies. Abi offered a tray of curiously decorated cupcakes while asking each person how old they were and if they owned any chickens because her cousins had chickens and for the last week she'd collected the eggs.

Suzy, Eric noticed, began guiding one of the owners in his direction. It wasn't someone he recognised; a tall blonde lady, only about his age, with her hair held back by a green bandana.

'Eric, this is Penelope. Penelope Hamilton,' Suzy said, then added, 'P. Hamilton,' when Eric still drew a blank.

'P. Hamil– oh yes.' Eric's eyes widened, his brain finally engaged. 'Of course. P. Hamilton. Penelope. I'm so, so sorry. I mean, I can't describe how terrible I feel. Of course, your greenhouse. I will reimburse you immediately. Get the new one ordered today.'

Penelope gesticulated in a similar vein to the queen. 'Please call me Penny. And don't fuss. It's not a problem. Accidents happen to the best of us. Your wonderful wife here was just telling me what a tough time you've been having with it. Running back and forth between here and London. And of course, losing your father.'

'Well ... umm. I suppose it's been an interesting start to the year.'

'Well, anything I can do to help. And really, don't think twice about the digger incident. Water under the bridge already.'

Bewildered, Eric drifted from one person to the next and found the conversations eerily similar. Even Mrs Maddock with her damaged prize-winning damsons was ardent to discuss her change of heart.

'There was a big storm you see, that night. So, when I got there, and my tree was broken I thought it must have been you with your digger. But thinking back on it now, I think it must have been the storm, as you were right over the other side of the allotment.'

'Well, I did think —'

'To be honest, I'm not sure how I could have thought it was your digger. Think it was the trauma you see. Shellshock, they call it.'

It was remarkable how many situations could suddenly be explained by the raging storm that had apparently attacked Burlam allotment a week last Thursday. Particularly remarkable given that he could see no evidence of this mini-typhoon whatsoever.

'What did you say to them?' Eric asked when he finally managed to get Suzy away from the endlessly babbling bean growers. 'What did you tell them?'

'Only the truth. That you'd been finding balancing the allotment with work tricky. And you really want to do your father justice as you know the place meant so much to him.'

'That's it?'

'That's it. Well, I might have thrown in a few lines about Abi's school struggling with her ADHD and offered to do a reading at next month's book club.'

Eric studied his daughter. She was currently balancing on one foot, using half a bean pole as a sword while smearing green butter icing across her cheeks as war paint.

'Abi doesn't have ADHD,' Eric said.

'Does she not?'

An hour later and the new greenhouse had been ordered and paid for and a more reasonably priced shed selected from the B&Q website. The shed owner, a stubbled and greying Richard, had decided since his initial email that several of his tools were still in fine working order. He also explained that he'd found his gardening gloves in his coat pocket, discovered that he'd lent his hose to one of his neighbours and confessed, rather sheepishly that his electric strimmer hadn't worked for several years. After sitting down and tallying up the total, Eric agreed to pay him five hundred pounds. He suspected he'd have settled lower, but he wanted to make sure there was enough in the kitty for the Roberts Radio; he'd hinted enough, and he probably deserved it for the mess.

By midday, all business was dealt with and Abi was higher on sugar than Willy Wonka after a trip in the Great Glass Elevator. The crowd had dispersed completely, either to their respective plots and greenhouses or else home for lunch and a nap. Eric yawned. His head thrummed with numbers and names, but his shoulders felt like a fifty-kilo dumbell had been lifted from them.

'So,' he said to Suzy, while Abi licked the crumbs from the bottom of one of the cake tins. 'What now?'

'Now? You take us back to Lydia's.' The weight on Eric's shoulders landed back with a wallop.

'Really?' he said. 'I just thought that, well you know.'

Suzy smiled.

'Our bags are there. We'll need all our things if we're going to come home.'

Eric stepped across a newly ploughed trench and took his wife's hand. Then he kissed it and kissed it and kissed it again.

'Urgh, you two are so gross,' Abi said.

Then they pulled her in and kissed her too.

It wasn't until he was standing by Sally, about to head off to Lydia's, that Eric remembered the other source of his nerves. His stomach plummeted.

'Crap,' he said.

'What?'

'I didn't ask about the eviction. I guess it still stands. After all, the seven days is done, and all I succeeded in doing was ruining two other allotments. I guess they've got all the reason they need to get rid of me now.'

He gazed at the lights and reached out his hand to brush the bonnet. They had had some good memories together, Eric recalled. Great memories. Like the first time his father let him get behind the wheel when his provisional licence arrived. How many teenagers could say that the first car they ever got to drive was a limited-edition Aston Martin DB4? Not many, he was sure of that. Eric had had to get straight As in his GSCEs first, and solid A-level predictions of course. And spend every weekend for the five years before his seventeenth birthday polishing each and every square inch of the car with a six-inch square chamois leather. A deep set, heavily rooted gnawing built behind his sternum.

'I was talking to Penny about that,' Suzy said, bringing Eric out of his daydream.

'Penny?'

'Penny. Penelope. P. Hamilton.'

'Oh, right? What did she say?'

'Not much. She said she hadn't heard anything about it. But she wasn't a member of the committee.'

'Well I'm sure she'll hear soon enough then,' Eric said. And went back to basking in his eternal misery.

※

Despite awaiting the inevitable loss of Sally, Eric skipped through the next week at work. He left early each morning after he'd brought Suzy her cup of tea in bed and was out the door the minute the clock struck five. Other people managed it; even some of the senior associate directors managed it. It was all a matter of prioritising, Eric told himself, and finally, he was getting it right. During office hours, he'd become beyond efficient. He stuck a tacky plastic mini whiteboard – the type you'd find in a primary school or displaying the daily specials in a cheap sandwich shop – on his back wall and crossed off his to-do list with a thick black line. He got coffee from the machine, rather than heading out, and apart from the one working lunch he couldn't avoid, he ate at his desk or skipped lunch altogether.

Three times that week they cooked at home as a family, which they hadn't done since he started earning enough not to break into a cold sweat at the cost of a takeaway. He helped Abi with her homework on Tudor clothes, and while it was a topic he knew absolutely zero about, he was still more effective at scouring the internet than Abi and therefore maintained the important parental position of omnipotence. It was a great week until the email came through from Cynthia.

Fortunately, the email had come through on the Friday night, giving Eric only one evening to mull and muse before they drove down together in the Audi on Saturday morning. David Bowie's greatest hits blared out of the speakers as they battled the morning rain.

'This music's so old,' Abi said, crinkling up her nose in disgust as her father bellowed out the chorus to *Life on Mars*.

'Yes, it is,' Eric said. 'And it's stood the test of time.' He continued with his singing at double the volume.

'You're so annoying.' Abi huffed, digging out her iPad, and plugging in her headphones.

Suzy smiled and took Eric's hand.

'We don't mind coming with you,' she said. 'If you want an extra pair of hands? Or some moral support?'

'It's fine,' Eric said. 'I'd rather you weren't there, to be honest. I'm not sure how this works. Or why we have to meet at The Shed. I expect I'm not allowed on the property anymore or something ridiculous like that.' A knot tightened around his kidneys. 'This is stupid. I don't even know why I'm going. What can they say in person that they couldn't write in an email? Unless they've decided I was responsible for the mythical typhoon of Burlam that wiped out Mrs Maddock's damson tree after all.'

Suzy squeezed his hand. 'Perhaps it's positive. Perhaps they want to give you another month.'

'I doubt that.'

'Well, either way, we're only a train ride away if you need us. Or I'm sure Tom could drop us down. Just let me know. We'll be there if you want.'

As they turned the corner and drew up outside his in-laws' house Eric squeezed his wife's hand back. 'Thank you,' he said.

Eric didn't get out the car. He was going to, briefly, then he caught sight of Lydia's glare and her look of daggers aimed directly at him. Suzy may have forgiven him over the lying incident, but it was clear he had a long way to go with her sister. Last time Eric upset Lydia, he ended up being given a crocheted toilet roll doll every Christmas for three years, complete with an almost new roll of toilet paper. Nuances had never been part of Lydia's toolbox.

❦

GRIFF MOTIONED to the back room as soon as he saw him.

'They're already waiting for you,' he said. 'Do you want me to bring you a Wimpy Git through? Or a bacon sandwich?'

Eric shook his head. 'Just a black coffee,' he said. His stomach never coped well with nerves, and for some reason, he was incredibly nervous. The Shed was filled with its normal aromas of pig fat and coffee, but the walls and hallways felt exceptionally dark and narrow. As Eric made his way through to the back room he paused, one foot resting at the bottom of the tiny staircase, the other at the top. The *back room*. Despite frequenting The Shed several times in the last few weeks, he'd not been back to the back room since his meeting there with Christian Eaves. Eric thought back to the letter, now stuffed somewhere in a box with old postcards and passport photos. What was it he said about misgivings? And deluded ideas of success? Eric shook his head clear and focused on the situation. Then he stretched his neck until it clicked and marched forwards into the back room.

With the chairs arranged in one big circle and many of the places already taken, Eric felt as though he'd walked into the world's oddest AA meeting. There were several familiar faces, including Janice, Cynthia, and Rich as well as several unknowns, many of a similar or younger age to himself. The committee was a big one, yet they all had one thing in common. Regardless of their age, race, or choice of breakfast beverage, all the members fell silent when Eric entered.

'Eric, please, come sit down, sit down. Have you ordered some food? Would you like anything? They do a lovely black pudding.' Cynthia ushered him forwards through the chairs.

'I'm fine, thanks,' Eric said. 'I've already ordered a coffee.'

'Great, well sit down then. We're almost ready to get started.'

Eric hovered awkwardly in the centre of the circle. There were three seats free, one on either side of Janice and one next to a face he didn't recognise. After a moment's hesitation, he took the one next to the unknown and quickly quashed his twang of guilt. Today wasn't a day for small talk. There was another moment's fuss when Hank – an exceptionally stocky pensioner with a Sailor Jerry tattoo, a limp, and a three-legged whippet – entered. He politely motioned to his leg when Janice pointed out the available seats beside her, then a moment later caught Eric's eye and winked.

After Hank had settled himself against the window ledge, another, longer silence fell between the group. Eric watched as eyes darted between one another, along with knowing glares and disgruntled tuts. Eric was surprised by how many people he didn't recognise. There was what appeared to be a young married couple with an overly hairy toddler playing with cars around their feet, and several people a generation or two older, most of whom possessed hair of a silvery-grey pigmentation. A few people coughed, some genuinely, others as a more obvious evidence of boredom.

'Well?' A man Eric thought was called Peter was the first to speak. 'What are we going to do? Just sit around here in silence until he turns up?'

'If he turns up.'

'He has to turn up. He's the chairman. And he's never missed a meeting before.'

'He's never done a lot of things before.'

All eyes, Eric's included, fell on Cynthia. She straightened her back.

'What, you think I have some control over him? A likely chance.'

There was a moment's pause until someone said, 'So what are we going to do then?'

The conversation descended into a mass of noise, through which every person was attempting to make their point heard. Eric's head went from one side to another, trying to make sense of the situation until a loud wolf whistle cut clean through them all. Still leaning on the window, Hank raised his hands.

'Look,' he said. 'Is the consensus going to change whether he's here or not?' A resounding *no* was emitted from the mass of shaking heads. 'Right then. In that case, I say we get on with this. No point keeping us all here for no reason. Agreed?'

There were more grumbles, though this time the resounding sound of a *yes* came out from the fog.

'He'll be pissed,' someone said.

'Then you can blame me. But let's get this over and done with. Cynthia?'

Everyone's eyes returned to Cynthia, who this time nodded demurely and rose to standing, her gaze focused solely on Eric.

Eric's insides churned. A juddering sensation vibrated around his appendix and, judging from the motion in his abdomen, his liver had been infested by a welt of hyperactive flatworms. He took a microsecond and closed his eyes. Ripping off the Band-Aid. That's all that was happening here. Ripping off the Band-Aid, blindfolded, using your teeth, while performing a one-handed cartwheel on a marble covered floor.

'Eric,' Cynthia said. 'First, I would like to apologise. After the incident with the digger, I'm afraid a few of my fellow alloties,' she shot some accusatory glares around the room, 'tried to take advantage of your good nature.'

'It's fine.'

'That is very kind of you to say, Eric. I, however, disagree and feel some action should be taken, but that's another matter, not for the here and now.'

Eric's shoulders dropped in relief although his insides squeezed tight. The last thing he wanted was to relive all that again, let alone be the centre of its fallouts. There were already some very disgruntled rumblings making their way in his direction.

'The next thing is the matter of the Unsatisfactory Cultivation Order you received.' Cynthia paused. 'As a committee, we hold the decision on many matters, including Unsatisfactory Cultivation Orders. In fact, all Unsatisfactory Cultivation Orders are supposed to go to the committee. However, in this particular incident, it appears that that step was missed.'

This time it was Cynthia's turn to blush.

'What do you mean?' Eric said. 'How was it missed?'

'Well,' Cynthia's redness was deepening, although she managed to maintain her aura of decorum and calm.

'On this occasion, it appears our chairman deemed it fit to take on the issue independently of the committee,' she said.

Eric took a moment to think through what he was hearing. 'So, what are you saying? That the order doesn't count? Is that what you're saying?'

'Well, it didn't previously count because it hadn't gone to the committee.'

'But it has now?'

'Yes?'

'So now it does count?'

'Well ...'

'Good God, woman. You don't half beat around the bush.' Hank had forced his way into the circle and opposite Eric. 'It's fine. You're fine. Provided you get it sorted in, say, the next two months?' He turned to the rest of the circle. 'Now can we get out of here?'

There was a reverberating concurrence around the room.

'Great,' he said. 'Scout needs his walk.'

He turned to go, his scruffy mongrel at his heel, but turning was as far as he got.

There was a figure standing in the doorway. His fingers were gnarled, and his shoulders hunched, and his stare went straight through the circle and through to the back of Eric's skull. Eric shrank into the chair. He tried to meet the man's eyes, his obscenely green eyes, and to look him squarely and not cower where he sat, but at that moment it was completely impossible.

'Well. It's nice to see how much my opinion counts around here,' Norman said. Then he grunted, spun around, and hobbled back outside.

CHAPTER 21

SEVERAL PEOPLE ATTEMPTED to follow Norman, but Cynthia stopped them all.

'Let me deal with this,' she said. 'This was my doing. I called the meeting. I spoke. He just needs a bit of time, that's all.' There were lots of ifs and buts, hushed voices, and sideways glances, but Cynthia was steadfast. 'Leave him to me, it'll be fine,' she insisted.

Eric was not among the concerned do-gooders. If anything, his sense of jubilation over the decision to let him keep the allotment – and therefore Sally – was only amplified by Norman's behaviour. This served him right for trying to set Christian Eaves and the bailiffs on him. And for goading him enough to tip the water butt over the plot. After the initial moment's shock, Eric was practically levitating in his seat watching the others fret over the miserable bastard's mental wellbeing. It was a couple of minutes before he managed to grab Cynthia's attention and gesticulated his farewell. She offered a smile and nod as he left.

Eric skipped his way to the allotment, and it was only when he reached the corner of Colombia Avenue that he remembered to call Suzy and tell her the news.

'That's fantastic,' she said. 'As long as you're happy?'

'You know what, I am. I'm glad I get to keep Sally at least. And strangely the allotment.'

'Poor Norman, though. It sounds like a horrid mess.'

'He abused his position on the committee,' Eric said. 'If I were the other members, I'd want him off.'

'You don't know all the details. I'm sure he had his reasons.'

'I know enough.' There was a brief silence in the conversation.

'Well,' he said. 'I'm just hopping over to the plot, making sure he hasn't drenched the ground with engine oil before I get there.'

'Play nice.'

'Not a chance,' Eric said and very much meant it.

As such, it was a stomach-plummeting disappointment to discover that Norman wasn't at the allotment. Gloating was an almost impossible task unless the person you were aiming to aggravate was within visual or auditory range. Still, there would be plenty of time to bask in his triumph later.

Now that the longevity of Eric's relationship with the small patch of ground had been determined, he wanted to get the remainder of the groundwork done. As long as he could get it to the point where the only maintenance required was to pull up a few straggling weeds each week, his part of the deal should prove easy to hold up. Half-an-hour a weekend at most. Unfortunately, with less than a third currently clear and weeds the size of birch trees occupying the remainder, it was going to take a little work to get there. He picked up his fork and got started.

❧

MONDAY ARRIVED and was its normal hectic self. It hit like a ten-tonne bull elephant and dragged Eric along with it, regardless of how much he wanted to curl up under the duvet and hide. Suzy had an event with her publishing house in Glasgow, which meant Eric had to pick up Abi from school at four. Under normal circumstances, and with his new ultra-efficient routine, it would have been fine. Only things at work weren't exactly normal.

The problem with having a boss like Jack Nelson – who even at the tensest times appeared so calm you'd think he'd just spent a week in a Japanese onsen listening to the entire Norah Jones back catalogue – was that seeing him even slightly flustered was, to put it mildly, troublesome.

On Monday, there was a sense of unease, by Tuesday people were notably agitated, and by Wednesday the tension was so palpable that Greg went home at lunch and reappeared in a pinstripe shirt and tie. Fingers tapped at keyboards with extra force and simple questions were met with snappy retorts. Jack progressed from pacing and hovering to slamming doors and banging his fist against various desks. After thirty-five minutes of marching in and out of his office, traipsing in and around various cubicles, and barking orders at unsuspecting interns, he appeared at Eric's door.

Eric's windpipe constricted.

'Do you mind if I ...?' Jack said as he poked his head into the room.

'No, no, not all,' Eric said. 'Come in, sit down.'

In a dirge-like walk, Jack crossed the office, then hovered, hands on the back of a chair, opposite Eric. It was a solid two minutes before he pulled out said chair and actually sat down. Eric, with his hand having adopted an unexpected quiver, abandoned the email he was writing and focused his full attention on his boss. He swallowed hard.

If anything, the extra lines nested around the corners of Jack's eyes and forehead added to the debonair spirit he carried so well. A touch of Clint Eastwood, perhaps. An older George Clooney. Jack scratched his temple, then his eyebrow, then finally lifted his gaze to meet Eric's.

'Eric,' Jack said. 'You've been at this firm a long time. A very long time.'

'Yes. Yes, I have. I mean I suppose I have.'

'And you've seen a lot of people come and go?'

'Well, I suppose so ...'

'And I bet you've heard a lot of things on the grapevine. A lot of things that maybe people wouldn't like me to hear.'

'I don't know. I don't think so. I mean ... I'm not exactly sure what you mean.'

Eric's pulse rose, sweat forming along his hairline. He really didn't know what Jack meant, and he definitely didn't know where the conversation was about to head, but it was looking less and less likely that Jack had come in to award him the company's very first employee of the month award. Jack leant back on the seat. He took a deep breath in through his nose and rested his fingertips against his brow bone. When he looked back up, he'd aged a decade.

'Sunday was my thirtieth wedding anniversary,' he said. 'Thirty years of marriage to the same wonderful woman.'

'Oh. Congratulations,' Eric said.

'And I forgot it.'

'Oh.'

'Yup.' Jack nodded. 'Thirty years of marriage and I forgot it.'

'Well.' The word came out of Eric in a long, drawn-out gust, expelling the tension that he'd been holding in his lungs since Jack's arrival. 'I'm sure if you do something nice. Buy her a nice present, perhaps? Does she like jewellery?'

Jack shook his head. 'Used that one up. Harry Winston, Bulgari, Cartier. She doesn't even open the boxes anymore. I think this is it. I think I've really blown it this time. She reckons all I care about is the business and the money.'

'What about a trip together then?' Eric grinned as he tried to keep the mood jovial. 'Somewhere special, exclusive. Romantic?'

Jack's head shook again. 'Tried that last year. Took her to Necker, she barely even cracked a smile.'

'Necker?'

'Little island, Richard Branson, and all that. Nice, but what's another beach holiday when she already spends half the year at some resort or another?'

Eric scratched his head. It was clear from this point that Jack had not come in to discuss any matter of impending business doom, yet it was also becoming apparent that he was not planning on leaving until he'd figured some solution. Another email pinged on Eric's screen. The to-do list was mounting, and there was no way of staying late with Abi to sort out.

The silence prolonged past a point of neutral contemplation, and Eric considered telling Jack that a little over a fortnight ago his wife had moved in with her sister on account of his lying and perhaps he'd be better taking his quandaries to Greg, who was clearly far savvier than himself when it came to handling cases of the opposite sex. He reconsidered, however, deciding that perhaps that wasn't the type of information Jack wanted to hear right now. Wishing to speed up the process as much as possible, he did what he often felt he should do in these situations, but never normally managed to master. He channelled his inner Suzy.

'What about going small then?' he said, after a moment's reflection.

'Small?'

'Back to when you first met. I'm assuming she didn't always get twenty-six weeks holiday a year?'

Jack smiled a sad half-smile. 'No, that she didn't. And you're not including the ski-season.'

'Well, why not plan something you'd have done before you had money? Just go for a drive in the car and see where the road takes you. That's what Suze and I used to do, before Abs of course.'

Jack raised an interested eyebrow.

'Go on?'

'You could go to the cinema. Or watch a movie at home with a take-away?' Eric scoured his head for other ideas. 'What about you take a class together? Like a dance class, or a cookery class?' Jack's head cocked to the side. Eric kept on, not wanting to stop now that he was on a roll. 'Wine tasting? I hear there are lots of wine tasting courses. And brewery ones too. Or you could go on a picnic. Take the train down to the coast, book in at some cheap B&B? What about going to a museum? Or grabbing a load of board games and spending a weekend playing Monopoly?' He paused and noted Jack's somewhat bewildered expression. 'What I'm saying is that I'm sure all you have to do is show her that you're still the same man she married, and she'll forget all about the millions you have squirrelled away in the bank.'

Jack jumped to his feet, nodding his head enthusiastically. 'You know what, I think you're right. I know exactly what to do. You're a genius, Eric, you really are. And that wife of yours is one lucky lady.'

Eric glowed inside and out. 'My pleasure, sir.'

Jack bounded across the room and swung open the door. He was partway to his office when he spun around on the spot and bounded back. 'You won't tell anyone of this conversation, will you?' he said, an unusual air of trepidation in his voice.

'Of course not.'

'Just checking,' he said and disappeared again.

With a new sense of accomplishment and motivation, Eric turned back to his computer screen, finished off composing his last email, then stopped. There was a florist on the way home, opposite Abi's school, or at least there had been a few years back. He picked up a Post-It from the pile and a biro from the pot and beneath a memo about staff turnover scribbled down, *Buy Suzy flowers*.

CHAPTER 22

FEBRUARY MELTED INTO March and signs of spring began to appear. In the city, knitted hats and thick woollen scarfs were abandoned in favour of more lightweight versions, and although Easter eggs had graced the shelves of the supermarkets since the second of January, their presence was now highlighted by the countless adverts of over-smiley people gorging themselves on foil-wrapped goodies. In Burlam, the changes were more subtle; bare trees budded with green, boats began to move up and down the estuary. The allotments were the busiest Eric had known them.

Finally, his plot was clear. It had taken more than a little hard graft, during which Eric had discovered several sets of previously dormant muscles, most of which he'd be perfectly happy never to encounter again. However, when all was said and done, even he had to agree it was worth it. The sixty by forty parcel of land was now a serene patch of smooth brown earth, ready for digging and planting, although until this misadventure Eric had never truly understood the misery of weeding.

Weeding for Eric had previously consisted of blasting the Islington patio with a twice-yearly glug of Weedol and occasionally plucking the stray survivors from the fence line. It had been a chore, but then jobs around the house usually were. Weeding in Burlam was never going to be that simple.

During the previous two Saturdays, Eric had spent over three hours clearing the ground, pulling up every root, stem and leaf he could, only to find that when he returned the following weekend they'd returned en masse and brought with them several of their more stoic friends. Eric considered it a genuine ecological mystery that despite slicing, maiming, and uprooting, they kept managing to reappear. The option of weed-killer was highly frowned upon, not only by his fellow alloties but also by Suzy. Suzy was all about organic; organic milk, organic eggs, even organic shampoo, and she sure as hell wasn't going to let Eric grow vegetables in compost filled with more chemicals than the periodic table.

So digging it was. Abi had started to show more interest in the plot and had even become somewhat of an asset when it came to dandelion extraction, albeit in the hope of stockpiling enough to persuade Eric they had to get a rabbit.

One corner of the plot which proved particularly stubborn when it came to weeds was the patch where the old greenhouse had stood. In a burst of inspiration, Eric decided an easy way to rectify this was to put another one in its place. He also purchased – with a sizeable discount given the greenhouse – a small shed. By the end of March, Sunday mornings had developed into an unnerving routine involving traipsing around garden centres and pining over the excessively expensive accessories one apparently required to grow a batch of carrots.

It was Sunday evening and Eric was lying in bed. Suzy had been out for over an hour beside him. The pages of her book lay crumpled between her face and the pillows as a soft semi-snore buzzed from between her lips. The scent of fresh earth clung to her hair; evidence of their family day at the plot.

'Gotcha!' Eric shouted.

'What? What is it?' Suzy jerked awake and flicked on her light. 'What's wrong?'

'Raised beds.' Eric waved his book at her.

'What?'

'I can do raised beds. We can make them out of old timber, line them, fill them with compost, and boom. Then the rest of the earth we can pave over and nuke with enough weed-killer to flatten the Amazon.'

'I'm sorry,' Suzy rubbed her eyes and stretched before she relocated her crumpled book to the side-table. 'Are you talking about the allotment?'

'Of course, what did you think I was talking about?'

'What time is it?'

'I don't know. Half eleven maybe?' Eric glanced at the clock beside him. 'Twelve forty then. What does it matter?'

'You're right, it doesn't.' Suzy groaned, switched the light back off and buried her head back into the pillows.

'So?' Eric insisted. 'What do you think?'

'About the fact it's twenty to one?'

'About the raised beds?'

Suzy muttered something, almost certainly uncomplimentary about raised beds, into her pillow and drifted back off to sleep.

Still, it was such a good idea that the next morning, and afternoon, it remained lodged at the forefront of Eric's mind. During the marketing team's meeting, his thoughts were fixated on what type of wood he would use, and where, of course, he could source it. During his working lunch with Greg, he was wondering whether the leftover crusts from his thin-pan goat's cheese and artichoke heart pizza would make for good compost. On the way home, he struck gold.

* * *

'WHAT THE HELL ARE YOU DOING?' Suzy asked when she glided past the dining room that evening and came to an abrupt stop. Eric was crouched down on the floor among nails, hammers, and various offcut planks. A decrepit wooden door lay flat on the dining room table, the paint chipped and peeling, and emanating a scent reminiscent of blocked drains and day-old kebabs.

'Don't worry, it looks worse than it is.'

'I very much doubt that,' she said.

Noting his wife's obvious disdain, Eric rose to standing and surveyed the situation himself. There were flecks of paint working their way into the beige carpet, and a long streak of mud marked the door's entry route into the room. Four more doors were resting against the wall, a spirit level was on its side propped against a pack of eighteen-inch stakes, and dozens of nails were sprinkled like confetti, marking out a clear silhouette of where Eric had been sitting. Charging by the plug-socket was the old Philips electric screwdriver they'd been given as a wedding present.

'I'll admit, it looks a bit of a mess now, but by bedtime you won't even know I've been in here.'

Suzy didn't move. Deciding it was best to get back to work, Eric started to shift smaller pieces of wood onto bigger ones until he found what he was looking for. A small bag of nails.

'You know we have a garden?' Suzy said. 'We have a perfectly good garden you could do this in?'

'I did think that. But it was already getting dark when I got all this, and I didn't want to waste any more time fumbling around not being able to see properly.'

'We have patio lights,' Suzy stated, and Eric had to admit he couldn't think of a response to counter that.

'What exactly is all this?' Suzy said. 'And where did you get it?'

Eric beamed at the question. 'You're going to love this,' he said.

'Really?'

Eric's smile stretched across his face. It was a face evocative of the expression a teenage boy would use to tell his friends he'd finally gone and popped his cherry, radiating satisfaction and pride from every pore.

'I got them from a tip,' he said.

'Pardon?'

'A tip. That grubby yellow builder's tip. Just down the end of the road. Can you believe that?'

'To be honest —'

'It's saved us a fortune. It's brilliant. I reckon I'll be able to make five beds from this lot. Maybe even more.'

'I'm sorry, you're doing what?'

Eric was about to reply – rather bluntly given that in his mind they'd already discussed the matter at length last night in bed – when Abi bounded in through the door, waving a two-foot-long, matte grey, steel crowbar.

'Is this what you wanted, Daddy?'

'Perfect.'

Eric grabbed the crowbar and jammed it into a gap between two planks of wood. He tensed his biceps and flexed his arm ready to wrench. He stopped and turned to his wife.

'Sorry, darling. Was there something you wanted me to do?'

Suzy's line of sight went from the dining table to the crowbar and back several times.

'No,' she said. 'Nothing at all.'

Despite Suzy's concerns, Eric deemed the dining room a most suitable location for the separating and sorting of the wood and timber, although even he couldn't deny it wasn't ideal for building the actual beds. They needed to be secured into the ground as they were built, and the only way to do that was to be on site. After a brief discussion with Suzy, he decided to book a room at the Sailboat for the following Saturday night.

'I know it was a bit chintzy,' Eric said. 'But even if we stay at your sister's, it'll be ten before we're down there and then we'll have already lost half the day. Besides, I looked on their website and it says they have family rooms, so at least we won't be so cramped.'

Suzy agreed. 'You'll have to take Abi for a couple hours on Sunday, though. I need a bit of time in the morning to get some work done or I'm going to miss these deadlines.'

'That's not a problem. I've got the perfect job. You can go find worms for my compost heap can't you, Abs? You'd like that, wouldn't you, going and finding lots of long wiggly worms?' Abi screamed in delight as her father chased her around the house, wiggling his fingers and making apparently wormesque noises. When Eric eventually collapsed on the sofa from exhaustion, Abi continued to spend next five minutes jumping on the sofa singing 'We're going to eat some worms at the weekend!' to the tune of *Daddy's Taking Us to the Zoo*. Their weekend was decided.

❧

WHILE THE OLD Philips screwdriver had served them well in their twelve years of marriage – if Eric's memory served him right, it had hung at least fourteen photo frames in that time – he decided he needed something with a bit more oomph for the amount of drilling and screwing he'd planned for the weekend. So, en route to Burlam, he detoured into Chelmsford and Lewis at Tools4U.

'You have to be kidding,' Lewis said when he saw him. 'You know you've lost your deposit on everything you've hired from us so far?'

'Which is why you should be even more grateful for my custom. You have insurance. You're raking it in. Besides, I'm not hiring anything today.'

'No?'

'No, my wife is.'

Lewis rolled his eyes.

'And I guess she doesn't need instructions on how to use these tools either?' he said.

'That'd be like cheating,' Eric replied and waited for him to fetch the power tools.

It was amazing the difference a month and a few good days of weather could make. Late Saturday morning, the allotment bustled with activity, and even Janice was too busy raking parallel lines in her topsoil to look up and announce Eric and the family's arrival. Either that or he was now too commonplace to be worthy of her high-level greetings. Suzy decided she needed to clear her head before she got to work and so took Abi for a walk along the river in search of seals while Eric unloaded the car. As well as the Black and Decker cordless drill, Eric had also borrowed – in Suzy's name – a workbench and a small jigsaw from Lewis at the shop. It wasn't until he'd unloaded all the wood and was setting up the workbench that he noticed Norman.

Eric had kept a peripheral eye on the pathway the entire time, for the exact reason of noting Norman's arrival. As such, he was unsure how he'd slipped past without his notice.

Two months had done nothing to ease the tension between the two, although Eric had made a conscious effort not to engage Norman in any form of eye contact at the risk it may turn into a conversation. Thus far the plan appeared to have worked. As Eric glanced up from his workbench, he accidentally caught the old man's eye across the plot. His stomach dropped. He was left with no option other than to offer a quick, obligatory nod.

'Still here then?' he said to Eric in a gravelly, lung-crackling growl.

'Not going anywhere, I'm afraid.'

'We'll see,' Norman said, then hobbled back into his shed, to return several minutes later with a trowel and a cup of tea in hand.

It was slower work than Eric had anticipated and more physically demanding, but by the time Suzy called to ask if he wanted to meet them for lunch, he had one planter fully built and lined and another four with pilot holes drilled, ready to be assembled.

'I noticed the little cinema in town has opened up again,' Eric said to Suzy as he chewed on his crab roll. 'I don't suppose they've got anything good on, but I thought we could take a look?'

'That sounds like a great idea,' Suzy said. Abi was too busy feeding her roll to the seagulls to reply.

Once lunch had been devoured, it was back to the allotment. Eric finished off one more of the planters before packing everything up and locking it in his shed. It was a cold evening, but a gentle cold. The type that made you feel grateful you had a nice warm coat and thick socks but didn't turn your fingers to ice or cause you to sprint for the radiator as soon as you got inside. The weeds had sprouted yet again, and he spent a scant half hour plucking what he could. It was only a half-hearted effort and more for appearance's sake than anything else. Drilling and sawing may have been the necessities of the day, but it didn't make him look any more of a gardener, unlike Norman who had spent all afternoon on his hands and knees digging around in the dirt, coughing up dozens of alveoli in the process.

The cinema was a pleasant surprise. While the white facade of the building advertised films a good six months old, inside played a surprisingly updated schedule. With Abi the controlling factor, they opted for the latest Pixar movie. A third of the way in, Eric's phone beeped in his pocket. When Abi and Suzy shot him simultaneous glares, he took it out and switched it off without so much as a second glance at the screen.

Abi was practically sleepwalking on the way back to the Sailboat. While Eric carried her up the narrow stairs – trying not to disturb her as he manoeuvred around the bannister and unlocked the door – Suzy went to the off-licence for a bottle of gin and some tonic.

'You know,' she said as they sat cross-legged on the pink satin sheets and clinked their glasses. 'I don't think I've seen you this relaxed for years.'

'Really?' Eric said. 'I can think of how to make me much, much more relaxed.' Then he put down his glass and began to nuzzle.

CHAPTER 23

AS PROMISED, ERIC took Abi in the morning so that Suzy could get on with some more work. With no proper desk in the room, she took herself down to The Shed, where Griff sorted her out with a space in the back and a double-shot macchiato to get her going.

With all the sawing done, Eric just had to assemble the remaining planters. He knelt on the ground, drilled into his salvaged planks, and noted how many of the pieces were tattooed with the hapless doodles of a child with a biro. One of the planks even had horizontal markers and names etched next to the notches. This was far better than buying something prefab, he decided. This planter had a life, a soul. And weren't plants meant to like things like that?

Abi spent a solid hour digging for earthworms. She'd collected quite a few, although the receptacle she was using – a plastic saucer – was highly inefficient in its function. As a result, she spent most of her time moving the same half-dozen worms back onto the plate from wherever they'd managed to slither to while her back was turned. Eric thought he should possibly inform her of the issue but at the same time, it was keeping her quiet.

'Look, Dad. Look what I've got,' she said after a particularly quiet twenty minutes. 'Look what Aunty Cynthia gave me.'

Eric lifted his head. 'Aunty who?'

Abi stood in front of him. Her nails were black with dirt, as were the knees of her dungarees and the end of her scarf. In her hand, she held a little white packet.

'Aunty Cynthia.'

'Sorry.' Cynthia stood behind her, grey roots peeking out from her red hair, an apologetic smile creasing her eyes. 'Aunty Cynthia. Force of habit. We're Aunty and Uncle to all the little ones around here.'

'Cynthia will do fine,' Eric said.

'Of course. Of course.'

'Look, Daddy. Look at what she gave me,' Abi held out her hand. 'They're seeds. Scallywags seed.'

'Scallions,' Cynthia clarified. 'Spring onion seeds.'

'And Aunty Cynthia says I can grow them in the greenhouse. Or I can grow them at home too, but then I have to put them in the greenhouse when they're bigger. That's right isn't it?'

'That's right. You remembered that perfectly.'

'Can I grow them at home, Dad? Can I? Then I can take them to school when it's my turn at Show and Tell.'

'Why don't you put them in the greenhouse? We can bring some pots down next weekend. And then your mum won't get annoyed with all the mess.'

Abi's face fell. 'But then I won't get to take them into Show and Tell. And I'll end up taking something rubbish in, like a doll, or one of mum's books. And Harry Nini will think that's rubbish because he gets to take his rat in and he's taken it in four times now and I've never taken in anything that good, not even once.'

Glossing over his eight-year-old daughter's reoccurring interest in Harry Nini, Eric made one last attempt.

'But we don't have anything in the greenhouse. And it's the only empty greenhouse on the allotment. Your spring onions can be the first things that grow in it. Don't you think that's cool? Don't you want your seeds to be the very first thing that's ever, ever been grown in this greenhouse? Ever?'

Abi contemplated for a second, took another admiring glance at the packet in the hand, then said, quite definitely, 'No.'

W㎎ all was done for the day, Eric stepped back to survey his kingdom. Six glorious planters of approximately the same size and nearly straight edges sat flush to the earth below. Even without any soil, or plants, or bean poles, they looked impressive. The multi-coloured stains of the pre-loved wood gave a romantic patina; a vintage feel to them. First stop Burlam, he thought, next stop Chelsea Flower Show.

'So, next week, it's sowing, right?' Suzy said. 'I thought your book said you should have already planted all your beans and whatnots by now?'

'The beans should be okay,' Eric said. 'But we've probably missed asparagus for this year. Shame though. We'll have to remember next year.'

'Next year? Good God, you're taking this seriously.'

'I'm just following my father's orders,' he said.

Abi was currently with another group of children crouched around a small cardboard box.

'I guess we should get her and get going,' Eric said. 'It's a pain I've got to go to work tomorrow. I feel like I've had a mini holiday.'

'Well you've still got all your holiday days racked up,' Suzy reminded him. 'I'm sure Jack wouldn't mind if you rang him now and said you wanted to take a couple of them last minute.'

Eric shook his head. 'No, I couldn't do that to him at the minute. He's been a bit stressed out lately.'

'That doesn't sound like Jack?'

Eric was about to tell her about Jack's missed wedding anniversary, when someone coughed, loudly and with obvious force, directly behind him. Eric swivelled around.

Norman's beard was a truly impressive feature, particularly from this distance. The tight white hairs coiled and spiralled into a thick nest that stretched all the way from his temples to his breastbone, narrowing down into a thin, pristine point. His lips and nostrils were lost entirely to it, and his eyes, though visible, were currently set down, and thus greatly obscured by his massive white eyebrows.

He coughed again, although this time the cough was genuine.

'I wondered if you might have a moment for a word,' he said.

Eric exchanged a glance with Suzy.

'I need to go get Abi,' she said to him. 'I'll see you in a minute, by the gate.'

'I'll only be a minute,' Eric said, then braced himself.

With Suzy gone, Norman continued to stare at the ground. His hands were in his pockets as he shuffled from one foot to the other.

'Did you want something?' Eric said, surprising even himself with the churlishness of his voice.

Norman looked up. He ran his tongue over his top lip, pushing some of the white whiskers momentarily to the side. He cleared his throat again, with a few more catarrhy coughs, then mumbled with his mouth half-closed.

'I 'spect that maybe –'

'Sorry, can you speak up?' Eric said. 'I'm afraid I can't hear you.'

Norman's eyes flashed, and his nostrils flared widely, although just the once. He closed his eyes then opened them again straight away and began to speak.

'I know we didn't get off on the best foot an' all —'

'With you trying to get me evicted you mean?'

'— and I 'spect I was a bit hasty with my actions, like. But I would like to try to make some 'mends.'

'Pardon?' Eric said.

'I said, I'd like to make amends. Apologise.' He glanced over his shoulder, where Eric spotted Cynthia. She was urging him onwards with encouraging nods.

He turned back to Eric, sucked in a deep lungful of air, held it in his chest, and stretched out his hand.

Eric examined the hand in front of him. It was creased and cracked like no hand he'd ever seen. Every crevice was brown, sealed in years of mud and soil, and there were splits in the fingertips, red and raw and centimetres long. That was before he even got to the dirt that covered them. Eric thought about the situation in front of him. He had no desire to shake hands with this man, particularly when the hand looked like an extra from *The Walking Dead*. But behind him, Eric could feel Suzy watching him, willing him to do the right thing. He held his breath, gritted his teeth, and stretched out his hand.

They had barely touched fingertips when Norman withdrew his hand and plunged it back into his pocket.

'I got you something. For your greenhouse like. Can't be having a greenhouse like that, all new with nothing in. Someone'll steal it. Or smash it. Need to be growing something in it.'

He pulled out a small packet of seeds, not dissimilar to the ones that Cynthia had given Abi earlier in the day.

'Dutch coriander,' he said. 'Start it off at home, I would. Too delicate with the weather being what it's like at the minute. One frost even in your greenhouse'd see it off.'

'Oh,' Eric said, unsure of what else he could say.

'Be best to bring it down 'ere start o' April. When they're nicely sprouted. Then you can put it in your greenhouse. You'll have some lovely plants.'

'Well, I don't know what –'

'Don't want to eat it raw, though. Not like that other stuff. No, you bring it down here come April and I'll tell you the best way to get cooking it.'

Eric took the packet and tipped a few of the seeds onto his palm. They were seedlike; seed-shaped, browny green. He almost expected his hand to start fizzing, not placing it above Norman to douse them with acid or some caustic sap, but nothing happened. He poured them back into the packet.

'A late housewarming, if you will,' Norman said.

What followed was an exceptionally awkward silence in which Eric experienced a peculiar gnawing around his large intestine. His mouth grew dry and his Adam's apple swelled. Norman waited, eyes wide and feet rooted to the spot.

No way, Eric thought to himself. *Not a chance.*

But Norman wasn't budging. Eric's palms grew sweaty. There had to be another way, there had to. But there wasn't. There was only one thing Eric could do, and he hated himself for it. If only Suzy wasn't watching. If only he could just walk away. Swallowing hard Eric took a deep breath and said it as fast as he could.

'Thank you,' he mumbled at his feet.

'What was that?'

'I said thank you.'

Norman smirked.

'I shall get some compost and seed trays and plant them next week,' Eric added for good measure.

Norman shook his head.

'I've got plenty of compost in my shed. And trays mind. Why don't you plant 'em now? It'll only take two minutes.'

'Well, I need to get Abi home,'

Norman huffed away his excuses.

'She can help you. Besides, Cynth has got a few seed trays she wanted to give her for those spring onions. Couple weeks and you'll have a full 'erb garden up 'ere.'

'Well ...'

'Two minutes. Let me get you those trays.' Then he added, 'I can tell you all about the mole fiasco while we're at it.'

It took less than five minutes to get all the seeds potted, and when they left to head back to London, they had four plastic containers of Dutch coriander and spring onions ready to sit on their kitchen window sill.

'Well that was lovely,' Suzy said. 'Give it a few weeks and you two will be thick as thieves.'

'I sincerely doubt that,' Eric said.

CHAPTER 24

THE FIRST THING Eric had felt was an icy blast as the covers were whipped off the bed, exposing his semi-naked body to the air. Next had come the vigorous shaking of the shoulders and the ear-splitting shriek.

'Daddy! Dad! Dad! Daddy! Daddy! Daddy! Dad! Dad! Are you up? Are you awake? Are you awake yet?'

'I am now.'

'It's today, Daddy, it's Tuesday.'

'Really? Are you sure? I thought it was Monday. It's Monday isn't it, Mummy?'

Suzy rolled over and curled herself up into the remainder of the duvet.

'You know what. I think you're right. I think it's Monday.'

'It's not! It's Tuesday,' Abi yelled. 'And you promised. You promised you'd come. You're still coming aren't you, Dad?'

Eric leant over the side of the mattress and hoisted Abi up onto the bed.

'Of course I'm coming. I promised, didn't I?'

April had arrived with its stereotypical showers and less typical frost, and as such, Eric's lovingly crafted planters remained sparsely populated with compost, old newspaper, and earthworms, but as yet, no vegetation. However, his greenhouse was faring a little better.

A sizeable variety of flora were germinating away in their little plastic pots, and as well as the usual suspects – lettuces (romaine and cos), chard, potatoes, Brussels sprouts, courgettes – he'd also tried his beginner's hand at a few of the more exotic specimens, such as aubergine and artichoke. His expectations were low, impressively so, although with every week that passed, something that could have been akin to anticipation bubbled away inside.

This upcoming weekend – frost depending – was transplant weekend, when everything that could and should be grown outside was going to be moved. In preparation, Abi had spent the last fortnight using the allotment as her inspiration for the Reduce, Reuse, and Recycle project at school. The results were an imposing sight. Along with the stereotypical DIY gardening effects you would expect from a eight-year-old – bird feeder, row markers, hanging baskets, and seed boxes – Abi had also proved herself to be quite the engineer. With the help of Google, Suzy, and Eric, she'd created a drip irrigation feed system out of plastic bottles – enough to place several in each of Eric's planters – and even her own mini polytunnel, created from densely glue-gunned empty coke bottles. Today was Show and Tell at school, and everything was going in.

Abi had been in a fit of excitement for over a week. So much so that on Saturday, Cynthia had had to take her down into town to get her an ice cream so that Eric could get five minutes productive sowing in. Suzy had offered to keep Abi for the morning, but he knew she had deadlines looming and keeping Suzy happy was still paramount on his list of agendas.

Eric's affection for Cynthia had done nothing but warm, and after his initial misgivings, he'd relented to the title of Aunty Cynthia. The prefix of uncle, however, still made him gag when used in reference to Norman.

It remained a mystery to him how Cynthia had managed to suffer Norman and his indignation for so long. He skulked around from one side of his plot to the next, hacking phlegm over all the beds as he coughed and wheezed, grunting obscenities under his breath at almost anyone who attempted to speak to him. There were a few exceptions, of course, Hank being one. Eric, however, was still firmly off the list. So, when Norman initiated small talk with Eric on the subject of Abi's Show and Tell, he was rather taken aback.

'Taking in all her seeds too, she says.'

'Um, well yes, that's the plan. The ones we've grown at home, anyway.'

'And that'll mean you taking a morning off work then, will it?'

'Well yes.'

'That's something I suppose.'

Eric continued to tell Norman a few facts about Abi's school; highly focused on the arts, and an international exchange programme that ran throughout Europe and South-East Asia.

'A choice of six languages to study from Year One.'

'Sounds grand,' Norman said. 'Can she say deadly nightshade in French?'

'What? Why?' Eric frowned.

''Cos it looks like she's just picked a load from that bush.'

Over by the edge of the allotment, Abi was studying something in her hand.

'*Abi!*'

Eric bolted towards his daughter, trampling over several allotments en route, and leaving great gaping footprints in the soil. Abi had her hand millimetres from her mouth. Dozens of beads glistened black in the sunlight, piled high in her cupped palm. With his heart in his throat, Eric lunged, diving across the air. He swung his arm towards Abi knocking the berries out of her hand a millisecond before they touched her lips.

'Dad! What did you do that for?'

Eric collapsed on the floor, panting. He grabbed his daughter by the wrist.

'You must never eat those berries, Abi. You hear me? Never. Not even one. Not ever.'

'What? Why?'

'They're poisonous. They'll kill you. They could have killed you.'

Abi crinkled her nose.

'Those berries,' Eric pointed to the glistening spheres now scattered on the ground. 'They're called deadly nightshade. And they're very, very dangerous.'

'No, they're not.'

'Abi, I'm not messing about.' Eric pulled himself up to feet. Now that the immediate threat was over the surge of adrenaline transformed into anger. 'You eat deadly nightshade berries and you'll end up in hospital, or worse. You hear me? Do you understand?'

'But they're not —'

'Abi will you please listen?'

'*You're* not listening to me.'

'No. You're not listening to me.'

'No,' Abi insisted with a stamp of her foot. 'You are not listening to me. That,' she pointed to a bush a little way behind Eric, 'is deadly nightshade, although it doesn't have any berries on yet and won't for another four months or so. Those,' she redirected her pointed finger to the black baubles in the dirt by her feet, 'are jellybeans.'

'What?'

'Jellybeans. They're jellybeans, see.'

She pulled out an open pack from her pocket. The crumpled bag was three-quarters full of little red and black spheres. 'Uncle Norman gave them to me. Just before he told me about deadly nightshade. And he said there's a badger somewhere in this hedge too. Have you seen it anywhere?'

Eric returned to his plot. Norman was resting against his pitchfork, his lips pursed in a whistle, a glint of satisfaction in his eye.

So, Eric had taken the morning off work. Jack had been fine about it. Since their heart to heart, nothing more had been said about the state of his marriage, although more than once Eric had knocked on his office door to find him giggling on his phone and using a series of endearments more commonly uttered by a sixteen-year-old girl.

As well as all the recycled articles, Abi also wanted to take in her spring onion plants, which were now proudly sprouting two inches above the soil, and Eric's Dutch coriander, which was demonstrating equally impressive growth. Mostly though she wanted to take in her dad, and Eric had at last relented.

Eric wasn't sure when he'd last stepped past the reception of Abi's school. *Mamma Mia* had taken place in the auditorium and he'd missed the Easter parade a few weeks before due to a meeting. Despite Suzy's insistence that this parade was an important educational milestone for their daughter, it seemed to Eric more of a trident display of parents' arts and crafts ability as opposed to anything to do with the actual children. As such, he suffered no remorse whatsoever for missing that one. As for parents' evenings, he'd told himself that he'd start to go when they actually mattered; GCSEs and above. Before then, there was nothing a teacher could tell him in a seven-minute meeting, cramped on a tiny child's chair in a room that smelt of poster paint, that couldn't be expressed more succinctly in a nice written report.

Show and Tell took place in the Key Stage One library. Only it didn't look like a library, it looked like a living room, or a play centre, or the hybrid mix if a genius child of the future had designed a living room with only play in mind. Rainbow beanbags were scattered across the floor while sizeable TV screens glowed with animated versions of Grimm's fairy tales and Julia Donaldson stories. Along one wall was a bank of computers, while on the other were half a dozen little cubby holes. Three-feet deep and the same wide, each of the cubby holes was padded with cushions, set with dim lights and a curtain, and also fitted with a television, iPod, and a set of headphones. There was a water fountain, a snack desk, and a little plastic box labelled *Ideas*. It was definitely not a library, it was Google HQ in the making. In fact, the only thing that really gave away the scholarly nature of the place was the perfectly procured aroma of pencil sharpenings and the rather voluptuous lady behind the desk who wore her thick-rimmed glasses on a chain around her neck.

Bang on ten, Abi's class arrived. Six other children were doing Show and Tell that day, and four of them had at least one parent there. They, like Eric, had clearly been dragged under duress, although unlike Eric they did not have such an active role in the performance aspect. Instead, they viewed their child's presentation through the screen of their iPhones, while attempting to reply to messages as subtly as possible and make sure they didn't miss the correct time to applaud. While Eric in no way considered himself unbiased, the other children's contributions could be considered, at best, dismal.

There was one vaguely decent attempt in which a boy with a straight fringe and sticky-out ears had recycled an old shoebox to form an elastic band guitar. The neck was made from toilet rolls and he'd even cut out some little cardboard pegs to stick on the end for authentic value. It looked good in the sense that it looked like a pile of absolute crap that an eight-year-old would make as an extended task that meant their teacher avoided any actual marking for a week. Eric was quickly reminded why he hated these types of things.

With the shoebox guitar the highlight, the rest of the offerings failed to hit anywhere near the mark. There was another shoebox, this time marketed as a reusable tissue box. From the clapping and applause the child received, it appeared to Eric that the rest of the audience had failed to grasp the fundamental flaw with the design, being that tissues did, in fact, come in their own box. There was a pencil case made from a toilet roll with one end cardboarded over and no evidence of decoration, and a coke-bottle rocket, imaginatively embellished with fins and blasters, that could apparently fly, only the child's parents wouldn't let him bring in the pump to prove this. Then it was Abi's turn.

Eric's pulse ratcheted up a knot as Abi took to the front of the class. Her arms were stretched wide around the makeshift mini polytunnel as she chose her footing carefully between her classmates. Once at the front, she set the object down on the teacher's desk before dashing back to the classroom to get the rest of the items. After three return trips, she had everything she needed.

'Good morning 2P,' Abi said to the class.

Her eyes darted to her father. Eric's stomach fluttered, and his heart thumped against the wall of his rib cage. He offered her an encouraging smile, but she didn't move. She'd frozen.

'Go, on,' Eric mouthed to her. 'You can do this.'

A thin bead of sweat meandered down past Eric's collar. Pep talks were one of those many facets that did not fall under his capacity as a parent. Pep talks at work were fine, but as a parent, he always missed the mark; a thump on the arm while telling a four-year-old child to buck up their ideas and focus on the big picture was apparently not always the required response. Neither was telling them not be such a wuss.

Abi's eyes still hadn't moved from her father, and several other children were now looking at him too. The one bead of sweat on Eric's neck was quickly joined by others. Channelling his inner Suzy, he shut his eyes, tilted his chin up, and took a deep yogic breath. The air hissed as he sucked it in through his nose. *You can do this*, he said in his head, praying the words would somehow transfer to Abi and she'd get the idea of following his lead. He opened his eyes and smiled.

'You've got this, kiddo,' he mouthed to her.

Abi closed her eyes, took a long inhale, then flicked her eyes open with a glint. A swish of her hair and she turned her attention back to the class.

'At the end of last year,' she began, 'my dad inherited an allotment. Inherited means when you get someone's stuff because they're dead ...'

Abi's speech went by in a flash. She explained in detail how she'd managed to join the bottles together to make the polytunnel and how to weight one side of the bird feeders so it wouldn't just spill out as soon as a bird sat on it. She described how the irrigation system meant you could get the water right to the roots of the plants, which was where it needed to be if the plants were going to grow, and when one child asked for a demonstration, she had no difficulty instructing her teacher to go and fetch the necessary water and an empty plastic bucket.

For her *finale* she passed around the seedlings, allowing the students to prod and poke at them at their will.

'Can we eat this?' one child said when handed Eric's Dutch coriander.

'I don't think so,' the teacher said, then looked to Eric as if for confirmation.

Eric shrugged. 'Um, I don't know. It's not fully grown yet. And I think you're meant to cook it first. It's probably better not to.'

The teacher conveyed this information to the child with a look. 'Pass it on for now,' she said. 'I'm sure Abi will bring some in when it's grown.'

At the end of the presentations, the children stood up then, clattering and chattering, went back to their classroom. Abi swung her arms around Eric as she passed.

'Thank you for coming,' she said.

❦

'SHE WAS INCREDIBLE. I mean, she's such a natural speaker in front of a crowd. Did I tell you she sent the teacher out to get some water when one of the children wanted a demonstration?'

'You did,' said Suzy. 'Twice.' She pecked him on the cheek. 'But it's great that you're so proud of her.'

Eric pulled three plates out from the dishwasher, then grabbed a handful of cutlery. He thought he might have overshared a bit at work too, as for the first time he could remember it was Greg who had to ask Eric to leave his office as he wanted to get some work done, as opposed to the other way around. Fortunately, he ran into Jack two minutes later, who was more than happy to listen to Eric regale him with tales of his daughter's ascension to social science guru.

Abi skipped into the kitchen and hopped up at the table.

'I was just telling your mum how fantastic you were again,' Eric said, laying out the crockery.

'Dad, you don't have to keep going on.'

'I'm not.'

Suzy spooned out the biryani while Eric doled out equal portions of pappadams.

'I thought I might see if I can leave early Friday,' Eric said as he sat down. 'It'll mean working late for a couple of nights, but I thought we could head down to Burlam in the evening again. I seem to get a lot more done that way.'

'Sounds great, only I have to work. I'm behind on this book. I honestly don't know where the time has gone. I thought if you were driving down Saturday, you could drop Abi at Lyd's on the way? You wouldn't mind that would you, hun?' Suzy looked at Abi, who shrugged in response.

Eric shook his head. 'It's fine. I'll take Abi down with me on Friday. That way you get the whole evening to work. Then if you want, you can come and join us Saturday. If not, Abi and I'll just work on together. There's a lot to get on with. We've got a state-of-the-art recycled irrigation system to set up, don't you know?'

Abi beamed.

'Yay! I'm coming too,' she said.

'That's settled then,' said Eric. 'I'll ring the Sailboat and book our room now.'

CHAPTER 25

ERIC'S FATHER-DAUGHTER bonding weekend didn't get off to an ideal start. He had somehow mis-communicated to Suzy that he'd been planning on taking Sally down to Burlam, and while the law was on his side in regard to taking a child in the back seat of a vintage car, Suzy was not. Forty minutes of his afternoon was spent going back and forth via text, email, and finally voice call between himself, Suzy, and Ralph before he finally conceded. It was a tough loss to take, but they could have been there until midnight otherwise. As it was, it was gone three by the time they'd finally packed up the Audi with their plant paraphernalia. Twenty miles of moderately light traffic through London and then, less than half a mile onto the A12, they hit a tailback that left them in stationary traffic for over three-quarters of an hour. Eric could sense a pressure headache developing beneath his temples. He gave Abi her headphones, told her she could watch whatever she fancied, then switched on Radio 4. Rachmaninov did little for the traffic but did at least manage to abate a migraine.

They arrived in Burlam just after six. With Abi and Eric both at the stage of hunger that meant either one of them may have thrown themselves onto the ground, hammering their fists at the slightest infraction, they parked up directly outside the chippy and went straight inside. After food, the evening consisted of an old-school Disney marathon with *The Little Mermaid*, *The Jungle Book*, and one-third of *The Lion King*, all watched in bed on Eric's laptop and thus absolving him of any guilt over not checking his emails.

Abi's eyelids fluttered as he lifted her up off the double bed and transplanted her into her own. *She looks so much like her mum*, Eric thought, brushing her hair out of her eyes. 'Sleep tight, princess,' he said and tucked her up in the duvet.

Saturday was brisk, although in the sun the heat was strong enough to make you want to remove your jacket and perhaps even consider wearing just one layer, long sleeved of course. Out of it and you were quickly reminded that April in the UK was definitely spring and nowhere near summer, and that your vest and cargo shorts should remain well and truly at the bottom of the wardrobe for at least another two months.

When they arrived, Hank was the only person there. Abi wanted to get there even earlier, having laid out all her labels and water bottles before the Disney-athon the night before, but Eric insisted they have breakfast first. While Abi ate a fairly substantial Chubby Little Bugger, Eric had his first Fat Bastard. All ordering was done by pointing at the menu, as even Eric wasn't naïve enough to believe Abi wouldn't pass on every detail of the weekend to Suzy, including a detailed and itemised list of each and every profanity he used.

At the allotment, Eric tipped bag after bag of garden-store compost into his planters, packing it down lightly onto the bin bags and newspaper as he prepared to transfer the bulk of his seedlings from the greenhouse.

In recent weeks, he'd come across the idea of companion planting. It was an appealing concept that involved planting different combinations of fruit and vegetables together in order to deter pests from one another and help maintain an organic crop without the use of pesticides. Suzy was all for it, and while Eric wasn't against it, the only issue was the amount of time he'd spent figuring out the logistics of the arrangements within his six by four raised beds.

Potatoes, for example, were compatible with several vegetables including lettuce, beans, and cabbage, but combative if planted with tomatoes. Whereas onions were ideal planting partners for carrots, beetroot, and strawberries, the effects were far less desirable when placed next to peas and beans. Radishes apparently deterred cucumber beetles while tomato leaves could repel the insects that munched their way through cabbages. But did he really want to plant his radishes next to his cucumbers or would they be better next to spinach, which they insulated against bugs, or lettuce, which would apparently make the radishes a delicious entity in their own right as opposed to an unelected buffer against the harsh insect world that awaits all home-grown, chemical-free vegetables?

Eric had studiously worked out places for most of his items although a few he intended on leaving in the greenhouse until they'd gained a little more growth. For no other reason than sentimentality, he also felt it only fair to give the spring onions and Dutch coriander seedlings a little time to acclimatise in the greenhouse before thrusting them out into the British climate after spending several weeks in a cosy London kitchen. With the plants spread out in their proposed positions, all that was needed was for Eric to pick up his trowel and dig the first little trench.

'Aunty Cynthia! Uncle Norman!'

Abi bounded across the allotment, brandishing her irrigation system as she went. The couple walked hand in hand through the rows. Eric did a double take. He had always thought of Cynthia as a rather youthful pensioner, but from this distance, she looked decidedly old. Her shoulders slumped, and her gait dragged as a heavy bag weighed her down on one side. Still, she shook off the years and smiled enthusiastically when she saw Abi bounding towards her.

'You're down here early,' Cynthia said.

She dropped the bag by her own shed before ambling over towards his. The scent of Dettol and blackberries shrouded the air around her.

'Abi and I came down last night. An important day today. Lots to do.'

'My, my, yes. And this must be your watering invention,' Cynthia said to Abi. 'Goodness me, it looks very technical.'

While Cynthia crouched down to listen to Abi's tales of her school presentation and a detailed scientific explanation of how to use a compass to pierce holes in a coke bottle, Norman cast his eyes over the allotment.

'So, you've started planting at last?' Norman said.

'Just about to,' Eric said. As he spoke the muscles in his neck turned taut, and a strange yet familiar sensation whorled its way through his abdomen. He held his breath and waited.

While the majority of Eric's functioning sense cells wanted nothing more than to tell Norman that he could keep whatever opinions he had about Eric's current horticultural layout to himself, the other part of Eric was in conflict. Seeing his seedlings sprout up through the soil over the last three weeks had been something akin to when Eric discovered he was going to be a father. He hadn't felt a great need to celebrate each shoot with a bottle of Moët and had been much more candid about the exact processes involved than when Abi had asked him how babies were made only four weeks back, but still, he'd done a simple act and created life. He was a miracle maker. The fruits of his labours were burgeoning around, and all he could do was watch and wait in wonder. And yet, until that life was fully grown and slapped up on a plate in front of him – the sentiment had been slightly different in regard to Abi, obviously – a nervous trepidation simmered constantly away in his belly. He'd found himself with a less than hospitable gut these last two nights and was well aware as to the root of the cause. The last thing he needed was the male-midwife of the vegetable patch coming over to tell him that he'd failed as a plant parent before his seedlings were even out of their pots.

'Overpaid for that compost,' Norman said and nudged one of the seventy-five-litre bags with his toe.

Eric decided to take a step back, bite his tongue, and await the verdict.

Norman's eyes scrutinised the freshly composted beds. The hair above his top lip wobbled as he exhaled in heavy grunts. He looked first at the potatoes with their flat, rounded bract, then the lettuce, then the tomatoes. In fact, Eric was certain Norman had examined every single specimen before his gaze finally settled on the greenhouse. He took several strides between the beds, slid the glass door open, then stepped inside. Eric followed, a nervous twitch running down the side of his left leg.

'I thought I was under watering them to start with.' Eric felt an unusual and insatiable urge to fill the silence. 'But then I read up and it said that with herbs, provided they weren't going yellow, I was probably giving them enough. Although I couldn't find anything about this one in particular.' Norman ran the back of his index finger against one stem of the Dutch coriander. He took a toothed leaf between his fingertips then bent down and sniffed.

'They've come up nice,' Norman said, then quicker than a dog in a Vietnamese restaurant swivelled on his heel, marched out through the open door, and disappeared off into his shed.

'It was nice talking to you,' Eric called after him.

❦

BY EARLY AFTERNOON, Eric was ready to go home. The middle of his back throbbed from constantly leaning over, his trousers chafed where the sweat had pooled between his thighs, and Abi was doing his head in as she ran in and out of sight chasing Hank's three-legged whippet. In Abi's defence, every time she stopped chasing it, the whippet slowed, doubled back, then pawed at her legs until she started again. Hopefully, Eric considered, she'd sleep the entire journey back. Deciding it would be stupid to stop when there was only one planter left to fill, he began to sow his carrot seeds. He was halfway through the planting act when a polite cough made him halt.

'Mr Sibley?' the woman said.

Eric turned and found himself momentarily stunned.

The voice had come from a petite lady with bright blue eyes, narrow lips, and a fair brushing of bronzer swiped across her brow. With her stature and complexion – and some favourable lighting – she could have easily passed for early twenties, though Eric suspected that she was a decade or so older. Her hair was scraped back in an authoritative manner, and she was the type of woman who, under normal situations, Eric would have found attractive, only in this particular instance he was rather taken aback, not at her sudden presence on his allotment so much as the uniform she was wearing.

'Mr Eric Sibley?' Her expression was neutral as she repeated his name.

Eric fumbled. He wiped his hands on the seat of his trousers, then stretched one out as a greeting, grimacing at the amount of earth under his nails.

'Yes, yes. I'm Eric Sibley,' he said.

His hand hung unmet in the air for a few seconds before he retrieved it and tucked it back away in his pocket.

'How can I be of help? If it's gardening tips you're after, I suspect you've come to the wrong place. I'm a first-timer I'm afraid.'

'Mr Eric Sibley,' the attractive police officer said. 'I am arresting you for possession of illegal substances, with intent to distribute.'

CHAPTER 26

THE NEXT FEW seconds disappeared into a thick, dense haze of brain fog. Eric's mind was numb, yet swimming. He felt both nauseous and faint and downright furious all at the same time. The police officer reached around and unclipped the handcuffs from her waistband. Behind him, Eric heard Abi's shriek followed by much energetic barking.

'You do not have to say anything, but anything you do say may be used in a court of law. Do you understand?'

'What?' Eric shook his head and blinked. 'Now you hold on.' He stepped backwards, catching his heel on the wooden edge of the bed. 'I think we need to take a second here. There's obviously been some mistake.'

The woman remained impassive. 'Mr Eric Sibley, of Albany Road, London? That *is* you? Yes?'

'Yes, but —'

'And this *is your* allotment. One that you inherited from a Mr ...' she took a small notebook out from her pocket and flicked through, 'George Sibley. Is that correct?'

'Yes, but if you give me a minute —'

'And this *is your* greenhouse?' She pointed to Eric's under-plenished greenhouse, the yellow plastic of the tomato grow-bags glinting through the glass.

'Yes, it is.'

'And your daughter,' she glanced down at the notebook for confirmation, 'Abi. She goes to St Andrew's the Apostles?'

'What has that got to do with anything?'

'I'm afraid there has been no mistake, Mr Sibley. I will need you to come with me to the station.' She pulled the handcuffs from her waist and held them out. 'We can do this the hard way or the easy way. There's no need to make a scene.'

A rush of heat burned all the way up from Eric's feet. 'I'm not making a scene,' he said. 'In fact.' He pushed his shoulders back. 'I think I'm being very calm about your accusations.' The officer didn't flinch. The cuffs dangled motionless from her fingers and her eyes remained on Eric, strong and fixed. Eric took this as a sign to carry on.

'You said an illegal substance?' He spoke at half his normal pace if not slower. 'What illegal substance? What exactly is it that I'm supposed to have done?'

The police office smacked her tongue against her teeth.

'I'm afraid talking about this anywhere other than the station goes against protocol.'

'You have to be kidding me?' Eric heard the volume of his voice but did nothing to lower it. 'You want to arrest me, but you won't even tell me why?'

'I've told you.' The officer took a long breath in. She moved to speak, but a fiery blast of barking cut through the air. A chorus of shrill laughter followed straight afterwards.

A rush of adrenaline surged through Eric's bloodstream. This time, his voice came out much quieter. And sounding much more panicked.

'Look, is there somewhere we can go to talk about this, other than the station? My daughter's over there. The last thing I want is for her to see you waving those things at me.' He motioned to the handcuffs. The officer looked at them. She wavered.

'Please,' Eric said.

With a sigh, she tucked them back into her pocket.

'We can talk in your greenhouse,' she said.

'The greenhouse? That's hardly —' Her look rendered him momentarily mute. 'The greenhouse is perfect.'

The greenhouse was substantially stuffier than it had felt that morning. The police officer was wearing a perfume, something fruity and strong, that added to the humidity and, combined with the growing tightness in his throat, made it increasingly more difficult for Eric to think straight. He moved himself to the far end of the shed, trying to find an angle from which he could view Abi, without being too conspicuous.

'Mr Sibley,' the officer was back on task. 'Am I correct in thinking that all the plants on this allotment are owned by you and have been grown by you?'

'Yes, of course.'

'The ones inside this greenhouse, as well as outside?'

'Yes. Well, except the spring onions. My daughter, Abi, she's grown those.'

'Excellent. And could you please tell me what this is that you're growing here? What will these plants be when they are fully grown?'

She pointed to the yellow plastic grow-bags that lined one inside edge of the house. A dozen seedlings averaged four leaves each. Two small, jagged, inner leaves and two large, smoother ones that extended a centimetre or so farther.

'They're tomatoes,' Eric said. 'This end bag here has Gardener's Delight. These here are cherry, and the ones on the end are meant to be San Marzano, although to be honest, I think I may have a few cherry ones in. I let Abi help, and she wasn't very good at —'

The officer lifted her hand to silence him.

'Good. Thank you. And these?'

She redirected her pointed finger to the first shelf.

'They're my daughter's spring onions,' Eric said. 'She'll be planting them outside next week, only she wanted to do it herself and she's been a bit preoccupied today. Also, we thought it might be best to give them a little time to acclimatise to the outside air. You know, like you do when you buy a goldfish?'

The police officer continued to stare at the spring onions, ignoring Eric's question about goldfish which, he realised on later reflection, probably hadn't been the most helpful comment. After a second more of staring at the various pots and plants, the officer reached into her pocket and pulled out her phone. Eric felt the tightness loosen in his gut. Clearly, she was messaging in that this had all be some horrid mistake. A few minutes of her apologising and he could be back to his radishes. He would need to plant fast though, as the clouds had adopted a decidedly purple tint.

'Mr Sibley,' the officer looked up from her phone. 'Do you recognise this plant?' She tilted the screen towards him. A small image took the centre of her phone. Eric leant in. The plant in question was a seedling of vague familiarity, but combined with the ever-increasing temperature and cadaverous odour that he'd just noticed emanating from his underarms, Eric was having a hard time focusing.

'To be honest, I'm probably the last person to ask about something like this. Perhaps we could go outside. If you want an expert opinion —'

'No, Mr Sibley, I want your opinion. Do you think that this plant, the one I'm showing you on my phone, bears any resemblance to anything you have grown in the last three months?'

'Well, I suppose ...' Eric considered.

'You suppose what, Mr Sibley?'

'I suppose it looks a little like the Dutch coriander.'

Eric studied the photo then the plants. The seedling on the photo must have been at least a week older, but there was the same leaf orientation. The same razor-edged leaves set at right angles to one another. Actually, it looked a lot like it. Eric turned to the police officer.

'Yes. I'd say it's probably Dutch coriander?'

'Dutch coriander.'

'This one here, behind you.'

In an attempt to conceal his ripening body odour, Eric pinned his arms to his side as he squeezed back into the tomatoes and gave the officer space to turn around. With one prodding forefinger, she inspected the coriander, then her phone. Then back again. After one final glance, she reached into her pocket and withdrew her handcuffs.

'Mr Sibley,' she said. 'You have openly confessed to growing the Class B drug, marijuana, in a public space. I have no choice but to bring you down to the station immediately. If you'd like to collect your daughter and advise me as to someone who can take care of her until her mother arrives, I will give you a moment to do that?'

'I ... What?'

'I can assure you I will talk to the judge personally. Clearly what we're dealing with here is a heavy case of drug addiction.'

'A what?'

'Reckless behaviour, obliviousness to the truth, an obvious lack self-hygiene, neglect of children —'

'She's playing with a dog!'

'They're signs, Mr Sibley. I've seen it all too often. Men in powerful jobs. Thinking it's just a way to relax. It starts as a casual thing. Just a spliff to take the edge off the day. Then you can't sleep without it. Then, before you know it, you're skipping work to try to deal your shoddy product to eight-year-old students at your daughter's overpriced private school and spending the weekend turning your dead father's allotment into a crack den.'

'What?'

Eric was standing in a tomato plant, but he couldn't feel it. He couldn't feel anything. His mouth was arid, his chest in a vice, and the only part of his nervous system that appeared to be working were his sweat glands. Even his eyes were having difficulty making sense of the situation. Marijuana? How? This made no sense.

And then it did. Then it all made perfect sense.

He barged past the police officer — pushing her to the side against his ornamental marigolds — and out through the door, sprinting across to the next allotment.

'You!' The tip of Eric's finger was barely an inch from Norman's wheezing chest. 'You did this.'

'Pardon?'

Norman stepped back from his runner beans. His long beard had a splattering of compost in it, darkening the white hair. He stretched himself up to standing, met Eric's gaze for less than a second, then turned back to his plants.

'This is the man.' Eric flayed his arms wildly. 'He gave me the seeds. Dutch coriander. That's what he said. Dutch coriander. This is the man you should be arresting.'

The police officer ambled across the grass, her handcuff swinging wistfully from her waistband.

'Well? Aren't you going to do something?' Eric insisted. 'Take him down to the police station. He's the one who did this. He's the one you need to arrest.'

Eric fought the urge to hurl himself across the allotment, grab the handcuffs, and do the bloody job for her. As she reached the corner of the allotment she stopped, tucked her phone away, and began to re-tie her hair.

'What are you doing?' Eric said. 'Arrest him. Arrest him!'

'You need to calm down,' Norman said.

'Calm down! I'll give you calm down!' Then to the officer. 'Why aren't you doing something?'

The police officer's eyes glinted. The corner of her lips quivered, and one eyebrow tilted up at an angle. She looked from Eric to Norman and back again.

'You're right,' she said. 'He is highly strung.'

'What? Who is? What are you talking about?'

But the officer wasn't talking to Eric. She wasn't even looking at him. She was looking past him and the rows of runner beans, to the scruffy haired geriatric with a smile cracked so wide across his face his jaw could have been dislocated.

'Maggie, my treasure. You did an old man proud.'

The two met together in a wide-armed embrace, the old man absorbing the little officer in a giant, bearded bear hug. Eric watched on, his own jaw barely above his feet.

'Uncle Norm,' the girl said when they broke apart.

'Did you film it?'

'No, I didn't. That'd be more than my job's worth.'

'Ahh, well I'll have to hope I don't lose my memory then. That one's going to keep me warm for very many nights.'

'You? Lose your memory? Chance would be a fine thing.'

Norman's face beamed. His cheeks glowed, and he continued to keep one arm around the officer.

'Eric,' he said. 'I'd like you to meet my niece, Maggie. She's a police officer. And also one of Burlam's keenest Amdrammers.'

'Amdrammer?'

Maggie stretched out her hand.

'We're doing *The Full Monty* at the town hall in the summer. Let me know if you fancy coming. Tickets are selling pretty fast.'

Eric was rigid. Speechless. Every muscle from his toes to his scalp burned, yet at the same time he was frozen to the spot.

'You're his niece?'

'Sorry about that. I can never say no to Uncle Nor. Particularly where a practical joke is involved. Friends?' She kept her hand hanging in the air between them. Eric made no attempt to meet it.

'A joke? Are you telling me that was a joke? Pretending that I'm being arrested? Pretending that I'm growing marijuana —'

'You got off lightly. He was actually going to give you marijuana when he first started.'

'Cinderella 99,' Norman said and kissed his fingers as though talking about some exquisite tasting delicacy. 'Now that would be a present.'

Eric's cheeks burned. His fists were clenched in balls and his nails dug so fiercely into his palms he wouldn't have been surprised if his hands were bleeding. He fixed his glare on Norman.

'You,' he said. 'I'll get you for this. You and all your prize-winning parsnip gang. Don't think you're safe because your niece is in the police.'

It was then, without warning, that something started happening in Eric's intestinal region. It was a cross between a spasm and twitch. Something deep and painful just below his abdomen that caused his diaphragm to lurch upwards and his chest convulse. His pulse rocketed as he attempted to force the motion down, but before he knew it he was doubled over, knees bent, eyes streaming, the uncontrollable paroxysm accompanied by a loud rasping sound that erupted from his lungs.

'You bloody git.' Were the only words that Eric managed to articulate, although they were repeated several times. 'You bloody, bloody, git.' Soon Norman was doubled over too, tears streaming down his tissue-paper skin and pooling in the whiskers around his chin. Maggie, who managed to stay upright for a minute or two longer, soon gave into the urge and allowed her body to be consumed by the convulsions. When Abi turned up five minutes later, the three-legged greyhound hopping behind her, she stared at the three adults and scratched her head.

'Why are you laughing?' she said. 'What's so funny? Tell me. I want to know.'

It was over a minute before Eric managed to control his breathing well enough to stand upright and wipe away his tears. 'One day,' he said, ruffling Abi's hair. 'I'll tell you one day.'

He slapped Norman on the shoulder, hugged Maggie goodbye, and got back to planting his radishes.

CHAPTER 27

ERIC HAD BEEN praying for good weather all week, but the statistics were not favourable. For the last month, it had been as though nature was mocking them. Weekdays had been your stereotypical April weather. Grey, windy, and interspersed with some traffic-seizing showers, but it was nothing you wouldn't expect from the UK in April. Provided you had a brolly and the sense to pack a spare pair of trousers, you were fine.

Weekends were a whole different matter.

In fact, every weekend from the middle of April to the start of June, it poured down. On his trips down to Burlam, the water pelted the windscreen harder than the wipers could keep up with. The car – the Audi, as taking Sally was most definitely off the cards – crawled through rushing torrents that sprouted up from the drains. Eric cursed every second of the journey down. He leant towards the glass, unable to see anything other than headlights in the blurred prospect. Praying for a break between the unending downpours, Eric repeatedly cursed his father and the ridiculous stipulations of his inheritance.

It didn't matter when he went down – Friday night, Saturday morning, Sunday afternoon after a vegan nut roast at Lydia's – and it didn't matter when he got there. Every weekend, the results were the same: monsoon season.

At the allotment, everything was wet. The ground, the air, his planters; they were all soaked. His newly sown seedlings stood limp, bobbing in the waterlogged compost, while rain poured off the greenhouse and shed roofs and gushed in eddying streams towards his little patch of land. Of course, the ground was slanted in a manner that meant the first allotment to flood was his. His rhubarb and carrots were drowning, and his sparkling new greenhouse had already sprung a leak.

Still, at least there was a little escapism.

Without a doubt, Norman's shed was the last place that Eric had expected to find equanimity, particularly with Norman there for company, but there it was. In the weeks since the incident with the Dutch coriander, the two had struck up a firm friendship. The foundations of this friendship, although still a little shallow on the ground, were built primarily on talk of old cars, vegetable growth, and Cynthia's homemade shortbread. If Eric arrived first, he'd do what he could in his Hunter wellies and a Barbour jacket, squelching around in the mud until his fingers reached a state of prunage usually associated with Suzy and the bath. At that point he would disappear into his greenhouse and prune the surplus leaves from his tomato plants until he spotted Norman hobbling up the path. After that, it was a case of waiting to see which dried out first, the conversation or the weather. Eric wasn't allowed in the shed, but the veranda was more than big enough for the foldable deck chairs and cups of steaming tea.

Some days the men had extra company – Hank, Cynthia, a few other names Eric couldn't remember – but mostly it was just the two of them. Their conversation was generally light, although once or twice Eric used it as a chance to unburden some of his work stress over plans of a merger and rumours of jobs cuts. Norman tended to ignore Eric's rants, or else divert the conversation back to the weather and how this was nothing compared to sixty-eight. The one topic they avoided, starkly, was Eric's father.

On the two occasions that George's name had arisen – both times through Norman, not Eric – Eric cast an immediate detour and swerved the conversation off into another direction. Still, the brief mention caused residual shudders to echo down Eric's spine.

As it was, the weather had entirely restricted Eric in his desire to take Norman out in Sally. Each week he'd had to postpone his plans, desperate that the following week would be better when inevitably it was worse. And so, he'd taken a risk.

When Eric received the notification through the owner's club he'd passed the idea by Suzy. When she deemed it a good one, he'd mentioned it to Cynthia. She too gave her approval. And so, weather providing, they were all good to go. Eric went to bed that Friday night with butterflies in his stomach, checking the day's forecast in three different counties on his phone. One day's good weather. That was all he needed.

He was woken the next morning by Suzy. It was an unpleasant awakening as Suzy threw off the duvet and Eric's immediate reaction – besides yelping with shock at the cold – was to grab his phone in order to once more check the weather situation.

'You don't need that.'

Suzy plucked his phone from his hand before striding over to the window and drew the curtains. She was wearing a tiny cotton night slip, and any other Saturday he would have delayed his plans by at least six minutes, but today time was too important.

'Coffee's waiting for you downstairs,' she said, then threw him a towel off the radiator. 'Don't forget to say goodbye to Abi. I told her she could have a lie in, but she'll be gutted if you don't pop in.'

Eric drank his coffee, showered, and dressed, then poked his head around the corner of Abi's door.

'I'm off,' he said. 'I'll see you tonight. Look after your mum.'

'Dad?'

'Yes, pumpkin.'

'I hope Uncle Norman has fun today.'

'I'm sure he will. See you later.'

'Love you.'

'You too, princess.'

The drive down from London to Burlam was all that Eric could have hoped, with empty roads and not a drop of rain in sight, but the cornflower blue skies and spun-sugar clouds did nothing to alleviate the niggling nerves. This was England. Sunshine in the morning may be nice, but it didn't guarantee a thing. Eric had informed Cynthia of their early start at the beginning of the week and she'd suggested he swing by the house and collect him, saving them all a journey to the allotment.

Norman and Cynthia lived on the outskirts of Burlam where the big houses dominated but before the new-builds started. Eric cruised around the bends and passed the Welcome to Burlam sign, then signalled left down towards the quay. His stomach churned.

It was over a year since he last took this turn. New cars graced the driveways and many of the hedgerows were higher than he remembered, but other than that, everything was the same. The wych elms, the cedar cladding. The oversized windows and red brick chimneys. It was the same as last year, same as the year before, and every year Eric could remember from his childhood. He slowed to park up outside Norman's front gate, hesitated, then kept going for another fifty yards until he reached the last house on the road.

It was impossible to ignore the glaring green *For Sale* sign with its deliberately askew *Sold* placard nailed over the top. Eric climbed out of Sally and took a step towards it. The grass in the front garden had all gone to seed, and the windows were veiled in ochre dust. Through the glass he could make out the shadows of the curtains, though there were no longer the rows of photograph frames sat on the ledge, there from his mother's time. He wondered first how much the house had gone for and second, who it had gone to. The who it was gone to question lingered longer in his mind. A family probably. A well-off one. The type where both parents work, and the kids are brought up by a nanny. Perhaps a family trying to escape the rat race of city life. Perhaps they'd come into their own inheritance lately and that was how they managed to afford it. Behind him, the elms rustled in the breeze. Eric came back to the moment, turned around, got into Sally, and headed back up to Norman and Cynthia's.

Cynthia answered in her slippers. A pink cardigan was draped over her shoulders and a pastel flowered button blouse. For a second Eric thought he may have had the wrong house, and it was only then he realised he'd never seen Cynthia without her sturdy green wax jacket and a pair of wellies.

She frowned, equally confused for a moment, before shaking her head clear.

'Oh, I'm sorry. I completely forgot. Oh dear. It's today, isn't it? Oh, what a nuisance.'

'Is he ready? We've got quite a journey on us. If we can get going now, we can hopefully avoid the traffic.'

Cynthia bit down on her bottom lip. Eric waited.

'To be honest,' she said, 'today's not too good. I'm so sorry. Had I remembered, I would have called you. Saved you the journey.'

'Is everything okay?'

'Oh yes, yes. Fine. Just his cough. Had him up a lot of the night, you see. It's so nice of you to offer to do this, but I'm not sure he's up to —'

'Cynth? Who's at the door?' Norman's holler barked through from the back of the house. 'If it's those bloody internet —'

'No, no. Don't worry. It's only Eric.'

'Eric?' Then after a pause. 'What does he want?'

Eric was about to offer a reply when Norman shuffled out into the hallway. His home attire consisted of plaid flannel pyjama bottoms and a long blue vest that made him almost unrecognisable from Eric's gardening mentor. He walked with a hand against the wall, scuffing his feet against the carpet as he coughed and spluttered. Eric's toes fidgeted in his shoes. This wasn't quite what he'd expected.

'Sorry to drop in on you,' Eric said. 'Cynthia said you weren't feeling great.'

'Nothing wrong with me bar being nagged constantly,' Norman grunted.

'Well, I should probably head back, anyway. Suzy could do with having me at home. Abi seems to be developing her teenage genes five years early.'

Norman grunted towards Eric then peered his head around him. His eyes widened.

'Is that what I think it is?'

With an implausible change of pace, Norman pushed his way past Eric, out the front door, and across the drive. Both Cynthia and Eric did a double take and by the time they'd reached him, Norman was standing barefoot on the pavement in his pyjamas, cheek flat against Sally's bonnet, pawing at the metal work with his hand.

'She gets more beautiful every time I see her,' he said.

'Norman, what are you doing? You'll catch your death. At least go and put some slippers on.'

Norman turned to Eric, tactlessly ignoring his wife. 'Are we going for a spin? Give me five minutes for a cuppa and I'll be good to go.'

After he finished speaking, he promptly broke into a coughing fit that saw flecks of saliva fly out onto the windscreen.

'Well, I'm not sure ...'

'Oh, don't worry about this,' he attempted to wipe the spittle away with the bottom of his vest. 'Had this cough for the last thirty years. It's not killed me yet.'

Eric turned to Cynthia. Outside the house and without the guise of her jacket, she'd shrunk to a person of Lilliputian proportions. Eric imagined her, next to Janice, together in a small house built into the stump of the tree. She looked from her husband to the car, a heavy sigh built between her lips.

'Since when have I been able to stop you doing something?' she said. 'But you need to take it easy, mind? Rest. And none of that junk food either. I'm making you both a salad sandwich to take while you get dressed.'

While Norman showered and dressed, Eric sat at the breakfast bar watching as Cynthia buttered slices of bread and filled them with home-grown produce. It must have been a beautiful house once, and it still was to some degree; it certainly kept with the same fastidious sense of order that Eric had come to associate with Norman. But it was tired. The kitchen was in need of a refit, with its faded lino flooring and veneer edging peeling back from the corner of the cupboards, and from what he saw, the rest of the house was in a similar state. Smells of homemade jams and piccalilli abounded around him, while through the window a view stretched all the way down to the river. Eric sipped at his cup of tea as Cynthia worked. It was peculiarly weak.

'How long have you been here?' Eric asked.

'Forty-seven years,' Cynthia said proudly.

'Wow.'

'Bought it off the plot. We probably should have moved at some point, you know, got smaller, moved closer to town, something like that. But when you're young you don't think about being old, and when you're old, you don't have the energy to do those type of things.'

'Still, forty-seven years, that's impressive.'

She folded aluminium foil around the sandwiches.

'There aren't very many of us originals around here anymore. Until a few years ago, we were still going strong. Then one by one, it's nursing homes and retirement villages. Of course, we've been to a fair few funerals too.'

'I can't imagine you and Norman settling into a retirement village just yet,' Eric said.

'No.' Cynthia smiled. 'Neither can I.'

Her gaze drifted off, and Eric was thinking of some way to break the silence when Norman's voice boomed through.

'Well then, are we getting on the road or not?'

Norman stood in the doorway to the kitchen. His shaggy beard had been brushed straight, along with his mane of hair which was lying flush to his head, glistening with water in perfectly combed lanes. He had on a tweed jacket, which hung well in the arm but a little loose around the middle, and carried a matching tweed flat cap in his hand. Eric stood up and straightened his own collar, feeling decidedly underdressed. 'I guess we should be getting on then.' He kissed Cynthia goodbye, then turned to Norman.

'I'll be right behind you,' Norman said.

THE CAR SHOW smelt of petrol and hog roast. There was a bouncy castle on one side of the field while on the other side a small stage was set up. As they arrived, a troop of boys were performing what Eric could only assume was a breakdance – disturbingly choreographed – while the poster promised the best Elvis impersonator in the UK as the afternoon entertainment. Following the arm signals of the men in hi-vis, they crawled across the grass and parked up next to a classic red 1955 Spider and a slightly less classic silver Porsche 924.

'It's been a long time since I've been to one of these,' Eric said, dodging the quagmire as he stepped outside. 'I don't think I can even remember the last time.'

''Spect it was around your O-levels. Your dad said you stopped going to things with him after then.'

The comment came matter-of-factly out of Norman's mouth and caught them both by surprise.

'I suspect it was,' Eric said, thinking about it. There was a minute's pause before he spoke again.

'So, what do you want to do?' he said. 'I've got chairs in the back, so we can sit out here, although I hear there's a 1954 300S somewhere in the grounds and a couple of E-types if you fancy going for a wander?'

Norman sucked in a breath with a wheeze. 'I think I'll stay with the old girl for now, if that's all right with you? Although.' He paused. 'I wouldn't mind you picking me up one of those hog roast rolls if you have a mind.'

'What about your sandwiches?'

'You know what? I think I forgot to pick them up.'

CHAPTER 28

ERIC WEAVED HIS way between the metal work and rubber. Norman was right, he thought. It must have been his A-level year the last time he came. After a few more minutes' contemplation, he was certain. Joining a queue for coffee, he raked through years of well-repressed memories. Of course it had been during his A-levels; it had been this time of year too, possibly even this show. He remembered it now because of how fiercely he didn't want to go. Exam season was upon him, and the pressure to get as far away from Burlam and his father was ever increasing. His father had turned up at school unannounced, on a Sunday, and expected Eric to drop everything and go with him.

'I've got work to do. Revision. Exams,' Eric had said. 'They start next week. I can't spend a whole day away.'

'Revision, *pff*,' his dad had harrumphed. 'With soft subjects like you're doing? They're not going to get you anywhere. Anyway. I've told your housemaster you're coming, so you're coming.'

Eric had taken his books with him and spent the whole time sitting outside the car. Whenever anyone approached Sally, he buried his head deeper into the pages and offered disgruntled grunts as answers to their questions. He ate the bacon butty his father brought, but only because his stomach was growling so loudly he was finding it difficult to read. In the car ride back, he rested his head against the window and pretended to sleep. Four long hours of his revision lost, not including the drive there or back. That was how he had viewed it then.

The clouds were making a play for centre stage, and Eric shivered against them as he took his drink. The coffee was far better than he'd expected for a standard boot-sale food truck, and he made a mental note to come back to the same truck later. While the paper coffee cup heated up his hand, he wandered between the cars. Abi would like it here, he thought. And Suzy too.

Treading down the long grass, Eric admired the paintwork, leather interiors, and restoration projects. He ambled at leisure, moseying about with no fixed pattern or system to his route, revelling in the luxury of no children or deadlines. Once or twice he thought about heading back to check on Norman, but for now, he figured, there was no rush.

It was about fifteen minutes into his amble when Eric realised that he was now part of a strange and apparently obligatory club; one that he appeared to have settled in with remarkable ease and enjoyment.

He also soon noted that he, and other members of said club, followed a somewhat predictable pattern.

First, he would stop by a car and run his eyes over the body, or wheels or some other such feature. Next, an owner would appear by his side.

'Only sixty-five of this colour ever made,' they might say. Or, 'Did all the restoration work myself.'

Sometimes Eric would find himself the first to speak. 'Beautiful looking car you've got there,' he might say, or, 'What year is this?' Or if he were really absorbed, a simple 'Hmmm' of appreciation was all that was needed. They would talk, he would listen, then he would offer his own input, exchanging names and handshakes and pointing people in the direction of Sally. Generally, he'd tell them a bit about her and inform them that he'd be there until four-ish and they should pop over for a gander if they had the time. He was surprised to find he meant it.

It turned out that Eric had had no need to drum up a crowd, as, by the time he returned to Sally, Norman had already amassed quite a congregation of his own. Eric squeezed his way between exceptionally complimentary onlookers and handed Norman his hog roast roll.

'I was just telling them how I used to badger your old dad to let me drive her,' he said. 'Damn git wouldn't let me anywhere near that wheel. Rest his soul and all.'

'He was rather possessive.'

'Possessive my arse. Thought I might drop dead behind the wheel.' He broke into an interlude of coughing as if to confirm Eric's father's reasoning. 'Let me ride in the back often enough. When 'e got that old lad from the garage to take her out. Bit of a squeeze, but I'm hardly one to whinge.'

Eric raised an eyebrow. Norman shrugged and smirked.

For the rest of the day, the two men sat on the foldout picnic chairs making small talk with admirers and sampling the various food trucks on display. Generally, they were as helpful as possible and offered titbits of history about Sally and the DB4 in general. Other times Norman would draw on his family flair for dramatics. Through sheer determination and tenacity, Norman persuaded a young lady that this was the exact car that William had taken Kate Middleton for a drive in on their first date, and an older couple that it was where Fred Astaire proposed to Robyn Smith.

However, stranger than even Norman's never-ending imagination and silver tongue, were the offers of condolence that Eric received.

These condolences came from strangers who had known his father back in the days when he was a regular at these types of events. There were faces that knew Eric by name and apparently had met him and his mother several times in the past. And there were those that knew the car and George but had not heard of his passing. Those were the hardest. Eric smiled and thanked them all for their kind wishes.

By the time they left, the sky had turned opalescent. Between them, Eric and Norman had consumed three pork and stuffing rolls, two bacon sandwiches, four cups of coffee, five cups of tea, and an undisclosed number of freshly fried mini doughnuts. They drove out through the now churned and muddy grass and onto the road, ready for the long drive ahead.

Tiredness laboured Norman's breathing, and though he worried for his comfort, Eric knew better than to ask if he was okay. Still, when they stopped at a garage for fuel, he checked anyway.

'Do you want me to move the seat?' he said. 'I'm sure we can adjust the angle a bit, make it easy for you to breathe.' Norman shooed the idea away with his hand.

'I'm fine. Don't you go getting any ideas,' he said as Eric went into the shop to the pay for the petrol and buy himself a can of Red Bull.

It was only when he got into the car and started to pull down his seat-belt that he stopped. Twisting his neck, he turned to Norman.

'Do you want to drive home?'

'What?'

'I know it's only another half-an-hour to go. But if you want?'

Norman's coughing and laboured breathing subsided entirely into a vault of absolute silence.

'You're pulling my leg.'

'It's fine. You don't have to. Don't feel obliged.'

'Obliged my arse, you can get your scrawny girl's backside out of that seat now.'

Norman flicked his seatbelt off and was standing outside the driver's door before Eric had even managed to get his feet out of the footwell.

'I guess that's a yes then.'

Norman took each corner with the steering wheel firmly between his hands and his lips tightly pinched together. Although his palms were wrinkled and creased, each little bow and curve caused his eyes to glimmer like a child's, and every so often his tongue would flick out while his throat crackled with a cough. Eric sank back into the seat and stared out at the view. There really were some exceptional roads around Essex, he decided. He'd just never really had a chance to look at them before. About five minutes outside of Burlam, he closed his eyes and fell asleep.

When Eric woke, the street lights were glowing a butterscotch yellow above him. They were parked outside Norman's, the old man wheezing in the driver's seat next to him, the silhouette of his wife moving behind the curtains.

'How long have we been back?' Eric said.

'Only a couple of minutes. I was enjoying a second's peace, but you've ruined that now.'

Eric squinted and blinked.

'Well,' Norman said. 'I'd invite you in for a tea, but Cynth'll insist on making it and her tea tastes like dishwater.'

'That's all right.'

'Easy for you to say. How a woman can cook like she does and still not tell that her tea tastes like weak piss has been a mystery to me these last fifty years. I tell you, I'm giving her one more year and then I'm divorcing her. There's only so much crappy tea a man can take in one lifetime.'

Eric smiled.

'Well, I guess I should be getting back,' he said. 'I didn't realise it was so late. I should have thought ahead and booked a room at the Sailboat.'

'I can ring 'em if you like? Or there's always the sofa? I can sneak you in. Avoid the tea altogether.'

Eric shook his head. 'It's fine. Suzy and Abs are coming down with me tomorrow. Said I'd take them for fish and chips by the river.'

'Sounds grand.'

The two men sat in silence. After two minutes had passed and Norman had not so much as flexed a finger, Eric coughed as subtly as he could manage. Norman jerked upwards in his seat, then stared at Eric confused. Half a second later, the look had gone. He moved his hand towards the door handle then left it there, hovering.

'You know,' he said. 'Last year, when your dad's 'ands 'ad gone, and he used to get that young lad from the garage to take him, I came out with him quite a bit.'

'Did you?'

'Almost every week.' Norman paused. Eric waited. 'He would sit where you're sitting now, rest 'is head against the window and close 'is eyes. Whole drive, didn't matter if it was to the end of the road or all the way up to Scunthorpe, your old man never wanted to open his eyes when he got in the car. Not them last few months. Never fell asleep mind. Wide-awake, just had his eyes closed.'

'I suppose he was tired,' Eric said. 'And he liked to listen to the engine. He always liked to listen to the engine.'

Norman sniffed in a manner that made it clear he disagreed. 'Nah, that's not why he did it. It was you. You were the reason.'

'Me? Why?'

Norman pushed his head back so as to view Eric from the widest angle possible.

'If 'is eyes were closed,' Norman said, 'it was easier to imagine you were still sitting next to him.'

CHAPTER 29

EVEN IF ERIC could have made it down during the week, he doubted he could have kept up with the pace of his harvesting. July arrived and overnight his beetroot, lettuce, and mangetout had sprung out of nowhere. He already had such copious numbers of radishes and courgettes that he'd started taking bag loads into work and leaving them in a basket by the reception to let people help themselves. His tomatoes were out of control, his rhubarb had gone into overdrive, and if he had to have one more meal garnished with Abi's home-grown, organic spring onions he was likely to drive to the nearest garden centre, douse their entire spring onion seed selection in lighter-fuel, and toss a burning match very deliberately in its direction.

The last weekend of the month was Abi's ninth birthday. This year she'd opted out of the idea of a traditional party in some horrific hall with an extortionately priced entertainer, in exchange for a picnic down at the allotment with Eric, their newly extended green-fingered family, and her cousins. The news was both a financial and mental relief to Suzy and Eric, who in their nine short years as parents seemed to have suffered enough princess, pirate, superhero, farmyard, and soft play birthday parties to last them a lifetime. It was particularly good news for Suzy, who last year had stayed up until gone midnight trying to construct the perfect princess castle cake. With its phallic towers jutting out at all sorts of ungainly angles, one could have been forgiven for thinking it belonged at a very different type of party. Abi was pleased with it though.

This year Lydia had offered to make the cake, so there was no baking to be done on Suzy's part at all. Cynthia had said she'd bring a quiche and sandwiches, and Janice was going to provide scones and jam. Eric whipped past Waitrose on his way down and picked up a couple of packs of mini scotch eggs, cheese, and some crusty bread and by lunchtime, they had their picnic blankets spread out under the sun and were well on their way into their second glass of Hank's sloe gin.

'If I'm honest,' Tom said, topping up his glass and ignoring Lydia's disapproving glare. 'I'm a bit jealous of this.'

'Why?' Eric said. 'You've got exactly the same at home. Better. And you don't have a three-hour round trip every week just to go and get a punnet of cherry tomatoes.'

'That's the part I'm jealous of. You can hardly pretend you've spent all day out digging the ground when your wife's been watching you sitting in your deck chair listening to Radio 4 from the kitchen window all day.'

'That's what a shed's for,' Norman piped in.

'Aye, only ours has been recently converted into an outside laundry, so guess who's always coming in and out?'

'There's an answer to that,' Lydia called from over by the greenhouse. 'Clean your own dirty underpants.'

The banter and chatter went back and forth, through midday and beyond. After cake and candles, the children continued to chase Hank's dog, Scout, around and the adults discussed the various benefits of home-grown produce over the shop bought equivalent. Eric had vacated his usual chair on the veranda in exchange for a place on the mat next to the scotch eggs. He glanced across at his wife and caught her eye. 'I love you,' he mouthed.

'You too,' she mouthed back.

He leant back onto the rug and smelt the fresh evening air drifting in. On a normal Sunday, he'd be thinking about heading off at this time. Tomorrow, he'd be back at work and today would seem like months ago. For now, though, he wanted to stay in the moment, the here, and now with his family. In the distance, he could hear Hank telling the children how Scout had come to lose his leg while displaying his own mechanical appendage. The children *oohed* and *ahhed* and asked the type of inappropriate questions that only children could come up with.

Maybe they could look at buying a little place down here for the holidays, Eric thought. There was a static caravan site down by the marina. The places weren't exactly state of the art, and some of the folk looked like they were the result of one too many dalliances with some close relations, but the caravans would be more than suitable for weekends and school holidays. Then again, they could always get a second mortgage if Suzy preferred. Not for a lot, but probably enough for something small. Perhaps he'd talk to her about it later. After all, she'd always liked Burlam too.

At five, the children had hit their limit. Sugar lows struck. Lydia and Tom took their two home after Hugo locked his younger brother in a greenhouse and told him it was an anti-oxygen tank and that he only had four minutes to get out before he suffocated to death. Half-an-hour later and Abi was curled up on the picnic blanket, one arm draped across Scout, the other clutching the personalised trowel she'd been given for her birthday by Janice. Suzy was talking to Hank about the difficulties of having a dog in the city while Eric and Cynthia picked up the remaining few paper plates and cups that had not made it into the rubbish bags earlier.

'You go,' Eric said. 'I can do this.'

'Nonsense,' Cynthia said. 'We're nearly done. Besides. I'll take it with us. We can drop it in the recycling bins at home.'

'Are you sure I can't give you a lift? It'll take me five minutes to run you up there, then I'll come back for the girls.'

Cynthia shook her head. 'No point wasting an evening like this in a car. Not while my legs still work.'

'If you're sure?'

'I am.'

Eric straightened up and shook the rubbish down to the bottom of the bag.

'Well, I think we're done,' he said. 'I guess we better wake the other two up.'

'Seems a shame when they look so peaceful, doesn't it?'

'Like butter wouldn't melt.'

Behind Abi and Scout, Norman was sitting in his chair. His head was tipped forwards, his glass of sloe gin half full on the ground beside him. Eric gathered up the coats and bags, bent down and scooped Abi up in his arms.

'I don't want to go home yet,' she yawned, rubbing her eyes and wrapping an arm around her father's neck. 'It's my birthday. I want to stay with Scout. It's still my birthday,' she dozed. Suzy appeared beside them.

'Scout's got to go home now too,' she said. 'It's time for his bed.'

'Aye, and if I don't feed him soon, he might 'ave my other leg off me,' Hank added.

'You ready?' Suzy said to Eric. 'Have you got everything?'

'I've got the bags, the coats and this one,' he said, nodding to Abi. 'Just need to say goodbye to Norman and we're ready to go.'

Eric turned to Norman. He was no longer sitting with his head forwards, but instead it slumped to one side. Cynthia was beside him, but rather than standing she was kneeling on the dirt. Her face was buried in his lap.

※

ERIC TOOK a week off work and spent the Monday to Wednesday down in Burlam. He didn't know what use he'd be, but he wanted to be on hand, just in case Cynthia needed him to take her anywhere. Maggie was busy with the play and work. She'd said she would drop out, but Cynthia had insisted she didn't. After all, she had said, what would be the point in letting people down, it wasn't going to change anything.

It hadn't come as a surprise to other people. Apparently, the fact that he'd made it to the summer at all had been a bigger one. He had everything in place, funeral arrangements, instructions for his ashes, all deeds, investments, and bank account information ready for Cynthia. He had even included a pamphlet for a local driving school that ran an intensive two-week course and a letter in which he'd said there'd be no excuse for not learning now, not with all the extra time she'd have on her hands. Everything was sorted.

Eric wasn't surprised at Norman's military organisation on the matter of his own death. He was the only person in the allotment who arranged his tomatoes bags according to the average growth height and had a rigid rotation system in place to ensure all areas of his allotment received nitrogen-fixing legumes at least once every three years. Perhaps it was the fact it made him feel so useless he found hard.

'It's easier when you haven't got children,' Cynthia said to Eric as they sat around the kitchen table. Norman had been right, Eric learned; her tea did taste a little like dishwater. He had driven Cynthia down to the church to speak with the minister in regard to hymn choices, only to find, once again, that the matter had been dealt with in advance. Eric was convinced that Cynthia would have been happier to walk the mile down into town on her own, but he had insisted, and so she'd said yes. Then he felt even more guilty. A seventy-year-old woman had just a lost her spouse of nearly fifty years and she was altering her plans so as not to hurt his feelings.

'Don't get me wrong, we'd have loved children,' Cynthia said, back home and oblivious to the insipidness of the tea. 'But at least you don't feel so bad about the fact you've got to move on at some point. I've seen my sisters. The way they fuss over their girls, terrified what will happen when they're not there to look after them. But kids are tough. And Maggie's hardly a baby. Thirty-six and a superintendent. She'll be fine. No, it's harder on us, I'm sure it is.'

'So, what will you do now?' Eric asked. 'If you knew this was coming, and Norman had everything in order, I assume you've made plans?'

A sad smile trembled on Cynthia's creased lips. Her eyes began to glisten.

'Norman was the planner,' she said. 'I was more concerned with making the most of the time together, while we still had it. But I've got some ideas. Some things I'd like to do. Places I'd like to see.'

'Like where?' Eric asked.

'Just places,' she said and smiled again, this time without the tears.

✦

'WHAT DO you think she'll do?' Suzy asked when Eric got home that Wednesday night. He had thought about going back again, and had he not missed Abi so much he probably would have done. Work emails were incessant in his absence yet having made the situation clear to Jack, he'd made the conscious decision to ignore them. There was nothing that couldn't wait. No deal he couldn't postpone for another three days. The world wouldn't collapse if he didn't get his spreadsheet of figures to Greg until Friday instead of Wednesday.

'I've no idea,' Eric said. 'Apparently Norman's got family over in Australia or New Zealand. Perhaps she'll go and visit them.'

'What about the house?'

'I think he wanted her to sell it. Move into one of those new retirement properties over by the school.'

'Do you think she will?'

'No idea. It's a lovely place. It could be great, but it needs an awful lot of work.'

Eric went to the fridge, pulled out a can of tonic and topped up their two large measures of gin.

'Abi wants to come to the funeral,' she said. 'She asked if it would be okay.'

'What did you say?'

'I said it would be up to you.'

'What do you think?'

Suzy shrugged. She took a large gulp of her drink. Eric did the same. He winced. There was strong and strong. Suzy spoke next. 'She knows what happened. She knows a funeral's where people go to say goodbye. I think if you're okay with it I am.'

'I'll probably hang around after, just for a bit, if that's okay? See if I can help out at all.'

Suzy took another sip of her drink. When she drew the glass away, she pressed her lips together in a flat straight line.

'What?' Eric said.

'Nothing.'

'No say it. You think I'm interfering, don't you? Poking my nose in where it's not welcome, but I'm not. I'm only trying to help.'

'I know that.'

'Then what is it?'

Suzy placed her glass on a coaster. She tucked a strand of hair behind her ear and drew in a deep breath.

'I think you're doing all this, keeping yourself busy, because it stops you thinking.'

'Thinking? About what? About Norman?'

'No,' Suzy said. 'About your dad.'

Eric frowned and took an extra-large gulp of his gin. He winced again then shook his head and took another mouthful.

'Why would I be thinking about my dad? I already went to his funeral.'

'Well,' Suzy said. 'You have to admit that for quite a while there, your relationship with Norman was pretty similar to your relationship with your dad.'

'That's ridiculous. Norman was Norman. My father was my father. And the only thing the two had in common was being old and having neighbouring allotments. Oh, and loving a car more than people I suppose.'

'That's not entirely true, is it? I mean there's the small factor of Norman making your life a living hell for six months —'

'I wouldn't say —'

'And your desire to prove them both wrong —'

'Again, that's not exactly how —'

'And the fact that deep down all you really wanted was their respect.'

Eric didn't reply. He exhaled in a huff through his nostrils. 'I'm a grown man, Susan,' he said.

'I know that, Eric. But as far as I can see, the one major difference between Norman and your father is with Norman, you got the time to work through your issues.'

Eric went to take another swig of his drink only to find his glass empty. He reached over and grabbed the bottle.

'I guess you've got all that psychobabble nonsense from a book or something,' he said and was kind of grateful when she didn't reply.

CHAPTER 30

THE FUNERAL WAS on the Thursday of the following week. Eric, Suzy, and Abi had all gone down the night before, having reserved their room at the Sailboat in advance. To try to make dinner a less sombre affair, they bought their fish and chips and headed down to the river, but after ten minutes of dive-bombing seagulls and an unseasonable chill to the air, they abandoned the idea and took them back up to the hotel room. Eric dumped their wrappers in the bin by the door and as a result, they arrived at the church the next morning with a subtle yet distinct bouquet of vinegar in their wake.

The church was already three-quarters full when Eric, Suzy, and Abi arrived. All the pews were occupied, though the number of occupants varied from as many as a ten to as few as four. Eric shuffled in with his eyes down and cursed himself for bringing Abi. Funerals made him feel funny. He hadn't been to that many, perhaps that was the issue. When you are approaching forty and the only funerals you'd attended were your parents' and grandparents', they take on an even weightier prospect. No child should attend a funeral, not even if they ask, he decided. Eric glanced at his side. Abi had chosen her outfit herself – a knee-length navy brocade dress and dark woollen cardigan. On the plus side, Eric thought, if she did take a turn for the worse, he could always insist that he be the one to take her out for some air. Suzy would understand.

Keeping his eyes down, Eric led his family down the aisle, apologising as they slipped into a pew, two rows from the back.

'Are you sure you don't want to go nearer the front?' Suzy asked.

'It's not a rock concert,' Eric replied. 'Besides. That's where the family are.'

Forgetting his eyes-down-in-churches rule, Eric glanced towards the altar. As if sensing the moment, Cynthia turned around from the front and caught his eye. Eric did a double take. She was a far cry from the figure he usually saw at the allotment and the old lady he'd seen that morning at her house. For starters, she looked at least a decade younger. Her hair was loose around her shoulders, now dyed a glistening champagne blonde and from the look of it freshly permed. More striking still was that rather than donning the traditional black attire expected of the widow in these events, Cynthia had opted for a sunflower-yellow dress, complete with a patterned blue shawl and hat, both of which were adorned with fresh tulips. Had he not been certain of the date, time and persons in attendance, Eric may well have found himself thinking he'd gate-crashed a wedding. Or perhaps Abi's Easter parade.

It was a few moments later that Eric realised Cynthia was not the only one in what he'd have considered inappropriate attire. The immediate family appeared to have coordinated to ensure that every colour of the spectrum was covered, while elsewhere floral patterns and paisleys, men in bow ties and boaters, and women with fascinators, cardigans, and enough fresh flowers to have their own stand at Chelsea Flower Show, graced the pews. The flowers on the altar were not lilies like at his mother's funeral, but massive bouquets of sweet peas, peonies, astrantia, and cow parsley.

Eric turned to Suzy, who also appeared to have noticed their error.

'I think we may be a little underdressed,' she said.

The dress code wasn't the only surprise of the service. There were speeches, many that Eric considered extremely inappropriate, a slideshow of Norman's most revered practical jokes, and the only song sung by the congregation was a Karaoke version of Lou Reed's *Perfect Day*.

Eric's lungs quivered. This Norman, the Norman that people had come to pay their respects to had been so much more than the man Eric had come to know. He had been quick-witted and fashionable. First to laugh at himself and the first to help others. He had been a teacher and a student but also a son, an uncle, and a husband. He had, if these speeches rang true, always been the last to get a drink in, but the first to pick up the tab at the end of the night. Most of all, though, he'd been a family man.

The last surprise came as the casket disappeared. It was a slight click that started it, then a short riff that, although Eric must have heard a thousand times in his life, took him a full ten seconds to place. By the third chorus, every member of the congregation was on their feet swinging their hips and lip-syncing to The Jam's 'Going Underground'. Tears streamed down people's cheeks, with Eric unsure whether the cause was grief or the downright ridiculousness of the situation. As they left the church, Abi was holding her parents' hands, swinging between them as she continued to whistle the tune.

'That was great,' she said. 'Can we go to another funeral tomorrow?'

Eric didn't stay long at the wake. Despite the drizzle, people were already spilling up the stairs and out into the backyard. There were lots of "How long did you know him?" and "Where did you meet?" and Eric wasn't really in the mood for talking about the allotment or his father's death, or anybody's death for that matter. He spotted Cynthia and made a beeline for her.

'I'll be back down at the weekend,' he said, clasping her hand. 'Just let me know if there's anything I can do before then?'

'You've done too much already,' Cynthia said. 'And I'm sorry I didn't mention Norman's *magical not melancholy* dress code to you. I thought you'd already know.'

'It's no problem. I'll see you on Sunday, at the allotment then?'

Cynthia paused. Her bottom lip twitched slightly, then her eyes did a quick scan of the room. Deciding the coast was clear, she moved in next to Eric and whispered in his ear.

'Not a bloody chance. They're a bunch of obsessives, the lot of them. More concerned with the straightness of their cucumbers than anything else. Present company excluded of course.'

Eric laughed. 'But I'll see you soon?' he said.

'Of course you will.'

It was only by chance that Eric saw the email that night. He had switched off his phone before the service then forgotten about it, only remembering when he climbed into bed and went to set his alarm.

He sat upright, pulling the duvet up and over his chest.

'Well, this is it. Jack's announced the meeting's tomorrow. Hartley's coming in too. All directors at nine. Team debriefs after that. All other meetings to be postponed.'

'What do you think it's about?' Suzy folded the corner on her book and put it back on the nightstand.

'It's the restructuring. It has to be.'

'So, what will happen next? You don't think Jack will let you go?'

Eric put down his own book and switched off the bedside lamp.

'What will be, will be,' he said. 'No point worrying about it now.' He only hoped that the lack of light and fact he was facing away from his wife may have been enough to convince her he wasn't lying straight through his teeth.

CHAPTER 31

EVERYWHERE ERIC LOOKED people were huddled in little groups, whispering to one another. Eyes darted frantically around the room, all making sure that nobody was in possession of a tiny snippet of information that they did not yet have.

It was a scorching day. Shirt collars clamped around the men's necks. Most of them had loosened their ties; several had removed them altogether. The women fared little better in the tailored dresses and shirts, although Eric did spy one or two who had sensibly opted for something looser and a little more aerated. He was infinitely envious.

'Perfect fucking timing.' Greg was sitting on Eric's desk, chewing on the end of Eric's favourite ballpoint. He stopped, studied it for a second, then moved to place the pen back in Eric's pot.

'It's fine,' Eric said. 'You keep it.'

'Sweet,' Greg said, pocketing the pen. A split second later, he pulled a new pen out of the pot and was chewing on that.

'I asked Emily to move in with me last night,' he said with a look of gloom.

'You did what? The intern? I didn't even know you were dating.'

'Well. We weren't and then we were, and then it turns I actually quite like her. Anyway, it won't matter. She's hardly going to want to stay with me if I don't have a job.'

'It won't come to that.'

'It might.'

Eric stayed silent. He didn't want to offer too much false optimism; he barely had enough for himself as it was.

At eight fifty-five, Eric and the other directors huddled into the boardroom, each one adhering to their own, individualised tics. While Greg was busy gnawing his way through an expensive-looking fountain pen, one of the senior associate directors was unabashedly chewing his nails and spitting out the off-cuts. There was also shoe-tapping, lip-picking, and hand-wringing to add to the mix. Eric realised his own foible was to stare intently at every other person in order to pick out their idiosyncrasies while avoiding any admission of his.

Jack Nelson and Alistair Hartley were both smiling as they entered. Jack, who was wearing a bottle green suit, took his laptop over to the screen and made eye contact with each person in the room. Hartley sat down and got his phone out.

'So,' Jack began. 'Let me start by saying thank you for your patience. But I'm not going to beat around the bush. Let's get down to the reason we're all here.'

The meeting was a first in that every senior and associate director remained absolutely silent until they were certain Jack had finished speaking. The nail-biting had stopped, as had the pen-chewing and the people judging. No one knew where to move or look and certainly not what to say.

'I know you will all have a lot to discuss,' Jack said. 'And I shall catch up with all of you later. For now, I'll let you think over what we've just said.'

With that, they left.

It was Greg who was the first to speak, finally breaking the minute-long silence that had engulfed them.

'Did anybody manage to follow that?' he said.

'I think it means we're screwed,' said one of the associate directors.

'Not all of us,' someone else chipped in. 'Just some of us. Just some of us are screwed.'

Eric kept his thoughts to himself as he too tried to decipher exactly what they'd all been told.

Yes, there was to be a restructuring. Yes, there were to be job cuts. Yes, they were to be part of the process. No, even though they were directors, it did not mean they were safe. Yes, they would answer all their questions. No, they wouldn't do that now. Yes, every situation would be viewed in a personal, case-by-case scenario. No, they couldn't discuss that with them now either. Yes, there would be one-on-one meetings. No, the order that these meetings happened wouldn't mean anything. Yes, they would be required to fire people. Yes, it would probably get unpleasant. Yes, this was all extremely necessary in order to bring the business forwards.

Eric's insides churned. Fifteen years at *Hartley and Nelson*, and he'd fired exactly four members of staff. And each one had been deserved. The thought of calling someone into an office to tell them that he was stripping them of their entire financial security was enough to make him nauseous. Then again, perhaps he was already out the door. Perhaps Nelson and Hartley had already deemed him unstable, and he'd be one of the first to pack his bag, collect whatever little bundle of redundancy they deemed him worthy of, and trundle off down the treacherous road of unemployment. Fortunately, it wasn't too long a wait to find out.

The meetings for the directors were to start after lunch. While the majority of the possibly condemned huddled together in the communal area for moral support, Eric waited at his desk, blinds drawn down. His stomach was in a bad enough state already. The last thing he wanted to do was drive himself mad seeing who had been called in first and second, how long they took, or how ruffled they looked when they reappeared.

At 5.00 PM, when he still hadn't been summoned, Eric messaged Suzy to tell her that he'd be late home. She replied to wish him luck. He then messaged her again at seven to apologise and wish Abi a good night, and yet again at eight to tell her not to wait if she wanted to eat without him. Suzy replied to all the messages and said she'd wait for him to get home before she ate. She then sent another message immediately afterwards to say that she'd order food early though as the delivery time at the Sichuan could be hellish on a Friday night. When his phone buzzed for the third time, Eric almost ignored it until he glanced at the screen and saw Jack's name flashing up behind the glass.

Come in when you're ready, it read.

There was little that could rival the view from Jack's office. As nine o'clock approached and the summer sun sank low into the horizon, Eric stepped into the room and drank in the scene. Through the windows, the sun clipped the roof tiles and cast them in a cloud of berry pinks and indigo. Below them, the Thames glinted and reflected every colour it was offered. It was a perfect scene; peaceful, serene, intelligent. But for some reason, while gazing at the plush white carpet and aged leather desk, Eric transported himself back to the little office of Christian Eaves. This was it, the furthest away from Burlam that any man could get. And it wasn't just the furniture or the carpet or the view. Jack's office smelt successful. It smelt of polish and wood and the air had a minty – almost caustic – tang that was impossibly far removed from the sea-blighted offerings of the east coast. This office was everything Eric had dreamed of, and from where he stood, he felt a very long way away.

'Why don't you sit down?' Hartley said. Eric turned to Jack, who offered one sombre nod.

'THAT'S CRAZY,' Suzy said, chewing on a spring roll. 'Insane. I mean. Not that I doubted you, but wow. Really, wow.'

Eric chewed on his chow mien. It was after ten when he got home, and Suzy had reheated the noodles for him in the microwave. They tasted okay, but the texture had altered to something resembling polystyrene foam tubes. He munched the mouthful the best he could, then swallowed.

'Education is where they want to focus, apparently. Schools, colleges, universities. Apparently, they want to slim down and specialise.'

'So, Director for Education. How does that feel?' Suzy said.

'Bizarre,' Eric admitted. 'Jack wants me over in Norwich next week, then Glasgow, and Birmingham over the weekend. Not exactly sure how I'm going to manage that.'

'You'll find a way if it's what you want to do.'

'I know,' said Eric.

CHAPTER 32

AT FIRST, ERIC thought Greg was the reason he couldn't sleep. Despite sending him three messages asking how his meeting had gone, he'd heard nothing.

'He's probably out celebrating,' Suzy groaned. 'That's what people do at this hour. Celebrate, or sleep.'

'Maybe,' Eric said.

While Suzy shuffled about under the covers, Eric's mind continued to race.

'Maybe I'll just give him a quick call,' he said and climbed out of bed.

It took two gin and tonics and several episodes of *QI* for Eric to decide not to call Greg. Calling someone at three in the morning, even if you did have their best intentions at heart, was not something a man like Eric did. Forty-five minutes later, he was staring at the ceiling wondering how he'd never noticed all the cobwebs up there before and whether it would be a good time to try to get them.

Two hours later, he gave up trying to sleep. Suzy was out cold next to him, offering scarcely a murmur as he switched on the bathroom light and grabbed his unwashed jeans from the laundry basket. He wrote two notes – one for Suzy, one for Abi – pinned them to the fridge door, and got a cab round to Ralph's.

Given that it was barely dawn, Eric hadn't expected a response when he texted Ralph to inform him he was taking Sally for a drive. In truth, he only sent the message so Ralph didn't freak out when he woke up to find the garage empty. As such, he was surprised to find his former housemate standing outside the front door, a wide-awake baby bouncing on his hip while tugging at his newly formed beard.

'Nine-month sleep regression apparently,' Ralph said. 'Before that, it was the six-month and the four-month one before that. When's he not in a bloody sleep regression? That's what I want to know.'

Eric tickled the baby under the chin. It gurgled happily.

'I won't be gone long. Perhaps if I get back early enough, we can go for a spin?'

'That'd be great,' Ralph said. 'First time I'll have had a nap in the last seven years.'

'I'll try my best,' Eric said.

If anything, the journey muddied Eric's thoughts further as opposed to clearing them the way he'd hoped. It was only when he started the engine and checked the side mirrors he remembered that the last time he'd driven Sally, Norman had been in the passenger seat. Together, they'd twisted through the lanes around the back of Burlam discussing their possible entrants for the autumn show while ridiculing Eric's disastrous attempt at making tomato chutney. It had been a short spin, less than fifteen minutes. Eric had been in a rush, but Norman had been in a grump all afternoon, whinging over the weeds and cursing the insects, all the while whining about how it was too hot and too hard and too everything. Eric had thought that maybe a drive would help bring him out of the funk. And it did a bit.

Now Eric wished it could have been longer, that they could have laughed at more of his gardening failures, that he could have asked him a bit about the past. As he drove past the sign and the old garage where they held Sally after George's death, Eric took the right turn, down the cul-de-sac lined with elms, and parked up outside Norman and Cynthia's bungalow.

A blue *For Sale* sign punctured the newly mown lawn. Eric felt a stab in his gut. Obviously, Cynthia wanted to move out quickly; the place must be red raw with memories. Still, Eric thought, she might have wanted to give it a little time first. Then again, if Norman had anything to do with it, he'd probably placed the listing the week before his funeral.

A glance at his watch told him it was far too early to call in and pay her a visit. Eric put his foot down on the clutch, twisted the key in the ignition, and took another glance at the doorway. He was about to pull away when Cynthia dashed out into the drive, dressing gown slipping off her shoulders, madly waving her arms.

'Eric, Eric!' Realising he'd seen her, she slowed to a walk, then stopped, panting. Eric cut the engine and climbed out the car.

'Sorry,' he said. 'I didn't mean to disturb you. I didn't realise the time. Thought I'd pop in later instead.'

Cynthia dismissed his apology.

'I'm glad you did. I'm heading out with Maggie this afternoon. She's got the day off, so we're going to check out some old folks' villages together. I take it you've noticed my news?' She motioned in the direction of the *For Sale* sign.

'I did,' said Eric. 'Is this his doing or yours?'

'Oh, this is all my doing. He'd have approved mind, but no, it's me who wants to get out of there. Can't even clean my teeth without seeing him in that bathroom, combing his beard.'

Eric laughed.

'That'd be enough to make anyone want to move house,' he said.

Eric stopped, took a moment, then moved towards the car. 'Well, I should be getting on. I want to get as much time in as possible.' He paused then added. 'Actually, I have a bit of news too. I got a promotion at work.'

Cynthia clapped her hands then reached around him for a hug. 'Oh, that's wonderful. Well done, you. I hope it means you get to spend a little more time with the family?'

'Well, I'm not sure, exactly,' he said.

'Oh, I'm sure you've got it all worked out. A smart lad like you.' She stopped and scanned him up and down. Her eyes widened as a sudden thought struck. 'Hold on one sec. I have something for you. Can you hang on a minute?'

Without waiting for his reply, Cynthia dashed into the house. She hurried back out a few moments later although her hands were seemingly empty of whatever it was she'd gone to retrieve. It was only when she uncurled her fingers and reached out her palm towards Eric that he saw the key.

It was an entirely unspectacular specimen. A little under an inch long, flat and flimsy with a thin loop of wire attached to the top. It was the kind of cheap-looking key that you'd get with any hardware shop padlock.

'It's for his shed,' Cynthia said. 'He wanted you to have it. Well, what's inside it anyway,' she added. 'I think he decided it would be easier to leave the actual shed on the plot. Of course, if you want it, I'm sure it wouldn't be a problem.'

Eric couldn't speak. A large, obtrusive lump had forced its way up his throat and was causing difficulty breathing.

'He's given me his shed?' Eric said.

'Only if you want it. I think he thought you'd find the tools useful. There's a lot of other junk in there too, mind. Might have found yourself more work than you bargained for. But I'm done with that place now. I've got my memories and they're more than enough for the next few years, so if you come across anything you don't want, either you pass it on or you bin it. Either will be fine by me.'

Eric nodded. His eyes were still fixed on the key, uncertain what would happen if he moved them. In a swift motion, Cynthia tucked the key into his top pocket and tapped it there.

'Well,' she said. 'We should both be getting on. And just because I'm taking a break from the allotment, doesn't mean I'm going to stop cooking. You get too many carrots, you pass them this way. I'll have a vat of soup and a half a dozen cakes for your freezer by the end of the week.'

Cynthia retreated to the front porch where she stood and waited, then waved until Eric had driven out of sight.

Eric was grateful the drive to the allotment was short. His legs had become decidedly wobbly and the lump in his throat had swelled so large that it was causing his eyes to water. Here was a man he'd known for less than a year. A man who had caused him torment and torture and insufferable frustration, and yet in one large swoop all that had disappeared. Norman Kettlewell had thought of him. He had thought of Eric beyond his own life in a way that his father never had. There were no conditions to this inheritance. No rules he had to abide by. True, it was only a shed, not an eight-hundred-grand house, or a five-hundred-grand car, but it was

Norman's palace and he'd bequeathed it to Eric. Eric's flood of gratitude was hit by a sudden surge of anger towards his father. So much for thinking the twisted inheritance would bring them closer together.

The allotment was empty and the large metal gates pulled closed. Eric pushed them apart. It had been a long time since he'd been the first person there. Those were the days when he'd arrive as early as possible in order to leave as early as possible. When work was at the forefront of his thoughts and Suzy and Abi somewhere around the back, along with important dental hygiene and renewing car insurance. A sadness swelled inside him; it would be like that again soon. In early, out early. No time to stop and natter over the compost heaps or indulge in lingering brunches at The Shed. He would have to be as productive as possible from now on. Only fourteen months, Eric told himself as he plucked a raspberry from a bush. He could manage fourteen months of juggling. After that, he'd have it all: the car, the job, the perfect house. Fourteen months and his life would really be complete. Although even as he said it to himself, he had great difficulty believing it.

The air smelt of greenness; of wet grass and dewy moss and freshly harvested vegetables. The powder-blue sky was littered with grey-white clouds, making the greens even brighter and bolder. Eric shut the gate and began to take his normal path towards his own little patch. It was well trodden and muddy and he could walk there with his eyes closed, but when he reached the first crossroad – straight ahead for his, left or right for who knows what – he stopped. Nine months he'd been here, and yet he'd made no real attempts to visit the other plots. He knew some of course – Norman's, Hank's, and Janice's to an extent – but had no real idea what lay beyond those little boundaries of turf, turnips and six by fours. Fighting against the power of practice, Eric turned right.

There was much of a muchness of course – runner beans, greenhouses, large blue water butts, and sheds with little brass padlocks – but there were also hidden gems among the sprouts and parsnips. Whole plots laid to wildflower. Not uncultivated, not full of weeds, but bursting at the seams with thyme and foxgloves and honeysuckle and lavender, the scents of which spilt upward and tickled Eric's nose as he leant in and sniffed. There were giant greenhouses again filled with flowers, but this time of a more cultivated variety. Roses, lilies, varieties that Eric had assumed you could only get at a florist, supermarket, or at a push, a garage service station, but had never assumed you could actually grow yourself. There were several beehives, birdhouses, and even some garden ponds. Each plot had a story and personality, and at each one, he found something different to admire. When he'd exhausted every route possible and was certain that he'd at least glanced at every plot that the Columbia Avenue Allotment had on offer, he arrived at the plot with the neat rows all labelled with plastic markers, the turf trimmed to an even an exacting level and the tomatoes ordered according to height.

Already the grass was growing up around the corners of the beds.

'Ten minutes with the secateurs and I can sort that out,' Eric said to himself. Then removing the key from his pocket, he stepped up on the wooden veranda of Norman's shed.

CHAPTER 33

INSIDE THE SHED large pots and plants obscured the light from the windows and caused a damp sticky heat to fill the air. The space smelt of ash, with a heady, woozy undertone that took Eric a second to place.

'Cinderella 99. What else.' He lifted his eyes up to the roof and said, 'If this is some kind of elaborate plan to get me arrested again, I'm going to use your ashes in a punching bag.'

Eric strained around until his eyes found the light switch. Hoping that Norman was as particular about his electrical skills as he was the rest of his allotment, Eric flipped his switch. A millisecond later he stood in the light, squinting but thankfully not electrocuted.

On the wall nearest the door were Norman's tools. Each one hung on its own specific nail, the outline drawn onto the wood behind it, indicating the exact angle from which it should be hung. Below the window was the plant life. Most of them were seedlings, but a few plants were more substantial. Eric ran his fingers between them. They were familiar, but nothing more than that. He'd need a couple more years at this before he could tell what plant was what from a two-and-a-half-inch sprout.

In the corner sat a small kettle while a half-sized fridge buzzed rhythmically below it. Inside was a blue and yellow cake tin. Eric picked it up, flinched against the cold, and shook it. When it rattled, he opened it to find half a loaf of Cynthia's carrot and walnut cake, green spores of mould beginning to flourish on the surface.

The last side of the shed was more like something you'd find in an office than a gardener's retreat, and Eric needed to take a step back to view it in its entirety. The desk featured a set of shelves loaded with pictures and frames and four drawers set beneath them. Sitting in front of the writing area was a heavy wooden rocking chair, complete with a padded cushion. Maybe Eric could get a rocking chair at work, he wondered. Maybe that would make evenings away from the girls more bearable. He picked up the cushion and turned it over in his hands. It smelt of lanolin and earth and hard work. There was nothing exceptional about it, and it was probably harbouring a dozen unknown pathogens, but it caused an ache to spread through the upper region of Eric's torso. He put it down on the chair, took a step to the side, and turned his attention to the picture frames.

The largest images faced out. There were wedding anniversaries and birthdays. Photos of Norman and Cynthia smiling, centre frame, cutting into cakes, surrounded by grinning children and adults. There were graduation photos of people Eric could only assume were nieces and nephews as well as Christmas shots around the tree and one or two christenings. Eric recognised a few faces – faces from the funeral – and Maggie featured in several, but mostly they were strangers to him. He continued to browse though, trying to place dates by the length of Norman's beard, or the style of the women's dresses and men's hair.

Behind these images were stacks of cards. Certificates. Mostly they came from the village show but there were a few with *National*, written in bold letters in the title. Best in show, second place, highly commended; carrots, cos lettuces, kohlrabi, cabbages. Largest onion. Three salad vegetables on a dinner plate. It appeared that every item in Norman's harvests had at some point been placed and prized. And not just him. Cynthia was there too. Her carrot and walnut cake appeared numerous times, as did her elderflower wine and her pickled shallots. Eric glanced at the dates. Two thousand and five. Nineteen ninety. Nineteen eighty-four. He flicked through, seeing how far back they went. Nineteen seventy-nine. Nearly four decades of knowledge and green fingers, commemorated by nothing more than slips of paper. Eric wiped the dust from them and placed each one back where he had found it.

The top drawer of the desk was filled with nails and screw plugs, but in the second one, Eric found more photos. He blew them clean, causing a billow of dust to fog up the air in front of him. The papers they were printed on were no bigger than postcards, and the sepia tones had faded with time. On many, the edges had bent and torn, and little speckles of dirt veiled the image like a veneer. Eric turned the top print towards the light.

The picture had been taken on a seafront, with a pier behind and a carousel off to the right. The couple in the centre had their arms around each other, although the young girl had her eyes closed, scrunched shut as if caught unaware mid-sneeze. He put the photo to the back of the pile and began to work his way through the rest. There were hundreds of monochromatic and tea-stained images. Some had stuck together with damp, many faded so much they were indecipherable, but still, there were countless left for Eric to look through and muse upon. Mostly they were images of Norman and Cynthia. A young Norman and strikingly beautiful Cynthia, both with long hair, thin waistlines, and wrinkleless faces that lifted out of the paper with their smiles. There were animal shots; a black and white cat lying on a window ledge beneath a hanging basket; a shaggy-furred dog with its tongue hanging out and a patterned bandana around his neck. One by one he worked through the pile, absorbing everything he could until the image of Norman and Cynthia at the carousel reappeared at the top.

There were only two more drawers left. In one was a toolbox. Rusted, grey, and locked with another cheap little padlock. Eric gave it a light shake, and a jangle rang out from within. No doubt more nails and screw plugs. He opened the last drawer.

The photo inside was face up but stuck at a jaunty angle which made it impossible to see what was on it until Eric had pulled it all the way out. The layer of dust on the frame was thin and the glass itself mottled with fingerprints as though it had been looked at recently. Twisting it towards the light caused his heart to lurch. Eric had seen the photo once before, all those months ago. Even so, it caused the tears to prick behind his eyes.

The photo was taken in front of the town hall with the clock tower clock clipped off the top. It consisted of three rows of people, several holding certificates, several more holding fruits, vegetables, and flowers, all arranged underneath a dated banner decorated with drawings of fruits and veg.

Eric ran his eyes along the back row. Hank stood at the side, his right leg out of view but Scout's tail just made it into the shot. Next to him stood Penelope Hamilton – from the excavator incident. Moving to the middle row, Janice, Cynthia, and another lady who was holding the most impressive spray of flowers stood in the centre between another dozen faces. Norman was on the front row, sitting on a chair. Several certificates were propped up against his feet and a few more on his lap, their corresponding prize winners next to them. However, for the first time since Eric had entered the shed, Norman was not the focus of Eric's attention.

Guilt struck behind Eric's sternum. It was solid and fast and caused his lungs to constrict and eyes to water. Still, he didn't change his gaze. His father was laughing. The flat cap on his head pulled firmly down. Eric had not once seen his father wear a flat cap, yet there it was.

From the date on the banner, Eric knew this was the last show he could have done. September, only a month before he died. Eric stared at the image of his father. Had he really looked that old? Not that Eric ever remembered. Perhaps it was because he was sitting down. People always look older when they're seated, Eric convinced himself. It's the way their posture slumps. His cheeks had hollowed too, sunken in and sallow. His hands were crossed on his lap, his fingers and wrists bent at strange looking angles. So, it wasn't just talk, his hands really did go.

Trying to ignore the intensifying heat building behind his eyes, Eric took the photo and placed it flat on the writing desk. He would keep it, he decided. Abi would like to keep it. Glancing back down, he saw that once more, the photo was refusing to lie flat. Assuming it was some problem with the frame, he turned it over to check the back.

Something stiffened behind Eric's belly button. His stomach twisted and churned while his eyes were locked on a small white envelope stuck with masking tape to the back of the frame. The name *Eric* was scribbled across the front. Gently, Eric peeled the tape away and ripped open the envelope. Inside he found a small metal key.

THE SMELL of soil and thickness of dust had become too much for Eric, and he carried the toolbox outside and onto the front of the veranda. He lowered himself into one of the chairs only to realise almost instantly that it was Norman's chair he'd sat in. He jumped up, wiped it down, and moved across to his usual place.

Eric's hands were back to shaking as he pinched the padlock between his fingers and racked his brain for what could be inside. Seeds? he thought, then dismissed the idea. Why would anyone keep his seeds under lock and key? Eric's pulse answered. Illegal seeds? He swallowed hard, held his breath, and turned the key.

CHAPTER 34

IT HAD BEEN ten years since Eric and Suzy had last shared a spliff, and he was certain it must have been more exciting back then. It had to be. Right now, all he was feeling was sleepy, clumsy, and like his nostrils had been held against a biofuel exhaust pipe. Still, there was only the one joint tucked in the bottom of the toolbox, and by the end of the evening all evidence of Eric's adult dabbling in narcotics would be over and done with.

'Do you think it was for the pain?' Suzy said, drawing in a long deep drag then blowing it out over her shoulder, and out through the open window. 'At the funeral, a lot of people said he was in pain.'

'I think they said he was *a* pain,' Eric attempted to clarify for her. 'He was definitely a pain.'

Suzy passed him the glowing roll up and rested her hand on her husband's knee. She leant in with a slight sway.

'But truthfully, how do you feel?' she said, 'About everything?'

'About everything? You mean the weed? Or the fact that I can see two tiny Erics in your pupils?'

'Eric ...' Suzy shuffled back accordingly.

Eric sighed. He offered the joint back to Suzy, who shook her head. He dropped it into a half-empty tonic can and flopped down on to the sofa.

'Truthfully? I have no idea. I mean, how am I meant to feel? It's nice, I suppose. Finding out my father isn't a complete and utter bastard and didn't entirely despise me.'

'He didn't despise you —'

'But that doesn't change the fact that he was an arsehole for most of my life. And even when he was dead.'

Suzy glanced down at the floor. The toolbox was open, the contents scattered out on the carpet. She riffled through for a second before selecting a tea-coloured newspaper scrap.

'Local Students Perform Outstanding Charity Concert,' she read.

'You didn't tell me about doing this,' she said, reading down the column to find Eric's name.

He shrugged. 'It wasn't anything big. It was just a local thing, I can't even remember what it was for. Probably an old people's home or something.'

'It says here it was for the Life Boat rescue.'

'That would make sense.'

'And your dad obviously thought it was a big deal, he wouldn't have kept it otherwise.'

'Well, he seems to have kept everything else.'

The contents of the toolbox were a walk through Eric's childhood. There was his hospital bracelet, impossibly small and written in the type of curved handwriting that transcended modern day penmanship, along with a photo of the three of them, standing on the hospital steps. Baby Eric's eyes were invisible in his full throttle wail and had there been colours to the image, Eric suspected his face would have glowed in phosphorescent purple. There was a letter Eric had no recollection of writing, in which he'd told his parents all about his first day of school, a picture of him sitting on his mother's knee, reading books, and another of him standing on a stool in the kitchen, reaching up to stir some giant bowl on the worktop. There were several other photos too, half a dozen of them out in the garden and various ones involving birthday candles, but most of the photos had a running theme.

Eric could map his age from toddler to teen, sitting behind the rim of Sally's polished steering wheel. Unlike the others in the photo, she had not aged a day, but in each one Eric's face glowed as he gripped the wood and gazed out of the windscreen, grinning. Sometimes his father was beside him, other times he was on his own. There were photos in the summer, a seascape and seagulls drifting in the background behind them. There was Eric in his school uniform, with his tie hanging loose and his hair sticking out at wayward angles. There was the day that he'd passed his driving test, where he stood on the driveway, one hand resting on Sally, the other holding onto a slip of paper, pouting in a sullen sulk. He could remember that one being taken. He was meant to be meeting friends to celebrate with, but his father had insisted they get a photo first. They had gone out in the cold only to discover that the camera was out of film, so he'd had to wait forty minutes for George to go into town, queue up in the post office, and get some film. Eric's mood had been made even more unbiddable by the fact he wasn't allowed to drive Sally there on his own. A little thing like insurance irrelevant in the mind of a hormonal seventeen-year-old boy.

Photos took up the majority of the toolbox. There was also his mother's jewellery; nothing fancy, her engagement ring, now dated with its gold floral setting and tiny diamond, and a few other pieces with it, like a locket which Eric opened to find a picture of himself and his father. There were bank account details. Accounts not specified in the will, for they were not in George's name. There was one in Eric's name – small, but not insubstantial – and two in Abi's, which Eric had to get Suzy to double check the figures on twice before he was satisfied his eyes weren't playing tricks on him.

And then there was the letter.

'Right,' Suzy said, standing up with a slight wobble. 'I'm going to bed. What are you doing?'

'I'll just check we're all locked up. And have a bit of a tidy up first,' Eric said as he stood. 'You go up, I'll join you in a minute.'

'Don't be too long,' she said and kissed him on the forehead.

Eric strolled around the house. He checked the back door and kitchen windows and, on finding the living room still humming with the scent of weed, opened all the windows as wide as possible. Heading back into the kitchen, he poured himself a large gin and took a seat at the dining room table.

He sat in silence, making no motion for the television, or paper or even the letter. After a couple of minutes, he downed the drink, shut the windows, and went upstairs to Suzy. It was time they talked.

※

It was the right decision. He was positive it was, and if he'd needed any clarification on this matter, it came when he told Jack the news. Losing his professionalism for only the second time in Eric's company, Jack pulled Eric towards him and slapped him hard on the back, then pulled away with tears in his eyes.

'I couldn't be prouder of you,' he said. 'I couldn't be more pleased.'

'I'm not sure how I'm meant to take that,' Eric said.

'Oh, I think you're barking. Completely barking. And you'll be back in six months without a doubt.'

'Thanks for the vote of confidence,' he said.

Jack slapped him on the back.

※

They had three sets of people view the house the first day it went on the market. Within five days it was sold, and six weeks to the date they had the movers at the door.

'You sure you're not going to regret this?' Suzy asked him for the hundredth time. The sun was out although the chill was enough to make them keep their jumpers on. The scent of peonies drifted in from somewhere up the road. Abi was at Lydia's. She was going to stay there for a few days until they could get the place in order. Eric took Suzy's hand in his and lifted it up to kiss her knuckles.

'No,' Eric said. 'But then who says regret is a bad thing?'

THE MOLE FIASCO

A Peas and Carrots Short Story

CHAPTER 1

GEORGE AND NORMAN stood shoulder to shoulder staring out at the plot.

'This is not great, is it?' George said.

'It's not ideal,' Norman agreed. 'Not ideal at all.'

For George, owning an allotment had never been about growing vegetables, although he had come to enjoy the pastime substantially. After his wife, Gloria, has passed away, he had found himself thrust into solitude and for the first time in his life, George Sibley had been truly lonely. It was true, he probably hadn't helped himself in the matter. Maybe if he had made more of an effort to keep in contact with friends from his younger days, or perhaps if he hadn't been so stern with his son, Eric, when he was growing up, they would have a better relationship now. Perhaps, if that had happened, Eric's visits would have been more than biannually. Maybe he'd have considered moving a little closer. He'd never leave London now though. George was certain of that.

There was, of course, Sally. She had been in his life longer than Eric, and the majority of the time, there was no place on Earth George would rather be. However, more and more, as he found himself getting older, George felt a distinct need for a little human company.

He had initially applied for a plot at the Columbia Avenue allotments only a month after Gloria's passing. At which point he had been told the wait would be a minimum of five years.

'That's an estimate of course,' the woman had told him on the phone after the lady at the library had found a contact number on the internet. 'It all depends you know. Sometimes people move. Some of our older tenants they tend to ... well...'

'Die?' George answered for her.

'Find the work can become a little too physically strenuous.'

George huffed. 'I don't remember my mother having to wait that long for her plot,' George said, verbalising his thoughts. 'She wasn't exactly patient. And I can't imagine more people wanting a plot now than they did then.'

A shallow lip smack rattled its way down the line.

'Did you say your mother had a plot there?' the lady asked. 'At Columbia Avenue?'

'That's right, from when I was about fifteen until the day she died.'

A pause filled the space.

'Well.' The woman spoke with noticeable hesitation. 'We might be able to get you sorted a little quicker. There's a little more flexibility when it comes to heirloom plots. Let me see what I can do. I'll get back to you as soon as I can.'

George grunted his thanks into the receiver. 'That would be grand,' he said.

It took another seven months before a letter came through the post, informing George of his assigned plot. And while seven months was still substantially longer than he had anticipated having to wait, it was also considerably better than the five years he had initially been told. And so, by George's standard, he was happy.

George continued to be pleasantly surprised when he went to inspect his plot the following day.

'You've got a good one here. Plenty of sunlight. Lots of windbreaks. Can be a bugger if it floods, but generally speaking, it's never been that bad.' His neighbour Norman stretched out his hand. 'And I'm always here if you need to check anything. Unless you want to gossip. I'm not a man for gossip.'

'No worries of that from me.' George met Norman's hand and gave it three firm pumps. 'George Sibley.'

'Norman Kettlewell.'

That was two years ago, and George had learnt a lot in that time. He had learnt when was the best season to plant his salad greens to ensure they didn't go to seed, and how using plastic tubing with sand in was the key to getting straight carrots. He had made friends too. Possibly more than at any other point in his life. Although the excellent placing of his near corner plot meant that he could easily avoid stumbling into quick questions that lengthen into two-hour conversations.

Yet while the action of growing vegetables was only secondary to George's purpose in being at the allotment, he couldn't help being miffed when something disrupted it.

'I'm assuming you've come across this before?' George said to Norman, although his eyes remained fixed on the fresh brown mound of earth rising from the centre of his feathery carrot leaves.

'Aye.' Norman puffed out a breath of cigarette smoke as he contemplated the question. 'A long while ago, mind. Not a lot of fun from what I remember.'

'Well, what should we do? Is it going to eat all my crops?'

Norman shook his head as he continued to blow smoke into the air in front of them.

'Probably best to wait a couple of days,' he said after a pause. 'He might move on. Could be gone by tomorrow.'

George's eyes remained on the mound.

'And if he's not?'

'Then we'll have to bring out our shovels.'

The following day, two more perfect molehills cast a shadow on George Sibley's plot. The day after there were yet another three, along with a further two poking out by Norman's neighbouring bean house.

'He's right next to my beans. That's what he's going for. I can tell you that now. He's going for my beans.'

'Oh dear,' said Cynthia, Norman's wife, as she came and stood beside them. 'That doesn't look good.'

'You don't say,' Norman grunted.

She rested a hand on his shoulder. 'I've spoken to Janice, and Hank – you know, the new chap – none of them have got any problems.'

'Typical. Of course it's only here the bloody thing chooses to wreak havoc.' Norman dragged on his cigarette as he paused for a thought. 'I guess I'll be sitting out with a shovel tonight.'

Besides him Cynthia bristled. 'You will be doing no such thing.'

Norman stuck out his chest indignantly. 'What do you expect me to do? Let it ruin everything? That thing moves underground. You know that, don't you?'

'I am well aware how moles travel, thank you Norman. All I am saying is that if you expect me to keep baking you chicken pies and making your cups of tea every day, you'll find an alternative.'

'But I —'

'But you nothing. The mole lives. You'll have to find a different solution.'

With that she pushed back her shoulders and made her way back across to their shed, leaving Norman to grumble under his breath.

'Her tea tastes like piss anyway,' he muttered. 'But God damn it, I love those chicken pies.'

George smiled to himself gratefully. As an adult, he had only one memory concerning moles, and it involved his father, a shovel and two years-worth of nightmares. While he had aged considerably in the time since the incident, he couldn't help but worry that the nightmares would have returned if Norman had had his way. Thankfully, due to Cynthia, he hadn't had to sound like he was going soft.

'I guess we ought to start looking at our options,' he said.

Norman huffed, drew yet another cigarette from his pack, and stared at the ground.

'Chilies.' Janice was practically bouncing as she imparted her pearl of wisdom. 'Not the type you grow here mind. The dried ones. The spicy ones. You know, like they use in all that Indian food. And not just a little bit,' she continued. 'You'll need a bag full. And not just a little bag. Oh no, you going to need ...'

With her miniature features and oversized glasses, the member of the committee had immediately reminded George of a woodland creature; a shrew perhaps, or maybe an owl; she was as smart as one, about that he was certain.

'I heard whiskey works,' someone else added their input into the conversation. 'Doesn't have to be good stuff. Just lots of it. They can't stand the smell. Either that or they get blind drunk and can't make the hills anymore. I can't remember which, but it's definitely whiskey. You definitely need to feed them whiskey.'

A small crowd had gathered around Norman's and George's plot, although other than the whiskey and the chilli, all others had been in agreement with Norman that there was only one way to rid yourself of a mole.

'No point telling me,' Norman grunted. 'My hands are tied.'

'Trust me. Go with the chillies. That'll definitely work,' said Janice, forcing her advice upon them yet again.

George and Norman exchanged a glance.

'I guess we're going shopping then.'

In the supermarket, the checkout girl eyed them sceptically.

'Some kind of cocktail?' she said, nodding at the two litres of cheap whiskey and the three bags of dried chilli.

'Moles,' George replied.

The girl's eyes widened. 'You mean garden moles?'

'Well he don't mean the moles on your behind,' Norman responded. The girl ignored him.

'Oh, well you don't need all this. You just need to grab yourself a handful of those.' She pointed across the counter to the strategically placed rows of chocolate bars and sweets.

'Mars bars?'

'No, chewing gum.'

'Chewing gum?'

'Uh-uh.' A queue was forming behind them, but the checkout assistant showed no indication of having noticed. 'Got to be the juicy fruit one, though. Can't be any other. You stick it in the top of the hills, and around them, you know, where the tunnels are and stuff. They don't like the smell you see. Can't stand it. My gran had them for years. Tried all sorts of things to get rid of them. Never worked. Then she tried this and, poof, just like that. It's the smell you see.'

George turned to glance at Norman. He shrugged.

'I guess we could throw some in,' he said, then pulled a handful of yellow packaged chewing gum from off the shelf and dropped it directly on to the conveyor belt.

'That'll be twenty-eight pounds sixty,' the girl said.

Norman and George gulped simultaneous.

❧

THAT AFTERNOON they got to work.

'Do you think we're meant to unwrap it?' Norman asked as he opened his sixth packet of chewing up. 'Cos I don't want this stuff getting into my top soil messing up all my seedlings next year.'

'Didn't she say it was the smell?' George unscrewed the whiskey and sniffed, before coughing as the fumes caught at the back of his throat. 'Surely we have to unwrap it if we want them to smell it properly. I suppose we'll just have to remember how many we put down. And where they go.'

'Or we could just start with them on your plot,' Norman suggested, ripping the foil off a stick. 'You think we're meant to chew it first?' Without waiting for an answer, he removed the cigarette from between his lips, stuck out his tongue and licked the pale white stick of gum. He grimaced, twisting up his features so that his lips and nose were lost entirely in his beard. 'We'll just use it as is,' he said, then took the stick of gum and plugged it straight into the earth next to George's tomato plant.

While Norman got about distributing the gum into the earth around the mole hills, George busied himself sprinkling the chillies. When they were both done, they took out of bottle of whiskey each. Norman's eyes twinkled as he sniffed the bottle.

'Would be rude not to, don't you think?' he said.

'Perhaps just a small one.'

'I'll just go fetch us some glasses.' When Norman reappeared from his rust red shed, he carried two well chipped mugs. 'Bottoms up then?'

George took a mug from Norman and proceeded to pour himself a miniscule measure from his own whiskey bottle. He was not one for drinking. Never had been. His mother and father held to the belief that alcohol was needed only for the slowest of minds, so as to obscure their senses enough for them to consider themselves intelligent. The older George got, the more he had begun to agree with the notion, particularly given how much his son, Eric, drank. But Norman enjoyed a tipple, and George enjoyed Norman's company.

'Seems like a waste to me,' Norman said, pouring himself another glug after finishing the first. 'But as long as one of these works, I'll be happy.'

Then he put his mug down on the ground and wandered around the plot drizzling the whiskey as he went.

A moment later, George followed suit.

CHAPTER 2

'YOU'VE GOT TO be bloody joking?' Norman fumed. 'Is this a joke? Is this a bloody joke?'

George and Norman had come down to the plot together the following morning. While George was excited to see whether the fruits of their labour had worked, they had not arrived until mid-morning, having decided that he would take advantage of the good weather and head out for a spin in the car. As had become customary over the last few months, Norman happily invited himself along.

'If you ever need a passenger, in that car of yours ...' Norman had said, only a couple of weeks after George had arrived at the allotment. 'She's a '68, right?'

''69,' George had corrected him.

'Course. Well, if you fancy some company ...'

'I generally prefer the quiet.'

The next week Norman changed tactics.

'I saw you took her out again this weekend. Does it not put her off balance only having someone in the driver's seat?'

'No. No, she's just fine. Like every other car.'

Eventually, George had had to give in, if only to stop Norman's useless attempts at discretion.

'You are not to smoke within six feet of her. You are not to smoke for two hours prior to setting foot in her. You are not to wear your gardening shoes in her, and you are not to touch any other part of her other than the seat. Do you understand?'

'Every word,' Norman replied.

Despite insisting he had been listening to George's speech, Norman obviously thought he was joking. He had turned up and George's house – surprisingly close to his own home, considering they had never crossed paths before the allotments – cigarette in hand.

'Nope.' George slammed the driver's door shut and switched on the engine.

'You have to be kidding.'

'I do not kid,' George had said, reversing passed Norman with his window down. 'Not about Sally.'

'But ... but ...' But George was already down the road; Norman whipped from his thoughts by the wind.

It was another two months before George gave Norman a second chance. This time he had shown up smelling of soap and old spice aftershave. It was only marginally better, but George didn't want to go back on his word. He had made it a quick spin though, twenty minutes. And he had put his foot down on the bends hoping that perhaps a little nausea would put Norman off asking to come again. He had known the truth though; he knew from the twinkle in his eye. Norman was hooked, from the moment he sat inside.

'If you kick it before I do, I'll buy her,' Norman had insisted, going to wipe his hand on the polished wood interior, only to have George slap it away before he could make contact.

'You know she's worth almost as much as your house.' George slowed for a zebra crossing, shooting a glare at the young woman and her pushchair who had made him stop. 'Besides, you'll be lucky to make the end of the year if you keep getting through those cigarettes the way you do.'

'You don't know what you're talking about. Besides, we could live in a caravan,' Norman continued. 'Cynth wouldn't mind. She'd probably like it. And it'd be less space. Means we couldn't have all the damn nephews and nieces over all the time.'

George had chuckled sadly. Being overrun by family visits wasn't something he had ever had to concern himself with. In fact, their current situation at the allotment was the first case of being overrun he could recall in a great many years.

There were now too many molehills to count. It was impossible; akin to a severe outbreak of chickenpox across the two plots. Dotted amongst the piles and piles of overturned soil were little white strips of chewing gum. Hank, one of the newer members of Columbia Avenue, was standing beside them while his dog, a boisterous whippet, was running up and down between the rows, kicking a ball between his two front legs.

'You went for the chewing gum trick then?' he laughed. 'Never really worked out why people fall for that one. Honestly, moles are more than happy to burrow beneath your strawberries or underneath raspberry plants. Why people think artificial pineapple would put them off is beyond me.'

George twiddled his thumbs. It did seem rather silly, now that he thought about it. But it wasn't like they had any better ideas. Other than brutally murdering the mammal. The night before he had had nightmares about a family of giant moles intent on seeking revenge for their youngest by stalking George around the dark aisles of the local hardware shop. He had been forced to hide among the rawl plugs and drill pieces and had only just got away unscathed. Thinking back on it, it had been ridiculous, although he had woken in a cold sweat at the time. If a shovel was the only way forward, Norman would have to be the one to do it, George decided. There was no way he could kill an animal like that.

'Sound is what you need to try,' Hank continued, breaking George's musings, and by the look of it, Norman's too. 'Moles aren't bothered by smells as much as you think. It's sound they don't like. Makes the earth vibrate you see. They can't work out which way they're going. What you need to do is get yourself a big set of speakers, and some good old-fashioned heavy metal. That'll get rid of them.

'Heavy metal? You mean that loud banging stuff?' George replied.

Hank nodded. 'Doesn't have to be metal, but the louder, the better.'

George's head moved as he contemplated the idea. It certainly sounded more humane than the alternative, although he had no idea what heavy metal music was, let alone how to get hold of it.

'Actually,' Norman said. 'I might know someone who could help us with that.'

After further discussing which genre of music would be most likely to repel the mammal in question, George could do nothing but wait. Norman had insisted he would see to all the details, namely sourcing a loud enough portable stereo system and the music to rid them of their unwanted visitors for good.

'No point doing anything until it's dark,' Norman said. 'You might as well go home and get yourself some dinner. I'll get everything sorted. We can meet back here at, say, eight?'

George pursed his lips and cast an eye back of the multitude of molehills desecrating his land.

'Do you think this'll work?' he said. 'What if we're out here all night and it doesn't help?'

'You got somewhere better to be?' Norman's massive hairy eyebrow rose a fraction.

George didn't respond. They both knew the answer. No, he didn't have anywhere better to be. He didn't have anywhere else to be full stop. So, whether or not this heavy rage metal, rage, thrash music, worked or not was irrelevant.

'Besides, this is it,' Norman assured him. 'This is the only other thing I'm going to try. If this doesn't work, then tomorrow night we're camping out here with shovels.'

George's pulse rose. 'What about Cynthia?'

'Oh I can handle her,' Norman said confidently, although George couldn't help notice that his fingertips gripped ever so slightly tighter around his cigarette.

At 7:30, George headed out from home and down to the allotment. It was only a twenty-minute walk, but George was always one for being punctual. Besides, Norman had been on the phone before he left the plot earlier and whatever plan he was hatching, George wanted to be there to see it in its entirety. Walking out of the driveway and onto the street, he continued to struggle to get his gloves on straight. If Gloria had still been here, she would have made him go to the doctors by now. So would Eric too, probably, if George actually told him anything of importance. But what could the doctors tell him? He was getting old. He didn't need to waste half a morning sitting in a waiting room full of sick people to hear that, thank you very much. No, his hands would be better in the summer, when the damp didn't get to his joints quite so much.

Continuing to mull over various issues, mainly from his past, he arrived at the allotment to find that not only was Norman already there, he was not alone.

'Uncle Nor? Are you listening to anything I'm saying?' she said.

The woman with Norman was, George supposed, in her twenties or possibly still in her late teens. The ambiguity in her age came partially from her petite structure and youthful features, and partially from the fact that her hair was dyed a rainbow of pinks, blues, yellows. Despite the freezing weather, she was dressed in ripped jeans, with her midriff fully exposed, and all up the sides of her ears hung an array of studs and hooped earrings.

'George, 'ave you met my niece, Maggie?' The girl looked up from the object in her hand and grunted. 'She likes to pretend she's a hooligan most of the time.'

Her eyes came up once again, this time in a scowl. 'Whatever Uncle Nor. Do you want my help with this or not?'

As her head went back down, Norman pulled a face behind her. Something sad pulled in George's chest. He remembered when Eric had first turned from a helpful child into a moody and sullen teenager; a phase which he'd yet to grow out of in George's opinion.

'Well,' Norman said, scanning his eyes across the rest of the allotment. 'I guess now might be time for a little aperitif. I'll just go fetch us one.'

George followed Norman over to his shed, and took a seat on one of the chairs. The sun had set while George was walking down, but there was still enough residual light to make out where things were, including the dozen small boxes between the mounds.

'Are all of those speakers?' he said to Maggie, who continued to fiddle with what George now realised to be her phone.

'They are.'

'But where are all the wires? How are they going to work without wires?'

A sympathetic smile rose on her lips.

'Don't worry about it grandad,' she said. 'I've got it all sorted. Just need to make sure they're all connected and ... that's it. We're good to go.'

A moment after Maggie made her announcement, Norman reappeared from the shed, a sizeable hand-rolled cigarette between his lips.

'Hey,' Maggie frowned, looking at her uncle with concern. 'That better not be my payment you're smoking.'

Norman waved her silent. 'Keep your hair on woman, assuming all that dye doesn't make it fall out, that is. You'll get what I promised you. I thought it might be nice to have something to accompany our impromptu little music festival, that's all.' Maggie's frown stayed fixed in place.

'You'd better be sharing,' she said.

'Let's see you get this lot working first.' Norman proceeded to sit down in the chair next to George and light his cigarette.

'All right,' Maggie said, moving between the allotments and lifting her arms as if she were about to start a drag race. 'Let's get this party started. It might be a bit loud. I haven't checked the volumes with this music at all. But hey-ho. Pretend you're at a concert.'

'A philharmonic one?' George asked hopefully. Maggie chose not to reply.

'Any final words?' she asked with her finger hovering above her phone.

Norman looked to George, who contemplated the question for just a moment. He was thinking about saying something deep and meaningful about the coexistence of all life on earth and the land belonging to the mole too, when Norman got there first.

'Bugger off and good riddance,' he said. And with a nod to Maggie, she pushed play.

The sound emitted by the speakers just moments after Maggie pressed the button was not music. In fact, George decreed, it was as far from music as he had ever heard. Music, in George's mind, was something with a melody. Something that you could dance to, or be absorbed in, or sing along too. This was not music. This, was a noise so vile and heinous it felt as though his very bones were shaking.

'Good Lord. What is this?' he said.

'Do you like it? It's Rage Against the Machine.'

The answer regarding the origin of the music had not, as George had expected, come from but Maggie, but from Norman, who was sitting back in his chair, smoking his cigarette, seemingly oblivious to the racket that was going on around him.

'How do you know what this stuff is?' George attempted to make himself heard over a low pitched repeated phrase, that gave the impression that the singer could either no longer remember the complete words to the song, or that the song had been written by a lyricist incapable of finishing a sentence.

'Relax,' Norman said. 'Here, have some of this.'

The smell that drifted from the end of Norman's hand-rolled cigarette had, until that moment, remained on the periphery of George's senses. There was undoubtedly something different about it; more of an earthy, citrusy tang than the normal packet specimens he coughed his way through. More calming. More herbal. Still, it was only when Norman stretched out his hand and offered it to George, that it clicked into place.

'You're smoking marijuana!' George's pulse skyrocketed. 'An illegal drug. In a public place.'

Norman chuckled. 'It's hardly public,' he said. 'Who's going to know out here?'

'But I'm right aren't I? That is marijuana?'

Listening on the edge of the conversation, Maggie swept it and pinched the spliff from Norman's fingers, before taking a long, deep inhale.

'Too, right it is.' She breathed out a lungful of smoke which mingled with the condensation in the air in front of them. 'And no one grows it better than Uncle Nor.'

'Oi, you go steady on that one.' Norman reached up and tugged it back out from Maggie's grip. 'You've got your own. And don't you dare tell your mother about this.'

'As if.'

'Well if she does find out she better not know it came from me.'

Maggie bent over and kissed her uncle on the cheek before taking the joint back from between his lips.

'You know I'd never do that to you ... again,' she laughed.

George didn't know where to look or what to say. Of course, people did drugs, he saw images of them on the television all the time. But they were young people. Young and poor and unpleasant. People who didn't wash and dropped out of school and didn't live in nice middle-class towns like Burlam.

'Sorry,' Maggie said, clearly confusing his look of sheer aghast for something else. 'Here you go.'

She thrust the joint between his fingers and without a moment to think, George Sibley suddenly found himself in possession of an illegal narcotic. It was too much for him to take.

'I ... You ...' he stuttered.

'It's all good stuff. Like the girl says, grew it myself.'

George sensed that Norman's words were intended to comfort him, although he doubted anything could manage that at that precise moment. His head was swimming and, in the darkness, the shadows appeared to move without his control.

'Good God man, what's a matter with you?' Norman's expression cleared. 'Nooo.' He extended the word until it lost itself in the air. 'Never? Really? But you're older than I am.'

George shifted around in the deck chair. The illegal spiff was still aglow in his hand although he doubted whether that was the source of the burning in his cheeks.

'How is that even possible?' Norman was now grinning from ear to ear as he sat forward, the heavy boom of the music out on the plot now a faint drumming compared to the hammering of George's pulse in his ears. 'You were alive in the sixties.'

'And working hard in school to ensure I didn't waste my life.' Norman and Maggie exchanged a look. The heat in George's cheeks intensified. Pushing himself out of his seat he strode over to Norman's chair and held the spliff out.

'Here, you can have it back.' He waited. The song on the speakers came to an end. The next one started. 'Well?'

Norman pressed his lips together.

'Go on,' George said, waving the joint only inches from Norman's face. 'Take it.'

When it became clear that Norman was being deliberately obtuse George turned instead to Maggie, a suppressed grin twisted on her lips.

'Sorry.' Her grin widened as she spoke. 'I'm good for now.'

The rage building in George's chest doubled with every passing moment.

'You think this is funny? Do you? Making me an accessory to your debauchery?'

'It's a little bit funny,' Norman muttered.

'It is not! It's is not funny at all.'

A tense pause, that was not in the slightest bit silent due to the horrific baseline that now thumped from the speakers, floated in the air around them.

Finally, with his lips pressed so tightly they had been lost to his beard, Norman stood up and rested a hand on his neighbour's shoulder.

'I'm sorry,' he said. 'Let me take that from you.' With a sigh of relief, George held the contraband roll-up out towards Norman.

'Just one thing ...' Norman said.

'I will drop this in the mud.' George reiterated.

'No need for that.' Norman's voice was calm and mischievous. 'I said I'll take it from you and I will. Just the minute you tell me why.'

'Why what? Why I don't want to be involved in your illegal no-goodery?'

'Why are you so worried? What are you so scared of? Why can't you relax, for one bleedin' evening?'

'I am perfectly capable of relaxing.' George's shoulders were rigid and he could feel a tension headache twisting around his temples.

'He doesn't look like he relaxes.' Maggie piped in from her position, now dancing around Norman's carrots.

'Just because I don't choose to fill my lungs with illegal narcotics, doesn't mean I can't relax. I have Sally remember. She helps me relax. I let go with her.' A small, almost undetectable nod, tipped Norman's chin.

'Okay.' he said. 'Alright.'

George's muscles tightened. 'What do you mean, *alright?*'

'I mean alright. I'll 'ave it back now. What did'ya think I was going to do? Bully you into trying some. You're a grown man. Older than grown. You can do what the heck you want with your life.' He stretched his hand out. 'Like I said, I'll have that back here thanks.'

George looked down at the item in his hand. Was he really afraid of letting go? Yes, of course, he was. He always had been. It had gotten worse when Eric was born, and then as he had got older even worse still. It was a matter of control. He knew that. Life was easier to handle when he was in control and there were no nasty surprises waiting around the corner. But how had that worked out for him, really? There were no surprises waiting around the corner, that was for sure. There was nothing waiting at all. Nothing but living the next few years thinking about all the things he could have done differently. And then, without giving himself a chance to think, George lifted the joint up to his lips and took a nice deep inhale.

CHAPTER 3

'PICK A SONG, any song. She's got 'em all on there, don't you, Mags my love? Any song in the world. What's that thing called? The thing that stores all the songs in the whole world.'

'It's called the internet.' Maggie looked, with a decidedly unimpressed expression, at her uncle. 'As you well know.'

'*Ahh*,' Norman nodded his head as he sighed. 'We didn't have that in my day.'

Norman wasn't the only one who had drifted away into his thoughts. For the previous half-hour, the past was all that George could focus on.

'I just wanted him to be successful, you know?' He spoke to the air, not really caring if anyone was listening. 'He never knew. Never had to grow up seeing what it was like having nothing. I just wanted him to succeed that's all. Is that so wrong? I just wanted him to work hard and succeed.'

He paused and glanced over at Maggie and Norman.

'You chose the last two songs. It's my choice,' said Maggie.

'You're not choosing again. Knowing your taste, you'll probably bring a whole bleeding family of moles over here.'

'I am not listening to another —'

'Here,' George left his thoughts and snatched the phone from them. 'I'm choosing. Now how do I find what I want to listen too.'

Norman grumbled something and backed away.

'You just type it up here. In the search bar. That's it.'

Half a minute later and the melodious tone of Frank Sinatra's *Fly Me to the Moon* bellowed out through Columbia Avenue.

'Now this,' George said, 'is music.'

It was as though he had been transported back through time. Above him, a slither of moon had escaped from the clouds and shone down on the three of them.

George danced from one side of the shed to the other as he sang along with Sinatra before Norman joined him. Taking each other by the hand they began a two-stepped between the plots.

The scene was made even more bizarre by the fact that George hated to dance; he had not even wanted to dance at his wedding.

'Then I'm going to need to marry someone else,' Gloria had teased. 'Because I will be dancing.'

'But you know I'm not any good at it,' George insisted. 'I'll just end up standing on your feet.'

'Then I shall be a happy woman with bruised feet.'

He had given in of course. He always gave in when it came to her. With guests around them, the pair had stood in the centre of the local village hall, George's arms fixed like lampposts around her waist while she swayed graciously. He couldn't figure it out. He was the one who'd hit the jackpot, with this beautiful, funny woman agreeing to marry him, and yet she was there grinning like the cat that had got the cream. If only she'd looked at him like that forever.

It hadn't been a bad marriage, not by any stretch. When Gloria passed away forty-eight years later it felt like his whole world had crumbled. She had been his everything; best friend, confident. unending supporter and harshest critic. Particularly when it came to parenting. There was no denying that George was not a natural when it came to children. The way they spoke and thought and acted; he couldn't fathom it. Nor could he fathom how he had ever been one. Parenting, that was the one place he knew he had really let Gloria down. He pushed the thought to the back of his head and continued on with his dancing. Norman had retreated to the shed with Maggie and the *Fly Me to the Moon* had been replaced with another Sinatra track. The cold breeze rushed against his skin as he twisted and twirled. They should have nights like this more often. Musical mole nights. And they could be themed, he considered. A Frank Sinatra night, obviously, then maybe a Tony Bennett one. Or a Nat King Cole. George was still considering what other possible themes they could have for their musical mole evenings when a throat cleared behind him.

'Excuse me, sir, are you the one responsible for this?'

AT 63 YEARS OLD, George Sibley had had exactly one run-in with the police. Technically, he didn't consider the incident a run-in, given that the notice came through the letterbox, in the form of a speeding ticket.

'Why would they put a speeding camera on that bend?' he'd grumbled to Gloria at breakfast after receiving the fine. 'Everyone speeds on that bend.'

'Which is probably why they put a speeding camera on it,' a teenage Eric had mumbled into his cereal.

'If I wanted your opinion, I'd have asked for it.' George snapped back. 'And don't think you're going to spend this weekend lazing around in your room. I've already told Mrs. Winters, at number 42, that you'll mow her lawn.'

'Dad!' Eric slammed his spoon down on the table sending droplets of milk flying across the placemat. 'You know I have work to do. I need to prepare for my exams.'

'Well you'll need to move fast then, won't you? Because I've said you'll do number 28 as well.'

Eric huffed as he stood up from the table, dropped his bowl into the sink and span around ready to leave the room.

'And don't think your mother is going to go picking up after you either. You'll be eating your dinner out to that bowl if it's not washed out properly.'

George's heart burned with a blend of regret and self-assurance every time a memory like that crept its way to the surface. Eric hadn't turned out badly, not really. He managed to get himself a good job, a nice house. And Suzy, despite George's initial reservations, had turned out to be a damn fine wife. But George saw so much of himself in his son. And it wasn't the good parts.

'ARE you the one responsible for this?' the police officer asked again, this time in a far less relaxed manner. 'For this disturbance?'

'Disturbance?' His wrinkled face crinkled further as he frowned. 'Oh, you mean Frank?'

'Frank?'

'Frank Sinatra. He's helping us get rid of the mole.'

It was the officer's turn to frown. She shook her head slowly as if trying to process what she was hearing. Then she stopped, nodded once, indicating she had found the answer, and smiled. She reached her hand outwards as she stepped forward.

'Do you live near here, sir? Is there someone I can call? Someone who might be a little worried that you're out so late on your own?'

'I live by myself, I ... I ... I'm not senile!' George exploded. 'We're trying to get rid of a mole.'

'A mole?' she shook her head again. 'I'm sorry, I'm not following.

'It's the sound. We're trying to get rid of it with the sound.'

'And who is we?'

George looked over his shoulder for support only to find that both Norman and Maggie scarpered into the shed, their soft titters of laughter echoing over to him.

Realising he was currently on his own, George took a deep breath and tried again.

'There is a mole problem. It keeps on digging hills on our allotments. We tried whiskey and chilli and that didn't work, so instead we're trying to play music. Apparently, they don't like the vibrations.'

'Is that right?' the officer said sceptically. 'And so you were the one responsible for the other music too? Because if you don't mind me saying so sir, you don't exactly look much of a hard rock fan.'

'It's not hard rock, it's metal!'

The voice came amid a squeal of laughter and a clattering of tools. George felt his chest drop with relief as the officer's eyes finally moved away from him, and towards the shed.

The police officer narrowed her eyes.

'You're not alone here?' she asked.

'No,' George weighted his answer heavily. 'I am not.'

With a deep inhale, the officer put her hands on her hips and strode toward the shed. They were substantial strides, George contemplated as he watched her walk. The strides of someone who was not in the best of moods. She stopped square in front of the door to the shed and spoke.

'My name is Special Constable Clarke. I need you all to exit the building now,' she said.

George's heart drummed in his chest. He wasn't in any trouble, he told himself. Not now. He couldn't possibly be. After all, it was Maggie's music on the speakers. And Maggie's speakers. There were the drugs to consider, but really, how much had he had. A fraction. A tiny fraction. Besides, the music he had chosen to play was perfectly pleasant. Probably far nicer than whatever the people in the pebble-dashed houses were listening to anyway. No, he was an innocent bystander. If anyone was going down for this it was Maggie and Norman. He was having no part in it.

'I will ask you one last time,' Officer Clarke said. Maggie and Norman's laughter had grown louder inside the shed. She ignored it like a seasoned professional. 'If you do not come out now. I will be forced to take you both down to the station.'

'What for?' Maggie's voice bellowed out into the night.

'Refusing to cooperate with the police. Obstruction of justice. And by the smell of it, possession of a Class B drug.'

Whispering made its way out through the wood. The officer rested her hand by her sides and smiled. Thirty seconds later Norman and Maggie appeared out on the veranda, Officer Clarke's suppressed grin gone in favour of a tight-lipped frown. She cast her eye from Maggie to Norman and back again.

'Do I know you?' she asked, her gaze fixing on Maggie. Maggie shrugged. Her bottom lip protruded out above her chin in much the same way George had seen his three-year-old grandaughter do.

'Margaret isn't it? Margaret Moore?'

'So what if it is?'

George shuddered. So, he saw, did Norman. Another sign of how far the youth of today had deteriorated, he thought. Speaking that way to a police officer was not something someone would have done in his day. Well, not unless it had been at a picket line or a protest. He had seen

Gloria speak to police officers in that manner plenty of times in situations like that, and although he had grimaced at first, he had quickly discovered it was an almost expected response back then. But not on a one-on-one situation. Not like this.

The officer ran her tongue along her bottom lip.

'Margret Moore,' she said again. 'You're getting yourself quite a name at the station, aren't you, young lady?'

'I don't know.' Maggie spoke in loosely enunciated grunts as oppose to clearly syllabic words. 'I'm not the one there, am I? Why don't you tell me?'

'Minor vandalism. Graffiti. Selling counterfeit items without a permit? Does that sound familiar?' Maggie's pout deepened. The office sniffed deeply. 'Oh yes, and possession and use of an illegal drug in a public space.

George shifted uncomfortably. *Perhaps I should just slip off*, he thought. It seemed silly to stand there and listen now that the officer was clearly aware of where to lay the blame. After all, she hadn't even asked what his name was.

'Do you know this girl?' Officer Clarke said to Norman.

Norman grunted and shook his head. 'Nope. Never seen her before in my life. Just showed up 'ere this afternoon with these bloody stereo things. Got no idea who she is.'

Maggie kicked him square in the shins. 'I'll tell Mum you said that. And I'll tell her that you're that one who gives me —'

'You will do no such —'

The officer cleared her throat, bringing the conversation back to its original source.

'Sorry.' Norman, lowered his head a fraction. 'Yes, she's my niece.'

'And this is your plot? Your allotment?'

'Yes. Well 'alf of it is. The other 'alf is his.' He nodded his head toward George, who had, by that point, managed to move a full four paces back. Sheepishly, he shuffled forward again.

'The smaller part's mine,' George added. 'The speakers are mostly on his part. You know I only —'

'Right.' The officer lifted her hand indicating she had clearly heard enough, most probably from the lot of them. 'I'm willing to cut you a deal, but first things first, can someone please turn that bloody music off.' She paused. The rest of them waited. 'Now,' she added.

'Oh, right.' Fumbling for her phone, Maggie quickly swiped her finger across the screen. The entire allotment fell silent.

'Thank you. That's the first of the issues sorted. Now, you,' she turned to George. 'I didn't catch your name.'

'My name?' George swallowed.

'Yes, what is it?'

'What is it?'

Officer Clarke arched her eyebrow upwards.

'Sorry,' George said hastily. 'It's George. George Sibley. I live at twenty —'

'That's fine Mr Sibley. All I wanted was your name. Now you said you were playing the music to stop moles. Is that true?' This time she posed her question to Norman.

'Aye, it's the sounds you see. We tried stopping them with smells, like. Gum and chilli —'

'That's fine,' she lifted her hand again to silence him. 'I don't need to hear the whole thing again. Now I don't know whether music stops moles or not, and quite frankly I don't care. Because even if it does, you cannot do this again. Do you understand? If I catch you making a public disturbance again, I will take you all down to the station. Consider this an unofficial caution.'

She turned her gaze to George who nodded hurriedly. Unofficial caution. That definitely counted as his most severe encounter with the police. And one he didn't fancy replicating anytime soon. His lungs quivered from the adrenaline of it all.

'Now there is just a small issue of the marijuana.'

'Marijuana?' Maggie and Norman's eyes simultaneously widened. Norman shook his head, wafting his great beard from side to side. 'Now I'm sure there's been —'

'Why would we have had —'

'Seriously?' The pair fell silent. 'Here's the deal. I will give you a choice. Option number one is that I go into this lovely red shed, find the marijuana I am almost certain is growing in there and book both of you for possession and the nervous one over there as an accessory.' George's pulse rocketed. 'Then you'll all be out of my hair and I let the courts deal with you. I suspect with your track record you'll be looking at possible custodial sentence this time around Miss Moore.'

While Norman seemed perfectly at ease with this decision, George was most definitely not, and it was clear to see, even in the dark, that neither was Maggie. Her skin had paled to near translucent and her previously protruding bottom lip was now tucked firmly under her top teeth.

'The other option...?' she whispered.

'The other option is that we have three open-days, at the police station next month. You know, give people a chance to see what the job is about, what we do around the community.'

'So?'

'So I want you to attend. All of them.'

'You are joking right?'

The relaxed demeanour the officer, disappeared. She reached for her waist and pulled off her handcuffs. 'Fine, have it your way. I'm sure you'll be absolutely fine. Although I'm not entirely sure how well your uncle and him over there will manage at their age in prison. Men's prisons in this country aren't exactly known for their kindness to the elderly.'

'Okay, okay,' Maggie stepped in front of Norman blocking the line between him and the officer. 'I'll sign up. Where can I do it? I'll sign up now. This isn't Uncle Nor's fault.'

A satisfied smile appeared on the Officer Clarke's face.

'Brilliant, that's exactly what I hoped you'd say.'

CHAPTER 4

THE NEXT MORNING, George choose to forego his normal walk to the newsagents, and decided instead to catch up on the news via the radio. He still couldn't believe it, the ridiculousness of it all. He, George Sibley, nearly arrested for smoking marijuana. Not to mention being a public nuisance. He couldn't imagine what would have happened if Maggie hadn't agreed to take the deal. He would have been forced to call Eric to come and bail him out most probably. No, he took a gulp of his tea and a bite of his toast. He would never have lived that down. He would have had to just spent the night at the station, or prayed that Cynthia would bail him out too when she came down for Norman. He took another bite of his toast, then opened the bread bin and put another slice of bread in the toaster.

He was starving, ravenous, and had been since he had woken up. He'd already eaten through three days worth of bread in sandwiches and toast, and his stomach was showing no signs of filling. It was going to completely put him out for the week.

While he waited for his sixth slice of toast to pop, George turned up the volume on the radio. Listening to the news on the radio just wasn't the same as reading it in the paper he decided. You couldn't get the same level of feel for a story. With a paper, a headline grabbed you and all you had to do was follow the instructions and turn to page seven. Then voila, another six columns on the story telling you everything you wanted to know. No such luck on the radio. You listened to the stories they wanted, and that was it. And they talked so fast nowadays, always trying to cram the information in before another weakly developed song started. You couldn't ask the lady to repeat something here and there because your hearing was deteriorating or the kettle chose that exact second to whistle out that it was done. No, the radio had its place, but when it came to the news, he would always choose a paper. Of course, a radio didn't have a crossword in either.

The lack of a walk, and then lack of a crossword to occupy his morning, thoroughly threw George and rather than spending his mid-morning sat at the kitchen table working out a seven-letter mammal from the southern hemisphere ending with an S, he spent half an hour pacing around the house, rearranging his cutlery draw and emptying the filter in the tumble drier. By the time he found himself a book and settled down in his armchair to read, it was nearly midday, and he was ready for lunch.

Standing at the hob, George stirred his soup while it heated. Every few minutes his eyes glanced toward the phone. When Eric had called he'd mentioned that he was going for promotion and although that was over a month ago, George was still waiting to hear whether or not he had got the job. Gloria used to keep track of the number of days it had been since she and Eric had last spoken. They averaged once a week, normally a Saturday afternoon. If ever it went longer than that George would notice the change in his wife.

'Let's not go out,' she would say if George suggested they go for a drive in Sally. 'I feel like staying in today. But you go if you want to go. I'm more than happy by myself.' And sometimes he did go out on his own, because it was easier that way, away from it all, than sat at home watching his wife pining at the telephone as his thankless son failed to call.

George, however, did not count the days. He refused to. Because if he did, he would have to admit something to himself. He would have to admit that his son didn't want to speak to him. Perhaps it was his own fault, George mused as his soup began to boil, and not just because of the difficulties he had had with Eric growing up. George hadn't made life easy for him where his son was concerned, even in the more recent years. One particular point of tension stuck in his mind.

When Suzy had fallen pregnant, Eric had suggested that George should get a smart phone, so that they could send him photos of Abi, after she was born. He even offered to pay for it. But George wouldn't have it. Oh no, he saw that trap a mile off. How long would he have had to listen to Eric go on about how much he had spent if he accepted that offer? Years probably, if not longer. There was no way he wanted to be indebted to his son like that. So, George had said he was fine without the phone and made it perfectly clear he would not receive any gifts of such a sort graciously.

Of course, back then, Gloria had still been alive and so Eric's visits had been more frequent and George had got to see far more of Abi. But when she passed away the visits became less and less. Now it was down to three times a year at a push. The camera phone had played on his mind continually, up until a point last year where he drove into Maldon, parked up and marched into the nearest phone store determined to buy one.

'What kind of tariff are you looking at?' the woman had asked him. 'Do you need a sim, or just the phone?'

'A sim? I just want to receive pictures?'

'*Ahh* okay, are you looking for unlimited data? Will you want roaming included?'

'Roaming?'

'Do you have anything for upgrade? And were you thinking of paying over 24 months or 36? What monthly rate were you thinking of?'

In the end, he had walked out with an armful of pamphlets he didn't understand, which he promptly deposited in the nearest bin. He would have to carry on without a camera phone, he had decided there and then. Recently he had started debating the possibility of asking Eric to come shopping with him the next time he visited. Assuming there was a next time.

He tipped the soup into a bowl and moved it over to the kitchen table. He had just pulled out the chair and sat down, when the telephone rang. Groaning, he put his spoon down and headed out into the hall.

'Have you been down the plot today?' Norman bellowed down the line.

'No, why?'

'According to Cynth, the buggers have been at it again. Not been down, myself, feeling a bit chesty today.'

George sighed.

'I'm done,' Norman continued. 'Sod what the rest of them think. We need this thing finished now. You and I, we'll get it done.'

'What are you —' George stopped talking, the line already dead.

Muttering to himself, George made his way back to the kitchen and his soup. It was slow eating. A painful tingling spread down his wrist every time he gripped the spoon. He clenched his fists, trying to eradicate the sensation, but only made it worse. Perhaps the late-night antics and being out in the cold was the reason why they hurt so much. Perhaps it was just old age catching up with him. Either way, it probably wasn't worth trying to take Sally out to day, he decided. He would stay in today. See how he felt tomorrow.

Once he had finished his soup he washed and dried the bowl and stacked it back in the cupboard, before ambling through to the living room. He always walked at half his pace in the house, George realised a few months ago. It wasn't an intentional thing, but he always did it; a slow laborious lumber, weighed most probably by the thousands of memories that echoed around him.

The living room had a chill. The windows had been replaced when Eric was still in school, but not since and spots of damp speckled the paint around them. George had considered getting them sorted, but what would be the point. When he died Eric would just sell the place to the highest bidder and they would strip everything from it there and then. And there was no point having the heating on, not in a house this size, not when there was only him living it. He took a blanket off the back of the chair and wrapped it around his shoulders, then settled himself down into the seat. Sleeping away the hours, that was another thing George had gotten much better at since Gloria had passed away. Sleeping away the days.

❦

A LOUD BANG jerked George awake. Jumping from his seat, he rubbed his eyes and tried to make sense of his surroundings. The light in the living room was muted and dusky; he had exceeded his normal length nap by quite some way. That stuff last night really had played havoc with him, he considered, although this time it was no wonder his stomach was growling. He had most certainly missed his four o'clock snack and may well have passed dinner time too. A bang rattled through the house for a second time and then a third. It was only on the fourth bang, that he realised there was someone at his front door.

'You ready? You don't look ready.' Norman was standing outside George's front door in full winter gear, with a puffer jacket, fleece gloves and woolly hat that, in combination with his beard and scarf meant that his vivid eyes were the only visible part of him.

George rubbed his eyes, trying to wipe away the fog of sleep.

'What are you doing here?' he said. 'What do you mean *ready*? We can't do the music again. You know we can't. She said she'd arrest us.'

Norman grunted into his scarf. 'Who said anything about music? What's wrong with you, we discussed it on the phone? Remember?'

'Did we?'

'Aye, we did. Sod Cynthia, I've done everything I can. This is it. You and me, remember?' Norman nodded to the back of his car, where two large shovels, poked out of one of the windows.

'Now have you got another couple of those blankets?' Norman added ''cos we're gonna need them.'

George didn't know why he agreed. He wasn't entirely sure he had. The passage of time, in between Norman arriving at his house, telling him it was time to leave and the pair of them arriving at the allotment, kitted out with blankets, earmuffs and three layers of socks seemed to have been lost to haze.

'Are you sure we can actually sleep here?' George asked as Norman attempted to lay his two garden chairs as flat as they would go. 'You don't think we are going to get arrested again?' There was no denying that the sound method of mole eradication had worked at a similar level to the chewing gum method. More hills had spread across the plots, and not just large rounded ones, but other ones too. Flat patches or dirt, like the mole had attempted to burrow back in through a different route. Maybe George could ask the committee if it was possible to change plots the next time a new one became available. That way they could all be left to do their own thing in peace.

'Firstly,' Norman had finally managed to get the back down on one of the chairs, 'we didn't get arrested and if you keep on going on like that, I'm going to do something that will get you banged up for good, just to shut you up. And secondly, we're not going to be sleeping. Not a chance. That rodent is not going to get the best of us again. No, we're going to stay awake until that bastard pops up, and it's gonna be the last time his twitchy little nose ever sniffs fresh air.'

George gulped. 'I'm not sure I'll be able to stay awake all night,' he said, tucking the blanket in around his shoulders. A small grin appeared on Norman's face, pushing his eyes up into two tiny downward crescents, George's stomach fluttered.

'Don't you worry, I got that one sorted too.'

It was, without doubt, the strongest smelling drink George had ever encountered. He wasn't ignorant to the ways of fizzy drinks. He himself was quite partial to the odd lemonade or even Coca Cola at the pub now and again. And growing up he had been all about the ginger beer. The stronger the better. This stuff though, this was a whole different board game.

'More caffeine than fourteen cups of coffee apparently,' Norman said as he handed George his second can. 'It's probably not great for the old ticker, but it's not like you and me 'ave got that many miles left on the clock anyway.'

'Then why aren't you drinking it too?' George questioned, noticing that Norman's hand was still lacking a can.

'Can't,' Norman said with a sigh. 'Cynth made me go to the doctor's this morning. Put me on these drugs for me chest. Off the caffeine, and the beer, and the cigarettes. Fortunately, he didn't say nowt about the other stuff,' he motioned with his head to his shed behind him. 'So I figure I'm fine on that one. Don't worry, I'm not going to sleep anyway. I'm not going to leave you on your own.'

George took the second can and sniffed, before pretending to take a large gulp. There was no way he was drinking anymore. Even disregarding the smell, there was the fact that it was the exact colour of toxic waste.

'Supposed to be pineapple flavour,' Norman commented.

Where do they grow their pineapples? George wondered to himself. *Chernobyl.*

The effects had been almost instant. After half of the first can he felt like his chest was going to explode. Every heartbeat, every breath felt like 1000 trains rushing through him. There was no chance he could have another can, or even sip, without risking a heart attack. But he didn't want to tell Norman that. He was already terrified Norman was going to make him be the one to hit the mole over the head when it finally appeared and he didn't want to let him down on this matter either.

There was nothing for it but to pretend. Pretend to keep drinking the drink, and pray that he didn't fall asleep. He shouldn't need to fall asleep, he thought to himself. Not after the nap he had had that afternoon. He shouldn't really have had any problem staying awake all night at all. It was a clear night and thousands of stars twinkled down on them from above. George gazed upward, before he pretended to polish off the second drink.

'You can shut your eyes if you want,' he said to Norman, who was already hunkered down beneath his blankets and scarf. 'I've got this.'

WHEN GEORGE WOKE, it was to the sound of birdsong. Not distant or muted, the way it normally was when he woke, but loud and piercing, like it was right beside his ear. He must have left the window open, he thought. That would explain the draft too.

'What the ... you fell asleep?' Norman's voice caused George's eyes to ping open in surprise.

'What ... where ...' he stuttered.

'You said you'd got this. You said you wouldn't fall asleep.' Norman was still in his seat, bent double as he commenced a fit of hacking coughs.

George rubbed his eyes. 'I don't understand. Did I fall asleep?' he said.

'What do you mean, *did you fall asleep?* Of course you bloody fell asleep. What time is it?' Norman glanced at his watch. 'God damn it, it's nearly nine o'clock. Cynth'll be having a bleedin' heart attack.'

'I thought ... I think ...' George was having trouble processing things. The cold air had seized around his thoughts and his joints. He pulled up his blanket, accidentally knocking one of the cans by his side. The toxic yellow liquid ran out toward Norman's feet.

'You ... you ...' His cheeks were red with rage.

'I can explain,' George said as he desperately tried to think of some way to justify his treachery. 'I was saving it. I didn't want to use it all —'

'There you are.' The two men stopped silent and turned their heads. 'Excellent, this saves me a trip. George.' Cynthia nodded in his direction. 'I trust you had a good night's sleep? Norman ...' Her tone changed. 'We'll discuss this later. First, I want you guys to meet Andy.'

Until that moment George had been too flustered to register the stranger at Cynthia's side. He was a young lad, probably similar in age to Eric, although kitted out in work boots, a plaid shirt and a thick pair of gloves, indicating he was much more willing to get his hands dirty, than Eric ever would be.

'Andy here is from Humane Pest Removal.'

He stretched out his hand, first to shake George's hand and then Norman's. 'So you're the one with the mole. Hopefully we've put an end to that now. But, I guess we should go check the traps. Sometimes it can take a couple of days.'

'Traps? What traps?' While Norman's beard bristled with confusion, George's eyes were fixed solely on Cynthia. A small, knowing smile, edged its way up on the corner of her lips.

'There are no more hills since yesterday morning by the looks of it,' Andy said as he walked. 'That's a good thing. We'll check the outer ones first, though they don't normally have quite as much luck. We've used a lot though, your wife had wanted me to put them everywhere,' he said to Norman. 'Quite insistent we get this problem solved as quick as possible.'

There, in the third trap they checked, was the small, dark, bane of the last few weeks. His tiny eyes squinted closed, as his feet grappled against the hard metal of the cage.

'He's a feisty little thing,' he said, pulling a cloth from out of his bag and draping it over the cage, plunging the mole into darkness. 'No wonder he caused you so much trouble.' He put the cage down on the ground. 'It's nice to get it sorted like this, quick and easy, no fuss. Honestly, you wouldn't believe the lengths some people go to trying to get rid of these things.'

'No.' George and Norman exchange a look. 'We probably wouldn't.'

I HOPE you enjoyed this short story and the little insight into George Sibley. Don't forget to read the continued adventures of his son, Eric, and his family in **Peas, Carrots and a Red Feather Boa**. Available to buy HERE

PEAS, CARROTS AND A RED FEATHER BOA

Book 2

For Mum and Dad

CHAPTER 1

ERIC YELPED AS he missed the nail and hammered his thumb for the fourth time in half as many minutes.

'Bugger,' he said.

It was the evening before Christmas Eve. Outside the air tasted of early winter; of ice and grey clouds and wood smoke drifting up from red brick chimneys. Inside it tasted of sawdust, drill bits, and pent up frustration.

'This is ridiculous,' said his long-suffering wife, Suzy, as she took the hammer from Eric and smacked the nail in perfectly on her first try. 'I'll call Lyds. I'm sure she'll be happy to host.'

'Not a chance.' Eric took another piece of carpet track and positioned it along the floor, ready for Suzy to nail in place. 'That's what she wants us to do. You saw her face when I said they should spend Christmas at ours. She's just waiting for me to screw up.'

'That's not true at all,' Suzy said, although her eyes didn't quite meet his as she spoke.

Suzy's sister, Lydia, had had a hard time forgiving Eric for an escapade involving a mini-excavator earlier in the year; although it wasn't so much the excavator she'd had the problem with, but rather the lying that had gone alongside it. In Eric's defence, he had been under a lot of stress at the time. It was shortly after receiving the conditions of his inheritance, when pressure at work was high, and the tyrannical, bearded busybody with the allotment next to him was a long way from becoming the friend that Eric now so desperately missed.

As a result, for the few last months, Eric had been the picture of husbandly perfection, and while Suzy was never one to harbour a grudge, the same could not be said for her big sister, and so he had invited them over for Christmas. Not just dinner, not even the whole day, but the whole event; Christmas Eve, Christmas Day, Boxing Day. The lot. Lydia, her husband Tom, and their two boys were to descend on Eric's beautiful home for three whole days, and he would graciously accept any carnage that prevailed.

Only Eric's home wasn't beautiful. Not even close. It was a building site. Lifting his head up from the task at hand, he took a moment to survey the chaos before huffing and slumping back down onto the bare floorboards where a protruding nail promptly impaled his left buttock.

'Sod it. Let's leave this room,' he said. 'We don't even need it anyway. We can eat dinner in the kitchen. Or on our laps. Lots of people eat Christmas dinner on their laps. It'll be casual. Funky.'

He puckered his lips and moved his hands in an attempt at a robotic dance move. The results looked about as funky as a hand-knitted mankini. Suzy raised her eyebrow sceptically.

'Fine then,' Eric said. 'We won't eat on our laps. But there's no reason we can't eat in the kitchen instead.'

'I thought you didn't want anyone in the kitchen? I thought you said the kitchen was the scourge of the house?'

'I didn't say that. Why would I? The bathroom is the scourge of the house. Then the staircase, and our bedroom and the front garden. They're the scourges. The kitchen is more a blemish. A repulsive, abhorrent, ulcer-inducing blemish.'

Suzy pouted, her eyebrows still butting up to her hairline. Eric offered a half-smile, using only one corner of his mouth. He added a wink and finally her expression relaxed. A long sigh rattled out from her throat. Part way through it transformed into a yawn.

'How about we take a break?' she said. 'Let's go into the other room and have a drink, then we'll do half an hour more before we head to bed.'

'A large drink? Like, four normal drinks in one glass?'

'A medium drink,' Suzy said. 'Though in fairness it might make your aim a little better with that hammer.'

It had seemed like such a good idea taking on Norman's house after his passing; the big bay windows, the garden, the views out over the river. Even now, with the dining room carpet rolled up in the living room, their teak coffee table upturned and getting damp in the conservatory, twenty-year-old peach cabinets gracing the kitchen walls, and a bathroom that caused Eric to weaken when he happened to pass it, he was sure they'd made the right decision in packing up London life and moving to the quiet riverside town of Burlam. Still, it hadn't been easy.

Technically it was Cynthia's fault the bathroom had been a disaster, although in Eric's opinion, Norman could shoulder a fair bit of the blame too. Had Cynthia – Norman's widow – not made a flippant comment about seeing Norman's reflection in the mirror every day, then perhaps Eric would have been slightly less hasty and considered the problem a little longer before he began to tear away at the fixtures and fittings. They had been in the house a week when he decided to take on the task and attack the tiles. After all, he told himself, he had renovated a bathroom before. How naïve he was.

Each day, a new issue appeared; be it corroded pipes, layers of lead-based paint, or old tiles set in enough cement to refill all the potholes from Burlam to Chelmsford. Water leaked from places where water shouldn't have been and bare wires twisted and sparked through gaps in the walls. His daughter, Abi, had been spending every weekend at Tom and Lydia's, and only now, with Eric having spent every hour from dusk to dawn working on the project, were they anywhere close to having a fully serviceable bathroom. Only now, of course, it was Christmas and the plumbers didn't work Christmas.

'I'll do it myself,' Eric had said three days ago, when the finish line was so close he could practically taste the sealant. 'How hard can it be? I'm intelligent.'

Suzy's eyebrows had lifted to their accustomed position of doubt. 'Have you forgotten what happened with the downstairs toilet?'

'That was an entirely different situation,' Eric pouted. 'I just miscalculated, that's all. Anyway, you're the one who's always on about saving the environment. What's more environmentally friendly than baking soda and vinegar?'

Suzy didn't flinch.

Eric had relented on the bathroom, although he had put his foot down at the dining room carpet and refused to pay for someone to fit that, insisting instead that he could do the work himself.

As he sipped on his gin and cast an eye over the half-finished room, he began to regret that decision.

At twelve-forty the pair finally went to bed. Eric's eyes stung from the dust and the strain, but the carpet was down, the table repositioned – with chairs – and even one or two Christmas ornaments laid down the centre.

'What do you think?' he said, slipping his arm around Suzy's waist and pulling her into his chest.

'I think it's shaping up to be a very good Christmas,' she replied.

***

IF ERIC HAD THOUGHT Christmas Eve in the countryside would be less stressful than in London, he was bitterly disappointed. At 9 am, with the Audi heaters blasting on full power, he crawled along the lanes towards Maldon and the nearest big supermarket. It was a last-minute decision to go, and he had stupidly agreed to take their nine-year-old daughter with him, giving Suzy a chance to wrap all the presents.

Although they'd left in plenty of time, the queue at the petrol station, urgent toilet stop – for Abi, not Eric – and now being stuck behind the world's slowest salt truck meant they were already an hour behind schedule.

In the supermarket, herds of Christmas-crazed adults barged their way to the front of the chiller cabinets and grappled for the last ready-washed, giblet-free turkey and discount Buck's Fizz.

'Can we get one of these?' Abi said, picking up a pack of battered and broken mince pies.

'I guess so.'

'And these?' Grabbing half a dozen chocolate oranges off the shelf. 'These are my favourite.'

'Fine.'

'Oh, oh, oh! I love—'

'Just put them in the trolley,' Eric said.

Ninety minutes and seventy pounds later, Eric left with four bags of shopping, a sugar-high nine-year-old, and a novelty headband that had transformed his daughter into a Christmas elf, complete with oversized ears and a hat. All he had gone in for was some chestnuts and a galia melon.

When they finally arrived home, Tom and Lydia were already there.

'We thought we'd come a bit early,' Lydia said. 'See if we could help with anything?'

'That's very kind. You shouldn't have. You really, *really* shouldn't have,' Eric said.

Suzy shot him a decidedly evil eye.

'But we're very glad you're here,' Eric added, then wrapped his arms around his sister-in-law for the longest sober hug he could recall.

'Yes ... well ...' replied a flustered Lydia as she brushed herself down. 'Anyway, I suspected your house might be a little bare, so I've bought some paint and a few little bits and bobs and thought the children could spend the afternoon making some decorations? Make it feel a bit more, you know, Christmassy.' And there it was, disguised as helpfulness, the subtle dig Eric had been expecting since the moment the invitation was sent out. But he had prepared. If Lydia wanted Christmassy, she would see Christmassy.

Eric pushed his shoulders back, a wide grin shining from his face.

'I think you need to come into the drawing room,' he beamed, 'and see our tree.'

The seven-foot Norwegian spruce was truly an example of nature at her finest. Procured by Hank – one of Eric's recently acquired allotment friends – through some black-market tree dealer, the emerald needles were illuminated with tastefully subtle white lights and decorated with a select choice of handmade wooden ornaments. Eric had spent a full day positioning every bulb and bauble, pruning and shifting until absolute perfection had been achieved.

'Oh,' Lydia said, her eyes scanning up, down, and then all the way back up again. 'It's very ...' she pondered for the right word. 'Minimalistic?'

On reflection, the arts and crafts activity was an excellent time filler.

While Eric prepared the turkey for its final salty bath, Tom peeled and prepared the vegetables, and Lydia and Suzy helped the children in their construction of cork Christmas tree decorations and papier mâché antlers for Rudolph.

'And you've grown all of this?' Tom said as he scrubbed the dirt from a nine-inch parsnip and tossed it onto the pile of clean vegetables that were accumulating on the draining board.

'It's all come from the allotment, but not all of it is mine. If I'm honest, a lot of it's from Norman's plot.'

After what was initially a very shaky start to their relationship, Norman had very much taken Eric under his wing as he'd attempted to breathe life back into his late father's allotment. It was for this reason that Eric had felt duty-bound to take over the maintenance and upkeep after his passing.

Eric stared at his hands as he shifted the turkey around in the salt solution. A large ache spread up from just below his sternum and caused his eyes to prick. Even dead, the man managed to grow better vegetables than he did.

'So, what's happening with that?' Tom said, his voice puncturing Eric's moment of reflection. 'I'm assuming they won't just let you carry on using it?'

Eric shook his head.

'No, unfortunately not. Although to be fair, it's tough enough trying to get down there for an hour a day at the minute, even not working. By the time I've taken Abi to school, got the shopping, then done a bit of work on this place, it's almost time to pick her up again.'

'The trials of being a man of leisure, eh?'

Eric laughed. 'I suppose I've got it pretty easy.' He opened the door and slotted the turkey-filled container into the ready-cleared space at the bottom of the fridge. 'But as for Norman's allotment, I'm still not sure what will happen. I was hoping Cynthia would take it over. I know she said she didn't want to, but I thought perhaps if she'd had a bit of time to mull it over …'

'So that's not going to happen?' Tom said.

Eric shook his head.

'No. I don't think so. I spoke to her last week, and she'd just booked a round-the-world ticket. Paris to Malaysia, then on to Australia and New

Zealand to visit the relatives, and finally Peru for a twelve-week tour of South America.'

'Wow,' Tom said.

'Yeah. I think she's worried about what will happen if she stays still too long.'

'It doesn't sound like that'll happen.'

'No, it doesn't.'

Out in the conservatory, someone shrieked. It was followed by several more squeals, then an unmistakable yell from Lydia.

'I'd better go and see if she needs some help,' Tom said, wiping his hands on his apron before slipping it off over his head. 'Though if it's the bloody superglue again, they can stay like it. You have no idea how ridiculous we looked at A&E last year.'

Tom, still grumbling about cemented fingertips, ambled out to the conservatory while Eric continued his military style preparation for tomorrow's dinner.

With the turkey ready, Eric started on the Brussels sprouts. He peeled the outer yellow leaves and threw them into the green-lined bin. The draining board was already full of veg, as were the two colanders on the worktop and the large saucepan waiting on the hob. By the looks of things, they were going to have enough food to feed the entire company of Burlam amateur dramatics society, although, on the plus side, he was going to be getting some great compost next year.

AT FIVE O'CLOCK, Suzy appeared in the kitchen. Eric, now onto the final stages of preparation, was wrist deep in a mixture of bread, onions, and herb extractions. He squeezed the pulp together with a satisfying squelch.

'If you want a shower, you're going to need to grab a quick one now,' Suzy said. 'I've told the kids to go get their warm things on. I want to leave in fifteen minutes.'

Eric squeezed the mixture again and let out a long groan.

'You're not serious about this, are you?' he asked.

'Yes, I am. You said you wanted to be part of a community. This is a community.'

'I meant a fun community,'

'For goodness' sake, Eric. It's one day a year.'

Eric pouted.

'Until Easter. Then you'll say it's only two days a year.'

'Fine. Two days a year.'

'No, because then there'll be Mothering Sunday, and Holy Tuesday, and Harvest-bloody-Festival where not only will you force me to go to church, but you'll take half my tinned goods to boot.'

'Where's your sense of fun? Your Christmas spirit?' Suzy said.

'Fun? If you think going to church is my idea of fun, you don't know me at all.'

Suzy sniffed, scowled, and then planted her hands on her hips.

'Well, tough. You're coming because it's your fault we have to go in the first place. You were the one who said to Janice I'd do a bloody reading.'

'Ha! So you don't want to go either. I knew it.'

Suzy's eyes flashed.

Eric stuck out his bottom lip in a pose that was scarily reminiscent of Abi.

'Fine,' he said. 'But I'm not having a shower. The only people who'll be there will be miserable old folk with nowhere to go and the local drunks who've been lured by the promise of free mulled wine.'

'And I'm sure you'll fit in equally well with both,' Suzy said.

CHAPTER 2

GIVEN THAT BURLAM played host to four churches, it was unsurprising that Eric found himself in one of the three he had never set a foot inside before. While Suzy abandoned him to find out the particulars of her reading, Eric was forced to lead the rest of the family to a place on one of the pews. Fortunately, a few steps in, Lydia decided to take the lead.

The church was not what Eric had envisioned, with lots of pine pillars, a large glass-fronted door, and stereo speaker system that would have been the envy of almost any teenager. Aromas of glass cleaner and cloves mingled with the dominating scent of ivy. The green vine had been liberally plastered on the pillars, seats, and lectern. The whole lot sparkled intermittently with thousands of multi-coloured fairy-lights. Sunday school decorations, consisting of toilet roll angels and paper plate snowmen, hung from a fifteen-foot tree that made Eric's Norwegian spruce look like a bonsai in comparison. The room was modern, sleek, and bordering on stylish.

Maybe it wouldn't be that bad, Eric thought.

Despite the variation in décor, Eric's estimation for the service and the congregation were pretty much spot on. Next to him, Janice warbled 'O Come All Ye Faithful' a full semitone sharp while the organist varied the pace according to the congregation's singing ability of each particular bar.

Rather than attempting to decipher the size eight font projected onto the screen in front of them, Eric substituted the actual words for a mumbling of *dums*, *dees*, and *tralalalalas*. Suzy read beautifully, as she always did, flashing smiles and glances at everyone as she spoke, while Lydia, who apparently knew every Christmas carol ever written, attacked the descant parts with the prowess of a castrated guinea pig. When the collection tray came around, Suzy placed a crisp, new twenty-pound note on the top of the pile.

'It's Christmas.' She grinned at him, as though that were a reasonable explanation for insanity.

'Can we go and play?' Abi asked, the moment she was sure the service was over.

'Ask your mother,' Eric said.

'Fifteen minutes,' Suzy replied. 'We need to get home in time to put out Rudolph's food.'

In a blink, Abi and her two cousins had disappeared into a large gaggle of children hanging around the nativity scene. A moment later, Suzy was strong-armed by Janice, the allotment's most well-meaning and meddlesome resident, into meeting various members of this committee and that committee.

'I'm just going to have a quick word with the pastor,' Lydia said, following in the direction of her sister. 'I want to congratulate him on his excellent choice of decorations and hymns.'

'Well then,' Tom said, as he and Eric were left standing by themselves. 'I guess we should go get some mulled wine then.'

It wasn't long before one glass turned into two, and two turned into a competition to see who could get the most cups of cinnamon-spiked Christmas spirit down their gullet before one of their wives caught on. It wasn't bad as far as mulled wine went, and whatever they put in it was certainly stronger than the average watered-down stuff Eric was used to at these types of events. Four cups in and the room had adopted a healthy warmth; as had his cheeks.

Thirty minutes in and they were level pegging. It didn't help that they stood right next to a large crowd. Even with his apathy towards religion, Eric couldn't bring himself to pick up more than one cup at a time or drink one in less than four mouthfuls.

Sensing the need for a new plan, Eric dropped his latest empty in the bin and made his way to the other end of the table. He placed himself strategically in a corner, away from any sociable looking folk while still within arm's reach of the refreshments. Tom had tried to follow suit but had drifted into part of a group and was being forced into conversation. If Eric was going to break into the lead, this would be the moment.

He was about to pick up his fifth paper cup when Suzy strode over towards him. Eric swallowed, assuming he had been busted. He opened his mouth to protest his innocence when Suzy smiled, stepped to the side, and revealed a slight, brunette woman behind her.

'Eric, this is Fleur. She moved here from Kensington last week.'

Fleur was narrow shouldered, half-a-head taller than Suzy, and wore a camel knit shawl. Eric gave an obligatory nod, slipped another mulled wine off the table, and let Suzy continue.

'I was telling her that we've only been here a few months ourselves,' his wife said. 'I suggested we get together for dinner sometime after the New Year. Perhaps we could go to that tapas restaurant we keep saying we're going to get to?'

It took a solid fifteen seconds of silence before Eric realised he was meant to say something in response. He jolted, sloshing his drink.

'Oh, right. Yes, brilliant. And congratulations,' he said to Fleur. 'Have the regrets sunk in yet or are you still high on the scent of marshland?'

Suzy glowered.

'Sorry, Fleur. Please ignore my husband. I think someone may have had one too many.'

'Oh, it's fine,' Fleur said. 'I'm high on a whole barrel load of things at the moment. I'll take anything I can get.'

Eric spluttered a laugh.

'So, what made you make the move?' he said. 'No, let me guess. All the usual clichés? Ridiculous working hours? Tired of the rat race? Desperate to relax in a cosy armchair to the sound of water lapping outside your window?'

'Throw in the extra clichés of a mid-life crisis and a messy break-up and you've hit the nail on the head.'

Eric downed drink number five and picked two more off the table. He handed one to Fleur.

'Well, welcome to the club. I'll drink to that.'

He knocked his cardboard tumbler against his new-found comrade's and brought the drink to his lips. A millisecond later it was whipped from his hand.

'I'll have that,' Suzy said. 'I think you've had enough.'

She finished his drink in two elegant draws.

'Besides,' she said. 'Tom had another three while we were having this conversation.'

Suzy patted Eric's shoulder.

'There's absolutely no way you're going to win now.'

While Suzy rounded off her conversation with Fleur, Eric was sent off to round up the rest of the clan. The children were sitting in the nativity scene, giggling while draping tinsel over the anatomically correct donkey while Lydia continued to chew the pastor's ear off about whether he was using energy efficient bulbs in all his lighting arrangements. Tom, who was looking a little worse for wear, stumbled into a table and sent a tray of mince pies flying, at which point Lydia broke off her sentence mid-way to turn and glare in disapproval. That half-second was all the pastor needed to make his escape, and by the time Lydia turned her head back, he was off into the vestry, a full jug of mulled wine in hand.

It still took another ten minutes to find their coats, draw the children away from the now lewd nativity, and venture into the bracing Christmas Eve air.

The walk back home was an unexpected treat. The cold breeze nipped at the tips of Eric's ears and the scent of imminent snow infiltrated his senses as he wrapped his arm around his wife, swaying in her wake. He had never believed it when people said they could smell snow in the air, but tonight he could. Tonight, *all* he could smell was snow. It was crisp and cold and icy white, yet it carried a warmth that spread up through his stomach in much the same way the mulled wine had.

Life is good, Eric thought as his feet trampled the verge.

Abi was up front, babbling away about Father Christmas.

'I've seen it on the computer. He's real. He has to go really fast, though. Super-fast. Faster than the Flash even. He has this really clever map to follow. Daddy says it's even better than Google Maps. First, he's going to head to New Zealand, and then India. But it's ...'

Her cousins, Hugo and Ellery, grinned.

'Abi,' Hugo started with a smirk. 'You don't really think that Father Christmas is—'

'Hugo ...' said Lydia with a look so stern that even Eric found himself cowering.

'What?' Abi said. 'What don't I think?'

Hugo scuffed his shoes against the ground. Lydia's look lingered.

'Just ... just ... well it's the reindeer, isn't it? That's why he can go so fast. You didn't think it was Father Christmas.'

'Well, of course it's the reindeer,' Abi said, rolling her eyes.

The warmth in Eric's abdomen spread. Suzy's family weren't that bad, really. In fact, as far as in-laws went, he could have done a lot worse.

'What are you grinning at?' Suzy said, her breath misting the air around them.

'Life,' Eric said.

Suzy chuckled. 'You're drunk.'

'No, I'm not.'

'Yes, you are,' she said kissing his ear, dotting it with a moment's warmth. 'And at a church service. Really, you should be ashamed.'

Eric nibbled her ear in return.

'I am not drunk. And even if I am, am I not allowed to be happy? I have the perfect wife, perfect daughter, an almost perfect house.'

'Perfect in-laws,' Tom said as he lolled about in front of them.

'Exactly,' Eric said.

The two men collided in a half-stagger, half-embrace, and stumbled along the verge, tripping over the clumps of grass and onto the road every few feet. When they reached the end of their road, they began singing 'Auld Lang Syne'.

'Just a little early there, boys,' Suzy said.

It was about a hundred yards from the house that Eric stopped, slipped out from under Tom's arm, and pulled Suzy back to him. While the rest of the family traipsed up ahead and into the driveway, Eric held Suzy back.

'What?' she said 'It's freezing. And we have presents to wrap.'

Eric put a finger to his wife's lips.

'*Shh*,' he said. 'I want you to hear this.'

'You *are* drunk,' she said again.

'So what?'

Suzy brushed back her hair and shivered. She smiled. It was the type of smile that caused Eric's heart to stir and his body to emit a hoard of post-adolescent hormones.

'It's freezing out here,' Suzy repeated.

'*Shh*, just listen.'

Eric lifted his gaze upwards. The sky was black, but so heavily lit by stars that it appeared closer to a deep violet. Snuggling his arms around his wife, he studied the scene and wondered how many constellations he could remember from evenings spent stargazing with his mother. He would teach the stars to Abi this year, he thought. Perhaps they would get a telescope. He should get her one for Christmas, he contemplated, then quickly realised it was probably a bit too late for that this year.

'What am I meant to be listening for?' Suzy asked, nestling deeper into Eric. 'I can't hear anything.'

'Exactly,' he said.

Then he kissed her the way he always forgot to do when he was sober. It was a long embrace, the type that was almost always reserved for drunken occasions. Eric squeezed his wife as close as he could and wished, in spite of the freezing cold, that the moment would never end.

'Shit!' said Suzy, breaking off the embrace.

'What.'

'They haven't got any keys.'

She wriggled out of Eric's arms and started up the road.

'They'll be freezing.'

Eric attempted to run behind. The tarmac glistened with ice crystals that crunched as he stumbled haphazardly forwards.

'Sorry,' Suzy said, stopping mid-stride as she turned into the driveway, causing Eric to run into the back of her. 'We just got caught—'

'What the hell?' said Eric, staggering backwards.

It was the contrast between the adults and children that was most startling. While Abi, Hugo, and Ellery bounced up and down in front of the porch squealing and clapping their hands, Tom, Lydia, and Suzy were frozen. Their mouths hung open, eyes wide in disbelief.

Suzy tried to speak. So did Lydia, but neither of them could manage any actual words. Eric wondered if it was an hallucination, a result of mixing dodgy wine with puritanical singing. It was only when the children stepped away from the front porch and a figure stepped out between them that someone finally spoke.

'Well, girls? Aren't you going to come and give your mother a hug?'

CHAPTER 3

YVETTE PARKER-NEWBURY had a flamboyance and floridity that transcended both of her daughters. It may have been eight-fifteen in the evening and sub-zero in Burlam, Essex, but Yvette was dressed for the Wam Bam Cabaret at the Royal Albert Hall. And as a performer, not a member of the audience.

'Darlings, darlings, darlings. Come and give your mother a hug.'

She opened her arms, sweeping wide the long feather boa that was draped around her neck.

'Oh, my little princesses. Don't just stand there. Come, come!'

Lydia and Suzy edged forward, exchanging a look of mutual trepidation. When they were three feet from Yvette, she pounced.

'*Mwah, mwah*. Oh, my beautiful babies, look how long your hair has grown. *Mwah, mwah*. What an interesting choice of colour you've gone for there, Lyd-Lyd.'

More kissing noises and several minutes of commotion passed before the daughters were pushed aside and the next targets located.

'My boys,' Yvette reached her extensive fuchsia nails out towards her sons-in-law. 'Come and give your mother-in-law a hug.'

Eric, having sobered up with miraculous speed, stepped in before a staggering Tom was pulled into the plum-coloured abyss of his mother-in-law's bosom.

'Why don't we go inside first?' he said. 'It's far too cold to be standing out here. Let's get in the warm and you can tell us all what you've been up to. I'm sure you've got lots to tell. *Like why the hell you're here?*' The last part he'd muttered under his breath.

Nobody else said a word.

Yvette was ushered straight into the decorated front room. The rest of the family scurried around in blind panic.

'But we want to see Granny,' Abi protested as Eric stripped her coat off and sent her to get into her pyjamas. 'She's got presents.'

'And you can have them tomorrow. Right now, you need to get into bed.'

'But it's Christmas Eve. I haven't put carrots out for Rudolph. I've got to. I've got to. If I don't put them out, Father Christmas won't come and then I won't get any presents.'

Her bottom lip wobbled, and her eyes began to fill.

'Fine,' Eric said, taking Abi through to the kitchen and grabbing one of his pre-cut carrots from the fridge.

'He won't eat that. It's not a real carrot.'

'Of course it's a real carrot. He prefers them cut up like this. They're cleaner. And easier to eat.'

Abi scowled.

'Okay,' she said, and Eric moved to place the carrot sticks into the centre of the table.

'It needs to go on his special plate,' Abi said.

'What?'

'The one I made with Aunty Lydia. Otherwise, how will he know it's his?'

Eric clenched his fists.

'Fine. Run and get it. Fast.'

Abi bolted through the door and returned less than a minute later with a papier mâché monstrosity. Eric tore off a piece of kitchen roll, which he placed on the table, before placing the plate on top. The table was in a bad enough state as it was without adding a smearing of PVA glue into the mix.

'There,' he said. 'Now up to bed.'

'But what about Father Christmas? He has to have a mince pie. And a drink too. He won't come down the chimney otherwise.'

Eric closed his eyes and took several deep calming breaths. A minute later he began rummaging in the cupboard until he found that morning's purchase of mince pies. Inside was a mass of shattered pastry cases and mincemeat crumbs. Eric tipped one out next to the carrot. Abi's face fell.

'They're fine.' Eric insisted.

'All the crumbs will get stuck in his beard,' Abi said.

'Then maybe he'll lose a bit of weight.'

Once again, her bottom lip began to wobble.

'Fine,' Eric said. 'We'll leave him two. That way he'll have plenty even if some does get stuck in his beard.'

Abi's lip turned into pout.

'Okay, but he still needs a drink.'

'Don't worry. That part, I have not forgotten.'

Eric took the gin from the cupboard, poured a double measure, and took a substantial sip from the glass.

'Daddy! That's for Father Christmas!'

'Which is why it's incredibly important that I check it's not poisonous,' he said.

❦

WITH ALL THE children in bed, the four parents shut themselves in the kitchen.

'Don't look at me,' Lydia said. 'I haven't spoken to her properly since March.'

'March? Why did you speak to her then? You didn't tell me that,' Suzy said.

'No, well I didn't want to bother you. You were going through a difficult time,' she said, shooting Eric a less than subtle glare.

'You told her about that? Seriously, Lyds.'

'Well, that's not why she's here, obviously. Anyway, I thought you spoke to her when you moved in here?'

'I did, but I have no idea how she got the new address. I'm sure I didn't give it to her. I vowed not to after that incident at the last place with the hair removal cream.'

There was a pause. Muffled sounds of the television floated in from the lounge. Something twigged in Eric's memory.

'Ohhh ...' he said.

All eyes turned to him. His stomach had become decidedly tight, and there was some definite constriction going on around his throat. He pressed his lips together and avoided any form of eye contact.

'Eric?' The word lilting upwards as Suzy spoke. 'What did you do?'

Eric swallowed. He could feel Suzy and Lydia's eyes boring into him. Even Tom had sobered up enough to get a grasp on the situation.

'She said she wanted to send Abi a present. She said she bought something in Venezuela or somewhere. It was an email; she sounded friendly. I didn't know she was going to turn up on our doorstep on Christmas Eve, did I? Anyway, let's look on the bright side,' he added.

'What's that?' Suzy said.

Eric downed the rest of Father Christmas' gin.

'Well, she appears to have forgotten a significant piece of baggage.'

The fire was lit in the lounge, illuminating the Norwegian spruce and filling the room with a scent of burning maple. The flames crackled and fizzed and would have filled the silences that may have existed had Yvette not been in the room. As it was, no one could get a word in edgeways.

'Well, it was all very last minute. I was wrapping Abi's present, thinking of her little face when she unwrapped it, and I thought, Christmas is a time for family. Why am I here teaching someone else's granddaughter to do a shoulder to shoulder, open hip twist, when I haven't taught my own granddaughter? So I stopped wrapping and went straight to your father and said I wanted us to come and see you. Well, of course, he was delighted and went straight to the captain to plead our case. Naturally, there was a lot of jiggling about to be done. Some of the guests are very particular, ask for me in person, you see, but anyway, your father insisted, and *voila*, here I am.'

'Here you are indeed,' Eric said.

Yvette coughed, then sniffed the drink in her hand.

'Well, it's a lovely surprise having you here, Mum, but where's Dad?' Suzy said. 'Is everything okay? Surely he can't be working without you? I thought you always danced together?'

'Oh, we do, we do.'

Yvette downed her sherry and shook the glass towards Tom. He took the bottle from the shelf and refilled the drink.

'Don't be stingy, Thomas,' she said, shaking her glass as he went to replace the top. 'I'll have a full glass please.'

When it was suitably topped up, she returned to Suzy's question.

'Daddy's very upset he can't be here. Very upset indeed. He was all ready to come, suitcase packed and everything. Then one of those silly little chorus boys went and sprained an ankle. Really, they have no stamina, these youngsters, none at all. In my day, you danced through a sprained ankle. Not now. Two weeks ice and bedrest. *Two weeks*. Well, what can you do? You can't run a cruise ship without dancers. They were desperate. What could your father say? And make no mistake, your father has got plenty of Fox Trots left in him. Never met a man of his age with such stamina. As I said, he's devastated, absolutely devastated, but I'm sure he'll make it up to us as soon as he can.'

Lydia yawned and rubbed her eyes. Eric suspected from the amplitude and expanse of her yawn that it was highly exaggerated, if not entirely fake; nevertheless, he was grateful. He made the most of the pause and turned to his wife.

'We should start thinking about stockings,' he said. 'The children will probably be awake by four, and the last thing we need is for Abi to wake up and think Father Christmas has forgotten her.'

Suzy stretched her arms above her head and imitated her sister's yawn.

'And talking of sleep,' she said. 'We're going to have to work out where we can put you, Mum. We're a bit short on beds I'm afraid.'

'Oh, I'm sure you'll think of something,' her mother replied, switching her gaze to Eric.

Before they'd moved to Burlam, Suzy had suggested they trade in their trusty old Lawson sofa – with its worn cushions and modest proportions that made it perfect for snuggling – in favour of a sofa bed. They were moving from a six-bed to a four-bed house, but with one of the bedrooms already a designated office space for Suzy, that put them down to only three sleepable bedrooms.

'We'll need it for when we have visitors,' Suzy had said about the sofa bed.

'When do we ever have that many visitors?' Eric had replied. 'We still have a spare bedroom. We can use a blow-up mattress if we need to. I'm not having my only sofa in the house some ugly wire contraption that digs into my backside whenever I want to sit down. I like the sofa we have, it's stylish, it's classic, it's staying.'

Christmas Eve night, Eric repeatedly and vocally rued his decision. Never had he consciously, and now almost soberly, spent an entire night on the sofa. Now he was waking up to the full consequences while his mother-in-law and Suzy enjoyed the comfort of his deluxe mattress.

The arms were too high to be a pillow but too low to offer the same support as a headrest, and every way he turned he found himself in possession of an excess limb, be it a spare arm or superfluous bony ankle. Thirty minutes after finally finding a viable position and falling asleep, he was woken by an icy draft and the realisation that the fire had gone out. It took less than ten minutes to get the new logs lit and burning, but the chances of getting any more sleep were well and truly scuppered.

CHAPTER 4

THE STOCKING UNWRAPPING had been brief and brutal. Metres and metres of wrapping paper had been torn and shredded, while plastic casings and cardboard boxes were demolished and thrown aside, all to a chorus of 'Wow!' 'Amazing!' and 'Why do you think Father Christmas got me this?'

By eight o'clock the family were gathered in the kitchen where the tried and tested aroma of fried bacon rose from the pan. Abi and the boys were playing a game of Dr Who Top Trumps at the table – which Father Christmas had knowingly purchased for Abi's stocking – while Eric stuffed the turkey and Tom aided Suzy with the breakfast.

'Well, I was doing a bit of totting up on the way over, and I've actually got an awful lot of holiday saved,' Yvette said.

Eric cringed.

While all the children were delighted at the appearance of their elusive grandmother, none were as enamoured as Abi. She perched herself on her grandmother's lap, pawing at her tassel-lined top, only looking up to the game when the boys demanded she do so.

'They're so pretty,' Abi said, now flicking Yvette's chandelier earrings and causing a spectrum of light to glint across her grandmother's ears. 'Can I borrow them?'

'Of course, my darling. My jewellery box is yours for the raiding. We'll need to take you to get your ears pierced first, though. These aren't your Aunt Lydia's silly clip-ons.'

'Mummy,' Abi shouted over the table. 'Granny says she'll take me to get my ears pierced.'

'That's brilliant,' Suzy said without raising her head from the frying pan. 'You've only got another four years to wait.'

'But, Muuuum.'

'You know the rules. No ear piercings until you're thirteen.'

'But Granny said—'

Suzy raised her head and fired a look over from the fried mushrooms. Abi pressed her lips together in a pout.

'Any more of that Buck's Fizz, Eric?' Yvette said, as Abi continued to sulk over her lack of pierced ears.

Eric, distracted by the fact his hand was once again submerged in a turkey's anus, glanced over towards the one and a half litre magnum.

'That was the end of that bottle, I'm afraid,' he replied.

'Then let's open another one,' Yvette replied. 'It *is* Christmas.'

'It's still pretty early.'

'Can't an old lady enjoy Christmas? Goodness me, I didn't realise I'd raised a brood of teetotallers. No offense, Lyd-Lyd.'

Lydia dutifully swallowed down whatever retort was burning on the tip of her tongue.

Shimmying Abi off her lap, Yvette stood up and glided over to the fridge, where she pulled out another bottle of prosecco and promptly popped the cork.

'Do you want some orange juice with that?' Eric said as she began to fill her glass.

'No,' she replied in a curt and defiant manner.

'I noticed you only brought a small bag with you, Yvette,' Eric said, moving the conversation back to the topic of her stay. 'I guess that means you're not planning on being here long?'

Yvette raised her eyebrows.

'Still that same need for control I see, Eric,' she said. 'And I thought you'd have loosened up a bit moving down here.'

Eric sucked in a short sharp breath and forced his lips upwards as he spoke.

'Oh, I'm wonderfully loose, Yvette, perfectly flexible,' he said. 'Although I'm not sure how long I'll stay that way sleeping on the sofa.'

Suzy gave him a stern look. Eric winced inwardly before trying a different tack.

'I suppose you must be missing Philip, though?' he said. 'I don't think I've ever seen you two apart before.'

'I'm a grown woman. Philip and I are quite capable of—'

'Of course,' interrupted Eric with his most butter-melting smile. 'I only meant that as wonderful as it is having you stay, I can't imagine that it's very pleasant for you here, particularly with the house the state it is. All this dust and dirt, it's hardly the five-star standard you're used to.'

Yvette took a gulp of her drink.

'Oh, don't you worry about me. I think it's marvellous. Rustic. Takes me back to my youth.'

She turned to her daughters.

'Did I ever tell you about the time I spent at a naturist commune on the east coast of Bulgaria before your father and I got married?'

'No,' Lydia said. 'I'm fairly sure that's something I'd remember.'

'Very interesting time. My goodness, they have a lot of good ideas on these communes. Splendid it was. And you see, there are lots of things you don't know about me. I wasn't always accustomed to the level of sophistication you think I was. Why, if you can undertake the Kama Sutra on a rusted pallet bed with a drove of Vietnamese pot-bellied pigs watching you ...' She paused just long enough for the execrable image to take form in Eric's mind. 'Anyway, what I'm saying is I can make myself at home anywhere. Just you wait and see.'

'Well, that's fantastic,' Eric said. 'Absolutely fantastic.'

While the rest of the family chowed down on the culinary masterpiece that was wholemeal bread, bacon, and brown sauce, Yvette gave her sandwich several dubious sniffs then pushed the plate away. The first sniff Eric tried to ignore, as he did the second one, but on the third sniff Eric felt his muscles tense all along his jaw. *Don't play into her hands,* he told himself. *That's what she wants.* He glanced around the table, trying to catch someone's eye, and praying they could hear his telepathic thoughts. Two seconds later and it was Tom who opened his mouth.

'Everything all right with the sandwich, Yvette?' he said. 'You've barely touched it.'

Eric groaned.

'Pardon, deary?' said Yvette widening her eyes in feigned surprise. 'Oh, oh, yes. Don't worry about me. It's not an issue. Not at all. It's all fine.'

'What's not an issue, Mum?' Suzy said.

'It's fine,' Eric said. 'She said not to worry. Let's leave her be.'

Eric received a withering look from Suzy and wondered briefly if these less-than-subtle looks were to be the only form of communication the couple would have while his mother-in-law resided in their house. With an entirely audible sigh, he relented.

'Can we get you something else, Yvette?' he said. 'Do you want me to make you another sandwich without the brown sauce? I think we've got some ketchup somewhere if you'd prefer that?'

Yvette wrinkled her nose.

'No, no,' she said. 'Don't be silly. I'm fine, I'm fine.'

'Are you sure? I can make you something different if you'd like?'

'I'm fine, honestly,' she paused. 'Well, perhaps if you have a piece of fruit, that would be lovely.'

'A banana?' Eric offered.

Her nose stayed crinkled.

'Perhaps something a little more locally sourced?'

'Locally sourced?'

'Yes. It's my constitution, you see. I'm on a macrobiotic raw food diet.'

'Macrobiotic?' Eric said, then cursed himself internally for his stupidity.

'It's a marvellous philosophy, really it is,' Yvette said, beaming at his sudden interest. 'The yin and yang of health and vitality. No more chemicals, no more harmful pesticides. Honestly, my cells have rejuvenated since I began.'

'That sounds great, Mum,' Lydia said.

'Oh, it is, it is. No, there won't be any more processed foods entering my body for a very long time,' she said, settling back into her chair with a satisfied grin.

'I'm guessing fermentation doesn't count as a process,' Eric replied, deliberately avoiding making eye contact with his wife as he made a quick exit to the lounge. 'Come on, kids. Let's go play Monopoly.'

THE TURKEY WAS out of the oven and resting. Beautiful, golden brown, crispy skin glistened, the potatoes continued to roast away in gallons of fat, garlic, and rosemary, and the myriad of vegetables, long since peeled and prepared, were ready and waiting in salted water as the bread sauce thickened at a surprisingly rapid rate. Despite the detailed organisation and relative success so far, by one o'clock, Eric was ready to throw in the towel.

The kitchen was a furnace. Condensation gushed down the newly replaced double-glazed windows while Eric stripped off his top and worked only in jeans and an apron. The rest of the family were supposedly halfway through their second game of Monopoly – an apparently accidental board flip by Hugo bringing the last game to an abrupt end – although Eric was certain that the only game they were actually playing was seeing who could cause him the most annoyance. Every minute it was another head around the door.

'Is it ready yet?'

'Do you need any help?'

'*Ooo*, can I try a bit of that skin?'

'We're all getting really hungry in there.'

'You don't mind if I pinch one of these, do you?'

'Do you not want to leave it in a bit longer? I like mine a little darker.'

'Did you not leave that in a bit long? It looks rather dark.'

'Perhaps if there was something we could nibble on while we wait?'

Eric snapped. His arms were marked with burns from the oven, and sweat covered his entire neck and back. His skin itched from spitting fat and the smell that emanated from his armpits was similar to the fur on Tom and Lydia's Old English sheepdog. Throwing off his apron, he marched out of the kitchen and stood in the doorway to the lounge. Noticing him in the doorway, the family put down their game pieces and looked up expectantly from the floor. Abi's mouth was wide open and drooling. Lydia's boys, Hugo and Ellery, were pawing at the ground, ready to run.

'No,' Eric said. 'It is not ready yet.'

Faces fell and a chorus of groans buzzed in the air. Eric placed his hands on his hips and huffed.

'And it won't be ready as long as you lot keep coming in and out of my kitchen every thirty seconds while I'm trying to get things done. Fourteen times,' Eric tried to show the number on his fingers, but then realised he was four digits short and dropped his hands back down. 'Fourteen times in the last ten minutes. That is not reasonable. That is ridiculous. How do you expect me to cook if you won't let me get on with it? From now on, the kitchen is out of bounds for everyone other than me until I say so. Do you get that?'

Suzy cocked her head and nodded encouragingly.

'I mean everyone,' Eric reinforced.

There was a small pause which Eric allowed to extend until he was satisfied that his message had been suitably conveyed. With a final nod, he turned to go, and was part way through the door when Ellery – whose face was already smeared in selection box chocolate – offered a small cough and raised his hand. The room was stiflingly silent. Eric could feel his pulse racing in his neck, the twinges of tension spasming in his shoulder. Slowly, he turned back. In a long, considered motion, he studied his nephew from top to bottom.

'Ellery,' Eric said in the calmest, quietest voice he could muster. 'I'm one question away from throwing the entire meal, turkey, stuffing, Brussels sprouts, the whole lot in the bin. Now this may sound like an empty threat, I get that, but I can assure you, this threat is very, very real. One wrong word, just one, and you and the rest of the family are going to be joining your grandmother in eating nothing but raw carrots, spinach, and a jar of Tesco's finest cranberry sauce for your Christmas dinner. So, think carefully, Ellery. Think very carefully. Whatever this question is, do you really, *really* need to ask it right now?'

The child remained motionless. There was a twitch at the corner of his mouth, followed by a flick of the tongue, after which his hand lowered back to his lap, and his head shook fast enough to make his cheeks wobble.

'No. It's fine, Uncle Eric,' he said.

'Good. Then I suggest you all finish your game of Monopoly, and I will call you when lunch is ready.'

Despite a further two near meltdowns, lunch was called only eighteen minutes later than planned, at which point the family stormed the dining room with a force comparable to a Genghis Khan led siege. The honey roasted parsnips were the show stealer for Eric, but the chestnut stuffing won an equally high number of accolades from the other diners. In addition, Janice's homemade cranberry jelly proved a much tarter and more refreshing alternative to the shop-bought equivalent. While Yvette munched on a salad of beans, radishes, and pumpkin seeds, the rest of the family gorged themselves on roast potatoes, bread sauce, and succulent turkey meat. After the main course came the trio of desserts, courtesy of Lydia, followed by the cheese course and port. By the end of the meal, Eric had to go upstairs and select a more generous pair of trousers to wear.

'Is it presents now?' Abi said the moment her plate was clear.

Even her bouncing was restrained due to the kilos of pavlova lining her stomach.

'We always do presents after lunch. Please. Please!'

The boys began to join the chorus of pleading. Eric turned to his wife.

'Did you get Abi anything for Christmas this year?' he said.

'Me? I thought you said you were buying her present this year?'

'No, I thought you were.'

'*Urgh!*' groaned Abi, throwing her hands in the air. 'You do this every year. And I know you've got me something. So you can stop pretending.'

'You know, do you?' Eric said. 'How's that exactly? Perhaps if you've been sneaking around, we shouldn't give you anything.'

'I wasn't sneaking. It was at breakfast the other day. And you said to Mummy "have you put the *you-know-what* somewhere safe?" And *you-know-what* means present.'

'Does it?'

'Uh-huh.'

Eric's eyes met his wife's. A smile flitted between them.

'Well, if that's the case, I suppose we'd better go and get the *you-know-whats*,' she said.

'You need to put your shoes on, though,' Eric added.

'What about us?' Hugo said. For a thirteen-year-old, he was an even messier eater than his younger brother and had somehow managed to get Yorkshire pudding stuck in his hair. 'What should we do? Do we get our presents now too?'

'I guess you should get your shoes on too,' Lydia said.

The boys squealed, tumbling over one another as they darted out of the dining room, through the conservatory, and over to the back door.

The presents were lined up in ascending height order, each one decorated with a bow tied to the handlebars, flapping about in the breeze.

'Awesome!' the children shrieked and clambered on to the saddles.

'Mine's the biggest,' Hugo said. 'Look, it's got twenty-one gears and everything.'

'Is this a bell?' Abi beamed. 'Can I ring the bell?'

'It's your bike, my darling, you can do whatever you want. Only,' Eric paused, 'no riding without helmets on.'

The children stopped and looked at one another. Their grins dropped.

'We haven't got any helmets,' said Ellery.

'Have you not? Oh, well, you can just look at them for now then,' Eric said.

Abi and Ellery's eyes began to fill with water. Even Hugo with his teenaged machoism was having a hard time disguising his disappointment.

'It's a good job I found these then,' said Tom as he came out of the back door, three boxes piled high in his arms.

The children leapt off their bikes and rushed towards them. 'Careful, careful,' Tom said as he bent down.

'Abigail, honey, this one's for you. Hugo, give that one to your brother. Good, now make sure all the straps are done up properly before you get on the bike.'

It was picture perfect. Squeals and giggles pealed through the air as the children rode around and around creating a noticeable track on the bare lawn. Eric slipped his arm around his wife and watched the scene evolve in front of them.

'Merry Christmas, my darling,' he said.

'Merry Christmas.'

CHAPTER 5

IT TOOK NEARLY an hour to get the children indoors, and even then it was only for a clothes change.

'It's far too cold to be out here dressed like that,' Suzy insisted. 'If you want to stay out, you need to go and put some more suitable clothes on. Otherwise, I'm getting the bike locks out.'

The three children dropped their bikes on the grass, ran inside, grabbed the required garments, and were back pedalling in less than two minutes. Another ten minutes later and they were dragging Eric's flower pots across the lawn in an attempt to set up a suitable obstacle course.

'How about you go out onto the front?' Suzy suggested.

Eric frowned.

'Don't you think that's a bit dangerous?'

'They'll be fine,' Suzy said, and then to the children. 'You can ride down towards the dead end, but make sure you can still see the house. Okay?'

'And no fast pedalling,' Eric added. 'And Abi, you have to stay on the pavement.'

'But, Dad—'

'And boys, you have to keep an eye on your cousin. You understand?'

They assured him several times they did.

'She's not allowed on the road,' he called again as they disappeared out of the driveway.

A moment later Yvette was by his side. 'I'll go and watch them,' she offered.

'You don't have to do that,' Eric said.

'Nonsense, what else are grandparents for?'

'Well, if you're certain?'

'I am.'

Eric gave an audible sigh of relief.

In the lounge, and despite Yvette's supervision, Eric continued to watch from the window, his body tensing every time Abi wobbled or jolted.

'I thought you wanted her to ride to school?' Suzy said. 'She's going to have to learn to ride on the road at some point.'

'I know, it's just this damn road. You know what it's like.'

'It's really not that bad.'

Eric huffed and continued to watch them. Clearly Suzy had been too busy with work to realise the potential dangers that awaited them in their calm little corner of the British countryside.

While their street was, for the most part, exceptionally quiet, at least twice a week Eric would be startled from his current chore by the screech of rubber against tarmac, as some preoccupied speed-freak took the turn assuming it was a shortcut to the centre of the village. Inevitably, on discovering that it was, in fact, a dead end, they would be forced to make an abrupt stop before attempting an ungainly three-point turn, often using Eric's, or someone else's, driveway to help increase their turning circle.

'Perhaps I'll get on to the council again. See if they got my last email about replacing the *No Through Road* sign,' he said. 'Maybe even persuade them to put up a speed limit sign at the junction as well.'

'That sounds like a wonderful idea,' Suzy said, pulling him away from the window.

With the children occupied it was time for the adults to exchange presents. A mixture of nerves and excitement bubbled their way through Eric's abdomen. For the first time in more years than he cared to admit, he had broken his no present rule and had bought something for Suzy of his own choosing. When he'd found it in the shop, he had thought it was perfect, but now it was in her hands, about to be unwrapped, his throat was feeling uncharacteristically tight.

'It's lovely,' Suzy said, turning the gift over in her hand. The polished wood glinted in the light.

'It's engraved. See,' Eric said twisting one side of the pen over to face her.

'To my beautiful wife,' Suzy read.

'It's for your book signings,' Eric said. 'It's made from wych elm, so I thought it would remind you of here when you're off on your trips. And the wife part is there so you can show it to any overly amorous fans.'

'It's perfect,' Suzy said as she planted a kiss on his lips.

The nerves transformed into pride as Eric looked on at his gift. He'd done well.

From Tom and Lydia, they received the obligatory homemade hamper.

'We've updated it a little,' Lydia said. 'Go on, have a look.'

Intrigued, Eric opened the top of the hamper and rummaged through. There was enough sugar to keep them in stock through until Easter, with salted caramel sauce, hot chocolate in a jar, and two types of brownies in a jar, not to mention a bottle of homebrew, a bottle of elderflower cordial, a homemade foot scrub – packaged in a re-purposed hummus tub – and half a dozen homemade bath bombs.

'This is incredible,' Eric said, as he picked up one item after another.

'We figured Suzy could do with a little more pampering this year,' Lydia said.

'Well, it all looks delicious,' Eric said.

Try as he might, he failed to get all the items back in the basket, and so the bath bombs and foot scrub were left perched on top. For Tom and Lydia, Suzy had bought an afternoon tea at one of the nearby stately homes.

'Now from me to you,' Suzy said to Eric. 'I'm afraid it's not the most thoughtful present of the day, but hopefully you will find it useful.'

Eric took the neatly wrapped rectangle.

'What could this be?' he said as he tore into the paper that was so obviously covering a book.

When the title came into view, Eric laughed.

'Brilliant, exactly what I need.'

He turned it around to show the title and cover to Tom and Lydia.

'*Backyard Poultry*,' Tom read. 'I didn't know you were planning on keeping chickens?'

Eric flicked through the first few pages of the book.

'It's still just a bit of an idea really,' Eric said. 'I've got to go through the committee first.'

'You want to have them at the allotment?'

'I'd prefer to. I guess I could always have them up here if they say no, but I've been through the allotment handbook, and I'm fairly sure it should be okay to keep them there.'

'Well, let me know when you get the go ahead,' Tom said. 'I've got half a dozen pullets you can have, that'll make lovely little layers.'

'Pullets?' Eric said.

'You should probably start reading that book,' Tom replied.

※

AT SIX O'CLOCK THE children and Yvette returned indoors just as Eric had finished constructing a platter of sandwiches.

'Who fancies a turkey sandwich?' Eric said before quickly pre-empting any complaints from Yvette by producing a macrobiotic crumble he'd whipped up using some hazelnuts from the back of the cupboard.

With the leftovers dished up, the family settled down for the *Doctor Who Christmas Special*. All in all, Eric considered, the day had been a success. Only one more to go, and he would be home and dry.

※

ERIC WAS DREAMING OF SPRINGTIME. Him and his harem of pullets – which in his dream were small, sprite-like creatures with exceptionally long fingers – were fishing for eggs from the stream. It started off easy enough; they reached their hands into the gently flowing water and plucked out one smooth, round ovule after another. But then the stream grew faster and their hands started being dragged down by the current. A moment later and the stream was a roaring river, crashing into eddies, its bellow so loud Eric was forced to cover his ears from the noise.

He threw off the blanket in a cold sweat, taking a moment to orientate himself. He was back on the Lawson, the fire in the front room still aglow with a soft tangerine hue. No more sprites, no more eggs, although the sound of running water was almost as loud as it had been in his dream.

'Shit.'

Eric leapt off the sofa. He knew they should have sealed the bathroom shut. With his head still foggy from one too many nightcaps, and his mouth tasting of chestnut stuffing, he bounded up the stairs. How much was this going to cost him, he wondered? Another grand? Two? It was bound to be Ellery who had used the toilet. How many times had he told him it wasn't plumbed in yet? Eric was halfway up the stairs when he froze. Holding onto the rickety banister – and attempting to steady his breath – he listened. A second later he bolted back down into the kitchen.

'What the ...?'

Eric stopped in his tracks.

The kitchen was a far cry from the scene he had left when he fell asleep. The taps were on full blast, rushing into a bubble-filled sink with white water spraying up and over the wooden countertop. On the kitchen table appeared to be every item of crockery, cutlery, and kitchen utensil they owned, plus some he didn't even recognise. The room smelt of citrus and baking soda, and everything from the plates to the lino gleamed.

'Yvette?' Eric said.

Eric's mother-in-law started and blushed.

'Eric, darling. Did I wake you?'

Eric blinked.

'What are you doing?' he said.

'Oh, I couldn't sleep,' Yvette replied. 'It's the stillness you see. I'm used to the sea. The motion. I like my bed to have a little sway to it.'

She shook her hips as she spoke.

'Oh,' Eric said, rubbing his eyes and still not sure he was seeing straight.

'Anyway, I thought I'd put myself to use,' Yvette continued. 'But then I finished the washing-up, so I thought, why not give the place a bit of a spring clean?'

'In December?'

'No need for sarcasm, Eric.'

Outside was dark. Through the trees, Eric glimpsed the moon, a buttermilk sliver in the sky.

'What time is it?' he said.

Ignoring his question, Yvette turned off the taps, the mountain of froth having broken free from the confines of the sink.

'Why don't you go back up to bed with Suzy?' she said. 'You can't have gotten any proper rest on that sofa. I'm not going to go back up now.'

'It's fine.'

'I insist. The mattress is far too soft for me, anyway. It's not a surprise you all have such poor posture when you spend every night on a marshmallow.'

Eric hesitated. Going upstairs to his actual bed sounded like heaven, but the last thing he wanted was to fall into one of his mother-in-law's traps.

'Are you sure?' he asked again. 'I don't want to kick you out.'

Yvette waved him quiet.

'I'll sleep when I'm dead,' she said. 'And don't worry about the children in the morning. I'm more than happy to keep an eye on them. You and Suzy have a lie in.'

Something squirmed around Eric's kidneys. Still, a couple of hours back in his own bed was too much to resist. He would deal with the consequences in the morning.

※

WHEN HE AND Suzy finally surfaced, it was gone ten. They had been awake for over an hour, just lying in bed, listening to the sounds of the children at play drifting in through the sash panes of the windows.

Eric and Suzy's bedroom was the largest in the house. It was also the most dated. Seventies-style brown and orange wallpaper hung on three of the four walls, the fourth having been decorated with a peculiar burnt-umber paintwork. The carpet was worn through to the underlay, and a string light-pull dangled down in the centre of the headboard. At first, Eric had been horrified when he noticed spores of mould populating the area around the window ledge and had sworn to rectify the situation immediately. Now, after numerous dousings of bleach, they were just another thing on the endless to-do list.

'I thought you might want to head down to the allotment today,' Suzy said as she climbed out of bed and pulled on her dressing gown. 'I can't believe it's been a year since we all first came down here.'

'I know,' Eric said. 'Seems like a lifetime ago.'

He reached for a pair of socks. Gone were the days of luxury, flat-knit hosiery, or cashmere hound's-tooth. Nowadays, he was all about warmth, and the thicker the socks the better. Sludge green, bark brown, the colour was irrelevant.

'Perhaps I'll take Tom down after lunch,' he said. 'We're still going to the Shed, right?'

'Sounds good. Although I can't stay long. I've got a pile of work to get through.'

'We won't stay long,' Eric assured her.

THE SHED WAS one of Burlam's longstanding establishments, and despite a very relaxed attitude towards contemporary cuisine, or modernisation of any kind for that matter, it remained steadfastly busy all year round.

Eric suspected that at least eighty-five per cent of their Boxing Day clientele were there with the sole purpose of abating their hangovers. Several heads offered him the obligatory welcome nod as he entered, although several more were face down on the table, hands clutching triple-shot coffees. The usual aromas of bacon fat and fried mushrooms wafted around them, mingling with the odd puff of cigarette smoke and spray of alcohol breath.

Griff, the establishment's eternally jovial owner, found them a table facing out over the river.

'Look at that,' Yvette said, flicking her hair in the direction of Griff. 'The best seat in the house. How ever can we repay you?'

Griff, with three days' worth of stubble and his apron covered in grease, beamed.

'Always do my best to please,' he said and trotted away with a wide grin on his face, promptly returning with the menus.

While the boys and Abi giggled at the uniqueness of the meal names, Lydia did not.

'I thought this part of the world was meant to be sophisticated,' Lydia said.

'What's wrong with a Whiny Bitch?' Eric said. 'I thought you liked omelettes?'

'I like omelettes. I don't feel it's necessary to lower the tone in order to eat one.'

'It's called humour,' Eric clarified. 'Besides, this is sophisticated. You should hear what the dishes were called before people complained.'

'I'd rather not.'

Griff took the orders. Two minutes later he returned with a tray of drinks.

'My goodness, what big muscles you must have, carrying trays around like that all day,' Yvette said, removing her feather boa like it was part of a burlesque show. 'Excellent core strength, I suspect. Do you do Pilates?'

Griff blushed.

'Just good old-fashioned walking's all I need to keep in shape,' he said.

'Of course, the old ways are always the best. Nothing keeps the body limber like good old-fashioned exercise. Of every type.'

Eric shuddered.

'Mum?' Suzy said, waiting until Griff had scurried away for the second time. 'Is everything okay?'

'What?' Yvette was wide eyed. 'Yes, dear, everything's quite all right. Absolutely fine. What a quaint place this is. And fantastic service. If you like that kind of thing.'

Her eyes followed to where Griff was crouched down by the counter, exposing a small but textbook example of a builder's bum.

Eric pressed his lips together and locked eyes with his wife. The shuddering was mutual.

When the plates were licked clean, Suzy, Lydia, and the children decided on a Boxing Day stroll down to the Yacht Club.

'Are you sure you don't want to come with us, Mum?' Suzy asked.

Yvette shook her head.

'I said I'd call your father this morning. You know what it's like with the time difference. He'll be ever so upset if we don't get to speak.'

'Why don't we come back with you then?' Lydia suggested. 'I'm sure the kids would love to speak to Grandad too.'

'And I'm fine to head back and get on with some work,' Suzy added.

Yvette brushed the suggestions aside.

'Perhaps tomorrow. He won't have much time before he has to get back. Such a busy time for him, darlings. Such a busy time.'

'As long as you're sure. We won't be long. And make sure you give Dad our love.'

'Will do, my darling. Will do.'

'Well,' Eric said to Tom as he waved Abi and Suzy off. 'I guess we should get going too.'

CHAPTER 6

THERE WAS SOMETHING refreshing about winter time at the Columbia Avenue allotments. The bare trees and spindled bushes acted as a literal fresh start; whatever you had or hadn't achieved last year was irrelevant. Soon it would be spring, and everyone would start from the same point of seeds and seedlings. You would all be beholden to the same weather, the same number of sunny, workable days, and if, come June, your neighbours' tomato plants had been bested by late blight, you could bet your bottom dollar yours would be too. The allotment was a great leveller of man, Eric considered. It didn't care about your age, your education, whether or not you were a good person even. All it cared about was how hard you worked and how well you turned your compost.

'So, I'm planning on entering the village show this year,' Eric said as he and Tom strolled down the path towards the allotment entrance. 'I'm not too sure what with yet, and I don't suppose I have much of a chance, but I've got to give it a go. It's a bit of a big deal here.'

'Oh, you don't need to tell me that. And you've got as good a chance as anyone. You're not exactly a novice anymore.'

Eric raised an eyebrow.

'Last year the winning stump carrots were over three feet long. And apparently it was a bad year. Unless they have a category for most phallic shaped vegetable or biggest caterpillar found on a cauliflower, I'm probably not in the running.'

'Perhaps you need to start with something a little smaller then? Go for tomatoes. Everyone can grow tomatoes.'

They ambled onwards between the empty beds and full water-butts. Eric offered numerous greetings and gesticulations towards the various figures hunched over the ground or squirrelling away in their greenhouses. To those farther away, he extended his arm in a wave, and when Scout bounded up to him and rested his stumped leg on Eric's knee, Eric crouched down to give him a substantial rub.

'I'd love a dog,' Eric said, scratching the soft fur of Scout's tummy.

'Then why not? Suzy likes dogs, doesn't she?' Tom said.

'She does. But I think she's got enough on her plate at the minute.'

Tom hummed knowingly.

'You still coming over for New Year?' Hank, Scout's owner, shouted over from his plot.

'You bet,' Eric called back.

'Don't forget it's bring a dish.'

'I'm already on the case,' Eric lied, then made a mental note to tell Suzy they needed to cook something for the event.

Hank was one of the first friends Eric had made at the allotment, and since the death of Norman and the move to Burlam, they'd become firm partners in crime. Only ever a phone call away if a quick pint down the pub was in order. He had also taken on Norman's role offering Eric advice for his plot.

After giving Scout one final belly rub, he pushed himself back up.

'Ouch,' Eric winced as a sharp pain shot through his shoulder.

'Everything okay?'

Eric rubbed the spot, just below the base of his neck.

'I guess I need to stretch a bit more,' he said.

'You're getting old, old man,' Tom laughed.

Eric chose not to respond.

They were approaching his own corner patch with its raised beds – that Eric had lovingly built himself – and small, prefabricated shed when Eric stopped abruptly. Something felt different. A cool breeze of uncertainty prickled the hair on his arms as he scanned the view from side to side. His plot was fine, nothing broken, or damaged; no evidence of the Burlam youths who a few weeks back had taken to using the allotment as a local BMX park. The committee had had to go to the school principal with CCTV evidence, after which the problem was resolved quickly enough; no doubt the youths had found a new way to stir up trouble in the village since. Eric was just about to brush the funny feeling off as paranoia when he spied the neighbouring shed, its rust-red door six inches ajar.

Something uneasy coiled its way around Eric's insides. He stepped towards the shed.

'Everything okay?' Tom asked.

Too distracted to reply Eric racked his mind over the previous state of the shed. He had long since emptied it of all of Norman's sentimental keepsakes, though he had continued to keep the tools inside. They were left to him, an inheritance he had used frequently since Norman's passing, and there was no point moving them into his own shed, not when they all had a place so orderly mapped out in Norman's. Perhaps he had forgotten to do the padlock up last time he was there. The winds had been strong a few nights back; it was possible that the door had just blown open. He took another step forwards then stopped. Lying beside the seating on the small, covered veranda sat a pair of shiny bolt cutters.

It was at the precise moment of glancing down that Eric saw the shadow moving inside the shed. His pulse ratcheted a notch higher.

'Did you—'

'*Shhh!*' Eric whispered, silencing his brother-in-law.

Tiptoeing across the plot, Eric crouched down and took the bolt cutters in his hands. The drumming in his chest grew louder and louder as his heart inched its way up his throat. With the bolt cutters in his hand Eric positioned himself with his back against the shed wall. The shadow moved again. Eric lunged.

Lifting the bolt cutters high into the air, he flung open the door.

'Got you!' he shouted.

'Eric?'

The bolt cutters froze in the air above his head as Eric squinted into the darkness. The face inside stared at him, doe-eyed and confused, but still smiling.

'It is Eric, isn't it? Suzy's husband?'

'Um, well, yes?'

There was an awkward thirty-second pause during which Eric tried to place the woman's face. She was certainly familiar with her brunette hair and big oval eyes, but he was finding it impossible to say why.

'Fleur? From Kensington. We met at church before Christmas?'

Eric still drew a blank.

'Church ... mulled wine ... Suzy ...' she continued.

'*Fleur!* Of course!'

In an attempt to throw off the embarrassment, Eric stretched out his free hand for an enthusiastic handshake.

'Sorry, I'm awful at names. Useless.'

'It's no problem, really.'

'Fleur, this is Tom, my brother-in-law. Tom, this is Fleur. She's just moved here from Kensington.'

Tom stumbled across the barren beds and shook her hand.

'Pleased to meet you. So, you're a green-fingered one as well, are you?'

'Hoping to be. I only got the go ahead to take this place over a couple of days ago, so I'm keen to get started. I'm guessing from the warm welcome you'd not been informed yet.'

Eric blushed.

'No, sorry about that,' he said as he lowered the bolt cutters to the ground. 'I've kind of been looking after the plot. I thought you might be looting the place.'

Fleur laughed.

'No, I think if I were to take up larceny, I'd pick something slightly more impressive than a dead man's bunch of cruddy old tools to steal. I'll be lucky if I don't get tetanus from these. Although I suppose it's good that they're here,' Fleur continued. 'It's an all right set to get me started. I guess I'll just bin them when I'm done.'

Eric shifted uncomfortably.

'Actually, they're not with the shed,' he said. 'They're mine. I mean, they are with the shed, but not the plot, if you see what I mean. They're still in there, but I left them.' Eric was acutely aware he was babbling, but he couldn't stop. 'Norman, the man who had this plot before you, when he died, he left me the shed and tools, and I suppose I should have really moved them, but with them being just—'

'Oh, I'm sorry,' Fleur said. 'Of course, take them. I didn't mean to—'

'No, no, it's fine,' Eric said. 'I mean you're welcome to borrow them, of course. Only the thing is—'

'I completely understand.'

'It's just that—'

'I will buy my own tools.'

'I don't mean to—'

'Fleur,' Tom cut Eric short. 'How did you manage to get your name on this place? I thought the waiting list was years?'

Eric offered Tom a grateful glance; for a moment he had thought the polite apologies might last them all the way through to New Year.

'Actually, yes.' A second later he turned back to Fleur, his thoughts of embarrassment very much distracted. 'I thought the wait was up to eight years. How did you do that?'

Fleur's eyes darted from side to side. She stepped forwards as if even the clear lack of proximity wasn't enough to ward off any souped-up hearing aids that might be listening in from the bushes.

'Let's just say,' her voice barely above a whisper, 'that money can't buy you happiness, but it can buy you a small allotment on Columbia Avenue.'

Eric let out a tiny, but audible, gasp.

※

'I DON'T THINK you're really one to talk,' Suzy said over dinner. 'Not when you think of all the tricks you tried to pull.'

Tom and Lydia had left late afternoon. After ensuring that all the children had the correct presents and that no one had left behind so much as a single head-light from a Lego Battleship, Eric, Suzy, Abi, and Yvette had waved them off down the road until they were out of sight. Eric was exhausted but satisfied; three days, five guests, zero disasters.

The four remaining family members were sitting around the kitchen table, three of them munching on battered sausages, cod, and chips. The refrigerator bulged with cold meat, Brussels sprouts, and a half-eaten ham hock, but the thought of another turkey sandwich had almost been enough to push them all onto Yvette's macrobiotic regime. So, while Eric cleaned up the last of the mess, Suzy and Abi had headed down the road to pick up fish and chips. Yvette ate a satsuma and half a bowl of blanched almonds.

'Oh, I'm not criticising her,' Eric said, dunking a chip in the curry sauce. 'According to Fleur, her donation will cover the entire cost of the drainage system. That's massive. I just feel guilty, I suppose. Another year gone and once again, the only allotment that becomes available goes to someone who is not even on the waiting list.'

'That's not your fault. You didn't ask to be left yours.'

'I know but still.'

Eric popped his curry-dunked chip into his mouth. The sauce was far spicier than he had anticipated. With the chip still in his mouth, he reached for his drink. An empty beer bottle later and his mouth was still uncomfortably warm.

'Another drink, Eric?' Yvette said, rising from the table.

Eric nodded mutely.

'You stay where you are,' she said, resting a hand on his arm. 'Let me fetch that.'

Whistling a tune, that to Eric sounded distinctly sinister, Yvette grabbed a beer from the fridge, flicked off the top, and handed it to him.

'Thank you.'

'My pleasure.'

Thirty seconds later and his mother-in-law was still hovering by his shoulder. Eric tensed. A hovering Yvette always made him nervous.

'I thought I might take a little jaunt into town tomorrow,' she said. 'A proper town, I mean. I wondered if I might be able to borrow the car to head to Maldon? Just the little run around, obviously.'

'What is it you want to get?' Suzy said. 'I can take you. I've got some writing to do, but if you—'

'No, no, it's no problem. I thought I'd get out of your hair. Just do a little food shop. Have a potter. You know. It's been a long time since I've had my feet on dry land. I thought it might be nice.'

Eric chewed on a mouthful of battered sausage.

'The only thing is you're not insured,' he said. 'Otherwise, I wouldn't have a problem with it.'

Yvette clapped her hands together.

'Well, that's marvellous then. Simply marvellous.'

Two minutes later, Eric's laptop was fired up and Yvette was typing his credit card number into the first insurance website she found.

❦

'Do you not think you should ask her how long she's staying?' Eric said as they snuggled up under the duvet. With Tom and Lydia gone, Yvette had decamped into the spare room and Eric was back, stretched out under his duck-down quilt. In place of a book, Suzy was marking red lines on a stack of manuscript papers, the bedside lamp casting peculiar shadows on one side of her face.

'And I was thinking,' Eric continued. 'Where is your dad at the minute?'

'Not sure. South America, I think Mum said. Mexico perhaps?'

'So it doesn't make any sense her calling him at midday? It'd be six o'clock in the morning there.'

'Perhaps he has some early lessons.' Suzy sighed, shuffled the pile of papers into one neat stack, placing them on the nightstand. 'If you're that bothered, ask her tomorrow, but she'll be gone by the end of the week. She always is.'

'I suppose you're right,' Eric said. 'I suppose you're right.'

CHAPTER 7

YVETTE WAS NOT gone by the end of the week. As Eric and the rest of western civilisation sank into the abyss that was the twenty-seventh to thirtieth of December, Yvette became more and more settled into a daily routine. While the unprecedented surprise of having a live-in babysitter had undeniable advantages, Eric would have been hard pushed to say he was enjoying his new living arrangement.

'Homemade granola,' Yvette said, waiting in the kitchen as Eric traipsed down the stairs.

A scent of dry oats, burnt nuts, and something vaguely coconutty confused his taste buds as it rose from the oven.

'I thought I'd have a bacon sandwich actually,' Eric said.

Yvette balked.

'Think of your body, Eric. Think of your cells. Where's the goodness in a bacon sandwich?'

'In the taste.'

'Well, I've thrown it away. It smelt funny.'

Eric frowned.

'Don't blame me.' Yvette shrugged. 'Perhaps if you hadn't quit your job and left Suzy to pay all the bills, you'd be able to afford more than cheap fatty bacon from the local village shop.'

'That wasn't exactly what happened, Yvette, as you know—'

'I'm just calling it like I see it, Eric.'

While Eric brooded over his lack of bacon, a bowl of freshly made granola was placed in front of him, along with a jug of distinctly brown milk.

'What's this?' he sniffed, turning his nose up at the smell.

'That, Eric, is hazelnut milk. Honestly, how you can continue supporting such barbaric acts as dairy consumption is beyond me. Do you read none of the research? Those poor calves snatched from their mothers. Not to mention what it's doing to your body.'

'I eat perfectly healthily, thank you, Yvette. The occasional bacon sandwich is hardly going to give me a heart attack.'

'Tell that to your middle-aged spread.'

Eric harrumphed and patted his middle. It was true, the slender days of his youth were gone, but he didn't consider himself out of shape. Stewing over the reality of his middle-aged lateral growth spurt, Eric scooped up a spoonful of granola and began to chew. The taste was one of year-old cardboard, although unlike cardboard the presence of saliva and moisture did nothing to help the disintegration process. Two minutes into the chewing process and his teeth continued to work at the same rock-hard fragments of oats.

'See, you can feel the goodness working, can't you?' Yvette said.

'Hmm,' Eric said.

If Yvette stayed, they were going to have to get a dog; it would be the only way he was going to survive her meals.

Making the most of Yvette's one redeeming feature, Eric decided to leave Abi for a couple of hours and head down to the allotment. It was a five-minute drive at most, but on the spur of the moment Eric opted to take Sally. The precious Aston Martin DB4 had been his late father's pride and joy, and getting his hands on her, for that matter, had been no easy task, so it made sense to make the most of her. Besides, she'd been cooped up for weeks, and after a summer of long drives and twisty lanes she was in need of a little attention. Somehow, with Christmas, the house, managing Abi around Suzy's manic work schedule and now Yvette, Sally had been pushed to the bottom of his to-do list.

Inside the car a smell of warm leather pervaded the air. A thin film of dust had built along the steering wheel. Eric wiped it clean, spilling the motes into the air around him. How much had he given up for this car? His job, his sanity. And he would do it all again in a heartbeat. He checked the indicators, tweaked the mirrors, and reversed out of the garage.

'Wait! Dad! Watch, watch!' shouted Abi, flapping her arms from the other side of the road. 'Watch what I can do.'

She was dressed in a Christmas jumper and a striped bobble hat. Eric smiled. Whatever qualms he and Suzy had had about moving her out of her crazily priced prep-school had long since evaporated. This was the type of life a child should have, he thought, not glued to an iPad doing homework until eight o'clock at night.

Eric pulled up behind her at what he considered a safe distance and kept the engine running. While he loved his daughter more than life itself and the whole point of moving to Burlam was to spend time with her doing things like this, if she scratched the paintwork on Sally, he could not be held responsible for his actions.

Abi straightened her helmet, placed her hands on the handlebars, and began to pedal. Ten metres down the road, her hands flicked up away from the handlebars. She shrieked, slammed her hands back down, and skidded to stop. The climactic moment lasted less than a quarter of a second, at most.

'Did you see that? Did you see that?' screamed Abi, pedalling back down towards Eric and the car. 'I went no-handed! Did you see that! Wait until I tell Harry Nini what I can do now!'

Eric wound down the window and blew his daughter a kiss.

'Very impressive,' he says. 'You'll be a stunt rider in no time.'

'You think?'

'Just stay on the pavement please. At least until the council puts the sign up. You know how fast those cars can go.'

'I know.' She sighed and pedalled off down the pavement, practising her no-handed milliseconds.

With Sally parked up in her usual spot, Eric trundled down the path towards the allotment. The patches of earth were a hive of activity, although apart from a quick hello to Hank, Eric kept his head down and headed straight for his little corner. He had too much to do to waste away the day listening to Janice prattle on about her bunions. About thirty feet away from his plot, Eric paused, frowned, and listened.

Loud noises – hedge-trimmers, chainsaws, and God-forbid, mini excavators – were not unheard of at the allotment but were usually confined to the more temperate months. These sounds however, were far less mechanical in their nature, and sounded like they were coming directly from his plot. Thumping, grunting, and occasional thwacks reverberated into the air. It was only when Eric approached the final corner that he saw where the sounds were coming from.

'What are you doing?' he said, picking up his pace and running towards the crumbling structure.

Sheets of chicken wire twisted as the pillars fell, the bean poles inside Norman's carefully constructed beanhouse reduced to nothing more than oversized splinters.

'That was ... that was ...'

Fleur poked her head out from behind the dismembered beanhouse.

'Sorry,' she said, wiping the sweat from her forehead with back of her hand. 'Did you say something?'

Eric opened his mouth.

'The ... the ... beanhouse,' he choked out.

With her sleeves rolled up and scarf around her neck, Fleur looked every bit a modern-day Felicity Kendal. Her large doe eyes blinked with endless lashes as she wiped her brow for a second time, then glanced at the massacre behind her.

'Oh, yes, nearly got rid of it. What a massive waste of space that was.'

Eric coughed and spluttered.

'It was a masterpiece. The beans Norman used to grow on them were—'

'Oh, I have no doubt it was very good at what it was meant for but really, beans? Runner beans? Who even eats them nowadays?'

'I ... I ...'

'After the war perhaps but not now. No, I'm sorry, this whole village show mentality, it's bonkers. In this day and age, the space needs to be utilised properly. All that worry going into growing a perfectly round onion when there are people starving. We should be growing food that people will eat and getting it to those in the community who need it.'

A lump formed in Eric's throat.

'Well, I—'

'Cooperative living, it's the way we've all got to head.'

She bent down and yanked a nail out from one of the planks.

'I figure I can repurpose this all one way or another. I was a bit of dab hand at DIY at school. Then I got married and well,' she paused mid-sentence, then looked up at Eric and smiled. 'Well, that's for another time. Anyway, what I'm saying is, I didn't pay what I paid for this plot to do some half-arsed attempt at pruning. I paid that money to grow vegetables and make a difference, and that's what I'm going to do, and I'll tell that to anyone who says otherwise.'

She bent down to the ground and plucked a two-foot hacksaw from the frosted grass. Eric swallowed.

'IT'S NOT that I don't respect the idea.'

Eric had gone back to the house for lunch. Abi had come inside for a snack break, and Suzy had also decided she needed a rest from staring at a screen.

'She's got some balls about her. Norman would like her, for sure. It's just the way she's gone about it. Smashing up someone's hard work with a sledgehammer. It's hardly respectful.'

'But like you said, if she's not going to use it, how else would you expect her to dismantle it?'

'Well.' Eric pouted and chewed on a stale mince pie.

He hadn't stayed long at the allotment. He couldn't concentrate. It had been harder than expected, seeing someone else in Norman's space, digging up the ground and trampling over the beds with complete disregard for the perfectly trimmed rows he had taken years to cultivate. Every time the shed door opened, Eric had expected to see him, hobbling out, coughing over his tea and fruit cake.

'Perhaps I'll focus on the house for a bit,' Eric said. 'Give her time to get her bearings down at the allotment. I don't want to come across as some possessive nutter. Particularly as she seems like a fairly normal person.'

'Well, I'm glad you like her,' Suzy said, passing him a bowl of soup and removing the plate of mince pies from under his nose. 'Because I bumped into her at the Co-op and arranged to go for dinner tonight. Mum's agreed to babysit.'

'That wasn't exactly what I had in mind,' Eric said.

'It'll be fun. And we're going for tapas.'

A cold chill spread down Eric's spine.

CHAPTER 8

TAPAS WAS ERIC'S idea of a social nightmare. While bacon stuffed with dates and spicy chorizo stews easily topped his list of all-time favourite foods, it was the dining experience that caused him so much anxiety. There was no security to tapas; it was a free for all in the worst possible way. You had no control, no guarantee. Just because you ordered a portion of fried goats' cheese with organic honey drizzle and a traditional Spanish tortilla, there was no way to ensure you would actually get to eat any of them. Even tapas with Suzy could swing either way. The only way for Eric to guarantee he got what he wanted was to over order. By a lot. Either that or order food he knew Suzy didn't like, and that just made him look like a prick. Going for tapas was a minefield and in Eric's mind, one that should definitely be avoided with new people. Particularly new people you were trying to avoid. But the table had been booked, and so tapas it was.

Eric's stomach was already rumbling as they pushed open the door. Shrill Latino music assaulted him from every side. He took a moment to scan the restaurant floor. The dining area was generically decorated with bright yellow walls, patterned accent tiles, and enough pieces of crockery to stock the nearest Tesco homewares department. Coloured glass bottles were strung from the ceiling as light fittings, and an upturned ham took centre stage on the bar, hoof and all.

'Look, there she is,' Suzy said, and pointed to the farthest of the four occupied tables.

Fleur was sitting with her back to the room, her head bent over the table, apparently reading her phone. Behind her, the kitchen door swung open and shut as members of the waiting staff busied themselves with orders and empty plates.

'Fleur?'

Fleur jolted from her seat, spinning around to face them.

'Sorry,' she said. 'I didn't see you there.'

Although immaculately dressed – in a mustard coloured cowl and jeans skinnier than Eric's forearms – her eyes were red rimmed, and a blotchy pinkness mottled her skin. Fleur grabbed a napkin off the table and blotted her cheeks. Suzy went straight in for a hug. Eric felt his body involuntarily recoil. Crying women took his tapas nightmare to a whole new level; he could only pray that the blotchy face was nothing more than an allergy to desiccated hydrangeas.

'Is everything okay?' Suzy asked, withdrawing from the hug and pulling out the seat closest.

'Oh, yes. I'm sorry. You just caught me by surprise.'

'We can always rearrange if now isn't a good time?'

'Really, I'm just being silly,' she said as she pushed back her seat and rose to standing. 'Everything's fine. Please, sit down.'

Eric quickly chose a seat, so he could see the food coming out of the kitchen.

'I wasn't sure if you'd want beer or sangria, so I ordered a jug of both,' said Fleur.

While the women chatted and poured the drinks, Eric *umm*ed and *ahh*ed in a half-listening manner. The menu had a good selection of food with all the classics; calamari, gambas al pil-pil, and a few unique items too, although Eric's mind was focused not on the dishes themselves, rather on portion sizes. Since their arrival at the restaurant, his stomach murmurings had gone from relaxed grumbles to angry snarls. It needed filling.

How many did they need? Eric pondered, his eyes still wandering up and down the list of small plates. Nine? Ten? The menu offered no indication of what was clearly a crucial piece of information. There was a deal on if you bought six plates, but that was definitely not going to be enough, and yet twelve between the three of them seemed greedy.

'Are you ready to order?' asked the waiter in his crisp white shirt, an iPad in hand.

'Yes, I—'

'Oh, we've barely looked,' Fleur said. 'Would you mind giving us another minute?' she smiled to the waiter.

'No problem.'

Eric's stomach growled in protest. A little of the growl escaped through his lips. Suzy shot him a glare. As the waiter retreated back behind the bar, the ladies turned their attention to their menus. Eric continued to scowl.

'It all sounds delicious,' Suzy said. 'Do we want to get our own meal, or should we just share a few dishes?'

'Oh, I'm more than happy to share,' Fleur said. 'I had a late lunch, so I'm really not that hungry at all.'

Eric's stomach loosened a little.

'Well, that's great,' he said. 'Shall I order then? Patatas bravas, meatballs, chorizo, jamon iberico. We definitely want two of the dates in bacon.'

Suzy frowned.

'I think that's a bit excessive.'

'Trust me, they'll be delicious.'

'Hmm, I'm not sure. I'm not exactly a date fan.'

'And I'm really not hungry,' Fleur reiterated.

'Just get one,' Suzy said. 'It'll be plenty, neither of us will eat them.'

Reluctantly, Eric gave in, although he insisted on a few more items to bulk the selection out. When the waiter came over and took the order, there were a total of seven dishes. It wasn't exactly a banquet, but provided the portions were reasonable sized it would be fine.

When the first dish came out, Eric was pleasantly surprised. The beef meatballs were firm but not dry and the sauce well-seasoned, although after a few mouthfuls he found himself even more hungry than before he began eating. The patatas bravas filled a hole, and the calamari had a good batter even if the squid was little on the chewy side. Then came the dates in the bacon.

Layered in the small ceramic dish sat five perfectly tooth-picked ovals. Caramelised and golden, the flavours of crispy fried bacon and sweet datey goodness spiralled up with the steam. Eric swallowed down a mouthful of saliva as the waiter placed them down in the centre of the table.

'They look good,' Fleur said and stabbed her fork into the one on top. Without a millisecond's pause the toothpick was discarded and the bite size delicacy devoured. Her eyes closed as her lips smacked together.

'*Umm, ohh*. Suzy, Eric, you have got to try these.'

More than willing to oblige, Eric readied his cutlery, but before he could raise his fork, Fleur pulled the dish out from beside him and placed it next to Suzy. Suzy delved straight in without a second's glance at her husband. It was like a dagger in his chest.

Eric winced in distress and considered his options. The plate was diagonally across from him, and stretching over for one would mean reaching directly across Fleur's plate. It wasn't exactly polite, but then she hadn't shown great manners when she stole it from under his nose either. He hesitated a moment, then went to speak.

'Could you—'

'Wow. They really are good,' Suzy said.

'I know.'

'I really didn't think I liked dates either,' she continued.

'Would it be possible for you to—' Eric tried.

'And they're really moreish.'

'Can I—'

Suzy's fork was poised for a second helping.

'I'm definitely coming back for more of these.'

'Could one of you please—'

Eric flinched as the prongs speared the bacon. She was his wife and the love of his life, but as she lifted the fork and placed it between her lips, he hoped she'd spear her tongue on it. The blood pulsed in his temples. The fork trembled in his hand. It was an unreasonable reaction. He knew it was. Then again, they hadn't even wanted to order them.

It was Fleur's turn to go in for second one. Neglecting the fork, she went straight for the toothpick. Her cleanly shaped nails inched towards the bowl for her second helping. Maybe she'd even grab two. Eric panicked. Maybe there would be none left for him at all.

He reached across the table, swiped the plate from under her hand and tucked it well and truly out of anyone else's reach. Then, stripping one of the dates from their toothpick mediator, he stuffed the penultimate tapas into his mouth. When he looked back up, both women were staring at him, mouths agape.

'I thought you weren't hungry,' Eric said.

After four minutes, an extended silence, and an excessively forceful kick on the shin for Eric, Fleur left to go to the bathroom.

'Well, that was just embarrassing,' Suzy said. 'What the hell's got into you?'

'You said you didn't want them.' Eric pouted his response. 'And then you were eating them all. And she said she wasn't hungry. And they are my favourite.'

'Are you five?' Suzy said.

Eric pouted.

'You're a grown man. You could have ordered some more, for Christ's sake. God knows what Fleur thinks. Honestly, Eric, would it hurt you to think of someone other than yourself for once?'

Eric continued to sulk. Admittedly, the idea of ordering more had escaped him at the time, but he couldn't possibly do that now. The remaining date sat turning cold in the dish, the crisp bacon fat congealing into white jelly as it cooled. Eric poured himself another glass of beer.

'You seem to forget, I need friends too,' Suzy said, her face stern, but then her voice came out a little softer, sadder. 'It's fine for you, you have your gardening gang, you have your weekly get together at the pub. And Abi seems to know every child under the age of fifteen in the place. But I don't have anyone. I sit in my little room all day, trying to meet my deadlines. With you not working, I don't even meet the mums at the school gates. Fleur could be a real friend for me. Please don't ruin that.'

Eric's pout loosened. He lifted his gaze from the congealing tapas.

'Sorry,' he said.

'I need you to think of me now and again,' she said. 'Or at least try to.'

'Sorry,' he said again.

Two minutes later, and after deciding that a cold date in bacon was substantially better than none, he spoke again.

'Do you think she's all right?' Eric said. 'She's been gone a long time.'

'She's probably waiting to see if you're going to bite her head off again.'

'I should probably apologise for that.'

'You think?'

It was another two minutes before Fleur appeared from the bathroom. Eric was polishing off the last of the lager from the jug.

This time the evidence of crying was far less subtle than blotchy cheeks. Thick lines of mascara streaked her face while clear snot dribbled from her nose.

'What's the matter?' Suzy said rising, from her seat.

Her new friend buried her snotty nose in her shoulder.

'It's ... it's ...' She could barely get a word out before dissolving back into more hysterical tears.

Eric stood up and backed away. He watched on, unsure whether he was meant to input some form of support to aid Suzy, or merely reassure the rest of the diners that this emotional outpouring was the result of an over-fried frittata.

'Well,' he said. 'Perhaps I should leave you ladies to it.'

Suzy glanced over Fleur's shoulder and gave him an approving nod.

'Suze, I'll see you at home in a bit. Fleur ...'

He moved forward just far enough to tap her shoulder with his outstretched arm.

'Sorry about the dates.'

※

'Well,' Suzy said, later that evening. 'It's all about the ex.'

They sat in the lounge sipping their gin and tonics. Eric had walked back home via the chip shop and treated himself to a fully loaded chicken kebab. It had been a worthwhile indulgence, even if his stomach now felt like it had been spread with butter and deep fried in a pan of boiling chip fat. Yvette had been meditating in the conservatory when he returned, although one whiff of the chili sauce and mayonnaise was all it had taken for her to retreat upstairs to the spare bedroom. Occasional thumps echoed down from above him, although Eric deemed them quiet enough to assume his mother-in-law had not yet collapsed from her yogic exercises.

The lights blinked on the Norwegian spruce. Despite its outwardly dense appearance, the needles were starting to drop at an accelerated pace.

While the deterioration of such a magnificent tree was saddening to watch, Eric had been told that the needles made excellent mulch for strawberries to sit on. Another entry for the village show, perhaps?

'Apparently, she'd given him an ultimatum, and it had not gone to plan,' Suzy elaborated, rousing Eric from his daydream of coloured rosettes and certificates. 'She's devastated, obviously. Eight years they'd been married. Together another five before that.'

'It's a long time,' Eric said, offering what he thought was a reasonable response, while continuing to mull over the best way to remove the rest of the needles for his strawberry mulch.

'I know. Being alone like that after all this time. It must be so hard.'

'Uh-uh.'

'I know what it was like when Pete and I split up. It was tough, really tough.'

Eric's ears pricked at the name Pete. It wasn't often that Suzy mentioned her ex-husband's name, but when she did, it caused an irrational heat to build up through Eric's belly, much the same way it did when someone prohibited the eating of his favourite tapas.

'Well, that's all done and dusted now,' he said attempting to steer his wife away from the topic of her Pete. 'I'm sure Fleur will be better off in the long run.'

'Maybe. I hope she's all right. Maybe you could do a little digging while you're at the allotment? See if there's anything you can do to help,' Suzy said.

'Digging at the allotment, eh? And you say you're not a comedian.' Eric grinned.

Suzy rolled her eyes and handed Eric her glass.

'One more before bed?' she said.

※

THURSDAY WAS New Year's Eve, and in complete contrast to the previous year's festivities – during which Eric was so high on painkillers that one brandy near enough floored him for the best part of January – he took no shame in indulging in Hank's homemade beverages from the moment they arrived. It was a social event, with what appeared to be two-thirds of the village in attendance. Fortunately, Hank and Jerry's five-bed detached house sat just six doors down from their own, well within stumbling distance.

From elderflower champagne and black currant liqueur, to pumpkin ale and liquorice stout, Eric left no stone unturned. In his defence, he wasn't entirely to blame.

'Now this one is from two thousand and twelve,' Hank's husband Jerry said, handing Eric a glass of something purple. 'Don't be put off by the bit of residue. I'm telling you, it's an absolute corker. And when you finish that one off, I've got a corker of a scrumpy for you to try too.'

Suzy had invited Fleur along to the bash, but after less than an hour she decided she really wasn't in the mood for a party.

'You don't mind, do you?' she said, resting her hand on Eric's shoulder as she said her farewells. 'I'm sure I'll see you down the allotment soon.'

Eric would have waved her goodbye, but that would have risked spilling one of his drinks. Yvette had also accompanied them for part of the night, although she too slipped out just before midnight.

'We've never spent a New Year apart you know, your father and I,' she said, swishing her feather boa around her neck as she prepared to leave. 'Not in forty-two years. No, he's terribly down about it. Terribly down.'

'We understand.'

'You won't hold it against me, will you? Poor Abi. I'd said I'd dance with her at midnight, I was going to teach her to salsa.'

'It's fine, Yvette, honestly,' Eric reassured her. 'There are plenty of us here to look after Abs.'

'Just give Dad our love,' Suzy added.

'I always do,' she said, and she glided out the front door, her tinselled tiara glinting as she went.

'Peculiar woman, your mother-in-law,' Jerry said, watching the front door close. 'Just offered to show me how to do the Argentine tango.'

'She's a dancer,' Eric said.

'In the bedroom,' Jerry replied.

CHAPTER 9

ERIC WAS WOKEN by the smell of coffee wafting temptingly beneath his nostrils. There was an intense fuzziness to his head that was somewhat disorientating. He rolled over, clicking the joints in his back and his neck. He wasn't in his bed, he could tell that, but the actual knowledge of where he was, or how he got there was almost entirely missing. His eyes flickered beneath their lids.

'Freshly made,' Suzy said. 'Colombian. Your favourite.'

Her voice hit like a sledgehammer. Eric gasped and jolted upwards. Five seconds later and there was still a reverb echoing around between his temples.

'Woah ...' Eric covered his ears as he struggled to sit himself up, finding it rather more difficult to maintain his balance than expected.

A few seconds later, he opened his eyes.

'Why's it so bright?'

He grabbed for a pillow, but underestimating the distance between his hand and the cushion, he fell back onto the sofa with a thud.

'It's not bright,' Suzy said. She pushed him back up into a seated position, pulled his shirt back down over his middle, and placed the mug of coffee in his hand. 'That's what happens when you drink for six hours straight.'

'My head hurts,' he said.

'That's not a surprise.'

Eric blinked and attempted to move his eyelids again. The pain of a thousand needles puncturing his skull and impaling whatever grey matter lay beyond shot through to the back of his head.

'Oh my God. How much did you let me drink?'

'*Let you?* Since when did I *let you* do anything?'

'*Urgh*, this cannot be real.'

The room was spinning. Suzy's choice of baby-blue coloured walls that had once seemed bearable now caused waves of seasickness. The aroma of the coffee, undoubtedly freshly ground and Colombian, went instantaneously from mouth-wateringly appealing to gut-wrenchingly nauseating.

'I'll just leave this here for you, shall I?' Suzy said, then moved the coffee table a good ten inches closer to Eric before she took the coffee cup back from his grip and placed it down on the table top.

After twenty-minutes of lying perfectly still, Eric found that if he focused his attention on one single point, he could slow the room's motion enough to move his coffee mug, but any accidental sideways glances and he was back to where he started. As such, he decided that the gap from the table to his mouth – although substantially reduced due to Suzy's kind heartedness – was still too far to risk. He lowered himself off the sofa and onto his knees. In a carefully considered movement, he lifted the mug up to his mouth for a sip. The drink was stone cold, but the response was instant. As well as a double shot, the coffee had been spiked with several spoons of sugar and a good-sized glug of rum. She was a good woman, his wife, Eric decided.

He was half a mug in before he found the spinning had lessened to a more controllable level.

'Drink this too,' Suzy said, returning to his side with a glass of water. 'And take these,' she added, passing him two small painkillers.

While Eric tried to decide whether the swirly pattern on the ceiling was an optical illusion or just another result of his ridiculous lack of balance, Suzy perched on the end of the sofa.

'I'm worried about Mum,' she said.

'You're always worried about your mum,' he slurred.

'I know, but this is different. And I can't get through to Dad either.'

'I thought Lydia was dealing with him.'

'She's tried. He just says he's really busy and gets off the line as soon as possible.'

'Perhaps he *is* really busy.'

'Perhaps.'

'Look,' Eric said, sensing his wife's need for support and recalling their conversation at the tapas restaurant only days earlier.

He pushed himself a little higher in the seat and immediately rued the decision. The speed of his action resulted in a spiral head rush. Images of dancing with Jerry to 'Radio Ga Ga' surfaced from some recess of his mind. Closing his eyes, Eric took several deep breaths before deciding he was stable enough to move again. He took one more substantial breath, opened his eyes, and tried to muster his most sensible husbanding voice.

'Your parents are adults,' he said, attempting to fixate on only one of Suzy's several sets of moving eyes. 'If something was up, they would have said. Perhaps they just need a little break from one another? They live on a boat together. They probably need a little space now and again.'

'They live on a six-hundred-foot cruise liner. It's hardly like they live on a barge.'

'Still, it probably gets claustrophobic now and then. Where is your mum, by the way? Please don't make me eat that granola again. I can't do it. Not today.'

'She's taken Abi sale shopping.'

'You mean we have an empty house?'

'We do,' said Suzy with a smile.

Eric and Suzy took immediate advantage of the empty house. After a *very* brief discussion on the merits of indulging in a little X-rated adult-only time, Eric instead went back upstairs to sleep off some more of the alcohol in his system while Suzy tucked herself away in the office and carried on writing. It seemed like a much more productive use of time, considering Suzy's impending deadlines and Eric's horrific hangover.

BY MIDDAY ERIC found that he could open his eyes without thinking he was going to vomit. He showered, cleaned his teeth with a double swill of a mint mouthwash – which he regretted instantly given the menthol schnapps tang still clinging to his tongue – and took another two paracetamol before heading back downstairs.

'What did you have planned for today?' Suzy said. 'I thought if you had time, we could pick out colours for the bedroom.'

'As long as I don't have to think.'

'You very rarely do,' Suzy answered.

It was slow work, narrowing down the hundreds of sample colours to one final choice. It was particularly hard work given that Eric was having extreme difficulty understanding exactly why thirty-six different shades of white were necessary, and if there was actually any difference between light white, pristine white, and perfect, bright white. But it was time spent with Suzy, and in the recent months that had been hard to come by.

The pair were sitting at the kitchen table, with Suzy deliberating between a buttercup and primrose yellow for the kitchen and Eric picking at various scratches, gouges, and encrustations that covered the ancient table top, when the slam of the front door echoed through the house. The single noise was followed by the rustling of paper and much excited shouting.

'Mum? Daddy?'

'In here,' they called in unison.

Eric took a large gulp of his coffee and debated whether it was too early to risk yet another two paracetamol. Given that the previous two had been swallowed only minutes before, he decided it was probably not a good idea.

Abi emerged through the doorway submerged in a sea of paper and plastic. Her hair was draped around her shoulders and a new, purple handbag dangled from her arm. Her striped bobble hat had been replaced by a canary yellow beret, which perched on her head at a jaunty angle. Around her wrists jangled three inches worth of metal bangles.

'Granny and I went shopping,' she said.

'I can see,' said Suzy.

'We bought stuff. A lot of stuff.'

'I can see that too.'

There must have been forty bags of every colour, shape, size, and texture ever manufactured. Yvette followed Abi into the kitchen, equally cloaked in bags, and complete with a matching canary yellow beret.

'Well, what is a grandma for?' she said.

'Look at these,' Abi said as she pulled out her fifth pair of shoes in a row and piled them onto the mountain of clothes already built up on the kitchen table. 'They're tap shoes. Granny's going to teach me tap dancing, aren't you, Granny?'

'I am.'

'As well as ballet, jazz, and ballroom?' Eric said.

'Children need a well-rounded education, Eric. And there's nowhere around here she can learn.'

'And wait until you see this dress, Daddy, it's amazing.'

Abi bent down to rummage in the shopping bags around her feet.

'Which one is it in, Granny?'

'Is it over there?'

As Abi leant to the side, reaching for a yellow, polka-dot bag, something glinted in the light.

'What's that?' Eric said.

Abi bolted upright.

'Nothing. What? There's nothing.'

She flattened her hair down against the side of her cheek. Another glint snuck its way out from underneath. Eric jumped up from his seat.

'There,' he said. '*What* is that?'

'Dad!'

'What the hell have you done to yourself?'

'Dad, get off!'

'You get here right now, young lady.'

'Eric!'

Abi squirmed and wriggled as Eric tried to get a hold on her. A two-minute wrangle later and he had his daughter bent over his knee, her hair tucked behind her ear, the tiny gold studs sparkling in her ear lobes.

'You have got to be kidding me,' Eric said.

Abi slipped out of his grip and ran over to her grandma.

'Eric, please,' Yvette said.

Eric's eyes flashed.

'You? You are behind this. You mutilated my daughter.'

'It's not a big deal, Dad. All the girls at school have it done.'

'If all the girls at school got a tattoo of a leprechaun on their faces, would you do that too?'

'What's a leprechaun?'

Eric couldn't answer. The blood pounded in his veins. Every muscle quivered. He took a step towards his mother-in-law.

'Eric, leave this to me.'

The coldness in the voice stopped Eric in his tracks. Suzy was standing behind him. Her hands were relaxed, hanging loosely at her side, and her lips were held in a soft, upward curl that, if you didn't know her, may lead you to believe she was perfectly at ease with the current situation. However, Eric did know his wife, and the cold look that simmered deep behind her pupils caused an icy chill to run all the way down his spine; a sensation he saw reciprocated in both the youngest and oldest member of the family.

'Abigail,' Suzy said with a voice so calm it prickled the skin on Eric's neck. 'Go upstairs to your bedroom please. Daddy and I need to have a word with your grandmother.'

Abi turned to go.

'But don't think you're off the hook either, young lady. I will deal with you later.'

Abi offered her grandmother a last apologetic look before darting off up the stairs.

'Shall we sit down?' Suzy said, her voice still dangerously quiet.

Yvette stiffened and sucked in her cheeks.

'I tend to find my back gets a little—'

'Sit,' Suzy said.

Eric shot down into a chair.

Despite causing the initial uproar, Eric felt it was best to sit back and let Suzy administer the reprimand. He did, however, offer his support through strategically placed coughs and unwavering glowers at Yvette.

Two minutes into Suzy's carefully procured silence and Yvette's lips began to twitch. As did her feet, then her fingers.

'What's wrong with a grandmother spoiling her granddaughter?' she said, finally obliterating the silence. 'Is it that wrong that I want her to be happy?'

Suzy pursed her lips a little but emitted no sound. Yvette's blinking grew more rapid. Eric could see the sweat beading along her brow line.

'So, I might have gone a little overboard. I got carried away. You can hardly punish me for that? I hardly see her. And you move her to this backward little town where they don't even have dance lessons. I mean what kind of parent—'

'Our parenting is not what's being questioned here. You knowingly went against our wishes,' said Suzy. 'You knew she was not allowed to get her ears pierced. You deliberately undermined Eric and me.'

'I wouldn't say—'

'You turn up out of the blue and knowingly disrespect our wishes.'

'All the girls—'

'Mother!' Suzy slammed the palm of her hand against the table, causing several pairs of diamante-studded tights to fall to the ground.

Suzy took a deep breath in through her nose. Eric followed suit.

'Here's what is going to happen. Tomorrow, you and Abi are going back to Chelmsford, and you're going to return every single item you bought—'

'Susan—'

'This is not up for debate. You will return every item on this table. And if it can't be returned, you will give it away. Red Cross, Salvation Army, I do not care. You will make Abi explain to every single shopkeeper that the reason she is returning them is because she deliberately disobeyed her parents. You will record every single exchange and send me the video as it happens. If you do not—'

'You can't seriously—'

'If you do not,' Suzy continued. 'I will ring up the Barbican Centre and tell them exactly who was responsible for the vandalism of the ladies' toilet in 2004.'

Yvette's jaw dropped.

'You wouldn't dare.'

'Wouldn't I? I have the photos, remember? And from what I recall, they're not taken from your most flattering angle.'

Yvette swallowed.

❧

LATER THAN NIGHT, Eric sat on the bed, the handful of Polaroid photos having nearly burnt a hole through his cornea.

'Apparently it was a protest against modern art,' Suzy said.

'She doesn't look like she's protesting,' Eric said. 'Why did you show me these exactly?'

'I've had to bear the burden too long, it's only fair you should have some of it too,' she said.

Somewhere in one of the walls a pipe growled.

'Oh, that reminds me,' Eric said. 'The plumber called. He can't make it until next week.'

Suzy let out a groan, which transformed part way through into a yawn.

'What's another couple of days?' she said.

CHAPTER 10

ON THE TUESDAY, Abi went back to school. While it gave Eric more space to deal with things like mould-riddled floorboards and paint stripper, Suzy was having to spend the week up in London; an April deadline appearing infinitely closer in January than it had only days before in December. This meant that Eric had an even more undiluted Yvette to deal with. By Friday, he had reached his limit.

Every corner he turned she was there, offering to help, be it stripping the hallway carpet or offering to whip him up a nut roast.

'I can run that to the tip, if you like?' she said as Eric worked on the staircase.

Starting at the top, he yanked the first part of the banister away from the railing. It wasn't just a case of aesthetics when it came to the staircase. Since the moment they'd moved in, Eric had been paranoid that the banister was going to collapse, and Abi would end up in A&E as a result.

'Won't take me a jiffy,' Yvette continued. 'And you might as well make the most of this insurance you're paying for.'

'It's fine,' Eric panted as he moved upwards before throwing another piece down with a clatter. 'I'm going to be repurposing the wood.'

Eric busied himself with the next balustrade.

'I saw some lovely bar stools made from old belts,' Yvette continued. 'And picture frames made from toilet seats. You can do some wonders with just a little imagination and lacquer. What were you thinking of doing? Something for the house, I assume, although I suppose you could make something for that little allotment of yours too.'

Eric groaned inwardly. After the earring incident, Yvette had been on her best behaviour, even to the extent of baking vegan lemon drizzle cake to try to appease them. She spent the days running around with the vacuum, washing all their laundry in organic non-biological liquid and soap nuts. Four days of Yvette's constant *helping* had seen his patience grow increasingly thin, but her attempts to help with the DIY were the most trying. So far, Eric had managed to deter her, mainly by sending her on endless errands to the shops.

'Well, I think that's a marvellous idea. Make do and mend. That's what I say.'

'Yes, well, that's the plan,' Eric mumbled. 'Sorry, Yvette, was there something you wanted?'

'Silly me. I'm in the way again, aren't I?'

'Well ...' Eric smiled apologetically.

'Don't say another word,' she said. 'You won't hear a peep out of me for the rest of day. I promise.'

Without so much as a goodbye, she trotted off downstairs whistling a Rodgers and Hammerstein melody. Eric waited for half a minute before casting his gaze down the length of the staircase. It really was a mess. He had hoped he could just remove and replace the worst of the balustrades, but now he wasn't so sure. There seemed to be more wonky parts than straight. Squinting, he cocked his head; it was difficult to get a clear picture of how bad it was from where he was standing. What he needed was to be on the other side.

Without giving himself a chance to rethink the action, he slipped his leg over the banister onto the outside of the staircase, hoping the different angle might throw up a better solution to the problem. His foot wobbled precariously as he tried to balance his weight.

'Peppermint tea?' Yvette asked, suddenly materialising at the foot of stairs and causing him to start backwards. 'It's organic.'

Eric grabbed the handrail and pulled himself tight in, his heart racing.

'Yvette!'

'Is this not a good time?'

'Clearly not.'

'Oh, yes. I hadn't noticed. You want to be careful standing like that. You could really hurt yourself if you fall.'

'You don't say?'

Yvette reddened and crouched down, placing the mug on the steps. 'Perhaps I should just leave it here.'

Eric took a deep breath in. When he exhaled, he forced his mouth into a smile.

'Why don't you take it into the kitchen? I'll be down in just a minute.'

Yvette picked the mug back up.

'Well, perhaps I'll do us a little something for lunch.'

'That would be great,' he said, the smile now so forced it was making his cheeks ache. 'I'll be down in just a minute.'

The moment her footsteps disappeared into the kitchen, Eric leapt back over the handrail, bolted down the stairs, and raced out the door, picking up his car keys as he went.

***

THE GREASE WAS GOOD. When his Wimpy Git was finished, Eric ordered another side of black pudding and a cappuccino with extra froth and chocolate sprinkles. He didn't even feel guilty. He had earned it in dry breakfast cereal and zero-taste nut milk. While he was finishing off his second beverage, a familiar barking piped up outside. Hank waved through the window. A minute later he hobbled in and sat down next to Eric.

'How've you been?' he said, helping himself to one of Eric's slices of cold toast. 'Not seen you since New Year? Still got the mother-in-law with you?'

'Yep, and for a while longer, I suspect.'

'Must be nice to have her about though. Some help with Abs and all?'

Eric raised his eyebrow. Hank laughed.

'Fine,' he said. 'Enough said.'

Griff walked past, and Hank paused to order himself a builder's tea and a piece of shortbread.

'You've not been down to your plot this week at all?' he said.

'No, I need to get down there though, sort out my sowing if I'm going to get anything decent for the show. I was thinking I might go in for spring onions. Abi grew some great ones last year.'

'Think you'll be in with a grand chance then? Have to say it's all about the runners this year.'

'Oh?'

'Well, old Norman had that one in the bag, didn't he? Nine years in a row. Can you imagine? That beats my sloe gin.'

Eric laughed.

'Now everyone from Janice to that doddering old Wilf on plot twenty-two thinks they're in with a chance.'

'That feels like a bit too much competition for me,' Eric said.

'*Ahh*, but I got an ace. Norman told me his secret last year, you see. Knew he was moving on obviously. Guess he didn't want anyone else stealing his legacy.'

Hank leant back in his chair and slipped a piece of toast down to Scout.

'Not a chance one of them's gonna beat me.'

Eric downed the dregs of his cappuccino.

'So, what is it? This secret?'

Hank threw back his head, emitting a nasal half-snort as he did.

'You'll have to wait until I'm on my deathbed,' he said.

THE CONVERSATION WITH HANK, combined with his unwavering desire to avoid Yvette, resulted in Eric heading down to the allotment rather than straight back home. It had been a little over a week since his last trip there. Thick frost had built in layers over the untilled earth and the scent of camping stoves and heaters filled the air.

At Eric's plot, things were not as good as he had hoped. During the first week of December, he made the decision to lay thick fleece on his outdoor beds to protect his parsnips from the icy mornings. The last time he had checked, he thought it was doing its job, but on closer inspection the lack of attention and bad weather had taken its toll. Eric pulled up handful after handful of black-ringed rotten roots; carrots, turnips, and in another couple of days his leeks would have been past saving too. Hoping that an emergency relocation session – or *heeling in* as he had recently learnt the correct term to be – would save the majority, and aware of the limits on his time, he knelt down and started digging them up.

'*Psst*, Eric, over here.'

Eric was a quarter of the way through the digging up process when the voice caused him to stop. Brushing the soil from his hands, he glanced upwards and then, unable to see anyone, rose to his feet and looked around.

'Eric, over here. No, this way. This way! Towards the bush, yes, that's it. Over here!'

Eric frowned and stepped towards the tall hedgerow that marked the edge of the allotment.

'Is someone there?' he asked, feeling more than a little embarrassed. 'Maggie, is that you?'

Maggie, Cynthia and Norman's niece, was Burlam's local police constable and resident prankster.

'If this is one of your tricks—'

'No, no it's Fleur.'

'Fleur?'

'Yes.'

She spoke hurriedly.

'Could you give me a bit of hand? There's a gate just in here—'

'A gate? Are you sure?' Eric stared into the hedgerow, seeing nothing but nasty looking thorns and berries.

'Yes, of course I am. Look, I'm going to push it open from the other side. But I'm going to need you to give me a hand. It's pretty well welded in with all these branches. If you could just grab hold and give it a tug—'

'I'm not sure—'

'Here I go. Three, two, one—'

Eric sprang back as a wall of thorns thrust outwards towards him. Behind it he could just make out the thin wooden planks of a gate.

'Can you grab hold of it?' Fleur asked. 'That's all I can do from my side.'

Eric stared at the bush and shook his head.

'It's not going to move. Why don't you come around the normal way? And how did you even know there was a gate here?'

There was a short pause.

'No, I need to come this way. Maybe you'll need to cut back a few of the branches?'

'I'm not sure—'

'There's a pruning saw in my shed. That should do it, shouldn't it?'

'I don't understand why—'

'Look.' Her voice was sharp, but only for a second. A moment later it was a smooth as melted butter. 'It'll take five minutes. That's all. I promise. And I promise you'll like what I'm going to show you.'

Eric hesitated. The last thing he wanted to do was waste all his allotment time helping Fleur, but then Suzy had asked him to be nice. Chopping down hedgerows had to constitute nice.

'Five minutes,' Eric relented. 'But if I can't get it open, then you'll just have to come in the normal way.'

'You're an angel,' Fleur said.

It took substantially more than five minutes for Eric to free the gate from its well-embedded nest in the holly bush. The prickly leaves were firmly twisted around the hinges and handle. When the last branch finally snapped, and the wooden gate sprang all the way open, Fleur leapt through the gap and wrapped her arms around him.

'Oh, you superstar,' she said. 'I knew you could do it.'

Once released, Eric peered over her shoulder into the space beyond.

'Whose garden is that?' he said.

Fleur shrugged.

'Some young couple. Jenny and Dan? Ellie and Stan? I can't quite remember. Wasn't it a find though, this gate? I spotted it the other day.'

'And they are okay with you doing this? Jenny and Stan, or whoever?'

'Oh, yes. I mean, they didn't even realise there were allotments back here. And when I offered to pay them with eggs—'

'Eggs?' Eric interrupted. 'Why would you pay them with eggs?'

The corner of Fleur's mouth rose in a tight-lipped smile. Her eyes darted about as she gave the surrounding area a quick once over. When she was sure the coast was clear, she stepped forwards out of the gateway revealing a large metal crate behind her.

Eric gasped.

'Eric,' Fleur said, her voice a sweet mixture of mischief and excitement. 'I'd like you to meet the girls.'

CHAPTER 11

'YOU'VE GOT CHICKENS,' Eric stammered out for the third time. 'How have you got chickens?'

Eric's stomach was both squirming and fluttering. The crate was uncomfortably full with at least half a dozen large, brown hens. A mass of feathers and claws poked out at various angles, and as Fleur approached, their squawking crescendoed to a new level.

'Can you give me a hand?' Fleur said and beckoned Eric to take hold of the crate. 'Honestly, you're a lifesaver. I don't know what I would have done if you weren't there. I would never have got that gate open without you. I'd have probably had to keep them in my kitchen. And I'm not sure what my neighbours would think to that. Those old cottages don't exactly come with soundproofing.'

'But where …? How …?' Eric stammered numbly as he moved through the hedge and into the garden.

It was a smallish backyard, crammed with a four-foot pond, child's swing, and small patio set left to rust in the winter air. His insides continued squirming as he took hold of the crate, and they maneuvered it back through the hedge, into the allotments, and across to Fleur's plot.

'I can't believe you've got chickens,' he continued to mutter.

Eric had the unfortunate job of walking backwards. It was a short trip, thirty metres at most, but the metal dug into his fingers and when he finally dropped it down beside her shed, a blast of air escaped his lungs.

'Poor things,' Fleur said crouching down beside the crate. 'Aren't they beautiful?'

Eric took a step back. Beautiful was not the word he would have used. On closer inspection, he suspected that beautiful was the last word he would have used. The beady-eyed birds glowered up at him with feathers more like vicious barbs than soft down. Their heads and backs were pink and raw, and when they opened their beaks, it was with a squawk that he was fairly certain was chicken talk for *We're going to murder you all*.

'They were battery hens,' Fleur said, reaching her hand through to stroke them. There was a flash of yellow as one of the hens flew for her. Oblivious, Fleur continued to fish for its affection while it clawed at her hand.

'If I hadn't taken them, they were going to be killed. Just because they're old. Isn't that terrible? They're completely healthy still, and more importantly ... laying.'

As Eric glossed over the words *completely healthy*, another thought struck him.

'What about the committee?' he said. 'Have you told them? You're not supposed to have chickens until they've been cleared by the committee. No one's got any at the minute, they might have even changed the rules.'

Retrieving her hand from the bird cage equivalent of a piranha tank, Fleur planted it firmly on her hip.

'Eric, did you not hear what I said? They were on death row. I'm sure those old dodderers won't mind skipping over a tiny bit of red tape when they learn it was a matter of life and death.'

Eric glanced into the cage. One particularly scrawny specimen had its beak and foot somehow trapped in the same wire loop. It squawked pitifully before Fleur noticed and pushed its appendages back inside. Survival of the fittest appeared not to apply in this situation.

'Anyway, they're not going to cause any problems,' Fleur said, moving across and opening up the door to her shed. 'I'll keep them in here for a few days while I finish off their hut—'

'A few days?'

'—and sound it out with the committee in the meantime.'

A tightening sensation was spreading its way across Eric's chest.

'But surely you could have told the committee before bringing them here. Surely you could have checked?'

'Eric, you of all people know that sometimes it's better to seek forgiveness than ask permission.'

She opened the cage from the top, took hold of one of the hens, pulled it out, and dropped it into Eric's arms. His muscles seized.

'Don't you think you should tell someone they're here now?' he said.

Ignoring his comment, Fleur stepped back, trampling on Norman's neat borders.

'Smile!' she said and whipped her phone out of her pocket for a photo.

Eric shuffled nervously trying to avoid both the razor-sharp talons and beak as she snapped away. After the impromptu photoshoot, she put her phone away, retrieved the chicken, and pushed it into the shed.

'Besides,' Fleur continued. 'You can hardly go and squeal on me. After all, you're my main accomplice.'

'Accomplice?' Eric paled.

Fleur grinned.

'Well, of course. It was you that hacked the hedge apart so that I could get them inside.'

'You asked me to!'

'And I'm fairly sure that cutting hedgerows without the RSPB's permission is illegal.'

'Illegal?'

'And it was you who trespassed on that poor couple's garden in order to sneak them in.'

'Trespassed?'

Eric felt even more blood drain from his extremities.

'I thought you had permission.'

'*I* did. Did *you*?'

ERIC WENT STRAIGHT to the pub, where he promptly ordered himself two pints. After finishing the first at the bar, he relocated to a corner table where he waited for his heart rate to lower fractionally before starting on his second. His hands were still quivering, and his throat felt as though he had swallowed several of the battery hens' mangy feathers.

'You all right?' the barman asked when he brought over a complimentary bowl of mixed nuts. 'You're not looking too great.'

'Never been better,' Eric said, shovelling the snacks into his mouth and spraying bits of saliva-covered nut onto the table as he went.

'Right then,' said the barman, stepping back cautiously. 'I'll leave you to it.'

It took until he was halfway through his second pint for his pulse to reach a point where he was no longer feeling it pounding in his chest. He sipped slowly as he mulled the situation over. A few days, that was when Fleur said she'd tell the committee. But what did a few days mean? Two days? Three? Four? A week? And what if someone had seen him helping? What if they told the committee in the meantime? If Eric lost the allotment plot, he wouldn't be able to uphold the bizarre conditions of his father's will and he would lose Sally too.

Eric shook his head clear. No, he couldn't bear the burden that long. He would go to the committee and tell them about the chickens himself. That was bound to be his best course of action. He would tell them. It wasn't as if Fleur had a leg to stand on. She'd already proven herself untrustworthy in how she'd come by her plot in the first place.

What Eric really needed to do was talk it over with Suzy. She was good with words. She would tell him how to phrase it, so the committee understood he had been misled. It was a pain not having her at home whenever he needed her, he mused. Eric had always known Suzy worked hard before they moved, but with him always at the office, he'd never really noticed *how* hard. Now it felt like he never saw her, particularly when she was working back in the city.

Hopefully, she wasn't going to be too late tonight. He would cook dinner; make sure there was no stress waiting for her when she got home. He pulled out his phone to check the time.

'Shit!'

Eric jumped up from the table, banging his knee and sending the remaining contents of his glass sloshing around.

'Everything all right?' the barman asked as Eric bolted past, throwing a ten pound note down on the bar as he went.

❦

ST JULIAN'S Primary School sat on the edge of the river with a view out over the estuary and a playground that had diminished from a football-pitch sized patch of land to little more than a tarmacked jungle gym in the last decade. In place of the school field stood a myriad of luxury apartments, along with a twenty-four-hour gym and yoga studio, inside which Eric had never seen more than three people at any one time.

He sprinted across the playground and into the reception area where he propped himself up against one of the brown chairs and attempted to catch his breath. It was the exact opposite of Abi's last school, where flat screen televisions took you through a virtual tour of the school upon entry. Here the reception was decorated with hand printed paper plates and a series of jungle animals made from recycled egg cups and tin cans. A school dinner aroma of baked beans, breaded chicken, and highly concentrated orange-squash clung to the air. It was only after a quick wipe of his forehead and a scan of the room that Eric realised the place was entirely empty.

He stepped up to the desk and rang the little metal bell. His heart was thumping in his chest, partly from the exertions of the run, partly from his own stupidity. A minute later a woman appeared. Mid-twenties and yawning widely, she appeared to have chosen her outfit from the *How to Dress like a Primary School Teacher* manual, with a colourful blouse and cardigan paired with a woollen skirt and thick tights. She offered Eric an acknowledging nod, then covered her mouth for one more quick yawn, after which she smiled apologetically.

'Sorry, Mr Sibley. I can't believe we've only been back a week. I feel like I need another holiday already. Is everything all right?'

'I'm so, so sorry I'm so late. Is she next door? I'll grab her things now.' Eric moved towards the classroom.

'Mr Sibley?'

'I completely lost track of time. Abi! Come on, hun, sorry I'm late.'

'Mr Sibley—'

Eric opened the classroom door. A series of patchwork paper elephants were scattered across the blue-green carpet, and a strong scent of PVA glue invaded his senses.

'Abi?'

The teacher appeared beside him. 'Sorry, Mr Sibley. I was trying to tell you. She's already gone.'

'Gone? With who?'

'With your mother-in-law. I thought you knew?'

❦

THE SOUND of cartoons drifted out through the open window. Eric's stomach twisted. There was no way out. He would have to go inside at some point. And better now than when Suzy was at home. Better to take one berating at a time; at least that way he may be able to get a word or two in for his defence. Not that he could think of any at that precise moment.

He took a couple of steadying breaths, then turned the key in the lock.

'Eric, is that you?' Yvette's voice sang through from the kitchen, the melodious twang a blade to his ears.

Abi was sitting on the living room floor, absorbed by the screen in front of her, mindlessly pulling crisps from a packet and popping them into her mouth.

'Good day at school, sweetie?' Eric said, his twisted insides contorting even further.

'Uh-uh,' Abi said, not moving her eyes from her screen, then she turned and added, 'and Granny's mad at you, by the way. She had to pick me up.'

'I'm sure she's not mad as such,' Eric started.

'She is.'

Eric stepped towards her and took one of her crisps.

'I'm really sorry. Did you have to wait for ages?'

Abi shrugged.

'It was fine. I played Jenga with Paul Cotral from Year Six. He's really good. He showed me how to make it really tall. And he has a BMX bike. He said maybe I could meet him at the park on Saturday, and he could show me how to do some stunts.

'Year Six? I'll teach him a thing or two about—'

'Eric?'

As timely as ever, Yvette's voice cut through the air. Eric shuddered.

'Could you come in here for a second please?' she called. 'I would like to have a little word.'

Eric swallowed. Abi shot him a half-hearted shrug.

'Good luck,' she said and went back to her crisps as Eric headed to the kitchen.

Yvette was waiting. Until that moment, Eric had assumed the phrase *grinning from ear to ear* was merely an expression. However, seeing his mother-in-law's face as she sat at his crappy kitchen table immediately dispelled that misconception. The woman had more teeth than any one human should ever have. Any power he had held over the previous week had evaporated in an instant.

'We all get caught up now and again,' Yvette said, her cheeks stretched almost to translucency. 'I'm sure it happens to everyone. Even when they don't have a job.'

'I was only a bit late,' Eric mumbled.

'A bit? My goodness, I'd like to know what you consider late then. The poor girl was distraught. Practically in tears.'

'She said she was playing Jenga.'

'No doubt to epitomise her crumpling spirit at the abandonment. Goodness knows what would have happened if I wasn't there to pick her up.'

'I suspect they'd have rung my mobile. Or Suzy's. It wasn't like they were going to throw her out into the Calais Jungle to fend for herself.'

Yvette tutted.

'Well, it just goes to show what I said all along. Men are just not up to the job of running a household.'

'Pardon?' Eric said feeling his eyes bug.

'Oh, it's not just you, Eric dear. It's all men. You don't have the genetics for it.'

'Excuse me?'

'At least when you were working, you were doing something. You were hardly a prize-winning husband, but at least the money was good. Now I'm not even sure why Suzy keeps you around when it's perfectly clear she'd be much better off without you.'

Eric's jaw hung slack. His stomach was positioned somewhere between his knees and his ankles. For a moment all he could hear was the blood pumping in his ear canals, and all he could see was a dirt brown, tomato-topped meatloaf.

CHAPTER 12

'NOBODY IS LEAVING this table until I find out exactly what is going on.'

Suzy had her hands on her hips. Her coat was still on and her handbag dropped at her feet where she stood. Abi was poised behind her, tentatively peering around her mother, not precisely sure what was going on, but judging by the expression on her face, well aware that the shit was about to hit the fan.

'Now is someone going to explain this to me or am I going to have to ask twice?'

Eric was red faced and red fingered. The tomato sauce from Yvette's meatless meatloaf – which had been lovingly prepared for the evening's supper – was smeared over his hands from where he had shovelled it out of the cast iron pan and lobbed it at his mother-in-law. Yvette, in turn, had gone at him with the bag of pine needles he had collected for the compost heap and had thrown the whole thing over his head. His back itched like hell as the needles stabbed between his shoulder blades, and dug into his collarbones, but there was no chance he was going to give Yvette the satisfaction of showing her that. Instead, he jostled his shoulders from side to side in hope of dislodging as many of the needles as possible. Yvette's grip was currently on a paper bag full of coffee grindings; the ultimate nitrogen fix for his compost. Eric gritted his teeth. Those things were like gold dust down the allotment.

'Mum? Eric?' Suzy spoke again.

Eric refused to lower his gaze.

'He forgot to pick up Abi,' said Yvette poking her finger pointedly in Eric's direction, spraying the ground with the precious black dust.

'You forgot to pick up Abi?' Suzy said.

'I was *late*,' he reinforced the word the best he could. 'And *she* said you would be better off without me.'

'Well, you would, Suzy darling!' Yvette continued.

'Says the mother who visits once a decade –' countered Eric.

'Well, I'm here *now*, aren't I?'

'Yes. You most definitely are. And why exactly is that? What are you hiding? What—'

'Children!'

Suzy's voice silenced them both. Eric's back molars ground together. The sound reverberated through his skull. Some of the pine needles had slipped down the back of his trousers now. A couple more inches and his itchiness was likely to take on a whole new level.

Suzy tried again.

'Will someone please tell me what is going on?'

'She started—'

'He started—'

'Please!'

Eric's bottom lip wobbled.

'Right, Mum.' Suzy once again had both hands on her hips. 'I want you to take Abi outside please, I need to have a word with Eric.'

'But—'

'And then I expect you both to clear up this mess and have the kitchen ready for dinner, is that clear?'

Yvette's nostrils flared. Her jaw jutted forward.

'You'll get your chance to speak, Mother,' Suzy pressed. 'But right now, I'm going to talk to Eric.'

Yvette's shoulders flopped with resignation. Reluctantly, she dragged her feet forward.

'Don't believe any rubbish he tells you about being at the allotment,' she whispered into Suzy's ear as she passed her. 'He stank of beer when he came in.'

Yvette shot Eric a final sneer as she moved towards the door. He responded with his best glare.

Silence filled the air between Eric and his wife. He skulked over to the sink and washed the tomato sauce from his hands before finding a cloth and beginning to wipe up the floor. Suzy pulled out a chair. She rested her elbows on the table and dropped her head into her hands.

'Did you really forget to pick up Abi?' she said, her voice tired and heavy.

'It was a genuine accident.'

'Were you at the pub?'

Eric dropped his gaze. Suzy sighed.

'This was your idea, this move, Eric. And I'm trying to do everything I can to make it work. I don't have a problem with you not working, really, I don't. But I can't do this. I can't work all day and come home to you and Mum screaming at each other.'

'We weren't ... it was just that ... it was only ...' Eric stammered before realising he could find no way to finish the sentence.

Suzy let out another groan and levered herself back up to standing. 'Look, I'm going up for a shower. Whatever the problem is, can we just get dinner sorted, get Abi to bed, and then talk about it afterwards.'

Eric nodded.

'Okay.'

Suzy's nose crinkled. Her eyes scanned the room.

'What is for dinner, by the way? It smells good.'

A ripple of guilt rumbled through Eric's spleen.

'Veggie meatloaf,' he said and lowered his gaze to the red soaked cloth in his hands. Suzy emitted her third sigh in as many minutes.

'Take away it is then,' she said.

Dinner came from the Thai where Yvette ordered a fish-free som tam. It was a mostly silent affair, after which Abi was sent upstairs early with the promise of an extra half-hour iPad time before lights out. After piling the dishes into the dishwasher, Yvette announced that she was going for walk.

'It's zero degrees outside, Mum. Don't be ridiculous.'

'The fresh air will do me good,' she said. 'And I don't want to be an intrusion.'

'You're not an intrusion, Mum.'

Suzy glanced at Eric for support. He sipped his drink. He had been forced to apologise in front of Abi, as had Yvette, and they'd both done so, but it was obviously under duress. Neither of them actually meant it. He most certainly didn't.

'It's fine, it's fine,' Yvette said, pulling on her coat. 'I know when I'm not wanted.'

'Mum—'

'Honestly, it's not a problem. I was going to go down to the Yacht Club, anyway. They are taking all the Christmas lights down tomorrow, apparently. I thought I might get a few photos before they're gone.'

'The Yacht Club is miles away.'

'It's fine. Honestly. Anyway, I don't suspect I'll be welcome here next Christmas. I want to make the most of it.'

Eric sighed internally. He desperately didn't want to get drawn in, but if he didn't do something, it would be next Christmas by the time they finished the bloody conversation.

'Why don't you take the car then?' he said, finally giving in. 'It's silly for you to go walking all that way in the cold.'

Suzy smiled gratefully.

'Well, if you're sure?'

'You're already insured on the bloody thing. You might as well.' Suzy's smile evaporated as her jaw set.

'Eric, darling,' she said in a tone that made his blood run cold. 'Why don't you take Mum in Sally. That would be a lovely treat for you, wouldn't it, Mum?'

Yvette beamed.

'Really?'

Eric balked.

'Well, it's not exactly the weather—'

'I've never been in a—'

'A ten-minute drive is hardly going to wreck her,' Suzy continued with a glint in her eye that was growing ever brighter by the second. 'Besides, you were saying the other day how you needed to give her a quick run out.'

'Yes, but—'

'You can think of it as an apology for throwing Mum's delicious meatloaf all over the floor.'

Suzy's mind was set. There was no way around it. Eric looked at the drink in his hand.

'Don't worry,' Suzy said. 'I'll have a big glass waiting for you when you get back. You better get going though, you don't want to get stuck behind one of those gritting lorries.'

SUZY DID NOT HAVE a big drink waiting for Eric when he got home. At first, he assumed she'd gone for a soak in the bath, or perhaps an early night. When he did finally find her, she was in the dining room with only the standard lamp on for illumination and two hundred pages of paper sprawled over every inch of wood, carpet, and table top.

'Isn't this what an office is for?' he said.

'Sorry.' Suzy shifted one pile of paper on top of another. 'I ran out of room. And I didn't want to disturb Abs with all my clunking about.'

'Anything I can do to help?'

'Stop fighting with my mother.'

Eric took a deep breath in.

'Don't worry,' he said. 'I was on my best behaviour. We had a lovely ride.'

'Good.'

It was the truth. The ride had been fantastic. He had gone at breakneck speed at every possible corner. Each gasp or sharp inhale from Yvette had been counted as a win on his part, and each time she'd begun to open her mouth he had gone just a little bit faster. By the time they stopped he could see her knees trembling.

'Sorry about the corners,' Eric said, helping his mother-in-law out of the seat. 'It's just the way these old cars drive.'

For once, Yvette was speechless.

In the dining room, Suzy's gaze was off in the distance. The end of her pen had disappeared into her mouth.

'I just want a week without a drama,' she said. 'A week where I can concentrate on my work, where you pick up Abi from school on time and eat my mother's vegan curry puffs for dinner. Is that okay? Can I ask for that?'

'Of course.'

'Because it feels like every day, there's something. And I don't want to be a nag, really I don't.'

'I know you don't. I'm sorry.' Eric bent down and kissed his wife on the top of her head.

He thought back to earlier in the day. He had been desperate to ask Suzy's advice on the issue of Fleur and her battery hens. He still was, but it would be one more problem that she felt she had to fix. One more problem of his making. No, Eric decided. Now was not the time to burden Suzy with the hens. He would have to deal with this on his own.

'No more drama,' Eric assured her.

When he went to bed that night, the *Backyard Chickens Handbook* was on the bedside table. Eric took it from the stand, dropped it into the bottom drawer, and pushed the drawer shut.

TWENTY-FOUR HOURS LATER, he and Suzy were tucked up together in bed and Eric's promise of no drama had lasted a full day. For a full day, everything had run smoothly. He had woken up early to make her a coffee, juice, and sandwich, which he left in the fridge for her lunch. He had taken Abi to school and picked her up – on time – and spent the hours in between adding art deco style coving to the lounge and dining room. At dinner, he had graciously eaten Yvette's Vietnamese tempeh and noodle pho despite the fact it felt like his mouth was being voluntarily filled with half-set plaster, and after that he had washed up, put Abi to bed, and poured them drinks, which he brought to Suzy while she worked away in the dining room. He had even picked up some organic, fair-trade, vegan, and gluten free chocolate for Yvette from Tesco despite the fact it cost four times more than the next most expensive bar in the shop.

'Thank you for today,' Suzy said as her head nestled into the pillow. 'Let me get this deadline out of the way. Then I'll be able to help out a bit more.'

'It's no problem.'

'Honestly. I feel like I'm chasing my tail the whole time. There just aren't enough hours in the day at the minute.'

Eric *umm*ed sympathetically. He remembered that feeling, where every half-hour not at work had felt like a half-hour wasted, and he didn't miss it one bit. Still, today had been good, and he would keep it up. Do everything in his power to make Suzy's life as easy as possible. Maybe he would try some new recipes. Suzy said she'd been missing the Lebanese from back in Islington. Surely hummus couldn't be that hard to make. Or tabbouleh. And he was pretty certain they were vegan too. Eric was deliberating over the difficulties of shawarma chicken when his phone beeped beside him. He picked it up and swiped the message open.

'What the?'

It took less than a heartbeat for Eric's cool demeanour and dreams of baba ganoush to vanish, leaving nothing but a cold sweat in their wake.

'You sneaky cow.'

'Eric?'

He snapped upright in bed, blood pulsing in his veins while his eyes bulged at the image, glaring at the screen.

'That vicious, conniving, sneaky little ...' He could barely spit the words out. His heart was racing, his throat completely dry. 'Just you wait. Just you—'

'Eric! What the hell are you going on about?'

'This!' he said.

Every nerve from his ear to his toenails still quivered with anger as he handed Suzy his phone. Wrinkles appeared across her brow.

'This is a cute photo of you,' she said. 'When was it taken? And whose chicken is that?'

'Look. Look at what she said. Look at the title.'

He watched as his wife's frown lines deepened.

'I don't get it. *Fowl Accomplice?*'

'She thinks she's being funny.'

'Who does? Eric you're making absolutely no sense.'

Eric snatched back his phone and threw it in the bottom drawer along with his *Backyard Chicken Handbook*.

'It's fine,' he huffed, folding his arms and flopping back down onto the mattress. 'You said you didn't want any drama.'

'And this is no drama?'

'Honestly. It doesn't matter. You said it yourself, you need friends. Just forget I said anything.'

Suzy expelled a lungful of air, pulled herself into a sitting position, and flicked on the bedside lamp.

'Eric Sibley. What have you done this time?' she said.

'Me?'

At that point, Eric felt he had absolutely no choice but to explain the previous day's scenario and why he was, most unequivocally, not to blame.

'She's just playing with you,' Suzy said, chuckling to herself as she settled back into bed. 'I don't know why you're so uptight about this. I think it's funny. She's funny.'

'Playing with me? I could lose my plot if the committee finds out about this. She could completely ruin my chance of having chickens there too.'

'Then have chickens up here. We've got plenty of room.'

'That's not the point.'

'Then what is?'

Eric huffed. Suzy rolled back over and propped herself up on one elbow.

'Look,' she said. 'If it's that much of a deal, talk to Hank. Tell the committee. I'm sure Fleur will get over it. She doesn't seem the type to hold a grudge.'

Eric mumbled something into the pillow. His insides still roiled, and his temperature felt like it had risen twenty degrees in the last ten minutes. He would be talking to Hank. He would very definitely be talking to him. Fleur could count on that.

CHAPTER 13

THE FOLLOWING MORNING was the first time Abi had taken her bike to school. She had ridden along the pavement – not strictly legal, but necessary given the speed cars travelled through Burlam – while Eric padded behind with her school bag on his shoulder. It had started easily enough, but halfway there Abi finally found her confidence. And with it her speed. By the time Eric arrived outside the school gate, he was dripping with sweat, red faced, and out of breath. Anybody passing would have been forgiven for thinking he'd come directly from the gym next door if it weren't for the fact that nobody in Burlam actually used the gym. Fortunately, his own radiating heat made the air a little less biting. As such, Eric decided to jog his way back home.

There had been a harsh frost overnight that made the village look like a picture from a Christmas card. Even when he was back inside the house working on the dilapidated staircase, Eric's breath fogged in the air in front of him.

'You need some draught excluders,' Yvette said. 'I should have brought my sewing machine. I could have sewn you some. I bought some gorgeous fabric when we were in Peru. This little market stall just off—'

'I'm sure we can buy some,' Eric said.

Yvette had been in a goading mood all morning. He had heard her on the phone in the early hours – most probably to her husband, Philip – and she had been wearing a face like a giraffe sucking a pear drop since breakfast.

'Of course,' Yvette grunted. 'Just buy some. Why not? I mean, if it's someone else's money you're spending.'

Eric bit his tongue and focused on the ailing staircase.

'You look rather unwell,' Yvette said, grimacing as she leant in and sniffed Eric's sweat soaked T-shirt. 'I hope it's not catching.'

'I'm just a little out of shape, that's all,' he said, refusing to rise to the bait. 'If Abi is going to keep up with this cycling thing, I should probably dig my own bike out of the garage.'

Yvette harrumphed at his lack of comeback.

'And do you have any idea when the plumber is coming?' she said. 'It is really not convenient having four of us sharing that one tiny bathroom.'

'That's strange because it was absolutely fine when there were just three of us.' Eric smiled.

Still scowling, Yvette skulked off into the kitchen. *Eric one – Yvette nil*, he thought as he continued to pull nails from the rotting wooden struts of his staircase.

It was an hour later – when Yvette had gone to Chelmsford to restock on adzuki beans and nori – that Eric decided it was late enough to call Hank. His time working on the banister had been entirely unproductive. His shoulder was playing up again, and every now and again a sharp and sudden pain struck deep into the muscles. When he wasn't distracted by the pain of his ageing ligaments, images of battery hens and official allotment eviction notices flashed through Eric's mind. If he was going to get anything done, he needed to sort out this business with Fleur and the committee as soon as possible.

Sitting on the bottom step of the staircase, Eric dug out his phone and searched through his contact list.

'I was just thinking about you,' Hank said when he answered.

'You were?' Eric said, his palms becoming immediately slick with nervous sweat.

'Aye. Had an interesting phone call yesterday from the committee, 'bout your new neighbour.'

'You did?'

'Aye, but I 'spect you already know what about.'

'You do?'

Hank's chuckle reverberated down the line.

'Don't worry. She explained everything.'

'She did?' Eric was well aware of his duo-syllabic responses but was having difficulty expanding on them.

'Aye,' Hank said.

Eric's stomach did something between a quake and a clench. He gripped the phone a little harder.

'What was that, exactly?' he said. 'What did she explain?'

Hank's laugh deepened.

'She said you were rather worried about the chickens. No need. Committee's fine. People have had chickens on the plots for donkey's years. Not had any for a while, mind you, but there's no problem. To be honest, she thought you'd have already rung to tell us. Think she was a bit disappointed.'

The queasiness in Eric's stomach lessened.

'Be good to get a bit of livestock up there again. Some fresh eggs would be lovely. Shame Cynthia's not here. I imagine she could whip up something grand with a few fresh yolks.'

Eric's chest flickered with guilt. Despite living in her house, Cynthia had barely crossed his mind these past few weeks. He should really call Maggie, he decided. See if there was a forwarding number he could call. Or at least an email.

'Well, I'm going to be heading down there this morning,' Hank said, his tone having changed to one that clearly wanted to finish the conversation. 'Will I see you there?'

Eric gazed around at the bomb site in front of him. The banister was half finished, the coving in the dining room needed a paint, and he still had no idea whether the bloody plumber was coming this week or next. There were a thousand things he needed to do around the house.

'Of course,' he said. 'I'll see you there in a bit.'

❦

ERIC'S JUSTIFICATION was the leeks. He had begun the heeling-in process last time, but with all the distraction of the chickens he was barely a third of the way through. If he didn't get them dug up and replanted somewhere with a bit more wind protection, they would be rotting pillars of mush before they'd even had a chance to grow.

Gardening in near zero-degree conditions had never been Eric's idea of fun. By the time he'd walked the distance from the car to the plot, his toes were numb and his fingers had the distinct tingle of appendages about to turn blue. Once there, he double layered his gloves, a thin, warm cashmere pair underneath his bulky, Gore-Tex-lined gardening pair. While this pairing undoubtedly helped abate frostbite, it made pulling up vegetable stems doubly arduous. He would get hold of one of the leeks only to have it slip through his fingers as he tried to pull it up each time. Replanting was a bit easier, but still not what he would have considered fun.

He was a third of the way through relocating his final row when a throat clearing behind him made him stop. He braced himself, then twisted his head around.

'Eric,' Fleur said. Today she was dressed entirely in green, including her ankle boots and gloves. 'I'm glad you're here. I was going to pop by the house and see you otherwise.'

'Were you?' he said.

Eric dropped his trowel, stood up, and very deliberately locked his eyes on hers. Fleur, apparently oblivious to the animosity Eric was trying to display, moved in and kissed him on both cheeks.

'So, good news about the hens,' she said. 'I'm so relieved.'

'Uh-huh.'

'And thank you so much for your help with that.'

'Uh-huh.'

'I told the committee how understanding you were. And how you wanted to make sure I followed their rules.'

'Uh-huh.'

Fleur stopped. Her eyes ran up and down his body. When she'd finished her study, a small crease appeared between her eyebrows.

'But you're mad at me, aren't you?' she deduced. Eric chose not to respond. 'Is this about the message? I was only joking. I'm sorry. I thought you'd see the funny side. I was only winding you up.'

Eric dug the toes of his boot into the soil. 'Well, I—'

'Oh, Eric,' she said and then in an entirely unexpected move, wrapped her arms around him and squeezed.

She smelt of lemons and bramble with undertones of London smog, although Eric barely managed a single intake of breath. Instead he remained absolutely rigid for the entirety of the hug, which lasted substantially longer than he would have anticipated. It was only when – about thirty seconds in – a strange trembling began to rattle down his shoulder that he realised what was going on. He stepped back, out of her arms and came once more face to face with a tear-streaked Fleur.

'I'm sorry,' she said, wiping her sleeve. 'I always go and do things like this. Get carried away. I think I'm being funny you see, and then ... and then ...'

'There, there.' Eric patted her shoulder from arm's length, trying to keep himself at a suitable bolting distance.

'This is exactly the type of thing he was on about,' Fleur sobbed.

'Who?' Eric asked, then cursed himself for being drawn further into the drama.

'My ex-husband. He'd always go on about how I didn't think before I acted. And he was right. At work and home. And now here.'

The sobs had reached a new volume. Eric looked rapidly around, trying to ensure people didn't think he was the one responsible for the woman's wailing. The standing still didn't help matters either. He had now lost all sensation in his ears and was starting to suspect his nose had taken on a purple tinge.

'Why don't I make you a cup of tea?' he said. 'You sit down on one of your chairs, and I'll bring it over.'

'I need to feed the girls first,' Fleur whimpered.

'That's fine,' Eric said. 'By the time you've done that, the kettle will be boiled.'

Then, before she could say anything else, Eric dashed across his plot, into the shed, and shut the door behind him.

※

IT WAS a peculiar sensation sitting on Norman's veranda, seeing the allotment from this angle again after all those months. A sad ache blossomed within him. He was grateful that Fleur hadn't sat in Norman's chair and that he was the one who got it instead, although that felt equally wrong, if not more so. Norman would never have let him sit there when he was alive.

Through the shed door behind them came the clucking of hens.

'I need to get their coop finished so they can go outside really,' Fleur was saying. 'But I don't suspect they mind being inside that much. Not in this weather. I've put in plenty of blankets to make sure they're warm enough.'

'I'm sure they're very comfortable,' Eric said.

He hated conversations like this, the type where he felt he had to talk. He had stayed in his shed as long as possible but eventually, he realised, he had to come out. Better to do it with a tea in hand and attempt to win some well-needed brownie points with Suzy than make a dash for it and end up with another disaster like the tapas.

'You must think I'm completely unhinged,' Fleur said, still not having taken a sip of her tea.

'Not at all.'

Fleur raised her eyebrow, which she followed with a grateful chuckle.

'I'm really not that crazy,' she said. 'It's just at the minute. Well, you know, midlife-crisis, messy break-up ...' She swallowed the last word and brought the mug of tea to her mouth.

The steam had dwindled into a thin spiral, but from the way she took a second and third sip it was still warm enough to drink.

'Do you ever regret it? Your move down here, I mean?' she asked.

'Not yet. I won't say it's been easy. But for the most part it's been worth it.'

'And does Suzy think the same?'

'I hope so,' said Eric, his mind drifting off into the past when his wife would spend the evenings massaging his feet and bringing him gins as opposed to working every hour God sent. 'I really do hope so.'

He was still dreaming of those evenings when he felt Fleur's hand slip into his. She squeezed it once, firmly, then let go.

'You two will be just fine,' she said. 'I can see that. You're special.'

CHAPTER 14

ERIC WAS WALKING with a spring in his step. His breath still misted the air, but the midday sun had cleared the sky of clouds, resulting in a blue so luminous it could have easily passed for summer in the tropics. Nothing could ruin his mood, not now he had a plan. And it was a great plan, an insanely great plan. He kicked a fallen twig with his foot and turned the movement into a short little skip.

It was the first really good idea he had had since moving out there and buying Abi a bike for Christmas, he decided. And it made perfect sense too. True, Yvette was not what he would consider the ideal housemate, but she was brilliant with Abi, and it was ridiculous not to take advantage of having her there because while they joked about the fact she was never going to leave, deep down they knew the drill. Any minute now she would pack up her things, flap her feather boa goodbye, and sail off into the sunset for another half-decade. They needed to make the most of it while she was still around.

Eric scanned the Internet on his phone as he walked. After finding what he was looking for, he pressed the home screen and rang his wife. The ringtone rang once, then twice. The excitement tingled in his belly.

'Eric?' Suzy answered just as Eric was about to hang up. 'Eric, are you there?'

'Yes, sorry. It's me. I'm here.'

'Is everything okay? Is Abi all right? Is everything all right with Mum?'

'Yeah, yes. Everything is fine.'

'Oh, okay.' she sounded flustered.

Through the line he could hear the tapping of keys and simultaneous rustling of paper.

'What's wrong? Please don't tell me this is to do with chickens because honestly, Eric, I'm up to my eyeballs in it here.'

'No, no it's not that at all,' said Eric, his excitement dwindling. 'Nothing's wrong. Look if this is a bad time …?'

'No, no, it's fine. I just need to be quick that's all. Two of the contributors for next month's piece have pulled out and I'm a little bit stressed that's all.'

'Oh.'

'So, what is it? What did you ring for?'

Eric inhaled through his nose. It had seemed like such a good idea two minutes ago, and he had been certain of Suzy's reaction. Now he wasn't so confident.

'Eric? Honey? If this can wai—'

'Paris,' Eric blurted out.

'Pardon?'

'Paris. I thought you might like to go?'

There was a pause down the line. Eric's chest tightened.

'*Erm*, maybe. I mean—'

'This weekend,' Eric interjected, realising he had missed an important piece of information from his announcement. 'I thought you might want to go this weekend. As in tomorrow.'

There was another pause. The tightness constricted further around his ribs.

'Eric, this is really not a great time. In fact, it's probably the worst time you could possibly pick.'

'I knew you were going to say that, but just listen. I thought we could get the train across. There are some really good deals at the moment, and that way you have the entire trip there and back to write or edit or do whatever you need to do. I'll even book my seat in a different place than you, so I don't disturb you.'

'Eric—'

'We'll only be gone one day.'

'It's just—'

'Listen. You can do as much work as you want while we're there. All I ask is that you have dinner with me by the Seine. That's it. One dinner and the rest of the time you get to spend working in Paris.'

There was another pause and the tightness around Eric's chest was still there, but it was looser, this was a thinking silence, rather than a cross one. He could tell.

'Darling, it's a really sweet idea but—'

'Don't say no. Please don't. If it's money you're worried about, there's no need. Honestly, what's the point of having savings if we don't treat ourselves now and again? And you love Paris.'

'Eric—'

'And when are we going to get another chance like this? In a couple of days your mum will disappear, and the joy of a live-in babysitter will be just a memory. Do you know when the last time we went abroad on our own together was? Do you?'

'Eric—'

'Nine years ago. Nine years, Suze. And all I'm asking for is one night.' He waited for the answer.

'When did you want to leave?'

'Yes!' Eric mouthed the word silently as he fist-bumped the air. 'We'll leave tomorrow morning. I can even meet you at the station, if you want to stay up in London tonight?'

'And you've run it by Mum?'

'Of course, she'd love to,' Eric lied.

'Have you booked anything yet?'

'No, not yet. I wanted to run it by you first.'

'Look, can you give me a couple of hours? If I can get these jobs sorted by then, then maybe, okay?'

'I'll—'

'This is not a yes. This is a maybe.'

Eric hung up the phone before she could change her mind. A second later and it rang again.

'Sorry,' Suzy said. 'I forgot to say the plumber rang.'

'He did?'

'I don't know why he didn't call you. Anyway, I sent Mum a text. She said she'd deal with it, but I forgot to let you know.'

'Okay. Don't worry. Let's see what extra problems he can discover to charge us for today.'

'Have fun,' Suzy said and this time she hung up.

Eric skipped his way back to the house. Even the sudden appearance of grey clouds and distant rumblings of thunder did nothing to dampen his spirits as he strode onwards. He would look up restaurants when he got back to the house. Last time they went to Paris they'd eaten every night at the same little joint behind Notre-Dame, although he suspected that place was long gone now. If not, he would definitely be making a reservation.

A quick glance at his phone told him it was one-thirty. In another hour he would have to start walking back down to pick up Abi. That left just enough time to run in, grab a sandwich, and a shower, and fix a fraction more of the staircase. He would need to find a hotel too, he thought. Greg, an old work colleague from his London days, had recently got back from honeymoon travelling across Europe after a shotgun wedding. Four weeks from Vienna to Barcelona by luxury trains, each place documented with a perfectly posed selfie and a grossly overly-revealing caption. If he went on Facebook, Eric was certain he'd be able to find where they stayed in Paris. It would be perfect.

Eric stopped outside the driveway and looked up at the house. The roof tiles were frosted white and the red paint on the front door peeled off around the hinges. The paving slabs that covered the driveway were black and engulfed by moss, and in the middle of the lawn stood a stone bird-bath, although the stone was chipped and weathered, and the onslaught of algae meant that any bird which ventured in for a dip was rewarded with a decidedly green hue. If they could get the inside sorted through winter, he thought, then they could start on the outside of the house when spring arrived. Twelve months from now, Eric considered, and he would be looking up at his second greatest achievement to date. Eric gave the garden one last look over then headed inside.

Upon entry into the hallway, Eric was greeted by a banging loud enough to shake the downstairs light fittings. His stomach sank. In the world of business and recruitment, Eric had had no problems seeing through peoples' crap in order to get the best possible deal. He could bluff and barter and hold a poker face or stony silence with the best of them, be it in a Michelin-starred restaurant over a complex business lunch negotiation, or down the end of an exceptionally tense telephone call. Even Jack Nelson, Eric's old and beloved employer, had always been impressed by Eric's ability to call people out on their bullshit in order to secure a contract. But that was when he was dealing with people in suits; people like himself. When it came to tradesmen, he was useless. All they had to do was throw in a few combobulated terms like *internal baffles* and *DWV systems* and he was reaching for his chequebook. He liked to think he had got better with age, but truth was, this was Suzy's domain. She was the hard-baller when it came to things like this. With no choice but to face the inevitable, Eric began to climb the staircase.

A few steps from the top, Eric began to appreciate what a labour-intensive job plumbing truly was. The banging had not let up since he had set foot in the house, and now he could hear the grunting that was going along with it. Whatever the job involved, the plumber was certainly putting his back into it.

Should he wait for a break in the banging, Eric wondered. He didn't want to burst in, surprise the guy, and cause him to put a twelve-inch wrench through the newly finished vanity stand. Eric shook himself. Plumbers were used to people walking in on them on the job, it was that type of profession.

By the time he was outside the bathroom, Eric had decided that he should probably go in and offer to give the man a hand before he ended up bursting an artery. He placed his fingers on the newly fitted chrome door handle, twisted, and went inside.

'Hi,' Eric said. 'I don't want to interrupt but ... oh God.'

The moisture evaporated from Eric's mouth. He stumbled back towards the door.

'Oh God. Oh, good God. What the ... what the hell?'

CHAPTER 15

THE BLOOD RUSHED from his head. His legs gave way as he stumbled backwards, knocking him from one wall to another as he tried to shield his eyes and still find the exit, all without vomiting all over his newly grouted tiles.

'My God. I'm so ... so ...'

So what? He didn't know what he was. Scared, that was for certain. Repulsed, absolutely.

'Hey, dude. Sorry about this. It's no problem though. No problem.'

The plumber took his time, pulling his trousers up from around his ankles. He slipped his belt around his waist and pulled it up along the notches, lifting a foot onto Eric's seven-hundred-pound ceramic claw-foot tub as he did. Once he had completed this part of the dressing ritual, he slowed further, taking his time to find his T-shirt from the ground, apparently in no rush to cover-up his perfectly chiselled abdominal muscles. Muscles that would be considered obscenely tanned for anyone, let alone someone who lived in a country lucky to get fifty days of sun a year.

'I think I'm blind,' Eric said as he clutched his stomach and tried to find a place to avert his gaze. His eyes fell upon a thin strip of black underwear. His mother-in-law's hand reached down and snatched them up from the ground.

'Well, I'm sure we've all got lots to be getting on with,' she said, smiling as she caught Eric's eye.

'You?' he said.

'Eric, please—'

'You stay there.'

'Eric—'

'Don't you dare.'

'Dude—'

Eric's attention flipped back to the plumber.

'And you? How old are you?'

'I'm—'

'Nope, don't answer that. This is unbelievable. And I mean that. This is literally unbelievable. What the hell is going on? Tell me this is some kind of nightmare?'

'Eric.' Yvette approached, only to stop at Eric's sudden recoil. 'Chad came around to sort out the plumbing.'

'Chad? You're serious. No one is called Chad. What are you, a pool boy?'

Chad's engorged pectorals jiggled.

'No, I'm the plumber,' he said. 'But I do have a landscape gardening business on the side.'

'Of course you do.'

Yvette's eyes darted nervously around the room. Chad had still yet to find his shirt.

Eric's gaze locked on to the young plumber.

'I assume you're done?' he said.

'With what?'

'With the bathroom? What else would I mean? Oh God, please don't answer. Just get out, will you? Just leave now.'

'Du—'

'Don't you even think about *duding* me. I'm not your dude.'

Chad's tongue ran along his top teeth.

'Look, it's cool, du— it's cool. I'll just get my tools, and I'll be out of your hair in a minute.'

He reached for his shirt.

'Turns out it was a really quick job, actually. Only took a few minutes. If I had known, I could have come over during Christm—'

'Just get out,' said Eric grabbing a handful of tools from the floor and stuffing them into Chad's bag. 'Out. Out.'

He pushed him through the doorway and out into the landing. Two steps down the stairs and Chad turned around.

'What?' said Eric.

'Sorry. It's just I haven't been paid yet. Your ... Yvette said you'd pay me when you got home.'

'Pay you? For what?'

'Dude.'

Chad's face wrinkled in disgust. He shook his head and let out a series of deep tuts.

'For the plumbing. God. Some people. No respect at all.'

<hr />

THEY CANCELLED PARIS.

Eric had rung Suzy and asked her to come straight home. He had had such difficulty speaking that she thought he was suffering a heart attack. When he finally managed to get out the word *Yvette,* Suzy presumed the worst and began to hyperventilate down the phone line. In the end, Eric hung up and sent a text telling her everything was fine, just to come home. However, the message still took a solid five minutes to write due to the shaking in Eric's hand, which he now assumed was permanent.

He took an overnight bag for Abi to the school gates and rang one of her friend's parents on the way.

'Are you sure that's all right?' he said. 'I don't want to intrude, it's just a bit of a family emergency.'

'I hope everyone's okay?' they'd said. 'Is it Suzy's mother? I'd heard she was staying over.'

'It's got something to do with her,' he said nodding. 'Yes.'

By 6 p.m., Eric, Suzy, and Yvette were once more sitting around the grubby kitchen table. Eric was already on his second gin and had instructed Suzy to down her first the moment she entered the house. Her knuckles shone white around the glass as her gaze went searchingly between her husband and her mother. Eric, by contrast, looked only down.

As if to contradict the afternoon's events, Yvette was dressed in a buttoned-up blouse and full-length skirt that Eric was convinced she'd gone and bought at the charity shop just then in order to make his side seem even more preposterous. Her hair was swept back too, and her typical fuchsia lipstick swapped out for a far more mellow peach.

'I don't understand,' Suzy said, when Eric had finally relayed the tale. 'Mum? How did this happen?'

Yvette cleared her throat.

'Well, you sent him round,' she said. 'And he really was a very polite young man.'

'Young?' Eric said. 'He was barely out of school.'

'Nonsense. He was twenty-five and a half,' Yvette replied.

'Twenty-five and half? Who measures their ages in half years other than children?'

Yvette tutted.

'What? Are you saying that just because I'm old, a younger man can't find me attractive?'

'No, Mum. We're saying that you can't go around shagging plumbers in our bathroom. For Christ's sake. What about Dad?'

A muffled mumble rose from Yvette's pouted lips.

'What was that? Did you hear me? I said what about Dad?'

'I heard you. I said what about him,' Yvette snapped.

'Mum?'

Yvette's expression was changing. The pout on her lips was giving way to a quiver, and the hard, fixed glare she'd had since they sat down was starting to gloss over with the sheen of tears. An uneasy sense of compassion stirred in Eric's gin-filled belly.

'Yvette?' he said, reaching his hand across the table and placing it on top of hers. 'Is there something you want to tell us?'

Yvette snatched her hand back.

'No.'

'Mum?'

In a swift motion, evocative of the elegant dancer she was, Yvette sprang up from her chair.

'I know what you're thinking. I know what you're both thinking. That I'm just some batty, old woman. That I don't know what I'm doing.'

'Mum, that's not—'

'Well, screw you. Screw the lot of you.'

'Mum!'

In a half-chasse, half-grapevine, she spun out on her heel and raced up the stairs. A moment later the spare room door slammed shut. Silence dangled in the air. Eric lifted his glass and downed the lot, leaving the ice cubes to jangle in the bottom.

'Well, this can't be good,' he said.

※

SUZY HAD TRIED to do some work afterwards; tried to distract herself with something else, but it hadn't worked. Less than twenty minutes after starting, Suzy abandoned the papers in the dining room and began pacing the downstairs of the house.

Eventually she'd gone up to speak to her mother. There had been several hours of sobbing, not to mention wine, hot chocolate, and the devouring of more than one bacon sandwich; Yvette's commitment to veganism apparently as shattered as her marriage.

Eric listened from the safety of the landing as the wails rattled through his newly laid coving.

'And with that little wench, of all the girls on the boat. Honestly, the way she strutted around the deck like she owned the place, even the captain would be all, "*Yes, Katrina; no, Katrina; anything you want me to do, Katrina.*" And it's not as if he'd get a job without me. Oh no. Do you know how many scrapes your father has got himself into? How many situations I've had to pull him out of? It's me who got us that job offer in the Caymans, not to mention the one on St Lucia. Oh no, your father has quite the temperamental streak to him at work. I bet you didn't know that, did you?'

She paused. A trumpetous blow of her nose followed.

'He once dropped a soufflé on a captain's hat. He did. Oh, that man. He wouldn't have a chance of getting another job without me. Just you wait and see. He'll be out on the street in no time. I don't suppose *Katrina* is going to cart him around with her for the next twenty years. After all I've done for him. After everything I've done. And now he won't even answer my calls.'

That was as much as she could take. For the next fifteen minutes, the only sounds that managed to escape Yvette's lips were a stuttering, juddering nonsense.

In the end, Suzy had run her mother a bath in the newly plumbed bathroom, filled it with bubbles, and lit the candles that she'd kept in storage for the last two years after deeming them far too pretty and expensive to burn.

'It only seems right that you christen it now,' Eric had said only to be greeted by one of Suzy's looks. 'What? I'm just saying that I'll never be able to set in foot in there, that's all.'

Yvette had started sobbing again as they both left her to her bath and went downstairs.

'So according to Mum, the first part of what she told us was true,' Suzy said, curled up on Eric's shoulder. 'One of the younger dancers pulled his tendon or something. Only it didn't happen just before Christmas. More like months ago. Anyway, Dad replaced this guy and was partnered with this girl. She's twenty-four, apparently.'

'Ouch.'

'Yeah. And it seems like the whole ship knew before she did.'

'Poor her.'

Eric pulled his wife in closer and ran his hand across her hair.

'So, what now? I mean, does she still have a job? Has she ever worked without your dad?'

'Not since she was twenty-one. I don't even know if she wants to work without him.'

'Jeez.'

'Yup.'

'And I don't know about him either. Mum's not lying, I know he's got into some right scrapes over the years. He's going to be hard pushed to find a job without her.'

'I guess he'll stay where he is until he retires. Can he do that?'

'I have no idea.'

Eric swilled the ice around in his glass.

'Has anyone actually spoken to him? To your dad? Do you think you ought to call him?'

'Me?' Suzy's eyebrows rose to her hairline. 'I think we've suffered enough. No, we've had to handle Mum in all this. Lydia can be the one to ring Dad. She's the oldest. She can deal with him.'

CHAPTER 16

WHEN ERIC CAME downstairs the next morning, it was as though a switch had been flipped. Yvette stood at the hob, spatula in hand as a pan of sausages sizzled and spat. She was dressed in her nightdress and gown, both pink and floral, with her hair dangling uncombed and not a scrap of jewellery or make-up in sight. Deep bags hung beneath her eyes, evidence of last night's tears still clearly visible.

The aroma was both sweet and savoury. As well as the sausages, there were mushrooms frying, eggs being scrambled, and a large tray of biscuits browning in the oven. The kitchen table was covered with a confetti of chocolate wrappers while the bin had failed to close properly due to the empty family-sized tub of non-vegan ice cream that had been stuffed into it.

'I suppose you heard all that last night?' Yvette said, spearing a sausage directly from the frying pan and taking a bite. 'I suppose you know what a stupid, old fool I've been.'

'Why would you be the fool?' Eric said. 'He's the fool.'

'Right under my very nose.'

'No one thinks you're a fool, Yvette.'

She smiled sadly and picked up another sausage, which she dropped onto a plate, before scooping on some eggs and mushrooms.

'I suppose you want me to move into Lydia's?' she said, still holding the plate close to her chest.

'What? Why would you think that?'

She shrugged. Her eyes glistened.

'No one wants me anymore.'

Eric hovered uncomfortably. He could feel the moment closing in. Any second now and he would have no choice but to hug his mother-in-law. Unfortunately, his attention was still focused on the plate of food in her hand. His stomach growled. He would have to remove the plate before any type of hugging occurred. Preferably, he would get to eat it first too, but that seemed a little callous. He was still deliberating his best course of action when the sniffing started. A second later came the shakes. Knowing it would only be seconds until the full-blown blubbering, Eric leapt across the room. Grabbing the plate from his mother-in-law's hands, he placed it on the draining board behind them and embraced Yvette in a squeeze just below smothering point.

It was a messy cry, with gulping breaths and plenty of snorts, and only when Eric was certain that he was in the hug for the long-haul did he loosen one arm, stretch across Yvette's back, and grab a sausage.

'Please don't make me go and stay with Lydia,' she wheezed out between snotty sobs.

'*Ufffcoursenot*,' Eric mumbled through a mouthful of pork.

'Their spare room smells like sheep,' Yvette said.

Eric smiled. It did. It really did.

***

SUZY HAD DECIDED to work from home.

'You don't need to do that,' Yvette insisted. 'You think that because I've finally told you, I'm going to have some massive nervous breakdown and set fire to your house or something ridiculous?'

'Well, we hadn't until now,' Eric said.

Suzy glared.

'It's for me, Mum,' Suzy said. 'I won't be able to concentrate if I go. I'm better off being here, where I can pop in and check that you're all right. Anyway, it's Saturday.'

'But are you sure you'll manage to get your work done?'

There was a moment's pause. Eric tried to look down, but he wasn't quick enough. One second of eye contact was all it took. Suzy nodded at him. Forcefully.

'Why don't you go to the allotment with Eric?' Suzy said, when Eric had still not taken it upon himself to speak. 'You've been saying you'd like to go down since you arrived.'

'No, no. I don't want to impose.'

'You're not, Mum. Eric's offering. Aren't you?'

Eric looked up in feigned surprise as if he had only just become aware of the conversation.

'It's going to be quite hard work today,' he said. 'I was planning on carpeting the spuds and carrots.'

'Then it'll be even better that you've got an extra pair of hands, won't it?'

'Well ... I suppose ...'

'It's fine,' Yvette waved. 'You don't need to babysit me. I'm perfectly fine. And don't worry, I won't get in your way either,' she said to Suzy, then turning to Eric she said, 'but perhaps you could wait for me to get dressed and run me down to the centre? I thought I might spend the day trawling the charity shops, now that I'm unemployed and all. No more Karen Millen for me.'

'Mum—'

'And don't worry about Abi. I can pick Abi up from her friend's house.'

'Mum, you really don't—'

'*Tsk*. Let an old woman feel like she's useful, will you? Particularly when she ruined your romantic weekend away.'

❈

'THAT'S SO TERRIBLE. I can't imagine how she's feeling. When Quentin and I—' Fleur stopped mid-sentence. 'Let's just say it was very difficult for both parties. Sometimes you just have to bite the bullet. No matter how difficult it might seem.'

'Maybe.'

'And it's such a shame you had to cancel your weekend.'

Eric sighed.

'I know, but Suzy didn't feel like she'd be able to focus if she was away. I understand.'

Another sigh was building in his lungs. Fleur caught it just in time.

'On the plus side, you've managed to get all this done,' she said.

Suzy had been right. Two pairs of hands were definitely better than one when it came to laying down carpet between the rows, and Eric had been impressed in Fleur's willingness to get her hands dirty. In exchange for her time spent kneeling on the ground with her hands between his potato plants, he had offered to help her finish off the chicken run.

'I think they're getting a little restless in there,' she confessed as a stream of squawking rattled the windows on Norman's red shed. 'And there was a very near miss between one of them and a pick axe. The sooner it gets finished the better.'

'Shouldn't take too long,' Eric said.

Not too long turned out to be the best part of three hours. While Eric admired Fleur's commitment to using all recycled material, trying to fashion a serviceable door out of battered timbers and offcuts from an old steel drum was more of a health risk than he had bargained for. Particularly given the peculiarity of the run shape so far.

'Measuring it just seemed too fastidious,' Fleur confessed as Eric attempted to join two pieces of two by four, set at a seventy-degree angle. 'I prefer to go with how I feel.'

Eric swallowed back his retort and soldiered on through the morning.

'Oh, it looks marvellous,' Fleur said flinging her arms around him when he finally presented a fully functioning chicken coop. Despite only being involved in the penultimate stage of the construction, Eric was impressed with his handiwork, in particular, his addition of the sliding hatch feature for easy access to the eggs.

'The girls are going to love it,' Fleur said, pawing at a wonky joint. 'Do you think I can move them in now?'

'Hold on, you're not done yet,' he said. 'You need to set your ground first. Lay chicken wire.'

'What, under the whole thing?'

'You could do. Or you might want to just put a trench around it. That should work as well.'

Fleur's eyes narrowed sceptically.

'You seem to know an awful lot about this?'

'I've done a bit of research,' Eric said.

'I guess that makes you my *go to* man on chickens,' she said, then reached up on her tiptoes and pecked him on the cheek.

❈

WHEN SUZY MET Eric at the front door to the house, he knew it wasn't good. He had left Fleur searching for the best way to lay chicken wire and driven home, grabbing a few items for a late lunch en route. As he climbed out the car, hands laden with cloth bags, he was greeted by his wife, thin lips pursed and eyes flitting nervously.

'What is it?' Eric said. 'Is everything okay? Where's your mum?'

Suzy stepped forwards and took his hand.

'Okay, so you're not allowed to freak out.'

Eric stepped back, the words enough to send his pulse into overdrive. 'What? What is it? What has she done?'

'This is just part of the healing process, that's all,' Suzy said trying once again to take Eric's hand.

Eric pushed past his wife and into the hallway.

'What has she done?'

'Eric—' said Suzy as she followed him into the house.

'Yvette! Yvette! If you've got—'

'Daddy! Abi appeared at the top of the stairs, an iPad in one hand a large pair of scissors in the other. 'Do you want to see what I'm making?'

'Not right now, honey. Do you know where your grandmother is?'

Abi's expression crinkled briefly before cracking into a wide grin.

'She's in the garden, dancing.'

'She is?'

'Yes, she's with all her friends.'

'Her friends?'

Eric's pulse did a peculiar double take as if it wasn't sure whether this was good news or not. As he turned to move, Suzy caught hold of his hand.

'Don't say I didn't warn you,' she said.

It was then that Eric noticed the sound reverberating its way through the walls of the house. Something between a chant and a song – rhythmic and vocal, but not words as such. At least not ones that he knew.

'The back garden?' he said, slipping out of Suzy's grip and moving with increasing pace through the house.

'This is not a big deal,' Suzy called after him. 'This is not a big deal.'

When he reached the kitchen, he stopped. The bags containing his lunch dropped from his grasp as he looked through the window into the back garden. His jaw hung open, and judging from the deafening silence that engulfed him, his heart had decided to stop beating altogether.

When he finally did find his voice again, it was croaky and hoarse and felt entirely disconnected from his body.

'This is a big deal,' he said to his wife who now stood next to him. 'This is a very, very big deal.'

CHAPTER 17

ERIC HAD LOST count of the number of times the three of them had sat in silence around the kitchen table. Had he known the prominence that this particular piece of furniture was to have in his day-to-day life, he would have probably put more effort into varnishing it, or at least made some attempt to sand away six-year-old Abi's scribblings. Now, he deemed, it probably seemed a better idea to burn it. The thought of fire threw his mind back to the vision in the garden.

'She can't stay,' he said. 'Not now. This is the final straw.'

'Eric—'

'Why on earth would you do that?' Eric implored, speaking directly to his mother-in-law. 'Why on earth would anyone?'

'Eric,' Yvette said, in a slow voice that seemed to imitate TVs first lady of the psychic, Mystic Meg, best known for her newspaper horoscopes and segments on the *National Lottery Show*. 'There is so much hostility in your voice. Come now. I hardly think I'm the one who needs to apologise for this situation.'

'You don't?'

'Why, no.'

'You do realise—'

'I was not the one who—'

'Mum!'

Smug satisfaction rose through Eric as his mother-in-law received her – albeit lax – scolding. He bit his tongue and avoided giving an unwanted jibe. It was going to be tough, though. He was definitely in the right on this one. Definitely.

Abi had been sent to her room with the bribe that she could watch cat videos on YouTube, although several times, Eric had noticed a small and distinctly human-shaped shadow moving in the hallway. Cat videos were exciting, he reasoned, but nowhere near as exciting as listening to your grandmother explain why she was dancing naked with a bunch of strangers in your back garden, or hearing your father trying to justify running into the garden screaming, while swinging frying pans madly at a load of naked pensioners.

On the plus side, Eric had been allowed a two o'clock gin and Yvette was now dressed, although she appeared to have found the matching twin to one of Lydia's batik Indian bedspreads. The bedspread-cum-dress, which was wrapped around her waist and then swept across her shoulder, emanated the same unusual aroma as her daughter's original. Paired with an enormous beaded necklace and a threadbare jumper, she looked like she was on day release from a Woodstock Festival re-enactment troupe.

'Mum, I'm sure you can understand why Eric was a little bit upset.'

'We were merely giving thanks to mother nature.'

'Is that what you call it?'

Yvette's eyes flashed. 'The fright you gave everyone. Really. You could have caused some permanent damage.'

'That was the idea. It was half one in the afternoon. And you were naked!'

'I didn't realise you were so ashamed of the human form, Eric.'

'Mum—'

Eric knew she was goading him. He knew it, but still felt himself rising to it.

'You know all the neighbours saw, don't you? You know there's probably going to be a police report about this?' said Eric.

'Please. We've done no harm.'

'Don't *please* me.'

'We were—' Yvette tried.

'*We?*' Eric slammed his fist against the table. 'Who exactly are *we?*

Where did they all come from? Did they give you the keys to the local loony bin?'

Yvette stiffened.

'*They*,' she caught her rise in tone and lowered it to the more equable alternative, 'are my coven.'

Eric coughed into his gin. The sudden output of alcohol caused a burning in his nostrils that spread upwards to his eyes causing them to tingle, then water, then stream.

'Are you okay?' Suzy asked.

'I'm going to the pub,' Eric said as he scraped back his chair and stood up.

Suzy frowned.

'No.' Eric was firm in his tone. 'I will take a lot of things. Really. I will. Vegan fudge, piercing holes in my daughter's ears, I'm even coming to terms with shagging the plumber in my newly fitted bathroom only twenty-four hours ago. But naked dancing in the back garden in broad daylight. No, I need a beer, I'm afraid. I need a very large beer.'

Ignoring Suzy's pleading looks, Eric grabbed his coat and headed straight out of the door.

※

HE HAD MESSAGED Hank on the way down, and by the time he reached the pub a cold pint was waiting on the corner table.

'Jerry's at choir practice,' Hank said, slipping a crisp off the table for Scout. 'I'm guessing this has something to do with the wicca weirdos doing a *sans clothes samba* in your back garden?'

Eric gulped back a third of his pint without breaking for a breath.

'You've heard already?'

'Oh, everyone's heard,' replied Hank.

'How? It was less than an hour ago.'

Hank shrugged.

'Village life, I suppose. I have to say I particularly liked the part when you started swinging the frying pan at the fella with a hearing aid.'

'What?' gasped Eric. 'You mean there's a video?'

'Four hundred and fifty hits already.' Hank passed him his phone.

After five seconds Eric handed it back.

'Well, at least they missed the bit where I fell over the washing line.'

'That's on another clip.'

Eric polished off the rest of his beer.

'You just need to have a little patience,' said Hank when they were securely into their third pint. 'It can't be easy for her.'

'I am being patient. I am. But this isn't normal.'

'What do you want her to do, get herself a Tinder account or go speed dating? She's an old woman.'

'Then she should start behaving like one.'

Hank shook his head and tutted. It was the type of *tut* Eric had regularly heard from his father, or more recently from Norman. It was the type of tut that someone was only allowed to administer when they were a minimum of fifteen years older than the person with whom they were conversing. Eric wanted to be old just so he could use that tut. He would use it a lot.

'It's not like getting divorced when you're young. Or like your generation that does it more often than laundry. She's invested her whole life in someone. She probably doesn't even know who she is without him. You say they worked together too?'

Eric grunted into his beer.

'Well exactly. God, I could imagine it would be easier for her had he died. At least then she wouldn't feel so abandoned.'

'I suppose,' Eric admitted.

'Can you imagine feeling so alone? The person you trust more than anyone in the world deserts you. Without any warning.'

'But ... but ... jumping over sticks naked—'

Eric was clutching at straws and he could feel it.

'Oh, tosh. Thank God you weren't around when I was young. You couldn't go for a walk along the river without seeing some old codger's todger while he prayed to this that or the other. Free spirits they used to call it then.'

An uncomfortable twisting was wrapping its way around Eric's insides. He redirected his attention to Scout.

'How's Suzy doing?' Hank asked.

'Suzy?'

'Well, it can't be easy for her, can it? I mean, I know she's not a kid, but no one wants to see their parents go through something like this.'

Eric's eyes fixed on Scout as he racked his mind. Had he asked Suzy how she was feeling? He must have done. He couldn't remember explicitly as such, but he would have asked her. He was sure he would have. Despite his internal reassuring dialogue, the churning in Eric's stomach intensified.

'She's okay. She's tough,' he said, finally lifting his hand from Scout. Hank raised an eyebrow.

'You know what,' Eric said, rising to his feet and downing the rest of his pint. 'I should probably be getting back.'

'Just have a bit of patience,' Hank said again. 'You've got a good family there. Trust me. The kooky ones are the ones you want to keep hold of.'

Eric took out his wallet, dropped a twenty on the table and gave Scout a rough farewell. 'That should cover me,' he said.

'See you tomorrow at the plot?'

'Maybe,' Eric said as he opened the front door and exposed the pub to the freezing Burlam air. 'Maybe.'

Whether it was the beer, or thoughts of his wife spurring him on, Eric raced home almost fast enough to stop his fingers numbing. Once there, he flung open the door and unsuccessfully threw his jacket onto the hook.

Suzy was in the dining room again. The mountain of paper had doubled in size. It was only after several loud raps on the door that she looked up from her pile. Dark circles hung beneath her eyes. When she didn't speak, Eric stepped inside.

'Can I get you a drink?' he said.

Suzy looked at the mountain in front of her and shook her head.

'I shouldn't. It'll send me straight to sleep.'

'Can I get you something to eat then? Are you hungry?'

Suzy straightened her back and put her pen down on the desk. Her eyes lingered on Eric just long enough to make him squirm.

'Sorry, Eric,' she said eventually. 'Is there something you wanted? Just I'm really busy, and if you've come to hav—'

'No, no,'

'Then would you—'

'I'm sorry,' Eric blurted out, falling onto his knees by her chair. 'I'm really sorry.'

Suzy stiffened in surprise, and she let out a deep sigh.

'You don't have to be sorry for anything,' she said.

'I do. I've made you come here and uproot your life, and I haven't been supportive—'

'Eric—'

'Please, let me finish. I haven't been supportive. I mean, I've tried to be, but I haven't tried that hard. Not really. I mean Paris was a stupid idea—'

'It wasn't—'

'And I didn't even think about the strain on you, having your mum here. I just assumed you were fine.'

'I'm fine. I'm just tired.'

'But are you sure? If something was wrong, really wrong, you would tell me, wouldn't you?'

'Eric, what are you on about?'

'I just don't want you to feel like you can't talk to me. I know I'm useless and I don't ask you if you're okay enough, but I don't want you to wake up one morning and feel like you and Abi are better off without me.'

'Eric ...' Suzy's eyes glistened.

'I love you so much,' he said.

'I know.'

Still in a kneeling position, Eric wrapped his arms around his wife.

'I'll be better,' he said. 'And if you want Yvette to live here, then that's what we'll do. We've been talking about getting the garage converted since we bought the place.'

'Eric—'

'I just don't want—'

Suzy lifted his head up so that his eyes met hers.

'I'm not going anywhere,' she said.

Eric took a deep inhalation of relief, which he followed with another shorter sniff and then a third. A smoky, but not unpleasant aroma was wafting about him. He sniffed again.

'Can you smell that?'

Suzy's lips twitched.

'What the hell is she doing now?' Eric said.

CHAPTER 18

MONDAY MORNING AND the house still smelt of incense. Suzy was already locked away in her study, with a *do not disturb* sign on the door by the time Eric rose, and downstairs Abi was tucking into a bowl of Cheerios at the kitchen table. Yvette sat next to her, tying flowers around a piece of wire. Incense sticks were now burning in the kitchen too, making the air smell like a blend between a Chinese medicine shop and a tub of vapour rub.

'Why aren't you dressed?' Eric said to Abi, as she spooned cereal into her mouth.

'Granny says I don't have to go to school today. She said I can go to her lessons instead.'

'Her lessons?'

Eric turned his attention to his mother-in-law. Having finished the flowers, she placed them like a crown on her head. Yvette, Eric mused, now appeared to own an unending supply of batik bed throws, although where she could have purchased them in Burlam was beyond him. One was wrapped around her waist as a skirt while another was tied tightly around her head as a bandana.

'Some of the coven and I are going to a crystal healing course,' she said. 'Nature at its most powerful. Lots of them take their children along. They said it would be fine if Abi came.'

Eric scoffed.

'Yes, well lots of them live in caravans, have court orders for not sending their children to school, and consider their second cousins distant relatives,' he said before turning to Abi. 'Go and get dressed. You're going to be late.'

'But, Dad—'

'Now,' he said.

After slurping one more spoonful of milk, she jumped off the chair and dashed upstairs. Eric took her place and helped himself to the remainder of her breakfast.

Yvette had started to thread flowers onto another loop, a smaller one that Eric suspected was designed for Abi. The flowers she was using were already wilting and dropping orange-brown petals onto her place mat.

'Must have patience,' Eric muttered to himself.

'What was that?' Yvette said, lifting her eyes from her handiwork.

Eric coughed.

'Perhaps at the weekend,' he said.

'Pardon?'

'Perhaps at the weekend. If one of your course things goes on over a weekend, then you can take Abi. But not if there's any nudity in it. Or drugs. You are not allowed to get my daughter spaced on some natural hallucinogenic.'

'That would be lovely,' Yvette said, smiling before adding, 'The course, not the hallucinogenic.'

The school run was hellish. Eric had assumed that all his work at the allotment would have helped him build up a baseline level of fitness; after all, it was the most digging and lifting he had done in years, not to mention walking. Unfortunately, all this manual labour had been negated by endless after-allotment trips to the pub, and he thought nothing of polishing off a Fat Bastard down at the Shed. As such, Abi's new-found cycling skills were putting Eric's body to the test.

'Slow down,' he yelled to Abi. 'You know you need to be careful on these roads.'

Perfectly timed to reinforce his point, a white minivan sped around the corner. Abi wobbled, wavered, then put her foot down and balanced herself.

'See,' she said, turning back to her father. 'I'm okay.'

Eric grunted. Behind him he watched as the minivan came to an emergency stop before reversing back, performing a U-turn, and speeding back past them. He would go to the next council meeting in person, he decided. That way they would be forced to listen to him.

Once they reached the school, Eric waited long enough to see Abi's head appear through the window of her classroom before he headed off towards the allotment. It was a perfect morning for gardening. The overnight rain would have caused the earth to soften and hopefully coax out a few worms for his compost heap too. It also meant that he was out of the house. As much as the kitchen countertops needed dismantling and the carpet on the staircase required laying, he was trying to give Suzy the thing she needed most. Peace and quiet.

Halfway to the allotment Eric stopped and rubbed his thighs. The tops of his legs had stiffened and ached from running after Abi on her bike, and a side stitch was creeping its way up beneath his ribs. The thought of digging and turning the soil was getting less and less appealing by the second. Perhaps, he thought, there was a better way to spend his morning. He stopped, turned around, and headed back home.

Like the rest of the house, Eric's garage – excluding the area where Sally was kept, securely covered and protected – was a work in progress. Boxes of things without homes were stacked up against the walls, along with samples of paints, a dilapidated lawnmower, and a variety of tools he kept meaning to sort through and take down to the allotment.

Half of the boxes were still sealed shut and Eric, for the life of him, couldn't think what was in them. One day he would find out though, just as soon as he got the dining room, kitchen, bedroom, staircase, and front lawn sorted. The smell of the garage was an amalgamation of aromas, with potato peelings, car wax, and grass cuttings all making it high on the list. Bizarrely, Eric quite liked it.

Eric pulled out the lawnmower, scraping the blades on the concrete. It had belonged to Norman. Cynthia had asked if Eric wanted to keep it after he bought the house. It was an old petrol mower with a rusted frame and often took three or four yanks of the chain to start, but it would do for now. There was no need to buy a new one when it still did the job. With that in mind, he reached over and grabbed hold of another well-cobwebbed metal frame.

It was difficult to remember exactly when Eric and Suzy had purchased their bikes; definitely before Abi was born. Ambitious plans had been discussed at length over late-night dinners with London friends, Ralph and Sarah. Trips round the Cornish coastline or head up to the Scottish Highlands, maybe even Land's End to John O'Groats. As it was, the farthest Eric had managed was a brief cycle around South Wales when Suzy had gone there for a book tour one year. After Abi was born, the bikes were packed up in the store cupboard along with his golf clubs, Suzy's sewing machine, and a Scalextric set Eric had bought on a whim. He had passed it on to Ralph when they moved in the hope that one of his children got to have a bit of fun with it.

Eric picked up his bike first. The once-pristine metal was now speckled with rust, and the shiny gears were now a brownish-grey network of cogs. Holding it off the ground, he spun the front wheel, followed by the back. There was a little resistance, but nothing that a bit of oil wouldn't fix. He tried turning the pedals. Same deal. Nothing seemed too loose or too tight and there were no bits – at least that Eric could see – dangling precariously about to drop off.

Satisfied that all was in good enough working order, he checked through Suzy's bike in the same novice manner. After which, there was only one thing left to do.

It had been several years since Eric had ridden a bike, but two minutes practising and it felt like it had only been yesterday. He was probably gripping the handlebars a little tight and was reluctant to bump himself up and down the curb, but he was on his third attempt at a wheelie when Suzy's head appeared out of an upstairs window.

'What are you doing?' she called.

'Look, they work.' Eric wobbled as he went one-handed to offer a wave. 'I thought we could start going on family bike rides. We always said we wanted to do that, right?'

'Hold on a second,' she said. 'I'll come down.' The upstairs window rattled shut. A moment later the front door opened.

'I'll give them a proper oiling,' Eric said as he stopped a few feet in front of his wife. 'I should probably get someone to give them a once over, just to check the brakes are okay too, but all feels good to me.'

He pointed to Suzy's own bike, propped up against the side of the house.

'You want to have a go?'

'I'm not sure I'm suitably dressed,' Suzy said, motioning to her skinny jeans and slippers.

'Don't feel you have to stay out,' Eric said, anticipating the *it's time I got back to work* line, and getting there first. 'Honestly, go inside, get your work done. We'll have plenty of time for bike rides in the summer. I need to get to the allotment, anyway.'

Suzy shook her head and smiled.

'Give me two minutes,' she said, and dashed back in the house.

❦

WITH SUZY RIDING BEHIND HIM, they headed out of their road and onto the main road before taking two successive left turns, leading away from the village and out into the marshland paths. From that point on, they rode side by side. Clouds sped off in the distance while pheasants ambled across their path. The night-time rain had given rise to the sweeter scents of the earth, like sycamore and chestnut. Eric pedalled against the chilly air. Sometimes he would speed ahead a little and force Suzy to chase after him, laughing. Other times he would slow, giving them both time to drink in the view.

They had been riding for close to forty minutes when they finally stopped. Eric had grown used to Essex, with its miles and miles of flat, brown earth and near absence of hills, but as he stared out at the vast flatness of the marshes, something changed. Even out driving in Sally, he had never really appreciated the remoteness here before or the quiet. There was something about riding through it all, being part of it. They would do this more often, he promised himself. Suzy slid into place beside him and took his hand. For a minute the two stared out together, the only sounds coming from the wind in the long grass.

He had wanted to take a slow ride back, perhaps stop at the pub on the way, but he saw Suzy's mouth twitch nervously at the thought of her looming deadlines.

'We'll come later in the year,' Eric said, cutting her off before she could start apologising again. 'It's getting a bit nippy. And I want to get to the allotment before picking Abi up.'

'Mum can pick Abi up. If she's going to be sticking around, we might as well make the most of her,' she said before pausing as a frown crept onto her face. 'You don't mind her staying, do you? I mean, really? I know there is always Lydia's, but—'

He kicked up the stand on his bike, swung his leg over, and was about to start pedalling away, when he noticed that Suzy hadn't moved. She was standing in exactly the same spot, staring out at space.

'Suze? Are you okay?' After no response, he tried again. 'Suze?'

With a deep-set frown, she turned and faced him.

'Sorry, did you say something?'

'I asked if everything was all right?'

The frown remained fixed in place.

'You know I love our life, don't you?' she said. 'That I'd never do anything to mess that up. To hurt you.'

'Of course I do.' Eric kicked the stand back down and swung his leg back across the bike. 'Where's this coming from? Is there something you want to talk about?' He moved towards her and took her hand, which had fallen limp by her side. 'Suze—'

'It's just sometimes I feel lost. Like I keep on losing all the things I'm trying to hold onto.'

'Suzy ...' Eric tugged at her hand, trying to move her around to face him. 'Where is this coming from? Is this because of your dad? You'll never lose me, or Abi. You know that.'

'My life before never made sense, you know.' She continued staring out at the fields as she spoke. 'All the things that happened. Everything I went through ...'

A slight breeze tickled the hair on Eric's neck. It spread down his spine as a shudder.

'Suzy. Is something wrong? Has something happened?'

The wind picked up as she moved her head and met his gaze for the first time since she'd begun. Eric's pulse quickened, Suzy's deep green eyes swallowed him whole. They always did. How many times had he stared into them, he wondered. How many times had he truly appreciated how perfect they were.

'Eric, I—'

The bicycle came down with a clatter behind them. Without a second thought, Eric dropped Suzy's hand and darted across to pick it up. He returned within the second although Suzy's frown had all but disappeared. A small smile lifted her lips in its place.

'Sorry.' He lifted her hand back into his. 'Was there something you wanted to tell me?'

She shook her head. 'Ignore me,' she smiled. 'I'm being dramatic.' Then she walked across to her own bike, securing her helmet beneath her chin as she went. 'Parents, hey. Who'd have 'em?'

※

AT THE ALLOTMENT, it took him a moment to figure out what was wrong. The scene was so familiar yet so out of place. It was as though his plot had been transported to the same parallel dimension that hippie Yvette had come from. His greenhouse was still standing, as was his shed, but despite the carpeted greens and neat rows of raised beds, he was certain it wasn't his plot he was staring at. It couldn't be his plot. His plot had newly heeled leeks ready to prep for next year's village show. His plot had clean, raked lines in the soil and clearly labelled markers at the end of the rows. His plot was ordered and structured, exactly the way he liked it, and it was definitely, most definitely, not covered in chickens.

'Fleur!' Eric yelled, leaping into one of his raised beds and spraying the air with soil as he went.

Squawking feathers flicked up around his ankles. One of the hens lifted her head from the ground, a long green stem fixed securely between her beak.

'Get off. Get off that!' Eric said and grasped hold of the leek. He pulled back and tugged, lifting the hen up into the air with the leek.

'Fleeeeur!'

'Eric?' said Fleur as she appeared from around the back of her shed.

Her hair was swept back, her flowing winter jacket dusted with chicken feed, and her make-up had a well-polished yet worn look to it that reminded Eric of an advertisement for a countryside organic clothing brand or some other middle-class necessity. She cocked her head with a peculiar, puzzled expression, before her eyes widened in shock.

'Oh no. Girls! Girls! Come here. Come here!'

While Eric still wrestled for his lost leek, Fleur bounded in, arms opens, as if she were mother nature and all the hens were going to leap straight into her bosom for some massive embrace. When that didn't work, she began deer-hopping about, trying to herd the bemused chickens back into their coop, all while trampling Eric's greenery into the ground.

'Girls, please come back.'

'I'm going to wring their bloody necks.'

It took several false lunges and a dive before Eric got hold of one of the hens. She wriggled under his arm while another one moved in to start an attack on his feet.

'You come here,' he said and swept down to pick up his second chicken.

'Get their coop open,' Eric said. 'And grab some food to get the others.'

One of the birds in his grip was pecking incessantly at his knuckles while the other was attempting to bury her head into the pocket of his jacket.

Fleur sprinted across to the coop and lifted the lid. Eric dropped the squawking hens inside.

'Two down, four to go,' Eric said.

It took a further ten minutes to corner, catch, and deposit hens three, four, and five.

'It's Margo,' Fleur said. 'She's still missing. We have to find her. She could get eaten by a fox or a cat, or she could starve to death. She's the dearest hen in the world. It's not safe for her to stay out.'

'She's just a blo—' Eric stopped himself as he saw Fleur's big doe eyes begin to fill.

'Is this what you're looking for?'

Eric turned his head.

Janice was hobbling up the pathway. In her arms she carried a red-feathered, bald-headed hen.

'Oh, Margo,' Fleur said, running to retrieve the bird. 'I thought I'd lost you. I thought I'd lost you.'

Margo – the dearest hen in the world – then proceeded to peck and scratch at Fleur's cheeks and forearms from the second she was taken until the moment she was dropped back into the coop with the other escapees.

While Janice offered a consoling, *there, there,* to an emotional Fleur, Eric went around the makeshift hen house, checking for possible escape routes. By the time he was back to the start he was scratching his head.

'I just don't understand how they got out?' he said. 'Everything looks completely secure. You didn't leave the back-hatch open, did you?'

Fleur pulled her arms away from Janice. Her cheeks had deepened in colour and her eyes focused on anything apart from Eric. Slowly the penny dropped.

'What?' he said. 'What did you do?'

Fleur wiped her eyes.

'I just thought they looked a little cramped, that's all.'

'A little cramped?'

'Like they wanted some more room.'

Eric could feel the blood rushing to his head. Janice, probably wisely, retreated a few steps behind the chicken coop.

'They are chickens, not children,' Eric enunciated slowly.

'I know, only—'

'They don't need room.'

'They need space—'

'They're bloody battery hens.'

Fleur stiffened.

'They are not. They are free range, free to roam, and they deserve a quality of life with plenty of room and the freedom to forage—'

'Not in my bloody allotment they don't!'

Eric stopped. He inhaled, held the air in his lungs, and then expelled it in a long hiss.

'I'm sorry,' Fleur said, her tone decidedly more muted than it had been. 'I didn't realise they'd go so far. I just thought they deserved a bit of time out in the open, that's all. Feel the wind in their feathers. I know it's silly, but I ... I ...'

'It's fine,' he said with a sigh, but it was too late. The waterworks had already resumed.

'This is me all over again,' Fleur sobbed. 'Running in head first. Not thinking about anyone but myself.'

'Well, it's—'

'Are they all ruined? Is everything spoiled?'

She moved across to Eric's plot. A moment later, she was on her hands and knees in the remnants of his leeks.

'Really, Eric, did they ruin everything?'

'Please don't do that,' Eric said, cringing at the sight of a grown woman crawling around in his dirt. 'Honestly, it's fine. It doesn't matter.'

'I'm sure there are one or two here that can be saved,' she said. 'I don't think they did that much damage.'

She pulled up a thin, green stem. A thick, claw-shaped gash was slashed down the middle.

'What can I do? I can give you the money. I can pay for the damage.'

With Eric now too embarrassed to move, it was Janice who pulled her back to her feet.

'Really? After what he did with that bulldozer? Don't you worry, dear, nothing to fuss about at all.'

'Are you sure?'

'Quite sure. Aren't we, Eric?'

It wasn't just the tone of Janice's voice that surprised Eric. There was a dark glint to her eyes, and Eric strongly suspected there was only one answer to her question.

'Of course,' he said to Fleur. 'No harm done.'

Eric picked up his trowel and began to rummage through the debris.

CHAPTER 19

'I'M VERY PROUD of you,' Suzy said as they sat at the dining room table. They had ordered Thai takeaway for dinner. It wasn't anything like their local in Islington, but they'd worked their way steadily through the menu and had now settled on a few firm favourites, including the Cantonese fried noodles and chunky French fries, although Eric had a strong suspicion that neither of those were genuine Thai delicacies. Yvette had managed to find some form of balance between her extreme macrobiotic righteousness and downright gluttonous carnivorous state and had opted for a vegetable fried rice. After the events of the day, food from the allotment was about to get a whole lot scarcer.

'Old Eric would have lost it if someone's chickens had destroyed his vegetables. Maybe you really have changed after moving down here.'

'Maybe I have,' he said. 'Although had Janice not been there, we would probably be having roast for dinner instead.'

Suzy laughed. Eric's stomach fluttered. After the bike ride this morning, he had driven past the farm shop and picked up a spray of wildflowers. They sat on the windowsill, their aroma a tangible memory of their brief adventure. He didn't bring Suzy flowers often enough, he had thought. Once a week from now on, minimum.

'How was your crystal healing class?' Suzy asked her mother.

Yvette swept her hair from across her face. She was still dressed in dubious clothing, with a violet headscarf and massive hooped earrings which could have easily been pilfered from one of the local gypsies. However, she was fully covered, and for that Eric was grateful.

'It was wonderful. Really wonderful. So much more than crystals. Honestly, I learnt more than I could have hoped for. Like how to resonate with my real centre, my spiritual centre.'

To demonstrate this new-found spirituality, Yvette shut her eyes and poured deep breaths in and out of her nose and onto the dining room table.

'Daddy, can I show you something?' Abi said, breaking the awkward silence that had begun to swell around Yvette's impressive respiratory display.

Eric, entirely bemused, squinted at his mother-in-law.

Fearing she hadn't been heard, Abi raised her voice. 'Daddy, Mummy, can I show you something?' she said again. She was sitting forward on her chair so that her face was only inches from Eric's.

'What's that?' Eric said.

'I want to show you something. But not now. After dinner. I want to show you all something after dinner, if that's okay?'

'Okay.'

'And I think we should probably go into the conservatory.'

'The conservatory?' Eric said. 'It's not very nice in there, Abs, the flooring's not even down.'

'I know. That's why I want to go in there.'

Yvette's eyes finally reopened. A knowing *hmm* buzzed from her lips.

'This all sounds very mysterious,' Suzy said, joining the conversation.

Abi caught Yvette's eye. Her grandmother's skin wrinkled and creased as her smile broadened.

'I guess you'd better show us after dinner then,' Eric replied.

With the plates and glasses piled into the dishwasher, the adults were instructed – under Abi's strict orders – to head to the conservatory and wait for her there.

Eric and Suzy sat together on the wicker sofa while Yvette hovered by the doorway, occasionally perching on the arm of one of the chairs. Several bangs and clatters rattled down from above, followed by multiple expletives that Eric was certain he must have misheard because there was no way in hell his nine-year-old daughter would be using that type of language.

'Do you know what's going on?' Suzy asked her mother after nearly ten minutes of waiting.

'I might do,' Yvette said.

A series of clumping footsteps announced Abi's arrival downstairs.

'Granny,' she called through the unvarnished door. 'I need you.'

'Just coming.'

Yvette hopped up and disappeared out into the next room. A minute later, she reappeared, the twinkle in her eyes a good degree brighter.

'You're in for a treat,' she whispered.

'Everybody ready?' Abi called.

'We're ready,' Suzy said.

'Granny?'

'Ready when you are.'

Yvette reached down beside her and picked up a small speaker. Two seconds later the music began.

When the door first opened, it was hard to tell that it was even Abi at all. She was dressed in skimpy black shorts with a white shirt and bow tie. Her hair had been tied up and tucked under a black top hat and in her hand, she held a white-tipped cane which swayed masterfully as she walked.

'May I present,' Yvette spoke over the music. 'Ms Abigail Sibley.'

Abi's feet, tapping heel and toe as she went, clicked and shuffled across the room. Her arms and hips swung and snapped as her feet whipped up, forwards and back and side to side. When the music slowed, so did she, and when it grew more intense her feet flicked back and forth, creating a series of clicks and taps and sweeps that Eric wouldn't have even thought possible. Her cane flew through the air, from one side to the other, always in time with the rhythm. For a show stopping finale, she pirouetted twice in the air, before finally coming to stop, cane in her hand, arms open wide.

'Wow!' Eric leapt to his feet, clapping his hands vigorously. 'That was incredible! I mean incredible! How did you learn to do that?'

'Granny's been teaching me,' she said. 'I'm getting better, aren't I?'

'You're amazing.'

Eric took hold of Abi's hands and swung her around.

'She's a natural,' Yvette chimed in. 'Picked that up far quicker than I would have done at her age. I honestly can't believe it.'

'She's obviously got a great teacher.' Yvette beamed at the compliment.

'I forgot how much I enjoy teaching children,' Yvette said, gazing adoringly at Abi. 'I always got the middle-aged ones on the ship. They give the rich old folk to the attractive young ones, obviously, but we still never really got to do the kids. I suppose it was because your father didn't like teaching them.'

Her face began to fall.

'Perhaps you could do some teaching here,' Suzy jumped in just quick enough to stop her mother falling too deeply into the abyss of marital memories. 'Something regular.'

'Perhaps,' Yvette said, although her eyes were still in some far-off place that Eric suspected looked very much like a cruise ship.

Eric put his daughter down and cast his eye once more over the impressive – and scarily mature – outfit she was wearing. He turned his attention to Yvette.

'Hang on a sec,' he said, stepping back and examining the pristine condition of Abi's tap shoes, shorts, and shirt. 'Didn't we say you had to take all of these things back to the shop?'

'You did,' Yvette said, placing her hands firmly on her hips.

'Well, then where did all this come from?'

Yvette shrugged. A sly grin crept its way onto her face.

'You never said I couldn't buy more.'

⁂

As JANUARY CREPT INTO FEBRUARY, the sky grew greyer and the roads and ground turned icier. After only two trips cycling to school together, Abi and Eric had returned to walking or more often taking the car. Suzy had taken her bike out twice too – once down to the shops and once to meet Fleur for a coffee – but besides that, she was too busy to leave the house.

'Why don't you come for a walk and clear your head,' Eric said one day mid-month, when his wife had barely left her study in twenty-four hours.

She shook her head.

'You wouldn't mind if I ate my dinner in here tonight, would you? It would just give me a little more time.'

'I'll make you a sandwich,' Eric said.

When he came back into the study two hours later, Suzy was asleep on her laptop, the sandwich untouched at the side of her desk.

The allotment at least, was substantially less stressful than it had been the year before. With little hope of saving his leeks after the chicken attack, Eric took on a more maintenance-centred role at the allotment. He had enough to get on with in the house, and more time spent away from the allotment meant more time spent laying carpet and skirting boards. By the end of February, Eric had managed to strip and re-wallpaper his and Suzy's bedroom, fix the banister, and was part way through tiling the fireplace in the living room.

'It sounds like you've done an amazing job,' Fleur said, when Eric described the escapade that was laying carpet on a crooked and curved staircase. 'I'm not even sure I'd know where to start.'

'YouTube,' Eric said. 'You always start with YouTube.'

Fleur chuckled.

The last Monday in February was as grey as the first had been, and only slightly milder.

'You'll have to come around and see it,' Eric said while knee-deep in U-shaped fencing staples. 'But not until we've got the kitchen sorted. If we ever get the kitchen sorted.'

'You'll get there,' Fleur said. 'And I would love to come around. It would be nice to see a bit more of Suzy too. She seems so busy at the minute.'

'She is,' Eric replied.

For the last two months, it had felt like every time Suzy got one deadline out of the way another two sprang up. Hopefully a few more months and they would manage to find some sort of balance. If not, he would seriously have to rethink the length of his loosely defined sabbatical.

Fleur handed him another sheet of wire, which he laid on the soil and began to roll out flat. Since the chickens' escape, Eric had become acutely aware of the size of their coop. Fleur was right. It was too small. For weeks, their irritated clucks and pitiful cheeps had distracted him as he turned his compost and dug his trenches. So, in the spirit of good-natured neighbourliness, Eric decided to help Fleur build something more substantial. Not only would he stop feeling bad about the woeful state in which Fleur's hens were living, he would get the chance to hone his carpentry skills for when the time came to build his own chicken run. Now he knew the allotment committee was fine with it, his only major decision was whether he should wait until spring and buy some in chickens or splash out on an incubator of his own and let Abi experience all the fun of things that way. Either way, he would be building their accommodation himself, so Fleur's run was a great chance to practise.

'This is so kind of you,' Fleur said as she pulled the tape-measure along the wire.

She snipped a hole in the metal to mark the correct length.

'I can't believe how quickly it's all come together. The girls and I are ever so grateful.'

'It's no problem,' Eric insisted, nailing the sheet into place against a three-by-six plank. 'And thanks again for the eggs. Yvette made a fantastic quiche with the last lot.'

'I've got another dozen for you, if you want them? Honestly, there are more than I could ever eat. How is she doing, by the way? Your mother-in-law? Suzy says she still won't talk about her father.'

'I think she's doing better, actually,' Eric said. 'She was away last weekend on some course or another. A reiki retreat, I think? Anyway, she seems like she's doing okay.'

'No more naked dancing?'

'Not at my house.'

Fleur chuckled.

'And she's doing wonders with Abi's dance lessons. Honestly, I can't believe how well she's doing.'

'And what about you?' Fleur said, leaning in to help him keep it all aligned. 'It can't be easy for you having your mother-in-law there the whole time, looking over your shoulder. Particularly not with Suzy as busy as she is?'

Eric hammered in another nail.

'Yeah.' He sighed. 'Yvette's not that bad. She's brilliant with Abi. She grows on you. It's a little like a fungal infection, actually. I guess at some point you just get used to the itching.'

Fleur laughed again. Her cheeks rose up, creasing her eyes.

'Well, if you ever need to escape, my diary is pretty free. Mine's the cottage with the tangerine fence. Honestly, some people's taste.'

Eric laughed. 'Maybe when I'm finished with the chicken run, I'll have to come around and paint it.'

※

AT HOME, Eric and Yvette had come to a peaceful truce. Her dance classes with Abi had continued and progressed to include Jazz and Modern. Modern was Eric's least favourite form of dance and involved his daughter writhing around on the floor as if under attack by an overly amorous poltergeist. Abi was loving it. She had done several performances for her class, and no visitor could escape their house without a complete hat, bow tie, and cane show first. While Eric was happy to allow Yvette all the freedom she wished for when it came to Abi's dance lessons, he was far more reluctant when it came to the crystal healing courses.

'It's all very calming,' Yvette insisted. 'Exactly what she needs.'

'And it means I can do spells while I tap dance,' Abi said, waving her arms above her head in a supposedly mystical manner.

'I'll do a spell if you carry on like that.' Eric scowled in mock annoyance.

'Honestly, it's such a peaceful environment. So beneficial. Perhaps we should all go together?' Yvette suggested. 'I'm sure you'd all learn something.'

Eric rapidly shook his head.

'Pleeeeease,' Abi begged, with an exaggerated extension on the vowels. 'Please can I go?'

'What do you think?' Suzy said, posing the question to her husband.

Eric sucked on the corner of his lip.

'As long as she knows that this is not actually science,' Eric said. 'Lumps of rock can't actually heal people.'

'I think you'll find—'

Yvette quickly changed her mind and stopped speaking. Learning when to pick their fights was something she and Eric had worked on in the last month.

'So, I can go this weekend? Can I? Can I? Can I?' Abi jumped up and down. Suzy and Eric exchanged a deliberately long look.

'I guess so,' Eric said eventually.

'Yippee!' cried Abi, leaping into the air. 'I need to text Harry Nini. I need to tell him I'm going to be a witch.'

※

THE NEXT MORNING, Eric and Abi left late for school. Although Yvette had taken over Eric's role as Suzy's personal barista – which should have theoretically freed up at least five extra minutes – somewhere between Abi picking up her rucksack and getting to the front door, she lost both her homework and her lunchbox. Fifteen minutes later and both were located hanging on the back of the door in the downstairs toilet.

'Have a good day,' Eric called back into the house, before grabbing the car keys and telling Abi to buckle herself into the back.

With no other parking spaces available, Eric pulled up outside the gym.

'I can walk by myself from here,' Abi insisted.

'No chance.'

'But other kids do. Other kids walk all the way here.'

'If other childr—'

'Pleeeasse?' begged Abi pressing her hands together. 'Pretty, pretty please?'

Eric eyed the distance between the gym and the school. It couldn't have been more than fifty metres.

'You need to wave to me when you reach the gates, you got it?'

'Thank you, Daddy. Thank you.'

Abi's seat belt was off, and she was out of the door before Eric had chance to say goodbye.

It was as Eric sat waiting for Abi to reach the school gate that he caught sight of the sign pinned to the gym noticeboard.

Yoga, gym, dance space to rent. Contact inside for details.

A small smile curled on Eric's lips.

※

'WHAT DO YOU THINK, MUM?' Suzy asked over a dinner of sweet potato mash and fish fillets. 'You said you missed teaching children.'

'But I wouldn't know how much to charge. And what if I couldn't get enough children? I'd end up being out of pocket.'

Like her food habits, Yvette had recently found a middle ground with regard to her clothing choices. While she still tended towards the hippie side of things – crystal pendants, floaty skirts – the colour, as well as the sheer quantity of garments she was wearing at one time had diminished considerably. Her make-up had also taken on a much more relaxed routine, without the need for false eyelashes or vibrant lipstick, and Eric would have had a difficult time saying she didn't look better for it. In fact, he thought, she looked the best she ever had since he'd known her.

'I don't think you'll have a problem getting the numbers,' he offered. 'Plenty of parents at the school said they would be interested when I mentioned it to them.'

'You've already mentioned it?' Yvette said.

'I didn't have much choice. Abi's been harping on about her dancing Granny since the start of term.'

Yvette beamed at her granddaughter.

'So, Mum. What do you think?'

Yvette pursed her lips. Her eyes narrowed and pinched before spreading out widely across her face.

'You know what,' she said. 'Why the hell not? Let's do it.'

A whoop of laughter erupted from the table as Suzy wrapped her arms around her mother in a hug.

'Well, I think we should celebrate,' Eric said, rising and heading over to the fridge.

From the fridge door he pulled out a bottle of bubbly, then gathered together glasses from the cabinet.

'Can I have one too?' Abi asked.

Eric and Suzy confirmed their opinions with a glance.

'A very, very small one,' he said, and picked another glass off the shelf.

Pointing the cork up to the ceiling, he opened the bottle with a pop, then filled the glasses, barely making a mark in Abi's.

'Yay!' Abi called.

'Cheers, everyone.'

Something warm swelled in Eric's stomach. This was it, he realised. This was life. So what if things didn't always go as planned? Planning didn't get them here. It didn't get him to where he was now, and at this single point in time, he couldn't remember being happier.

'Here's to unexpected pathways,' he said, and went in for another clink.

By Wednesday morning, everything was sorted. Yvette had booked the space, and with Abi's help, had created posters on the computer advertising two lessons a week; one on Thursday afternoon and one on Saturday morning, starting in a month's time. Eric had distributed them all around the village, even sticking one up on the allotment noticeboard next to a flyer informing people of red setter puppies for sale. Eric had been right, they hadn't had to wait long. By Friday evening, as Eric prepared Suzy a G&T, Yvette had nearly a dozen confirmed students.

'Much left to do?' Eric asked as he took the drink into Suzy's office.

'Always.'

She pushed her glasses to the top of her head, accepted the drink, and took a long, considered sip.

'You missed a good film tonight,' Eric said.

Friday nights had become family film night. While Yvette sorted snacks, Abi rearranged the cushions, and Eric worked, and usually failed, on drawing his wife away from her never-ending pile of work.

'I'm sorry,' Suzy said, after a second pull at the drink. 'Did Abi go down okay?'

Eric nodded and smiled.

'I feel like I haven't seen anyone in weeks. And I don't know when I last left the house. I've got so much work to do I feel guilty about going into the kitchen and taking a ten-minute break.'

Eric sighed sympathetically.

'You need to get out more,' he said. 'Find people to go for a drink with.'

'When do I have time?'

Eric's insides wrenched as he tried to think of something helpful to say.

'Anyway,' Suzy said, shaking her head. 'How's Mum doing? Any more enquiries today?'

'She's doing great,' he said. 'Five more confirmations today, I think. And two more asking if she'll do adult ballroom lessons too.'

'Will she?'

'I think so. At this rate, she'll be teaching every day.'

'That's great, she needs this.'

Eric took a moment to think. He had been toying with the idea of a garage conversion in earnest for the last few weeks. He and Suzy had discussed the possibility before they bought the house and once or twice – half in jest – when Yvette had first turned up. But now that his mother-in-law looked set to stay, and with the dance school idea looking like a viable source of income, it seemed like the perfect time to take considerations to a more serious level. Eric was about to mention this when the doorbell cut straight through his thoughts.

Suzy eyed him quizzically; it was after ten.

'Are you expecting anyone?' she said, downing the dregs of her drink in one impressive sweep.

Eric shrugged.

'Hank had just finished off a batch of sloe gin and was going to pass some on. It's probably him. He's probably just trying to get away from Jerry's singing.'

Suzy rose and glided effortlessly across the room. A few seconds later came her footsteps on the stairs and the clunking of the front door lock. Eric lifted his glass to his lips as he listened for the sound of Hank's voice. A gust of cold air whipped its way into the house.

'Suze?' Eric called. 'Tell him to come in. I'll get another glass.'

Something akin to a muffled yelp drifted out from the hallway. Eric stood up and followed Suzy downstairs.

'Suzy, who is it?' he said.

He was about to say something else, probably about shutting the door to stop all the heat escaping or something more curt if it turned out to be more damn travellers trying to sell more tat under the ruse of it having mystical powers when he stopped dead in his tracks.

'No ...' he said.

CHAPTER 20

PHILIP DEVONPORT HAD the most picture-perfect smile Eric had ever encountered. So much so that if he hadn't heard the man speak, Eric would have been certain that he was American or Italian or any one of the dozens of nationalities that had better dental hygiene routines than the majority of Brits. He was well dressed, in a double-breasted grey overcoat and a thick scarf wrapped multiple times around his neck. And despite his thinned – and clearly dyed – jet-black hair and the abundance of wrinkles crowding the corners of his eyes, his perfect teeth and the generous twinkle in his eyes were more than enough to keep his roguish good looks afloat well into his sixties.

'Dad?' Suzy was the first one to speak. 'What are you doing here?

'Is there any chance I could come in?' Philip said. 'I'm not really used to this kind of weather.'

An overly dramatic shudder was accompanied by a sly grin. Suzy didn't move. Eric, who could feel the static buzzing in the air, followed his wife's lead entirely. Philip sighed and shook his head.

'She's here, isn't she? I just want to talk to her; that's all. I just want to see her.'

Adhering to her usual rule of impeccable timing, Yvette's sing-song voice echoed through from the kitchen.

'Suzy? Eric? What's going on? Who is it?'

Philip offered his daughter a pleading look, but Suzy's glare refused to falter.

'I think you'd better come out here, Mum,' she said, her eyes still fixed like stone on her father.

As Yvette stepped into the corridor, Eric shifted himself to the left. A small gasp burst into the air.

'Philip?' she said.

'Oh, my little Vetty,' Philip said.

Yvette's jaw dropped momentarily down before she brought it back up with a snap.

'What are you doing here?' she said.

With a theatrical sniff, the old man dropped his bags on the ground and buried his head in his hands.

'I'm sorry,' he said. 'I'm so, so sorry.'

❦

ERIC FELT like he was twelve years old again. With Suzy squished next to him, the adult pair were perched together on the top step of the staircase, straining to listen in on the grown-up conversation going on downstairs.

'We need to know what they're doing,' he said. 'We can't just sit up all night, waiting to see if they want us to make up the sofa. Perhaps your mum is waiting for us to interrupt.'

'Mum's a grown woman. She can get us if she needs us,' Suzy said.

The pair fell back into silence. Eric dug his toes into the carpet.

'Then again ...' Suzy said.

A minute later and they were both downstairs. Suzy knocked twice on the door.

'Mum? Dad? Is it all right if we come in?'

A short pause followed. Eric glanced at his wife, who shrugged.

'Mum?' she said again.

'Of course, of course, come in,' Yvette's voice filtered through the wood.

Suzy opened the door just enough to peer through. Unfortunately, that meant Eric was left out on the hallway standing on his tiptoes to try to assess the situation from there. He assumed, from his lack of view, that the pair were sitting.

'Mum, Eric and I are going to go to bed. Do you need us to do anything? Only we haven't set the door alarm or anything. We didn't know what Dad's plans were?'

Another pause followed.

'Oh, I'm not staying. I hadn't realised the time. No, I'll be off now,' Philip finally piped up. 'But I'll come again tomorrow, if that's all right?'

Eric didn't need to see them to tell that the question was directed at Yvette.

'Great,' Philip said conveying Yvette's apparently positive response.

A moment later and Eric's father-in-law appeared in the hallway. There was a brief meeting of eyes, barely enough for a blink before he scuttled out of the front door without another word.

Suzy turned to Eric. She was paler than he expected, and a series of lines and wrinkles criss-crossed her brow. She met his gaze and offered one short and stately nod. Eric smiled sadly.

'I'll see you in bed in a bit,' he said, squeezing her hand before he reached over and kissed his wife on the forehead. 'Let me know if you need anything.'

Upstairs, Eric spent an extra moment watching Abi as she slept. What a right old mess, he thought.

※

Philip was already in the kitchen when Eric came down the next morning. Yvette was standing by the oven, a pan of eggs sizzling away on the hob, her body draped in purple tie-dye dressing gown.

'You're here early, Philip,' Eric said, noting how his father-in-law's nose twitched at the state of the kitchen table. 'Everything okay?'

'Yes, fine, fine. Is Susan not coming down?'

'She's already started work. Locked herself straight in the office, I'm afraid, but she'll come down for lunch, I suspect. Unless you want me to go tell her you're here?'

'No, no, don't be silly,' said Philip shaking his head. 'And I hope you don't mind me being here. Yvette was telling me all about the allotment and insisted I try some of these eggs.'

He looked up at Yvette and smiled, his infinite teeth gleaming as if they were under ultraviolet light.

'No one makes scrambled eggs like my Vetty.'

Yvette reciprocated the smile. It was wide and stretched across her cheeks, but her skin was tight, and her eyes remained rigid. Something uncomfortable twisted in Eric's insides.

'So, Philip,' he said, deciding there was no point beating around the bush, and noting that Yvette had managed to polish off all of Fleur's eggs for her estranged husband's breakfast. 'What are your plans then? Any idea how long you'll be staying?'

'Well,' Philip said. 'I've rented a little cottage for the next week. It's over towards Maldon.'

'So, you'll be staying the week?'

'It depends,' he said as Yvette placed down a plate of eggs in front of him.

'On what?' said a voice from the other side of the kitchen.

All eyes swivelled to the doorway. Suzy was dressed in jeans and a grey jumper, with tortoiseshell glasses perched on the top of her head. Philip shuffled in his seat.

'What does it depend on, Dad?'

'On whether I've persuaded your mother to come back with me by then.'

Suzy grunted and turned her attention to her mother, who was now at the sink washing-up.

'You don't have to do that, Mum. Why don't you go upstairs and have a bath? I'll finish off. I need to make myself a coffee.'

Yvette opened her mouth to speak, but Philip got there first.

'That reminds me, Vetty,' he said. 'I brought a bag of your clothes with me. You left with so little. And judging by those horrible things you're wearing, this place doesn't offer much in the way of quality apparel.'

Yvette looked down at the purple swirls of her dressing gown and smiled meekly. Her hand reached down and brushed the glinting mirror mosaics on the pockets.

'Thank you,' she said.

Eric and Suzy exchanged a look.

'Grandad!'

Abi bulldozered into the room, her hair a matted mess, complete with pyjamas a good two inches short in the leg.

'Abikins.'

Philip knelt down and swept his granddaughter up in his arms.

'Eric,' Suzy said while Abi continued to shower her grandfather in hugs. 'Do you think you can help me with that thing upstairs?'

'Thing?'

'You know. The *thing*.'

Another lingering look followed before Eric finally clicked.

'Ah, the thing,' he said, nodding his head vigorously, despite the fact that only Suzy was watching him. 'Most definitely.'

Leaving Abi to demonstrate all her newly acquired dancing skills to her grandfather, he hastily retreated upstairs after his wife.

'I just don't know what I'm supposed to do.' Suzy closed the door to her office.

Eric wasn't normally allowed in the room for such menial purposes as a conversation, but the door was thick, and Suzy wanted to make sure the pair weren't overhead. So while Eric took the swivel chair, Suzy paced from one side of the room to the other.

'What are you meant to do in this situation?'

'The best thing we can do is leave them to it,' Eric said using the most grown up and self-assured voice he could muster. 'Your mum's not a fool, she's not going to take him back unless she has forgiven him.'

'I don't know. It's just recently ... it sounds silly, but she's been kind of ...'

'Nice?' Eric suggested.

Suzy offered a sad snort in response.

'You know,' she said. 'I never thought my parents would separate, but now they are, I'm not sure I can imagine them back together.'

Eric stood up and wrapped his arms around his wife. She smelt of pencil lead, washing powder, with an undertone of coffee.

'You get on with your work,' Eric said. 'I'll take Abi to the allotment. Lock yourself in here and give them a couple of hours peace. You never know, by the end of the day, your mum may well have sent him packing.'

'I don't know why this is so hard. I'm an adult,' Suzy said.

'It's hard because you love them,' Eric said.

Suzy stayed suspiciously silent.

❧

'My goodness,' Fleur said as Eric told her how their evening had unravelled. 'What a lot of drama. What do you think they'll do?'

'I have no idea,' Eric said as he watched Abi chasing Scout over on Hank's allotment. 'But as long as it doesn't end up with more naked dancing or Abi getting her bellybutton pierced, I'll be happy.'

It was the type of day Eric hated at the plot. A light drizzle filled the air, amplifying the aromas of compost and mildew and rendering everything damp. At least with proper rain you could justify hiding away in your shed and greenhouse, but on a day like today, you looked weak if you turned up and didn't dig the dirt for at least an hour, particularly if, like today, the allotments were heaving.

With less than half a bed to go, Eric leaned over to grab a trowel from the floor. His fingertips were inches away when it struck.

'Ow,' he said as a sharp pain spasmed across his shoulders.

He straightened himself up to standing. The pain fired again.

'Ow, ow, ow.'

'Are you okay?' Fleur appeared at his side. 'What happened?'

'Argh,' Eric said, attempting to rub away the throbbing at the top of his neck. 'I guess I must have pulled that damn muscle again. Bloody hell, that hurts.'

'Here come and sit down.'

'No, I'm – ow!'

'Come,' Fleur insisted, leading Eric over to Norman's shed – he wasn't sure he'd ever be able to call it Fleur's shed.

'Now, where did you say it hurts?' she said, lowering him down into one of the chairs.

'Just, ow, there,' Eric said, flinching as he attempted to show her. 'But I really don't think you can touch, ow, ow, ah ... ahhh.'

Fleur's fingers kneaded their way into Eric's muscles. She poked and prodded while he rubbed at his neck, feeling the nerves stretch and straighten as he did.

'How? What?'

'Just give me another minute,' Fleur said as undercurrents of expensive perfume wafted up from her hands while she worked. 'You are so tense. I'm not surprised with all that's going on. You need to take better care of yourself.'

Eric closed his eyes. He really was tense. He could feel it now, all across his back and shoulders. All down his neck and spine. He breathed in deeply and let Fleur work her magic. By the time she'd finished, he was near enough asleep.

'Where did you learn to do that?' he said, stretching himself upwards and wiggling joints he doubted had wiggled in years.

'I did a course, years ago mind you, when I was travelling in Thailand. I went to this tiny little village near Chiang Mai and spent three months there, just learning about massage and meditation. One of the happiest times of my life. A little sad, right? Twenty years later and I still haven't topped it.'

Eric continued to rub his shoulders, amazed by the miraculous disappearance of the pain.

'You should go into business. Honestly, you'd make a fortune. You could set up a little station. Although you'd probably have to deal with Janice's bunions.'

Fleur laughed.

'I'd pay you,' Eric said.

'Surely Suzy gives you massages at home?'

'She does,' Eric said. 'But with everything that's been going on ...'

Fleur nodded knowingly.

'Besides,' Eric said. 'They were never like that.'

Fleur left shortly after the massage, leaving Eric to get on with some well-needed weeding. His shoulder, he thought, had not felt better in years. In fact, he felt so good he decided he'd treat Abi and himself to fish and chips for lunch.

As Eric opened the front door to his house, he and Abi were greeted by a caustic citrus scent that could mean only one thing. Yvette was on a spring clean.

Once they'd removed their coats and boots, Abi ran into the front room and turned on the TV while Eric gave his shoulder a quick once over and ambled into the kitchen. He found his mother-in-law elbow deep in soap suds.

'Everything all right?' he said.

'Oh, Eric.' Yvette jumped.

Various saucepans, cakes tins, and casserole dishes – that had almost certainly not been used since her previous cleaning frenzy – were spread out, drying on tea towels around the room. The windows were glistening, the oven door transparent, and even the dining table had been scrubbed of some of the lesser scribblings and stains.

'You don't mind, do you?' she said.

'You go ahead,' Eric replied. 'Just let me know if you need anything.'

She smiled sadly, narrow and tight lipped.

'Thank you, Eric dear. I will.'

Shortly afterwards Philip arrived at the house. With a spray of fresh roses, a box of chocolates, and his normal yet freakishly luminous smile, he swept into the hall as if it were a ballroom.

'Grandad!' Abi shrieked, delighted to see her grandfather again so soon. 'Are you going to live here now too?'

Philip bent down and lifted Abi up into his arms.

'We shall have to see, my little *mon amie*. We shall have to see.'

Eric rolled his eyes. Yvette saw.

Dinner was non-stop talking. All of it Philip.

'Do you remember that time in Ecuador,' he said, chowing down on Yvette's homemade, veggie meatloaf, 'where they handed us those guinea pigs?'

'As pets?' Abi said.

'Not exactly,' her grandfather replied. 'And what about that time in the Cayman Islands with the stingrays? Now that was something really special, wasn't it, my love?'

It was as though he was running through a back-catalogue of every good thing the pair had done together over the last forty years.

'And Verona? What year was that? Sixty-four?'

'Sixty-eight,' Yvette corrected him.

'Sixty-eight, of course, you're right. Still, *Violetta*.' Philip kissed his fingers, then flew them from his lips. 'What a girl, what a voice.'

Fortunately, Philip's incessant chatter and Abi's constant barrage of questions distracted from the obvious animosity within the room.

'Is everything all right, dear?' Yvette said, bringing Suzy's silence to both Abi and Philip's attention. 'You seem rather quiet.'

'Just thinking,' Suzy said.

'About what?' Yvette said.

Suzy didn't reply. After twenty-seconds of silence, a cold swell engulfed the dining room and everyone's eyes, Eric's included, became suddenly distracted by the table-top etchings. The silence expanded, and a deep-rooted gnawing drilled away at Eric's insides. This was familiar. He had sat through family dinners like this before. Silent, awkward, uncomfortable. He remembered them well. But they'd always involved his family, not Suzy's, and more often than not the cause for the tension had been Eric himself. Eric took a deep breath and prepared himself to be a grown up.

'This meatloaf—'

'So, Dad,' Suzy said, clipping Eric's sentence while spearing a potato with her fork. 'How long are you planning on staying?'

'Like I said, I'll stay as long as—'

'But what about work? Surely they can't keep your job open indefinitely?'

'Well,' Philip lowered his fork to his plate. 'I'm on holiday at the minute. And we've got plenty of time saved up. Besides, I don't think indefinitely will play into it, will it dear?'

He grasped his wife's hand and squeezed it. Yvette's timid smile flickered.

'I was looking,' he said, 'and there's a position going in the Maldives. Senior dance instructors at an all-inclusive. I know it's not what we're used to, but I thought it might make a nice change. Get off the boats. Try something new. And you have always loved the Maldives, haven't you, dear?'

'Maybe,' Yvette said.

'Or Iceland. I saw a position going in Iceland. And Grenada. There were two there. Didn't you have a friend who worked in Grenada, Vetty? Perhaps he could put in a good word for us?'

'Perhaps,' Yvette said and pushed a piece of meatloaf around her plate.

Philip grinned his talk-show host grin.

Eric feared another silence was once again about to consume them and was considering what other polite topics – other than the meatloaf and weather – he could use to break it when Philip dropped his knife on to the plate with a clatter.

'I almost forgot,' he said, brushing his hands on the thighs of his trousers and pushing his plate into the centre of the table. 'I've got a bit of a treat for you.'

'For me?' Abi bounced in her seat.

'Not this time, I'm afraid. This one's a treat for your grandmother.'

While Abi sank sulkily back into her chair, Suzy stiffened.

'Box tickets,' Philip continued, oblivious to their reaction. 'To see *Hamilton*. It's a matinee performance. I tried for the evening, but they were completely booked up. I had to call in some favours just to get these. I thought we could go down next Friday, book ourselves into the Ritz, make a weekend of it.'

'The whole weekend?' Yvette asked.

'Of course. That is all right, isn't it?'

Yvette's bottom lip disappeared under her top row of teeth.

'Granny,' Abi said, following her grandfather's example and dropping her cutlery with a clatter onto her plate. 'I thought you were going to take me to one of your lessons next weekend.'

'Well, I ...'

Philip reached over and stroked his granddaughter on the shoulder.

'Don't you worry, she'll have plenty of time to give you some dance lessons when she gets back. Maybe I can teach you, too. How does that sound, a bit of ballroom dancing with your grandad?'

Abi pouted.

'We weren't going to a dance lesson. We were going to a magic lesson.'

'Magic lesson?' Philip frowned.

Yvette blushed.

'Crystal healing,' she said. 'It's a crystal healing course.'

Philip's face tightened and pinched before cracking open into a full smirk.

'Good God, it looks like I came back just in the nick of time,' he said. 'First hippie clothes, now crystal healing. Another week and you'd have been jumping over sticks naked in the back garden.'

CHAPTER 21

FOR THE REST of the week, Philip continued to invite himself over for breakfast and dinner. Eric would have liked to have made his own presence as minimal as possible, but it was tough. Every time he caught Yvette's eye, there would be a sharp tug behind his ribs and he would feel obliged to stay and offer her some form of moral support. Particularly with Suzy barely making it downstairs most days. While Eric would never question the amount of work she was currently submerged beneath, he suspected that her father's presence in the house was also playing a large part in her absence.

'Has your mum mentioned to you what she plans to do at all?' Eric asked one night when Suzy crawled into bed, well after midnight.

'Not a word,' Suzy said. 'But if she's staying or leaving, I wish she'd just make up her mind. One way or another.'

When Friday arrived, Yvette readied herself for their trip to London.

'Are you sure you don't want me to give you a lift to the station?' Eric said. 'I really don't mind at all.'

Yvette shook her head. 'It's fine, honestly. I like the fresh air.'

'I can run you down?' Suzy said, having left the shackles of the laptop long enough to bid her mother farewell.

Once again, Yvette declined. 'Honestly, I'm perfectly fine walking by myself,' she insisted.

Eric examined his mother-in-law as she slipped her handbag over her shoulder. Some days, the wonderment of how she could ever have raised Suzy and Lydia was beyond belief. Other times, the three of them were so clearly cut from the same cloth. Today, it was difficult to tell. Yvette was dressed in her old clothes, with a feathery scarf and chandelier earrings all set off by the massive emerald ring of her grandmother's that she'd refused to let Eric use to propose, but there was something not quite right. The bright lipstick didn't seem to suit her so much anymore and made her mouth droop downward; the false eyelashes made her face look tired and small.

'I hope you have a wonderful time,' Suzy said, kissing her mum on the cheeks.

'So do I,' Yvette replied.

In place of missing her crystal healing course, Eric had arranged for Abi to go for a sleepover at Tom and Lydia's for the night. They would keep her there for the morning, then he and Suzy would go and join them for dinner on Saturday night. That meant that for the first time in as long as Eric could remember, they were going to have the house to themselves, all Friday night and Saturday morning.

'What's the most romantic thing someone has ever done for you?' Eric asked Fleur as he composted the last of the rotten parsnips from the crop.

It was such a waste. Next year, he decided, he would be planting more manageable amounts. Different varieties, that was the key. Make sure he didn't end up with any gluts.

'Me?' Fleur said.

Her hands were placed in a tight grip around Margo as she stroked her feathers. The chicken, it appeared, was not too keen on this, as indicated by its constant cawing and clawing at Fleur's skin.

'I'm not sure. My ex took me on holiday once. It wasn't a surprise though. I had to book it. And pay half. I'm not sure if that counts as him taking me on holiday or not? Chocolates. Fancy hotels. Ed Spencer made me a heart shaped card out of jellybeans when we were in primary school. Although I couldn't eat the jellybeans as they were covered in glue, which seems like a waste now I think about it. I guess that's it, really.'

'Hmm,' Eric mulled. 'Suzy's not a big fan of jellybeans. But what about in the house? Would you find the whole rose-petals-on-the-bed-thing cheesy? Or a candle-lit bath? What would be the most romantic thing ever?'

Fleur put the chicken back in the run and mulled the question over.

'My cat was a present,' she said. 'Not from a boyfriend though, but it's still the most thoughtful gift I've been given. I'd just moved up to London. Never lived by myself before. Never even been on my own.'

'I didn't know you had a cat.'

'Colin. He died last year. He was sixteen, so he'd had a pretty good life.' Her gaze wandered off into the distance. 'I still miss him, actually. Weirdly he was my best friend, keeping me company when I didn't know anyone. In a way, I suppose he kept me sane. I guess I probably shouldn't say that out loud.'

With her head still lost in her thoughts, Fleur reached into the run and retrieved another hen.

'I'm guessing that Suzy wouldn't want you to get her a cat as a romantic gesture?' she said, ignoring the onslaught of talons into her wrist.

'No,' Eric said as an idea began to formulate in the back of his mind. 'She most definitely would not want a *cat*.'

Suzy had mentioned wanting a puppy since they first met. She had never had pets as a child, due to the sporadic nature of her parents' living arrangements, and later because of her ex-husband Pete's litany of allergies, although Eric suspected his aversion to commitment also played a part. The garden in London was nothing more than a concrete box and they'd both decided that it just wasn't fair to bring up an animal when they were both so busy working. But they were home now, a lot. And how often had Suzy mentioned being lonely in the last few months? How many times had she wished she had an excuse to get out of the house and go for a walk? A dog was the ideal excuse. She could meet people with a dog too, take it out for walks, rides even, now that they were both using their bikes. It would be perfect.

Eric strode over to the allotment entrance. Yvette's dance class flyer was in the exact same position he had pinned it nearly two weeks ago, and next to it the same A4 sheet of paper.

Red Setter Puppies For Sale, the notice read.

Eric didn't bother taking a photo of the sign. He typed the number directly into his phone and rang them straight away. Romance was not something to ruminate on. Romance required action. When the phone was answered, and the availability of a puppy confirmed, he launched into full operation mode. Everything had to run according to plan.

BY SIX-THIRTY ERIC'S nerves were shot. Suzy had left with Abi to go to Tom and Lydia's around five. He had also persuaded her to pick up a takeaway to give him a little more time.

'Please can you go and get it?' he whinged. 'They always get the delivery wrong over the phone.'

'Mine's never wrong.'

'Yours might not be, but mine always is. They always give me chicken instead of beef. And they never listen when I say no onion unless I'm actually there to say it.'

'Then you go and get it, Eric. I've been sitting all day, the last thing I want is to sit in the Chinese after dropping Abs off.'

Eric pulled his best pleading face.

Suzy frowned, clenched her jaw and then relaxed it.

'Fine. I don't care. I'll go and get my boots on.' She called up the stairs, 'Come on, Abi, we're leaving now.'

'Drive safe,' Eric shouted after her, waving as she pulled the Audi carefully out of the driveway. It was time to put the plan into action.

'ALL KENNEL CLUB REGISTERED,' the owner had told him as Eric stood in the puppy filled kitchen. 'Only got bitches left I'm afraid.'

Eric had gone straight from the allotment to Tesco earlier in the day to stock up on puppy related paraphernalia. He had arranged to meet the owner at her house – just a few miles outside of Burlam – at two o'clock.

'Litter was fourteen, but these five are all that's left. And I've got another two people coming to look tomorrow, mind you. I wouldn't be surprised if they were all gone by Sunday. They've had all the jabs, of course. Fine to socialise if you have other animals.'

'That one,' Eric said, not having listened to a word the woman had just said. 'I want that one.'

His chosen pup was lying down, apart from the rest of the litter, and since Eric's arrival she'd done nothing but stare at him. Her deep brown eyes drooped down and her paws – four times too big for her body at least – stuck out from under her chin. Every now and again she would cock her head as if trying to figure out what was going on inside his.

'That one?'

'That's the one.'

Eric took a tentative step forwards, then stopped. For a brief second, he thought she might bolt and scurry back to the safety of her siblings. But her head cocked, her eyes blinked, and less than a heartbeat later her tail was thumping hard against the floor. Only when Eric put his hand down to stroke her did she close her eyes. A soft hum vibrated through him as she nestled herself against his palm.

'This is the one,' Eric said again.

He picked her up and cradled her in the crook of his arm. This little girl was going to make everything right.

After handing over a ludicrous amount of money, the next stop was Hank's.

'It'll just be a couple of hours,' Eric assured him. 'As soon as I get Suzy out the house, I'll call you.'

※

'YOU NEED TO BRING HER NOW,' Eric said, having started the call to Hank before Suzy and Abi were even out of sight. 'And don't forget the food and the bed. And the chew toy. Don't forget the chew toy, I think it's her favourite one.'

'It's all packed and ready,' Hank assured him.

'Don't bother knocking, just come straight round the back, all right?'

'Got it.'

'Okay, see you in five.'

Eric was about to hang up when he remembered one last thing. It wasn't the most important element, but he did want to do things properly.

'I don't suppose either of you two have a bow, do you?' he asked.

After a fair bit of consideration, Eric had decided that the conservatory would be his room of choice when it came to his wife's surprise. The cloudless night sky added a constantly changing background of stars while the lack of soft furnishings would also offer the least chewing opportunities for the as-yet-unnamed puppy. Also, it had direct access to the garden where it would be necessary to house the puppy for the short time until his big reveal.

He was two-thirds of the way through lighting mountains of cathedral-style candles when Hank and Jerry appeared in the back garden. Eric waved them in.

'Good God,' Eric said, on surveying his newly purchased puppy. 'What the hell is that?'

Around the puppy's neck was tied a lime green bow tie, the magnitude of which Eric had never before encountered. The frilly lace material looked like it was something off one of Yvette's dancing get-ups, and the knot alone was almost double the size of the poor dog's head.

'I had a few props left over from last year's Halloween party. I think this was used for somebody's pumpkin costume,' Jerry said.

'I guess it'll have to do.'

Eric stretched out a hand and scooped her out of Hank's arms.

'It's all right, little girl,' he said. 'You're back with Daddy now.'

Just like Suzy, Eric had never owned a dog before. Growing up, his father had never been keen, and with all the weekend trips away in Sally, he didn't think it would be fair. Still, Eric saw himself as a dog person. He could see it now, walks along the river front, the puppy's neckerchief fluttering in the wind. Winter evenings curled up in front of the fire, his slippers obligingly delivered. She was everything he imagined and more. Before now, Eric had only believed the concept of love at first sight to exist on a purely biological level, but now he wasn't so sure. Her wet nose burrowed in under his chin, and the smell of earth and lanolin rose from her fur.

'Have you had a setter before?' Hank said. 'Lovely dogs. Lovely temperament.'

'No, I haven't,' Eric said.

'Oh, she'll be grand. Great for Abi too. Obviously, she'll be barking.'

'You mean loudly?'

'Oh no, I mean *barking* as in *crazy*. Setters, they're bonkers, the lot of them.'

Eric looked at the bundle his arms. The ball of fluff rose and fell, and a slight whimper escaped from her lips.

'Not this one. She's perfect.' And almost as if she'd heard him, she lifted her face towards his and gave him a long, slobbery kiss on his cheek.

Eric felt bad locking her up in the shed, but it was only for half an hour at most, and the last thing he wanted was her knocking over one of the candles or shitting in the middle of the room before Suzy got back. He'd cornered off an area between his seed trays and power-tools and dropped her down with her blanket and her favourite toy. Then he gave her one last quick squeeze and hurried back to the house. Less than three minutes later the front door opened, and Suzy walked in laden with Styrofoam containers.

'Have you at least got the plates out?' Suzy called, smells of soy sauce and fried beansprouts accompanying her voice.

Eric raced into the hallway before she could get too far into the house and grabbed the bag of containers from her.

'I'll sort this out.'

'Are you sure?' she said.

'Why don't you go and sit in the conservatory. I thought it might be nice to eat in the air for once.'

'Why would we eat in the conservatory?' Suzy frowned.

'Why not? We have a big house, let's use it. Now, go sit down, I'll follow you in.'

Suzy eyed him suspiciously as she removed her shoes and coat. Eric watched on. His heart was beating at ten to the dozen, and it was taking all his self-control not to scream out, '*I got you a puppy,*' at the top of his voice. But that was for later. First came the romantic part.

Suzy's reaction was everything he hoped for. The moment she set foot into the conservatory, the whole space echoed with her gasp, and even Eric had to do a double take. It looked better than he had realised. The dozens of candles reflected off the glass walls, filling the whole room in a thousand tiny sparkles. Smells of vanilla and honeysuckle rose thick, and the air and the warmth and light surrounding them was both mesmerising and comforting all at once.

He stepped behind her and wrapped his arms around her waist.

'Eric,' Suzy whispered. 'What is all this for?'

'What's it for? It's for everything. For putting up with me, for coping with your mum, for never saying no to any of my silly schemes, and for always putting everyone else before yourself. I don't want you to think I don't appreciate it. We all appreciate it.'

'Eric,' she said again, her eyes brimming with tears.

'Come on,' he said, 'Let's eat.'

Eating proved more challenging than expected. Eric's eyes went back and forth to the shed as he attempted to chew his kung-po *chicken* and noodles all while feeling as though an army of genetically-modified giant millipedes were doing the Argentine tango in his intestine. It didn't help matters that Suzy was eating infuriatingly slowly.

'How's Fleur doing at the allotment?' she said. 'I keep meaning to catch up with her, but honestly, I don't know where the time has gone. Can you tell her to give me a call the next time you see her? Maybe we could arrange to go for tapas again.'

'You don't mean with me, do you?' Eric said, blanching.

'No, definitely not with you. Don't worry. I learnt my lesson.'

Eric's gaze went once more back to the shed. It was a warm night, the warmest it had been so far that year, and he had put plenty of blankets in the shed, but he still felt bad. The place they'd got her from kept her inside, by the fire, and she probably wasn't used to being in the cold for that long. The last thing he wanted was to follow up his surprise with a trip to the twenty-four-hour emergency vet's.

When Suzy had only a few forkfuls left on her plate. He began to blow out some of the lower candles.

'What are you doing?' Suzy asked. 'They looked pretty.'

'It was starting to get a bit hot for me,' Eric said. 'And I don't want to set the place on fire.'

'Oh, okay.'

'Don't worry,' Eric said, noting Suzy's distinct pout. 'I have another surprise for you.'

'You do?' she said, her pout blossoming back into a smile.

'I do.'

Deciding that saving the puppy from the freezing cold was far more important than Suzy finishing her meal, he took her plate and put it down on the floor next to his. Then he bent down on the ground and took her hands.

'I know this year hasn't got off to the greatest start for you,' he said. 'What with your mum, and work and now your dad.'

Suzy gave a sad, half-laugh.

'And I know that it's been harder here than you thought. I know you feel like you've been in the house on your own a lot, and you don't really get a chance to meet people. I know you don't like feeling so cooped up like this all the time. And—'

'Eric, where is this going?'

'Well, I was trying to think of a way to tackle things, at least some of them. And I think that I have.'

Suzy straightened up in her seat.

'What have you done?' she asked.

Eric sprang to his feet.

'Just wait here,' he said, 'and close your eyes. You can't open your eyes until I say.'

Suzy gave Eric one more quick look.

'Okay,' she said, and scrunched her eyes closed, a slanted smile twisting on her lips. 'But I hope you've not done anything stupid, Eric.'

CHAPTER 22

IT HAD NOT gone well.
'A *puppy?*' Bolted upright, red faced, hands on hips, looking miles and miles from the blissful, grateful wife he had imagined. 'What on earth did you get a bloody puppy for?'

'For you. For company. To get you out of the house.'

'Do you have any idea how much work a puppy is?'

'But she can stay with you during the day,' Eric stuttered. 'You'll have company.'

'I'll have another bloody chore. Do you know how much walking one of these needs? Do you?'

'Well, I—'

'And who's going to toilet train her? Have you thought about that?'

'Well, *erm*—'

'And what about when I'm away on book tours or have to fly off last minute?'

'I'll still be here, I can take her to the allotment.'

'So that she can get covered in mud and trample it all over the house?'

Eric squeezed the puppy tightly in his arms. The big brown eyes were still gazing up at him and piercing through the exact point in his sternum that led to his heart.

'I'm sorry,' said Suzy, softening her voice and lowering herself back down into the chair. 'But you do understand where I'm coming from, don't you? Maybe in a year's time when this book is all sorted, and the house isn't a complete mess, and Mum and Dad have sorted out whatever Mum and Dad need to sort out. Maybe then we can think about getting a dog. But not now. This can't work now.'

'So, you want me get rid of her?'

There was a strong heat building behind Eric's eyes; he would have liked the cause to be anger, but it wasn't. It was her. This little red bundle who had already stolen his heart so completely. She didn't deserve to be tossed back to that place. To the cold, dog-eat-dog world of puppy sales. Who knew who might take her home? Gypsies, drug-addicts? What if no one took her home? What would happen then?

'She needs to go back,' Suzy said again.

With his throat clamped tight Eric sniffed his way through a nod.

'But she can stay tonight, can't she? I'll take her back in the morning but not now. She's tired. And it's a long way back to where I got her,' he lied.

Suzy lifted her hand and ruffled the scruff of her neck. 'She can stay tonight,' she said. 'But first thing in the morning ...'

'First thing in the morning,' Eric repeated.

<hr>

ANY HOPES ERIC had harboured about Little Red — as he had covertly named her — changing Suzy's mind overnight were quickly eradicated when the howling started. At first it was just a whimper, a quiet sound that was easy to dismiss, much like the wind rattling through the windows or the hum of a fan in the summer months. Then it got louder; the whimpers became whines, the whines grew longer, and soon the only option Eric had was to go downstairs, curl up on his ridiculously uncomfortable sofa, and stay by her side. When she did finally fall asleep, it was in the crook of Eric's arm. When he woke it was to a wagging tail and an onslaught of licks. His heart ached. At least if she had pissed all over him, he would have felt a bit better about returning her, Eric thought as the puppy wrestled on the ground with one of Abi's dance shoes. But she wouldn't do that. Little Red was perfect.

'She needs to be gone before Abi gets back,' Suzy said. 'I'm not having you two siding against me on this.'

'Fine,' Eric agreed. 'You know it's not like a pet shop, I probably won't get the money back.'

'Then you won't get the money back. I'm not changing my mind. And maybe it's best if I pick up Abi myself. Give us a bit of time. I'll tell Lydia you're sick or something.'

Eric didn't bother with a reply. He was far too busy tickling Little Red's tummy.

With Suzy heading out early to pick Abi up from Lydia's, Eric decided to make his remaining time with Little Red special. He packed up her toys, along with a small bag of sausages, and readied himself for the allotment. He was halfway out the door, both dog and sausages in hand, when the house phone rang.

'Hello,' Eric said, pinching the phone between his shoulder and ear as he tried to hold the squirming dog in place.

'Is 'e there?'

Eric took a moment.

'Sorry,' he said. 'Who's calling?'

'Is *he* there?'

The tone was efficient to the point of curt and the accent, thick London. An unnatural tension roiled its way down Eric's spine.

'Who's speaking please?' Eric asked.

'You tell that little *pipsqueak* that I know where he is, and what he's done, and I'm coming for him.'

'Sorry, who is—'

The phone clicked dead.

Under his arm, Little Red yapped.

'I've no idea,' Eric said. 'Probably a wrong number.'

He considered that he should probably tell someone that the Burlam youths had graduated from performing wheelies in the station carpark to making sinister prank calls.

Together the pair strolled down to the allotments, Little Red trotting out front on her lead. There was something special about her, about their connection, Eric mused, as once again he had to pause to allow her to pick up a stick and toss it around between her paws. She was certainly more intelligent than the average dog, he was sure. After all, how many other dogs would respond to the name after less than twenty-four hours?

'Red?' he called, just to check it wasn't a coincidence.

Her little ears pricked as her tail thwacked the floor. Eric's chest throbbed.

Tossing her stick aside, they continued on.

'So,' Hank said as he saw Eric approach. 'How did it all go? What did Suzy think to the newest member of the family?'

Eric shook his head.

'What?'

'She said we can't keep her. She said she's got to go back.' A lump was swelling rapidly in Eric's throat. 'I know it's ridiculous because she's only a dog, and she doesn't know me from Adam, but honestly, I feel like I'm losing a limb.' The lump forced its way up towards his voice box. 'The way she looked up at me this morning when I was eating my breakfast. I just don't feel like the house is going to feel the same without her.'

Hank took off one of his gardening gloves and ruffled up the pup's fur. 'They'll find somewhere good for her.'

'I hope so.' Then sadly, and solemnly, Eric trod the way to his own patch of dirt.

'Oh, my goodness, who is this?' Fleur swept over, lifting the dog out of Eric's arms before he even had a chance to say hello. After two minutes vigorous ear rubbing, she finally looked up at Eric.

'Tell me you didn't? Oh, you did, didn't you? Oh, my lord, she is gorgeous. Did Suzy love her? She must be thrilled.'

Eric raised an eyebrow and tilted his head.

'What?' Fleur said. 'Don't tell me she didn't love her? How could anyone not love her? Just look at those eyes. And those massive feet and those amazing floppy ears.'

'I know, right?'

With the puppy back in his arms, Eric strode across to Fleur's veranda – it was starting to feel more like Fleur's than Norman's – where he collapsed into one of the chairs with a sigh. Pursing her lips, Fleur lowered herself into the seat next to him.

'So, what now?' she said. 'What are you going to do?'

'Suzy said I have to take her back, so I guess I have to take her back.'

'No?' Fleur lifted the dog out of Eric's arms again and placed her squarely on her own lap. 'You don't want to do that, do you?'

'Of course I don't.'

The moment's silence was filled by the contented murmurings of Little Red, who had now climbed onto Fleur's shoulder in order to gain a more optimum ear chewing position.

'I just didn't realise I'd ... I'd ...' Eric could feel the tears welling in his eyes, yet again. 'I just didn't realise I would fall in love with her so quickly,' he said sniffing loudly and wiping his eyes with the back of his sleeve.

His emotional outburst was met with yet more silence. Once more Fleur's lips were pursed, although now her brow was crinkled in a thoughtful, contemplative way. The silence continued to expand around them.

'What if I took her?' she said eventually.

'Sorry?'

'I said, what if I took her? I've been thinking about getting an animal, cat, dog, whatever since I moved here. It just feels so empty now that Colin is gone. This seems like the perfect solution. I could bring her down to the allotment—'

'And I could still see her?'

'You could even pop round to the house now and then to take her for a walk if you wanted.'

Eric's heart was thumping. His cheeks were glowing with an uncontainable heat, and his smile stretched to its limit. He shook it away and frowned.

'No, you can't do that. You can't take on a dog just because someone else is abandoning it. That's no reason to get a pet. What if you got bored?'

'Of those eyes? Anyway, that's not why I'd be taking her. Like I said, I've been thinking about it for a while. And somehow this seems right. Like it was meant to be.'

Fleur lowered her gaze to where Little Red was now attempting to bundle herself beneath her jacket.

'Does she have a name?' she asked.

'I've been calling her Little Red,' Eric said.

Fleur grimaced.

'How about Lulu?' she said to the puppy. 'What do you think about that? Do you like that name? Do you like that name Lulu?'

As if she were aware of the entire conversation that had just taken place, including the sudden and abrupt change of her name, the little red setter wiggled her way back down onto Fleur's lap, then hopped down onto the floor, tail wagging. Fleur and Eric laughed.

'You don't know what this means to me,' Eric said, standing, and walking the two steps over to Fleur.

'Don't mention it.'

Eric wrapped his arms around her in a hug. Who would have imagined, he thought, all those months ago, that his sledgehammer-wielding, chicken-smuggling neighbour would be the one to save the day? After that thought he hugged her for another second longer because that's what it felt like you should do when someone had stopped you being separated from your canine soulmate. You should hug them.

CHAPTER 23

IN THE END, Eric had driven over to Lydia's for dinner. It seemed churlish holding onto a grudge when a fairly reasonable compromise had been obtained. Also, there was nothing in the fridge and he was fairly certain that Lydia was making one of her potato lasagnes.

When the front door creaked open, Suzy stepped outside and took him by the hand.

'Thank you,' she said. 'And I'm sorry you had to do that. It couldn't have been easy.'

Eric nodded. The image of Lulu trotting off into the distance echoed in his mind.

'Were they all right about talking her back? I'm sure they'll be able to find a good home for her.'

'I'm sure she'll end up at a very good home,' Eric said, recalling how he spent a solid fifteen minutes explaining to Fleur exactly where to rub behind Lulu's ears – and on her tummy and under her chin – to ensure that you got the biggest tail wag possible. He would try to pick up some treats to pass on to Fleur next week, maybe a pig's ear, or something else equally over-indulgent. He should probably get something for Fleur as well, he thought.

The children were eating separately.

'It's a special treat,' Lydia said to them as she dished up sizeable portions of shepherd's pie onto their plates. It wasn't lasagne, but it wasn't bad. 'You've been really good this weekend, and us grown-ups want to have a catch up.'

'That means they want to talk about Grandma and Grandad,' Ellery said.

Tom clipped his son round the ear.

'Go and eat your food,' Lydia said, before promptly shutting the door and turning to Eric and Suzy.

'So, has he said anything about this other woman? This twenty-four-year-old?'

Suzy shook her head.

'Not a thing. He's just swept in, apparently not taking *no* for an answer.'

'But that's a good thing, isn't it?' Lydia said. 'He's realised his mistake, and he's come to make amends.'

Suzy's nostrils flared in and out as she considered the questions.

'I'm just not sure,' she said. 'A month ago, I would have said yes. But it's strange seeing Mum on her own like this. She's never been like this before, and it's hard to explain, but it's almost as if without Dad she's, she's—'

'Nicer,' Eric finished for her. 'She's nicer without him.'

'I was going to saying *freer*, but yes, I guess in some ways she is nicer. Nicer and freer.'

Eric spooned a mouthful of shepherd's pie into his mouth, which he hastily followed by a second. Was it the celery, he wondered? Tom and Lydia seemed to use it in everything, and even he couldn't deny their food was good. Celery was easy to grow, perhaps he'd focus on that for next year's show. It was only going in for his third mouthful that Eric looked up and noticed the tension fixing itself around the table. Lydia's lips were pressed tightly together, disappearing into a straight line. Suzy's expression mirrored it almost exactly.

'What?' Suzy said, being the first one to break the silence. 'Whatever it is, just say it.'

'It's nothing,' Lydia insisted.

'Lydia?'

'Well, it's only ...'

'It's only what?'

Lydia leaned back in her seat and took a long deep inhale. Eric silently scooped another mouthful of mash. He wasn't entirely sure where the conversation was headed, but from the squirming around his intestines, he was certain it wasn't going to be pleasant.

'Let's be honest,' Lydia said, looking solely at her sister. 'You're hardly able to look at this from an objective point of view, are you?'

'Pardon?'

'Well, it's true, saying this stuff about Mum being freer and nicer, I just don't think that's coming from an objective place.'

'What are you on about? We see her every day, Lydia. I see her every day. I know exactly what I'm talking about.'

'I just think that maybe you're getting your emotions a bit caught up. Maybe you're not seeing this from a clear perspective.'

'Pardon?'

'Dad cheated on Mum, and yes, that was really wrong of him. But now he's come back and apologised, and Mum has obviously forgiven him, or at least she's going to if she's spending all this time with him. I just think it's wrong to tar Dad with the same brush as Pete.'

'Pete?'

He should have seen it coming from a mile off, but he hadn't. And from the way Suzy's face flushed with anger, neither had she.

'You think I'm mad about Dad cheating on Mum because my ex-husband cheated on me.'

'That's not exactly what I said.'

'Yes, it is, that's exactly what you're saying.'

'No.' Lydia paused for a sip of water. 'I think perhaps you're having difficulty seeing that Mum might be better off with Dad because your perceptions are skewed.'

'And I think you're a delusional forty-five-year-old with Daddy issues whose house smells like mountain goat.' Suzy was on her feet. 'Abi,' she yelled through into the other room. 'Get your things. We're going.'

'But I've not finished eating,' Abi called back.

'We'll stop at McDonald's on the way home.'

She marched through the door and grabbed Abi, leaving Eric sitting red faced at the dining room table.

'Great shepherd's pie,' he said, rising to his feet still chewing a mouthful as subtly as he could. 'I really must get the recipe from you at some point.'

※

BACK AT HOME, Abi was given instructions to go and practise her dancing or ride her bike or basically do anything that meant she wasn't in earshot of Eric and Suzy.

'Do you think she's right?' Suzy asked him, over a late afternoon G&T. 'Maybe I'm acting this way because of Pete.'

'Do you think you are?'

'I don't know. No. Yes. Maybe? I don't think so. The stuff that happened with Pete ... it was ... we were ... It's not the same as this. I can't imagine what it's like for Mum, after all those years, all those memories. She trusted him. She had built a life around him. I don't see how he could just ruin all that.'

'Perhaps it was just a silly mid-life crisis.'

Suzy *umm*ed as she sipped her drink.

'Maybe, but then *three months*. He stayed away for nearly three months. Why did he come back now? If he knew he'd made a mistake, he should have been on the first flight after her the moment she left. Why did it take him so long?'

'I don't know,' Eric said. 'That's something you're going to have to ask him.'

Suzy took another long draw of her drink. Eric followed suit.

'You know,' she said, when she placed the glass back down in front of her. 'I really am sorry about the puppy. It was an amazing gesture, and an amazing night. I'm sorry I ruined it. I just can't see how we can bring a puppy into *this*.'

Eric pushed his glass against his lips and forced his eyes to meet hers. Even glazed with tears, they were the most beautiful eyes he had ever seen.

'I should have asked. I should have thought it through a bit more.'

'Soon,' she said. 'Maybe next year we'll be ready for one.'

Eric closed his mouth and nodded. His mind flicked to his little red puppy and how willing Fleur would be to relinquish her responsibility after a full year. She would probably understand, he thought. Fleur was good like that.

※

Philip and Yvette returned from London the following day, weighed down with fancy cardboard bags and hat boxes. The smell of cigars and pastries wafted off their clothes along with something that smelt remarkably like whisky and back-alley kebabs.

'Granny.' Abi ran down the stairs to meet them. 'Did you get me anything? Did you? Did you?'

'Maybe,' Yvette said. 'I guess you'll just have to wait and see.'

'You two look like you had fun,' Eric said, unloading his mother-in-law.

'We did, Eric, we really did.'

Yvette was grinning. It was a giddy grin, the type often caused by an exacting quantity of alcohol. Eric recognised it rather well. One more drink could tip the scale either way. Still, it was good to see her looking so at ease.

Suzy glanced at her watch.

'It's pretty late,' she said. 'I'll guess you'll be wanting to head back to your place now, Dad?'

Yvette and Philip exchanged a look.

'Actually,' Philip said. 'I thought I might stay here, if that's okay?'

'Here?' Suzy said. 'What's wrong with your place?'

Yvette stepped forward.

'It's a bit of a drive. Your father's been coming in from Maldon each morning, and he can't really drive back now. He's had a few too many. It seems like a waste of money to pay for a taxi when there's more than enough space in my bed.'

'Eric can drive you,' Suzy said to her father, a distinct lack of question mark apparent in the tone of her voice.

Philip shook his head.

'I couldn't ask you to do that. Really, it's fine. It's absolutely fine.'

Eric could see the tension building around his wife. Her blinking had reached an unprecedented level, and her foot was tapping faster and faster against the floor.

'Yvette,' Eric said. 'Would you mind taking Abi upstairs and running her a bath? Perhaps you can show her what you bought today?'

'I'm sure her grandad would like to show her too,' Yvette said.

'Grandad will come up shortly,' Suzy said.

After a brief moment, Yvette took the hint and left.

The remaining adults were three steps away from the kitchen table when Eric stopped. He had had more serious conversations around the cheap, tatty pine table lately than he could even remember. He could barely sit at it without visions of naked Yvette or Abi's pierced ears jumping to the forefront of his mind. At that exact moment, it seemed to symbolise every disaster that had befallen them in recent months.

'Shall we go into the dining room instead?' he said to Suzy.

Suzy shrugged.

'Fine by me.'

It was immediately evident that the decision to use the dining room as their questioning chamber had not been a wise one. While Philip moved around the table to sit beside the fireplace, Eric and Suzy took the seats opposite. The immense length of the piece of furniture made it look like a board meeting, or a rather bizarre job interview.

'So,' Philip said, taking the lead in what was clearly his interrogation. 'What do you want to know?'

'The truth,' said Suzy. 'About everything.'

Philip nodded, although it was still another minute before he found a place to start.

'The truth,' he said, sucking in his cheeks and frowning. 'The truth is that I was an old fool.'

'Go on,' Suzy said.

He sighed.

'I wish I could tell you something original, something inventive, but the fact is, I'm just a cliché. An ageing man, flattered by the attention of a young girl, fallen foul of all his morals.'

'How long was it going on?'

'Going on?'

'The affair?'

Philip's eyes widened.

'An affair? No, it wasn't like that. I would never do that to your mother.'
'What then?'

Once again, Philip expelled the air from his lungs in a woeful gust. Eric's jaw locked. He knew this was an emotional time and probably difficult for Philip to talk about, but the number of sighs he had used to perforate the conversation had already tripled the length of their discussion.

'Your mother told you about me being reassigned, I assume?'
'She did.'

'And this was not my choice. I asked to stay with your mother. I really did, but there aren't as many men on the ship. Tis the burden of the artistic man.' He paused, and when he received no hint of a sympathetic smile from Eric or Suzy, he continued, 'It was just before Christmas, three or four days before I think, and we had just finished a big show. Katrina – that was the silly girl's name – said there was a party going on in her cabin and asked if I would like to come along. The only reason I said yes was to be polite. You understand that. You can't work with these people and live together and not be courteous. Anyway, there were drinks involved and later, after everyone left, she kissed me. I hadn't expected it. It was entirely out of the blue.'

'And then?' Suzy asked.
'Then?'
'Then?'
'Then ...'

Philip buried his head in his hands. Some whimpering noises – much the same as Lulu had made the night before – escaped from the cracks between his fingers. Eric turned to Suzy. Her skin was white, and her eyes were rimmed with the slightest tinge of pink, but she was holding it together. Of course, she was. This was Suzy. If this had been him and his father talking, Eric would have been across the table with him in a headlock before he had even had a chance to start speaking. Then again, Eric and his father had never had a particularly affectionate relationship.

'It was the one night, I swear. That's all it was.'
'But Mum said the whole ship knew. That it had been going on for months? Almost half a year she said.'

Philip scoffed dismissively.

'Ships and their gossip. Absolute nonsense. A load of tongue-wagging fishwives the lot of them. Never give a second thought to who they're hurting in the process. Believe me. I've seen it all.'

Suzy sucked on her bottom lip.

'So why stay away for so long?' she said. 'If it was, like you say, one drunken night of stupidity? Why did you not come after her? Three months, Dad, that's a lot of time to leave someone thinking you were having an affair.'

Philip massaged his temples with the knuckles of his index fingers.

'Perhaps that was wrong of me. Perhaps I miscalculated, but I thought she needed time. Space away from me. The last thing I wanted to do was badger her.'

'One phone call, Dad. Would that have been so hard?'

He lifted his hands, palms out in defeat.

'Like I said, I'm a fool.'

In the end, Eric made up a bed on the couch in the living room. Yvette protested vehemently.

'We're married adults for goodness' sake. Don't be so ridiculous.'

Suzy fixed her face with her most measured smile.

'This is my home, Mother. And while you're here you will abide by at least some of my rules. If that's a problem, I'm sure I can ring up the Sailboat Inn. They have lovely family-sized rooms well within walking distance.'

'The sofa sounds grand,' Philip said.

'WHAT DO YOU THINK?' Eric said, as he curled up in the bed. Suzy was facing the ceiling, her eyes locked on the place where the old string light-pull used to be.

'He sounds like he's sorry,' she said. 'And if it was just a one-night mistake, like he says ... I don't know, after all there was the incident with the plumber.'

'Oh God, Chad, don't remind me,' groaned Eric.

'But if he missed her that much, surely she would have heard something. Three months is a long time.'

Eric couldn't disagree. The previous year, he and Suzy had spent a week separated and every hour of it felt like a lifetime. He opened his mouth to offer some words of wisdom to help comfort his wife, only to quickly realise he didn't have any.

'I guess we just have to trust your mum,' he said.

CHAPTER 24

THEY WERE WOKEN the following morning by a stream of bangs and clatters. Eric's first assumption was that Yvette had once again decided a spring clean was in order. However, when he stumbled out of bed and down the stairs, with Suzy close on his heels, it was to the discovery of Yvette's suitcases, stacked by the front door.

'Mum?' Suzy asked as Yvette came out to meet them, hair stacked high above her head in rollers.

'I'm moving back in with your father,' she said. 'We've talked it through and we've both suffered enough.'

'Now? Don't you think that's a bit fast?'

'What would be the point in waiting?' Yvette replied.

When Suzy couldn't offer a response, Eric jumped in with one.

'Where are you going?' he said. 'Back to the ship?'

Philip flinched.

'No, no. Fresh start and all. We thought we might try somewhere different. Like the Dominican Republic. Vetty's got friends there. They've been trying to get us out there for years. This seems like the perfect time.'

'Sounds incredible,' Eric said.

He turned to his wife. Suzy's and Yvette's eyes were locked in a gaze.

'We're not going straight away,' Yvette said, a hint of apology lilting in her voice. 'Your father extended the booking and has still got another week on the rental place, so we thought we could pop back during the day if that's all right? See Abi a few more times before we leave?'

The thought of leaving Abi was clearly causing her some distress. She wiped her eyes before any of the budding tears had a chance to escape down her cheek.

'Of course,' Suzy said. 'She'd love that. Do you want me to wake her now, so you can say goodbye?'

'No, no, don't fuss. We'll see her tomorrow.'

Suzy reached in and hugged her mother. Eric stretched out his hand towards his father-in-law.

'*Adieu,* good man,' Philip said and opened the front door just in time to see a car speed past.

A second later came the sound of brakes screeching, followed by the familiar growl of a vehicle in reverse.

'Gosh, they come down here fast, don't they?'

'You have no idea,' Eric replied.

Five minutes later and the pair were packed in Philip's hire car, Yvette waving wildly through the window.

'You know,' Suzy said, wiping away the stray tears that tumbled down towards her chin. 'I thought I'd feel a bit happier about this.'

※

ABI WAS IMMEDIATELY aware of the absence within the house.

'But when are they coming back?' she asked, munching on a bowl of cereal. 'I've got a performance in assembly on Thursday. Granny said she was going to help me.'

'They'll be back for dinner tomorrow night,' Eric told her. 'And she's not leaving until next week. There'll be plenty of time for her to teach you everything you need to know by then.'

'But what about my friends? She was going to teach them too. She was going to teach us all.'

'I know she was, sweetie.'

Eric looked to his wife for support, but her gaze was gone, lost in some far-off place.

'Suze?' he said. 'Everything all right?'

There was a moment's pause before she turned to face him. Her eyes glinted sadly.

'Just a lot to be getting on with, that's all. Are you okay to get Abi sorted? I should probably head upstairs and make a start on things.'

'You go,' Eric said, lifting a coffee out from under the machine and taking it over to her. 'I'll get Abi to school.'

A smile tried to reach her eyes.

'Thank you.'

As she turned to leave, Eric caught her by the elbow.

'I forgot,' he said. 'I was going to pull out some of the kitchen cabinets today. But that can wait if you'd rather? There's plenty I can do at the allotment.'

Suzy frowned and bit her lip. Eric waited for a response.

'Suze? Cabinets or allotment? Are you sure you're okay?'

Suzy's frown deepened, and a moment of confusion graced her expression before it cleared.

'I'm fine,' she said. 'Honestly. Why don't you head to the allotment? We can make a start on this together next week. I could probably do with smashing some things.'

'Sounds perfect,' Eric said and leaned forward to kiss her on the lips.

❦

ERIC HADN'T BEEN LYING about having lots to do at the allotment. Given the overly wet winter, many of his greenhouse seedlings were ready to be transported out into his planters. He had several varieties of spuds that he wanted to make a start on, and if time allowed it, he wanted to clean out his big blue water butt. The water had been stagnant all winter and the combination of bird droppings, dead snails, and a multitude of wriggling creatures caused Eric's stomach to turn. He wanted it seen to as soon as possible; after all, he had first-hand experience at what happened when it was left even longer.

However, despite his extensive list of jobs, Eric had a hard time getting anything productive done at all.

'How's my best girl?' he said, rubbing a hand furiously on the exposed tummy of the red setter puppy. 'How's my favourite little girl in the whole wide world?'

'She's such a star,' Fleur said, picking up a rag-toy they'd been playing tug-of-war with. 'She barely makes a whimper in the night, she hasn't peed in the house once, and I think she already knows how to sit. Here, watch this. Lulu?'

The dog's ears pricked immediately up.

'Lulu, sit,' Fleur said.

Lulu wagged her tail.

'Sit,' she said again.

The dog's tail wagged even harder.

'*SIT*, Lulu.'

The dog leapt up onto her owner's lap and grabbed the tug-of-war toy in her mouth.

'Okay,' Fleur said. 'So maybe that's more of a work in progress.'

Eric sauntered over and plucked Lulu up and off Fleur's lap.

'There's just something so calming about dogs,' Eric said. 'It's like they make all your troubles disappear.'

After that he continued to mill about, faffing with his seedlings and pulling out the odd weed but would find himself stopping every ten minutes to play yet another game with Lulu.

At half-past-eleven, Fleur brought out bacon sandwiches.

'I made extra, just in case there were other people around,' she said, offering the plastic container to Eric.

He obligingly accepted.

'Brown sauce,' he said. 'Good call.'

'Right?' Fleur said, taking a substantial bite of her own. 'You know, it's only been a few months, but I can't believe how much clearer my head is now, living down here. It was a good choice making this move.'

'And illegally bribing the committee for an allotment?'

'That was definitely a good idea. Look at the amazing company I get to keep.'

She laughed and threw her sandwich crust into the chicken run. A mass of feathers ran towards the scrap, wings flapping and beaks snapping.

'We're going to need to get your run sorted soon,' she said. 'I thought you said you were going to have everything ready for your own chickens by April? We're well into March already.'

'I don't know where this time has gone,' Eric replied.

While Fleur continued to decimate the sandwiches, Eric surveyed his plot. The raised beds and ordered rows were unrecognisable from the condemned patch of hell he had inherited nearly a year and a half ago. That whole chapter of his life felt like a lifetime ago, yet at the same time, he had no idea how the time had passed so quickly.

'Well,' he said, bringing himself back to the present. 'I ought to get on with some actual work.'

He reached his arm across and scratched the short, soft fur of Lulu's ears.

'I shall see you tomorrow, little lady. And thank you,' he said to Fleur. 'For everything. I can't help feeling you're picking up a lot of my pieces at the minute.'

'What are friends for?' Fleur replied, and then she walked over and kissed his cheek.

<hr />

ABI WAS in a foul mood when Eric collected her from school. Nothing was right. No choice of food was correct, no suggestion of games she could play acceptable. She didn't want to help Eric sow seeds in the mini greenhouse he'd bought for the garden; she didn't want to practise her dance routine for assembly next Thursday; she didn't want to go outside and ride on her bike, nor did she want to see if any of her friends wanted to come over and play. The television wasn't showing anything she wanted to watch, and everything on her iPad was boring.

'What do you want, Abs?' Eric begged after thirty minutes of pre-teen meltdown. 'Tell me what you want to do?'

Abi's bottom lip jutted out above her chin.

'I want to see Granny,' she replied.

'Of course you do.'

Video calling turned out to be a suitable compromise.

'We'll be back tomorrow evening,' Yvette said on the phone. 'Your grandad and I just had a little bit of catching up to do. We'll go through all the routine then, I promise.'

'Are you coming back to stay?' Abi asked.

Yvette pursed her lips and avoided the question.

'Right,' Eric said, when he had finally persuaded Abi to hang up the phone. 'Now get outside. You're not wasting a nice afternoon like this watching television. And we didn't buy that bike so that it could sit in the garage.'

'Fine. I was going to go out, anyway.'

'Good. Just make sure you stick to the—'

'I *know*.' Abi rolled her eyes as she spoke. 'Stick to the pavement, don't go near the main road, make sure my helmet is done up properly. I know. I know.'

She stomped off outside and into the garage, leaving Eric to wonder exactly how he was going to survive the teenage years.

With Abi outside, Eric boiled the kettle and made a cup of tea. Four o'clock was Suzy's standard tea-drinking time, and the plan was that taking it up to her might give them a chance to talk.

'How are you doing?' Eric said, pulling out a coaster and putting the mug down next to Suzy's computer. 'Have you got much done?'

Suzy yawned and rubbed her eyes.

'Yes, I suppose. I don't know. Nothing feels right at the minute.'

'You're stressed. You need to take a break.'

'Probably,' she admitted. 'But do you know what I keep thinking about the most? There's all this stuff with Mum and Dad, and work, and Abi and do you know what the one thing is that I can't stop thinking about it?'

'What?'

'That bloody puppy.'

'The puppy?'

Suzy pushed her glasses to the top of her head and rubbed her eyes. 'It was the right decision. I know it was. There's no way we could have a puppy at the minute. Not with the house in the state it is, and me working all the time.' She paused for a second. 'But I should have been the one to take it back, not you. That must have been horrible.'

Eric shuffled his feet.

'Well ...'

'I know how much you always wanted a dog.'

'Honestly, Suze—'

'We'll get one. I promise we will. Next year, okay?'

Eric nodded, unable to offer a response for fear it might give him away.

'Maybe we should book that weekend away together?' he said, noticing the bags beneath his wife's eyes. 'Before your mum and dad disappear again. It doesn't have to be Paris, we could just drive up to Norfolk or the Cotswolds?'

'Maybe,' Suzy said. She exhaled heavily before her eyes switched from Eric to her work and back once again.

'I'll let you get on,' he said.

She was back tapping away on her keyboard before Eric had even reached the door.

Ten minutes later, Abi was back inside moping.

'What are you doing?' Eric said. 'Where's your bike? I thought you were practising going no-handed?'

Abi huffed and flopped down onto the sofa.

'I'm done,' she said.

'You've barely been out there five minutes.'

'The man in a car was weirding me out.'

'Weirding you out?'

'Yes, you know. Making me feel weird.'

'What man? What car?'

Abi pushed herself onto her knees, pulled back the curtain drapes and pointed across the road.

'That car. That man. He kept staring at me while I was trying to go no-handed.'

Eric followed Abi's finger. A black saloon was parked up directly opposite the house. It was an unremarkable vehicle to look at, something run of the mill, like a Toyota or a Ford. The type of car that regularly sped down their road thinking it was a shortcut to the village. But this one wasn't speeding. It wasn't even moving. A pair of sunglasses stared outwards from the driver's seat.

'Abi, you stay here,' Eric said. 'And lock the door after me.'

'How can I do that, if I have to stay here?' Abi replied.

Ignoring his daughter's last comment, Eric darted through the hall, out of the house, and onto the driveway. Perhaps it was a surveyor, he thought, or one of those door-to-door salesmen searching for old people to sell their house into some dodgy pension scheme.

His optimistic reasoning was quickly shattered. No sooner had Eric stepped foot out of the driveway when the car sparked into life. Eric picked up his pace, arms waving at the driver as the car pulled away from the curb.

'Hey,' Eric called.

The road was a dead end, and the car was facing the wrong way to get out. It would have to do a U-turn to get back out onto the main road. Eric ran into the road to get a better view. The car, having reached the dead end, came to an abrupt stop and began turning around. Eric stayed where he was; in the middle of the road. There was no way it would be able to get past him, Eric thought, standing squarely on one of the white lines. There wasn't room. It would have to stop. At which point, Eric would ask the driver to wind down his window and find out exactly why he was staring at his daughter. Nice car or not, that kind of behaviour was not all right. Eric stood his ground as the car came charging back towards him.

'Slow down,' Eric said, then, thinking that perhaps the man hadn't seen him, he begun to wave his arms. 'What the ...'

The black car hurtled towards him, engine roaring and music blaring from the speakers. Eric's heart pounded in his chest. It would stop, it had to stop. There was no way the driver couldn't see him, but he couldn't keep going at the speed he was, it would hit him. It wouldn't though. Surely not, not unless it deliberately intended to.

Eric dived out of the way in the nick of time. His elbow slammed against the curb, and small stones sprayed up around him.

'Daddy!' Abi ran out of the driveway, barefoot and ashen faced. 'Daddy, are you all right?'

Eric twisted his neck around as the tires screeched against the tarmac. He watched on as the black saloon turned right onto the main road. Right out onto the bends and away from Burlam. There was no chance he would be able to catch him now. Beside him, Abi was crying.

'It's okay, baby. Daddy's okay. Daddy's okay.'

The words echoed from Eric's lips, and it took him a minute to realise that they were true. Yes, his heart was still doing two hundred beats a minute and there was blood in his mouth – no doubt he had bitten his tongue when he threw himself out of the path of the car – but all his limbs were intact. Nothing was broken, at least not that he could tell. One thing was certain; that was not a regular lost driver.

Back inside the house, Eric bolted the front and back doors, then called the police. In less than ten minutes, Maggie was at his door.

'So, you didn't get the number plate?' she asked Eric, pen between her lips and notepad out on her lap.

'No,' he said. 'I wasn't looking. I just assumed he was going to stop.' He took a sip of his tea, then, finding it too hot, blew the steam off the surface. 'I still can't believe he didn't stop.'

Maggie had had to make the drinks. Given that the house had previously belonged to her aunt and uncle, she knew the place well, and neither Eric nor Suzy was in any state to handle boiling water.

'I can't believe you even went out there. You should have called me,' Suzy said.

'Or me,' Maggie agreed. 'That would have been the sensible thing to do.'

Eric's tea sloshed in his cup. His legs were still trembling with aftershock. He took another sip of his tea.

'I wasn't thinking. I was just going out to speak to the guy.'

'You're okay, that's the main thing,' Maggie said.

'What about the man,' Suzy asked. 'Do you think there's much chance of catching him?'

Maggie sighed and closed her notepad.

'I'm going to be honest. We haven't got much to go on. A man in dark glasses driving a black car that may or may not have been a Toyota or a Ford. I've put it out over the radio, but I wouldn't hold your breath.'

'We understand. Thank you,' Eric said.

'It might just be a huge misunderstanding,' Maggie said, tucking the notepad into her pocket and rising to her feet, 'but I don't think you should let Abi out there on her bike for a while. Not unless someone is with her.'

'Don't worry, there's no chance of that,' Eric said.

'Good. Also, I'll drop by the school tomorrow to let them know about the situation. See if they've heard of anything similar going on. You never know, he might have done this at a few places. It won't hurt us all to be a little more alert. We assume Burlam is this little bubble. And maybe it is, but there's a road in and out of it, and more and more stuff seems to be seeping its way in.'

Suzy crossed the room and pulled Maggie in for a hug.

'Thank you,' she said. 'Maybe we could get together at some point, under nicer circumstances? Perhaps dinner round here when we finally get our kitchen sorted?'

'That would be lovely,' she said. 'And don't worry. I can let myself out.'

She offered Eric one last pat on the shoulder as she went.

With Maggie gone, Eric and Suzy fell into a silence. Abi, shaken up by the whole event, had wanted to stick close. They had put the iPad on for her to watch and she'd curled up on the floor by Suzy's feet, but within ten minutes the stress had taken its toll and she was fast asleep. Eric picked her up, laid her down on the sofa, and pulled a blanket up over her shoulders.

'I just can't believe it,' Suzy said. 'I didn't think things like this happened out here. That was part of the reason for moving. So Abi could have more of a childhood. So she *could* play outside and not have to worry about things like this.'

'I know.' Eric combed his fingers through Abi's hair, tucking a strand or two behind her ear.

'And you didn't recognise him? You don't think it could have been some kind of prank?'

Eric scoffed. 'Definitely not a prank,' he said. 'And I didn't recognise him or the car.'

'Drink?' she sighed, bracing her arms against the chair.

'Yes, please,' Eric replied. 'A large one.'

After a minute, Suzy still hadn't moved. Eric wondered if she'd been implying that he was the one who was meant to get the drinks, and was about to ask as much, when she spoke again.

'I guess it's just a good thing Mum wasn't here. That would be the last thing she needed to hear after everything.'

'Uh-uh.' Eric thought it over.

On the sofa, Abi let out of soft childish snore.

'Perhaps we're better off keeping this to ourselves,' he said, standing up after finally deciding to get the drinks himself. 'The last thing we want to do is stir up a whole lot of fuss. After all, I'm sure it was just a one off.'

Suzy's eyes followed his, down to the top of Abi's head.

'Perhaps you're right,' she said.

CHAPTER 25

KEEPING THE NEWS of the mysterious black car to themselves didn't last quite as long as they'd hoped. At Abi's school, Eric had barely switched off the engine before he was accosted.

'We heard about last night,' a random parent told Eric as he approached the gate, Abi's hand firmly in his. 'In Burlam of all places. I can't believe it.'

'I won't be letting mine out on their own any time soon,' said another.

'This is terrible,' Abi's teacher said in the classroom. 'We're so glad that Abi managed to get away.'

'Well, he didn't actually try to grab her,' Eric said.

'Are you sure?' she said tilting her head, as if to imply Eric might be the one with the wrong information.

'Pretty sure, I was there, remember.'

'Oh, yes. Of course, you were.'

Her teacher wasn't the only one who seemed to have got an embellished version.

'I heard he pulled a knife on you,' said Janice cornering him the moment he arrived at the allotment. Her basket was slung over her shoulder, already half full of cut stems.

'No, no knives,' Eric said. 'Or guns, or any kind of weaponry. Apart from the car. I guess the car was a weapon, sort of.'

'Oh,' Janice said looking genuinely disappointed.

'He did try to run me over though,' Eric said, hoping that might cheer her up a little.

Janice shrugged and hobbled away.

'It really is terrible,' Fleur said as they sat on her veranda. 'You can understand why people are upset. Especially if they have children.'

'You don't need to tell me,' Eric said. 'I don't ever plan on letting Abi out the house again.'

'And in Burlam. It's so sleepy. You wouldn't think something like that was possible here.'

Lulu, who was undoubtedly blessed with some type of doggy intuition, had refused to leave Eric's side since she'd arrived at the allotment. Even when Fleur had called her, she'd fixed rigidly to Eric's ankles. Currently she was sleeping on his lap, the soft buzz of her snore vibrating down his knees.

'That's exactly what Suzy said,' Eric replied. 'This kind of thing was one of our reasons for leaving London in the first place.'

Fleur inhaled sharply.

'Where was Suzy when this was going on?' she asked. 'I thought she'd be home.'

'She was. She was upstairs, working in her office.'

'I see.'

'She's pretty snowed under at the minute.'

'Obviously,' Fleur replied, with what sounded like a tut.

Behind her a loud squawking cut into the air.

'Not again,' she groaned, levering herself up and out of the chair.

'Margo?' Eric questioned.

'Most probably.' Fleur chuckled, making her way over to the pen to deal with the clucking. 'She's probably got her feet stuck in the wire again.'

'How does she do that?'

'I've no idea. In some chicken circles, she'd probably be considered a genius.'

Eric thoroughly doubted that was true.

A little before midday, Eric packed up his tools and began the cycle home. He had left the car for Suzy, in case she fancied going out at all, although he knew the chance was slim. He was going to stop in at the police station and see if there had been any developments, if for no other reason than to put Suzy's mind at ease, but Maggie had promised she would call him directly if anything turned up, so he decided better of it. With this thought at the forefront of his mind, he was more than a little startled to arrive home and find their driveway blocked by a blue and white police car.

'Suzy?'

Eric dropped his bike against the wall. His keys fumbled in the lock.

'Suzy! Suzy!'

His legs carried him straight up the stairs to her office. He pushed open the door to find it empty. Racing back downstairs he ran into the dining room. Her extended office was strewn with papers and notepads, but, yet again, no Suzy.

'*Suzy!*' Eric shouted at the top of his lungs.

'Eric?'

With his eyes glazing from the panic, Eric turned to the voice. Suzy was standing at the entrance to the conservatory. In two strides he crossed the kitchen and flung his arms around his wife.

'Eric, what's wrong?' Suzy said, pushing herself back to arm's length and brushing a hand against his cheek.

'The police car,' Eric said. 'I thought ... I thought he'd come back. I thought ... I don't know what I thought.'

His head flopped into his hands as he attempted to shake his stupidity away.

'Maggie popped round is all, and we thought we'd talk in the conservatory. Since it was a nice day.'

'I'm sorry,' said Maggie as she appeared in the conservatory doorway. 'This is my fault.'

She was holding a freshly brewed cup of tea. Steam from the surface weaved up in spirals.

'I didn't mean to freak you out, only we got a bit of news and I wanted to tell you personally. I've only just got here. Literally, two minutes ago. Suze just put the kettle on so I could give you a ring. Probably should have rung ahead first, though.'

'That may have been a good idea,' Eric said, closing his eyes and exhaling in relief.

A second later his eyes pinged open.

'You've got news?'

Maggie's mouth twisted.

'Perhaps we should sit down?' she said.

Maggie led the pair into the conservatory. Still holding Suzy's arm, Eric lowered himself down into one of the chairs.

'Obviously we didn't have much to go on, but after I left yours last night I went up to Buchanan's, you know, the garage?'

Eric knew it well; it was where Sally had been stored after his father's death. It was situated half a mile up the main road past their turning.

'Well, I thought I'd ask Florence, the owner, if she'd seen anything. Miraculously, she said she'd seen a man and car who fitted your ludicrously vague descriptions, and she remembered it because he wasn't particularly polite. So, I asked if I could have a look at her CCTV and guess what?'

'You managed to get a plate number?' Eric said.

'I did.'

Eric's sigh of relief was as dramatic as it was audible. He turned to his wife. Suzy smiled back and squeezed his knee although the relief was short lived.

'What is it?' Eric said. 'What did you find out?'

Maggie steepled her fingers and rested her chin on the top of the spire. 'The car we identified, the one we *think* fits the description, is registered under the name of a Mr A. Carvay. Anton *Carvay*.' She emphasised the last name heavily, both times she said it, although Eric wasn't entirely sure as to why.

'Am I supposed to know who that is?' he said.

Maggie's head bounced on her fingers. It was more of a contemplative gesture than a nod.

'No, but we do. Not a pleasant chap. He's had a lot of dealings with the police in the past. Not around here though. Mostly around South London.'

Suzy frowned.

'And you're saying that this man, this Anton Carvay, is the man that tried to run Eric over?'

'It looks like it,' Maggie nodded.

'But why?' Suzy pressed.

'That's what we keep asking ourselves. I was hoping you might be able to offer some suggestions?'

'Suggestions?' Eric said.

'Well, I was thinking.' Maggie directed her questioning at him. 'I know you worked for a big company in the city before you moved down here. I wondered if that might somehow be linked to all this. I'm not sure. Perhaps someone might feel you have a debt to pay?'

Eric shook his head.

'I mainly worked with schools. The last two deals I secured were hiring extra physics teachers for schools in the Midlands. I can't imagine he'd have a problem with that. I know a lot of kids hate physics, but that seems a little extreme.'

Maggie offered a suitably humoured chuckle that faded quickly.

'What about you?' she said to Suzy. 'You can't think of anyone who might have a grudge against you?'

It was Suzy's turn to shake her head.

'Not unless they have a problem with mediocrely written chick-lit and articles on how to make the most out of overripe avocados.'

Maggie continued to nod thoughtfully.

'Okay, well I had to check.'

Maggie placed her mug down on the floor and stood up, causing Suzy and Eric to follow suit.

'You know there's a very good chance that this is all just some misunderstanding, and I'm sure it will all blow over soon enough, but just in case—'

'We'll bolt the windows, double lock the doors, and have you on speed dial,' Eric finished.

Maggie hugged them both before letting herself out.

IT WAS ONLY in the early evening when Abi came careering down the staircase in her full dance garb that Eric and Suzy remembered her parents were coming for dinner.

'Shit,' Suzy said. 'Have we got any food in?'

'Not unless you did a secret shop. I completely lost track of time. Sorry.'

As if sensing the conversation, the doorbell rang.

'Takeaway it is then.'

They were three steps away from answering when Suzy stopped. She knelt down to eye level with Abi, shooting Eric a quick nod en route.

'Abi, I think it's probably best we don't tell Granny and Grandad about the man with the car,' she said. 'I don't want to worry them.'

Suzy looked at Eric, who nodded his agreement, then turned once more back to Abi.

'Do you think that's all right, honey? Do you think you could keep it our little secret? Just for a bit. Not forever, just we don't want to tell them right now.'

Abi wrinkled her nose as if she were a rabbit mid-chew. After a second or so, she dropped the expression. A small light glinted in her eyes.

'Can I take the iPad to bed tonight?' she said, a smile creeping onto her lips.

Eric scoffed.

'No,' he said. 'Absolutely not.'

Abi sighed dramatically.

'I guess I'll have to tell Granny and Grandad about the strange man then,' she said.

Eric's jaw dropped.

'Abigail Sibley, are you blackmailing me?' he said.

The glint twinkled a little brighter in his daughter's eyes as she stared innocently up at her father.

'I'm not sure, does it mean I'll get my own way if I am?'

Eric was agog. Beside him Suzy cleared her throat.

'Twenty minutes, that's it,' she said.

Abi grinned.

'A pleasure doing business with you,' she said.

As Philip and Yvette swept through the hallway, it was like the last months had never happened. Yvette's coiffed hair stood inches above her scalp and a haze of floral perfume clouded the air around her. Sparkling jewels dripped from her ears and neck while her signature rings were back on her fingers. Philip looked different too. His skin appeared to be three shades darker. Eric had a recollection of there being a tanning salon just outside of Maldon. Clearly Philip had been making the most of his time on the land.

'Darlings, darlings,' said Yvette as she swung her coat from her shoulders and strode into the hallway, tossing the garment over to Eric en route. 'My goodness, it feels like I haven't seen you in years.'

She leaned forward and air kissed Suzy's cheeks.

'Granny,' Abi said, tugging at her grandmother's hand. 'I need you to help me. We have to practise. I'm dancing in assembly this week. In front of the whole school.'

'The whole school? Abigail, that's marvellous, simply marvellous!'

She crouched down to hug her granddaughter.

'Well then,' she said. 'We must practice.'

'Is takeaway all right for dinner?' Suzy said, taking her father's coat and hanging it on a hook next to Yvette's. 'We were going to cook, but I'm afraid time got away from us.'

'Takeaway sounds delightful,' Philip replied. 'Although not Indian. The chilli powder they use in these inauthentic meals gives me terrible wind. And not Thai either. My stomach bloats terribly with Thai. I suspect it's the fish sauce.'

'Chinese it is then,' Eric said. 'I'll be back as soon as I can, although I thought I might cycle down if you're all right with that?'

'Sounds like a great idea,' Suzy said.

Eric kissed Suzy goodbye, squeezing her shoulders for extra support.

'I won't be long,' he whispered.

'Ride safely,' she replied.

THE CHINESE WAS in the centre of the village, just three doors down from Eaves and Doyle solicitors, the firm who had handled Eric's father's estate after his death. A red-neon dragon flashed above the entrance, and the smell of deep-fried wontons wafted out into the street anytime someone opened the door. Said wonton aroma had many a time been Eric's undoing, and more than once he had indulged in a little pre-lunch appetiser of spare ribs and prawn crackers after visiting the allotment.

Suzy had promised to ring through the order from the house the moment he left but knowing how long it took Philip to make a decision about food, Eric suspected he would be waiting for the best part of half an hour. Normally this would have been a source of deep aggravation; however, as Eric propped the bike against the wall outside the restaurant, he looked through the window and smiled.

'Well, I didn't expect to see you here,' he said, pushing open the door to the sound of Chinese mandolins.

'I'm addicted to the hot and sour soup,' Fleur said. 'Don't tell anyone. It's my third takeaway this week.'

Eric laughed. From down below him came a small bark.

'Hey, you,' said Eric, kneeling on the linoleum flooring and bundling the little dog into his arms. 'Twice in one day. Aren't I lucky?'

The small dog slobbered all over his face, filling his nostrils with a smell of dog food and puppy breath. With a playful growl, Eric submerged his face into the wriggling mass of fur.

'Dog down, or dog outside.'

Eric lifted his gaze from the ground to be confronted by a decidedly angry-looking teenage girl.

'Sorry,' Eric said, still on his knees. 'My wife was going to ring through an order. Kung-po beef, spring—'

'I know your order. You need to put your dog down. Now.'

'Sorry, I was just—'

'Now.'

Eric caught Fleur's eye. The corners of his mouth twitched as he suppressed a grin. He could see her doing the same.

'Sorry,' Eric said and lowered Lulu back to the floor.

When the girl had disappeared back into the kitchen, he reached into his pocket and pulled out a dog biscuit. Keeping one eye on the door to the kitchen, he slipped the treat to Lulu. Her tail thumped the ground in response.

'So,' Fleur said. 'Any news from the police? Do they have any idea who it was that tried to run you over yet?'

'Actually, yes.'

'Really?'

'It's a bit of a crazy story.'

'I've got time,' Fleur said.

Eric opened his mouth and tried to figure out what to tell her. It was probably best to start with Maggie appearing at the house in the police car and his ensuing panic despite the fact it made him sound like a neurotic idiot.

'Well, after I left you this morning, I—'

'Number two-two-four?' yelled the cantankerous girl from behind the counter, stopping Eric's story before it had even started. 'Number two-two-four?' Reaching up, she dropped a bag laden with sealed plastic containers onto the counter.

'Lemon chicken, spare ribs, crispy seaweed, prawn crackers, hot and sour soup, sweet and sour pork balls, and chicken fried rice? Number two-two-four.'

'That's me,' Fleur said and levered herself to standing before walking over and taking the bag. She passed the girl two twenty-pound notes, which she took and planted into the till.

'So, tell me what happened?' Fleur said, returning to her place on the hard, white seat.

Eric shook his head.

'I'll catch you up in the morning. It's a long story, and it's not that interesting, really. You don't want to keep your company waiting.'

'Company?'

Eric glanced back down at her feet. Lulu was attempting to pilfer prawn crackers from the top of the bag.

'Oh, this. This is just for m—' Fleur stopped mid-sentence and blushed. She pushed herself to her feet again. 'Yes, this is for me and *my company*. I definitely have company. Right, Lulu?'

She smiled again, wider this time. It pushed the apples of her cheeks into perfect rounds.

'I guess that means I'm busted.'

Eric was still staring at Fleur's cheeks when she stopped talking. They were incredibly round he noticed, and absolutely symmetrical. Almost like golf balls.

'So … yes … well …' Eric started stuttering, suddenly coming back to the moment and hoping that he had started talking before Fleur noticed him staring. 'I'll tell you everything when I see you tomorrow.'

Lulu looked up at her previous owner. Her tail flopped between her legs.

'I know,' Eric said to the dog. 'But I'll see you tomorrow.'

She whined. Fleur looked at him apologetically.

'You know, I think she misses you,' she said.

'I miss her, too,' Eric said.

He sighed deeply as he offered Lulu one more hurried rub. A moment later the pair sauntered off down the high street. Eric's chest ached. There really was something special about that dog. A bond. Maybe he could talk to Fleur about letting him have her back next year when Suzy was a bit more settled.

'One kung-po chicken with extra onions,' the girl called across the room.

'Goddamn it,' Eric cursed.

ERIC MADE good time on the ride home. He'd kept at a fairly strenuous pace all the way until the turn-off to his road when he slowed down; the last thing he wanted was to come face to face with a lost car doing a U-turn straight into him. In a battle of car vs bike, there was only ever one winner. A few metres from the house and a voice caught his attention.

'No, that's ridiculous.'

There was something about the hushed urgency that made Eric slow.

'Why? ... You're panicking. It's understandable.'

For a second, Eric thought that Philip and Yvette had moved outside for a more private conservation, but as the one-line responses continued, he realised it must be a phone call.

'You shouldn't be calling ... We agreed. This is for the best. It's the only option, you know it is ... I would have heard ... I promise. Now stop panicking, you've got more important things to focus on.'

Eric's pulse was thumping in his chest. He couldn't stay out all night and listen, he needed to get into the house, but the last thing he wanted was for Philip to think he had been eavesdropping. With three metres left to go he pushed down hard on the pedals and sped into the driveway as if he had sprinted the whole way there.

Startled, Philip jumped back.

'Eric,' he said as he slipped his phone into his pocket. 'I'd just come out to see where you'd got to. Is that the food? Fantastic, I'm starving.' Then without another word he spun around and disappeared into the house.

Inside, the dilapidated kitchen table was covered in sequined lace and glitter glue. Hoping for another option, Eric peered into the dining room to see that table there was equally camouflaged, although in Suzy's paraphernalia as opposed to Abi's.

'Granny's making my costume,' Abi said.

'I can see. I guess it's a TV dinner,' Eric said.

'No, no,' Yvette said. 'We can clear all this up.'

She lifted a corner of the fabric only to spray the floor with glitter.

'I'll get the trays,' Suzy said.

'Why's it called a TV dinner when we're not allowed to have the TV on?' Abi asked as Eric opened the various containers. 'It should be called a lap dinner because we're allowed it on our laps.'

'Fine, it's a lap dinner,' Eric conceded, sensing what could potentially become an incredibly long conversation.

'Can I watch my iPad? Then it's a bit more like a TV dinner.'

'Nope, but good try,' Eric said. 'Anyway, we're not eating in the living room. I thought we'd eat in the conservatory for a change.'

After dishing up the food, Eric laid the spare ribs and prawn crackers on the counter top, instructing everyone to help themselves. In the conservatory, he took a place in the wicker armchair while Philip and Yvette squashed up on the sofa. The last time he had been in there, Eric thought, was with Lulu. The ache in his chest resurfaced and swelled. Clenching his jaw, he forced it back down. This was a nice room, he told himself. He couldn't let memories of his lost puppy haunt it forever. Particularly when there was a chance that one day, he might get her back.

Eric was reminded one mouthful in how he hated TV dinners. Even more than his crummy kitchen table and messy dining room. He found it impossible to eat on his lap without spilling something for starters, and the crick in his neck felt even worse hunched over.

'So, Mum, did you have a good day yesterday?' Suzy asked, sitting crossed legged on the floor, with her plate between her knees. 'Did you and Dad do anything nice?'

'Oh, we did lots of nice things. Lots of very nice things.'

The pair looked at each other and giggled. Eric shuddered.

'And we transferred all our money. Ready for the Dominican Republic.'

'So, you're definitely going through with it?'

'We are,' Philip said shuffling to straighten his already perfect posture. 'We even opened a Whole World Bank account. Our entire savings will soon be accessible in Dominican Pesos.'

'Wow, that's a big decision,' Eric said.

'But a good one,' Philip replied.

Next to him, Yvette smiled. Her eyes were still wary, Eric thought with a little sadness, but at least her smiles were making a dent on her features now.

'Eric's right. This is a big move,' Suzy said, fixing her eyes solely on her mother.

'Well, it's time we did something a little different,' Yvette replied. 'And it means we'll have a base. A place that Abi can come and visit us. You'd like that wouldn't you, sweetie?'

'Probably,' Abi said. 'I guess it depends what the food's like.'

The conversation continued with Philip at the helm again. Most of it was repeats of the previous night; which countries they'd enjoyed the most, where they would never visit again, and why Philip was so vehemently against going back to the cruise ships.

'It's claustrophobic,' he insisted, spooning up a forkful of crispy-shredded chilli beef into his mouth. 'You don't see it when you're in there, but no, at my age, *our age*, I think it's time for a change. Time to opt for a slower pace of life.'

'Is that right?' Eric said.

'Not to mention the lack of culture. No theatres, no art galleries, just crass, big budget films and the same cabaret night after night.'

'Do they have many art galleries in the Dominican Republic?' Eric asked.

The group fell into a food-fuelled silence. Eric looked at his wife. Even in her silent state, Eric could see the cogs turning. He only wished he knew what conclusions they were building to.

'Are there any more of those spring rolls?' Philip asked despite the fact his plate was still half full.

'I'll go see,' Suzy responded.

Eric placed a hand on her shoulder.

'You stay here. I'll go get them.'

She offered him an appreciative smile as he slipped through into the kitchen.

'They have dolphins in the Dominican Republic,' Yvette was saying to Abi as he went. 'You can swim with them there. Would you like that, Abi, dear? Dancing and swimming with dolphins.'

'Will they eat me?' Abi replied.

In the kitchen, as Eric piled up the remnants of the appetisers to take back through, he was suddenly jealous of Fleur's mountain of food. No matter how much they ordered, he never felt like he got enough when guests were over. Fortunately, he was in the exact position to remedy that. Halfway through sneaking one of the larger spring rolls into his mouth, the doorbell rang. He groaned and dropped the roll back on to his plate.

For a man that had previously prided himself on family privacy, moving to Burlam had thrown a complete spanner in the works. Most probably it was one of the neighbours, wanting to catch up on the gossip regarding the black car, or else add their own sordid explanation. A small internal smile flickered within him. It wasn't that bad, being part of a community. In fact, he rather liked it.

'I'll get it,' Eric said.

He was busy musing over which version of the story the caller would be here to deliberate when he reached the door and opened it without so much as a glance through the window.

'Hi ...' Eric began before running out of words.

In all of Eric's adult life he had never – bar one trip to Chicago where he watched an NBA game – considered himself a short man. At just shy of six-foot he had found his height highly acceptable for all jobs he could be required to do, including reaching items from the top shelf at a supermarket, spotting Abi and Suzy in a packed hall after a school production, and any general handyman type activities needed around the house or the allotment. In some situations, he had even considered himself tall. This was not such a situation.

It would not have been an understatement to suggest the man with whom Eric found himself face to chest with was at least a head and a half taller. With the breadth to match, he stood nearly as wide as the door, and Eric roughly estimated that one of the man's biceps would probably measure the same in diameter as both of his own thighs strapped together. However, neither of those features – height nor bicep size – concerned Eric quite so much as the item of sports equipment currently grasped in his hand.

The baseball bat struck the man's palm once, then again, and then a third time.

'Is he here?' the man said.

Eric winced at the glint of a gold tooth, more due to the cliché than anything else.

'Sorry? I think you may have got the wrong house.'

'I'm not going to ask you again,' the man said, eyes bulging in their sockets. 'Is *he* here?'

'Right,' said Eric and then took a deep breath in as he tried to muster his most polite and forceful response. 'I'm going to tell you again. I think you have the wrong house.'

With one swift elbow, the man shoved Eric to the side and pushed his way into the hall.

'Wait a minute, you can't just barge in here!'

The man planted one of his oversized boots into the living room door. The wood buckled with the force.

'What the hell?'

'I know he's here.'

The man spun around, swinging the baseball bat into the already busted living room door. The wood cracked with a sickening thud.

'Eric, what the hell is going on?' Suzy appeared in the hall in front of the pair. Her eyes blinked in disbelief at the sight of the man in front of her.

'Get out, Suze!' Eric cried to his wife. 'Get everyone out.'

CHAPTER 26

THE HOUSE WAS a blur. Confused by all the noise, Yvette, Abi, and Philip also appeared in the hallway with Suzy. The mammoth man with the baseball bat stood between Eric and his family.

'Go out the back door. Now!' Eric shouted, trying to see a way around the Goliath to get to his family. '*NOW!*'

For a moment, the group watched on as if the sight were too bizarre. In a flash, Yvette had bundled Abi up in her arms while yanking Suzy back into the kitchen. Seeing they were safe, Eric ducked back out through the front door. A minute later the four of them had regrouped in the driveway.

'Who the hell is that?' Suzy asked.

She, like Eric and Yvette, was panting, although the run could not have been more than a few metres.

'I have no idea. We need to call the police.'

'What on earth did he want?'

'Philip!' Yvette screamed.

Eric glanced around them, the road was lit up by the street lamps and hazy house lights. She was right, he realised. It was just them. In the confusion, his concerns had been solely for Abi, Suzy, and Yvette. He hadn't even thought about Philip.

'Grandad?' Abi questioned.

'He's still in there!' Yvette cried. 'We have to get him. We have to.'

Eric turned to Suzy. She stood a little way away clutching Abi, her phone pressed to her ear. A moment later she was walking towards him.

'Maggie's on her way, but we need to get her out of here,' Suzy said, motioning with her chin towards Abi.

Eric nodded. His voice taking a moment to catch up.

'Take her to Hank's,' Eric said. 'And take your mum too.'

Suzy nodded, although Yvette refused to move.

'Yvette, I need you to go with Suzy. I'll see to Philip. Are you listening? You need to go with Suzy and wait for the police.'

'Philip,' she muttered, seemingly oblivious to Eric's words. 'My poor Pipsqueak.'

A loud crash jerked Eric's attention back to the house with a shudder. The whole situation was insane. The man, whoever he was, was clearly deranged, and now Philip was trapped in there with him. A churning sensation roiled its way through Eric's gut. There was no way a man like Philip could hold his own against the Goliath-like intruder, and neither, Eric suspected, could he. But maybe if he could just find a way to keep the man occupied until the police came, that would be enough. He had no choice. He had to go back in.

'You can do this,' Eric told himself in a mini-motivational pep talk. 'You've got this.'

He closed his eyes, held his breath, and raced back into the house. His fists were up and balled, ready to strike, yet he had barely stepped inside when he froze.

'What the ...?'

Eric was confronted with what could easily have been a comedy sketch, the fast and nimble cat chased around the house by the lumping giant dog. Yes, the man with the bat had strength on his side, but fifty years of ballroom dancing meant that Philip was quicker on his feet than most men half his age. He ducked and dived and pirouetted out of the bat's reach, anticipating its movement with every swing. The bat came down with a *thwack* against Eric's sofa. Now they would have to get another one he thought. Although after this they were never having guests again, so a sofa bed was well and truly off the list. Another blow slammed down on the coffee table. Eric winced. Handmade Balinese teak tables were tough to get hold of at the best of times, and he had no idea how he would file this for the insurance claim. He couldn't look at the staircase; he didn't want to know what had happened to his beautiful balustrade.

'Eric,' Philip shouted when he saw his son-in-law appearing in the doorway. 'What are you doing?'

'I came back to help you. What are you doing? Yvette and the girls are safe. Get out of here.'

Suddenly aware of the additional target in the room, the giant stopped and twisted round to face Eric. Philip took advantage of the distraction. As if choreographed from a West End show, he leapt from the armchair and into the air. He planted his left foot on the arm of the sofa, sprang into the air, arched his back, and twisted upwards, sending his legs spinning. With one final flick of his foot, he struck square across the man's jaw. The baseball bat fell with a clatter. Dazed, or maybe dazzled, and confused, the man staggered backwards and then forwards again, his eyes wandering and wobbling wildly. For a second, he looked like he might go down, but then his gaze steadied and began scanning the floor. Eric saw what he was looking for just a fraction of a second before he did.

There was no choice in the matter. If the meat-head got his hands back on the baseball bat, it was likely that both Eric and his father-in-law, who was down and appeared to be suffering from his spectacular Bruce Lee impression, were going to meet the worst possible ending. Even without it, there was a good chance that this ended badly for them. Without allowing himself any more time to think, Eric lunged across the room and grabbed the bat with both hands. He gasped in both fear and relief as he rolled onto his back.

It was a peculiar position in which to face an assailant, Eric decided, his mind playing like a scene from a film unfolding in slow motion. The man was focused now, standing and looming only metres away from where Eric lay flat on his back, waving the bat furiously above him. The man-mountain moved forward.

Eric squeezed his eyes half-shut, blurring the figure in front of him. He had been knocked unconscious once before when he was eleven. His father had made him try out for the rugby team. A misplaced throw combined with a complete and utter lack of spatial awareness resulted in him taking a blow to the left temple. He had heard the crack for only a millisecond before everything went black. Hours later and the woozy feeling had failed to pass; he had a feeling this was going to be a lot, lot worse.

Eric waited, heart in his mouth. He should have told the girls he loved them before he ran back inside, he thought. But they would know that, wouldn't they? They would remember how much he loved them. His eyes were fully closed now, awaiting the inevitable, trying to remember the last time he had kissed his wife and daughter. He had just managed to recall the moment when a fizzing, electric static sound filled the air.

'Look out!' someone yelled.

Eric opened his eyes, gasped, and rolled to the side just in time to watch his Balinese teak coffee table disintegrate beneath the giant.

'But I don't get why he was even here?' Yvette said. 'Clearly he was insane? Had he escaped from somewhere? Do they have an asylum in Burlam?'

She was tending to a cut on the side of Philip's cheek. Everyone in the room, bar Maggie, was sitting, although on what remained questionable. The much-loved sofa no longer had functioning arms, and the coffee table looked more like one of Eric's failed DIY projects than anything else.

'No, Yvette,' Eric said. 'No asylums in Burlam. Except maybe this one.'

'We need to press charges,' she continued. 'Oh, my poor little Pipsqueak. You saved us all, you know that, don't you? You saved us all.'

Now that the adrenaline had worn off, the reality was starting to sink in. Every time Eric blinked, the vision of the bat swinging above his head came to the forefront of his mind, causing cold sweats to spill out over his face and neck. If Maggie had arrived even a second later, Abi could have found herself without a father. It didn't bear thinking about.

Once again, it had fallen upon Maggie to make the tea. Her colleague had taken the statements and headed back to the station after bundling the assailant into the back of a police car. Technically, Maggie had already clocked off, but she'd stayed to make the drinks and give the house another once over before she left.

'So, it was who you thought? That was Carvay?' Suzy asked.

Her hand trembled slightly as she clutched Eric's knee, although that aside, she appeared to be in a better state than the rest of them. She had rung Lydia and asked her to collect Abi from Hank's and had managed to answer most of the police questions despite seeing far less than Eric or Philip.

'It was,' Maggie replied. 'The man himself.'

'But why?' Suzy continued. 'What did he want with us? We don't even know the man.'

Maggie took a deep breath. She held it in her lungs as her eyes moved from Philip, to Suzy, and back again. Philip, Eric noticed, had been unusually quiet since their relocation to the living room, letting Yvette fuss and tend to him without so much as a word.

'Mr Devonport, I believe you and your wife were recently separated?' Maggie said.

Yvette stiffened.

'Only briefly. And that's all in the past,' she said, brushing off Maggie's comment with a dismissive wave of her hand. 'We're moving to the Dominican Republic. We've opened a bank account.'

Maggie smiled.

'Besides,' Yvette continued, 'What would that have to do with some random thug coming into my daughter's home and attacking us?'

'I have to agree, Maggie,' Suzy said. 'I'm not sure why the state of my parents' marriage has anything to do with a random attack.'

Maggie's smile remained in place, but it was tight and narrow and caused an unusual constriction around Eric's abdomen. He looked to Suzy; she could see it too.

'The thing is, I don't believe it was random. And I'm not so sure that this separation is entirely in the past, is it, Philip?' Maggie continued.

Yvette's cheeks flamed, and she threw herself up to standing.

'How dar—'

'Dad?' Suzy's quiet tone stopped her mother's outburst in its tracks. 'What's going on?'

All eyes turned to Philip, whose head was down and shaking while Maggie nodded knowingly.

'Philip? What's she on about?' Yvette was still on her feet. 'What does she mean, not in the past?'

Philip's gaze remained down, but even Eric, from across the room, could see the sheen of tears that began to glaze his eyes.

'I'm so sorry,' he said. 'I'm so, so sorry.'

In truth, Eric felt like he had missed half a conversation. Maggie was continuing to nod her head sympathetically while Philip buried his in his hands, and Suzy's whole face contorted in repulsion.

It was only when Yvette spoke that Eric realised he was not the only one who needed a few more blanks filling in.

'What is she talking about?' Yvette said, her gaze focused on her husband. 'What have you done, Philip?'

The clock in the hall was broken, smashed up by a loon with a baseball bat. Nonetheless, Eric couldn't help but hear a slow tick-tock as the seconds passed one after another.

'I didn't know,' Philip said, finally lifting his gaze. His eyes pleaded first to his wife, but then in turn he looked to his daughter, and Eric and even Maggie. 'I didn't know who she was. She was funny and charming and beautiful. She made me laugh. I felt like I was twenty-one again.'

He paused and smiled slightly as if waiting for someone to interject. When nobody did, he continued.

'She told me what her family did, who they were, but it didn't matter to me. She wanted out of that life. That was why she was on the boat. And I'm old, my clock's ticking. I was happy. We were happy. We were in love.'

Eric listened to his wife's repeated gulps as she swallowed back one tear and then another. Yvette was nearly translucent, trembling. Even he was having a hard time keeping his hands in his pockets and not balling them into fists ready to launch them at his father-in-law. The silence expanded. There was more to come; Eric could feel it prickling in the air, he just prayed in his heart he was wrong.

'We were going to raise it together,' he said. 'That was what she wanted, what I wanted too. We both did.'

Yvette yelped in pain. It took Eric a second longer.

'A baby? You got her pregnant?' he said.

Philip nodded soundlessly.

'We were going to be a proper family.'

'You're over twice her age,' Suzy said, her pale skin having now taken on an angry glow. 'You're old enough to be her father. Her grandfather even.'

Philip screwed up his nose as if Suzy had said the most disgusting, despicable thing possible, regardless of the fact that it was entirely true.

'Love doesn't care about age,' he said.

Eric felt a flash of heat rush to his cheeks.

'Are you insane?' he said. 'You had a family. A wife. You vile piece of—'

'What happened?' Maggie said, halting Eric before he actually lunged. 'I assume her family found out? Threatened you?'

Philip chewed his lip and nodded.

'Carvay, he's her brother. We knew it was just a matter of time, but we thought we could try to appease him. We thought if he saw how happy we were, then he wouldn't—'

'He wouldn't care about the forty-year age gap?' Suzy finished for him.

Philip sucked on his cheeks and pouted.

'The minute we made port, she made me go. I knew about his temper, about it all. Poor Katrina, she only wanted to save me.'

'So why come back here?' Suzy said, a jet-black glare in her eyes. 'Why come back to Mum with all these romantic gestures, trying to win her back?'

Philip lowered his gaze. Tears cascaded down his cheeks, but he made no attempt to wipe them away.

'Why would you do that, Dad? If you were happy with this girl, why did you come back at all?'

The room waited for an answer, and for the longest time none came. Tears flowed in unending torrents that slid silently down Yvette's face, though through it all she kept her posture upright and unyielding; never snivelled or sniffed. In fact, she'd been entirely silent since that first, painful yelp.

'Why, Dad?' Suzy asked again. 'Why did you come back?'

When a further silence followed, it was Yvette who cleared her throat.

'He needed me,' she said. 'That's right isn't it, dear? You needed me so you could get a job in some remote little place where no one would find you. That's why it was all about the islands. Am I right? Bora Bora, Fiji, Dominican Republic. Anywhere off the radar. I'm right, aren't I? You needed to get yourself as far away from this place as possible, and I was the easiest route out of here.'

All eyes were on Philip.

'What was the plan?' Yvette continued. 'Wait until we were settled then send word to your tart and ship her over? Give her enough time to get back in the leotard and slyly sneak her into my place. You're a has-been, and even if you weren't, no one was going to give you a job after this stunt. It's a shame that love can't pay the bills, isn't it, Philip? After all, who would employ a pregnant twenty-four-year-old dancer? I was your only chance.'

'Dad?' Suzy had gone pale again. 'That isn't true. Surely? That can't be true. That can't be why you came back?'

Philip's head remained bowed, and Yvette kept going.

'Were you even going to come with me?' she asked. 'Or did you just want to make it look like you'd gone? Perhaps if the rumour mill heard that you and I had disappeared to some remote little island, this Carvay would call off the dogs, and you could slip back to a life here with your twenty-something whore.'

Philip's head snapped up, his eyes flashing with anger.

'Katrina is not a whore.'

'No?' Yvette held her composure far better than Philip was managing, far better than Eric imagined anyone would do in such a situation. 'Maybe not. Maybe it is love, but everything else is true, isn't it? I was a decoy, a diversion, a sad little plot twist in your sordid little love story.'

Philip mumbled something as he ground his molars.

'I still love you too,' he coughed out eventually, the words somewhere between a choke and a splutter.

Yvette laughed. It was cold and heartless and sent chills straight down the length of Eric's spine. Eric stood up. He crossed the room, took hold of the door handle and opened the door wide.

'I think you need to go now, Philip,' he said.

※

The moment Philip left, the tears started in earnest. Maggie escorted him out while Yvette fell to the floor. Suzy tried her best to comfort her, as did Eric, but in the end, all they could do was guide her up to her bed. Two hours later and her sobs still echoed through the walls.

Eric had then left a message on the school answer phone – at nine-thirty at night – saying that Abi wouldn't be coming to school the next day due to personal circumstances. Suzy had messaged her editor about pushing back a deadline. They needed time as a unit, to support Yvette, that was clear. The decision was made that they would all go up to Lydia's tomorrow and make further plans from there. Hopefully some space away from the house would be enough time to get things clearer in their heads.

'I should get on with some work,' Suzy said, ignoring the hour. 'I'm going up to my office for a bit.'

'Are you sure I can't help you with anything?' Eric replied.

'I'm sure,' she said.

For an hour, Eric busied himself trying to fix some of the mess that the baseball bat had caused. The recently laid carpet was full of splinters, and the prized balustrades smashed to pieces. When his legs and mind could take no more, he went up to Suzy's office and rapped his knuckles on the door. When she didn't reply, he pushed it open anyway and peered his head through.

'Suze?'

She twisted around to face him. Her face was blotchy, red, and raw from where she'd been crying. On her desk lay her laptop and notebooks, all of them were closed.

'Suze,' he said. 'What can I do?'

She smiled meekly.

'Is there any work I can help you with? Or your mum? I was thinking about it, and we can start converting the garage next week if you want? I'm okay with that. Really, I am. She can stay forever if that's what you want.'

Suzy's smile broadened just a little. Eric moved closer. Bending down, he wrapped his arms around her. It was minutes before they separated.

'Can you message Lydia? See if Abi's okay.'

'Already done.'

She nodded.

'I just don't understand how he did that to Mum? To any of us,' she said. 'I knew he wasn't perfect, but to trick her like that. To use her. And now the baby. What, I'm going to have a brother or sister who's younger than my daughter? That's ridiculous.'

Eric stayed silent. There were no words he could offer that would be of any real comfort, and in the end he decided no words were better.

'I just can't get the image of Mum out of my head. She was so numb, so hurt. He broke her, Eric, I really think he broke her.'

Images of them all sitting back in the lounge flitted through Eric's mind. Poor Yvette, she'd hung onto his hand for so long, tending to his wounds, so desperate to believe it wasn't true, desperate to believe her darling little *Pipsqueak* still loved her.

Eric dropped Suzy's hands.

'Shit,' he said. 'He rang here. He rang here and warned me.'

'What? What are you on about? Who rang? What did they warn you about?'

'Him. Carvery or whatever his name is.'

'What?'

'He was saying something about *killing that little pipsqueak*. That's what he said, "tell that little pipsqueak we know where he is and we're coming for him." It was about your dad.'

Suzy's jaw was agape. Her eyes bulged. She pushed herself back in her seat.

'And you're only just telling me now?' she said.

Eric jerked.

'Well, I didn't know what they were on about. I thought it was some kind of prank call.'

'But you didn't think to tell me about it? That somebody telephoned and threatened my dad.'

'I didn't know they were talking about your dad. I thought it was just the village kids playing pranks again. I didn't even know your mum called him Pipsqueak.'

'But you should have said something.'

'I wasn't thinking,' Eric admitted. 'I was in a rush, and then it slipped my mind. This is a genuine mistake, Suzy, why are you speaking to me like I've done something wrong?'

Suzy was on her feet; her whole body was trembling.

'A man, with a baseball bat came into our home and attacked my family. Abi was here for Christ's sake, Eric. Abi was here.'

'I don't know what you want me to say. That's not my fault.'

'You could have stopped it.'

'I thought it was a prank!'

Eric's eyes were locked on his wife's, although at that moment they were utterly unrecognisable. Her nostrils flared as she refused to blink. Then, after what seemed like an eternity, she snapped back down into her chair and swivelled away from him.

'I think you should go,' she said. 'I have a lot of things to deal with.'

Eric stared at the back of her head, waiting for her to sigh, or cry, or offer some form of normal reaction.

'Suze?'

'Just go,' she said.

Then, slamming the door behind him, Eric did exactly as she suggested.

CHAPTER 27

ERIC WASN'T THINKING straight when he stormed out of the house. He wasn't really thinking at all. A stream of red-hot emotions hurtled through him as he grabbed the closest coat to the door and marched outside, oblivious of the weather that had drifted in since his father-in-law's departure. Even when he did notice the rain, he didn't care.

The best thing he could do, he thought, was ring Hank. Hank always made him see sense, always offered a reasonable, and well-balanced approach to any situation. Always helped him see both sides. Although at that moment, Eric realised, that wasn't what he wanted to hear. He didn't want to hear how hard the day had been for Suzy, or how she deserved a little slack. Hadn't he been trying his hardest? Hadn't he attempted to take some of the strain off her by doing every household chore under the sun. Hadn't he tried to arrange a weekend away where they could both relax and forget about the house and the allotment and all the ridiculous goings on in their life for a little while? Hadn't he let her turn the dining room into an extended office, and let her mother live there unconditionally with barely a hint of complaint? A car sped past, spraying water up onto the pavement and soaking Eric's trouser legs. He was not a shitty husband. He was doing his best.

No, Eric realised as the rain fell faster and began to splash up around his feet. He didn't need Hank guilting him into feeling bad about the situation, making out like he was somehow to blame when he clearly wasn't. Suzy was being unfair, and that was the truth of it. What Eric wanted, he realised, was to feel wanted. What he wanted was someone who would appreciate everything he was trying to do, the husband he was trying to be. Someone who would offer him affection without judging or asking questions. Someone who would be pleased to see him, no matter what. What he wanted, he thought, was Lulu.

Eric had passed Fleur's house with the luminous fence posts enough times to know which one it was. He had even waved at her through the window a couple times, but he had never actually knocked on the door. He stood there, the light rain now a full-on storm that poured down the back of his neck. It was only after he'd knocked that he glanced at his watch and realised how late it was. He hesitated, ready to turn and leave when the door swung open. Fleur stood there in a tasteful silk dressing gown.

'Eric, my God, what's happened? Come in, quickly come in.'

Eric staggered inside, his legs suddenly lead weights beneath his body. The cold of the rain had reached all the way through to his skin and his head was spinning with exhaustion and frustration and a hundred other emotions he couldn't quite place.

'Eric, is everything all right?'

'I needed to come. I needed to see—'

As if she knew, Lulu came bounding from inside the house, her tail wagging, tongue drooping. She wanted him, just like he knew she would. Lulu wanted Eric.

Eric dropped to his knees in the hallway as she bounced up and down on the floor around him. This was what he needed, he told himself, as she buried her nose into the sodden material of his coat. This was what he wanted. To be appreciated, to be loved, to be understood.

When or why the tears started, he couldn't be sure. At first it was just difficult to breathe, then his shoulders started juddering. Then the juddering spread and his breathing grew shallower, and before he had even realised, he was crouched down on Fleur's tasteful hall carpet crying as Lulu licked his ears.

When he finally looked back up, Fleur's brow was furrowed with concern.

'Do you want to come through?' she said. 'I have leftover Chinese.'

'Leftovers sounds perfect.'

The spare ribs were cold, and the prawn crackers soggy and chewy, but the food made an immediate difference. Half a plate in, Eric stopped chewing and began to talk.

'You poor thing,' Fleur said, having listened to his account of the entire evening, from their meeting at the Chinese takeaway to his subsequent arrival on her doorstep. 'Going in after him. You could have been killed. You must have been terrified?'

'To be honest, I wasn't really thinking about that,' Eric said.

He was sitting on a variety of towels, with one draped over his shoulders and a hot water bottle on his lap. Fleur had offered him the use of her shower, but with no dry clothes for him to change into, it didn't really make any sense.

'No,' Fleur said. 'I don't suppose you were. And now where is your father-in-law?'

'Gone back to this Katrina for all I know.'

Eric's fingers were sticky with sauce. As he reached them down for Lulu to lick, he winced at the pain in his shoulder.

'Your shoulder again?' Fleur said.

Eric nodded.

'Right, turn around.' Fleur moved from her seat across the room to the space on the sofa directly next to Eric. 'Let's have a proper look at this.'

'I'm soaking wet, you don't want to do that,' Eric said.

Fleur looked at him and raised an eyebrow.

'I think I can cope with a bit of rainwater.'

Eric was going to insist that he was fine, but the pain struck again, this time surging up his neck.

'Only if you're sure?'

Fleur pushed him forward on the seat and slipped in behind him. There was a funny sense of misplaced déjà vu to the act as she squeezed herself into the gap, placing her body tight against his, a powder blue towel filling the space between them.

'You really need to take some time for yourself,' Fleur was saying as she worked out the knots and the cricks with her fingers. 'Honestly, the month you've had. You deserve some rest.'

She smelt new, like peppermint or soap, and when Suzy's own aroma, of pencil lead and late-night gins, crept into his mind, Eric pushed it down. He didn't want to think of Suzy. Thinking of Suzy right now made him feel angry and disappointed and let down. After all he was trying to do for her, how could she honestly think he'd keep something like that from her deliberately? Everything he tried to do was to make life easier for her.

'This tension has gotten worse,' Fleur continued as she worked. 'I told you, you should have had it seen to.'

Eric sighed. His eyes were closed and his mind drifting off, and more and more Fleur's voice was fading into the background, like waves lapping on a distant shore. He focused instead on the pressure of her hands, the softness around his neck, the receptiveness of his muscles. An involuntary moan escaped his lips.

In hindsight, he could see it coming, and not just from that evening. Looking back, he could see that it had been building for weeks, if not months, but until that actual moment, the moment when it actually happened, he had been completely oblivious.

Fleur's hands squeezed their way around Eric's shoulders, before moving down to the tops of his arms. Another moan escaped him, and her hands slipped lower, falling into his, where their fingers entwined. At the time, he thought she was twisting him around, although later he would realise that was impossible. It must have been him who'd twisted or leaned in or at least turned a little. Probably, he thought, so that he could say something. Probably so that he had could thank her for the Chinese or the ear or for keeping the puppy that he had so desperately needed to see. But when he parted his lips, it was not to speak.

His lips were met by another pair. A pair that tasted of red wine and sweet and sour and were stronger than the usual pair that pressed up against his. By a force beyond his control, his mouth responded, and the two pairs of lips found a rhythm, a new, unexpected, exciting rhythm.

Eric snapped back into the room. With his pulse racing he sprang up from his seat, pushing Fleur to the side as he did.

'I ... I ...'

Fleur was on her feet, hand on his shoulder.

'Eric?'

'I can't do this, I didn't mean ... I didn't want to ... I ...' He was stumbling backwards, stammering as he went.

His coat, still sodden, hung across the back of a chair. He grabbed it with one hand.

'Eric, please.'

Lulu was at his feet now, barking and yapping and clearly confused by the sudden outburst.

'I just wanted to see the dog,' Eric said as he staggered out through the front door. 'I just came to see the dog.'

CHAPTER 28

THE LIGHT WAS on in the lounge, exactly what Eric had dreaded. The walk home had given him time to deliberate every eventuality. The best-case scenario was that Suzy was upstairs in bed. He would have to tell her. He had to tell her, but morning felt like a more suitable time. He could get up early, make her breakfast in bed, and then tell her. Then again, he thought, maybe that would be a bit strange. Maybe it was better if he just got it out the way now. Maybe it was a good thing that she was still up. And hopefully a bit angry. It would be much easier to tell her what happened if she was still angry.

He considered what words he would use to explain the event, if that's what he could call it. He had to call it something, but to say *kiss* made it sound lurid, sexual. Like he had cheated. And he hadn't. He was certain he hadn't. At least not deliberately. Three times during the walk back Eric had had to stop and steady his thoughts in order to prevent himself from throwing up on the pavement. He wanted to convince himself it was the Chinese. That he had just eaten too much, but he knew that was bullshit.

His stomach corkscrewed. It wasn't his fault, he reminded himself for the hundredth time in twenty minutes. He had gone there with good intentions. All he wanted to do was see Lulu and indulge in a bit of non-judgemental affection. If Suzy hadn't made him get rid of the puppy, he would never have gone around to Fleur's in the first place. If Suzy had just let him keep Lulu, none of this would ever have happened. Suzy definitely held some responsibility in the situation, Eric tried to convince himself, although as the squirming around his intestines increased, he realised he was not doing a particularly good job.

He had barely turned the key in the lock when the door sprang open.

'I'm so sorry,' Suzy said. Eric's feet were still firmly placed on the outside welcome mat as Suzy's arms squeezed tight around him. 'I'm so sorry. I was completely out of line.'

She had been crying, a lot, judging from the blotchiness of her skin. Her hands were cold, as if she hadn't thought to turn the heat up, and her loosely knotted hair messily framed her face.

'How were you to know they were after Dad,' she carried on. 'I wasn't thinking. I really wasn't. I wouldn't have known if I answered the call either. I'm so sorry.'

She backed up into the doorway, giving Eric room to slide into the house.

'Oh, my goodness,' she said, suddenly noticing Eric's state. 'You're soaked. Take these off, and I'll put them straight into the wash.'

'I'm fine.'

'You're not. You're not fine at all.'

The scene evolved as if Eric were a spectator, watching as his wife fussed about, apologising for something she really didn't need to apologise for. She took his coat and then his jacket and even made him remove his jeans standing there in their open hallway.

'I'll sort these for you now,' she said. 'You go get dry.'

She moved in for a kiss. Eric stiffened. A waft of red wine, which clung to his lips caught his attention. He turned his head sharply to the side.

'I'm just going to have a bath,' he said. 'Warm up a bit.'

Suzy's hands dropped. Fixing her gaze on him, she tilted her head to the side. Her eyes narrowed ever so slightly.

'Eric?' she said. 'Is everything all right?'

'Everything's fine,' he said and this time he held her gaze. He held it for all he was worth. He held it so firmly that his eyes began to water, and he could feel his pulse pounding with every passing breath. 'I just want to get clean and dry, that's all.'

For a moment, Eric was certain she knew. His heart thumped even harder in his chest, his pulse beat fiercely in his stomach. Perhaps Fleur had already called here. Perhaps this niceness was simply a ruse, and she'd taken his clothes simply to set fire to them before pushing him out stark naked into the night so that he could rot forever in accidental adultery hell. It was too much, he had to tell her now. He had to tell her.

Suzy dropped her gaze and smiled.

'Of course,' she said. 'You get in the bath. I'll bring you a drink up.'

WHEN SUZY CLIMBED into bed in the early hours, Eric pretended that he was asleep. He groaned, what he considered to be a reasonable amount, when she moved the duvet over to her side and mumbled in what he felt was a suitably incoherent, sleepy sounding manner, when she spoke.

'It'll calm down now,' Suzy said. 'I'm certain. We'll find our rhythm again. Everything will calm down again now.'

Eric couldn't respond. It was going to be a sleepless night he realised. An incredibly sleepless night.

Eric had tossed and turned all night, battling his wife for the duvet while racking his brain for the best way to explain that he had kissed – or had at least been involved in being kissed by – another woman. The room was hot, stiflingly so for the end of March, but even opening the window did little to alleviate the sweating. In the room beside them, Yvette fared no better. Her pacing and sobbing provided a constant ostinato to his own melodrama, which replayed over and over in his mind. Only when he had finally drifted off, and the early morning birds had just broken through the night-time silence, did Yvette's sobs turn into a scream that shattered everyone's fitful sleep.

'Mum?' Suzy jerked herself awake, her feet off the side of the bed before she had fully opened her eyes. 'What is it? What's happened?'

Eric bounded into the living room only moments after Suzy, to find Yvette blanched and shaking.

'The money. Our joint accounts, he's drained them.'

'What do you mean?'

'All the pesos. They're gone. That was the plan. That was always the plan.'

Three tabs for three different bank accounts were open on the laptop screen in front of them.

'He must have done it last night, as soon as he left.'

Together Eric and Suzy studied one page of Yvette's finances, and then the next and the one after. Each displayed a strikingly stark balance of less than a hundred pounds.

'How could he do this?' Yvette was trembling and her complexion constantly fluctuating between furious red and ashen grey. 'After everything. How could he do this?'

Suzy's complexion was also undertaking similar periodic variation.

'But he can't have,' Eric said, the only one who seemed to be able to find a voice in the situation. 'Are you sure you haven't made a mistake? That you're not looking at old accounts?'

Yvette flicked the screens to the on-screen statements, each of which showed massive transfers.

'We won't let him do this, Mum, we won't.' Suzy rested one of her hands on her mother's elbow, the other a clawed talon by her side. 'He can't do this. We'll get you a lawyer. The one in the village. We can call him now.'

Yvette shook her head.

'There's no point,' she said plainly. 'It was all shared. Everything. Our entire life. And now he's taken it all. What are they going to tell me, that I'm an old fool?'

Eric scanned through the statements, each one causing him to balk with more disgust than the next.

'But do you not have anything separate? Surely all your accounts weren't together?'

'Forty-two years.' Yvette clenched her fist for emphasis. 'Why would I have thought to change it after all this time? Besides, we thought it would be best for the move.'

She corrected herself.

'*He* thought it would be best if everything was in pesos. That way we could ... we could ...' She stopped herself just in time.

A few sharp breaths turned into another heavily expelled sigh. The tears momentarily abated.

'I have a little bit,' she said to Suzy. 'A little bit that your grandmother left behind. And my jewellery too, but I could never part with that. All our savings. All your inheritance. Oh, Suzy, I'm so sorry, that money was meant for you and your sister.'

That was all it took. Yvette collapsed into her daughter's arms, shuddering with tears. Suzy looked to Eric. Her eyes were pleading for support in a way they had done so many times across the years. Still he had difficulty holding her gaze, even now. Even with this.

※

'ARE you sure you can't come?' Suzy said later as they loaded up the Audi with an overnight bag for herself, Yvette, and Abi, ready to take to Lydia's. Yvette was shrouded in one of her batik quilts, all the healing crystals she owned draped around her neck and wrists.

'No, it's fine. There are things I can get on with here,' he said. 'I need to get the house sorted before Abi gets back. And besides, there's not enough room at your sister's for all of us.'

'And you're sure you'll be all right by yourself?' Suzy said.

Eric nodded.

'I'll be fine.'

When she kissed him goodbye, he thought he might just throw up. His hands were shaking, and there were so many causes it was almost impossible to identify the main culprit.

He was furious, that much was certain. Furious at Fleur. Who the hell did she think she was, kissing a married man like that? And her friend's husband to boot. Suzy had bent over backwards to welcome her to the village; taking her out for tapas, inviting her to Hank's for New Year's Eve. Did she have any idea how lucky she was to have a friend like Suzy? And look at how she repaid her. Fleur was a bad friend, a bad person, Eric decided.

He wandered back into the house and sighed. In the light of yesterday's events, there was still an excessive amount of clearing up to do. The bottom two railings of the banister were busted, as were the third, fourth, sixth, and ninth. In the living room, both the coffee table and the sofa were completely beyond repair. He carried on through the house. Fucking Philip. What kind of man would do that to his wife? To his children? Had

Philip not made such a catastrophic balls-up with his life, Eric would never have been at Fleur's. Had he just had the guts to leave Yvette, or tell her the truth, or just run off with his twenty-four-year-old girlfriend to Bora Bora or wherever the hell he was planning on taking her, then none of this would have happened.

He slumped to the floor, next to a broken photo frame. He should be tidying things up, he thought, looking at the sea of debris filling the floor around him. He should be doing as he said he was and making the place straight for when Abi got home. Only he didn't feel like tidying. He felt like the exact opposite.

IT WAS AN INCREDIBLE FEELING, swinging the sledgehammer into the scratched pine and hearing the wood splinter beneath him. How many years had they had that crappy piece of flat pack furniture, he thought. Too many. He changed his angle and struck one of the legs. The table buckled at the side. Another whack saw the whole side collapse to the ground. He didn't need that kind of crap in his life. He was still raining down blows on the now decimated table when the doorbell rang. Eric dropped the sledgehammer, wiped his brow with his sleeve and made his way over to the front door.

'You have to be kidding me,' he said and moved to close the door the moment he had opened it.

A hand pushed back against the pane, stopping it just before it clicked.

'Please, Eric,' Fleur said. 'I just wanted to apologise. I brought you these.'

She held out a basket of eggs. Eric scoffed in disgust and moved again to shut the door. For the second time Fleur caught it.

'Eric, I—'

'No,' he said, swinging the door open fully. 'I don't want to hear it. What the hell do you think you're doing coming around here? This is my home. Suzy could have been here.'

'I ... I ...' Fleur stuttered, the eggs in the basket rattled as her hand shook.

'You what?' Eric snapped.

'I was watching. I saw her leave.'

Eric balked.

'You were watching the house? What are you? Some kind of stalker now?' A small yap averted his attention before turning his muscles rigid.

'Please,' Fleur said. 'I was out of line, I completely misread the situation—'

'You think?'

'— but I don't want to ruin our friendship. Please, Eric, it was one silly mistake.'

Her eyes were welling, and her lower lip trembled; beside her Lulu had started to whine.

'I was just lonely, and you were kind and funny and I ...'

Before Eric realised what had happened, she was scrunched up against his shoulder, sobbing as the basket dangled in her hand. Eric's stomach loosened. The burning anger becoming a more bearable simmer.

'I messed up so badly, didn't I?' Fleur said. 'It's the same every time. I mess everything up.'

Eric sighed.

'Come in,' he said. 'I'll make you a cup of tea.'

In the kitchen, Eric discovered that his hasty demolition of the kitchen table may not have been such a wise move. With mugs of tea on their laps, Eric and Fleur sat on high-back chairs, facing each other.

Now that she'd stopped crying, Fleur was remaining unusually quiet. Even Lulu seemed to be eyeing Eric with some kind of suspicion.

'I really am sorry,' Fleur said. 'I was confused. The loneliness, our friendship, then you turning up like that, all soaked through and upset. It felt like something out of a romantic comedy, I suppose.'

'Or a horror movie,' Eric muttered.

'What was that?' Fleur said. Eric shook his head, and she let it go. A silence expanded between them.

'Have you told Suzy yet?' said Fleur, breaking the silence after several sips of her tea.

'No.'

'Are you going to?' It was a question he had asked himself multiple times. 'I mean, I won't tell her. I won't tell anyone,' Fleur said. 'Really. We can keep it a secret, keep this between you and me. I don't mind.

You don't have to tell her if you don't want. I swear, I'll never say a word.'

Eric stared at the mug in his hand. *Could he do that?* he wondered. His memory skipped back to the last time he had lied to her, the last time he had hidden the truth about where he was going and what he was doing. She had left him over it. She came back of course, but she had left him; packed up and gone to Lydia's for over a week and it had broken his heart. Not seeing Abi every day, not having Suzy next to him when he curled up in bed at night. Eric's stomach twisted and tightened. She had been under so much pressure recently; how could he add this to her list of things to worry about? The argument went back and forth in his mind. Besides, what if she didn't believe him about it simply being a kiss? What if she didn't believe that Fleur was the one responsible, not him? She wouldn't stick around, not after everything she went through with Pete. And then what would happen?

Eric placed his hand on the back of one of the chairs. The air in the room had thinned and the kitchen table had started to shift in and out of focus. It should be an easy decision to make, one side of his conscience was telling him. It should have been straightforward, and yet each thought in his head was countered by another even more convincing one. The dizziness was almost unbearable.

'Are you all right?' Fleur lifted her hand to his shoulder. Eric shook it away

'I can't,' he said.

'Can't what?'

'I can't have her leave me.'

A tangible silence filled the air between them. Eric's heart pounded in his chest.

'If you breathe a word—'

Fleur's eyes brightened, her head nodded rapidly. 'I swear I won't.'

'And you're not to see her, not to speak to her, not even to be friends with her anymore?'

'But I ...' Her lower lip trembled. 'Okay. I won't. I won't ever talk to her again.'

A deep breath filled his lungs with cold air. He was really going to do it, he thought. He was really going to keep the kiss from Suzy. The pounding in his chest has lessened by a fraction. It was for the best, the best for all of them. This way they could move on with their lives without any more shadows hanging over them. This way he could focus his attention on helping with Yvette and Abi, not waste all his energy trying to convince Suzy that he still loved her. Because he did. More than anything in the world, Eric loved Suzy.

'Okay,' he said to Fleur, his pulse steady for the first time all day. 'She will never find out.'

EPILOGUE

ERIC HAD TRIED to keep his word to Fleur. When they had spoken, he had been certain it was the right thing to do. But as the minutes passed, the old arguments rose in the back of his head, and finally, on the floor of a smashed-up kitchen, he accepted the truth. He couldn't keep it from her.

'I need to talk to you,' he said down the phone, the sounds of shrieking children echoing in the background.

'Can it wait?' Suzy said. 'Mum is still in a bad way.'

'No,' Eric said. 'I need you to come home now. I need to speak to you now.'

'Eric, is everything all right?'

'Please,' he said. 'Please can you come home? Just you, though.'

There was a pause.

'I'm on my way.'

Eric was staring out the window when her car pulled into the driveway. He had rehearsed his lines to himself multiple times, and provided she didn't interrupt, he would be fine. A lump was bulging in his throat constricting his airway and making it near impossible to swallow while sweat slickened his palms more by the second.

The minute her car door clicked open, he was on his feet.

'Eric?' Suzy called as she rushed into the house. 'Where are you? Is everything all right?'

He stepped out into the hallway. Suzy flung her arms around him.

'What happened?' she said. 'Did he come back? Did Dad come back? Did Maggie call?'

'No,' Eric said. Tension filled his whole body forbidding more than one-word answers.

'Then what? What is it?'

'I think you should sit down.'

'Eric, you're worrying me.'

'Please, Suzy.' He could feel the heat building behind his eyes. 'Please sit down.'

Suzy's brow knitted.

'Okay,' she said. 'Okay.'

With both the living room and kitchen out of action, Eric led Suzy into the dining room. The carpet, though a little more weathered, still exuded the new carpet smell and forced Eric's mind back to the night just before Christmas when he and Suzy had worked all night to get ready for Lydia's arrival. Their in-law invasion had only just begun, and Fleur hadn't even entered their lives. How happy the children had been as they rode their bikes up and down the road. It felt like a lifetime ago. So much had happened.

'Eric?' Suzy said, taking off her coat and hanging it on the back of her chair. 'What is it? Why did you need me to come home?'

Eric closed his eyes. He took a breath in through his nose for six long counts, before holding it, then releasing it to a count of eight. When he opened his eyes again, he tried to block out the thumping in his chest and focused entirely on Suzy.

'I need you to know, it didn't mean anything,' he started.

He had meant to sit down before he started, he had wanted them both to be sitting down, but now he was standing he had no choice but to carry on that way.

'I need you to know that,' he said again. 'It didn't mean anything.'

Suzy's eyes flashed and blinked.

'Eric?'

'It was, it was, an accident, and I know that sounds silly, but it really was. I really just wasn't thinking.'

'Eric, what did you do?'

'Had I known I would never have gone around there. I wouldn't have even thought about it.'

'Eric?'

'It was one kiss. And she kissed me, she did, I didn't know what I was doing, and I hadn't gone around there to—'

'Eric.' Suzy's voice cut a hole in the air around them.

Her skin was white, startlingly so, and Eric could see the tremble to her hands as she looked up at him. A heavy vice clamped around his chest. Suzy opened her mouth to speak and a single tear began to wind its way down to her chin.

'You kissed someone?' she said.

Eric stared at her. He could feel the blood pulsing in his veins, banging against his ear drums. Suzy was waiting, her eyes glistening, and wet as she stared up at him. He wanted to speak. He desperately wanted to say something, anything that would change the look currently affixed to her face. But he couldn't. There just weren't enough words.

'Who did you kiss?' Suzy said, her voice now embroiled with a bitterness that caused Eric's stomach to curdle. 'Who? Who did you kiss?'

Eric tried to swallow back the lump in his windpipe.

'Fleur,' he whispered. 'I kissed Fleur.'

Eric had expected a more volatile response. A yell or a scream or perhaps just a small gasp. Instead Suzy nodded. It was a slow nod, barely discernible at all, but every second of it caused an agony of inextinguishable flames to writhe around Eric's chest.

'At the allotment?' she said. 'Today?'

Eric shook his head. He could feel his own tears now, tumbling beyond control.

'At her house. Last night.'

'Last night?'

Eric nodded. His tears were now mingled with a streaming nose, and he wanted to say more, give her his pre-rehearsed speech, but suddenly all the words he could think of sounded hollow and feeble.

Suzy was shaking her head now.

'I don't understand. When did you go to Fleur's? Why? Why did you go to Fleur's?'

'After we fought. I just wanted to see her.'

'To see Fleur?'

'No,' said Eric as he stepped towards Suzy, but she stood up and backed away just as fast. 'I went to see Lulu. I just wanted to see Lulu.'

'Lulu?' Suzy flung her hands into the air. 'Who the hell is Lulu? What is this, one of Fleur's friends, was this some kind of sordid orgy—'

'No! God no. Lulu. The dog. My dog. Our dog. I just wanted to see our dog.'

Suzy's faced was crinkled now, scrunched up in confusion, and when she shook her head, it was with far more ferocity than before.

'What do you mean *our dog?*'

'Our puppy. Little Red. The puppy I got you so you wouldn't be lonely.'

'What? Why would she be at Fleur's? I thought you took her back?'

Eric's eyes shifted to the ground. It was small, but Suzy saw it. She grabbed her coat and moved for the door.

'More lies,' she said.

'Suzy, please,' Eric begged.

He reached for her arm, but she was already through the hall and at the front door.

'Suzy, listen to me.'

'You lied,' she said striding towards her car. 'You lied again. How many lies have you told, Eric? You promised. After last time.'

'I haven't lied. I'm telling you the truth now.'

'You told me you got rid of the dog—'

'I did, I just didn't—'

'It's just lies, Eric. Everything that's coming out of your mouth.' She stopped and looked him square in the eyes. 'You don't get it, Eric. Secrets. Lies. They spiral. You can't control them. You don't understand. You can't—'

'Suzy, you're not making any sense.'

'And now you're cheating on me. Kissing my friend—'

'No, I'm not cheating. I swear. It was one kiss.'

Eric was sobbing now. The words were coming out between gulping, gasping breaths.

'It wasn't even me. I just wanted to see the dog.'

'For God's sake, Eric.'

Suzy flung the car door open and got in.

'Please, Suzy. Please. It was a mistake.'

She wound down the window.

'Pack a bag, Eric, I don't want you here when I get back,' she said and began to wind the window up.

'Suzy, no, Suzy, please.' He clung to window, until his fingers were nearly squashed. 'Suzy!'

She turned the key in the ignition. The car choked and spluttered as it failed to start.

'Suzy, please.'

Eric hammered on the window. She turned the key again. This time the engine started, and she put the car into reverse.

'Goodbye, Eric,' she mouthed through the glass.

Suzy's eyes were still on Eric as she slammed her foot down on the accelerator. Eyes glistening with tears, he held her gaze, pleading with all his heart as she left without a moment's hesitation. She never once looked away, not even to glance in her wing-mirrors or her rear-view mirror, or even over her shoulder as she sped backwards into the road – the road Eric had complained about so many times. Had she looked, then perhaps she would have seen it coming.

Instead, Suzy's pale blue eyes still were fixed solely on Eric's when a dark red car sped around the corner and collided right into the side of their car.

'*SUZY!*' Eric screamed.

PEAS, CARROTS AND SIX MORE FEET

Book 3

For T and S, always brightening my day

CHAPTER 1

TWO SHARP KNOCKS rang through the door. Eric wasn't going to open his eyes. He couldn't. His head throbbed from tears and drink, and a smell that may or may not have been his own body odour was causing him to gag each time he breathed in. He was in no fit state to talk. Whoever was outside would go away, eventually. They always did.

'Eric, you need to get up.'

He opened his eyes, only to close them again.

'Eric, I know you can hear me.'

There was a pause. Eric rolled over and pulled a pillow over his head.

'I'll be back in ten minutes,' Yvette said. 'You need to get yourself sorted or I'm coming in there. You understand?' Another pause followed as Yvette waited for a reply. Eric smacked his lips together. His pulse thumped in his ears. She could wait all she liked, he thought. He was saying nothing. Finally, the sound of footsteps retreated down the hallway and into the bathroom. At the click of the lock, Eric opened his eyes.

The onslaught of light burned through his retinas. The curtains were drawn and the light was no more intense than an average May morning, but to him it was blinding. He squeezed his eyes shut again and tried to shake away the headache that was crushing in around his temples.

Eric didn't want to be awake. Being awake meant letting thoughts into his head. Thoughts that clamped around his chest and caused every nerve in his body to burn with a pain so furious and so overwhelming he didn't understand how he was still alive. How was it possible to be alive when you hurt this much? How was it possible to feel this much pain and survive?

Suzy was dead.

❦

SHE HAD BEEN next to him, the car's crumpled metal body keeping them separated. But he could see her. He saw it all. Behind him, the driver of the red car stumbling about, blood oozing on his forehead, struggling to stand. Eric didn't care about him.

'Suzy!' Eric had screamed as her head lolled to the side, a thin trickle of blood snaking its way from her nostril. Shattered glass scattered across her body and the hiss of the deflating air bag leaked into the air around them.

'God, no. No, no, no. Please. God. No. Suzy please.' Eric pushed his body through the shattered window, barely able to breathe from the invisible vice around his lungs. 'Suzy, you need to wake up. You need to wake up.' Eric reached through the glass, hands outstretched, but the man with the busted leg yanked him backwards.

'You mustn't touch her,' he said. 'You can't do anything. You need to wait for an ambulance.'

'No,' Eric screamed. 'Suzy, please wake up. Please.'

'You need to leave her there.'

'Get off me!' Eric swiped at the guy. The man held him firm. Eric swiped again and again.

'Get off. Let me go!' He could feel the tears and taste the salt. The man's face was contorted with pain as Eric fought against him, thrashing and kicking and thumping at him to let go. Eric elbowed his ribs, his groin, even his leg where blood was seeping through the denim of his jeans.

'She's my wife!' Eric screamed. Still, the man refused to let go. 'She's my wife. I need to get to her.' That was when Eric realised. Even if he did get to her, there was nothing he could do. He had already done enough. His vision went, followed by his knees.

❦

'Ten minutes is up. You need to get sorted.'

It took a moment for Eric to realise that the owner of the voice was not outside the room, but looming over him, with great feather earrings dangling from her ears.

'Eric, are you listening?'

He groaned and rolled over. His hand landed on something cold and smooth next to him. A bottle. He extended his grip only to have Yvette snatch it up before he could check if there was anything still left.

'Lydia's only taken Abi out for a short walk, they'll be back soon, and she can't see you looking like this.'

'Abi?' Eric snapped upright in bed. The effect was instant and nauseating. His head swirled as if his brain had been liquefied and its melted remains left sloshing about inside a hollow skull. The smell didn't help. There was no way that could be him he thought. No one could smell that bad. He steadied himself with a hand against the bed frame and frowned.

'Why are they coming back? I thought Lydia was going to take her? I thought they were going to do something together? Why is she coming? I said she couldn't come.'

'Really?' Yvette marched across the room and pulled open the curtains. Eric recoiled at the light. 'You're going to stop her going to her mother's funeral? And Lydia too? You expect her to miss it? To miss her own sister's funeral?' She tutted, but it was more than just the average tut. It was laden with disgust and disappointment, and Eric was certain that he deserved every bit of it.

She looked old, Eric thought as Yvette fixed him with a glare. Old and tired, and now she had to bury her daughter. And he had to bury his wife.

'Have a shower and sober yourself up or it'll be you who's not attending,' she said. Then added, 'I'll have breakfast ready in twenty minutes. Tom and Lydia are going to eat here too, and we'll all go to the crematorium together. The service starts at *two*.'

Eric bristled.

'You think I don't know that? I know what time my wife's funeral starts.'

Yvette pursed her lips, but for once didn't offer a reply. She had been talking less and less recently, to a point that even Eric could tell. She probably didn't think there was much worth talking to him about anymore.

Taking her silence as compliance, Eric reached down the side of his bed and felt around with his outstretched hand. When the floor offered nothing, he re-angled his body and pulled open the bottom drawer of his dresser; he had been keeping a store there, not loads, but enough, and away from Yvette's prying eyes and nosey do-gooding.

'If you're looking for your drink, it's all gone.' Yvette's cheeks pulled in as she spoke. 'I got rid of it. Again.' A dense silence stippled the air between them, which Eric took to mean she was either going to storm off and slam the door, or else lay into him yet again. Though instead, she sighed. The bags below her eyes grew visibly as she dropped herself down on the end of the bed. Her shoulders slumped and her hands rested in her lap. Another sigh was expelled from between her lips, even longer and heavier than the first. 'This has to stop, Eric. You've done your wallowing. You've got a daughter to think of.'

'You know I don't drink in front of her.'

'No, just around her constantly. You think she can't smell it on you? She's not an idiot, Eric, and you're pushing her away.'

'I am not.' His nostrils flared as the muscles along his jawlines tightened.

'So you think you're being supportive?' You think you're being the kind of father she needs in her life right now?'

Grumbling incoherently under his breath, he looked down at his hands and picked at some invisible dirt under his nails. This was why he preferred the screaming and door slamming, because every conversation he had nowadays ended with him feeling worse than he had before. Even when he didn't think that was possible.

Drawing a long pull of air in through her nose, Yvette levered herself up to standing before brushing down the small patch of the bed on which she had been sitting. She turned towards the door, then stopped.

'I don't suppose you'd be sober enough to tell, but have you seen a ring lying about anywhere? A diamond one?'

Eric continued his wordless mumblings. Yvette waited, lips pouting, eyes scowling.

'Well thank you for all your help,' she said, moving towards the door. 'It's much appreciated.'

When she was halfway down the stairs, she stopped and called back up to him.

'You need a shower,' she said. 'You smell disgusting.'

Eric picked up another pillow and held it over his face. Maybe if he smelt bad enough, she'd stop coming in and bothering him.

Despite the desire to while away yet another day in bed, Eric knew that today, of all days, it would be an impossibility. After one last check of the floor and bottom drawer, he grabbed a towel from off the back of the door and headed for the bathroom. If bathrooms could have talked, Eric knew for a fact he would have asked his not to. At the beginning of the year Eric had had the misfortune of walking in on his mother-in-law in a compromising position with a twenty-something plumber; an image he thought would be ingrained in his mind for the rest of his life. Occasional flashbacks of lacy underwear and spine shuddering groans still, now and then, leapt into his consciousness, but now there were other images seared in his memory; ones of twisted metal and angry tears and Suzy's lifeless body pulled from the wreck of her car. Those were the images that would be with him for all eternity, of that there was no doubt. Clenching and unclenching his fists, Eric focused on the task in hand. A shower. He could manage that.

As it happened, the shower did help with some things. It lessened the odour and the need to gag, and it cleared the crust from his eyes that had been hazing his vision for days now. But it sharpened other things, like his awareness of the need to shave and the fact he looked like absolute crap. It also sharpened his mind, his memories. A small coil of long blonde hair was slowing the flow of water down the plughole, and half a bottle of lavender and jasmine shower gel sat above the soap tray. Eric flicked off the lid, lifted the bottle up to his nose, and inhaled. A dull throb spread its way up through this sternum. Slowly the throb began to burn, searing through his skin until it was all he could focus on. It gripped and tightened around his chest and ribs, squeezing them. For a second he thought that his legs might buckle – the same way they had so many times in the last two weeks – but they held, and, with his hand trembling, he placed the bottle back on the shelf then adjusted its position until it was back in the right place. When he stepped out of the shower, he rubbed himself dry then picked up a razor for the first time since the accident.

※

THE AMBULANCE HAD COME with its sirens on, lights flashing as it turned down the street and raced towards them. The paramedics dashed from the front, bags in hand, but they were too late. Eric knew it.

'It's my wife, my wife. Please, please. She's my wife.'

One of the paramedics pulled him to the side as the other got to work. Someone else tried to drag him away, to stop him watching as they heaved her body out of the twisted wreck, but he pulled himself out of their grip.

'Do something,' he yelled at anyone who could hear. 'Do something. You have to be able to do something.'

'Sir.' Someone spoke to him, the voice floating and calm, like they couldn't see the chaos unravelling in front of them. 'Please sir, you need to come with us. Is there someone you can call? Is there someone you want us to call?'

'Call? She's my wife. She is my wife. Who else am I meant to call? There is no one else. There is no one else.'

※

ERIC HALF-HEARTEDLY RAN the razor across his cheeks. It was a surprise to see that the quick shave made the outside appear better even if the inside was still a train wreck. He returned to his bedroom, towel wrapped around his waist. Yvette had tidied, and judging from the job she had done, he must have been in there longer than he had thought. The window was open, filling the room with a cool clean breeze, while his bed and the clothes that were strewn on the floor had all been straightened up and all the empty glasses were gone. Hung up by the window was a freshly ironed shirt and his funeral suit. Eric stepped towards it and ran his hand down the seam.

He had worn the suit only three times; once for each of his parents, once for an elderly friend that had died the year before. Norman. After he died, they had bought his house. The house they lived in now. The house of dead people, Eric mused.

He had never had to go to a funeral for someone younger than himself. Never did he once suspect that the first time it would happen would be for his wife. Attending Suzy's funeral had always been an impossibility to him, like being a grandparent. Of course there was a chance it would happen one day, but at this point in his life it was all such an abstract concept he had never really given it a second thought. Now he was standing in the bedroom they had shared, preparing to say goodbye. Eric pulled his arm into one of the sleeves and stared at himself in the mirror. It wasn't just Yvette who had aged recently. His skin had taken on a greyish hue, his eyes were bloodshot and shrunken from all the drink. Had he passed his reflection on the street he wouldn't have recognised himself; he would have probably crossed to the other side of the road too. Still, he continued to dress, mindlessly moving from one garment to the next.

After knotting the tie around his neck, Eric stared some more. This was it, this was how he was going to say goodbye to his wife, to the love of his life, looking like an undertaker or a cheap wedding musician. He pulled on the bit of nylon around his neck. And in a skinny tie? Why did he not own a thick black tie? Why was the only plain black, funeral-worthy tie he owned from the days when C&A was still considered the height of fashion and men wore bell-bottoms in a non-ironic way? He tugged at the tie and loosened the knot before pulling it off altogether and throwing it to the ground. No chance. Not a chance in hell.

Opening the wardrobe, Eric rummaged through to the back. It was the first time in two weeks he'd had any kind of definite drive, and if what he was looking for turned out not to be there, he didn't know what he would do. He tossed one garment to the side, then the next before finally finding the item crumpled at the back, having slipped off its hanger. He sighed with relief, pulled it out of the wardrobe, and dropped it onto the bed.

Suzy had bought the shirt in Camden market years beforehand. Eric had never been a great fan of it.

'It looks like the Y-fronts my uncle used to wear,' he had said when she picked it out for him.

'I never knew your uncle was so fashionable,' she replied, holding it up to him to get a gauge of the size. 'It suits you.'

On reflection, it wasn't anything like the neon patterned underpants his uncle would strut around in, much to the disgust of Eric's father. Most of the material was black, it was a decent enough cotton, and the paisley pattern was thin and delicate.

'Please wear it,' Suzy would say, almost every time they went out. 'You look so good in it.'

'I said I didn't mind if you bought it. I never said I was going to wear it.' Eric replied.

Sometimes he would give in and wear it anyway – truthfully it wasn't the most offensive item he owned, throughout the years he had collected quite the array of novelty T-shirts and superhero socks – but at other times he'd put his foot down and opted for something more his own style; like plaid or stripes or just a good old T-shirt. He slipped his arms into the sleeves, then buttoned it up to the top before reaching for his black funeral tie. His hand hovered momentarily above it before he changed his mind. Another quick rifle through the wardrobe found a turquoise one; another of Suzy's gifts to him. She always loved turquoise. He wrapped it around his neck and took yet another glance in the mirror. It didn't match, not even close, and he didn't care at all.

Downstairs, Yvette was busy in the kitchen. A large spread was laid out on the dining room table, which had been moved into the kitchen after the visit from a baseball-bat-wielding thug. Countless varieties of cakes and sandwiches obscured the wood; easily enough for fifty people, if not one more.

'I thought you said it was just Lydia coming for breakfast?' Eric said to Yvette's back as she stirred a pan of scrambling eggs.

'It is,' she said.

'Then what's all this for?'

Yvette turned around to face him. She was dressed in a knee-length skirt with a floaty top. The style was typical of the fashion that Yvette had recently adopted, hippy with the mildest hint of seniority. The colour – black – was not. Eric watched as she scanned him up and down, from his jeans to his turquoise tie and back again.

'You look good,' she said. 'A much better choice.'

Eric glanced down at the table. His stomach growled, but the last thing he wanted was food. What he wanted was a drink. A large one.

'I've made some coffee,' she said. Eric's eyes went to the drink's cabinet. Yvette shook her head.

'We need all that for the wake. Besides. You're the host.'

Eric snorted. 'I don't think anyone's going to begrudge me having a drink after burying my wife,' he said.

'Maybe not. Then again, perhaps ...' Yvette let her sentence drift into the ether, where it sent prickles of annoyance tingling down Eric's spine.

'Perhaps what, Yvette?'

She turned back to the pan and began to stir.

'Why don't you go and check the order of service?' she said. 'You might at least pretend you had something to do with this funeral.'

The sudden change in tone pierced Eric, just as it was meant to. As he swivelled on his heel, ready to disappear back upstairs, the doorbell rang.

It was just the doorbell, no different to the hundreds of other times Eric had heard it ring over the last two weeks. It had the same pitch, the same ding-dong melody, and the same short reverberation time, yet with it came a cool draft that set off goose bumps on Eric's arms.

'You need to get that,' Yvette said. '*She* needs you to get that.'

Eric's heart drummed against his ribcage. The thumping rattled up through to his ear drums.

'I've forgotten something,' Eric said. 'I just need to run upstairs. You answer it. I'll be back down in a minute.'

In a flash Yvette had crossed the room. Taking his hand in hers, she offered one, heartfelt squeeze.

'No,' she said. 'I've seen her already today. She needs to see you. She needs you.'

Something constricted around Eric's throat. He wanted to say something, find a more viable excuse, defend his reasoning so that Yvette couldn't possibly say no. But he didn't have any reason. Other than being a coward.

'She needs you,' Yvette said.

He nodded, rendered mute by it all. In truth, he really was trying, but in the fifteen days since Suzy's death he had been failing as a father, and he knew it. It wasn't that he didn't want to be there for his daughter. He did. He desperately did, but how could he look at her after what had happened? How could he look at her and tell her he loved her and that he would do everything he could to protect her when he was the one who had done this? He was the one responsible for Suzy's death. Looking at Abi was too much to bear, and so he had started with the excuses. The house needed fixing up. The allotment needed seeing to. Not that he actually did any of these things; he couldn't recall the last time he had stepped foot on the allotment and he didn't even care. Every time Abi would ask to join him, and Eric would be forced to construct some feeble excuse about why she needed to stay with her grandmother or aunt or a neighbour even. Anyone but himself. He just couldn't face Abi, not yet. The scary thing was, he didn't know when he'd ever be able to again.

CHAPTER 2

ERIC COULD BARELY recall seeing Abi that afternoon in the hospital. He had rung Lydia in the ambulance – he couldn't remember what he had said – and she had arrived with Tom and the children, including Abi.

'Daddy!' Abi had run in to his arms. He lowered himself to the ground and wrapped his arms around her. He had tried to hold her as tightly as she deserved – as tightly as she had needed – but his arms were numb, leaden with disbelief and guilt.

'She'll wake up though, won't she, Daddy?' Abi had said, her big, pleading eyes the exact same shade as Suzy's.

'No,' Eric said. 'No, she won't. I'm sorry. I'm so sorry, baby girl. Mummy's gone. She's gone. She's dead. Mummy's dead.'

And that was it; that was how he had comforted his nine-year-old daughter in her hour of need. No sugar coating, no softening remarks about angels watching over us and being in a place where there's endless cups of tea and biscuits. He hadn't asked if she needed anything or given her the chance to wish her a final farewell. He just told her she was dead.

'We can take Abi back with us tonight, if you want?' Lydia said as they stood in the hospital waiting area. Green plastic chairs and a smell of antiseptic shrouded all of Eric's other senses. 'We can bring her back in the morning. Or whenever you need. You just let us know.'

Eric nodded mutely; it was Yvette who stepped in.

'No. She needs to be at home with us,' she said. Eric nodded again. They could have said anything. He was just going to keep on nodding. Still, when they left hospital, Abi was in her Uncle Tom's arms, not Eric's, and when her eyes lifted from his shoulder and for a brief second fell on her father, Eric lowered his gaze to the ground. Shitty husband, shitty father. All round shit. Since then they had been passing ships, and he was the one deliberately setting the course.

The doorbell rang again. Yvette had dropped his hand but had made no attempt to move to answer the door. She wasn't going to, he realised. This was all on him.

'Go on,' she said.

In tentative half-steps, he made his way down the hall to the front of the house where he lingered at the front door. A moment later he reached forward and opened it.

'Eric,' Lydia said, and grasped him in an embrace. It was far too tight – suffocating. He stayed there for what he considered long enough before he began wiggling his shoulders until she got the hint and let him go.

'Tom,' Eric reached out a hand to his brother-in-law, who took it, pumped it once, then also moved in for a hug. This one was thankfully shorter.

'Let's all go inside, shall we?' Lydia said, manoeuvring herself around Eric. He stepped back and gave them all room, keeping his eyes down as the children passed him.

Eric had already seen Abi that morning. She had climbed into his bed around three a.m. when the nightmares had started, slipping under the covers next to him and curling up in the crook of his arm. He'd pretended to be asleep, even when she spoke his name. Eventually, she had drifted back off and he had held her, trying not to wake her with his shuddering sobs which lasted until the dawn chorus broke the silence of the night. When Abi woke, an hour after the birdsong, Eric once more pretended to be asleep. Eric knew she would go to her grandmother. Yvette was better at these things than he was.

Now in the hallway, she had stopped directly in front of him. Her dress, Eric noticed, was turquoise.

'Good colour,' Eric said. 'Is it new?'

Abi shook her head. 'Mum bought it for me ... before.'

A dense lump forced its way up Eric's throat.

'We match,' he croaked out, and lifted his tie.

'We do,' Abi said.

The late breakfast was a near silent affair. Yvette had gone all out on the fry up, but the boys were the only ones who could manage to eat. Eric watched Abi as she pushed a piece of bacon from one side of her plate to the other while Lydia took endless sips of her orange juice without even pretending to touch anything on her plate.

'I invited Lydia, Tom, and the boys to stay the night,' Yvette said, when after five minutes sat around the table nobody had spoken. 'I hope you don't mind, Eric?'

'What? No. No, that's fine.' He was staring at an ink blotch on the wood. This table was meant to be their best. Their dining room table, but Suzy had been using it as a temporary office for the last few months. They had had such high hopes for moving to Burlam – more family time, less work – yet for the last two months of her life Eric felt like Suzy had been glued to one desk or another. His eyes began to water as he continued to stare at the ink splotch. She must have spilled something on it. He reached out a finger and touched the mark.

'Actually, Mum, we are going to have to leave after the wake I'm afraid. We'll help you tidy up and everything, but we've got to go to Birmingham tomorrow.'

'Oh?'

'Tom's mum has had a bit of a fall. Nothing serious, but she could do with us going up and helping out around the house.'

'Oh.' Yvette made no attempt to hide her disappointment.

'But if you need us to go and grab anything? Or you want to borrow the car before we go ...?'

Eric shook his head. 'We'll be fine, thank you.' He hadn't even thought about getting in a car, not since he watched his wife die in one. Even the sight of his prized Aston Martin would see his whole body roil in guilt and shame. 'Excuse me,' he said, pushing himself up and backing away from the table. 'I need to go and sort some things.' It was time to change all that.

IN HIS HIDEY-HOLE of the driver's seat, Eric turned the bottle around in his hand. He could see it would be bad taste arriving at his wife's funeral half-cut – even if he was the reason everyone had to attend a funeral anyway – so for now the lid remained sealed. Although after the funeral; that he would make no promises on. The brashness of the garage lighting was lost inside the cocoon of the car. Instead dappled light, muted by dust, clouded Eric's vision. He breathed in the smell of the woodwork and the leather and ran a hand across the dashboard before returning it to the neck of the bottle. Had Lydia not brought up the matter of cars at brunch, Eric probably wouldn't have remembered he had stashed a bottle away in here for emergencies. He couldn't even remember when he had done it. It was irrelevant now though; he had a replenished supply that Yvette would not be getting her hands on.

Sally, Eric's late father's limited-edition Aston Martin DB4, was Eric's most prized possession. What a ridiculous notion, he realised, prizing an inanimate object. As an atheist he thought religious people were off their rocker, worshipping great unknown beings with mystical powers that they might only see when they die. But how much better had he been? His car, his house. For so many years that number on the bank balance was what had mattered the most, and by the time he understood what was important, it was too late. It shouldn't have been too late, of course. They should have had longer together, but they didn't, and that was Eric's fault. Eric's mind wandered to Abi. It wasn't fair. No child should grow up without their parents. Not when that parent loved them as much as Suzy did. He had stolen that from her. No wonder he couldn't bear to look her in the eye.

It felt as though his ribs had been torn from his chest one by one. He glanced at the bottle in his hand. He knew he should talk to her. But what could he say? That Suzy would always be with them? That she was watching over them. It was bullshit. There was no one watching over them. How could there be? He unscrewed the lid and took a long sniff. Maybe the answer was in there.

'You don't need that.' Eric started as the passenger door to the car swung open. A moment later, Lydia squeezed into the passenger seat. 'Besides,' she said. 'It's already gone ten. If you really needed a drink, you'd have had one by now.'

'Speaking from experience, are you?'

'Yes.'

Eric raised his eyebrow sceptically. Lydia was every bit the condescending older sister, with her backyard hens and full organic lifestyle. The closest she ever got to letting go and breaking free was turning the central heating on three days before the start of December, and that only ever happened in cases of extreme frost bite. The chance of her understanding the need to lose yourself so completely was exactly zero.

'Whatever.' Eric shook his head and fixed the lid back on the bottle. Lydia took it from him and slid it down into the foot well beside her feet. When her head came back up, she was biting down on her bottom lip.

'It's true,' she said. 'First when I was a teenager. Something happened and I ... well ... It wasn't a long spell or anything, but it set the scene for future years. When Tom and I were first married, I had four miscarriages in two years. Then I was made redundant. We lost the first house we bought together. It wasn't a pretty time. I found an easy way to forget. That time was harder to dig myself out of.'

Eric studied his sister-in-law. Her face was set and steady – truthful.

'I didn't know that.'

'No, well it was before you were on the scene, and it's not something I tend to discuss.'

'Suzy never said anything.'

'We're sisters. That's what we do. Keep each other's secrets. Why do you think there's hardly ever alcohol in the house?'

'Because you're cheapskates?'

Lydia laughed. Eric felt his lips twitch too. He might have even managed a smile, had Lydia's laughter not come to such an abrupt stop.

'I get it must be hard,' she said. 'I can't imagine. I know how much I'm hurting. She was my baby sister. I was meant to protect her, always. That was the deal. And I failed again.'

'You never failed her. Not like this. She thought the world of you.'

'You have no idea,' Lydia said. 'Trust me, she deserved better that me.' Her eyes glazed as they drifted away and out of the car. A second later she sniffed and straightened herself, wiping her eyes with the back of her hand.

'You're breaking Abi's heart, Eric,' she said. 'You can see that, can't you? She's heartbroken.'

'I ... I ...'

'She feels like she's lost her father too.'

Eric's fist clenched around the steering wheel.

'That's not fair,' he said.

'I'm not trying to be fair,' Lydia replied. 'I'm trying to be honest. She's a little girl. A baby girl and she lost the most important person in the whole wide world, and now you're making her feel like she's done something wrong.'

'I'm not a good person for her to be around right now. I'm not in a good place.'

'You're the *only* person it's good for her to be around, Eric. The only person. You are who she needs.'

'Not like this.'

'Your worst is better than any of us can do. You see that, don't you? You have to.'

Eric loosened his grip around the steering wheel and dropped his head with a sigh.

'You need to do something, Eric. You need to show her that she comes first in all of this.'

'Of course she does.'

'Well it doesn't look like that. Not from where she's standing. Do something, Eric, please,' she repeated. 'Before it's too late.'

'I'll try.'

'Trying isn't going to cut it this time.'

<hr />

ONLY A YEAR AGO, stepping into Abi's bedroom had been like stepping into some fuchsia-invaded candy land. Pink unicorns and teddy bears, pink lampshades, curtains, bedspread, everything had been pink. Everywhere he had turned, Eric had been faced with yet another shade of rose, magenta, or blush. There had been the occasional train set or yellow toy stethoscope to add some variety to the mix, but it had been a little girl's room. His baby girl's room. Not anymore. There were still a lot of pink things of course, her ballet clothes and shoes, hung up on the outside of the wardrobe door, her favourite teddies, some of the pictures that Suzy had commissioned from her artistic friends, but the walls and bedspread were purple now. And white curtains hung from the rail. Jeans were currently the clothes in favour, with trainers and a hoodie, not frilly pink dresses.

Abi was lying flat on her bed flicking through the pages of a book. Her eyes lifted now and again with hints of a smile. Eric watched her from the doorway. She looked peaceful, almost happy. If he didn't speak, he thought, if he just left now then he could keep that image of happy peaceful Abi, and he wouldn't have to face the truth. He was on the ball of his foot, ready to turn and retreat to his own room, when Abi's head jerked up.

'Dad?' she said. 'Everything okay?'

'Abs ... I ...'

His first two attempts at speech got jammed somewhere around his larynx. On the third attempt, his eyes fell upon the book on the bed and a few words managed to croak their way into existence.

'What's that you've got there?' he said, taking one step into the doorway.

'Just something Aunty Lyds gave me.'

'Can I see?'

She shrugged.

Eric moved across to the bed. Just like his room, this one needed airing, and he had no idea when her sheets had last been washed. Hopefully Yvette was on the case. Even when Suzy was the only one working, bed linen was still on her household chore jurisdiction, meaning he had no idea when they would have last been cleaned. Shaking his head clear of dirty laundry, he leaned over Abi's shoulder to get a better look at what she was studying.

It was as if he had been dunked head first in salt water, with his eyes forced open. Eric gasped, audibly. Painfully. The images around him – the bed, the window, his daughter – all blurred into one peripheral haze. Tears were causing the haze, he realised. Tears that needed to be sucked back down before Abi saw. Tears he had to hide to prove to her that he was strong, that he could do this. But the lack of air was making it harder to do. The lack of oxygen in his lungs, the light-headedness that came with it. He was going to pass out. Or vomit. Or both simultaneously.

'This was her first day at school. Aunty Lydia told me.' Abi spoke with her eyes still fixed on the photo. 'She was so excited. Apparently, she went to bed the night before with her uniform on, just to make sure she wasn't late. She's even littler than I am. Look.'

Eric's heart hammered.

'Oh yes,' he heard the words emitted from his lips although he had no idea how he had managed to make them.

'And then she cried when Granny had to pick her up at the end of the day. She loved school.'

'Is that so?' He was trying to hide the quiver in his voice.

'She was pretty, wasn't she? She was really, really pretty.'

For the first time Eric looked directly at the photo. The edges had lost all their colour, but it was clear from the foreground that she was standing in front of a house. Her feet were pressed together, the laces tied in perfect bows. It was only when Eric managed to draw his eyes away from the faded images of a pigtailed Suzy, that he realised Abi was looking at him, waiting for an answer.

'What was that?' Eric asked attempting, yet failing, to swallow back the tears as they escaped down his cheek. 'Sorry, yes. She was beautiful. The most beautiful. Can I?' he said, indicating the space on the bed next to Abi.

Abi nodded mutedly.

She shuffled across, keeping the book firmly in her grip as she moved and made just enough space for Eric to lie down beside her, belly on the bed sheet. As he struggled to find a comfortable position, he remembered this was how Suzy read books with Abi at night. Eric preferred to sit up and avoid getting cricks in his back and neck, but the girls could lie belly down for hours, flicking through page after page, laughing at the rhymes they had memorised by heart.

'You look like her,' Eric said quietly, scanning his eyes up and down the page of photographs.

'You think?'

'Most definitely. Look, you have the same shape mouth, and eyes.'

A sad and slanted smile creased its way across Abi's lip and a thin glaze began to glisten in her eyes. She blinked it away with far more grace than Eric.

'There are some baby photos too. Do you want to see those?'

The pummelling in Eric's chest continued. 'Yes,' he said. 'I do.'

Abi flicked back a few pages to the front.

'This one's my favourite. I love the costume. I think Granny picked it out.'

'I agree,' Eric said, marvelling at the choice of feathers and sequins for a six-month-old baby. 'But who's the fat little boy?'

Abi thumped him on the shoulder. 'That's Aunty Lyds.'

'Eek,' Eric said. A small chuckle expanded in the air between them, only to evaporate before it had had a chance to really sound. Abi was still looking at him, Eric realised, waiting for answers he didn't have to questions he didn't want her to ask.

'I think I like this one best,' he said, creating a diversion from the silence and pointing to a small, black and white image of a baby. She was chubby and round, maybe three months old, and laid in a rocking chair wearing only a nappy. 'That one really looks like you.'

'Really?'

'Definitely.'

He had meant it as another passing comment, but the more Eric studied the photograph, the more he realised it was true.

'Look,' he pointed. 'She's got the same dimples that you had. And the same big ears.'

'I don't have big ears,' Abi protested, clamping her hands to the sides of her face.

'You did when you were a baby.'

'Let's see,' Abi said.

She flicked from the page of the smiling baby towards the back of the book. The corners of the pages, Eric noticed, were already well thumbed, with water marks and fingerprints littered across the paper.

'Are there photographs of you in here too?'

'Uh-huh,' Abi said. 'And you. And Granny and Grandad. There's everybody.'

'And Aunty Lydia made it for you?'

'Yes.' An ache rose through Eric's sternum. This was what he was meant to have done. Not Lydia. This was his job, but it hadn't even crossed his mind. He had been too busy worrying about himself.

'Oh,' said Abi, her face crestfallen as she landed on another page. 'I really did have big ears.'

Eric reached over and tucked a strand of hair behind her ear, tickling her skin a little as he did.

'Yup, you were my little Dumbo,' he said. 'And look, dimples too. You two could have been twins.'

Abi's eyes returned to the photo. 'I did look like her.'

The sadness in her voice echoed in the room around them, and it was only as her face fell, and the ache once more began to spread, that Eric realised he had been smiling.

'I miss her,' Abi said as tears rolled down her cheeks. 'I miss her and my heart hurts.'

'I know,' Eric said, unable to control his own surge of tears. 'I miss her too.'

'Will it get better? Will it stop hurting?'

'I hope so,' Eric said. 'I really hope so.'

CHAPTER 3

EVENTUALLY THE TEARS stopped. It wasn't that he wanted to stop crying, merely that he had run out of tears for now. His eyes and head and every part of him had been cried dry. Still, he lay there, cradling his daughter while she released her insatiable supply of heartache. Only when she was almost asleep, exhausted from all the pain, did she finally stop crying.

A light knock rapped on the door and brought them both back to the present.

'I'm sorry,' Yvette said, looking genuinely apologetic as she spoke. 'But it's gone one. I thought you might want to think about making a move.'

Eric manoeuvred himself up to sitting and noticed the damp patches spread across the now crumpled paisley shirt. It would dry, he thought.

'We'll just be a couple more minutes,' he said, motioning to Abi with a nod. 'Is that okay?'

'We'll be downstairs,' Yvette said.

Abi rubbed her eyes, then took the book and placed it onto her nightstand. She swung her legs over the bed, preparing to leave. Eric caught her by the hand.

'Wait,' he said. 'I have something for you.'

She turned back and tilted her head expectantly.

Now that he had said the words, Eric knew he couldn't go back, although his rattling pulse implied he desperately wanted to. He dug his hand into his pocket and clenched it around the small, cold item inside. It wasn't meant to be like this, he thought. This isn't how things like this were supposed to be passed on. But nothing about this was the way it was meant to be. Lydia's words were on replay around his skull. *Do something, Eric. Show her she comes first. Do something, Eric.*

'Do you know how I proposed to your mum?' Eric asked, picking Abi up by the waist and shuffling her into a position which faced him. 'Did we ever tell you that?'

Abi twitched her nose and considered the question.

'Wasn't it on a ferrous wheel?'

'A *Ferris* wheel, yes,' Eric said. 'Your mum loved Christmas, and I thought that would be a great place to ask her to marry me. On a Ferris wheel, high above the city where she could look out over all the pretty Christmas lights.'

'And she said yes.'

'She did,' Eric said. 'But you missed a step.'

Abi straighten her back and leaned a little closer.

'When you ask someone to marry you, you have to give them a ring.'

'Like a wedding ring?'

'Exactly like a wedding ring. Only you give it to someone before you marry them, so you call it an engagement ring.'

'An engagement ring,' Abi's head nodded as she whispered the word, her brow furrowing as if searching for a hidden memory. 'There's a photo of it in the book,' she said, reaching across for the thickly bound leather folder. 'Aunty Lydia said it was the biggest diamond she had ever seen. She said it was another word too. Ostend, ostend—,'

Eric gritted his teeth and said nothing. Abi found the page she was looking for.

'Look,' she said. 'That's it, isn't it?'

Eric's stomach lurched. It was a photo of the pair of them, taken outside in a pub garden. The image was a close-up on their faces but with their hands twisted together and resting on the table in front of him. Suzy's eyes were scrunched closed, head tilted back, and mouth wide open in a laugh. Eric gazed adoringly at her.

Summer '05, it said beneath it. The year before they married. Something dense began clogging Eric's windpipe and obstructing his breathing.

'Daddy, are you okay?'

Eric shook his head, then changed it rapidly into a nod, remembering the whole purpose of this conversation.

'Well that was the ring we got after I proposed,' Eric said, trying not to let his eyes get drawn down to the multitude of smiling photos he so desperately wanted to weep through. 'I let your mum help me choose that one. But the one I gave her when I asked her was different.'

The story was true. Eric had known he wanted to marry Suzy after the first month, possibly even the first date, which took place in a smoke-filled London bar, where a Duran Duran cover band were playing, and the menu was limited to chips, beer, and Babycham. He knew the chances of anyone of her calibre ever looking in his direction again was as close to zero as odds got, and he wanted to make sure there was a ring on her finger and a walk down the aisle before she realised how much better she could do. But trying to pick out a ring had been a nightmare.

He tried contacting Yvette and Philip, to ask for permission and discuss the possibly of using one of Suzy's grandmother's heirloom rings to propose with, but getting hold of the pair of them when they were on a cruise ship was about as easy as finding a torch and working batteries during a power cut. That, combined with Lydia's assurance that Yvette was not going to hand over those rings until she was six feet under, had forced him to try another route. He considered using his mother's, but the dated style would have never been right for Suzy. Friends had given widely differing opinions as to what she would want, but he knew Suzy; she'd never say she didn't like anything. She'd have accepted whatever he gave her graciously and lovingly. The last thing he wanted was for her to be spending the next fifty years walking around with a ring she thought looked like a gumball machine gift on her hand. With that thought in mind, Eric went directly to the nearest gumball machine.

'It's a mood ring,' he told Abi. 'The same ring I gave your mum, and it cost one pound.'

'A mood ring?'

'Yup, it means it changes colour when you're feeling happy or sad.'

Eric slipped his hand out of his pocket and opened his palm. The cheap metal was as thin and bendy as it had been all those years ago, although by some apparent miracle, still silver in colour. The round stone stuck out from the middle like a bubble blown from a bubble wand, with similar shades of blue and purple swirling on the top.

Abi stared transfixed.

'Is that it? Is that the mood ring?'

'That's the mood ring,' Eric said, trying to force down the frog in his throat. 'This is the ring I gave to your mummy when I asked her to marry me.'

Abi reached out her hand to touch it. Eric stopped her. He took her hand gently, holding her by the fingers.

'It's yours now,' he said slipping it onto her middle finger and squeezing the metal tight. 'You need to make sure you take care of it, you understand?'

Abi nodded. Silent tears tumbled down her cheeks as she continued to gaze at the stone.

'It's turning red,' she said. 'What do you think that means? What mood do you think that means?'

Eric drifted back to the memories where those same words drifted from Suzy's lips.

'It must mean we're in love, don't you think? Either that or I'm cross that you got me a cheap metal ring?' Suzy had said.

Eric laughed. 'It's love. Red has to be love.' And then he had kissed his future wife.

'I think red is what it shows when you're feeling strong,' Eric said. 'When you're feeling brave.'

Abi stared at the stone a little longer before shaking her head. 'I think red is what it shows when your heart hurts,' she said.

❦

THE FUNERAL WENT by in a haze of thanking. With Abi gripping his hand, Eric was jostled from one place to another. He thanked people for coming, for their thoughts and prayers, for their kind words. He thanked them for sending cards, for sending flowers, for sending wishes. Every other word that came out of his mouth was thank you, and every moment of it he felt like an absolute fraud. There was only one noticeable absence from the mourners; Philip, Suzy's father, although in truth Eric was relieved. He had enough drama of his own to deal with. When the service began, he fixed his eyes on the casket in front of him.

'Pack your bag, Eric. This is it.' The words went over and over on replay in his head. The last words his wife had said to him before she sped off in reverse without even a glance to the road behind her. He remembered something someone said to him when Yvette and Philip had separated. 'It would have been better if they'd died,' people had said. They didn't have a clue.

A kaleidoscope of emotions turned continually within him as he sat in the front seat and listened to Lydia, then Yvette, then a couple more friends talk about his wife. Not that he had a wife anymore. He was a widower. Alone. His heart went from numb to soul-searing agony and from disbelief to complete destitution a hundred times over. And then it was his time to stand up. His time to speak.

As Eric took to the lectern, his hands shook. His knees trembled, and his mouth and throat turned so dry that his tongue stuck to the back of his teeth. With a single piece of paper in his hand, he stared out at the mourners in front of him. If he had his way, he would pull this whole place down he thought, and make sure he was at the centre when it happened.

He coughed twice to clear his throat.

'Suzy hadn't planned her funeral,' he said. 'I guess she thought ... we all thought she would have a lot longer left with us.' A lump floated upwards in his throat. He swallowed it back down. 'So, with that in mind. I thought I would like to read something we had read at our wedding instead. I know some of you were there, but many of you weren't. This is what we wanted to be. This was how it started.' He glanced down at the paper in his hand. Reading the poem had been Yvette's idea. At the time of agreeing Eric hadn't really thought about what it meant, only that doing this, doing as Yvette said, would be one less thing for him to have to think about. She had printed him the paper too. Eric realised, as his eyes scanned down the lines of black ink, that he had probably not seen the poem since his wedding day.

'The Secret of Togetherness,' he said, 'by Peter Jefferson Clark.'

"Togetherness is tough.

Togetherness requires two separate people to remain individuals with each of them acting as one to support the one another."

He thought of the night before Christmas Eve, when Suzy was hammering in nail tack after nail, fixing their carpet to the floor. They acted as one then, sorting the house, but what about when she was working every hour, stuck up in her little office; or when he was working every hour in London? How much had he supported her then? How much had they acted as one back then?'

"Togetherness means letting go of the little things, so that the bigger picture can come into view.

Togetherness is always putting each other's mutual interests ahead of your own individual gain.

It is letting the other person know that your love is unconditional of mood or temperament or anything outside of yourselves.

It is always being there for one another."

Eric paused again. Did he do that? Did he let Suzy know that he loved her unconditionally? He was certain he did, but did he tell her? Had he told Suzy he loved her as she and Yvette had bundled off into the car to head to Lydia's? He couldn't remember doing that. What about on the phone when he told her she had to come home so he could talk to her and tell her what he had done? He definitely couldn't remember saying I love you explicitly then. No, he didn't. And would it have counted? How could it have counted after what he'd done? How can you promise someone that your love is unconditional after you've kissed another woman? The poem didn't mention that at all. It didn't mention anything about kissing anybody else. Eric's pause elongated. People were staring at him, of course they were, but not just because they were listening. One or two turned to another. Hushed whispers drifted their way to his ears. It didn't matter though, he would get back to the poem in a minute, he just had to remember the last time he told her he loved her. The night before, he thought, as tears weaved their way down to his chin, but again, he couldn't remember it. Why couldn't he remember? Why couldn't he remember the last time he told her he loved her?

"It is appreciating the little things they do for you and not holding grudges for the things you feel are against you." Eric's head jerked to the side, suddenly aware of the hurricane of tears that continued to stream down his cheeks and the pressure on his fingers. Lydia was at his side, holding his hand, reading his poem.

"It is laughing together at things which would otherwise break you apart.
It is knowing when to talk and when to stay silent.
It is understanding the difference in the silences you share ..."

With Eric muted, Lydia read until the end, then guided him back down to his seat on the front row. Another hand slipped into his. Abi's. She squeezed it as hard as she could. Eric let it go.

After the service came yet more thanks, from more people who Eric was forced to endure. While Yvette and Tom rushed off to sort the food, Eric lingered. The crematorium had been big, with various hidden nooks in which he could hide; there would be none of that when he got home. Even at the crematorium he'd had difficulty shaking one particular shadow.

'Why don't you go with your grandmother?' Eric said. Abi was staring at the ring on her finger, the colour having not changed from the same deep red all morning. She pressed her lips together and shuffled her feet along the floorboards.

'What? What is it?' Eric said.

Abi lifted her head. Her eyes full of tears.

'I want to be the last,' she said eventually. 'I want to be the last to go. I want to be the last to say goodbye.'

Something blocked the air to Eric's lungs. He nodded in quick succession.

'Me too, honey,' he said. 'Me too.'

Together they found a seat to the side. Silently they waited for the space to empty. When all the footsteps had faded, and the doors closed, Eric turned to his daughter.

'Are you ready to go home?' he asked.

Abi stayed motionless, eyes forward, fixed on the empty space in front of her.

'Another five minutes?' she said.

Eric sucked back the tears.

'Another five minutes.'

※

WHEN THEY ARRIVED BACK at the house, people were already tucking into Yvette's canapes. Eric crept in through the front door, his hands on Abi's shoulders as she walked in front of him.

'You hungry?' he said to her, while nodding politely to the sympathetic nods and pats on the back. Abi shrugged.

'Let's go into the kitchen. Your grandmother will probably be in there. And you should probably eat something.' Besides, he thought to himself, I need to get a drink.

It appeared that Yvette had not been the only one busy preparing food that morning. The table was far fuller than when he had left the house, with everything from cucumber sandwiches and wraps to homemade scones and jams.

Centre table, Eric noticed, was a large, loafed carrot cake. His heart flickered. Last time he had been to a funeral it had been for his friend Norman, and the loss had hit Eric hard. He hadn't expected the next one he attended to be so soon. He certainly didn't expect it to be in the same house. His eyes were drawn back to the carrot cake. It looked exactly like the one Cynthia, Norman's wife, used to make before she packed off to travel the world. Another friend he had lost.

'Do you want me to cut you a slice?'

Eric spun around. 'Cynthia?'

Her hair was back to vibrant auburn and a small smile lifted gently at the corners of her lips, although her eyes, like everyone else's, were laced with sadness.

'You came.' A dull heat burned in Eric's chest. 'You came back for this? I thought you were in Australia, or New Zealand?'

'I was. And I did. But it was time I was heading back, anyway. People to see. I can't run away from life forever, now can I?' Her smile faded, and deep crevices etched themselves around her eyes. 'I'm so sorry,' she said. 'I was heartbroken when I heard. Poor Abi. Are you holding up all right? Truthfully now, how are you doing?'

Eric took a deep breath in. The normal trope line, about surviving each day as it comes came to his lips only to disappear back within him.

'I feel like I'm dying,' he answered honestly. 'I have no idea how I'm supposed to get through this. No idea.'

Cynthia nodded sympathetically. 'I understand. I do.'

The two stood locked in silence. It was impossible to say when the pair had grown so close; probably after Norman's death although possibly before. There was something about the non-judgemental way in which Cynthia viewed the world that reminded him of his mother. An optimist and yet a realist. Compassionate to the core and ready to fight to the death for something she believed in. Eric was about to lead her through to find Abi when a small woman with a bleached crop of hair appeared at Eric's side. Her lips twisted apologetically before she turned to Cynthia.

'Sorry, you don't mind, do you?' she said, indicating her desire to steal Eric away for a conversation.

Cynthia shook her head. 'No, not at all. I was just about to disappear.' She looked at Eric. 'I'm keen to meet this mother-in-law of yours everyone is talking about. I hear she's quite a character. Perhaps we could arrange a get together later in the week?'

'That sounds great. I think you two will get along fabulously,' he said, then leaned in and kissed her on the cheek, after which she promptly disappeared into the sea of black.

'Eric.'

The woman Eric was left with was of elfin proportions. Her black sweeping poncho and skinny trousers were far too fashionable to be placed within a fifty-mile radius of Burlam. Still, it took Eric a solid minute to place her.

'Sam,' he said, taking her by the shoulders and doing the obligatory kiss on both cheeks that he had become so accustomed to in the last three hours. 'How are you?'

'Missing her,' she said. 'Every day I'm looking at my emails, waiting for one to come through from her. I don't know if I'll ever stop.'

'I know.'

'Fourteen years I've been her agent. Fourteen years, can you believe that? That's got to be longer than most marriages last, hasn't it?'

'Longer than mine,' Eric said. 'We only got to twelve.'

The woman's face flushed fuchsia. 'Eric, I'm so sorry. I didn't mean to imply—'

'It's fine. I was being flippant. Honestly.'

Her eyes hovered on his, the look of concern still at the forefront. Eric had had a lot of looks of concern over the past few days, and it was getting harder and harder to look each one in the eye.

'Well I just wanted to let you know that we're here if you need us. The whole team. Suzy was like family to us, and if you have a minute or you want to discuss …'

Eric's mind wandered off as Sam continued to talk at him. He scanned the scene, oblivious to the woman's heightened look of concern or actual words that she was saying. It was a bizarre mix of people that had come to pay their respects. Hank and Jerry were busy talking to one of Suzy's old school friends, while Tom and Janice exchanged solemn looks over cheese scones. Greg, his old colleague, was currently helping Ralph remove his two-year-old's hand from the fire grate. Fortunately, it was May; otherwise the kid would probably be requiring an emergency trip to A&E, although it wouldn't be the first time for Ralph and his brood. There were writers and artists from Suzy's old days, and mums and dads from the more recent years. A selection of men and women dressed in purple robes, who Eric assumed must have been part of Yvette's coven – he used the term loosely – were helping themselves to her vegan meatloaf, although Eric tried not to look too closely. The only other time Yvette had invited that particular group of friends over to their house, it had ended with a viral YouTube clip of Eric chasing naked pensioners across his lawn with a frying pan. Still, he was grateful they had come to support Yvette.

All in all, there must have been at least a dozen people crammed into their kitchen, and easily double that number spilled out into the dining room, living room, and conservatory, and Eric reckoned he knew fifty per cent of their names at best. There were teachers from the primary school and the entirety of the allotment committee, and if he knew this village at all, they weren't going to go until they were certain that his fridge was stocked, his carpets hoovered, and most probably his underwear ironed.

'So, what do you think?'

The abrupt silence that followed, caused Eric's eyes to fall back on Sam, who was currently looking up at him expectantly.

'Sorry?' he said. 'I missed that. What did you say?'

'I was just saying how it was such a shame that the—'

'What?' Eric's attention was severed again, this time as he caught a glimpse of chestnut hair and a flash of familiar blue-green eyes in the conservatory. 'You have to be kidding me. You have to be fucking kidding me.'

CHAPTER 4

SUZY'S AGENT, SAM, was entirely forgotten as Eric barged his way through the mass of black jumpers and jackets and plates of sandwiches and scones. He had to have been mistaken, he had to. He was exhausted; his mind must have been playing tricks. There was no way in hell she could possibly be there, he thought as he stood on yet another pair of polished black shoes. There was no way she would do that, not after everything. Not after the mess that she caused. His pulse was soaring, pumping the blood through his veins with such ferocity it pounded in his ear drums. Yet despite his reasoning, Eric knew what, or rather who, he had seen and the moment he was within touching distance, he grabbed her by the elbow. Maintaining as best an air of normality as he possibly could, Eric dragged Fleur straight out of the conservatory backdoor, into the garden, and down into the alley by the side of the house.

'What the hell do you think you're doing here?' Eric spat. He was shaking with anger. He could feel it, every single muscle in his body on fire.

Fleur blinked, her doe-eyes and lashes fluttering up at him.

'Eric? I don't understand?'

'You don't understand? What. The. Hell. Are. You. Doing. Here? This is my wife's funeral. Her wake.'

Fleur was shaking her head in confusion. A thin veil of tears building on her lower lids.

'I just came to say goodbye. Suzy was my friend.'

Eric laughed. It was harsh and bitter and sounded so unlike his normal voice he could barely recognise it. But he knew the sentiment was what he felt. Pure repulsion.

'You weren't her friend.'

'Eric?'

He was trembling so much he couldn't even manage to speak, and while Fleur was trembling visibly too, he didn't give a damn. She sniffed repeatedly as she cast her gaze to the sky, but despite her attempts to thwart the inevitable, in less than a minute the tears in Fleur's eyes reached their capacity and one by one escaped and slipped down her cheek. She wiped them away with the back of her hand.

'Eric,' she spoke through staggering breaths. 'I'm sorry about what happened. I am. I thought you and I ... I thought we—'

'There is no *we*,' Eric said, bitterness embroiled in every syllable. 'There was *never* any we.'

Fleur's mouth clamped shut. Her chin bobbed up and down in the rapid succession of a nod. Several times her lips puckered and pursed, like she was considering saying something again, but Eric was on her, less than a foot away, teeth bared and ready to draw blood.

'I should go,' she said, when she eventually opened her mouth again. 'I should leave.'

'I think that's the first sensible thing you've said in a long time.'

After offering Eric one last pleading look, Fleur crossed the patio and disappeared into the house.

'Argh!' he screamed, clenching his fist and bringing it down against the neighbour's fence. 'Fuck, fuck, fuck.' His teeth ground top and bottom, the heat of anger burning away in his veins.

'Fuck it!' The wooden spike of the fence post speared into his hand, a warm wet trickle of blood pooled within his clenched fist. He flicked his hand, marking the paving slabs with his blood splatter. 'Fuck it all.'

After a parting kick at the fence, he closed his eyes and sucked in a long deep breath of air. He expelled it, then took another. He could stay out here, he thought, for a couple of minutes at least. No one would miss him. No one would think any worse of him. He glanced at his hand, which stung as he flexed his fingers. It didn't look bad enough for stitches, but it needed cleaning. Perhaps a plaster or something too. With a rub of his knuckles he turned around, ready to walk back into the house.

'So, are you going to tell me what that was all about?' Yvette said. 'Or would I be better off asking for someone else's opinion?'

Eric blanched.

※

TEARS LEAKED down Abi's face as Lydia and Tom said their goodbyes.

'We're only a phone call away,' Lydia said. 'You can ring any time, okay? Day or night. And you can have sleepovers every other weekend if you want?'

Abi looked to Eric while she fiddled with the mood ring, still fixed fast on her middle finger.

'I'll be okay,' she said. Eric nodded his head, sensing for once what she needed.

'She'll be okay,' he said.

Shortly afterward she fell asleep on the living room sofa, the wake still in full flow around her.

Sam had had to disappear early too, waving her phone by means of an apology. By that point Eric was too disorientated to even lift a hand in response. It was as though his whole house was filled with a fog that only he could see. He knew people were talking – to him, at him, around him – but when their mouths moved it was as though they were detached from the sounds they were making, and their voices reached his ears as nothing more than a muffled hum. The only word he ever managed to hear was Suzy's name, amplified past all reason, blaring out like a foghorn at him. Finally, people dispersed, and numbers dwindled.

However, one of the strangest scenarios of the whole afternoon came when Eric headed back into the garage to retrieve his stash from Sally, only to discover someone else had got there first.

It was the sobbing noise that alerted Eric to the fact he was not alone, and he thought momentarily that Abi had slipped away for a little privacy. On reflection he realised that Abi had her own room to go to if she wanted privacy, and that her voice was a full octave higher than the one currently wailing away between his lawnmower and spare tyre set.

'Pete,' Eric said, discovering Suzy's ex-husband crumpled on the ground, with Eric's secret bottle almost a third of the way through. 'What are you doing?'

Pete's head came up from his lap. Snot and tears had dribbled down into his beard, while white chalk marks from the walls had dusted his black jacket.

'Eric,' he said, stumbling to his feet. 'I'm sorry, I didn't mean to cause any trouble. Is this yours?' He held the bottle out to Eric.

'You found it in my house, so the odds are fairly good, wouldn't you say?' Eric took the bottle and downed a mouthful. It was exactly what he needed; sweet and burning and numbing. He savoured the moment, then took another. In the twelve years Suzy and he had been together, Eric had never had the displeasure of meeting her ex-husband. He had heard about him, obviously, although not in the way he expected some women spoke about their lying, cheating ex-husbands. Rather than that, Suzy would tend to clam up when talking about Pete. A pained expression would form on her face, at which point Eric would always try to distract from the situation.

'I'm sorry.' Pete took the bottle out from Eric's hand before Eric had even realised. 'There were just so many people, you know, asking how I knew her. And it's hard to say you're the ex who screwed up her life, you know.'

Eric tensed. 'You didn't ruin her life.' He sucked on his teeth. 'Suzy had a perfectly happy life after you. We had a perfectly happy life. Abi, Suzy, and I. We had a great life.'

Sensing his error, Pete knocked back another double-shot's worth. 'All I meant was … I was just saying that …' With a press of his lips. 'I have two girls now. Did you know that?' He handed Eric back the booze and slipped his phone out of his pocket. 'Eleven and nine. I can't believe how quickly they grow. How quickly they …'

He stopped again, pressing his lips into a thin flat line.

'I should go,' he said. 'My wife's picking me up. She's probably waiting.' He turned and crossed the garage, placing his hand on the door handle before turning back to face Eric.

'Do you think she forgave me?' he said, his eyes shining with even more desperation than Fleur's had only moments before. 'I know what I did was terrible. I do. But I was young. We were young. Do you think that she ever really forgave me?'

Bile and whisky churned in Eric's stomach. What did he know of Suzy's forgiveness? That he didn't deserve any, that was for sure. Had that car not come hurtling around the bend, he might have ended up no different to Pete; a wasted ex, wallowing in all the mistakes he had ever made.

'She was Suzy.' Eric croaked out the one reply he desperately wished he could hear. 'She forgave everyone.'

<hr />

'How many of those have you had?' Yvette asked, gesturing to the whisky glass in Eric's hand.

Hank, Jerry, and Janice had been the last to leave, although Eric's ex-colleague Greg and his new wife stayed around to help with a lot more tidying up than Eric would have predicted. The whole thing had gone on far too long for his liking. After the incident with Pete he had headed back into the wake, armed with the remainder of the bottle. No one had said anything. No one would have dared. He never used to drink whisky before, only gin, but a love of gin was something that he and Suzy had bonded over, and even thinking of pouring a glass without pouring a second one to accompany it caused a blistering sensation to spread its way up from his sternum.

'Does it matter?' he replied, glancing at the glass in his hand.

Yvette pressed her lips together in a line.

'Well, everything's sorted in here,' she said. 'Are you going to stay down long, or do you want me to lock up?'

'I'm not sure.'

'Well, shall I lock up the back at least?'

'If you want.'

'And do you want to carry Abi up to her bed? She can't stay down here all night.'

'For Christ's sake, what is it with all the questions?'

Yvette recoiled. Eric didn't care.

'You honestly think I'm going to let her sleep down here all night?'

'I was just asking.'

A year ago, a visit from Yvette was about as regular as the bowel movement of a fried-chicken addict. Now she lived with them, he could barely go for a piss without turning around and finding her hovering over him.

'I'll carry her up now,' Eric relented with a sigh.

He moved to stand, only to catch his right foot on something invisible. His leg wobbled around before he managed to steady himself on the doorframe.

'Perhaps I should take her up instead?'

'For God's sake, Yvette, I'm fine. Will you just back off.' Still huffing, he marched out of the kitchen and through to Abi, seething every step of the way. He had carried her upstairs after far more drinks than this before and no one had ever batted an eyelid, he thought. Christmas Eves. New Year's Eves. How many other nights had Abi fallen asleep in front of a film and Eric and Suzy waited until they had polished off half a bottle before taking her upstairs? To imply he wasn't capable of looking after his own daughter ... who the hell did she think she was?

Striding into the living room, he swept Abi up in his arms.

'Eric ...'

'Back off, Yvette.'

He could feel her, watching him, even as he took the first step. He clenched his jaw and padded upwards. Each step louder and angrier than the last. When he reached the top of the staircase, he heard a sigh of relief expelled from down below. His shoulders tightened.

'*Let it go, Eric,*' he said to himself.

In the bedroom, he laid Abi down on the bed. She had already changed out of her funeral wear into a pair of leggings and a long-sleeved top so there didn't seem any point in waking her to put her pyjamas on, not when she was so fast asleep. Instead he simply pulled the blanket over her. As he turned to leave, he caught sight of the yellow and green photo album on the table.

It spanned Suzy's entire life; childhood photos, teens, and early twenties. Lydia's wedding, their wedding. The shell suits, the bouffant hair, hoop earrings, diamanté earrings, elasticated waists, and giant bum bags. Over three and a half decades of memories and bad fashion condensed to fit between two faux leather pages. Eric flicked to halfway; their wedding.

They had picked a day in early September. It was less clichéd than summer – and therefore cheaper too – and they'd hoped that the last of the mid-year sun would keep them warm through to the afternoon. It didn't. The whole day was wet and freezing, with winds like they'd never experienced before. Leaves were ripped from the trees, and the rose petals that were thrown as a replacement for confetti were hurled straight back into the eyes and ears of guests. At one point – as Suzy and Eric stepped outside for photos — a gust of wind whipped Suzy's veil up and over, wrapping itself around her throat. Strangled on her wedding day, they had joked. Married for twenty minutes. That would have been a record. The memory rose and churned up in his stomach. He flicked back to the front.

She did look like Abi, Eric thought again as he ran his fingers around the image of baby Suzy. Her eyes had exactly the same expression Abi had had when she was a baby too. She still had in fact. Quizzical. Questioning. Eyes that saw through to his soul. With the tears beginning to build again, he moved to another page.

Next came images of their first house in Islington, taken at a moving in party by the looks of things. Surges of nostalgia rolled through him as he perused the photograph. The house had been in a complete state when they had first bought it; not dissimilar to this place. Everything they had done themselves; well, not the electrics, but the flooring, plastering, plumbing. And it wasn't like they had YouTube to go to back then. Suzy would borrow books from the library, or else beg more manually minded friends to help them.

'No, no ... Mummy, Mummy.' Abi's whimpers rattled around the room and she twisted in the sheets. 'Please, Mummy. Please ...'

Eric closed the book and watched as Abi kicked the sheets from off her body.

'How the hell are we going to do this?' he whispered as he clumsily tucked her hair behind her ears. 'What the hell are we going to do?' He waited a minute or two, continued to rub her arms and shoulders until she fell into less restless slumber. Then he answered his own question by heading downstairs and opening another bottle of drink.

WHEN HE WOKE the next morning, there was a moment. Outside the birds were bringing in the dawn and the sheets rustled against his skin. Warmth filtered its way in through the curtains, the light from which dissolved the last dregs of his dream. What was it he was dreaming about? He couldn't quite catch the image. It was moving constantly away from him, teasing him. A clattering rang its way up from downstairs. Eric's stomach knotted. He should have got up first, he thought. It should have been him who got up first to make the coffee. Suzy never worked well until she had had her first coffee.

All it took was her name. The moment it flicked into his head, it was like a boot to the gut. Eric sat up, gagging, coughing, whisky-filled bile spilling out of his nostrils. His hand reached over to her side of the bed, still cold, unslept in for over two weeks now. The argument hit him next. The vehemence in her eyes, the distrust with which she viewed him as she reversed the car without so much as a glance in her mirror. That was it, that was how he had said goodbye to the love of his life. That was how he had driven her to her death. He leant over the side of the bed and searched for something to be sick in. When he found nothing, he reached down and grabbed his shirt from the previous day. Green, acidic vomit sprayed out of his mouth. He let the last bit dribble down his chin, before wiping it off and throwing the shirt back on the floor. He picked up the bottle and shook it. There was still a bit in the bottom; he must have passed out before he finished drinking. He pulled off the top and lifted the bottle to his mouth,

'Daddy?' Abi stood in his doorway. 'Daddy? Is everything all right ...?'

'Abi, my darling.' Yvette appeared in the doorway, sweeping Abi up into her arms. 'Let's go downstairs. I've just put some sausages in the oven. They'll be ready soon. We'll let your dad have a little more rest, eh?' Yvette's voice was epitome of calm and understanding. She ushered Abi out and directed her down the stairs, then glowered as she pulled the door to Eric's bedroom closed.

Eric stared at the bottle in his hand and sniffed. It wasn't like there was a lot there to drink. It was hardly going to get him drunk. He lifted the glass bottle-neck back up to his mouth and held it there. He hesitated, sniffed again, then downed the lot.

The alcohol hit the back of his throat in exactly the right spot. The vapours rose back up to catch in his nose. His eyes pinged awake. No harm done, he thought and tossed the bottle down the side of the bed. It clattered as it hit the floor. Eric looked down to find another one, flat against the carpet. It must have come from last night, he thought, although he couldn't remember drinking it then. Possibly it was earlier in the week. Groaning, he reached out and stretched his arms. The headache struck right behind the temples. It was a sharp headache, like twisting screws turning deeper and deeper into his skull. He rolled over and pressed his head against the pillow. He would get up soon, Eric told himself as he squeezed his eyes shut in an attempt to lessen the pain. Nothing did.

❦

'YOU NEED TO DO SOMETHING,' Eric told himself as the alcohol began to take effect on his thoughts. That's what people tell you, isn't it? That you need to stay busy? He conversed back and forth inside his head. He would tidy the room, he thought. That was a good place to start. Then he should probably head out of the village, get a change of scenery. Maybe even take Abi to the cinema.

Cinema. Another word that sent him spiralling down. A single word was enough to spark a thousand memories catapulting between his synapses. Their first trip to the cinema to see a horror film that Suzy had insisted she would like, only to scream all the way through it. Another cinema date, this time in their early marriage, where Eric had cracked a tooth on some hard-boiled pick and mix sweet. Suzy had been gutted, she had wanted to see the film for weeks. Instead they had had to leave the cinema and go in search of an emergency dentist. Then there was Abi's first cinema trip, and their first one to the cinema down here, before they had moved to Burlam. That had been a good time, all staying in the Sailboat's chintzy rooms, eating greasy fish and chips by the river.

A surge of adrenaline rushed through Eric's veins as he tried to remember the last film she had seen. They went to the cinema with Lydia and the boys about a month before Christmas, but was that it? Was that her very last trip? She had talked about taking Abi, or even arranging a girls' evening with Fleur – Eric flung the name from his thoughts before it had a time to take hold. How could he find out? It felt important, like it was something he needed to know. The adrenaline gave way to a crash of emotion. Everything Suzy had done over the previous few weeks had been her last and she hadn't even known.

The last time she brushed her teeth or swept her cheeks with blusher. The last time she had emptied the bins or stayed up past midnight typing away on her computer. Her last sandwich, her last cappuccino. Her last trip on a train, in a plane, in the passenger seat of a car. The list went on and on, swirling around in his head. The last time she had taken a glass of gin from Eric and put it to her lips. The last time she had pulled the covers off him in the night as he slept. The last time she had handed money to the *Big Issue* girl outside the Co-op. Eric's mind whirled. An infinite number of lasts and he wanted them all back, he needed them all back. He needed his last kiss goodbye. His last hang up on the phone call. She shouldn't have gone. She should never have gone.

'Eric?' Yvette knocked on the door, although she was in the room before he had even had a chance to stop his head from swimming. 'I'm going to take Abi out.'

Eric squinted, looking for his phone or watch.

'What's the time? It's still early.'

'It's ten,' she said. 'And I have my first dance class today.'

'You do?'

Yvette pressed her lips together. They stayed that way, pushed together at an awkward angle for an extended length of time, before opening by half an inch. Even then it was a full fifteen seconds before she spoke.

'Yes,' she said. 'I reminded you about it last night?'

Eric sat up. Something twinged in his shoulder. He bit down against the pain.

'Don't you think it's a bit soon?' he said, levering himself up to standing.

'Soon?'

'You, starting work today. You only buried her yesterday. And you want to start work? The day after your daughter's funeral?'

Yvette ran her tongue slowly across her top lip. She was playing the delay game, Eric could feel it. Trying to make him feel bad for something when he'd done absolutely nothing. Suzy was her daughter for God's sake, and she was acting like everything was normal.

'No,' Yvette's said. 'I don't think it's too soon. This is what Suzy wanted me to do, remember? She wanted me to start teaching these lessons. I am trying to carry on my life the way Suzy wanted me to. Can you say the same?'

Eric's jaw locked.

'I'll be taking Abi with me. We're going to Hank's for lunch. We won't be back much before three I don't suspect. It would be nice if you managed to stay sober that long.'

AS IT HAPPENED, Eric didn't manage to say sober that long. He had had every intention of abstaining, he even got as far as looking up the cinema times on the computer with a view to taking Abi that afternoon. He was still on the wagon when lunchtime came about and he took the sandwich Yvette had wrapped and labelled in the fridge for him. Then, deciding it looked like a warm enough day, and considering the number of memories enclosed in the house, he decided to eat outside. He had barely sat down on their planked wood picnic table when the thoughts started again.

It was the shed that had tripped the switch. The garden shed where Eric had hidden Lulu, the red setter puppy, for a full hour while he waited to surprise Suzy with her gift. Suzy had been surprised, but not in a good way. An argument had broken out and she had insisted that he take the dog back. And he said he did. He almost did. But instead he had given the puppy to Fleur. That was it. That was the start of everything. One little lie about returning a puppy and his whole world came crumbling down.

With a trembling hand Eric pulled open the shed door and scanned the inside. One of the toys he had bought was there on the floor, covered in dust-bunnies and spiders and goodness knows what else. Next to it he spotted a bottle of Hank's homemade moonshine.

'Almost like it's meant to be,' he said. The stuff was lethal, barely fit for human consumption, and exactly what he needed. Eric shook the bottle and gave it a proper swill about before tipping it back to his lips.

A puppy. That was what it came down to. If Eric hadn't got the puppy in the first place, he would never have been able to give it to Fleur when Suzy told him to get rid of it. If Fleur hadn't had the puppy then Eric would never have gone around to her place that night in order to see it. And if Eric hadn't gone around to Fleur's then the kiss would never have happened, and Suzy would never have driven off the drive in a full-blown rage, too upset to even look for any oncoming cars. Eric took another pull from the moonshine bottle. Even drunk it tasted like piss. Still, it was better than being alone with his thoughts.

❦

A COLD BREEZE roused him from his sleep. Eric shivered as he yawned, then frowned as he surveyed his surroundings. His head went from one side to the next, and on catching sight of the shed next to him, realised he was still outside. He groaned as the bottle of moonshine resurfaced in his memory. The sun was slinking its way over the horizon, casting the clouds in purple shadows, while smells of rushes and damp earth rose from the marshland behind. He stumbled to his feet and moved towards the back door. Only one step in and he froze. The moonshine bottle must have fallen out of his hand when he passed out. Shards of glass spattered the ground by his feet, causing his stomach to lurch. There had been much more glass then, of course, a hundred times more at least, but even one shard of broken glass was enough to send his mind spiralling back to the scene of the accident. This was what it was like nowadays. He had barely been awake a minute and was already desperate for the next way out. Knowing there was only one cure for his current situation, Eric made a move towards the shed, hoping that he might find another bottle of moonshine or two tucked away under the strimmer and the wall plugs. His fingers were on the handle when he stopped, listened, cocked his head, and listened again.

'Abi?' he said. The laughter was unmistakable, a low-pitched giggle that rattled with a heartiness of someone over five times her age. It made no sense and yet he heard it again and again. His heart leapt. Two weeks and he hadn't seen Abi so much as smile. Now she was laughing. He bounded towards the house, pushing back the throbbing behind his eyeballs, thoughts of moonshine gone. Yvette could be back to doing her naked Wiccan dancing for all he cared. If it meant hearing Abi laugh again. He twisted the handle to the back door and stepped inside.

Yvette was standing by the kettle, pouring herself a cup of tea while Abi was kneeling on the ground. The laughter had extended to an uncontrollable giggling fit. Eric looked down at his feet to see the cause.

'Isn't she beautiful, Daddy? Her name's Lulu. She needs a home. Can we keep her? Can we, Daddy?'

CHAPTER 5

ERIC COULDN'T FEEL his feet. He couldn't feel his hands or his stomach or any of his other organs that under normal circumstances he wouldn't have even considered being able to feel anyway. Still, at that moment he knew he couldn't feel them. It was like his body had separated from his mind. He was outside of it all, watching the colour drain from his skin, his eyes bulging from their sockets, while Abi rolled around on the floor, allowing the red setter puppy to clamber all over her and lick her face.

'Abi?' Yvette had stepped away from the kettle and was kneeling down on the floor next to the pair. 'Why don't you go and take Lulu upstairs to your room?'

'But I want Daddy to see her. Can we keep her? Please, please, Daddy? Granny said we could.'

'Upstairs, Abigail. Your daddy and I need to talk.'

Abi's eyes went pleadingly to her father. He stared, mouth open again, pulse racing, unable to find a single word.

'Come on, Abigail, my darling. I'll take you.' Yvette looked to Eric for some kind of response, but he offered none. A moment later, multiple footsteps pattered up the staircase before a single set padded back down and Yvette reappeared. Eric staggered to the fridge.

'I need a—'

'You need to sit down.' Yvette's hands were on her hips, her expression firm. Eric didn't care.

'Yvette, this is not a good—'

'Not a good time? You're going to say that to me? Honestly? I just buried my daughter. You remember that, don't you? I had to arrange my daughter's funeral.'

'Yvette—'

'No. Don't you dare *Yvette* me. Not again. Something is going on here. And I want to know what.'

'I lost my wife.'

'That's not what I'm on about and you damn well know it.'

Eric ran his tongue over his top lip. His toes dug into the floorboards as he avoided making any form of eye contact with his mother-in-law.

'I'm not going anywhere,' she said. 'I can stand here all night.'

'You're being ridiculous.' Eric stepped forward with the intention of shoving Yvette to the side, but he was drunk and she was far stronger than most women of half her age. He tripped backwards over his feet, barely managing to catch his balance on the table before he fell. Still, his knee smacked a chair leg which reverberated with a thud. When he looked up Yvette's scowl was still firmly in place.

'Maybe I should just go and ask that Fleur woman then?' she said. 'Maybe she'll tell me what's going on?'

A flash of fear shot through him. His eyes flickered up, accidentally meeting his mother-in-law's.

'So, I'm right then?' Yvette said. 'Well, you should know that whatever it is, it can't be any worse than I'm imagining. So, either I hear it from you, or I hear it from her.'

Eric stared at Yvette. The colour and heat drained from his cheeks, and the throbbing behind his eyes which had momentarily subsided returned with vengeance.

'I ... I ...'

'I'll get us both another glass then, shall I?' Yvette said.

His confession was met with silence. Yvette was staring at him. Probably only seconds away from standing up and slapping him, or worse, it didn't matter. He deserved it. He deserved everything he got. Eric Sibley was responsible for his wife's death. There was no punishment enough for him. He didn't know how he had expected Yvette to respond – he hadn't planned on telling her – but her silence was worse than any shouting could ever have been. That's what Suzy would have done too. That was why it hurt so much.

The silence expanded further. It stretched and stretched, elongating into an all-consuming bubble which he wished would swallow him up whole.

'So,' Yvette said, finally breaking the tension. 'You're to blame for Suzy dying?'

The words struck like a hammer to the chest.

He coughed. His throat narrowed. Yvette smacked her lips together.

'And you blame me too, then?' she said.

Eric blinked.

'What?'

'You blame me too? You think that I'm responsible?'

Eric shook his head, rubbing his temples with his palm. His mother-in-law was infuriating enough when he was sober. Apparently being drunk only made things worse.

'Did you hear me?' Yvette said. 'You think that I'm to blame for Suzy's death?'

'No.' Eric rubbed his temples a little harder. 'I just told you. It was my fault. If I hadn't kissed Fleur—'

'But if I hadn't have come here, that thug would never have rung the house. You and Suzy would never have got into the argument.'

Eric closed his eyes. The alcohol was still swimming in his system, causing his head to sway. Yvette was making no sense. Nothing was making any sense.

'If I hadn't come here,' Yvette repeated. 'Then that man would never have called the house.'

'That's ridiculous,' Eric slurred.

'No, it makes perfect sense. I mean, Philip, he has to shoulder a lot of this blame too, mind. If he hadn't got that silly girl pregnant.'

'No.' Eric rose to his feet. 'You're not listening.'

'Yes, yes I am. And it makes sense. All these things we did. I did, Philip did, they're why Suzy's dead. We're responsible.'

'No, you're not.'

'Yes, I am.'

'No. I am. I am responsible. I am the reason Suzy is dead.'

'So am I!'

'No, you're not! Stop doing this.'

Yvette sprang to her feet. She opened her mouth as if to shout, then closed it again a little.

'Don't you see,' she said, her voice not much more than a whisper. 'That if you're to blame, then so am I?'

Eric covered his ears with his hands, rocking back and forth. Yvette reached over and touched his shoulder.

'Eric,' she said. She tugged at his forearm, but he didn't let go. Whatever she was about to say, he didn't want to hear it.

'Eric,' Yvette said again. 'Please.'

'No, you don't understand. This is my fault.'

'This is no one's fault, Eric. This is nobody's fault. Please don't make it yours. And please, please don't make it mine. I can't take that. Not now. I can't, I can't ...'

Yvette stopped.

For more than a minute, Eric watched his mother-in-law. Twice, he reached out his hand in an attempt to comfort her but withdrawing before any contact was made. The third time he placed his palm against her shoulder. She lifted her head.

'It was an accident,' she said. 'A horrible accident.'

'But what I did—'

'Was stupid. What you did was stupid, that was all, Eric. You were a fool. I can hardly judge you for that. Not after how I went running back to Philip.'

Eric scoffed. 'I'm no better than him.'

Yvette's chin jutted firmly forward. 'He got a young girl pregnant, in our place of work, right under my nose. Then he won me back over just so he could steal all my money and run off with her and their bastard child again. You really think you're no better?'

Eric shrugged.

'No,' Yvette continued. 'We're not having any more of this. Do you understand? You were an idiot. And a crappy husband at times. That does not make you responsible for Suzy's death. Why was the driver going so fast in the first place? And how many times had you emailed the council asking them to put up a sign at the end of the road? You want to blame someone. Blame them. At least your anger would be a little better served that way.'

Eric's throat had constricted. No air was getting in.

'But—' he tried one last time.

'No more,' Yvette said. 'You hear me. No more.' She took their glasses, still both half full, and poured the remaining contents down the sink.

'Now then,' she said wiping her hands on the front of her skirt. 'What are we going to do about that dog?'

Eric took the steps slowly. Probably the slowest he had ever taken a staircase before. After Yvette had made them both cups of coffee – which to Eric tasted weak and bland without the presence of something to give it a little more kick – they had discussed the matter of Lulu.

'She can't stay, she can't,' Eric insisted. 'She has to go back to Fleur.'

'Fleur's gone,' Yvette said.

'What do you mean *gone*?'

Yvette gave a quick, single-shoulder shrug. 'Hank said she had decided to go back to London.'

'Because of me.'

'I think there's more to it than that. Something about not being able to find work down here. Although I expect your little dalliance didn't help.'

'It wasn't a dal—' Eric cut himself short. There was no point trying to defend himself. He didn't deserve it, anyway.

'Hank said he'd take on the dog until she could be rehomed properly,' Yvette continued.

'Well she can't be. Not here at least.'

'Fine, then you tell Abi that. Because I'm not going to be the one.'

Eric's back molars ground together. 'You were the one who let her bring the bloody thing home.'

'Because you were the one who was too busy being drunk and wallowing in his own misery to be a proper father. No, if you want to take that dog away from her, you're going to be the one to do it,' Yvette insisted.

A dull pain flickered in Eric's chest. For all his married life, he had insisted that Suzy was nothing like her mother. She certainly didn't look like her and was nowhere near as flamboyant, but at that moment all he could see was his wife.

'You need to do it now though,' Yvette said, 'before she gets even more attached.'

Eric grunted. It was the closest thing to an answer he could give.

Standing on the top step he listened.

'You'll like this house,' he heard Abi say. 'Granny makes really good cakes, and I'll take you out for walks every day. It's a shame you didn't get to meet my mum though. She would have loved you. We can look at photographs together though. I miss her. You must miss your mum too. Hank said you're not even half a year old yet. At least I had my mum when I was little. I wish I had her now though.'

Eric gulped. He twisted his shoulders, momentarily considering a retreat back downstairs, but he stopped himself. Yvette was right. The longer they were together, the more attached she would get. He knew what it was like for him. He had barely laid eyes on the red-brown ball of fluff before she had stolen his heart. Had she not, they would probably not be in this mess in the first place.

A burning reignited in Eric's chest. There was no way around it. The dog could not stay.

CHAPTER 6

'IT'S NOT HER fault,' Eric said to Yvette as they sat around the dining room table. He forced himself to swallow a mouthful of couscous. It was dry. Everything tasted dry. What he needed was some form of lubrication, preferably with a proof above thirty per cent, but he was trying, despite the headache and mouth that felt like the inside of one of Janice's gardening slippers.

'She's a dog. She can hardly be held responsible for what happened. Besides. Abi had already grown too attached.'

'So she's staying?'

'For now.'

Even with his hand on the doorknob, listening to Abi's coos and laughter, Eric had been firm with his resolve. There was no way that Lulu could stay. It wasn't possible. How could he keep an animal when every time he looked at her, all he thought about was the effect it had had on him and Suzy? How could he walk her every day knowing that his desire to see her had ultimately resulted in the betrayal of his wife? It wasn't possible.

'Abi,' he said as he pushed open the door. 'We need to have a talk.'

It had been instant. The flood of emotions he had expected came, but not, as he had predicted, with anger. Maybe it was the smile on Abi's face, or how seamlessly Lulu appeared to have found a position resting on her lap. Maybe it was the way her tail thumped on the ground, so absent-mindedly blissful. The reason didn't matter. His chest swelled and ached, and all the tears he had tried to drown through drink tumbled down his cheeks. The minute Lulu lifted her head from Abi's knees and looked him in the eyes he knew. The pair remained, eyes locked for nearly a minute. Lulu beat her tail on the ground twice.

'Dad,' Abi said, lifting her gaze from the dog to speak to her father. 'Are you okay?'

Eric coughed and sniffed, trying not to cry yet again.

'We're going to need to go and get some dog food,' he said.

ROUTINE PROVED the key to Eric's survival during the next three weeks. That and keeping himself busy. It wasn't easy. He woke up at 6:30 and let Lulu out into the garden before waking Abi up and making them breakfast. Cooked breakfasts worked better than cereal. It required his attention, and anything that kept him distracted from that first morning drink was a good thing. After washing up and checking that Abi had properly cleaned her teeth, he and Lulu walked her to school. With summer just around the corner there would be plenty of time before he needed to consider the prospect of a car again, which was a good thing, because at that precise moment he wasn't in the right mind frame to consider one at all.

From dropping Abi off at the school gates Eric then went for his long walk of the day, taking Lulu around the marshes. It was tricky, finding a place to go that didn't cause him to freeze with grief; anywhere he and Suzy had cycled together was out, along with any of the routes they had taken in Sally too, and that wasn't considering all the places they had walked in the years they had visited before they had taken the leap of moving to Burlam. Still, he found a couple of walks; across the railway line and down towards the marina, over the camping ground into the next village. He could escape for a couple of hours at least and while away the time, throwing sticks for Lulu to fetch.

His afternoon distractions came closer to home. In the house, he had started on the kitchen in earnest. Suzy had wanted to paint the room yellow, only Eric couldn't remember what type of yellow she had decided on. It might have been primrose, but then again, it could have been buttercup. Primrose and buttercup certainly sounded familiar, but that wasn't necessarily a good thing. 'Too sickly,' were the words she had used to describe some of the shades they had looked at, but had that been buttercup or primrose? Perhaps even both. Yvette thought primrose was the sicklier of the two, Eric thought it was buttercup, and Lulu sniffed at both the samples with equal displeasure. In the end he had gone back to the store and bought a large tub of lavender grey. That way he definitely couldn't get it wrong.

When he'd done as much as his shoulders could take, he would fix himself some food before picking Abi up from school and heading over to the fields for Lulu's second big walk of the day.

Lulu acted as a buffer, Eric discovered. He would watch over the pair as they chased each other up and down the fields, silently grieving for all the moments that Suzy would never see, but it was bearable. In the evenings he could talk to Yvette about a rabbit that the dog had seen and chased, or a throw Abi had done, which had forced Lulu right out into the estuary. He was surviving, which was better than he had hoped for at some points.

During one of his afternoon walks Eric was gazing out at the fields, remembering the first time he had brought Suzy to Burlam to meet his family. It hadn't gone well. His mother had welcomed her with open arms and gleaming smile. His father had commented solely on her divorce and lack of formal education. She had taken it all in her stride. She set the places for dinner, placing herself opposite George, and spent the whole time questioning him on everything from cars to carrots; he hadn't had time to get his insults in. Afterwards he commented to Eric that she was overbearing and over opinionated; Eric responded with a comment about pots and kettles.

'I heard you had a dog,' a voice said, disturbing Eric from his thoughts. By now Eric had become well accustomed to the greetings of fellow dog walkers and even knew a couple of dogs by name; for some reason recalling the animal's name proved infinitely easier to Eric than recalling those of the owners. This was one person, however, Eric hadn't expected to see.

'Christian,' Eric said and reached out a hand. The solicitor looked a far cry from his normal, badly suited self. Instead he was dressed in a pair of ripped board shorts and a 1994 Glastonbury T-shirt. His shoes were caked in thin layer of mud and the twist of a headphone cord dangled around his ears.

'I am so sorry about Suzy,' Christian Eaves said, reaching down and letting his spaniel off the lead to go crazy with Lulu. 'I came to the funeral. I hung around at the back if I'm honest. I didn't come to the wake. Didn't feel it was my place. I hope it was an okay occasion, as okay as these things can be.'

'It was,' Eric searched for the words, 'as expected.'

For a minute the pair cast their gazes out over the field. Eaves' spaniel had found itself a massive branch that Lulu now desperately wanted. Abi was playing umpire to the pair. From this view she could have passed for a normal, happy nine-year-old, although it was hard for anyone who knew her not to see the change. When he asked her about her school day, the only replies he would ever get were, 'It's fine,' or 'Okay'. Her love of play-dates had diminished and the only time she ever looked genuinely happy was around Lulu. Most of the time her head was in a book, no doubt her most plausible reason not to talk. And the less said about her temper, the better.

'So.' Eaves cleared his throat in a more business-like manner, shooting Eric back to his plywood furnished office and his father's will reading.

'I was looking through a bit of paperwork today,' Eaves said, his eyes still forward on his dog almost as if he were deliberately avoiding eye contact. 'And it turns out I got something a little bit wrong.'

'You did?' Eric said. 'What?'

'Well, it turns out there's a bit of ambiguity to you father's will.'

'Ambiguity?' Eric's temperature took an upward turn. The last time Christian Eaves had been informing Eric about his father's will it had been to explain all the various conditions and constraints it had come with. He had contingency after contingency put in place. It had involved beefed up bailiffs and had been an altogether unpleasant experience. As far as Eric knew, his father's wishes were anything but ambiguous, and the last thing he needed was more stress right now.

'Well, yes,' Eaves continued. 'As you know, your inheritance of the car came under the condition that you tend the allotment every week for two years.'

'I know that,' Eric said.

'Well ... initially, I assumed that the two years meant from when you started. From your first visit to the allotment.'

'And ...'

'Well the will doesn't actually specify that. It could well mean from the date that your father visited me to draw up his will. Or at the very least the date that he died.'

Eric shook his head, confused. 'I don't get it. What is it you're trying to say?'

Eaves pressed his lips together. He twisted his neck around to face Eric making eye contact for only the second time in their conversation.

'What I'm saying is that it's yours. I'm not going to check. No one's going to check. The last thing you need is this nonsense going on. The car is yours. You can do what you like with it. I'll bring around the paper work tomorrow.'

Eric blinked. He could feel his eyes filling.

'This isn't some sick joke?'

'No, I can assure you it is not.'

Eric pressed his lips together and gave a short sharp nod.

'Thank you,' he said.

Eaves' eyes were back on the field.

'Don't mention it,' he said. Then he put two fingers into his mouth and whistled at an impressively loud volume.

'Help!' he called. 'It's time to go home.'

'Help?' Eric said. 'You named your dog *Help*?'

'My family has a peculiar sense of humour.'

※

'THAT'S FANTASTIC NEWS,' Yvette said, when Eric told her about the car that evening. 'Maybe you and Abi could go for a drive?'

'And Lulu,' Abi said.

'Not a chance,' Eric said. 'I am not having her devalue my car by slobbering all over the upholstery.' As if understanding exactly what had been said, Lulu hopped up from below the table onto Eric's lap and planted a slobbering lick on his chin.

Yvette's cheeks sucked inwards.

'Talking about cars,' she said. Eric rolled his eyes.

Cars were on the list of topics that Eric had been actively avoiding, along with cash flow, work (his or Yvette's), summer holidays, and any moment further forward in time than the evening of the exact day they were on. However, currently, cars were on the top of Yvette's list. While summer in Burlam was fine, walking Abi to school in the mid-winter was far from ideal.

'The new one's arriving next Tuesday,' Yvette said, pulling a pan of something brown and sizzling out of the oven. 'I dealt with the insurance company myself. I thought it would be easier that way.'

'You did?'

Eric's muscles twitched. Yvette's meddling had been the bane of his existence since her arrival here, from piercing Abi's ears to changing the breakfast cereal. Here she was, at it again. A familiar, impulsive heat rushed through him and he opened his mouth, ready to read her the riot act about taking control of his life and sticking her nose in where it wasn't wanted, but he didn't. He closed the mouth and met her gaze.

'Thank you,' he said. 'Thank you for doing that.'

'You're most welcome.' She reached up into the cupboard and pulled down three plates. 'Before I forget. You haven't seen a ring lying about anywhere, have you?'

'A ring? Like mine?' Abi said, lifting her head up and holding out her hand, the bauble stone now a gentle amber colour.

'I hope you didn't wear that to school?' Eric said, lowering his cutlery to his plate. 'You know what I told you about keeping it safe.'

'I didn't, I promise. I put it on when I got home.' Her unwavering eye contact meant she was either certainly telling the truth or most definitely lying.

'Really?'

'Really.'

'Good. We can't get another one of those. If you lose it or break it, it's gone forever.'

'I know.'

'And I don't want you wearing it when you're messing about with Lulu, either. The last thing I want is her to swallow the damn thing and for me have to go sifting about in mountains of dog—'

'It's a diamond one,' Yvette said, steering them back towards the original source of conversation. 'With emeralds on the side. I thought it was in my jewellery box that I brought with me from the ship, but I can't find it and I can't for the life of me think where else it could be. You'd recognise it if you saw it.' Eric smiled internally. He was certain he would. It sounded like the exact ring Yvette had refused to give him in order to propose.

'You did leave the boat in rather a hurry,' Eric said, keeping his thoughts about the ring to himself. 'Any chance you could have left it there?'

A series of creases formed along her brow. 'I'm certain I was wearing it when Philip and I went to the theatre in London, but to be honest, the longer it's missing, the less sure I am.'

Eric frowned and tried to pick his words as delicately as possible.

'I hate to sound pessimistic, but you don't suppose he took it, do you? He did take the rest of your money after all.'

'Philip?' Yvette shook her head with absolute certainty. 'No. Definitely not. That was my mother's ring,' she added. 'Even Philip couldn't have stooped that low.'

'He did miss Suzy's funeral,' Eric reminded her.

'Yes, well ...' Searching for a new route to direct the conversation. She glanced at Abi's ring, finding the orange stone even brighter than it had been just a moment before. A small smile crept upwards on her lips.

'Abi,' she said. 'Do you know what else is that colour orange?'

※

YVETTE'S REASONING behind the bright orange convertible Beetle was that it would hold no memories of any sort, and to give her her dues, it was true. Eric had never in his life possessed such an outrageously coloured vehicle. The choice of car had initially jarred with Eric, mainly because he had never envisioned himself as the type of man who travelled around in a modern soft top let alone owned one.

'Really? You really want me to drive around in a car that colour?'

'Well if you don't want to, I'm more than happy to. Besides, it's not like you leave the house that often.'

'I think it's satsuma orange,' Abi said, ignoring the burgeoning argument as she ran her hand along the shiny new bodywork.

'Then satsuma orange it is.' Yvette clasped her hands together.

'And now we have an orange car *and* an orange dog.'

'We do indeed,' Eric replied. 'We do indeed.'

Lulu looked up from the ground and wagged her tail.

'I guess you and I might have to do some rally driving together girl,' Eric said.

When Abi was at school, Lulu would stick to Eric's heels like they were thick as thieves. She was there beside him at the kitchen table, ready to receive any scraps he may have going spare and more than once had followed him into the toilet to watch him do his business. Whichever room Eric was in, Lulu would be feet away. It was only when Abi came home that he realised Lulu's affection towards him had been a time filler; some way to pass the hours before her real owner got home.

'Did you let her sleep in your bed again?' Eric said a week after the car's arrival as he stripped the covers off his daughter's bed amid a cloud of red fur.

'She gets lonely on her own,' Abi replied indignantly.

'It's in the same room! And why have you got three of my socks in here? And why are they covered in drool?'

'Because she cuddles them,' Abi said and looked at Eric like he had just made the dumbest comment of any parent in the world throughout the existence of all parents.

Socks weren't Lulu's only penchant when it came to Eric's clothes.

'Abi!' Eric yelled up the stairs almost every other morning. 'Your dog has eaten one of my shoes, again!'

Abi would appear at the top of the stairs, Lulu at her heel, and both of them would look at Eric with their big puppy eyes.

'She's really sorry,' Abi would say. 'Granny says she likes your smell.'

'Well if she does it again, I'm getting a kennel and she'll be sleeping outside.'

'Okay,' Abi would say, rubbing Lulu's ears before skipping off to her bedroom. They were all well aware that that was as much punishment as either of them were going to receive. Eric hadn't so much as raised his voice to Abi since her mother had died. He couldn't, despite the fact he desperately needed to.

'You need to go in and see the head teacher,' Yvette said, after picking Abi up from school one afternoon.

'Why, what happened?'

Yvette pointed her gaze to Abi, who was currently looking only at her feet.

'Abi?' Eric said. 'What's going on?'

Abi shifted her weight from one foot to the other under his gaze.

'Nothing. I just hit someone, that's all.'

'You hit someone?!' Eric's voice hitched in surprise. Abi was the girl who rescued earthworms and cried at the cartoons whenever anything remotely sad or happy happened. 'Why? What happened?'

Abi's feet continued to shift about.

'Abs?' Eric pressed.

Abi sucked a lungful of air in through her nose before planting her hands on her hips.

'He's a bully. He'd stolen Kimmy's Kinder Egg and he wouldn't give it back.'

'So you hit him?'

'I asked him first,' Abi said. 'Twice. But he refused to give it back. And it wasn't like it was a hard punch.'

❧

THE NEXT MORNING Eric sat in the head teacher's office as he relayed what Abi had told him.

'From what I hear, Mr Sibley,' said Mrs Woodhouse. 'Abi didn't even say a word to the boy. She just walked up and punched him.'

'That doesn't sound very likely,' Eric said. 'From what I've heard, the boy is a bully. And a thief.'

'Mr Sibley, I have not called you in to cast aspersions—'

'But I am right, aren't I? What was it Abi said he stole? A Kinder Egg?'

'Well ...'

'And you weren't actually there to see if she spoke to him or not?'

'I can assure you—'

'This is ridiculous. I've been called in because my daughter was sticking up for her friend.'

'That is not why—'

'Perhaps you need to take a look at your bullying policies,' Eric said, pushing up from his seat. 'Because if it comes down to a nine-year-old girl to make sure that other children aren't being picked on, then it looks like there might be an issue.' He reached out a hand, which, after a quick hesitation, and a very sour expression, Mrs Woodhouse shook. After a couple of quick pumps, Eric moved to retrieve his hand only to find it still held firmly within her grasp.

'Mr Sibley,' she said. 'I like Abi an awful lot and I know what happened to her mother is going to have a tremendous impact. Have you thought about counselling for her?'

'Counselling?'

'I think it might help.'

Eric tensed. Not only had he been brought down here for no reason whatsoever, now, someone who knew absolutely nothing about their life was doling out their own, narrow-minded opinion. 'Abi's fine. She has me at home and her grandmother. There's plenty of people around her if she wants to talk.'

'Sometimes a stranger is far easier for people to talk to. And not just children. Think about it.'

She dropped his hand, but left her comment hanging in the air between them.

'Thank you for your time,' Eric said and turned and left, leaving the door wide open behind him.

CHAPTER 7

'CAN WE TAKE Lulu to Danbury Woods?' Abi asked her dad a week later. 'Pip Eddy says his family always do their dogging in the woods there.'

'I'm pretty certain that's not what Pip Eddy said,' Eric responded, making a mental note not to visit the wooded area for any late-night dog walking. Lulu had been with them a month and continued to keep them all busy. Chewing through the water pipe to the washing machine and flooding the kitchen, eating an entire pack of Abi's wax crayons – which resulted in days of what Abi referred to as *unicorn poo* – and even managing to get into the utility room cupboard, where Eric kept a series of incidentals, including small tools, masking tape, and boot polish. The latter had turned the pedigreed red setter into a black and brown mottled mongrel.

'She needs a shampoo,' Yvette pointed out, just in case Eric couldn't see.

'She needs to be put down,' was Eric's reply.

Two months after Suzy's death – when the label of *puppy* was losing traction where Lulu was concerned – Yvette brought up yet another matter Eric had been staunchly avoiding.

'I've been looking at the finances,' she said. 'With the house and things. You can correct me if I'm wrong, but it doesn't look good.'

Eric hummed. It had been a tough day, probably the toughest since the arrival of Lulu. Abi had performed in assembly for the first time since Suzy had passed away. The year group assembly was a special event, so special that the school had even managed to dig out some almost-full-sized seats to place at the back ready for the parents. It wasn't like they had deliberately set out a place for Suzy, but there had obviously been a fair fewer mums and dads than expected. Yvette had had a last-minute dance class request, and with money the way it was she couldn't turn it down. Hank had had to take Jerry for an eye appointment after an incident with a blackberry bush, and it was too far to ask Lydia to come just for a thirty-minute play. As it was, when the moment of the assembly arrived Eric found himself next to an empty seat. Every time Abi's eyes moved towards him, he could see the aching in her chest. The bare piece of folded plastic where her mother should have been sitting a tangible reminder of what she had lost. He considered moving, but then he feared Abi might have thought he had left altogether, and he couldn't do that to her. She got through it though, even managing to pull out a smile for her dance solo.

Then there was the incident with the new supply teacher.

'You must be Abi's dad,' said the sartorially stereotypical twenty-something. Eric had gone up to the front of the hall to collect Abi. Other children were dispersing, hugging their parents and grandparents and receiving endless accolades for their mediocre performances. Eric and Abi got cornered. Even before she had started talking, he could feel it wasn't going to be good.

'Abi talks about you so much. And her mum too. I heard all about her books and writing? I was really looking forward to seeing her. I thought that she'd come. Is she busy at work?'

Eric felt Abi tense beside him. Their jaws dropped simultaneously.

'*Uhm* ...' Eric struggled to find the words, caught so unaware by the comment. Abi, however, seemed to have found the exact thing to say.

'She's dead, you silly cow. Don't you know anything?'

TWO HOURS later and Eric was up in Abi's room where Lulu's fur was soaked from use as a pillow. He had been sent straight to the head teacher – obviously – and she had wanted Abi to be present as well. But Eric had insisted, and so Hank had abandoned Jerry at the opticians and come to fetch her.

'Am I going to get kicked out of school,' Abi said, up in her bedroom, still stuttering through the tears. 'I didn't mean it. I didn't. I was just angry. How could she not know? Everyone knows.'

Eric stroked his daughter's hair.

'You are not going to get kicked out,' he said. 'I spoke to Mrs Woodhouse. She's pretty cross. She said if anything else like this happens, she'll have to suspend you.' Abi's eyes filled.

'Does that mean they'll kick me out?'

'For a little while, yes.' Her mouth flew open in horror. Eric caught her before she could start sobbing again.

'But that's not going to happen,' he assured her. 'You will not get kicked out.' He stopped, taking a pause to consider his next wording. Abi noticed.

'What is it? I'm in really big trouble, aren't I?'

Eric took his daughter's hand. 'You are not in big trouble. But your teacher has suggested to me that you need to speak to someone.'

'Someone?'

'A counsellor.'

'Counsellor? What's that?'

'It's a person that you can talk to.'

'About what?'

Eric shuffled. 'About Mum. And about me. About school. About anything you want to. And you can tell them anything you want, and no one will get cross.'

Abi's fingers fiddled with the ring on her finger. Currently the stone was a pearly green. 'Do I have to go?' she said.

Eric nodded. 'I think you do.'

She continued to stare at her knees, pressing her fingers into the ring, possibly in an attempt to make it change colour.

'Can I take Lulu?' she said eventually. Eric smiled.

'I think we can make that happen,' he said, then he wrapped his daughter up in his arms and let her cry a little bit more.

'So,' Yvette said, forcing Eric away from his mulling and back to the conversation. 'Am I wrong or are finances an issue?'

Eric swilled his glass around. The drink was cola, but he had poured it into a whisky tumbler in the hope that it would lessen his desire for something stronger. It helped a little. After the meeting with the head he desperately wanted a drink, but thoughts of Abi pulled him back. Twice he opened his mouth to respond to Yvette's question, before closing it again. On the third time he managed to speak.

'It's not good,' he admitted. 'I've been looking at it as well. And now we're going to have to factor weekly counselling sessions into it too.'

'I just don't want to dip into Suzy's money. Her royalties are meant for Abi. For her future.'

'But without her money there's no income coming in, so what do you suggest?'

He returned to swilling the cola, before lifting his eyes away from the glass and up to his mother-in-law.

'I'm not sure. I've been thinking that maybe the best thing we could do is sell up and head back to London. I've spoken to Jack. He says there's a job there waiting for me if I want it.'

'What?' Yvette said, unable to disguise the surprise in her voice. 'Are you serious?'

'Possibly.'

'Then why didn't you say anything?'

Eric took a draw from his drink. The ice clattered against the glass.

'Because I'm not sure it's the right thing to do. Not right now. What do you think?'

'Me?'

'One day I think a fresh start is exactly the thing Abi and I need. No school problems, no memories of this place. The next day I think uprooting her is only going to cause more stress.'

Yvette slowly scratched her head.

'I'm inclined to think the latter. You going back to that job, working all hours isn't going to help her in the least bit.'

'But the upkeep on this place is massive. And money is money. We need some. More than we've got at least.'

'That is true.'

'And we don't need all this space. You know the ridiculousness of it is when Suzy was alive, and you were living here, the place felt so busy and cramped all the time. Like I could barely find an inch to myself. Now it feels like a bloody castle, it's so empty.'

'I know,' Yvette agreed. She picked up a teaspoon from her saucer and began to stir the tea. The bag had already been removed and Yvette never took sugar in any of her drinks, but she stirred away, eyes lost in the moving liquid.

'I did have another idea,' she said. 'It's not ideal, but it's an option.'

'I'm willing to hear anything,' Eric said.

'No.' Five minutes later and Eric's whisky tumbler now had a very large shot of whisky added to it. Yvette was still nursing her cup of tea, although her posture was far less relaxed than it had been a few moments before.

'No way,' he repeated. 'Absolutely not, under no circumstances.'

'It makes perfect sense.'

'We'll find another way. I'll work part time. I'll get a job at the Co-op.'

'Eric listen—'

'No. That is Suzy's office. Suzy's space. There is no way I am letting it out to some ... some yuppie for a few bucks a week.'

'But it's good money. Commuters would pay a lot for a room in a place like this. And it's not like her room is being used. It's just there, collecting dust, hanging over this place like a shadow.'

'No.'

'When was the last time you went in there then? Tell me that? Even if you don't let it out, the place needs sorting. You can't just leave all of her things there, pretending nothing's happened.'

'You think that's what I'm doing?'

'When it comes to that room, yes. And don't get me started on her clothes in the wardrobe. It's not doing you any good holding onto those things.'

'What are you suggesting, that I just throw everything away?'

'No. Not all of it. But, Eric, you've got to see sense. A lodger would bring in extra money. You would be able to take your time, find a job you want to do down here, and Abi wouldn't have to be uprooted.'

Eric shook his head. 'What kind of person would want to lodge in a house with a nine-year-old girl living in it? I can tell you exactly what sort.'

'Then let the room to a woman.'

'And look like I'm running some brothel?'

'Eric, you're being ridiculous.'

'My answer is no.' Eric finished his drink and slammed the tumbler down on the table. 'If you want to get a lodger, find your own bloody house to live in.'

He took the bottle upstairs with him and didn't even bother with the glass. His only intention had been to get drunk enough that he didn't have to think about things. He certainly hadn't planned on going inside that room. But now all he could think about were Yvette's words. How it needed cleaning, how it was a waste of space. How he was holding on and ignoring things. He pushed her words down with another gulp of whisky. It could never be a waste of space, Eric thought. It was Suzy's space.

The door creaked open, pushing against the carpet the way it always did.

'It'll be fine in a couple of months,' Suzy used to say. 'The carpet just needs to wear down a bit.'

'I could always trim it with scissors,' Eric would reply.

'You could bloody well not.' Suzy would laugh and then she would reach up her hand and wrap it around his neck and plant a kiss on his lips. But he never let it last long enough, he realised. He should have forced her to let him stay there with her. He should have forced her to stay. Visions of his wife, head down over a laptop, or else book in hand, scribbling away, swelled in currents through his mind as he bypassed the light switch, moved across the room and switched on the table lamp. He gave his eyes a second to adjust.

Yvette was right about one thing at least. The room had been collecting dust. Six weeks since Suzy's death and the spiders had claimed official squatter's rights. Dense cobwebs hung from the coving and a not-insubstantial layer of dust had settled on all the books. Her laptop, closed, was dull with its dusty veneer. A crack lengthened in Eric's heart. Suzy had always said she would write a horror novel one day; this would have been the perfect setting.

He pulled out the chair and slumped down in it. The seat was warm as if she had only just been sitting in it, and the longer he sat, the stronger the scents of lavender and pencil lead became. If he closed his eyes he could just imagine that she had popped out for an evening, perhaps gone up to London for a conference or something. No matter how tight money was, letting out this room was simply not an option, Eric told himself, and as long as he was the owner of this house it was going to stay that way. That meant there was only one other option on the cards.

❦

ERIC FELT like a money grabbing whore. Like some black widow who had deliberately murdered his wife in a bid to pocket her fortune. The day suited the mood perfectly. Heavy back clouds closed in around the street as he waited for the bank to open. More than once he considered heading home and coming back down in the afternoon when the rain had eased off a little and the bank would definitely be open. But he didn't. If he headed home, he knew there was more than a fifty-fifty chance of his cracking open a bottle of whatever he had hidden away from Yvette and not coming back out again for the rest of the day. And the fact was he needed to be there.

'Not long now,' he said to Lulu as she tugged on her lead. She was clearly confused by the detour to their usual routine.

Despite the conversation with Yvette, the sudden disappearance of digits in his bank account had come as an unexpected shock. To start with, there were the funeral expenses. While Eric's father and mother – the only two funerals in which he had a personal insight to – had both prepared in advance for the impending departure, Suzy had not. No money was set aside for such an event, no insurance policy set to pay out. Now that seemed ridiculous. So many times he and Suzy had had the discussion about this exact situation, but there had always been something more important to do, another bill that took priority, a new car, a new sofa. A new holiday so that they could all unwind a little. Add that to the fact they had clearly thought themselves invincible. Not anymore though. Eric had never been more aware of his own mortality.

His mainly inebriated state in the days immediately following Suzy's death meant that all purchases to do with the funeral had fallen on Yvette. Clearly not wanting to scrimp on her daughter, and despite having no funds of her own, she went all out. Eric hadn't asked for an exact figure, but he had noticed the increasing dent whenever he went to the cashpoint to withdraw more for his next drinking binge.

Then there were the house renovations. While their new bathroom suite was advertised at a reasonable two and half grand, Eric had learnt that that – fairly reasonable – figure had been entirely absent of everything other than the toilet, taps, and bath itself. It didn't include delivery or labour let alone the tiles, specific non-slip, high durability flooring, and major re-plumbing work that took over the entirety of their first floor. Thus, over the last few months his savings had taken a battering and with no job to replenish them, he had to make the decision to transfer all of Suzy's money to his account.

His nerves bubbled away as Eric took yet another glance at his phone. He was holding a briefcase. Brown leather, with a smell and patina indicative of a far wealthier time in his life. It had been an anniversary gift from Suzy although he couldn't for the life of him remember what year it had been for. Five years perhaps? Was that leather? Maybe it was ten. In the end, he decided it didn't matter and gave up thinking about it.

There was a time when holding a briefcase had felt like the most natural thing in the world to Eric; possibly even more natural than holding Abi's hand. But that was the old Eric. Now holding a briefcase felt awkward and clumsy, like he was wearing a costume he no longer fit into. After placing it down on the ground and stepping a little further under the eaves, he went back to staring at his watch, wishing that there was some way to swallow back the sea of trepidation that was currently swelling around his insides.

It wasn't like he was doing anything wrong, he told himself for the umpteenth time that morning. Suzy's will had specifically said everything would be left to him. And even if it hadn't, legally he was entitled to it. But that was semantics. He wasn't actually meant to spend Suzy's money. The plan was that he would put it away somewhere safe until such time that

Abi needed it. University fees, a deposit for her first house, that was where Suzy's money was meant to go. All Suzy's years of toil and endless royalties had been intended for that. Now they were needed just to keep the lights on.

Just one more thing for Eric to feel shit about, Suzy was even providing for them from beyond the grave. He would have laughed had it not been so utterly heart-breaking.

At three minutes to nine, a rotund gentleman with equally round glasses and a small metal name tag bearing the name Dennis Hopkins appeared at the door.

'Rather keen today, sir?' he said, turning the lock and pulling the door inwards to let Eric in. 'Some exciting cheques to pay in?'

'I need to see to my dead wife's account,' Eric responded.

The man's cheeks coloured to a perfect cherry red.

'Oh, I am sorry. Mr Sibley, isn't it?'

'It is.'

'Christian Eaves said you might be coming by.' There was a short pause, during which Eric tried to look as impassive as possible. Of course the lawyer had mentioned to the bank manager that Eric would be coming. He had probably done it over a plate of hash browns and black pudding at The Shed; after all, this was Burlam. Everyone knew everything.

'If you'd just like to come this way,' Hopkins said, leading Eric to one of the small partitioned offices at the back of the building. 'We'll get all this sorted for you. Have you got all her account numbers?'

Eric sat down and opened the small briefcase before pulling out a small bundle.

'This is everything I could find,' he said. 'All the other accounts are joint.'

'Not a problem, I can change those over to you too. Assuming you've got all the legal documents?'

Eric nodded and pulled out another plastic envelope filled with papers. He wasn't even sure what they said, only that Eaves had insisted he sign the bottom several times before he told Eric he would need to take them to the bank.

After ten minutes of tutting and tapping, Hopkins looked from his screen to Eric. 'I'll just get these things printed off for you to sign,' he said, then disappeared only to appear less than a minute later with a ballpoint pen and a stack of papers.

'Just at the bottom of this one.' Hopkins pointed to a line below an awful lot of small print. He whipped out the sheet before the ink had even dried. 'And if you can initial this one.' He pointed to another line. 'This one needs your initials and a signature. And if you could date this one. That one needs your name printed in capitals.'

It felt like an eternity of signing. No one ever told you that, Eric thought as he signed away. You expect it to feel like the world has ended when your spouse dies. You expect the loneliness and the hollowness and the endless supply of mediocre casseroles that people insist on bringing around at whatever time of day they feel appropriate. You expect the mass of flowers. None of that had come as a surprise. But the signing, that was a surprise. And endless.

'Great.' Hopkins stood up from his desk. 'Well that's it. We're all done here. The old accounts have all been shut down and everything has been transferred to a brand-new savings account in your name.'

'Thank you,' Eric said.

'It may take a couple days before you can set up internet banking and see the numbers for yourself, but if it's not all sorted by the end of the week, come in and we'll have a look at it.'

Eric's stomach squirmed. He really didn't want to say what he was going to say next. Not in the slightest. What he desperately wanted was to find some way out of it, some way to thank the bank manager, turn around, and deal with the whole financial mess in the privacy of his own home. But he knew he didn't have a choice.

His tongue felt like it had swollen to double its size as he attempted to get out the words.

'Would it be … could I, I mean is it possible—'

'Yes?' Hopkins' eyes were magnified in his round glasses as they peered at Eric expectantly.

Eric swallowed and tried again.

'Would it be possible to see the statements now?' he asked. 'I mean, I know you said I'll get the details through this week, it's just so I have a bit of an idea how much there is. I don't mean to seem crass, it's just, you know, with the funeral expenses and the house—'

'No need to explain.' Hopkins waved Eric's bumbling to a close. 'No need to explain. Of course, of course. Hold on one second, and I'll get those printouts for you now.'

Hopkins returned with a small stack of paper. Eric stared at the numbers on the bottom, his mouth growing drier by the second.

'Are you sure this is correct?' he asked. 'This doesn't make sense.'

<hr>

YVETTE HAD PURCHASED some dandelion and burdock drink at the local farmer's market. It was a disgusting beverage, sickly sweet and medicinal yet at the same time savoury and cloying. Her hope had undoubtedly been to alleviate some of Eric's desire for alcohol, although the only similarity it had with a decent Scotch whisky was the way it was most certainly destroying brain cells. Nonetheless, Eric took another sip. The vileness of the taste at least distracted from the spinning currently going on in his head.

'Well surely there's some mistake?' Yvette said, the reams of paper spread out across the dining room table in front of them all. If anyone had walked in, they would have been forgiven for thinking Suzy was on one of her editing sprees. That was unless they looked too closely and saw that the red ink had been used to highlight numbers and not words.

'It's not a mistake.' Eric assured her, hands around the burdock bottle. 'I asked for the statements too, every one for the last two years. They're over there.'

Yvette gave the pile a quick skim.

'What about other accounts? Did you ask about other accounts?'

'No other accounts,' Eric said. 'I got him to double check.'

'What about other banks then? She might have used another bank.'

Eric shook his head, momentarily forgetting what he was holding before taking a sip and being forced to fight down a gag.

'You know Suzy, she liked things simple. Ordered. One bank, that was it. No heading round town to every street corner or having to remember twenty different pin numbers just so you could check which account to pay for the shopping from.'

'Then what does this mean?' Yvette asked.

'I don't know,' Eric admitted. 'But there were credit cards too. Mostly paid off, but still a bit on them.'

The fact the numbers on Suzy's bank statements were barely any healthier than his own was only half the shock. More concerning was the lack of money going in.

'I've been through it all, and from what I can tell, the last time she had any sort of payment from the publishing house was nearly six months ago,' Eric said. 'Surely that can't be right, can it? I know they work on funny times in the book world, but six months? They can't expect a person to go that long before being paid, surely? How do they expect them to survive?'

Yvette shrugged. 'Maybe they froze her earnings when the accident happened?' she suggested. 'Could they have done that?'

Eric scratched his head. 'But that was nearly two months ago? And surely someone would have said something to me first?' He picked up one paper and then the next, hoping that the reasoning behind Suzy's distinct lack of funds would become obvious on the twentieth reading.

'So, what are you going to do?' Yvette said, coming to stand beside him and placing a hand on his shoulder.

Eric sighed, puffing his cheeks out as he blew.

'I'm going to have to ask the only person who may have a clue,' he replied.

CHAPTER 8

THERE WERE MOMENTS – getting off the train, elbowing his way through ticket barriers, standing in line for a skinny latte – that Eric could have believed he'd slipped back two years. Back to a stage when London was his life, one of the suited and booted who strode down the street with a phone to his ear, not giving a damn about who he walked into as he tried to make the dash to his favourite sushi restaurant. But he wasn't heading towards the office. He was heading somewhere he'd never been before.

During their wooing days, Eric had frequently met Suzy for lunch dates or coffee breaks, but given that they worked on almost opposite sides of the city, they had always picked somewhere central; convenient for them both. As such, in thirteen years, Eric had never once stepped foot inside her agency.

The butterflies in his stomach reminded him of a first date. A rather twisted and confusing first date. Fortunately, Suzy's agent, Sam, had been able to reschedule so that she could fit him the day after his visit to the bank. He was grateful. Sleep had been hard enough to come by since Suzy's death, but last night felt like a record. All night he had stared at the ceiling wondering what he was missing; was it just another bank account he didn't know about, or was Suzy really hiding something from him. Eric shook his head clear of the thought. This was Suzy, who prized honesty above anything else in a relationship. There was no chance she was hiding anything from him. Hopefully this meeting would get it all cleared up so they could get on with their lives without money troubles and mysteries hanging over them.

Sam appeared downstairs in the foyer only moments after the receptionist had rung up to tell her that Eric had arrived. Wearing a grey poncho and pointed shoes, she looked every bit as elfin as she had at Suzy's funeral, although here, in the streamlined waiting chairs and exposed filament lighting, she looked far more at home.

'Eric.' She reached up on tiptoes to kiss him on the cheek. 'It's so good to see you.'

He followed her lead to see how many kisses were required in this situation. They settled on two.

'Thank you for agreeing to meet with me at such short notice.'

'It's no problem at all. Come on up.' Sam waved at the receptionist, who, without appearing to move, managed to swing the glass doors open. 'I was surprised you called. I'm sorry I had to dash off like that at the wake. You looked like you had enough to deal with.'

'Please don't apologise.' Eric followed her into another lobby, full of elevators and posters on how to save the environment by bringing your own coffee cup to work. 'I had a few things on my mind.'

She offered the same, sad-eyed sympathetic nod he had seen a thousand times in the last eight weeks.

'Of course. How's Abi doing? It must be hard for her. For all of you.'

'It is,' Eric agreed. 'But we've got a dog. That's helping.'

'A dog?' Her lips pinched into an exaggerated O shape. 'I'm so jealous. One day when I move out of my apartment.' The elevator opened before them. Eric stepped inside. 'I've considered getting one plenty of times, but I don't think it's fair, keeping one all cramped up without a garden. And I want a proper dog, you know. Not one of those silly yappy things.'

No sooner had Sam stepped inside than the door closed. For once, Eric mourned the absence of elevator music.

'I'm just down here,' said Sam as they exited the elevator a few floors up.

Sam led the way down a series of corridors filled with people on phones or holding their refillable cups of coffee. From somewhere out of sight came a series of low rumbling laughs.

'This one's me,' Sam said, opening the door to her office and stepping back to let Eric pass. Eric took a moment to survey the chaos. No wonder Suzy and Sam got on so well.

The glass windows of the office had been entirely obscured by books that had overflowed from the bookcases and desk space. A buckled chair was propped against a wall, holding yet more books, and the carpet, or what space was available on it, seemed to have been decorated mainly with coffee mugs and china plates.

In any other situation he would have said it was a cesspit or at the very least a highly unproductive working environment, but it fitted with here, with Sam, with Suzy.

'Please, sit,' Sam said, clearing a pile of books off a chair and placing them on top of another already precarious pile. 'Sorry, it's a little untidy. One day I'll get around to sorting it. I guess I'm a bit worried what I'll find under some of these piles if I look too closely.' She laughed, though it was tight and faded rapidly. 'Tell me, what is it you wanted to talk about?'

Eric cleared his throat. He had practiced the conversation several times in his head and once to Yvette to ensure he didn't sound too pushy or confrontational but now that he was here, in the moment, the speech or at least the starting part of it appeared to have evaporated from his mind.

'It is about money,' he said.

Sam's lips disappeared as she pressed them together. The tension in the room rose notably after just four words, but there was no way Eric could leave without answers. So ignoring the drumming in his chest, he continued.

'I was given her bank statements from the bank, and well, it doesn't seem like she's been paid for quite a while.'

'Paid?' Sam's head tilted to the side.

'Yes, well like royalties and such. There doesn't seem to have been any payments from the publishers in quite some time.'

Sam's head remained at the same jaunty angle, although an added frown line had formed directly between her eyebrows.

'I'm sorry, Eric, you're going to have to help me out a little bit. I'm afraid you've lost me. What would you expect the publishers to be paying her royalties for?'

'What for? For her books, of course.'

'But they've been out of print for nearly a year.'

Whether it was the instantaneous whitening of Eric's skin, or merely the momentary thought that happened after the fact, it was apparent from the wide-eyed look of shock on Sam's face that she knew she had said something wrong.

'You didn't know?' She reached her hands across the table, although Eric mindlessly drew his own back.

'But how? Why, I ... I ...'

Sam reached yet further across the desk until her hands were firmly over Eric's. After a brief hold she released him, leaned back into her chair, and sighed.

'I tried, I can promise you I tried. But the industry's just not what it was.'

'So they just dropped her?'

'There just wasn't the market for them.'

'But ... but ...' Eric rubbed his temples. All the late nights working, the scraps of paper. None of it made sense.

'But she was working on things,' he told Sam. 'Editing.'

Sam lifted her hands. 'I know she was doing editing work, I was passing what I could on to her. And I think she got a couple of mentoring jobs from what I heard.'

'From what you heard?'

'You know what she was like. Stubborn. Didn't want people to worry.' She paused, her top teeth biting down on the top of her lip. 'Eric, I am so sorry. I am so, so sorry.'

He nodded mutely. The numbness of the last few weeks had at last been replaced by something new. Something fiery and hot and all consuming.

'She was lying to me.'

Eric needed headspace. He had stumbled out of Sam's office, barely even able to string together a coherent goodbye as his mind spun one way and then the next. There was no way around it. Suzy had lied to him. Lied to all of them, for nearly a year. He exited the building, dropped his briefcase on the ground and screamed.

'Argh!' His fist punched the air repeatedly. Several passers-by eyed him suspiciously before giving him a wider berth. 'How could you do this? How could you do this to me?'

His first instinct was to head for the nearest pub, but a quick glance at the London prices resulted in him getting on the first train back to Burlam. But he wasn't going home. He couldn't.

Despite the lies Eric had frequently told Yvette, that afternoon was in fact his first trip to the allotment since Suzy had died.

So much foliage had grown over the beds he couldn't even tell where he had planted his seedlings. Jerusalem artichoke was shooting up everywhere, and his tomato plants were so obscenely thick it was a miracle any of them had managed to get any sunlight at all. It was a good thing Eaves had let the condition of the will slide, Eric considered, otherwise he would be adding Sally to the list of loves in his life he now longer had. He picked up a trowel and half-heartedly began to dig around before changing his mind. He didn't want to tend things. He wanted to destroy things.

'You lied to me!' he screamed as his boot made contact with the edge of one of his DIY raised beds. 'You lied. You lied to me.' The ends of his once best work shoes scuffed and marked. 'Why didn't you tell me?' When his toes throbbed from kicking, he picked up the trowel and began to hammer at the wood. It didn't make any sense. The trowel wasn't going to break anything. But nothing made any sense. After all her self-righteousness, her fastidiousness for telling the truth, and she had been lying to them all.

'Bad day?'

Eric's face was in a snarl as he twisted around. 'This is not a good time, Hank.'

'I can see that. But I've got a sack full of potatoes for you here if you want them? Only babies mind. I was just getting out a few.' Hank limped over with Scout's tail thumping against his good leg as he walked. 'No chance of us getting through all of these. Seem to have hundreds of things on the way.'

'Then let them rot,' was Eric's reply.

Hank sniffed. 'Sounds like a bit of a waste. Perhaps you could pass them on to your sister-in-law. It's her that makes that frittata, isn't it?'

Eric's jaw was locked. Hank was normally the first person he could rely on for everything from babysitting to chewing his ear off at the pub. But today he clearly wasn't getting the hint.

Still oblivious to Eric's mood, Hank passed him a plastic carrier bag, stretched translucent by the weight of its contents, but when Eric took hold, Hank's hand remained there, gripping tightly but motionless. A silence expanded between them.

'You want to talk about it?' Hank said after a minute.

Eric continued to stare at the potatoes. There was probably more in the single bag than he would manage to get in a year. And given their current state of affairs, even he could see that refusing good food for the sake of stubbornness would not be his wisest decision.

'No.' Eric tugged the bag closer towards him until Hank released it. 'I do not want to talk.'

Eric did not change his mind about talking, and Hank didn't pester him with any questions. Instead he had stayed by his side, silent and stoic as they stood staring out at the plot.

'I thought about turning the whole thing over for you,' Hank said eventually, after what he felt seemed like a suitably meaningful and poignant passage of time.

They returned to conversation and the topic of choice was, as usual, Eric's allotment plot. 'It wouldn't take long to give the whole thing a good overhaul, only I didn't know what you wanted to keep. I know you had plans on the village show this year.'

'Somehow, that fell down the list of priorities,' Eric replied as he bent down and pulled out a fistful of weeds and threw it towards the compost pit.

'I thought as much.'

A contemplative silence fell between the pair.

'I thought this might help,' Eric said after a pause, his hand clutched around another mass of green stems. 'That it might clear my head a bit being down here.'

'And it's not?'

'No, it's not. Now I just get to see how another part of my world is falling apart or growing out of control in this case.'

Hank tutted. 'A few good days and you'll have this plot right as rain. At least it's not too late to put a few cauliflowers or sprouts in.'

'Maybe,' Eric said. 'But what would be the point? Maybe I should just let someone who wants it have it.'

'That'd be a right shame, after all you've put into it.'

Eric chose not to reply. He was considering his next move, whether to grab a spade and go the whole hog, or else head home and write a letter to the board handing his notice in there and then. Then again, if they didn't get some money in soon, they might end up living on his wonky carrots and substandard green beans. He was still considering the matter when Hank moved up next to him and rolled up his sleeves.

'I've got a couple of hours now. I could help you get this place sorted if you want?'

Eric smiled, trying his hardest to look genuine. 'Actually, I've got to head back to the house. I've got a delivery coming for the kitchen.'

'You have? No worries then. But call me. I'll get a group of us together. It'll take no time at all.'

'Thanks.'

'And if you need a hand putting some of those cabinets together, you just give us a bell.'

'Will do.'

※

THE KITCHEN CABINET delivery had only been a half-lie. They had been delivered two days earlier, but for now sat in the garage, boxed and unopened. They had been Suzy's choice. She loved a bit of DIY, and he knew how cross she would have been if he'd started putting them together without her even seeing them. But now she was never going to see them; that was the long and short of it. And did he even care if she was cross with him? The same thoughts whirled around and around in his head. How could she have lied to him like that? How? He hadn't a clue, not the vaguest idea. Did she not trust him? Was that what it came down to? Did she not trust that he would support her, understand her? He took a knife and sliced through the top on one of the boxes. Then he sliced through the next one and the next one and the next one. By the time Abi and Yvette arrived home, he had got as far as moving the unmounted doors to the kitchen although there was enough shredded cardboard in the garage to keep a family of guinea pigs happy for a lifetime.

'How did today's session with the counsellor go?' Eric asked Abi over a dinner of baked potatoes – courtesy of Hank – and value, unsalted baked beans. Any moment of silence offered an opportunity for his mind to wander in to dark recesses that he had only recently managed to drag himself away from.

'He's nice,' she said. 'And Lulu likes him.'

'That's good. Did you talk to him?'

'I guess.'

'What about?'

'What do you mean?'

'I mean, what did you talk to him about? What things did he ask you?'

She pushed a bean to one side of her plate and back again.

'You know, just stuff,' she said.

'Well did you tell him the truth?'

'About what?'

'About anything. When he asked you a question, did you tell him the truth?'

'I—'

'Because there's no point you going if you're not going to tell him the truth. You understand? There's not point lying about this, Abigail. Lying doesn't help anyone.'

'I'm not.'

'Because—'

'Eric!'

Yvette glared, her face scrunched in confusion. She looked again to his daughter. Her hands were gripping her cutlery and her already pale skin became visibly sallower.

'I'm sorry, Abs. Of course you're not lying. I'm sorry.' He closed his eyes, resetting his frame of mind. 'Enough about the counsellor. How is school going?' he asked.

Another non-committal answer was followed by the three of them sitting in silence and casting their gazes among the dismantled cupboards and chaos that was their kitchen. When the doorbell went, all three of them leapt to answer it.

'I'll get it,' Eric said to Yvette. 'You need to get ready for your lessons.'

'But I—'

'And you need to finish your dinner and have a bath,' Eric said, before Abi could offer any of her reasons. He suspected it was Hank, checking up on the kitchen progress, and the last thing he wanted was for Yvette to invite him in. At some point he needed to sit down with her and explain about the money situation, but it would have to wait until after her dance class. At least that would give him a little time to work out what to say.

With the plan of suggesting to Hank that they head out for a beer or two after Yvette's lesson – therefore delaying the inevitable conversation with his mother-in-law even further – Eric opened the door, surprised to find a young woman with dark brown hair and a bundle in her arms.

'Are you Eric?' she said.

Eric nodded.

'I'm Katrina.'

CHAPTER 9

'CAN I COME in?' the girl said, bouncing the bundle up and down as soft whimpers escaped from beneath the blankets.

Eric nodded and side-stepped to let her in. It would have made sense, he thought, to ask a little more about her, but the name had caught him off guard for reasons he couldn't quite figure out. The girl was pretty. Slight, particularly considering the baby in her arms. A minute later he would recognise it as a dancer's physique, but it wasn't until he had taken her coat and ushered her through into the kitchen that things began to fall into place.

'Eric, who was—' Yvette stopped and dropped the fork she was holding to the ground. It bounced and clattered and came to rest beside the chair leg. 'What in hell's name is she doing here?' She pushed back her seat and sprung to her feet. 'Is this a joke?'

'Yvette this is Katrin ... ahhh,' Eric said. A wave of realisation clobbered him over the head. That was why the name was familiar. Katrina. The twenty-something dancer who Yvette's ex-husband – Suzy's father – had got pregnant and run off with.

'Is he here too?' Yvette asked, her teeth bared as she spoke. 'Is Philip with you? Because if he's turned up now, after what he's missed, then I swear I will put a knife right thr—'

'No,' Katrina said, shaking her head. 'Philip's not here. I didn't come with him.'

'Then why did you come?'

The girl's eyes wandered around the room, falling fleetingly on Eric and then Abi and then the unpacked kitchen cabinets which were sprawled out on the floor.

Eric noticed his daughter, cutlery down, gawping at the situation.

'Abi, upstairs,' he said.

'What? No,' she protested. 'I want to know what's going on.'

'Nothing's going on,' he said. 'Now upstairs and run your bath.' He moved around the room and swept Abi up off her seat before ushering her out of the kitchen and up the stairs. Lulu scampered up after her mistress.

'I'll be up in two minutes,' he called, desperately hoping he was telling the truth. 'And don't forget tonight is a hair wash night.'

In the kitchen, the two women stood in silence. Yvette, frozen to the spot, continued to stare daggers at the young girl while Katrina, whose hands and knees shook visibly, continued to bounce the baby in her arms. A slightly musty smell of soured milk rose from the pair.

'Please, Yvette,' Katrina said, finally breaking the silence. 'I need your help.'

Yvette snorted. There was a harshness in the sound that Eric had never encountered from his mother-in-law. Katrina flinched visibly.

'You are joking, aren't you? You can't think I'm that naive?'

Eric's eyes scanned back and forth between the pair. Katrina refused to lower her eyes despite a definite sheen within them glistening in the light. Yvette's eyes, by contrast, showed only venom.

'Yvette.' The unease of the situation swirled in Eric's gut. 'Surely you can hear the girl out?'

'Hear her out?' Yvette's nostrils flared at the apparent insult. 'Whose side are you on in this?'

Eric opened his mouth, then closed it hurriedly and bit his tongue.

Even in her current state, it was easy to see what Philip had fallen for in the girl, with her cascades of ringlets and long, slender neck, although at that moment, with bags under her eyes and tears making a bid for freedom, she barely looked older than Abi. She held the baby at an angle in her arms as if she were not quite sure what it was, or whether it was safe to hold it. Her nails were bitten to the quick and her dry lips were chapped. This was a girl for whom things had gone very, very awry, Eric thought.

'Yvette,' he said acutely aware of the tremble in his mother-in-law's hands. 'You need to get to your dance lesson. You don't want to be late.' Yvette transposed the venom of her glare from Katrina to Eric. 'You know you have to go,' he repeated. 'You'll be late if you don't leave now.'

Without so much as a whispering breath, Yvette sucked her cheeks in tightly, narrowing her features to a fraction of their normal state.

'She better be gone by the time I get back.'

Then, without so much as a goodbye to Abi, she grabbed her handbag from the back of her chair and stormed out through the house, slamming the front door behind her.

The slam of the front door had a multitude of small effects. These effects, whilst on their own would have been insignificant and at worst mildly irritating, combined in the exact proportion that they were, resulted in an overwhelming cacophony of chaos. First, Lulu started barking, which resulted in the bundle in Katrina's arms wailing at full pelt. Katrina, in turn, burst into tears. Not one to miss out, Abi came storming back down the stairs, towel wrapped around her, and began shouting at the top of her voice that no one valued her opinions or considered her as a person. In one second, pandemonium had set in.

'That's not fair. Why did you tell me to leave? I shouldn't have had to leave. I'm part of this family. And there's a baby. And I love babies and you made me leave the baby and—'

'Abi, please—'

'I'm sorry,' Katrina sobbed, barely audible over the wailing baby. 'I'm sorry. She's just fussy. Sometimes when we're in new places she gets fussy. And old places. You can stop crying now. You can stop now. Please stop. Please stop.'

Eric turned his head, trying to find some direction in which to shield his ears.

'And you know I've always loved babies—' Abi continued to shout at him.

Lulu barked for good measure.

Eric closed his eyes, hoping that it might somehow help with the issue.

'And you say that you care about how I'm feeling bu—'

'Please, why won't you stop?'

'And this is my house—'

'All right. Enough! Stop it! Will everyone please just be *quiet*!' Eric's placed his hands over his ears as he bellowed.

The result was instant. In less than a second Katrina, Abi, and Lulu were all stunned silent, mouths wide, the final breaths of their words still hanging in the air. And while the baby continued to wail, even that was at a more diminished volume. Six pairs of eyes stared expectantly up at him. Eric exhaled with relief.

'Thank you,' Eric said, taking the moment of quiet to breathe before they started up again. 'Abi, you need to have a bath.'

'But the baby—'

'Needs some quiet.'

'Bu—'

'Now,' Eric insisted.

'But—'

'Now. It is late. You have school tomorrow, and tonight is a hair wash night.'

Abi pouted, squeezing her mouth tightly into a perfect circle.

'Don't make me ask again. Today is not the day you want to try to battle me.'

With her pout still in place, Abi narrowed her eyes, clearly considering whether the threat from her father was real or not. After a brief moment's contemplation, she huffed loudly and whistled the dog to her side.

'Well Lulu's coming with me,' she said.

'That would be wonderful,' Eric replied. With Abi still grumbling to herself, the pair stomped their way up the staircase. Eric sighed in relief; however, the volume of the room was once again on the rise.

Although Katrina continued her actions of rocking and shushing, it became increasingly obvious to Eric that they were having very little effect on the child. Within a minute the gentle sobs were once more full-blown screams, and the baby's olive-toned skin had now adopted an angry purple hue. Katrina's eyes blurred with tears.

'She's only just been fed. And I winded her. But she's so fussy. And she won't sleep at the minute. She never sleeps. She just never sleeps. And I can't ... I can't ...' Tears streamed down her cheeks. 'I can't ...'

Eric stepped towards her. She was pale to the point of ghostly, with dark bags weighing beneath her eyes. It wasn't just her nails and skin that were in a bad state. Her hair was more unkempt, knotted, and oily than he had realised at first, and the top of her jumper was mottled with whitish stains. Every attempt to speak was shorted by a deluge of tears or an ill-timed yawn. Still, she continued to stutter out her apologies.

'I ... I'm so sorry. It's just ... it's just—'

'Do you want a drink?' Eric said, trying to figure out what kind of helpful comment people usually used in this type of situation. 'We've got some tea?'

Katrina snivelled and wiped her nose with the back of her hand. Her chest shuddered with muffled sobs.

'Tea would be good,' she said.

It turned out that tea was the perfect solution in that it allowed Eric to busy himself and avoid any type of proper conversation. However, it was still more challenging than he had originally anticipated. With the expectation of making a simple cup of builder's brew, Eric found himself rather out of his comfort zone when he opened the cupboard and began to search for tea bags of which, he quickly discovered, there was a multitude.

'*Uhmm*,' he said, pulling one box out and then another. 'I've got peppermint tea—'

'That would be fine.'

'Or ginger and lemongrass? Or Earl Grey?' He turned a patterned box over in his hand. The carton looked more like something you would wrap Grandma's birthday present in than a tea box, with layers of multi-coloured flowers on. 'I'm not sure what this one is ...' He dropped it to the other side of the pile. 'But there's a liquorice and chamomile, or goji berry — is that a thing? — goji berry and grapefruit?'

'Peppermint will be fine,' Katrina replied.

Why did they have so many types of tea? Eric wondered. He didn't even drink the stuff. It had to be Yvette. There was no way Suzy would have had the patience to sort through all these every time she wanted a drink. Then again, it was starting to look like he didn't know Suzy quite as well as he thought he did. He found another carton, this time a selection box, with ten different types of green tea infusion.

'Or this says it's—'

'Peppermint would be great.' Katrina looked him in the eye.

'Peppermint it is then.'

No words were exchanged while they waited for the kettle to boil, and after he had poured the water, he took the mug in his hand and held it out. His throat had tightened awkwardly while his mind was having difficulty trying to process what type of etiquette should be displayed in such situations.

'Why don't you go drink that in the living room?' he said, suddenly aware that she had been in the house for nearly ten minutes and he had not so much as offered her a seat, despite the weight in her arms. 'You can sit down then. I'll carry the tea through.'

'A sit down would be good.'

'After you,' Eric said and pointed his hand out of the kitchen. He followed her out into the hallway before leading her into the living room and placing the mug down on their recently purchased, imitation teak coffee table.

'I should go and get Abi sorted,' he said. 'I'll only be a couple of minutes.'

'No need to rush,' she replied, her body sagging into the sofa.

Half an hour later and Eric had almost managed to get Abi settled in bed.

'Who is she?' she'd asked as she pulled on her pyjamas and took the toothbrush which Eric held out for her.

'She's a friend of Granny's.'

'It didn't sound like they were friends,' Abi said and raised a sceptical eyebrow. He flinched at an action that was scarily like her mother.

'Well they are friends,' he said. 'They just haven't seen each other in a while. They need to get to know each other again. Now I need to go and check if she's all right. So you need to go to sleep.'

'You know you shouldn't lie to me,' Abi said, her toothbrush by her side and her glare unwavering. 'Mr Joe says it's not healthy for you to lie to me, and I should say if I don't feel like you're being truthful.'

'I'm being truthful when I say you need to go to sleep.'

'Dad ...' Abi growled.

Eric sighed, taking her toothbrush and dropping it back in the pot. 'Okay, they aren't friends. But they were and maybe they can be again.'

'And that's the truth? You swear?'

'That is the truth. I swear,' Eric said. 'Now go to sleep.'

Abi shuffled into her room and up onto the bed.

'Can I read first?'

'Fifteen minutes maximum. And I mean that.'

'Love you, Dad.'

'Love you too.' Eric kissed his daughter on the forehead. She might look like Suzy, he thought, but she would always smell like Abi; earthy and new, yet somehow fizzy like sugar-coated cola bottle sweets. 'Sleep tight, my darling.'

He turned around to find himself toe to toe with Lulu. She looked up at him longingly from the floor.

'Fine. You too. Fifteen minutes,' Eric repeated and moved his arm to the side. Lulu bounded into the room and onto Abi's bed, where she promptly snuggled down next to her. He let out a sad little chuckle. There was no chance that dog was going anywhere, not on his say so.

It was only when he was halfway down the stairs and Abi's laughter drifted down after him that Eric realised this was the first time he had put Abi to bed without her mentioning her mother. He didn't know if this made him more or less sad.

In the living room, Katrina was asleep. The mug of peppermint tea sat untouched on the coffee table while the bundled-up baby lay silently in the crook of her arm. It was almost impossible to believe that only a short while ago the same child had been screaming loud enough to wake the entire street. A trail of milky spittle was trickling from her mouth. Eric lifted the corner of her muslin blanket to wipe the dribble away.

'Sorry,' Katrina jolted from her sleep. 'I must have dozed off.'

'It's fine. It's not a problem.'

'Is Yvette back?' she said manoeuvring herself upright. 'And Suzy? How long was I asleep? I need to speak to them. I have to speak to them.' Her panicked tone and sudden tensing began to rattle the baby who grizzled wordlessly in her arms.

'No, not again. It's fine. Go back to sleep,' she whispered. 'Please don't wake up.' Her voice hitched with distress. 'You need to go back to sleep. Please, please. Not again. I need you to go back to sleep.' Apparently, the baby was unable to hear the desperation in her mother's voice as her screaming did nothing but increase. Within seconds, the purple features had returned.

'I'm sorry, I'm so sorry ...' She aimed her flustered apologies at Eric. 'I don't know why she's like this.'

'It's fine,' he said. 'Honestly. We've all been there.'

'But she'll be coming home soon, right?' Katrina begged, bouncing the baby up and down at an ever-increasing pace. 'It won't be long?'

'She'll be back soon,' he said, without quite meeting her eyes.

Pressing his lips together, Eric glanced at his watch. Normally Yvette came straight home after her dance lessons, apart from on Thursdays when she went for a drink with a couple of the women from her seniors' class. Tonight was a Wednesday, which meant she should be home fairly promptly, although the squirming in his stomach told him he probably shouldn't bet on it. He tried not to show the doubt on his face.

Gradually the wail diminished into low grizzle. Katrina looked up at Eric.

'I think she needs feeding again,' she said. 'Honestly, it's non-stop. I don't understand what's wrong with her. You don't mind, do you? If I give her some food here?' As if reacting to the thought of food – and before Eric could offer a slightly wary *go ahead* – Katrina's stomach let out a loud grumble. She yawned and blushed simultaneously, before it repeated the sound, this time even louder.

'I've got a pizza in the freezer,' Eric said, rising to his feet. 'I can pop it in the oven if you fancy it?'

'I don't want to be any trouble.'

'It's not.'

Katrina nodded gratefully.

'Pizza would be great. Thank you.'

Eric scurried out of the living room, leaving Katrina to feed the baby.

He took his time in the kitchen, waiting for the oven to heat up before unwrapping the pizza from its plastic packaging and sliding it onto the top shelf. The dishes from dinner were sitting on the draining board, Abi's only half eaten, Yvette's fork still on the floor. Eric moved to place it all in the dishwasher, only to discover it full of unwashed plates and cutlery. Washing up it was then.

The plates had been cleaned, dried, and put away and Eric was just taking the pizza out of the oven when Yvette arrived back home. He had stayed in the kitchen the entire time, poking his head around the corner only once to ask if Katrina wanted another cup of tea or a glass of water, both of which she declined. Something was bothering him as he paced around the table and washed the suds off the plates, but he couldn't put his finger on it. Most probably though, he suspected it was to do with Abi; most things that concerned him were. Perhaps her comments about Mr Joe. He couldn't be certain, but all the while he was waiting for Yvette something was niggling away at the back of his mind, just out of reach.

'Tell me that's not for her?' Yvette said, dropping her bag on the kitchen table and scowling. 'Tell me she's not still here?'

Eric slid the pizza onto a plate and opened the drawer in search of a pizza cutter.

'Eric?'

He turned around with a sigh.

'What do you want me to say, Yvette?' He rubbed his temples in the vain hope of some relief from the headache he felt building. 'Yes, it's for her. Yes, she's still here.'

'Why?' Yvette's fist balled at her side.

'Because she wanted to speak to you.'

Yvette's balled fists tightened, whitening the skin on her knuckles.

'Eric, what that girl did to me—'

'Was unforgivable. I know, Yvette, I really do. But she's tired, and she's upset, and she wants to talk to you. It's obviously caused her a great deal of distress to come here.'

'A great deal of distress? What does someone like her know about distress?'

'Yvette, you need to be reasonable.'

Yvette threw back her head and emitted a high-pitched laugh.

'Me? Be reasonable? You men. All she has to do is bat her eyelids and utter a few sad, little words and there you all are running after her.'

'That is not the case.'

'I should have known you wouldn't be any better, not after what happened with that Fleur woman.'

The flash of regret was immediate, but the words had already been released. They shot through the air piercing Eric right between his ribs.

'Eric,' Yvette's hand flew to her mouth. 'I didn't—'

'No.' Eric silenced her. The sting of her words continued to resonate through his chest. He inhaled and forced it down the best he could. 'Yvette, I have barely spoken three words to the girl, but even I can tell she's a train wreck. She doesn't want to speak to me. She came here to speak to you.'

'I have nothing to say to her.'

'I understand, but she obviously has something to say to you. She wouldn't have come all this way, otherwise would she?'

'She's probably after my wedding ring.' Yvette huffed walking over to the fridge and pulling out a bottle of white wine. 'Or my liver. You can be cert—'

'*Yvette*. Please, talk to her. Give her five minutes. If, after that, you want to send her packing then that's fine. I'll drive her to the station. She doesn't deserve your time or generosity, I get that. But you listened to me, and I didn't deserve it either.' He moved forward and took her hands in his. They had aged too he realised as he wrapped his fingers around hers. The skin with thinner, colder, frailer. 'You're a reasonable woman, Yvette. You're a good woman. Don't let all these things that have happened change the fact that you're a good person. Be the better woman here.'

Yvette's eyes went to the ground. She shuffled her feet as if thoughtfully preparing for some intricate dance step.

'You should probably be there to referee,' she said eventually.

'I think that's probably wise,' Eric agreed.

THE BABY HAD FINISHED her feed and was lying across her mother's shoulder. With her bald head and plump chubby cheeks, she didn't look to be more than a few weeks old at most. Katrina was repeatedly patting the baby's back while shaking and shimmying her bottom. Occasionally the tiny lips twisted with the promise of wind, helping to distract from the adults' painfully obvious silence.

'She never wants to wind,' Katrina said, after five minutes jiggling. 'It doesn't matter what I do. I've tried all the stuff from the pharmacy, drops, syrup, and I've watched all the videos on YouTube about it. There's meant to be this special way you can hold them that brings up the wind straight away, but it doesn't work. Nothing I've tried makes any difference. Most of the time it makes her sick.' She upped the rate of her patting. 'I thought maybe it was colic, you know, because she cried so much. I took her to the doctor, but they said it's normal. It doesn't sound normal, though, does it? Does this sound normal to you?' Eric listened, but he could hear nothing other than the occasional gurgling of a recently fed baby. 'I wanted to go back to the hospital, but Philip said I was being ridiculous, but there has to be something wrong, doesn't there? Why else would she be like this all the time?'

Her eyes went from Eric to Yvette and back again. Eric cleared his throat and prayed the floor would swallow him up before he was forced to think of something to say to break the tension. He was trying to remember what Abi was like at that age, see if he could offer some words of advice, but before he had even recalled what Abi looked like back then, Yvette started in with her interrogation.

'What do you want, Katrina?' Yvette's voice was devoid of emotion. 'Why are you here? If Philip sent you for more money, there is none. He already took it.'

Katrina's pale skin blanched further.

'Philip doesn't know I'm here. In fact, I'm not even sure where he is.'

Yvette shifted her position. 'What do you mean he doesn't know you're here?'

Yet again, the whimpers from her shoulder began to rise in volume. Jiggling the baby up and down, Katrina's eyes glazed as she tried to hold back the tears.

'She never stops. It's all night, all day. Sometimes I think she knows. That's why she does it.'

'Knows what?' Yvette said. 'And where is Philip?'

'Because it's not right. No matter what the doctors say. It's not. I know it's not.'

'Katrina,' Yvette's voice was sharp, and out of patience. 'What are you talking about? You're not making any sense.'

Slowly, Katrina's gaze lifted. There was no subtle glaze to her eyes anymore. No attempt to hide it. Tears escaped and slipped down her cheeks in an ever-increasing torrent.

'I think she knows that I don't know what I'm doing,' she whispered in a staggered breath. 'I think she knows that I shouldn't really have had her. That I wish I hadn't had her.'

CHAPTER 10

YVETTE HAD TAKEN the baby and left it to Eric to find a box of tissues. After two minutes of searching for them, he gave up and plucked a half-full toilet roll off the holder and took it through into the living room. He passed the roll to Katrina, who ripped off a strip of squares and blew her nose, after which she used the same piece of tissue to wipe her eyes. Eric shuddered silently. It was the type of unhygienic move Abi would have pulled. No one had spoken since Katrina's previous statement, other than Yvette when she stretched out her arms and spoke in no uncertain terms.

'Give her here.'

Katrina had instantly obliged.

It was another three minutes before anyone felt able to speak again. That anyone was Katrina.

'I'm sorry.' A pile of damp toilet roll lay scrunched up on the arm of the sofa beside her. 'But it's so hard. It shouldn't be this hard, should it?'

Yvette laughed. 'It's always this hard. It's called having a baby.'

Katrina shook her head.

'No. This is different. I know what it's like to be around babies. I have friends with babies. Cousins too.'

'Then you'll know it gets better.'

Katrina bit down onto her bottom lip, causing it to swell out at the side. 'But I don't sleep. Most days I hardly eat. It's impossible.'

'That's normal,' Eric attempted to assure her. 'We were just the same. Everyone's the same. My friend Ralph reckons he hasn't had a full night's sleep in six years, so you're definitely doing better than him.'

From the look on her face, his assurances weren't doing much good.

'She doesn't like me. It sounds stupid saying it out loud, but it's true, I know it is.' Katrina turned her attention to the baby, currently swaddled in Yvette's arms, sucking on a dummy. 'She would never be like that with me.'

'It takes time,' Yvette said.

Katrina recommenced her head shaking. 'It's been four weeks, and it's getting worse. Not better. Every day I'm not sure if I'm even going to make it through to bedtime. And what difference does it make if I do? It's not like she sleeps. I'm not meant to do this. I'm not meant to be a mother yet.'

The baby emitted a muted murmur. Yvette manoeuvred herself out of the seat and began rocking her arms as she walked.

'It takes time,' Yvette repeated. 'You need to give it time.'

For a split second, the women's gazes met. Eric, holding his breath as he watched, felt his pulse rise.

'Where's Philip?' Yvette said, severing the moment and releasing just a little of Eric's tension. 'Why don't you know where he is?'

Katrina snorted. 'He bailed before she was a week old.'

'Bailed?'

She was struggling to stem the tears again. 'He left a note. And two hundred quid. Can you believe that? Two hundred quid. Do you know how much nappies are? And wet wipes and baby grows? Because they grow so fast. It's all gone. All the money. And I can't go to my family. I can't. I just can't.'

Yvette's head was still shaking. 'Surely not. Surely he wouldn't do that?'

Katrina shrugged. 'He did. Three weeks now. I've not heard a thing. I thought maybe you would know.'

It was Yvette's turn to snort. The bitterness reappeared in her eyes.

'Fat chance. If he turned up here, he'd be leaving in a coffin. What sort of man doesn't even come to his daughter's funeral?'

'Funeral?' Katrina's eyes widened. 'I don't understand.'

That was when Eric realised what had been wrong about before. Katrina hadn't just asked to see Yvette, she hadn't just wanted to know when Yvette was returning home. She had asked about them both. Yvette *and* Suzy. Eric's ribs began to burn the way they always did whenever he encountered someone who did not yet know the news. Katrina didn't know. Her expression conveyed that clearly enough.

'Suzy?' She turned to Eric, her mouth agape. He managed one, single nod.

'How?' The air in her breath cast the word into a long stream. 'I'm so sorry. I had no idea. Truly. I didn't ... I didn't know. I'm so sorry.'

Yvette's glare focused on the young girl.

'You'll forgive me for saying your thoughts mean very little to this family.'

Katrina's lips pinched. She looked to the ceiling and managed to blink away whatever tears were coming. When her gaze lowered back down, it landed on Eric. She met his eyes. He didn't want to look at her. He didn't want more sympathy, but he couldn't look away.

'I'm sorry,' she said. 'I truly am.'

He nodded once again, turned his attention back to his mother-in-law, and prayed he could keep himself together.

With the baby now silent and asleep, Yvette lowered herself back into the armchair. She lifted her elbow, making a cradle, and slid the baby down from her shoulder into the gap. A new, saddened silence expanded around them.

'Katrina.' Eric felt it necessary to break the silence, for fear it may go on all night. 'Philip isn't here. If you were hoping to find him—'

'No,' Katrina shook her head. 'I wasn't looking for him. I thought he might be here, but really, I was looking for you. For you and for ... for...'

'For Suzy?'

She nodded.

'Why?'

Seconds passed.

'I can't go back on the ships,' she said eventually. 'Not with her. And I don't have any other way of making money.'

'There must be some—'

'Dance is all I know. I can't do classes because of the money it costs me to rent a studio, and no one is going to hire me like this. I can't even get a part-time job waitressing or in a bar or something cos I can't afford the childcare. I'm trapped.'

'Even if we wanted to help,' Eric said, a pang of sympathy blooming within him. 'We're barely making ends meet.'

'No. I don't want your money,' she said, a small sound buzzing on her lips as her eyes were drawn across to the bundle in Yvette's arms.

'Then what do you want?'

'I want you to take the baby. I want you to adopt my baby.'

༺༻

Yvette and Eric had disappeared to the kitchen under the exceptionally weak ruse of making some more tea, leaving Katrina and the baby in the living room.

Yvette's hands, Eric could see, were shaking almost as much as his own.

'She needs help,' Eric said. 'Professional help. Clearly there's postnatal depression of some degree going on there. Not to mention all the family issues she's got. We know that much from when her psycho brother smashed the place up. She probably needs a good night's sleep or two as well,' he added.

He moved over to the cupboard, this time selecting the box of teabags closest to hand. Without bothering to look what they were, he dropped two into a pair of mugs before adding in hot water and placing them down in front of Yvette.

'I remember what it was like when Abi was born. It was horrific. Crazy. Like, the worst hangover of your life but without being able to enjoy the getting drunk part. No wonder she doesn't feel like she's coping. Particularly with Philip bailing. What a shit. What an absolute shit. And God, if that brother of hers is still on the scene. No wonder she's having trouble coping.' He went to the fridge for the milk. 'Maybe she needs to go back to the doctor? See if they can't offer her some sort of help. I'm sure she'd be able to make an emergency appointment for something like this.'

It was only as he went to add the milk to the tea that he realised Yvette had been entirely silent in the exchange. Her hands were resting on the mugs.

'Yvette,' he said. 'Is everything all right?'

Yvette turned to him, her hands still on the mugs.

'I would give anything for another day with my little girl. Anything. For one more lunch date, or afternoon gossip. To have seen one more of her school plays or read one more of her stories.'

Eric placed the milk down.

'I know,' he said.

'Both my girls. From the moment they were born, I would have run into a burning building for them without a second thought.'

'Of course you would have, you're their mother.'

Yvette shook her head. 'And yet she's in there, ready to hand her over?'

Eric scratched behind his ear.

'Well we don't know all the ins and outs. She's obviously under a massive amount of stress.'

Yvette tutted and muttered something under her breath. 'Asking a complete stranger to take her. That woman doesn't deserve a child. She deserves to rot in hell.'

Eric stepped back. He had seen his mother-in-law angry before. He had seen her bat-shit crazy, but this was different. The bitterness and venom that had cocooned her when Katrina had arrived continued to fizz below the surface of Yvette's skin.

'Yvette?'

'You should have thrown her out the moment you realised who she was,' she spat.

'Now hold on a second,' Eric said. He was surprised to find his finger pointing at her in a most outraged manner and his voice sounding uncharacteristically commanding. 'She's young. She's scared.'

'She's no younger than I was when I had Lydia.'

'But you had Philip.'

'So did she,' Yvette spat back.

'Obviously not quite the way she thought.' Lowering his finger, Eric moved over to the table. 'You were married, to a man you loved, you had family around you. Katrina's in a very different situation. Clearly her family are bonkers. She has no job. No partner.'

'I would have run into a burning building,' Yvette repeated.

Eric looked her squarely in the eye. 'And that's what she feels she is doing. Don't you see that? Asking us for help like this, that's exactly the same. She's doing whatever she thinks is necessary to save her baby. True, it's probably a little bit of a misstep, but that's what she's trying to do.'

Yvette's cheeks remained pinched, her eyes watery.

'Come on,' Eric said. 'You've got to see that. If someone as emotionally inept as me can manage to put that together, surely you can see it too?' He reached out his hand and placed it on top of his mother-in-law's. She tensed beneath his touch, before relaxing and expelling a long and breathy sigh, her shoulders and chest dropped with the weight of it.

'It hurts, Eric,' she said, her eyes full of pain and apology. 'Surely you understand that? Surely you can see that too?'

'Of course I can,' he said. 'I can't imagine what this is like for you. But I can't imagine what it's like for her either. We're not in her shoes. Look, we're jumping ahead of ourselves. For all we know, tomorrow morning, after a good night's sleep, she'll come to realise this was all a ridiculous idea, call Philip, and everything will be sorted.'

Yvette offered a half-grunt as a response. 'Philip wasn't much use when my girls were born either. Used to have an awful lot of rehearsals that always started around dinner and bath time. But I just got on with it. That's what you did. That's what you had to do.'

'And that's probably what she wants to do,' Eric said.

'It's what I tried to do. I swear, it's what I tried to do.'

Eric and Yvette's heads turned to the doorway. Katrina stood with the baby in her arms, bouncing it gently up and down. Her face was etched with tiredness and sadness and a hundred other emotions Eric couldn't begin to fathom, but on top of them all, she tried to smile.

'I realise,' she said, 'that I never told you her name. It's Mabel. Mabel Elizabeth.'

Yvette muscles tensed again. 'Elizabeth after Philip's mother, I assume?'

Katrina shook her head.

'After Elizabeth Bennett. From *Pride and Prejudice*? It was my favourite book growing up.' With a deep breath in, Katrina pushed back her shoulders revealing her dancer's posture for the first time since her arrival.

'I know what you're in here saying. I do. You think I'm just being weak. That I'm tired and I need to get on with things. You probably think that I deserve this for what I did to you and your family.'

'Pretty much, yes,' Yvette said. Eric shot her a glare even Suzy would have been proud of.

Katrina nodded. 'Maybe,' she said. 'But it doesn't change the fact. I can't do this.'

'You've barely tried,' Yvette said, lifting her hands to the air. 'It's an adjustment. You suck it up.'

Katrina chuckled sadly. 'I've tried. Believe me. At 3 a.m. when I can't sleep. At 6 a.m. when I'm searching for a job I can do where I can take her along, or some course I could complete, because I never finished school because I was just dancing. Dancing was always what I was going to do.'

'Having a baby is a sacrifice. You have to work at it.'

'I have tried. I am trying. I've tried talking to people, seeing if I'm the problem here. But it's not helping. It's not helping any of us. It would just be better if I could ... if I could ...'

'Give her up?' Eric said.

'I might not know much about raising children and families and taking care of a new-born baby, but I know what happens when someone has a child they don't want. When someone must pretend every day that this is the best thing in their life when it isn't. They resent it. They resent the child for being there and stealing their life. And they think they're doing a good job of hiding it and they think the child can't tell, but they can. They know. A child who grows up being resented will know it, and Mabel doesn't deserve that.'

'And you feel like that already?' Eric asked.

She tilted her head, her brow crinkled. 'Not all the time ... but sometimes, yes. And it won't get easier, I can feel it.' Her eyes looked up, pleading beneath her long, matted lashes. 'I love her. I do, with all my heart. She's perfect. But it's not enough. I can feel that it's not enough. But if I do this, if I give her away and if she's with a family who love her, some of the guilt will be lessened. Because there's so much guilt right now I feel like it's going to crush me. There's just so much of it.'

The pause at the end of her speech built into a silence. Yvette's face, Eric noted, had softened slightly. Only a fraction, but it was there, a modicum of compassion sneaking through. Meanwhile, his own thoughts and emotions on the situation remained a veritable yo-yo.

'There's always guilt,' Yvette said, her tone a fraction gentler. 'That's what it's like to be a mother.'

'But I don't want my baby to experience that. Not like this I don't.'

Yvette placed her hands on her hips.

'Why come to us?' she said. 'You must have known what kind of welcome you'd get. You have your own family.'

'We met them,' Eric added nodding to a dent in the wall where a baseball bat had been swung at it just a few months ago.

'So you understand why she can't go to them,' Katrina answered. 'Mabel can't be brought up with that. She can't. Like I said, I know resentment. Imagine the welcome she'd get there, being the unwanted bastard child of an already unwanted bastard child. And with a dad who's twice my age.'

'And the rest,' Yvette coughed under her breath. The other two ignored her. Katrina continued.

'And if by some miracle they don't resent her – which they will, believe me, I know my family – then everything's about money, about the business, that gang. I don't want my daughter growing up being part of that life.'

'You'd rather just give her away?'

Katrina prickled, but covered it well.

'I'd rather she was loved.'

'By someone who isn't her family?'

'*You* are her family,' she said.

Yvette's jaw clenched. The softening that had been occurring in her eyes took a sharp detour backwards.

'That child is no relation to me. That child ruined my life.'

'No.' Katrina shook her head. 'I ruined your life. Philip ruined your life. Mabel had nothing to do with that.' Yvette's pinched lips tightened until they vanished. Katrina continued. 'Whether you want to admit it to yourself, Mabel is part of *this* family. That's why I came here, that's why I thought Suzy and Eric would help me. Because Mabel is part of their family. Mabel is Suzy's sister.'

The statement was so simple. Katrina let the words hang in the air, filling all the spaces between them. And for a moment, all Eric could hear were those four words going around and around on repeat in his head. Mabel is Suzy's sister; it was entirely true. Suzy had even mentioned it, all those weeks ago when Philip had first told him about Katrina and the baby.

Yet until that moment, it hadn't even crossed Eric's mind. Philip, and Philip's baby, that had crossed his mind. Yvette, and the pain she must be going through in all this, that had crossed his mind too. But not Suzy. Not really. And yet this baby was Suzy's sister. He glanced down at the bundle in Katrina's arms, and for the briefest moment she opened her eyes and stared up at Eric with eyes of vivid green. Green. Just like Suzy's. It felt like Eric had been stabbed in the gut. Suzy's sister. Suzy's genes.

'No ...' Eric started, as his thoughts began tumbling in a helter-skelter downwards spiral. 'You can't use that on us.'

'I'm not trying to use anything. I just want you to see the truth, that's all. That's what brought me here.' She moved over to Yvette and handed Mabel to her. 'Your stories, Yvette. Stories of Suzy and Abi and you with your allotments and cars and holiday disasters. A family. A real family.'

Katrina's eyes went pleadingly from Eric to Yvette and back again.

'Photos you showed me, Vetty. Things Philip would talk about. I knew, even then, Suzy was the type of mother I never had. The type of mother I could never be.'

'Please ...' Eric said. The frequent mention of his wife's name was becoming harder and harder to handle. 'Please stop.'

'That's the life I want my daughter to have,' Katrina continued, seemingly oblivious to Eric's unravelling emotional state. 'A proper family. A life like Abi has with you and Suzy.'

'Well Suzy's gone,' Eric said, slamming his fist down on the table. 'Suzy's gone and so has that life.'

CHAPTER 11

THINGS HAD BECOME blurred after that. He hadn't passed out, at least he didn't think so, but he had come close to it. He couldn't focus. Thoughts and images swirled through his head. The green eyes, staring back up at him. Suzy spitting out her final words of hate at him. Abi, crying at her mother's funeral. The lies about the books and the money. In the end, Yvette had handed the baby back to Katrina and pushed Eric out the front door, then lowered him down onto the step and fetched him a glass of water before heading back into the house. It wasn't a great place to leave him, staring at the spot on the road where he had watched the love of his life die, but he tried not to think of that. Instead he lowered his head onto his knees and sat there until the unseasonable chill in the air grew too much to ignore. With his knees still weak, he had managed to get to his feet and headed back into the living room where Yvette and Katrina were sitting on the sofa.

'They're going to stay here tonight,' Yvette said, before Eric had had a chance to open his mouth. 'They've missed the last train, and they can hardly sleep on the street.'

'Okay,' Eric replied.

'And they can take your room. You can sleep on Abi's floor.' Eric nodded mutely. 'We'll empty out one of the drawers as a crib,' Yvette continued, now talking to Katrina, as opposed to Eric. 'That's how both her sisters slept for the first four months of their lives, and it never did them any harm.'

'Thank you,' Katrina said, and when the two women's eyes met, Eric felt something shift in the world around him and he wasn't entirely sure he was comfortable with it.

For over an hour he tossed and turned on Abi's floor. He had placed a couple of camping mats on the ground and taken the sleeping bag in too. At first, he tried to convince himself his lack of sleep was an issue with not having his own pillows. He tried taking one, then two of Abi's but it made no difference. He tried folding one in half to make something a bit sturdier, then he tried turning it over to make sure he got the cold side. None of it made a blind bit of difference. In the end, he gave up and went down to the kitchen to fix himself a drink. He carefully opened the freezer and took out some ice cubes.

'We need to talk about this,' Yvette said appearing out of the ether. Eric pulled a bottle of bitter lemon out of the fridge then closed the door.

'No, we don't,' Eric said.

'How can you say that?'

'This is not an abandoned dog,' Eric said, debating whether to add gin to his drink before finally deciding against it. 'This is a child.'

'Exactly. My daughter's sister. Abi's aunt. That baby is our blood.'

Eric groaned and flopped down into one of the chairs.

'It's late, Yvette. Can we talk about this tomorrow?'

'What if she's gone?'

'Then great, problem solved.'

'You don't mean that?' Yvette pouted.

Eric placed his glass down on the table and looked up at his mother-in-law.

'Yvette, be reasonable. The girl's knackered. She needs a break. You know as well as I do that tomorrow morning she'll realise this was a stupid mistake and run on back to London to do mummy and baby yoga classes or whatever it is they do nowadays.'

'And if she doesn't?'

'She will.'

'But if she doesn't? It's not the baby's fault her parents are useless.

What was it you were saying earlier? That the girl needs help. She is running into a burning building to try to save this child, Eric. Surely we should be there to try to help her?'

Eric sighed and massaged his forehead with his fingertips. 'I understand that. I honestly do. But suppose it is true – which it's not – suppose she actually wants us to take the baby. Look at us, we can't even keep ourselves together.'

'Speak for yourself,' Yvette muttered. 'I happen to be doing perfectly well.'

Eric sighed again.

'But it's not about you, Yvette. It's about this family. Only a couple of weeks ago we were talking about me and Abi moving back up to London so that I could get a job. Our only vague hope of being financially stable disappeared this afternoon.'

'What do you mean?' Yvette quizzed. 'What happened this afternoon?'

Eric inhaled through his nose, squeezing the bridge of his nose as he exhaled the air back out. Halfway through an entirely different discussion was not the way he had planned on telling Yvette about their latest disaster.

'The publishers took her books off their lists,' he told her, trying to make it sound as casual a statement as possible.

'What? Because she died?'

'No. Before she died.'

Yvette frowned, creating a deep crevice in her forehead.

'But I don't understand. If they had taken her books out of print, surely she would have told us about that? Surely we would have known?'

Eric was grateful for Yvette's use of the word *us* in her sentences. *Us*. He had always considered Suzy an *us*, but the truth was she had been lying to Eric for months.

'I had no idea,' Eric replied, his voice as void of emotion as his heart was full of it. 'She never said a word.'

His gaze went down to the kitchen table. From upstairs came the gurgle of water, the bathroom tap. Slowly, Yvette pushed his glass to one side, this time it was her turn to take his hands in hers.

'I don't think the baby would mind where it lives, as long as it has a family,' Yvette replied.

Eric pulled his hands away from hers. 'That is not the point and you know it.' He snatched his drink back off the table and downed the contents. 'Suppose Katrina does decide that's what she wants right now and leaves the baby with us. What happens when she changes her mind? What happens when two, three years down the line she realises she made a mistake and she wants Mabel back? Or worse still, in ten years, when she has another baby and realises she wants Mabel to be part of that family? What happens then? You haven't thought this through properly.'

'I don't need to think it through.' Yvette's tone was as exasperated and determined as his own. 'That baby is the last link I have to my daughter, and I'm not giving her up.'

'No, Abi is your last link.' Eric gritted his teeth. 'This is ridiculous, Yvette. The whole thing is a moot point. When we get up in the morning, I'll take her down to the station, pay for her ticket, and put her on the first train back home. I'm not having this conversation any longer.'

It hurt, seeing his mother-in-law so optimistic about something and having to come down on it like a sledgehammer, but he held firm, eyes fixed, hand locked on his empty glass.

'And just when I thought you'd learnt to put family first,' his mother-in-law said. With that she stood up and waltzed out the room and up the stairs. Eric sighed. Just one more thing to deal with.

※

LATER, he considered that Mabel going down without a sound should have been a sign. He and Yvette had had their debate in complete and utter peace, and even when Yvette had marched off upstairs and Eric had decided to pour himself a very short nightcap, everything in the house was perfectly quiet and still. It didn't stay that way for long.

It was possible that he and Suzy had just been lucky when it came to Abi and that she had been as perfect as he remembered; he certainly never recalled it being quite this traumatic. It was far more likely, however, that he had simply chosen to repress the hideous nights of endless wailing to the farthest recesses of his mind. There was no repressing this though. Not a chance. The minute he laid his head down on the sofa it started. Hour after hour of wailing came through loud enough to rattle the light fittings and set Lulu off barking.

'Is the baby staying the night?' Abi said, rubbing her eyes as Eric ushered her back into bed for the second time in as many hours.

'I hope so. Either that or an entire pack of banshees have taken up residence in my bedroom.'

Abi was either too tired or to confused to question the statement.

'Is she going to be staying for long?' she asked.

'Just for tonight,' Eric replied, pulling back the sheets and lifting her up onto her bed. 'She has to go home in the morning.'

'But we can play together for a bit first, right?' Abi yawned.

'We'll see,' Eric said, tucking her back in.

'I think she's sad,' she said, looking more awake by the second. 'Should I go in and check on her?'

'She'll be all right,' Eric said. 'She's just hungry.'

'She sounds like she needs some cuddles.'

'She'll be fine. She's with her mummy. Mummies fix everything.'

It was too late to take it back. The words clattered around the air, devouring everything else in the room. Abi's lips trembled.

She nodded quickly.

'We'll be all right too,' Eric said. He pulled back the covers, scooched her over and squeezed into bed next to her. 'We're going to be just fine.'

Somewhere around the five-fifteen mark, Mabel, Eric, and – he assumed – the rest of the house finally got to sleep. With Abi curled up on his chest and Lulu adding extra weight to his feet, it felt like the first time he had slept in a century. Even when Lulu began to stir and slivers of light shone through the blind, casting thick parallel lines on Abi's quilt, Eric managed to hide his eyes from the light and convince Lulu to lie down for just a little bit longer, so they could all get just a bit more shut eye.

※

A SHARP SHRILL ring of the house telephone was the next thing to disturb them. He pressed the pillow against his ears. It was probably Lydia calling to check that he hadn't slipped into some alcohol induced coma or allowed Abi to stay up late watching movies, she had that little respect for Eric's parenting skills, although given recent form it wasn't entirely unforgivable. Either that or some Mumbai call centre had got confused with their time zones. He let it ring out, then yawned and rolled back over to catch another five minutes shut eye.

The phone rang again.

'Eric!' Yvette called, her tone almost as sleepy and slow as he felt.

'Daddy ...' Abi groaned, rolling over next to him.

'All right, I'm getting it. I'm getting it.'

Rolling out of Abi's bed, and feeling every tiny ache in his body, he headed down the staircase and picked up the house phone.

'Hello?'

'Mr Sibley?' said a firm, yet concerned sounding voice down the end of the line.

'Yes.'

'It's Mr Heath here. From St Lawrence's.'

'St Lawrence's?'

'The school? Abi's school?'

'Oh, yes,' Eric said, his brain slowly starting to engage with the moment.

'I was checking if everything is all right with Abi?'

'Abi? Yes, why, she's fine?' Eric was squinting as he spoke. The light was unfeasibly bright and the endless interrupted sleep had resulted in an inability to think straight.

'It's just that she's not in school,' Mr Heath continued. 'And we haven't had any information from you about an authorised absence. We wanted to check that she was okay?'

'She's not in school?' He blinked again only to have his open eyes land on the hallway clock and the information that they had severely overslept.

'Ah, yes,' Eric said, trying to figure out how a house with a screaming baby, overactive dog, and alarms set on all their phones could somehow oversleep to such an impressive degree. 'I was going to keep her home today,' he said.

'So, she is unwell?'

'Um, yes.'

'Okay. Will you be able to bring in a doctor's certificate tomorrow?'

'A doctor's certificate?'

'It's school policy.'

'Well ... I ...' Eric's mind and voice stuttered. 'It's more of a stress thing. You know, with everything that's been going on. With her mother and all,' said Eric, instantly hating himself and mouthing a silent apology skywards to Suzy.

A pause echoed down the line.

'I completely understand. But you do need to make the school aware of these things in the future.'

'Sorry. I'll let you know next time,' Eric said.

Only when he had hung up the hall phone did he pick up his phone from the living room coffee table and glance at the time again. 10:20. That was probably a new record.

The phone call had woken up the rest of the house too, and it was less than a minute before Abi came bounding down the stairs.

'We're late,' she said, in a voice that sounded remarkably like her mother's. 'Why did you let me oversleep? I'm going to be late for school.'

Eric yawned.

'It's fine, I spoke to the school. They know you're staying at home.'

'I am? Why? What's happened?' Lulu trotted down to sit by Abi's feet.

'Nothing.'

'Is it something to do with the baby? What's wrong?'

'Nothing's wrong. I just thought you might like to spend some time together, that's all.'

'With you?'

It was the surprise in her voice that struck Eric so acutely. The glimmer of hope, barely allowing itself to become visible above the underlying sadness that had become ever-present in his daughter's features. A lump built in his throat. He knew he had been absent of late, but had somehow deluded himself that he had covered it well. Apparently not.

'With me,' he said. 'If that's okay?'

Abi nodded rapidly.

'I'll have to catch up on the maths I miss though,' she said. 'It's maths lessons on Thursdays.'

'I'm sure we can see to that,' Eric said.

The sound of the toilet flushing made its way downstairs. A moment later, Yvette appeared on the staircase, baby in her arms.

'I told Katrina to get some sleep,' she said, before Eric could begin to question her. 'I said I'd make some breakfast too.'

'Is she staying?' Abi said, her hand reaching up to brush one of the tiny fingers that peeked out of the swaddling.

'We'll see, darling,' Yvette replied. 'But we need to teach you how to change a nappy, just in case. Now run up to your bedroom and get a towel. We'll have to make do with one of those as we don't have a changing mat. Not that we ever had changing mats in my day, of course.'

'Actually,' Eric said, before Yvette could wheedle any more notions into Abi's head, 'you need to go and get dressed. We've got things to do.'

'We do?'

'We do. We're heading to the allotment.'

Knowing he had serious ground to make up with Abi, not to mention other distractions to consider, it seemed silly not to make the most of the May sunshine and head down to the plot. Eric had no doubts that being in one of the places that brought the family closer together was going to be hard, but if he didn't get on it soon then last year's hard work would all be a waste. While he wasn't even sure if he wanted to continue with the allotment at all at the minute, he did not want to be responsible for passing it on in the same derelict state as he had received it.

'It's going to be a tough day,' Eric continued, searching through the basket by the back door for Abi's gloves. 'The beds haven't been weeded in months and the greenhouse is probably full of rotten tomatoes. I suspect all your spring onions will need to be thrown too.' Having reached the bottom of the basket and having no luck, he tried the junk drawer. When that failed he turned to Abi. 'Do you know where your gardening gloves are?'

'I do, they're in my room. Why?'

'Why? Because I'm looking for them. Well?' he said, still waiting for Abi to move. 'Go and fetch them then.'

Abi didn't move. She stood, fixed to the spot, staring up at her father. Slowly, the edges of her mouth began to twitch, and in less than a heartbeat, she was standing, arms wrapped around her father, grinning. Beside her Lulu barked. Eric took in the moment. A lump had formed in his throat, forcing up what felt like happy tears. Whatever happened for the rest of the day, Eric told himself, this moment would be his memory.

AT THE ALLOTMENT, Eric turned his head from side to side and back again.

'I don't understand,' he said. 'This doesn't make sense.'

Abi bent down, picked up a stray dandelion, then stood up and shrugged.

'It doesn't look too bad,' she said. 'I thought it was going to be like when Grandad died.'

'Yeah,' Eric agreed. 'Me too.'

While his memory had been more than a little bit fuzzy of late, it would have been fair to say that the allotment looked substantially better than it had during his visit the day before. In the greenhouse, the tomato plants had been cut right back, revealing an abundance of ripe fruit. Four of the seven raised beds had been completely dug out, and the remaining three looked like a good weed would see them right, despite the dents inflicted by his outburst the previous afternoon. There even looked to be a bit of viable veg in the mix. Was it really just a day since he'd stood here with Hank? So much had happened.

'Is this courgette ready?' Abi asked, spying the patch just a second after Eric did.

'Looks like it. Snap it off and make a pile.' Eric said. 'And see if you can grab some of those onions too. They look about ready to go.'

'I guess Granny's cooking vegan tonight,' Abi said.

'I guess she is,' Eric laughed. With her head down and hands in the dirt, Eric couldn't help but think how proud Suzy would be at the sight of their daughter. At least that part wasn't a lie. Lulu found a patch of sun beside the greenhouse and took to lying belly up while the others got on with the job in hand. Eric had bought her a pig's ear, and every so often she would roll over and have another gnaw at the disfigured rubbery treat. Slowly his fingers found a rhythm in the earth, the birdsong, the mindless motion of it all. However, twenty minutes later their peace was rudely disturbed.

'Lulu,' Eric said as Lulu jumped to her feet and began barking. 'Stop it. That's far too loud.' He glanced around thinking that perhaps Hank had appeared with Scout, but there was no sign of them. *Doggy sense,* Eric suspected. They were probably walking through the gate, although when he looked back to Lulu, who continued to bark with an unwavering frequency, he saw that her eyes were locked on one place. Norman's, or more accurately and recently, Fleur's, shed. Draped on the outside chair was a pair of tailored women's gardening gloves. Eric's stomach plummeted.

CHAPTER 12

ERIC'S TEMPERATURE WENT from blazing to freezing and back again in the space of ten seconds. His pulse hammered as he turned to Abi, who was now on her feet and walking over to Lulu.

'What is it, girl?' she said. 'What's up?' Abi turned to Eric. 'Do you think she's all right?'

Eric couldn't respond. His eyes were on the shed door, slightly ajar, a slim silhouette moving in the shadows. He would never have come down had he thought there would be any chance of bumping into Fleur. Especially not with Abi. He cursed Yvette. He knew he shouldn't have believed her when she had said Fleur had left. Gone on holiday, perhaps, had enough of Lulu, maybe, but not left-left, the way he had thought – the way he had hoped – that she had gone. And now he was going to have to face her, with Abi right there with him.

Lulu was still barking by his side, tail thumping, and any second she would go leaping into the arms of her former mistress, of Eric's former ... whatever she was. The door shifted open half an inch, then further. He was going to be sick. He was definitely going to be sick.

'Auntie Cynthia!' Abi leapt from the ground and raced across to the neighbouring plot. A moment later and she was lost, enveloped in hugs and kisses. 'You're back. You're back!'

'I am,' Cynthia said, and lowered her to the ground.

Eric blinked. The figure he was staring at, while both a previous allotment owner and a woman, was not the one he had expected to be faced with. And while his chest ached, it was not with anger or fury, but with relief and joy.

'What are you doing here?' He followed Abi's lead and wrapped his arms as tightly around Cynthia as he could. 'I thought you'd moved on after the funeral? Why didn't you say you were back to stay?'

'Well, I did look at moving, but you know, then I got here and it's not a bad place to live. Not really.'

Eric went in for a second hug.

'You should have said. Why didn't you say anything?'

'I was going to. I just wanted to give you a little time. I didn't want to be pestering you.'

'You'd never be pestering. God, am I glad to see you.' A sudden realisation formed in Eric's mind.

'Are you responsible for this?' He indicated to his substantially improved allotment plot. 'Are you the one behind all this?'

She shook her head, modestly. 'I'm just a willing accomplice,' she said.

'Hank?'

She nodded. 'He had a bit of a ring around yesterday afternoon. Said he thought you needed a bit of a hand. Thought you looked like you needed a pick-me-up.'

Eric shook his head in disbelief.

'You didn't have to do that.'

'Don't thank me too much. I stole a couple of your courgettes for my Zucchini bread.' Cynthia winked. 'I wasn't expecting you to come back down here so soon.'

He laughed. Even with a team of them working, it would have taken a good few hours to have cleared the plot as much as they had. That type of thing would never have happened if they were still living in London. It would never have happened to him here a year ago, he knew that from experience.

'Where are you living?' he said. 'Have you got a place to say? We are rather cramped at the house, otherwi—'

'Don't worry, I'm sorted. One of my nieces was looking for a flat mate to help pay the rent.'

'Sounds fun.'

'It is. Movie nights, bowling. I even get invited out clubbing now too,' she said. 'Although I have put my foot down at the suggestion of Tinder. For the time being at least,' she said and winked at Abi, who looked totally bemused by the comment. Eric chuckled. 'And this must be Lulu?' Cynthia bent down to scratch the setter's ears. 'I've heard all about you from Janice.' Her eyes went back up to Eric in a roll. 'I have to say, I'd forgotten how much that woman could talk.'

'You wouldn't believe it, but if anything, I think she's got worse.'

'Oh, I believe it, but I think I might have actually missed it a little bit. And it doesn't half distract you from the weeding.'

Eric tilted his head. 'So, you've been down here a lot?' he said, only now turning his attention to Norman's plot. Fleur's chicken coop was gone and the edges of the beds were considerably straighter than they had been when Fleur was in charge of them. Still, it was surprising to see Cynthia behind the transformation. At Norman's funeral, she had been adamant that she would not be setting foot at the allotment now that Norman was gone.

'I thought you hated the place,' said Eric, teasingly calling her out on her previous comment.

'Hate is a strong word, I'm not sure I would have said—'

'No, I'm pretty sure that you said hate—'

'Hush now, let's not bring up silly things like that.' She laughed as she waved his words away. 'You know what they say; you don't know what you've got until it's gone.'

Eric did. He knew exactly what she meant.

'So, does that mean you've taken the plot?' he said, steering his thoughts away from Suzy.

'I know,' Cynthia spared a moment to glance down and rub Abi's hair. 'I'm a fool and I'm certain Norman's rolling around in his grave with laughter.'

'But how? I thought you had to be on the waiting list?'

'Well, as it turns out, when this woman – Fleur was it? – left, the committee discovered they hadn't actually handed the lease over at all. It seems there had been some very underhanded dealings, I have to say. Nothing like that would have happened under Norman's watch. Anyway, the plot was still in Norman's name. In our name. So, they rang up asked if I wanted to take it back. Turns out I said yes.'

Eric took a moment to consider what she was saying. Abi did not.

'We're neighbours?' she said, jumping up and down on the spot.

'We are.'

'For good?'

'Well, for as long as I've got left,' Cynthia said.

'I can show you all my dancing,' Abi said with glee.

It felt like a significant moment. Watching his daughter bouncing up and down, Lulu barking at her heels, and Cynthia's smile blooming from subtle and delicate to an outright grin. It felt like something good was being rebuilt from the ashes of his ruined life.

'Thank you,' he said, pulling Cynthia into his shoulder.

'For what, you daft fool?'

'For coming back. Thank you for coming back.'

'Well I'm here. Whenever you're ready to talk.'

As it happened, Eric discovered, he was ready.

Cynthia had done some renovating in Norman's shed, turning what was once his shrine to the village show into the perfect little artist's retreat, complete with moveable easel and a stack of storage. It provided an excellent distraction for Abi, who, after an exceptionally good harvest, was showing distinct signs of boredom.

'You paint away, Abi my love,' Cynthia said, settling her down into the seat and pulling out a pad of watercolour paper for her to use. 'And don't worry if you use up any of the colours. There's plenty more at the shops.'

She turned to Eric and opened a small Tupperware box, inside of which was a perfectly baked banana cake. Eric took a slice. The first time he had encountered Cynthia's cake he had been certain it had been poisoned, or at least spiked with something. It was strange to think how much their relationship had changed in less than two years.

'God, you're getting a rough end of it at the minute, aren't you?' she said, when Eric had finished telling her about Katrina and the baby. 'What are you going to do?'

'I don't know,' Eric said. 'To be honest, I think it's all a moot point. She's not going to give her up.'

'I happen to agree with you.'

'You do?'

'Yes,' Cynthia said, placing the lid back on the banana cake. 'I suspect the girl just needed to know that someone's there. That's all.'

'I agree. I just wish Yvette could see that. The baby's only been here a few hours, and she's let herself get attached. Her heart's going to be broken all over again when she goes.'

'And you?' she said, reaching a hand across and taking his. 'How do you feel about it?'

Eric considered the question carefully.

'I think my heart's got enough to deal with at the moment,' he said. Cynthia nodded knowingly.

'I don't want to speak out of turn, but do you mind if I said something about Suzy? About the money and the books?'

Eric shrugged. The likelihood of Cynthia ever saying something completely out of turn was slim to none. 'Go ahead,' he said.

'I suspect she was doing it to protect you. So you didn't feel like you had to worry about money or working.'

A sad chuckle floated in the air between them. 'I know that. It was my first thought too.'

Cynthia smiled with relief. 'So please don't hold it against her. She adored you and Abi. You know she did.'

'I do,' Eric said. 'But that's what makes it so hard. That she felt like she couldn't trust me with this. How could I have held it against her? Honestly?'

Cynthia tutted, although rather than the judgemental, condescending tutting sounds her husband had made, this was contemplative.

'We've all done silly things when we feel like we're backed into a corner. Remember that, Eric. It's a lot easier to see a picture when you're two feet away from it.'

❦

BY EARLY AFTERNOON, Abi had had enough of painting and Eric's stomach was suggesting they all head back for a late lunch.

'Are you sure you don't want to join us?' Eric asked Cynthia for a second time as he took Abi's hand and prepared to leave.

'It's all right,' she said and nodded towards his last two scruffy planters. 'I've got a little more tidying up around here I want to get done first.'

'You don't have to do that.'

'I know I don't.'

Eric placed a hand on her shoulder before reaching in for another hug. 'What would I do without you?' he said.

'You'd be just fine and you know it,' she said.

Abi's hand remained in Eric's for the entirety of the walk home. Her pace was quick, bordering on jaunty, and for the first time in months she seemed to have plenty of topics for conversation.

'I don't understand why everyone's not upside down,' she said. 'Aunty Cynthia showed me her photos and they're not. No one who lived in Australia is upside down.'

'Because that's not the way the world works.'

'But they are on the bottom of the world, right? And the world is round. So they should be upside down?' she reasoned.

'Perhaps that's a question you should ask your teacher,' Eric replied.

Abi hummed thoughtfully.

'She's not that bright,' she said. 'She thought hydroponics were a boat that went over water.'

Eric shook his head in mild amusement wondering how it was that his daughter understood what hydroponics was, but didn't seem to grasp the concept of gravity.

'Try googling it,' he suggested. She took a moment then nodded, clearly happier with that response.

'Will the baby still be at home when we get back?' she said, switching from one topic of conversation to another without a pause. 'Will Granny's pretend friend still be there too?'

Eric chuckled. 'I'm not sure. Maybe, but I'll probably be taking them to the station.'

Abi nodded her head.

'It's a shame you and Mummy didn't have any more babies,' she said.

'Pardon?' Eric stopped quickly, jerking Abi's hand as he did. A flash of shock flickered across her face. 'Why did you say that?' he said. 'What did you hear?'

'Nothing?' Abi shrugged. 'I didn't hear anything. I dunno. I was just thinking that maybe if I had a little brother or sister, I wouldn't miss Mum so much. That's all. I just thought I wouldn't miss her so much then.'

He nodded mutely before finding his own answer to the paradox.

'Maybe there'd be more of us to miss her,' he said eventually.

Any thoughts of an early lunch that Eric had been harbouring were whipped out from under him the moment he stepped into the house. He had barely taken his coat off when Yvette came thundering down the stairs, cheeks flushed, eyes wide.

'Abi, dear,' she said, helping Abi out of her shoes – something she hadn't needed help with for quite some time – 'That bedroom of yours is a tip. There's dog fur everywhere, all over the carpet.'

'I thought—'

'The hoover is already up there for you. Go on. Get upstairs.' Abi looked to her father, but his confusion was equal to her own. He shrugged.

'Granny, I'm not sure I know how to hoov—'

'Just switch it on at the plug and move it around a bit. You'll work it out. Make sure you do it properly though, don't just go over each bit once. You need to go over it plenty of times, make sure you've got it all. Plenty of times, you hear.' She shooed her up the stairs. 'You'll get the hang of it. Keep it going until I tell you when you can turn it off again.'

A moment later, Eric was pushed into the dining room. Baby Mabel lay flat out on her belly, her arms and legs sprawled out at her sides as she grimaced unhappily.

'She doesn't look very happy there,' Eric said, noting the way her mouth and nose twisted continually.

'It's tummy time,' Yvette replied. 'She needs it to build her muscles. She should be practicing lifting her head up.' She pulled the door closed and frowned.

'Yvette—'

'*Shh*,' Yvette said, tilting an ear upwards. She held her head in that manner, ear pointed to the ceiling, only bringing it back down again once she heard the vacuum cleaner whir into life above them.

'Yvette,' Eric said a little more forcefully. 'What is going on?'

'Sit down,' she said. 'And keep your voice down. I don't want her to hear us.'

'Abi?'

'Katrina.'

Yvette gave one more furtive glance towards the door, checking it was shut, then reached around into her back pocket and pulled out several sheets of paper, paper clipped at the corner and neatly folded.

'You need to look at these,' she said.

'What are they?' Eric said.

'I found them,' she said. 'In Katrina's things. You need to have a look.' She spread the papers out on the dining room table. Eric made no attempt to move.

'Yvette, what were you doing going through Katrina's things? And where is she now?'

'*Pff.*' Yvette waved a dismissive hand. 'She's upstairs asleep. And I was looking for some muslin cloths, that's all. Mabel's a very dribbly baby.'

'And those looked like muslin cloths to you?' Eric questioned.

She ignored his comment. 'Look,' she said. 'You need to look at these. You said you don't want to take this baby because it's all just a new mother's whim. Because Katrina giving her up is just a phase. You need to read these. You need to understand.'

Reluctantly he crossed the room and glanced down at the papers.

'What are they?' he said. 'What am I supposed to be looking at?'

Yvette's eyes lifted to meet him, glimmering with a fierceness he thought had gone forever over the last couple of months.

'They're adoption papers,' she said. 'This is an agency. And all the details are already filled in. She meant it. Katrina meant it. She's going to give that little baby away. And if we don't take it, then who the hell will?'

CHAPTER 13

ABI HAD BEEN allowed to stop hoovering her bedroom and instead been instructed to start on the living room and downstairs hallway. Eric had to admit it was a fairly genius idea on Yvette's part. Privacy from a prying nine-year-old's ears and the house cleaned to boot. However, that appeared to be where Yvette's good ideas finished.

Still, Eric was uncomfortable to put it mildly. It felt like he was a lead person involved in an ambush, and while he was certain he should try to do something to stop it, he wasn't sure how.

'What does this mean?' Eric said. 'What difference does it make to us? I'm sure Abi can still get to know her growing up. If that's what we decide to do.'

Yvette shook her head so hard her jowls wobbled.

'It doesn't work like that,' she said. 'If Katrina hands Mabel over to someone else, we will be out of her life forever. Abi will be out of her life forever. They might as well not exist to one another.'

Eric bit at his nails as he scanned up and down the papers. No matter what the situation, baby Mabel was Suzy's sister, and the thought of her being shipped off to some unknown family with no chance of him, or Abi, ever getting to see her again hurt more than he wanted to admit.

'How long has she been napping?' Eric said, jutting out his chin to indicate his reference to Katrina upstairs.

'About an hour I think.' On the carpet, Mabel emitted a small squeak of annoyance at her extended tummy time sentence. Before it could turn into anything more, Yvette swept her up and began bouncing her in her arms. 'Do you think I should go and wake her?'

'Katrina? No,' Eric said with absolute certainty. 'I think you've stuck your nose in enough.'

'I was simply looking—'

'That's enough, Yvette.'

To cope with the silence that followed, Eric began tapping his toe, which matched perfectly with Yvette's pacing.

'I'm going to wake her up,' Yvette said after four lengths of the dining room.

'You are not.'

'It's not good for her to nap for too long. It'll stop her sleeping at night.'

'She's an adult, Yvette. She can sleep as long as she wants to. And if last night is anything to go by, she's not going to get much sleep tonight.'

In the hallway the vacuum stopped. Less than a minute later, the doorway pushed open.

'I'm done,' Abi said, a surprisingly satisfied expression on her face at her accomplishment. 'I hoovered my bedroom and your room and downstairs too. Does this mean I'll get extra pocket money?'

'We shall definitely see about that,' Yvette said, before Eric could comment on their distinct lack of funds.

'Can I have it now?'

'Have what now?'

'The extra money.'

'Not right now, darling.' Yvette said, her eyes still on Mabel.

'But I want to put in my money box.'

'We don't have any money right now, Abs,' Eric interjected.

'But Granny just said—'

Abi's objection was interrupted by another figure appearing behind her.

'So this is where you all are.'

The sleep had done Katrina good. With her bright brown eyes and glossy hair, combined with a baggy T-shirt and tracksuit bottoms, she looked like a new person. A distinctly young one. Eric's eyes went from the baby to her mother. A sad churning shuddered through him.

'Thank you so much for looking after Mabel,' Katrina said to Yvette. 'I really needed that.' She looked down at Abi. 'Did I hear you say you just did all the hoovering? Wow, I don't think I could do that at your age. You'll have to teach Mabel when she's old enough.'

'Well, only if it gets me more pocket money. Dad's being tight.'

'Is that so?' Katrina laughed. She lifted her hand to her mouth, ready to cover a yawn, when halfway there her eyes widened. Her hand froze, four inches from her mouth, trembling.

'What is that?' she said.

Yvette paled. She shifted her feet, trying to block the line of sight between Katrina and the papers sprawled out on the dining room table.

'It's nothing. It's just—'

'You went through my things?' Katrina side-stepping around Yvette. 'You went through my things when I was asleep?'

Eric crossed the room to Abi. Placing his hands on her shoulders, he swivelled her back into the hallway.

'Abs,' he said. 'I just need you to pop upstairs for a minute.'

Abi spun back around and pouted. 'Why? I've only just come down.'

'I know. It's just I need you to go back upstairs.'

Her jaw clenched. Beside her, Lulu barked.

'Or take Lulu outside then,' Eric suggested with a definite curtness to his tone. 'She needs some air.'

Abi refused to move. Her fists clenched and unclenched at her sides.

'Why? Why do I have to leave?'

Eric's own jaw locked in response.

'Because I asked you to.'

'Then I'll do it in a minute.'

'No, you'll do it now, like I asked you to.'

'No, I want to stay here.'

'Lulu needs to go outside.'

'She's been running around at the allotment all morning. She doesn't want to go outside. She wants to rest.' As if understanding exactly what her young mistress was saying, Lulu flopped to the ground. 'See,' Abi said.

Eric's molars ground together. Katrina and Yvette were locked in a staring contest. Yvette's skin had paled to near translucent while Katrina's cheeks were growing redder by the second.

'Abi,' he said, his patience with the lot of them having just about reached breaking point. 'I need you to take Lulu outside now.'

'No.'

'This is not up for discussion.'

'I wan—'

'Stop being such a brat and do as you are told.'

He watched his words burn through her, her eyes quickly brimmed with tears. He wanted to swallow the words back inside, apologise and say he didn't mean it. He knew she wasn't a brat – if anything, she was the one who kept him on the ground – but within a flash she and Lulu had disappeared from the room.

'Abi, wait.'

Eric moved to go after her. Yvette caught him by the hand.

'Give her a minute to cool off.' Eric hesitated. 'Trust me,' she said, relocating Mabel into his arms and rendering him stuck. 'We have other things to deal with.'

'I'll say we have *other things* to deal with.' Katrina's face was like thunder.

Reluctantly Eric stepped back into the room.

'You went through my things,' Katrina said again to Yvette. 'And you let her?' She turned her rage to Eric. 'You let her go through my stuff?'

He jolted backwards, lifting his free hand up in defence. 'I wasn't even here. I had nothing to do with this. I was with Abi. At the allotment. I swear.'

Katrina sniffed, her eyes narrowing on Eric before switching back to Yvette.

'What were you doing in my room?' she said.

Yvette coughed. 'I was trying to see if you had any washing to do,' she said. 'I was trying to be *helpful.*'

'I thought you said you were looking for muslin cloths?' Eric said.

Yvette shot him a glare vicious enough to make him flinch.

'Anyway. That's not the point,' Yvette continued, shimmying her shoulders into a more authoritative posture. 'The point is, what are these?'

Katrina's eyebrows slanted upwards. She snorted at the comment.

'You already know what they are. They're adoption papers.'

'Well what were they doing in your bag then? This says it's from an adoption agency? That you'll be handing the baby over to complete strangers. You didn't say anything about that.'

Katrina stepped back, genuine confusion rippling on her face.

'Why would I? This is none of your business.'

Yvette flushed. She leant forward, pushing her weight down on the table.

'Of course it's our business. You came to us.'

'I came to *Eric* to ask *Eric* if he would adopt her. What do you think I was going to do if he said no? Just carry on the way I was? Just *get on with it,* as you like to put it?'

'Well ... I ...'

'What, you think this was some silly whim? You think that I just needed a good night's sleep? That I just got on a train one morning and thought, why not, let's go see what they say. Maybe I'll get myself a free frozen pizza out of it.'

'I ... I ...' Yvette continued to stutter.

'No, don't you dare try to justify yourself,' Katrina continued. 'I came here in trust. I thought you were trying to help me.'

'I wa—'

Katrina turned to Eric, cutting Yvette's words short.

'What about you?' she said. 'Have you got anything to say about this?'

Eric could feel his body temperature rising everywhere from his toes upwards. He looked at the baby in his arms and tried to figure out what he could say. *Yes,* he wanted to say. *I do have something to say.* But he didn't know what that something was. He wanted to say he was sorry, that much he knew. But what else he wanted to say, he wasn't so sure. Mabel gurgled up from his arms, causing a painful ache to spread through his chest. Suzy's sister. Suzy, who valued her family – no matter what was going on, he knew it was true – more than anything else in the universe, and he was about to cast her away. He wanted to say he would help Katrina, that he would do whatever she needed not to take Mabel away from them, from Abi. He knew he was meant to say something. He could feel that now was one of those moments, those times when what you say could change the whole direction of your life. But the words couldn't seem to form. In fact, no words could form at all. He clamped his mouth shut and shook his head.

'Clearly this is not the type of family I thought it was,' Katrina said, tears rolling downwards to her chin. 'Mabel will be better off with strangers. Better off with people who actually want her.' With that she reached forward, took the baby out of Eric's arms, and marched out the front door. 'I should have known.'

Two hours later and Abi was still refusing to let Eric into her room.

'Please, sweetheart, I'm sorry. Please let me come in and apologise. At least unlock the door. It's not safe like this.' Eric twisted the handle and tried again. She had wedged something underneath the handle, a chair most probably.

'Goddamn it.' Eric cursed Suzy for letting Abi read all those Nancy Drew type escapades that taught her to be so resourceful. She probably had a map with all the underground tunnels of Burlam on in there somewhere, along with a satchel full of hair clips ready to pick locks with. 'You need to eat, Abs. You haven't even had any lunch. Please, Abi, let me in.'

'You understand why I did it, don't you?' Yvette asked, standing beside him, her second glass of wine in her hand. 'You understand why I had to ask?'

'Right now, Yvette, I've got bigger things to deal with.'

'There's nothing bigger than this,' Yvette said.

'Yes,' Eric said. 'There is. My daughter. My actual daughter.'

'I'm not going to let you in. Not ever!' Abi shouted through the door. 'I'll stay in here forever if I have to. I am not opening this door.'

'Fine,' Eric said, and pushed past Yvette and onto the stairs. It was time for a different approach.

At thirty-nine years old, this was officially the first time that Eric had needed to scale a building to gain the attention of a girl he loved. Most of the books or films this happened in involved men half his age, and so he felt perfectly within his rights to use a sturdy, extendable ladder, as opposed to a drain pipe or vine leaves to help reach his goal. Abi's window was at the front of the house which, while offering a nice array of shrubbery should he happen to take a downward tumble, also meant that it was in full display of all the neighbours. He propped the ladder against the wall, securing the bottom beneath the hedgerow. After double, then triple, checking that it was steady, he began to climb.

'Abi,' Eric called through the window, his hands gripping the top of the ladder. 'Abi, sweetheart, please can you let me in?'

From this position he could see the chair, wedged masterfully at an angle beneath the door handle. Abi was on her bed, a familiar photo book in her hand, Lulu curled up by her feet. Eric tried again. He knocked gently on the glass.

'Abi. Please.' Abi's refusal to even bat an eyelid led Eric to assume that she was unable to hear him through the double glazing. Checking his balance, he lifted a hand and rapped a little harder on the glass pane. Abi's head lifted slightly. He knocked again.

'Abi? Please, Abs? Can you open the door?'

With her eyes wide, Abi's head spun around to face the window. For a brief second, her face registered only confusion before switching instantaneously back to anger.

'Go away. I don't want to speak to you.' Her gaze snapped back down to the book on her lap.

'Abi, please. I'm sorry I called you a brat. I didn't mean it. I was just under a lot of stress.'

Her bottom lip jutted out as she continued to stare at the pages of her book.

'Please, Abs. I don't want you to be mad. I climbed a ladder for you. Look. I'm like Romeo?'

'Who?'

'Rom— It doesn't matter. Please, just take the chair away. Open the door and come and get some food. We can talk about it.'

'I don't want to talk to you.' Abi's nostrils flared. Her cheeks glowed with heat. She jumped off the bed and marched across the room to the window.

'Please, Abi,'

'GO AWAY!'

In reality it was probably the surprise that caused Eric to fall, as opposed to Abi's hands striking against the glass – even a fairly strong nine-year-old would have had difficulty creating that much of a wobble.

However, at the time, it didn't look that way. Abi's eyes went from absolute fury to absolute fear in an instant as Eric felt both his hands and feet leave the ladder.

'*Dad!*' Abi shouted, her hand flying to her mouth in a silent scream, that Eric saw right up until the point he hit the ground.

CHAPTER 14

YVETTE HAD INSISTED on calling an ambulance, despite the fact Eric was certain he could stand and walk. He didn't however, deciding instead that lying on the grass and attempting to stifle the pain was better than Abi seeing her father screaming in agony if he discovered he had broken both his legs. It was a bizarre five minutes, listening to his wailing daughter while he stared up at the sky, Lulu's slobbering tongue licking everywhere from his forehead to his toes, while Yvette's flustered instructions repeatedly told him, *Do not move. Don't you dare move.* The neighbours had all appeared, each offering differing advice.

'We should check his airway.'

'His breathing's not a problem. We should put him in the recovery position though. In case he chokes.'

'That might paralyse him.'

'You think?'

'I don't want to risk it. Do you?'

Eric tried to block out the noise and focus only on the approaching sirens. Only when he had been lifted onto the gurney, neck brace in place, did Abi finally manage to speak.

'Don't die, Daddy. Please don't die,' she managed through the sobs as she sat next to him in the ambulance. 'I'm so sorry. I'm so sorry.'

'Abi, I'm fine,' Eric insisted.

'But your neck. That thing on your neck ...'

'It's a precaution,' Eric assured her. 'I promise.' He reached up and found the strap on his neck brace. 'Ow!' he shouted as a searing pain shot through to top of his shoulder. The paramedic leapt up from his seat and placed Eric's hand back by his side.

'Best leave that on until the doc has seen you,' she said.

'It's my fault. It's my fault he fell,' Abi stammered.

'Your daddy is going to be just fine.'

'But, but ...' Abi barely managed to get out a word before she once again dissolved into tears. Ignoring the paramedic's advice, Eric levered himself up to sitting. He twisted around as far as he could before the pain began to show.

'Abi, none of this is your fault.' He sucked in air through his nose, trying to stop his eyes watering. 'Do you understand? None of it. It was an accident.'

'But if I—'

'It was an accident.'

Abi nodded mutely.

'Good,' Eric said, and fell back onto the gurney exhausted.

⁂

'You were lucky,' the doctor said, clipping the X-rays to a mobile lightbox next to the hospital bed and showing Eric the resulting images. 'You could have done some serious damage falling from that height.'

There was no denying that he looked a mess. He had stitches in his ear where a bramble had torn through the top of it and several cuts and bruises around his left eye which could have been a lot worse had they been a fraction higher or lower. Every inhalation felt like he was being impaled by thousands of red-hot needles, and his swollen lip was making it incredibly difficult to talk.

'So, he's not going to die?' Abi said. 'You're sure?'

Her tired frame trembled as she held her father's hand. She had been with him the entire time, having not left Eric's side other than when he had the X-rays taken. During the three short minutes they were separated, he had heard her screaming through the doorway and when he reappeared, she clasped him so hard he thought he had heard yet another of his bones crack.

'No. He's not going to die. Not from the fall anyway.'

'I'm guessing something's broken though?' Eric said, taking a deep breath and causing his eyes to water from the pain.

'Ribs,' the doctor said. 'You've fractured six of them.' She pointed to the various positions on the X-ray. 'It's going to be fairly uncomfortable for a bit while they heal. And you've probably got a mild concussion. There's a bit of bruising around your coccyx too. But other than that, you were exceptionally lucky.' She flicked through the tablet in her hand. 'Falls like this often end a lot worse. What was it you were doing up on the ladder again?'

Eric looked to his daughter. Her skin was grey and her bloodshot eyes once again looked ready for an outpouring. Her lower lip quivered.

'I was just cleaning the window,' he said.

The doctor nodded. 'Well perhaps next time you should pay someone to do that.' She closed the protective cover for the tablet, indicating that their brief consultation had come to an end. 'Are you still set on discharging yourself today?' Eric nodded. 'I seriously advise you stay the night for obser—' This time Eric held up his hand to silence her protests. 'Well, do you at least have someone who can drive you home?'

'My mother-in-law is waiting outside.'

'Then I shan't keep you any longer.' The doctor stretched out a hand ready for Eric to shake. He went to move his own, only to gasp with the pain.

'I'll leave a prescription for some painkillers at the nurses station,' she said.

❧

THE DRIVE HOME from the hospital was silent. Abi fell asleep almost immediately on the back seat, her head flopping against her chin. Sobbing had commenced at seeing Lulu, who had bounded out of the car and into her arms, but it hadn't lasted long. She was drained, physically and emotionally. She wasn't the only one.

'I didn't mean to push things this afternoon,' Yvette said, her eyes on the road as she spoke. 'It's just, there's a bit of Suzy in that baby and I won't let it go without a fight.'

'I know,' Eric said, as he rubbed his ribs. The painkillers had numbed it all to a dull throb, yet he had the sneaking suspicion he was going to need several more to get through the night.

'It feels like fate,' Yvette said. 'Like this terrible thing happened to us, but something good will come from it. Something we didn't even think was possible.'

Eric didn't believe in fate and neither did Suzy. 'Too many bad things happen to good people,' she would say, and it was hard not to agree.

'We're a mess, Yvette. What makes you think we could bring a baby into this?'

'What makes you think we couldn't? Katrina said she wanted Mabel brought up in a family that loved her. Isn't that what counts the most?'

'Sometimes love just isn't enough.'

The rest of the journey they sat in silence. Eric rested his head against the window and shut his eyes, pretending to be asleep. Norman had told him something on one of their drives out in Sally. He had told Eric how his father had always closed his eyes when someone else was driving the car. That way, according to Norman, George could always imagine it was Eric driving the car. Until that moment, Eric had assumed it was nonsense; some sentimental tosh created by Norman to try to soften Eric's feelings towards his late father. But just then, with his thoughts dazed from the painkillers and overwhelmed by the events of the previous twenty-four hours, Eric let himself believe, just a little, that it was Suzy behind the wheel.

Only when they came out of the bends and drove past the *Welcome to Burlam* sign did he sit back up and take note of their surroundings. Yvette moved to turn on the indicators.

'Actually,' he said. 'Can you go straight on? I want to go to the station.'

'The station, why?'

'Just a hunch,' he said.

With her eyes still on the road, Yvette nodded and clenched the steering wheel a fraction tighter.

The engine had been switched off, and the inside light of the car turned on to compensate for the darkness. Eric had been resting against the door handle from the moment Yvette had pulled into the carpark, but so far, he had failed to move. From their position in the car he could see the silhouette of the pair, slowly rocking back and forth through the waiting room window.

'Do you want me to wait for you?' Yvette said.

Eric shook his head. 'I'll be fine.'

'It's a bit of a walk.'

'I'll be fine,' he repeated.

'You should probably get moving. She could be getting this one.'

Eric turned his head to the side. In the distance, he could see a blinking of lights moving behind the trees. Yvette was right; if she got on the train now, he would end up losing Mabel forever. Finally, he mustered the courage to step out of the car although discovered his fears were unfounded. As the train pulled to a stop, a handful of passengers disembarked. Katrina, however, remained in the waiting room.

Still standing outside, Eric rested his weight against the wall, watching as Katrina returned Mabel to her pram and rocked it back and forth with one foot while she scrolled through her phone. He should turn around and leave, he thought to himself, clenching his eyes closed as a spasm of pain darted down his side. How could he even think it was a good idea, messing with all their lives like this? But their lives were already messed up, far more than he would ever have anticipated. What difference would it make, adding one more spanner into the works? Gritting his teeth and hoping that the painkillers didn't wear off before he got home, Eric opened the door to the waiting room.

'You're still here?' he said.

Katrina's eyes turned towards him only fleetingly before returning to the phone on her lap. Her eyes were red rimmed, as was the skin around her finger nails. Any benefit she had gained by her extra sleep earlier in the day had faded.

'I left my things at the house,' she said, still looking at her phone as she spoke. 'My wallet and stuff. I went to get them, but no one was in. Can't buy a train ticket if you don't have any money.'

'Yeah, we had a bit of an incident.'

He waited for her to look up or ask for clarification. When neither happened, he hesitated, then moved himself to sitting.

'Shit!' He gasped in pain. Having cracked ribs apparently made it difficult to move every other bone in his body too, including his feet and knees. Katrina's head lifted from her phone. Her eyes widened, only to return to her screen less than a second later.

'What happened?' she said, attempting to maintain an ambivalent and uninterested air.

'Like a said, a bit of an incident.'

She shrugged.

'I was pretty lucky actually,' Eric continued. 'It could have been a lot worse.'

'Oh.'

What followed was an impenetrable silence, broken only by the buzz of the game on Katrina's phone, which she had left playing despite the fact her fingers were now motionless. Suzy could be like this, Eric recalled. She would never speak after an argument, not until she had considered every angle and found her own peace with all the possibilities. Trying to force her into talking only ever ended badly. Now he wished he'd forced her to talk more. There were undoubtedly things he and Suzy had needed to talk about.

'The train arriving at platform two will be the 18.12 to Liverpool Street.' The tannoy system sawed through the silence. 'Please stand away from the edge of the platform.'

Outside, the platform remained empty. The rumble of the train rattled the lines from the distance. When the train appeared, a handful of people exited. None, that Eric saw, got on.

'What are you doing here?' Katrina said, finally speaking. 'Did you bring my stuff?'

'No,' Eric said. 'I was just hoping we could talk.'

'Why?'

'Because I think we need to.'

'About what?'

'About Mabel.'

Katrina's bottom lip disappeared beneath her teeth. The screen to her phone had now gone black, although she continued to clutch it in her hand. Eric turned his gaze to Mabel. She had kicked the blanket off one side of her body and five tiny toes twitched as she slept. Eric went to replace the blanket, only to recall his difficulty in moving.

'From what I can see,' Katrina placed her phone down on the bench beside her, 'we don't have anything to talk about.'

'I believe we do.'

'Why?' The sound of sniffed back tears echoed in the small chamber of the waiting room. 'I expected some degree of respect,' she said, speaking through the snivels. 'Maybe I don't deserve it. Maybe you just see me as some stupid kid who got themselves knocked up. But I just thought, from everything I'd heard about you and Suzy—'

'Suzy's gone, remember,' Eric said. Katrina nodded mutely.

'I get that. I do. But coming to see you, it wasn't easy. Facing Vetty, after what I did. Can you even imagine how hard that was for me?'

'I can.'

'We used to be good friends, Vetty and I, back on the ship. Did you know that?' Eric shook his head, but it did explain why Yvette was so hurt. It wasn't just Philip's betrayal she'd had to contend with. 'I didn't want to come,' she continued. 'I didn't want to. And I'd have signed Mabel over to the adoption agency already, really, I was going to. Only, I wanted her to be part of a normal family. I wanted her to have that chance. You hear horror stories, you know, about kids who get lost in the system. Kids who fall in and out of foster homes, end up on the street, that type of thing. And I couldn't bear to think of that happening to Mabel. I wanted her to be with her family.' For the first time she lifted her gaze away from her knees and up to meet Eric's. 'I love my daughter, Eric,' she said. 'It might not seem like it to you. It might not look like that, but believe me, if I thought there was any chance I could keep her, and keep her happy, I would do that in a heartbeat. But I can't, I know I can't. That doesn't mean I don't love her. I am doing this because I love her.' Two tears trickled down her cheeks. Eric desperately wanted to wipe them away.

Eric sighed heavily on both the inhale and the exhale, both of which resulted in a painful throbbing around his chest.

'I know that.'

'You're only here because you don't want her to go off to strangers,' Katrina continued. 'If I said I was keeping her, or giving her to my mum, you wouldn't care then, would you? I heard you last night, listing all the reasons you weren't going to take her.'

'Maybe you're right,' he said. 'All those things I said last night, they're true.' Katrina's bottom lip disappeared back under her teeth. Eric continued. 'I'm not even sure that me taking her on will be a good idea. I'm not in a good place right now, none of us are. It would mean another disruption for Abi, and she is struggling at the minute. More than I realised.'

'I understand.'

'And this isn't something you could change your mind about. If you handed Mabel over, you wouldn't be able to come back in five years and demand to take her back. You would be giving up your right to her. You would be giving up your right to be her mother.'

'I get it. I do.' The tears had multiplied now. Try as she might, she couldn't wipe them away fast enough. 'I understand what you're saying.'

'No,' Eric shook his head a fraction of a turn. 'I don't think you do.' He inhaled as he tried to figure out the words to explain his feelings. 'This afternoon, after you left. I fell off a ladder.'

'Oh?' Katrina made no attempt to hide her smirk.

'I did, and I was lucky. But something serious could have happened to me. I realised that on the way to the hospital. If something ever happened to me, where would that leave Abi? She has no siblings. She would have no one to talk to about silly things her parents did when she was little. No person to visit on Christmas Eve.' He paused in preparation for sharing more of his soul than he was ever normally comfortable with. 'Suzy always used to talk about Abi having a sibling. She wanted another child, I know she did, but she found the pregnancy hard. After Abi was born, too. She hid it well, but it was hard. She struggled with talking about it. For a while there, she wasn't the wife I used to know. Maybe if I'd been a better husband I would have made her see someone, but I didn't. I ignored it. Did a few extra hours at the office, waited for the moment to pass. Which it did, eventually. But I didn't want to put that on her again. I didn't want to go through that again. So, every time talk of having another one came up, I told her I was happy with one. That we were a perfect family of three, and it was best not to upset things. But now I realise I was wrong. I've been wrong a lot.'

In her pushchair, Mabel began to grizzle. Eric reached down and placed her dummy back in her mouth.

'What are you saying?' Katrina said, a mixture scepticism and fear on her face. 'Are you saying that you'll do this? You'll adopt my baby?'

Eric fixed his eyes on Mabel's porcelain skin. Her lips twitched ever so slightly as she breathed, the tiny gust of air fluttering the edge of her blanket.

'I need to have a couple of conversations first,' Eric said. 'But yes, I think I am. I think I want to keep this baby.'

※

THE FIRST CONVERSATION went exactly as Eric expected.

'Yes, yes, yes, yes, yes. *Yes!*'

'So that's a yes then?'

'Definitely!' Abi bounced up and down on her bed swinging her arms above her head. 'I'm going to have a sister. I'm going to have a sister,' she sang, bouncing higher and higher with every rebound.

'Look,' Eric said, trying to rein in a little of her excitement. 'It's not going to be easy. Having a little brother or sister, it's hard work. They'll take up a lot of my time, and Granny's. You won't get to have your own way so much. And they cry a lot. And they stop you sleeping and they'll take all your toys.'

Abi's mask of excitement flickered. 'All of them?'

'Well, not all of them, but they might break one or two.'

Abi scratched her eyebrow thoughtfully. 'I'll just give her the ones I don't really like.'

Eric reached up to pull her down, only to wince at the pain. Concern flashed across Abi's face.

'I'm fine,' he assured her. 'I just need you to sit down and listen for a minute.' Substantially sedated at the sight of her father in pain, Abi sat back down on the bed.

'I need you to think about this carefully,' Eric said taking her hand. 'And I need you to tell me the truth. If you're finding things difficult at school still, or you don't think—'

'Dad,' Abi moved to place a hand on Eric's shoulder, before remembering and drawing it away. 'I understand. I do. It's going to be hard. You're going to be grumpy when she keeps you awake at night, and I probably won't get half as many new toys as I used to, but I think it's what Mum would want.'

Eric rested his hand on hers. 'You know what, I agree. But you're going to have be so grown up, and I don't know if it's fair to do that to you.'

'It's fine, Dad. I'll be fine.'

'What if you're not?'

'Then I'll talk to the counsellor. That's what he's there for, right?'

Eric removed his hand from hers and placed it instead against her cheek.

'When did you get so wise?' he asked.

So far, all was going perfectly to plan.

CHAPTER 15

'YOU CAN'T ADOPT the baby, it's not legally possible.' Eric's second meeting wasn't going quite as well as his first. He had been running late and forgotten to take his medication, and his brain was beginning to fog beneath a haze of pain. The bad news was taking longer to compute than expected.

'Are you sure?' he said.

'I'm sure.' Eaves crinkled up his nose and nodded his head as he spoke, indicating the ridiculousness of Eric doubting his statement. He was certain. This type of thing was his job. 'In the US, this whole private adoption thing is completely normal. Mums can even decide on who they are going to give the baby to before it's born.'

'But that's not possible here?'

'I'm afraid not.'

'Even if she's our relative?'

'But she's not, is she?'

They were meeting in the back room of the Shed. Since first encountering Christian Eaves, he had discovered that the lawyer much preferred to do business over a full English with a side of black pudding and a long white. Eric, who hadn't had much of an appetite these last few days, opted only for a bacon butty and cappuccino, but without the painkillers, simply lifting his hand to eat or drink was far from comfortable.

'So, what do we do? What's our next course of action? What if she hands the baby over to one of the adoption agencies and then we try to take her from there, would that work?'

Eaves shook his head. 'This process can take months, if not years, and you're not even in the system yet. There will be countless people ahead of you. Particularly with such a small baby. I think that would be an extremely poor decision.'

'Then what? What can we do to keep this baby?'

Eaves expelled the air from his lungs with an impressive amount of force.

'Your best bet would be to register as foster parents. You're not the baby's grandparents, so you can't take her into your care legally without being a registered foster parent first.'

'And how long will that take?'

'Normally about six months.'

'Six months?'

'But we might be able to push it through a bit faster, given the situation. To be honest, this is a little out of my expertise, but I'll give you my wife's details. She's a family lawyer.'

'She is?'

'Yup. Heads up one of the big firms in Chelmsford while I stick around here dealing with unpaid parking tickets and disputes over whose land a fence post is on. You're not the only one who's a kept man in the village.' His hand rose to his mouth as he realised his mistake. 'I'm sorry, Eric, I wasn't thinking.'

'It's fine.' Eric waved the apology away with a result of considerable pain. Fortunately, it stopped him thinking about the semantic of the matter too greatly. He had come to a decision that previous night, after a conversation with Yvette about Mabel and Abi and, of course, Suzy. He couldn't blame her for hiding the fact about the books. Chances are he would have done the same to try to protect her from the worry. For a little while at least. 'I forget she's gone half the time myself,' he told Eaves. 'I can hardly blame other people for making the same mistake.'

'Still.' Eaves grimaced apologetically.

'All right,' Eric said, his mind turning over all the information that he had just heard. 'But three months is still a long time. What happens in the meantime? What are we supposed to do? The girl's not in a good way, I can't imagine she'll take kindly to us telling her she needs to wait it out for another twelve weeks. And that's hardly fair on the baby, either.'

Eaves speared a piece of sausage.

'Well,' Eaves said, the fork hovering inches from his mouth. 'Do you have a spare bedroom?'

※

'They're going to live here?' Abi bounced up and down on the sofa as Eric disseminated the news. 'I'm going to get a big sister too?'

'We need to talk through a few things first,' Eric said.

'But they're both going to live here?'

'Quite possibly.'

'No,' Yvette said, having paced the length of the room at least a dozen times in a minute. 'There has to be another way.'

'It won't be forever,' Katrina replied to Abi. 'I won't be staying forever.' She turned to Eric. 'That's the maximum, right? I won't have to be here any longer than that? After that I can go?'

'Eaves reckons so, although we'll have to talk it through with his wife.'

'Surely there must be some other way,' Yvette directed her question solely to Eric. 'This can't be the best solution. It's ridiculous.'

'We're not related to the baby.'

'As good as. I can't believe she has to stay with us too. There has to be some other way.'

'If there was, the solicitor would have said, wouldn't he?' Katrina responded.

'Well perhaps we need to find another solicitor,' Yvette snapped back.

The tension was rising to a palpable level.

'Abi, darling,' Eric said, waving his arm to get Abi's attention, 'I think your room—'

'No.' Abi stopped bouncing at once and folded her arms across her chest. 'I am not going to go up to my room.'

'I thought perhaps Lu—'

'I am not going to take Lulu into the garden either,' she added. 'And I am not going to vacuum the whole house so that I miss out on everything you lot are talking about. I live here too. This is my home too. I deserve to know what's going on.'

All eyes turned to Eric.

'Abs. It—'

'I'm right, aren't I?' Abi said, with an authority that would have made her mother glow with pride. 'You wanted me to be a grown up about this. You said I would have to be. Well that means that you have to treat me like a grown up too. You can't just cut me out when you don't want me to know something. That's not fair.'

She placed her hands on her hips, eyebrows raised as she waited for an answer.

Eric offered one slow and deliberate nod. Like him, the other adults were looking at his daughter with an impressed mixture of awe and shock.

'You are right,' Eric said. 'You should know what's going on. But right now, I don't know. None of us know. That's why *we*, the *adults*, need to have a conversation about it.'

Eric watched his daughter flush with anger.

'I deserve to—'

'As soon as any decisions are made, you will be the first person to know.'

'No.' She shook her head, hands still on her hips. 'That's not good enough.'

'Abi.' It was Katrina's voice, louder and surprisingly more commanding than normal, that spoke next. 'Why don't we both go out into the kitchen? You, me, and Mabel. That would give me a chance to tell you what's going on, and I can answer any questions you might have. And it would give the adults a chance to discuss what the solicitor said.'

'You're an adult too,' Abi said, not quite ready to fall into some well-laid trap.

'Not really,' Katrina said. 'In fact, I'm pretty sure we wouldn't be in this state if I'd known how to behave like an adult in the first place.' She waited, studying the flickers of consideration as they worked across Abi's expression. 'What do you say? Would that be okay? Then we can come back and tell your dad and granny what we've talked about. Would that work?'

Once again she waited, holding Abi's gaze the whole time. After shooting a quick glare at Eric, Abi sniffed and then nodded.

'Okay, but I get to stay when you're talking to Dad and Granny next time, right? I am not being shut out of the room again.'

'Agreed,' Katrina said. 'You are not being shut out of the room again.'

'Agreed?' she said, turning the response into a question for her father.

Eric pursed his lips. He opened his mouth to object when a gentle voice rattled through his ears. *She's growing up, Eric.* Suzy's voice came through so clearly she could have been standing next to him. *You can't treat her like a baby forever.* Whether Suzy had ever said those particular words to him before, he couldn't be sure. But she had said similar and of the same sentiment, of that he was certain.

'I will not,' he began, 'shut you out of these conversations, unless—'

'No—'

'Unless your granny and I *both* agree it's a good idea.'

Abi's lips projected in a pout.

'But—'

'That's it,' Eric said. 'That's the best you're going to get. If your granny and I both think the conversation is too grown up, you can't be there.'

Abi's eyes went from her father, to Yvette, and eventually Katrina, who nodded forcefully.

'It's a good deal, Abs,' she said. 'I'd take it.'

Abi's pout remained. 'Fine,' she said. 'But if I find out you've been having secret meetings when I've gone to bed—'

'We won't,' Katrina assured her. 'If it's important, we'll wake you up.'

Finally, Abi looked satisfied with the response. She turned to Katrina.

'We should get talking,' she said. 'I have a lot of questions.'

The two girls slipped out of the living room door. In a flash, Yvette was back on her feet.

'You can't seriously be considering this. You can't be.'

Eric reached into his pocket and pulled out a blister packet of painkillers. He was trying to keep track of how many he took a day, although today, despite the fact it was barely midday, he had already lost count.

'Of course I'm serious. What else would you have me do?'

'Living here? You would have her living here, in this family, with us?'

'Yvette, it wouldn't be permanent. And you seem to be missing the point. If we want this baby in our family, this is the only thing we *can* do.'

Yvette shook her head. 'I refuse to believe it. Can't she stay somewhere close? In a hotel or something?'

'For three months? On whose money? We're barely making ends meet as it is. Yvette, you were the one who pushed for this. You were the one who begged me to come around to the idea of taking on this baby, and now I'm on board and I'm telling you that this is the only way possible.'

'I will not live under the same roof as that woman,' Yvette said.

'You'll have to,' Eric replied. 'If you want this baby to be part of this family, that's the only option you've got.'

CHAPTER 16

THE FIRST WEEK of cohabitation went better than expected on several fronts. Lulu had absolutely no issues with the new family additions and would frequently be found – particularly when Abi was at school – curled up in a ball next to Mabel's swing seat. Abi had come back from school each day singing – along with glowing feedback from her teacher on what a positive improvement she was showing. And, despite all the odds, Yvette and Katrina had managed to find a state of existence in which they were reasonably pleasant to one another – at least in Eric's earshot. It probably helped that Katrina spent eighty per cent of the time shut up in Eric's room and the other twenty per cent talking loudly on the phone about all the things she was missing. More than once she had burst into tears in front of Eric or Abi, although the triggers could be as varied as not being able to change channel on the television to worrying that her whole life was an utter failure.

'She's homesick,' Eric reminded Yvette several times.

'Like that's our fault. She should at least try to show a little gratitude,' Yvette huffed. 'All she does is sit about all day watching television and crying, yet somehow she makes more washing than Mabel.'

'Didn't you offer to do her washing for her?' Eric questioned. Yvette pouted and dug her hands into her pockets.

'Well that's hardly the point, is it?'

THE INITIAL MEETING with Helen Eaves – the family lawyer, who appeared to be far too intelligent, sophisticated, and elegant to be related to Christian Eaves in any way, let alone married to him – went well. Very well.

'I see no major issues as to why we can't push this through in the next twelve weeks. We'll need character references; neighbours, work colleagues, and a list of family members who Mabel is likely to be in day-to-day contact with, but from the looks of this you have a fairly strong case.'

'Even though I'm not directly related to her?'

'I don't think it will be too much of an issue. How is she coping living in the house with you?'

'I don't think it's her ideal situation, but she's coping,' Eric said.

'That's good.'

'And how are you coping with things?'

'Me?'

Helen rested her chin on her fingertips. 'I'm going to be blunt. Any judge is going to be impressed seeing how well you're managing this after all you've been through.'

'I ...'

'Losing your wife, taking on her father's child. To be honest, you're pretty much a hero in my eyes right now.'

Eric grinned. After everything they had suffered in the last couple of months, it was good to hear something positive.

'What about finances?' she added, just as Eric prepared himself to leave.

'Finances?'

'You'll need to be able to show that you can afford to take on another one. But judging by where you've come from, that shouldn't be too much of an issue.'

A dry, sandpaper-esque feeling lodged itself in Eric's throat.

'No,' he said, offering the widest smile he could manage. 'That shouldn't be an issue at all.'

'How much is that?' Yvette said, flipping over the price tag of the brand-new car seat Eric had decided he wanted to invest in. 'Can't you find a cheaper one? The trolley's already full.'

'It's got all the best safety ratings,' Eric told her. 'And she can stay in it until she's six. It's a necessity. And it's non-negotiable,' he reinforced. 'Unlike ... what is that you're holding?'

Yvette rolled her eyes.

'It's a tummy time roll. To strengthen her muscles. You don't want her growing up with a flat head, do you? It could lead to developmental delays.'

'Can't we just use a kitchen roll instead?' Eric said. 'I'm sure it would do exactly the same thing.'

Yvette glowered.

'Fine.' He sighed and plucked another item from the trolley. 'But do you really need these? What are they?'

'Black and white stimuli. The last thing we want is for her to struggle making attachments because we didn't buy her the right toys.'

'If she wants black and white stimuli, she can look at some of my bank statements. There's red on there as well to help stimulate her.'

Yvette frowned.

'No more toys,' Eric insisted. 'Essentials only from now on. Think. What else do we need? Cynthia said one of her nieces has got a stroller for when she's a bit bigger. And they've got a crib she can give us now.'

Yvette's eyes rose the heavens. 'You can't put a baby in a used crib, Eric. Do you not read any of the research? It's an absolute disaster waiting to happen.'

'That's nonsense. Abi had a second-hand crib that came from the boys and she's absolutely fine. And like you said, Suzy and Lydia slept in a drawer.'

'That was then. We put whisky in their milk too, for goodness' sake. It's a miracle they both survived.'

There was a moment of silence when it felt like the world might imploded in on them. Around them, happy couples picked up neutral coloured baby grows and pressed hands against swollen bellies. Yvette's lips began to quiver with the realisation of her words. Eric leant on the trolley and sighed.

'Well we're not getting them now,' he said pushing the mood away with his words. 'I can't lift another thing.' He placed a hand against his ribs to emphasis his point.

'Fine,' Yvette replied quickly in an attempt to avoid the tension returning. 'We've still got plenty to get though. We need nappies, gripe water, wet wipes. New dummies, a steriliser ...'

Eric groaned and turned over the unending list.

The decision to apply for a new credit card had come almost immediately after the decision to adopt a new child. While Eric had managed to secure a couple of freelance consultancy jobs through Jack, those weren't until next month, meaning that payday was still a long, long way off. Summer holidays were little more than a month away, and with Yvette's dance classes becoming more and more popular with each passing week, it didn't make sense for Eric to look for anything permanent until Abi went back in September.

'Right, then,' Yvette said, passing Eric his wallet back after burning a considerable sized hole it in. 'Next stop, Boots the chemist.'

BACK AT THE HOUSE, Abi was in full big sister mode, showing Mabel all her favourite dance outfits and teaching her the difference between a single buffalo and a shuffle move.

'She hasn't left her side,' Hank told them, having volunteered for babysitting duty the moment he heard Eric's news. 'She even changed her nappy.'

'Let's hope that's a habit that sticks.'

Eric had considered asking Katrina to watch over the pair for a couple of hours while they shopped, but had quickly decided against. While Abi's wish of a little sister was looking more promising by the day, her optimism over an older one had been quickly snuffed out. Other than when she appeared to raid food from the fridge, she saw little of Katrina. Mabel still slept in the room with her, although more often than not it was Yvette who got up to do the late-night feeds. Hence it was more than a surprise to see her bounding down the stairs to help with the shopping.

'Did you get everything you need?' she said taking the bags from Eric and marching through the house with them. 'It looks like there's loads here.'

'I think we got everything, *literally everything*,' he said, massaging his ribs as he followed her into the kitchen. 'Formula, nappies, more formula, more nappies.'

Katrina dumped the bags on the kitchen table.

'I don't suppose you managed to pick up those other things, did you?' she said.

Eric frowned, scanning the mountain of plastic and paper in front of him.

'In that bag, I think,' he said, managing to flex one finger towards a piece of plastic. 'I'm fairly sure I got everything you asked.'

Having abandoned the rest of the things, Katrina sifted through and peered inside.

'You are a star,' she said, pulling out several items before replacing them and picking up the entire bag. 'What would I do without you?' Reaching up on her tiptoes she kissed him lightly on the cheek before spinning on the spot and disappearing upstairs.

Behind him, Yvette coughed. Eric felt his cheeks colour.

'We should get on with putting this lot away,' he said, avoiding his mother-in-law's glare. 'Hank,' he called through. 'You fancy a cup of tea?'

◊◊◊

'What was that about?' Yvette asked later, when Hank had left, and Abi was attempting to explain to Mabel the subtleties of playing Top Trumps.

'What was what about?' Eric replied.

'Those things? *You,* buying gifts for *her.*'

'Hardly *gifts,*' Eric said, opening the fridge and fixing himself a ham sandwich. 'She just asked me to pick her up a few things: shampoo, deodorant. Stuff.'

'And is she going to pay you back?'

'I don't know. I doubt it. It's not like she has any money.'

'Well how much did it cost?'

'I didn't look.'

With a terse sucking noise, Yvette's eyes scanned across the room. Eric waited for the next comment.

'What?' he said, a full minute later when she was still staring pointedly with her eyebrows raised and lips twisted. 'You might as well say whatever it is you're thinking.'

'I'm not thinking anything.' Yvette pouted.

'Good,' Eric said, taking another slice of ham from the packet before laying the rest out on the buttered bread. He finished with the top slice of bread, then picked the whole thing up. 'Then I'm going to eat my—'

'I don't think it's a very good idea.' Yvette placed her hands on the table in front of her. Eric put his sandwich back in the plate.

'What isn't a good idea?'

'Buying her gifts. It doesn't look good.'

'I wasn't buying her gifts. I was buying her sanitary towels. And who's it going to look bad to, exactly?'

Yvette shimmied her shoulders. 'To the lawyers. Social services. It might look like we're trying to bribe her into giving us the baby or something.'

'That's ridiculous.' Eric turned towards the kettle and winced. He had never fully appreciated the role his ribs played in practically every aspect of his existence before now, and he was certain he would never take them for granted again.

'You'd rather I hadn't bought her them? Is that what you're saying?'

Yvette tutted into her peppermint tea.

'She's getting her feet under the table. You mark my word, she's playing you. She sleeps in your bedroom for goodness' sake.'

'While I sleep on the sofa.'

'Exactly.'

Eric sighed. The ham sandwich sat longingly on the table. His stomach was already growling. However, instead of reaching for it, he moved around the kitchen table, wrapped his arms around his mother-in-law, and kissed her on the top of her head.

'Look, the lawyer is happy. Katrina is staying out of your way. We've got this.'

'You don't know what she's like.'

'Then it's a good job I've got you to keep an eye on her, isn't it?' Eric kissed her on the head again and gave her his best sheepish grin.

Yvette shuffled as she tried to keep her glare in place, but her pout loosened ever so slightly.

'I'm watching her,' she said.

※

WEEK TWO MARKED a considerable milestone for Eric in terms of parenting although it hadn't come without its nerves.

'I still don't know if this is a good idea,' he said, his pulse already battering his ribs with alarming ferocity. 'We should give it a couple more days. Let her get more used to me.'

'You're being silly,' Yvette insisted. 'You were fine all last night with her.'

'That's because Abi was here. And we were in the house.'

'You're only going to be alone with her for ten minutes.'

'But what if she cries? I can barely pick her up.'

'It's a two-minute drive.' Yvette clipped the straps of the car seat in around Mabel before closing the door and stepping back from the car. 'You have everything you need. There's milk and nappies in the bag. And Abi knows which of her cuddly toys to give her if she starts grizzling.'

Eric counted to three as he took a deep breath in. It was a very cultured first outing; he was meeting Cynthia at the library for *Children's Hour*. Yvette was going to pick Abi up from school and drop her off before heading back for her dance class; that way Eric wouldn't have to keep getting Mabel in and out of the car and risk hurting himself. Driving with a new-born in the car when feeling less than on par did not feel like an auspicious start. He had also skipped his painkillers on the pretext that he did not want them to affect his reactions in the car. Katrina had gone for a long run, which, along with watching Netflix and old dance videos of herself, appeared to be her favourite hobby.

'Just take your time,' Yvette said. 'Take as long as you need.'

'Don't worry,' Eric replied. 'I will.'

Eric couldn't help but laugh at himself as he drove up the road in his orange kiddie wagon at thirty miles an hour letting everything from tractors to cyclists overtake him. Oh, how times had changed. When he arrived at the library, he checked on Mabel in the rear-view mirror before swallowing two of his painkillers and dropping his head down onto the steering wheel. A bang on the bonnet quickly brought him up.

'They're going to start soon,' Cynthia said, then raised her handbag and added, 'I brought us snacks.'

※

THE BOOK READING didn't go so well. Only four other children were present, all toddlers, who ran around chasing one another and refusing to sit down. Mabel managed to smush her hand into Cynthia's piece of apple pie when Eric wasn't watching and mashed it into the carpet, only to have one of the toddlers slip on it and go careering into the newly curated book display. Finally, a disgruntled librarian cornered off part of the room for them, making sure she pointed out the *no food* notice *en route*.

'She is beautiful,' Cynthia said, resting Mabel on her knees and blowing raspberries on her tummy. 'Is it me, or does she look just like Abi when she smiles?'

'That's what I thought,' Eric agreed. 'It's a bit scary. She loves Abi though. The pair of them, already, they're thick as thieves.'

'And she's sleeping okay?'

Eric waved his hands back and forth. 'Better than some of us. At least she has her own bed.'

Cynthia tilted her head and frowned. 'Have you still not got that sorted yet?'

Eric's gaze dropped guiltily to the ground. Katrina had been using the house as a bed and breakfast in between trips up to London for dance auditions and two-hour runs that Eric suspected only got as far as the local wine bar, but he still felt bad about turning her out onto the sofa. She was, after all, Mabel's mother, and the arrangement wasn't forever. Then there was the issue with Suzy's study.

'It's ridiculous.' Eric brushed some more pie crumbs off Mabel's hand before she deposited them in her mouth. 'I know it is. But I can't change her study. That room was her soul, as soon as I start messing with it that's it, she's gone forever. And I just can't do it. Not yet.'

'Speaking as someone who knows,' Cynthia said. 'It won't get easier with time. You're better off going up there when you get back, throwing everything you don't want to keep into a black bag, and sending it down to the charity shop. At least that way you'll have somewhere to sleep.'

'Maybe.' Eric chewed it over.

'At least get a pull-out bed for the girl to sleep on so you can have your bed back.'

'Perhaps you're right.'

'You know I am. Now if you want some help with the lifting, you just let me know.'

'Thank you,' he said. 'I will.'

ABI CAME and joined them at three-thirty. Within fifteen minutes, she'd signed Mabel up for a library card, withdrawn half a dozen books in her name, and had sat down on one of the oversized bean bags with her head buried between the pages of a book.

'She gets more and more like her mother every day,' Eric said, not sure if the comment made him happy or sad.

Mabel had had two grizzly moments, once when she needed milk and once when she needed her nappy changed, both of which Eric had handled with extreme deftness. Over the last two weeks he had mastered methods of managing the soreness from his ribs. These included burping Mabel on his shoulder, changing her on tables or sofas, and only picking her up if he knew he wasn't going to have to put her down again in less than ten minutes. He had also realised that while a large pushchair was incredibly helpful when it came to loading up the food, trying to push it up the hill on the way back was not worth the effort.

'I guess it's like riding a bicycle,' he said, pulling the Velcro tabs of her nappy back in place and fixing the poppers on her baby grow. 'Although it smells significantly worse.'

'I like riding my bicycle,' Abi replied, taking a moment to lift her head up from her book and join in the conversation. 'I do not like poop.'

By the time they headed home it was nearly six, and they had been out of the house for over two hours. Eric unclipped Mabel, handing her to Abi so that he could open the front door.

'It smells like Granny's been cooking,' she said as she waited for Eric to find the key. 'Do you think she's made meatloaf again? I already have leftover meatloaf in my lunch box.'

'I don't think so,' Eric said, opening the door and stepping back so Abi could go in. 'This smells good. Really good. Not that Granny's veggie meatloaf doesn't,' he added hurriedly with a substantially raised voice. 'Your granny's meatloaf is delicious.'

'She can't hear you,' Abi said, handing Mabel back to him so that she could take off her shoes. 'She'll be in the kitchen.'

The house was a menagerie of aromas, full of savoury tannins that resulted in the immediate production of saliva.

'I'm in the kitchen,' a voice called as the front door clicked closed.

Eric and Abi exchanged a look.

'Katrina?'

Tentatively, the pair made their way through the house. The table was laid and a series of pans bubbled away on the hob.

'I thought it was probably time I did something to help,' Katrina said.

A moment later and the click of the front door went again, this time announcing Yvette's arrival.

'We're in the kitchen,' Eric called.

Yvette entered with the flushed glow and relaxed air that always followed a successful dance lesson.

'A good evening?' Eric asked.

'Yes, it was. Honestly, that Jerry is such a cad. We managed to—' Yvette stopped. Her eyes shot quickly around the room. Her relaxed look rapidly faded.

'You've cooked? The chicken?' She clocked the lit oven, identifying the aromas that had been confusing Eric since his arrival.

Katrina smiled.

'Nothing special. Hank, is it? He dropped over some more potatoes from the allotment. A few other bits and pieces too. Some amazing parsnips. And there was the chicken in the fridge, so I thought I'd make a roast. I realised I may have been a bit antisocial, hiding away. I just figured it's best, you know. Not to get attached or anything.'

Eric sniffed deeply. Now that she mentioned it, it was obviously chicken. And it smelt damn good.

'You didn't have to do that,' Eric said. 'We understand. This is a strange time for all of us. But it smells amazing.'

'It's my aunt's way of cooking it,' Katrina continued. 'You brown off the chicken in a pan first then pour the juices over the vegetables before you roast them.'

'Ruining them entirely for the vegetarians among us,' Yvette responded. Katrina paled.

'I didn't think. I'm sorry. I can do you something different if you'd like?'

'Did you leave any of the parsnips? I can make a soup.'

Katrina's pale skin rapidly coloured to a deep red. 'There were only a couple. I can make you something else though,' she said, rushing over the fridge and swinging open the door. 'I'm sure there's plenty in here I can put together if you give me a second? There's a cauliflower ...' she said, riffling through the vegetable crisper at the bottom, "... and a couple of tomatoes.'

'Don't bother,' Yvette said. 'Just tell me you deboned the chicken first? I'd bought it to last the week. I needed it to make a stock, and I promised Abi I'd do her chicken wings over the weekend.' Once again, the colour flooded to Katrina's cheeks.

'I'm sorry,' she said. 'I didn't think of boning it.'

'That must be a first,' Yvette said. With a flick of her chin, she spun around and marched out of the room before Eric could even open his mouth and respond. Katrina, Eric saw, had once again begun to cry.

'I mess everything up,' she said. 'I always get it wrong.'

CHAPTER 17

Eric stood at the bottom of the stairs, fully armed; plastic crate in one hand, cardboard boxes tucked under his arm, and bin bags and packing tape stuffed in his back pocket. The plastic crate was for anything sentimental he wanted to keep, the boxes for books and anything else that could be donated, and bin bags for anything he could just throw away. He had taken up a full roll of bin bags, in the hope that he would simply be able to chuck most of it out, but he knew that was more than a little bit optimistic.

It had been a tough night. The two days following the chicken debacle had been tense, and that was putting it mildly. Katrina had locked herself away in his bedroom, while Yvette huffed about this, that, and anything she could think of. This would not really have been an issue had Mabel not repeatedly sicked up her formula, meaning Katrina was needed to feed her, placing the two women in less than ideal proximity. For forty-eight hours, the women had snapped back and forth with nearly every confrontation ending with Katrina in tears. Last night was the worst so far.

Yet again, Mabel had refused to settle. Katrina, exhausted from feeding, was of the mind to let her cry it out. Yvette was not.

'She's crying because something's wrong,' Yvette said. 'Did you wind her properly after her food?'

'I told you,' Katrina replied, 'she doesn't like to wind.'

'It's not a matter of liking it or not. You can't put a baby down if she's got wind. Just give her here,' Yvette said. Forty minutes later and the screaming had got even worse, and the bickering had reached an all new level. To make matters worse, it was all going on in the living room, which was currently doubling as Eric's bedroom.

'She's crying because she's overly tired. Put her down and she'll fall asleep.'

'She's crying because she's hungry. I told you, you should have given her some more milk.'

'She doesn't need any more milk. All she's done all evening is feed.'

'Because she's growing. That's what babies do when they're growing. Feed.'

Eric had tried his best to keep his nose out and eyes shut, but at twenty to one, something snapped.

'Right,' he said, whipping off his blanket. 'You two, upstairs.'

'But—'

'We—'

The women objected simultaneously, suddenly in agreement for the first time all night.

'Give me Mabel, and get out,' Eric insisted. 'I've got this. We'll be absolutely fine.'

'But you're—'

'Out.'

'But if—'

'Out. Now.'

Katrina didn't need telling again. With a final glance at Mabel, she shrugged her shoulders and headed straight off upstairs to bed, but Yvette lingered a fraction longer.

'I promise,' Eric said again. 'We'll be fine.'

'But if you need—'

'I've got this, Yvette. Go to bed. Get some sleep.'

Fine was perhaps an over exaggeration, but despite his own – well-hidden – reservations, Eric was certain he and Mabel would be much better off on their own than with the women quibbling every small decision about her. After Yvette left, Lulu decided to abandon her place next to Abi and join them downstairs. Having the dog there perked Mabel up for a full fifteen seconds, after which she commenced her screaming at a new, record volume. At that point Lulu rapidly retreated back upstairs to Abi, leaving Eric truly alone with the bawling baby.

Two poos and one major sick-up followed, but an hour after taking up the mantle on his own, Mabel had fallen asleep on Eric's chest, his arms wrapped around her, the talcum powder scent of little babies filling his nostrils. He should really move her, he thought, as her tiny body rose up and down with every inhale and exhale, but he didn't want to put her down in her cot only to have her start screaming and wake the whole house up again, and he didn't really like the idea of having to go into his bedroom while Katrina was sleeping. But mainly it was the thought of not being with her for the rest of the night.

'Tomorrow,' he said, whispering as quietly as possible. 'I'll sort you out a proper room tomorrow.'

So that was what he was preparing to do.

He had waited until Abi had gone to school, Yvette had gone out to one of her coven meetings – she had missed a fair few since Suzy's passing, but Eric had convinced her that a bit of crystal healing was just the thing she needed – and Katrina had got the train to London to follow up on some leads she had about dance jobs for when the fostering process was complete. Yvette was so pleased about hearing the news she had booked the train ticket for her.

Now Eric was alone with Mabel and Lulu, and all he had to do was get on with it. He started with a quick phone call to Hank asking if he could come around later to help him put any boxes in the loft and load the car.

'I can help you pack the stuff too, if you like? Gotta take Scout to the vet's, but other than that, I'm free.'

'It's fine,' Eric said, bouncing Mabel to sleep in her chair while using his spare hand to rub Lulu's fur. 'I think I need to do it myself.'

'If you're sure? Just give me a bell when you want me then. I'll be about all afternoon.'

'Thanks. I will.'

By the time he hung up the phone Mabel's eyes were beginning to droop. A few minutes later and they were properly closed.

'Of course you sleep now,' Eric said.

With a slight wince, he lifted the dozing baby out of the seat, carried her up the stairs, and placed her down in her cot.

'Sweet dreams,' he said and kissed her forehead, before checking the sheet was securely tucked in. He left the door open an inch. Outside the room Lulu was waiting.

'Just you and me then,' Eric said to the dog. Lulu barked. 'I guess we'd better get on with it.'

For the longest time Eric stared at the wood panelling of the door, remembering all the times he had stood there, cup of tea in hand, wondering whether it would be a good time to interrupt Suzy from her work. She rarely said she minded, even if Eric had disturbed her at the worst moment possible. She would always smile and respond to whatever menial problem he had before turning back to her computer, mentioning this deadline or that deadline and getting on with her tasks in hand. Now he wished he had disturbed her more. Or not disturbed her and simply sat there, watching. Although, that would have been disturbing in a slightly different way. Nonetheless, he wished he had done that at least once. A sad groan escaped from the region around his heart. He should have realised. All those papers spread out over the dining room table. When had Suzy ever done that before? Never, she had always worked in her office in Islington. And yet there she was, laying it all out in front of him, begging him to see. He should have noticed.

Nothing about the door had changed since Suzy's departure. There was the same rust speckling on the metal doorknob, the same bare patch of wood in the top corner where the paint had chipped off. Standing there, staring at the door, he tried to convince himself into believing nothing had changed. That life was the same as it had always been, exactly the same as it was meant to be. As if reading his thoughts, a slight whimper came through from the baby. He held his breath, twisted the door knob, and stepped inside.

The curtains to the study were open a chink, causing a thin shaft of light to spear into the dimness and illuminate all the dust motes in its path. Eric clicked on the light before crossing the room to open the curtains fully. He pushed open one of the windows, with the thought of letting in some fresh air. Various papers and notelets fluttered upwards from the breeze. Hurriedly, he shut the window again, before securing down the papers with books and paperweights. He opened the window for a second time, just a little though.

Despite the mugginess, the room was cleaner than last time he had visited. The dust was more thinly spread, the carpet less grey and the family photo on the desk had a fresh smudge mark on the glass, as though someone had kissed it while wearing lipstick. It wasn't hard to work out who. Eric picked up the photo and pressed his thumb against his wife's cheek. She was extraordinarily beautiful, he thought, as his eyes moved from her smile to her eyes and back again. He wished he'd told her more often.

Shaking off the nostalgia, Eric put down the photo and turned to face his challenge.

'Where do I start?' he said to himself. Lulu barked in response.

The room was big, with more than enough space for a double bed and the crib if he moved the desk and one of the bookshelves out and shifted the rest of furniture around a bit. It would be good to have a spare bed in the house again, and would certainly be perfect for the remainder of Katrina's stay, although the thought of further expenses caused the ever-present knots in his stomach to tighten. He would have to see if he could pick one up second hand, he thought. He could even put a notice up in the Co-op; the pinboard there was always full, from unwanted fridges to people seeking out cheap second-hand cars. That said, he didn't know how well the idea of a second-hand bed would go down in the house.

However uncomfortable it was, having Katrina camped out in Eric's bedroom reminded everyone that it was a temporary arrangement. Getting a bed for her in the same room they planned on being Mabel's nursery would no doubt ruffle Yvette's feathers even further. And Katrina's. Any mention of money had her biting at her nails and rushing with excuses to leave the room. Several times he had found her chowing down on a packet of instant noodles and reduced package salads to save them the expense of feeding another person.

Eric pushed aside the mountain of thoughts that rushed at him constantly. Bed or no bed, he thought, it would be something to deal with later. First, he had to get the room sorted. Preferably before Mabel woke up.

Given that Eric was standing next to the desk, it felt like as good a place as any to start. Solid oak with a leather top, it was one of the few things that Suzy had brought with her from her old house after her divorce. It had been the first item of furniture to lay claim to a room in the Islington house and again here. While Eric was not one to adhere to the concept of souls, particularly when it came to inanimate objects, there was something about the desk that exuded the very essence of his wife. He placed a hand against one of the drawer handles and flexed his fingers. A moment later he backed away to the bookshelves. Books would be easier, he figured, much less personal. Who knew what tear-jerking distraction lay waiting in the desk drawers; it was much better he tackled those later.

For half an hour he worked with remarkable detachment. One advantage of having spent so many hours awake the previous night with Mabel was that it had given him a chance to develop a system; one he stuck to with absolute rigidity. Signed books he would keep. Books he knew that Suzy had adored and would wish to pass on to Abi, he would keep. Anything else was to go in the charity shop box. Yes, it was ruthless. Yes, he was bound to miss a few favourites that they had never discussed over the dinner table so he didn't realise how much they had meant to her, but if he *ummed* and *ahhed* over every choice, he knew it could be Christmas before he had even managed to clear the first shelf. This was efficient and effective and most of all, stopped him getting drawn into any dark places. With a nod of reassurance at Lulu, he picked up the first book and began to sort.

When the first cardboard box was full, Eric pushed it out the room and started on another, each shelf proving quicker to sort than the last. Within thirty minutes the entire bookshelf had been cleared, with two boxes to go up to the loft and three to the charity shop. Nothing so far had been binned.

A small filing cabinet containing various invoices, receipts, and contracts sat tucked in one corner. A quick glance at the contents told Eric that it was well beyond his area of expertise and probably not stuff he wanted to risk binning. He scooped up the papers and placed them into the plastic crate. He could always pass it over to Eaves later, or else bin them in a couple of years when he knew they were defunct. An uncomfortable gnawing nipped him in his gut. Avoiding finances and receipts had become a speciality of his own over the recent weeks. He had contingences if he needed them; his dad had left a fair sum to Abi after he died, but dipping into that would be less than ideal. Particularly now he was a single father with possibly two lots of university fees to pay for in the future. Once again, he forced the issue back with the other hundreds of repressed memories and continued with sorting the office.

With the bookshelf and the filing cabinet seen to, the only remaining matter for Eric to deal with was the desk. The item he had already identified as Suzy's most intimate writing partner. He could leave it, he thought. Moving the bookshelf would make more than enough room for Mabel's cot, and he could make do on the sofa if he had to. He shook his head and stepped towards the desk. There was no point avoiding it any longer.

The first item Eric picked up off the desk was a pen. *To my beautiful wife*, Eric read as he picked up the last Christmas present he had given his wife and turned it over in his hands. The inscription seemed silly now; too predictable, too ordinary. He could have picked a thousand better adjectives to describe his wife; incredible, talented, stunning, caring, compassionate, extraordinary. Extraordinary, that would have been a much better fit. *To my extraordinary wife*. But he had picked beautiful. Was that the most important trait he wanted to remember her by? Of course not. Still, it was the last gift he had even given her. That meant something.

He slipped the pen back into its box then placed it inside the plastic crate. He would give it to Abi at some point, he thought, but not yet. Perhaps when she moved up to secondary school, or started university. Then again, maybe he would save it for another tough day when she needed something to bring her mother close again, like the mood ring had done. With a single item having taken nearly as long to deal with as an entire shelf, and aware that Mabel's nap was unlikely to last very much longer, Eric willed himself back into action.

There were various framed photos on her desk, the majority of which he decided to move to Yvette's room. She had frequently mentioned how she wished she had more photos of Lydia and Suzy growing up. While there was little he could do to remedy that exact issue, he figured the photo of Abi digging in the sand in Corfu when she was two and a half would give her something to look back on. He had thought about giving Abi the laptop as well, but she was a bit young still and he doubted it would stand the test of technological advancement for very long. However, he was reluctant to throw it, so it went in the crate to be dealt with another day.

With the top of the desk cleared — or near enough — it was time to tackle the drawers. A painful nervousness bubbled through him. This was it, clearing Suzy's desk drawers. The last, most concrete action to cement his wife's departure. After this there would be no mysteries, no unknown corners of the house, nothing not infected by his touch. He reached for the top handle, changed his mind, and pulled the desk a little out from the window.

The wires behind the desk were thick with cobwebs and acted as the exact distraction Eric needed at that precise moment. He passed his fingers through the gap only to have them return entwined with thick dense threads. He would need to bring the hoover up here, he thought. Clean it properly. Probably repaint the walls too. His mind drifted back to the first time he had had to prepare like this. For Abi's nursery, he and Suzy had opted for green walls having not known what they were expecting, but it would be up to Abi to choose this time, he decided. Abi could choose what colour room her sister had.

The word jumped into his head without any warning, but Eric let it sit there, mulling it around. Abi's sister. He liked how it sat. The words he had spoken to Katrina at the railway station a fortnight ago flitted through his memory. They were true, every one of them. He had lost count of the number of times he and Suzy had talked half in earnest, half in jest about having more children; giving Abi a companion, a comrade in arms when the teenage nightmare years arrived. But he and Suzy had been older when they married, and having Abi had been hard work.

In Suzy's defence, she wasn't the only one who had struggled with the adjustment to a new baby. Becoming a father had been mentally exhausting. The lack of sleep, the new responsibilities, having to play second fiddle, learning to prioritise — he had had particular difficulty with that one. Suzy had made Abi her entire world for the longest time after she had been born, and there was no doubt that Eric had felt more than a little rejected at times. But it had all been worth it, Eric thought to himself, stamping on the doubts before they could fully form. After all, could he imagine his world without Abi? Of course not. She was his world. Casting the sentimental moment aside, he clenched his fists against the blooming pain across his ribs and returned to the drawers. This time he was not stopping. No matter what.

He started at the top and was pleased to find that his extreme aversion and nervousness appeared unjustified. The majority of items filling the deep, solid oak drawer were junk. Old pens, pencils and scraps of paper. Notebooks were stacked almost to the top. Eric flicked open the first little notepad. *Possible plot?* he read. *Swapping luggage at the airport with drug dealer.* A big line had been scrawled through it, the words *cliché* written in the margin. *Possible plot?* was written again below it, this time with slightly more details about a woman with amnesia. Eric flicked through the pages. Fresh anger burned through his cheeks, but not at Suzy, at the publishing house. How could they do that to her? How could they abandon her after all her years dedicated to them? He scooped the notebooks up and put them away in the crate, again with Abi in mind. If she had her mother's talent for telling stories, then what greater way to share it together? And she would show those publishers a thing or two. Beneath the notepads he found photographs. Old photographs, from the days when people had to take film down to the pharmacy to have it developed. Their first holiday only four weeks after meeting; camping in Cornwall. Their wedding a year later. There was no way they were going in the bin.

Almost everything Eric found in the drawers ended up going into the plastic crate; magazine clippings of reviews or short stories that Suzy had had published early on in her career. Envelopes stuffed with invitations to book launches and parties and certificates for nominations. Large crowds and rapturous accolades were not something Suzy gravitated towards and he knew she would have turned most of them down, but they were still worth holding on to, he decided, for the time being at least. A tangible reminder for Abi, and now Mabel, as to who Suzy really was.

One of the last envelopes in the top drawer was considerably well aged. The thin paper was speckled with dust, and the glue on the back of the seal had turned a mustard yellow over time. Eric slipped his fingers inside, expecting another invitation or perhaps one of Suzy's earlier articles. Instead there was a photograph; a polaroid, once colour now faded to sepia.

Eric frowned at the image of a young girl. It was Suzy; that much was apparent. Looking a few years older than Abi, he estimated her age to be around fourteen, although he realised he could have been out by a couple of years either way. Her eyes were tired and her lips tight together as though she were forcing herself not to cry. She was clothed in what appeared to be a nightdress. But these were details Eric only noticed later on. Far more prominent than the way her hair was swept back in a ponytail, or how her nails were bitten down to the quick, was the item she was holding in her arms. A baby.

Eric's hands shook as his fingertips pinched the image. With his pulse beating out like a percussion kit, he held his breath and tipped the envelope over. A small sliver of plastic fell into his hand. Still trembling as he twisted the plastic over and read the label on the plastic bracelet.

Baby boy

S. L. Devonport.

'Susan Laurel Devonport,' Eric said out loud. Suzy had another baby. One that he knew nothing about.

It was like a sledgehammer to the stomach.

CHAPTER 18

ERIC TRIED TO keep his composure the best he could. It had been over forty minutes since he'd found the photo, but he still couldn't stop the shaking. Mabel had started crying while he sat on the floor, hypnotised by the image, and for a few minutes he had not even registered the sound. When he did, he rushed into his room to find her red faced and soaked through. It took a few false starts before he was able to get her new nappy on properly he was shaking so much.

Three times he picked up the phone and three times he put it back down again. On the fourth attempt, he realised it really was the only thing he could do. With every muscle in his body trembling, he found the name, made the phone call, then packed up Mabel for a walk while he waited out the time. There was nothing he could do, not until Lydia arrived. His best option was to keep himself as busy as possible.

He was half hoping to bump into Cynthia, or Hank, or even Yvette who could have assured him that this was all some silly misunderstanding and there was really nothing to be so worked up about, but after marching all the way to the allotment and seeing no one *en* route, or at the plots, he turned back around and went straight home. When he arrived, he unstrapped Mabel from her seat, carried her to the kitchen and poured himself a large glass of whisky.

'Don't judge me right now,' he said, as Mabel stared up at him with her massive green eyes. 'This is an emergency.' Mabel gurgled her response. Eric took half a sip, then another larger one.

'Oh we are in a pickle here, Mabel,' he said. 'We are in a right old pickle.'

He was still nursing the same glass twenty minutes later when the doorbell rang.

'Here we go,' he said, placing Mabel back in her seat before he answered the door. 'Wish me luck. It's time for you to meet your Auntie Lydia.'

Asking whether your wife had had a secret child, fifteen years before you met, wasn't the type of conversation Eric wanted to have over the telephone, but there was another – possibly even more awkward – issue to add to the mix. While it was impossible to distinguish one source of nervousness from the other, he knew which issue he had to tackle first.

Lydia was sitting with a mug of tea in her hand, although there was zero chance of it still being warm enough to drink. For nearly five minutes they had been sitting there, Eric listening to the sound of the clock as it ticked away, waiting for her inevitable outrage. Every passing second only made it worse.

'Do you want something stronger to drink?' Eric asked, eventually.

'Is that meant to be funny?' she said.

'Sorry,' he said, recalling her teetotalism too late. He himself was desperate for a substantial glug of Dutch courage, but having plied himself with painkillers he decided it may not be the best idea. His initial glass of whisky was sitting still half full on the table. Still, as Lydia's silence extended around the room, he seriously considered downing it in one.

'You're not serious,' she said eventually. 'You can't seriously be considering adopting this baby?'

'What else can I do?'

'Anything. Anything would be more sensible than this.'

Eric bit down on his tongue as he waited for whatever else she had to say. There was no chance Lydia would leave her opinion at just that.

Lydia's lips tightened and squeezed; a physical manifestation of the chewing action which was almost certainly rolling around and around in her head while Eric was finding it hard to look at her. Lowering his gaze, however, was not an option. Lydia was bound to see that as a sign of defeat, and this was something he was not going to be defeated on. Not ever.

'Eric.' Lydia spoke on a puff of exhaled air. 'This is not some spur-of-the-moment decision. You can't decide to take on a baby out of grief.'

'I understand that.'

'Do you? Really? Then why are you only calling me now? Surely that should have been one of the first things you did.'

'I needed some time to process things.'

'It's been over two weeks,' she pointed out.

Eric let his gaze drop momentarily to his feet. He raised it again only milliseconds after.

'There have been some things to work through,' he said.

'Oh, I don't doubt that.'

'But, please, you have to understand—'

'This baby is *my* sister.' Lydia didn't wait for him to finish as she played the line Eric had been waiting for since he first dropped the news. 'She is related to *my* children too.'

'I am aware of that, Lydia.'

'It doesn't feel like that.'

'Believe me, I am.'

He was. He was well aware. More than once it had crossed his mind that Mabel would probably be much better placed with Lydia and Tom in the house that smelt of unwashed sheep and with a woman that could only take a joke as often as a solar eclipse. That was part of the reason he had avoided ringing them. He had even raised the fact with Katrina, but she had been explicit in who she wanted to raise the baby, and that wasn't going to be an easy thing to say.

'I understand how this might look to you,' he said, placing his mug down on the coffee table only to pick it up again immediately afterwards. 'And I can't explain it, but it feels like it's meant to be. It really does.'

'Eric, two months ago you were barely able to get through breakfast without a drink.'

'And yet now, here I am, with a dog and a family, and things are going well.'

'And yet Abi's having to see a counsellor. And you ended up in hospital because of an argument between the pair of you.'

Eric gritted his teeth. 'I assume Yvette told you that?'

Lydia tried to smile through her sigh. 'I'm not trying to cause a fight here, Eric, really I'm not. But how can you think it's a good idea, turning Abi's life upside down like this so soon after losing her mother?'

'I have spoken to Abi. At length. She is happy about this.'

'On the outside.'

Eric rolled his eyes. At moments like this he had learnt it was better saying nothing at all, despite the desperate urge to do so.

Lydia leant back in her chair and shook her head. 'The baby would be better placed with me,' she said.

'Possibly. But that's not what her mother wants. And it's not what I want either.'

'This isn't about you, Eric.'

'It's about all of us.'

Through each second of silence, Eric felt his pulse pounding in his neck. There were so many things he could say, and yet so much he wanted to avoid saying at the same time. In the end, he threw caution to the wind and laid it all out in front of her.

'Look,' he said. 'The truth is, Katrina only turned up on my doorstep because she didn't know about Suzy. Because Philip hadn't told her.' As expected, Lydia's eyes grew wider. 'Perhaps if she had known about the accident, it would have been your doorstep she turned up on. Then all of this would be a moot point. But even when she knew about Suzy, she still didn't change her mind. We fit together, this baby and Abi and me. If you saw us together, you would see that. We are a family. This baby is my family.'

Through the quiet, Lydia emitted a soft and sad chuckle which filled the air between them, before disappearing like the last tendril of smoke from a snuffed-out candle.

'I always wanted a girl,' she said, when some minutes had passed. 'You know, having two boys and everything. I'm too old for any more. And it wasn't like it was easy for me, getting pregnant in the first place. This could be my chance. A little girl, my own flesh and blood to bring up.' Her eyes drifted off, like she wasn't really talking to Eric at all. 'I'd be doing something right.'

'So, what are you saying?' The muscles in Eric's neck twitched nervously. 'That you do want her? That you're going to fight for custody?'

Lydia pursed her lips.

'Eric, this is not a toy. This is not a puppy. It's not a case of wanting her. It's a case of wanting to do what's right for her.'

'I understand that.'

'Do you? You were a working dad when Suzy had Abi. You were away half the time.'

'That's not true.'

'It is. I'm Suzy's sister, remember? I'm the one she spoke to during it all. The one she called up and wept to when she was so exhausted, trying to juggle her writing and the baby and still be the picture-perfect wife.'

'It wasn't like that at all,' Eric said.

'Yes, it was. You may not have seen it, but believe me, it was. I don't think you know what you're getting yourself into.'

Eric straightened his back. It was not an easy action, given his current state of disrepair, but he managed it without so much as a visible wince.

'I understand, Lydia. I really do. Maybe I wasn't the perfect husband I imagined myself to be when Abi was growing up. But I'm not the same person anymore. I left that life. I changed, remember. I changed for my family. And this baby is my family.'

'And it was that easy?'

'No. But I'm not going back to how things were. Not now.'

Lydia crossed her hands on her lap and inhaled deeply. In the pause, Eric reached down for his drink. His hand wavered on the coffee before settling on the whisky. He took a slow considered sip.

'I don't know what you want me to say,' Lydia said when she spoke again. 'I don't approve, I can't. The whole thing is a complete and utter disaster. It's going to end badly, and I don't know why you can't see it. I don't mean to sound heartless, I understand why you're doing it. But I can't approve.'

This time, Eric flinched. It was more than Eric's ego that needed Lydia's approval. In the previous session with Helen Eaves, she had insisted that Lydia and Tom would be needed for character references. Without them on side, it could seriously jeopardise his chances of being allowed custody.

He held her gaze, breathing in and out while trying to work out how best to word himself. After a minute of silence, he leant forward and took his sister-in-law's hands. Bodily contact with Lydia wasn't something he was drawn towards, but he needed the personal touch, now more than ever.

'Tell me what I can do to change your mind?' Eric said, leaning further in, but keeping his grip loose. 'You want honesty? You want me to prove I've grown up? Well that's what I'm trying to do here, Lydia. The truth is that I'm going to need your support. When it comes to the courts and the fostering and the whole adoption process, I'm going to need you to be there. I've got a meeting with the family law specialist tomorrow, and I need to show that we can provide a solid life for Mabel. Friends, aunts, uncles, the lot. Please, Lydia, in all the years I have known you, I have never asked for anything. Not one thing. But I need this from you now. I need this.'

'You're still drinking?' she said, nodding to the glass on the table.

'Rarely,' Eric said and pushed the glass back behind the coffee mug.

'What about money? You don't have a job.'

'There's something in the pipeline,' he lied.

'What?'

'I'd rather not say just yet. You know. I don't want to jinx things.'

Lydia rolled her eyes. She sat back in the seat, pulling her hands out of Eric's grip. 'What happened to honesty? I thought that was what you were just saying? I want to support you, Eric, I really do. I know you love Abi and I know you can be a great dad when you w—'

'Stop there,' Eric said. 'I'm going to take that as *yes*.'

'Eric—'

'I am going to take it as a *yes*, and I am going to prove to you that I can provide for this baby, and Abi. I am going to provide them with everything they could possibly need.'

Lydia sighed. 'It's not a *yes*, yet, Eric. I need to think it over. I need to talk to Tom. You can't just spring this on me and expect me to be okay with it. You can't have thought that that would happen.'

'I guess not,' Eric admitted. 'But I'll show you. I will.'

'I hope so,' Lydia replied. She offered a smile. It was small and forced, but despite how he felt, Eric understood. He moved in to hug her when a glance at the table and the speckled old envelope brought him back to the other reason he had called her there. His stomach churned.

'There's something else,' he said.

His sudden change in tone was echoed by an uncharacteristic darkening of the room as the clouds crossed in front of the sun. The effect of both caused Lydia to stiffen slightly in her chair.

'What is it?' she said. 'It's not Mum is it?'

Eric shook his head. 'No,' he said. 'This is about Suzy. Before I knew her.'

He reached down and plucked the envelope from the table, then he crossed the room and sat down on the sofa beside Lydia. What seemed like an eternity passed before he handed her the photograph.

'What do you know about this?' he said.

The change was immediate. Lydia's flushed pink skin drained to a sallow grey.

'Where did you get this?' she said, rubbing her hands on the seat of her trousers.

'It was in one of the drawers in Suzy's office. This was with it too.' He handed her the hospital tag, the clear plastic now a grimy yellow.

'S. L. Devonport. Susan Laurel Devonport,' he repeated the name he had said so many times over the last hour. 'This is Suzy's baby, isn't it? Suzy had another baby when she was young?'

'Eric, please don't ask me this.'

He could feel the heat building behind his eyes. 'Lydia, this is my wife. I need to know. Did she have another baby? Did she have another baby and not tell me?'

Lydia brushed her fingers against the photograph, first her sister then the child. Inside his chest Eric felt his heart cracking. His wife, the love of his life, had another child and after all they had been through, all the years together, she had never trusted him enough to tell him.

'No,' Lydia said, whipping her gaze away from the photograph and wiping away the tears that had formed in one quick swipe. 'Suzy didn't have another baby.'

'But the photo?'

'She didn't have a baby. It's mine.'

Eric's jaw dropped. 'What do you mean?'

'I mean it's mine.'

Lydia's eyes went back down to the photo. Eric shook his head in disbelief.

'No,' he said. 'That makes no sense. The name on the tag is S. L. Susan Laurel.'

'Or Stephanie Lydia.'

'Stephanie?'

Lydia nodded. 'That's my first name.'

Eric's head was spinning as he reached for his tumbler only to change his mind.

'Your first name is Lydia. I would know if it wasn't Lydia. You were a witness at my wedding. I saw you sign your name. I've seen your address. Your post. Your name is not Stephanie.'

Lydia inhaled deeply. Her fingers were still gripping at the photograph although her eyes were looking directly into Eric's. She exhaled a large puff of air, blowing warm in Eric's direction.

'My full maiden name is Stephanie Lydia Devonport. But I never really liked the name Stephanie. Even before ... before everything. I could have only been about nine when I first tried to get the other children at school to call me Lydia.'

Eric raised an eyebrow.

'It's true,' she continued. 'I did. Back then, no one did, other than Suzy, and she did whatever I asked because she was my baby sister.' Her eyes drifted past him to a forgotten memory. Eric could see them both, running around the school yard, chasing one another, Suzy hanging on her big sister's every word.

'What happened?' Eric asked.

'What happened?' Lydia said, shaking her head as if waking up from a dream. 'I got pregnant.'

Eric's pulse drummed. 'That's it?'

'That's it.'

Eric pressed his tongue to the roof of his mouth. He should stop, he thought. A better man than him would stop her now, accept what she had told him and leave her in peace. But he couldn't. Something was gnawing away in his gut, and it wasn't going to rest, not until he knew everything.

'And the father?' he said, when the pause had grown too long to bear.

Lydia scrunched up her nose. 'He was no one. Older than me. Took advantage of my naivety. You know, same old story. I thought he was different. I thought he loved me. And well, you can guess what happened when I got pregnant.'

'He left?'

'He did. Joined the army, I think. Or the navy. Somewhere to get as far away from me and the baby as possible. He came back once a few years later. Wanted to give things another try; wanted to make up for what happened.'

'I assume you said no?' Eric asked.

Lydia's lips twisted. Eric sensed that was one question he better let lie.

'What happened then? Yvette and Philip, what did they do?'

Lydia shook her head rapidly. 'They didn't know. They were barely around, this dance show and that dance show and besides, I hid it well. I dressed in baggy clothes, big coats. I was a rake back then too, so it was easy enough.'

'So nobody knew?'

'No one did. The only person who knew was Suzy. She was the only person I trusted enough to tell. God, I wish we'd had that conversation earlier. I really do. Things could have been different. But it was left too late ...' She inhaled deeply through her nose and let the air out with a sigh. 'Anyhow, after I'd had the baby, well, I didn't want to be Stephanie anymore. I wanted to forget all about that girl. That naive little girl who deserved so much more. So, I dropped the Stephanie from my name altogether. This time I made sure it stuck. I got my friends, my school, everyone to call me Lydia. Teachers too. Refused to reply if they called me Stephanie instead. Mum and Dad were probably the hardest to come around to my decision, but they had chosen my first name so you could see why they would be a bit miffed.' She tried to make light of the matter, with a half-hearted chuckle at the end, but it didn't stick.

'And afterwards?' Eric said, unable to even fake a smile at what he was hearing.

'Afterwards, I tried to shut that chapter in my life. Block it out altogether. That's when the drinking came about. I told you I had some issues. Now you know why.'

Eric rubbed his temples and attempted to process all this information.

Lydia was staring at the photograph, broken. Her eyes were bloodshot, the colour drained from her lips and cheeks. He could tell he had made her relive one of the worst moments of her life; that much was clear. And that should have been enough. But, despite all she'd said, a slight niggling within him persisted. It was pride; he knew that. The fact that Suzy never told him. Even after all those years she didn't trust him enough to tell him her sister's secret. It didn't make sense.

'But the photo,' Eric said, hating himself for not being able to let it go. 'In the photo, it's Suzy. Why would Suzy take a photo of herself with *your* baby? And she's in a nightgown? It doesn't make sense.'

Lydia placed the photo down on the table in front of her, crossed her legs, and looked Eric straight in the eyes.

'She took a photo, because I wouldn't. I didn't want any photos. Any reminders. But Suzy did. It was part of our family, she said. She begged me, I suppose in case I wanted to have some reminder later down the line, so I allowed her to take this one. Just the one. But I wouldn't be in it. I couldn't.'

'And the nightdress? It looks like she's the one in the hospital.'

'Because she was. She turned it into an adventure.' Tears escaped and trickled down the side of her cheek. This time, she made no attempt to wipe them away. 'That night, when it happened, Mum and Dad were away, I couldn't leave Suzy and she wouldn't leave me. Anyway, she walked with me to the hospital, and made me laugh with terrible jokes so that I wouldn't think about the pain. The whole time she never left my side, never let go of my hand. When we arrived they gave us a room with two beds, even gave Suzy a fake hospital bracelet, see.' Lydia pointed to the photo and the thin barely visible sliver of a hospital tag.

Eric could feel his own tears now brimming over his lower lids and slipping down towards his lips.

'So then ...'

'So then I had the baby, and we took that photo and then they took him away.'

'A boy?'

'A boy,' Lydia repeated.

The tears were tumbling now. Eric glanced at the ceiling, attempting to keep them at bay.

'So Yvette and Philip—'

'Never knew a thing. And they never will.' Lydia uncrossed her legs and leant towards him. 'You have to promise me, Eric. You have to. Mum couldn't bear it. Not now. Think about Mabel. How attached she's grown to a baby that is no relation to her. Think how much worse it would be for her to know her own flesh and blood was out there. Another grandchild. A grandchild she never even knew. To know that we lied to them for all those years. It would break her heart.'

Eric nodded, trying to force down a lump that had swelled in his throat.

'And Tom? Tom knows about this?'

Lydia's eyes flickered, only ever so slightly, and the pain that flashed in that moment wrenched at Eric's core. She had told him before of the miscarriages; he couldn't imagine the pain the pair of them had suffered. A moment later and the flicker was gone and her eyes were back as steadfast and firm as they had ever been.

'Tom knows the truth,' she said.

The air had fallen stagnant between them, and the aching in Eric's chest grew with every heartbeat. He looked at his sister-in-law, a woman so full of strength, of tenacity, of downright stubborn bullishness and he had never had a clue, not in all the years he had known her.

'You will let this be, won't you?' Lydia said. 'For Mum's sake as much as mine.'

Eric nodded. 'I'm sorry I made you relive that.'

'I'm sorry I had to, too.' She stopped and gave one final glance at the photo before handing it to Eric. He took hold, but she didn't let go.

'I'll support you, Eric. You want this baby. I can tell that. You want this baby for your family and for the right reasons, and I will support you. We will support you.'

Eric studied Lydia's face, waiting for some kind of condition, some *but* to her statement. When none came, he reached over and wrapped his arms around her.

'Thank you. You won't regret this.'

Lydia pushed herself up from the sofa and brushed down invisible creases in her trousers. She handed Eric both the photograph and the tag.

'Do you not want to keep them?' he said.

She shook her head rapidly.

'I'd rather leave them here if that's all right. Somewhere safe.'

'Of course.'

A moment of silence was exchanged between the pair.

'Do you want to stay for dinner?' Eric asked. 'It would give you a chance to meet your sister.'

Lydia shook her head. 'I need to get back. I hadn't told Tom I was going, so I'll need to pick the boys up from Scouts or they'll all be wondering what's happened to me.'

'Maybe next week then?' Eric said. 'When I've sorted everything out with the lawyer, maybe we can have a little pre-fostering party and the boys can come down and meet their new cousin?'

'That's sounds ideal,' Lydia said, and she pecked him on the cheek before sweeping down to pick up her bag and gliding out of the front door.

Eric glanced down at the photograph in his hand. 'You could have trusted me, Suzy,' he said to the air. 'Why didn't you trust me?'

CHAPTER 19

THE HOUSE WENT from peace to pandemonium in a matter of fifteen seconds. Yvette returned home with Abi, which immediately set Lulu off into an excited barking frenzy, and that in turn woke Mabel, and all only moments before Katrina strutted through the door, arms laden with bags. After finding the photograph, Eric had postponed Hank's visit in order to speak to Lydia, meaning that the upstairs landing was littered with boxes which both Abi and Yvette began to riffle through without a second's thought to how much sorting they had taken.

'Can you leave those alone?' Eric said, hobbling his way up the stairs and flinching with every other step. The previous hour sitting had allowed the muscles around his ribs to seize up yet again and he was having difficulty even walking, let alone climbing the stairs. 'Hank's going to be around in an hour to help me put them in the loft.'

'But I want to keep this,' Abi said, plucking some random item from the top of one of the boxes. 'This was Mum's favourite.'

'I'm not getting rid of it. It's just going into the loft.'

'But I want to have it in my room.'

'You can, but not yet. You're too young.'

'I'm—'

'Abi?'

Whether luck or judgement, Katrina's voice came through at exactly the right moment, managing to stop the meltdown midway. Eric closed his eyes, relieved.

'I got you something in town. Do you want to see it?'

She was standing at the bottom of the stairs, staring up at them; more colour to her cheeks than Eric had seen since her arrival.

'A present for me?' Abi said. Immediately, she dropped the item in her hand onto the floor by the box and dashed down the stairs. Yvette – who had been silently rummaging herself – adopted a decidedly uninterested expression, then also replaced the item she was holding.

'Buying Abi gifts?' she muttered to Eric as she crossed him on the landing. 'Where's she got the money for that?' Still sporting a falsely blasé appearance, she sauntered down the stairs after Abi, leaving Eric to sort out the mess they had made. Two minutes later, with all the boxes once again packed, he joined the women of the family in the kitchen.

Had Eric not known better, he would have thought the early days of Yvette had returned. Numerous clothing store bags were scattered out on the kitchen table, with glittering items of costume jewellery and various soaps and smellies spilling out from their insides.

'You've bought a lot,' Yvette commented.

'I needed to,' Katrina replied. 'It feels so good to have some clothes that fit.' She lifted a handful of the bags off the table and placed them down on the ground. 'Honestly, since Mabel's been born I've hated it, trying to squeeze into all my old things. This will make the world of difference. It's impossible trying to audition for something when you feel that you look bad. Now ... where did I put them?' She continued to pull out several items and packages before finding what she was looking for; a small, cardboard bag, tied at the top with a pink ribbon.

'For you,' she said, handing the bag to Abi.

'For me? What is it?'

'Open it, so you can find out.'

Abi looked to Eric. He nodded. Tentatively her fingers tugged at the ribbon before pulling the folds of the bag open and lifting out a small box. Inside, she found a bracelet.

'It's beautiful,' she said. 'Can I wear it? Can you put it on me now, please, Dad?' She handed the piece of silver to Eric.

'It might be a bit big,' Katrina commented. 'It's for when you're older, really. But look, I got the same one for Mabel,' she lifted up another bag. 'And have a look at the charm. Can you see what it says?'

Abi took the bracelet back from Eric and twisted the charm around to face her.

'Sisters,' she said.

'Exactly. And Mabel's says the same. Sisters.'

Abi beamed.

'You didn't have to do this,' Eric said, his eyes half on Katrina, half on the bracelet.

'I know. But you have given up a lot for me. And I know, once I leave here, I probably won't see you anymore. I just wanted some way to say thank you, that's all.'

'Can you put it on now, Dad? Please. Can you put it on?'

Eric hesitated, before offering Katrina a single nod of gratitude before attempting to fix the tiny little clasp. After thirty seconds of fumbling, he gave up.

'Yvette, can you do this?' he said.

Despite asking for her directly, Yvette appeared not to hear. Even when Eric repeated her name for a second time, she remained motionless. Finally, after Eric's third attempt, she lifted her head.

'Yvette?'

'I thought you said you had no money,' she said, pointing her question at Katrina.

Katrina nodded thoughtfully.

'I did. Thank you, that reminds me.' She reached into her handbag and extracted her wallet, from which she pulled out four twenty-pound notes which she handed to Eric. 'That's for all those things the other day. And for food and things. Let me know if it's not enough?'

Eric stared at the money in his hands.

'That's ... uhmm... thank you,' he stuttered. His uncertainty was not coming from the money – which was undoubtedly a useful extra – but from his mother-in-law, whose face was growing more and more thunderous by the second.

'Yvette?' Eric said. 'Is everything okay?'

'I thought she was broke,' she muttered, before raising her voice and speaking once more to Katrina. 'So now you do have money?' Katrina bristled.

'It would appear that way.'

'And would you like to tell me where it came from?'

'Not particularly.'

Eric had to give Katrina her dues. A lesser person would have crumbled under Yvette's glare, yet this whippet of a girl was holding her own much better than Eric had managed under similar situations.

'I need to know where the money has come from,' Yvette said.

Katrina laughed. 'It's none of your business.'

'Actually, it is. You are living in this house, with my family.'

'For which I am grateful. That doesn't mean I have to tell you every last thing about my life.'

'I need to know where it came from.'

'No, you don't.'

Katrina reached down to the table and began to clear away the various clothes and items that had spilled out of her bags.

'The last thing they need is to be caught up in your family's dodgy dealings.'

A look of hurt flashed across Katrina's face. 'You think I'd do that? You think I'd involve you with them? Involve Mabel with them?'

'I wouldn't put anything past you.'

Katrina's expression hardened. 'I told you. I have nothing to do with my family.'

'Then where did the money come from? You're telling me it just appeared in your bank account?'

'I'm telling you that where my money comes from has nothing to do with you.'

'It does if you're living in my house.'

'It's not your house; it's Eric's.'

'This is my family.'

'And this is none of your business!'

'Ladies!' Eric stepped between the pair. There was still four feet separating them, yet he felt the need to stretch out arms to keep them apart. As Yvette moved towards him, he jerked an open hand towards her only to have a spasm of pain shoot straight down his spine.

'Daddy!'

'Eric!' The women dashed to his side. Panting through the pain he rested one hand on his knee and waved them away with his second.

'I'm fine. I'm fine,' he huffed. 'Just give me some space.'

Yvette and Katrina stepped back. Abi stepped closer by his side. Eric reached out his hand and took hers.

'I'm fine,' he said, holding her hand and looking directly into her eyes. She nodded mutely.

After a minute bent double, surrounded by a tangible silence, Eric pushed himself back up to standing. The women, Eric discovered, were still locked in a stalemate of stares.

'I'm sorry,' Yvette said, her tone sounding anything but. 'I just don't feel comfortable. You come into this house saying you don't have a penny to your name, and two weeks later you're buying Abi and Mabel expensive jewellery and refusing to tell us where the money comes from. Surely you can see that looks suspicious?'

'You could just trust me.' Katrina said.

Yvette laughed bitterly. 'Surely, you have to be kidding?'

'Fine,' Katrina placed her hands on her hips with a huff. 'If you must know, I sold something. I was hoping I wouldn't have to, but I decided in the end that it was better if I did.'

'What did you sell?'

'It's none of your business.'

'It must have been worth a lot of money?'

'It was,' Katrina replied. She threw back her shoulders in a huff. 'If you're that bothered, it was a ring. A ring that Philip gave me. One he wanted me to pass on to Mabel.'

Yvette stiffened. Something in the air changed.

'A ring?'

'Yes, a ring.'

'What type of ring?'

'It was just a ring.' Katrina replied.

Yvette's hands had begun to shake as the colour drained from her cheeks.

'Show me?' she said, her voice low and threatening.

'I can't. I've sold it.'

'Then show me a picture. Describe it to me.'

'I ... I ...' Uncertainty quivered on Katrina's lips. 'There were emeralds,' she said.

'And a diamond in the middle,' Yvette finished. 'About so big?' She indicated the size with her fingers. It was Katrina's turn to tremble.

'How do you—'

'My mother's ring. You stole my mother's ring!'

Katrina edged back.

'No,' she said, but Eric could see the doubt in her eyes. Her complexion was fading, like she was treading water and about to be engulfed by the mother of all waves.

'A square diamond?' Yvette said again. 'And rectangular emeralds either side?'

'He said it was his mother's. He said she left it to him.'

'You are a liar.'

'I swear ... I swear ...'

A moment later, Yvette lunged.

CHAPTER 20

THE TWO WOMEN were standing in the garden, water dripping from their hair and clothes. In the end it was Abi's quick thinking that cut the scrap short. Eric had been useless, with his flustered pleas of '*Stop, Stop*'. Abi had picked up Lulu's water bowl and had thrown its contents over the pair.

'They do that with dogs,' Abi told him. 'It stops them fighting.'

'The irony is not lost on me,' Eric replied. Abi frowned, confused.

Two seconds later, Eric had pushed them out of the back door to the position in which they were currently standing, dripping and shivering. Arms crossed, scowls the perfect mirror image of one another.

'That ring was an heirloom.' Yvette was still white with disbelief. 'It was my grandmother's ring. Then my mother's, it was supposed to be passed down to Abigail.'

'Philip said the same thing, but he said it was his grandmother's.'

'I don't believe you.'

'It's true, I swear.'

'He stole it from me. He stole it right out from under my nose.'

From inside the house came Mabel's cry.

'I'll go,' Abi said, disappearing before Eric could ask her, although she did appear in the conservatory a minute later, Mabel in her arms and just within earshot of the conversation.

Katrina pursed her lips together.

'I can give you the rest of the money.'

'I don't want the money.'

'Then we can buy the ring back. I can get a credit card. I can take the rest of the stuff back. We'll go first thing tomorrow,'

Yvette laughed, the low pitch snort embroiled with disdain. 'Do you have any idea how much it was worth? Do you? Because if you got anything less than the cost of a new car for it, you've been ripped off and we don't have a chance in hell of buying it back. Do you understand that?'

Katrina's slight frame was trembling and only partly from the cold of being soaked in the dog's water.

'I'm sorry,' she said. 'I really am.'

Yvette's eyes showed no indication of softening. She flicked her hair, spraying a mist of water much the same way Lulu did when she finished in the bath – and looked solely at Eric.

'I'm sorry,' she said. 'I can't do it. I thought I could rise above it. I thought I could cope with it, but I can't. She's there, in my kitchen, in my bathroom, flaunting herself around my family the whole time. I want this baby in my life, Eric, really I do. But I can't live under the same roof as that silly tart even one more day. I just can't.'

Eric lowered his gaze to his feet, then turned his neck slightly to the doorway. Abi was blowing raspberries on Mabel's belly. Every time she did, Mabel lifted her arms into the air and emitted a high-pitched squeal of glee. They were perfectly happy. Abi was perfectly happy. Slowly, he turned back to his mother-in-law.

'I am sorry to hear that, Yvette. Really I am.'

THEY HAD GOT fish and chips for dinner. It wasn't a very sensible idea. There was food in the freezer as well as the things Hank had brought around earlier in the week, but that involved cooking and Eric couldn't think about cooking right now. Katrina offered to pay, but given the situation, Eric didn't feel it wise. He would make up for it with a few extra frugal days later in the week, he told himself. Abi was happy to spoon down pasta and cheese for days on end. And there was always the credit card if it came down to it.

'I'm so sorry,' Katrina said, nudging her chips with a small wooden fork. 'If I'd have thought for one moment that—'

'This is not on you,' Eric said, reinforcing the words the best he could. 'Really it's not.'

'I had no idea. Honestly. Philip said ...' She shuddered as she said his name. 'If I'd have known. It's no wonder she hates me.'

Eric's response was non-committal. The morning felt like a million years ago. How was it possible that only hours beforehand he had been cleaning out Suzy's office, then talking to Lydia? Mabel was with Abi, who Eric had let eat in the living room, watching television, under the strict proviso that she did not give Lulu any chips. Truth was he didn't care what she did right now, she could feed Lulu the whole damn plateful as long as she wasn't making a fuss when she did it.

'Do you think it's true? About how much the ring cost?' Katrina said, apparently having replaced her silent sullenness of the previous weeks with a more vocal alternative. 'I should have known. The man at the shop was way too happy to take it off my hands. Do you think there's any way we can get it back? Claim that he tricked me? Go to the police even.'

'If everyone went to the police when a pawnbroker ripped them off, we'd need to triple the number of policemen,' Eric commented.

Katrina bowed her head. 'You know what the worst of it is?' she said, moving the chips around her plate. 'It's that I actually thought I was doing something right today. I really did. It was the first time since Mabel was born – other than coming here, to find you – selling that ring, getting myself clothes for auditions, even those presents. I thought I was starting to repair things in my life. Turns out I only ever make things worse.'

'It was an honest mistake,' Eric said, seeing more than ever the naivety of her youth.

Katrina nodded, thoughtfully, then speared a chip with her fork. 'Do you think she'll come back? She will come back, won't she?'

Eric lifted his eyes up from his plate.

'Yvette made the decision to leave. And she can go back on it at any time. I made that perfectly clear. This is her home for as long as she wants it. She just needs a little time to cool down, that's all.'

The tell-tale signs of another developing silence prickled the air around them. 'What about you?' he said, attempting to distract from the burgeoning tension. 'How are you doing? You're the one who's given up their life for the next three months.'

'I'm surviving.' Katrina glanced down at her knees with a sad chuckle, then raised her head again. 'Actually, I've thought about leaving once or twice,' she said.

Eric dropped his fork to his plate.

'What?' Today, it appeared, was going to find every bombshell currently in existence and throw them directly at him. 'Not with Mabel?'

Katrina's eyes glazed as she lifted them to the ceiling.

'Sometimes, yes. Mostly no,' she admitted.

'But why?'

'Why not? We're two weeks in, and Mabel would rather be with Abi than me.'

'That's a good thing.'

'It is,' she agreed. 'But can you imagine what that feels like? Maybe if I was away, it would be easier.'

Eric picked his fork back up from the table and moved it over to his plate.

'Do you think it would be better if you spoke to someone? Like Abi's doing?'

'What, a counsellor?'

'It couldn't hurt.'

'And where do I find the money for that?' she said.

Levering herself up, she lifted her plate off the table, walked over to the bin, and tipped the contents inside.

THE REST of the evening was a strange one. Katrina retreated into her room after dinner, leaving Eric to do the night time routine by himself. Apart from the walk to the allotment, Lulu had been inside all day. Not wanting to impose on Katrina to babysit, Eric called up Hank who was happy to take Lulu out for an evening stroll with Scout, leaving Eric very much by himself.

His eyes moved continually to the door, waiting for it to open and Yvette to flounce in. At all other moments, he was staring at the photographs on his phone.

'What have I done?' he said, as he swiped through the images one by one, wishing with every movement he'd taken more of Suzy and Abi together. So many photos of vegetables, and of house renovations. What a waste of time that was. It didn't feel real, he thought, pressing his thumb against a selfie of him and Suzy with their cycling helmets on; the last photo they had taken together. Even after all this time, even after everything that had happened to them, part of his brain just couldn't accept that she was truly gone. Only the constant searing pain through his heart assured him she was.

At eleven o'clock, when he could no longer face the prospect of another crappy sitcom on his own, he went upstairs to consider the bed situation. Yvette leaving presented him with the prospect of an actual mattress for the first time in weeks. It seemed wasteful not to take the opportunity.

Eric had not slept in the spare room before. When Yvette had arrived at Christmas last year, Lydia and Tom had also been staying, so he had been once again forced on the sofa. After that, Yvette laid a permanent claim on the space, and he rarely, if ever, went in there anymore.

Tomorrow, he told himself. Tomorrow he would finish getting Suzy's office sorted, and things could get back to normal. Well as normal as life could be when your wife was dead, and you had agreed to temporarily house her father's ex-lover before adopting their illegitimate child. He pushed open the door to Yvette's room and stepped inside, only to close the window, switch off the light, and head back downstairs to the sofa.

'I DON'T HAVE to go if you need me to stay.' Katrina said, standing by the front door, bag over her arm, raring to leave. Yvette had been gone for close to a week, and after the first three days Eric had realised that all phone calls and the messages he was leaving were doing no good whatsoever. It was quite clear at this point she was simply deleting the lot.

Phone calls and text messages were not the only attempts at contacting his mother-in-law Eric had made. He had considered heading to one of her dance classes and seeing her there, but he knew Yvette; her professionalism was one of the few things Philip hadn't managed to strip her of, and the last thing Eric wanted was to be the one to ruin that. However, he had spent extra time lingering around outside the Co-op on the chance he might catch her grabbing some groceries and had even asked at the Thai restaurant – where she had a soft spot for the Tom Kha Gai – whether they had seen her recently, only to discover they were more secretive about their clientele than a high-class escort agency.

'If I have to, I can probably catch a later train. It wouldn't be ideal but ...'

'We're fine,' Eric said.

Katrina looked around the hall and grimaced. It was, undeniably, chaos. Abi had lost her school shoes, and her school tie, and her jumper, and her favourite book which for some reason she simply *had* to take in that morning. Lulu on the other hand had managed to find several shoes, all of which were Eric's and all of which she had chewed past the point of repair.

'Honestly, you go,' Eric said ignoring his daughter's constant wails and stamping feet. 'I'm going to need to convince the lawyer that I can cope on my own tomorrow as it is. Plus, for something like this I really should be the one to take her.' He opened Abi's coat and turned to her, ready for her to slip her arms into it, only to find that she had now disappeared and was playing peekaboo with a screaming Mabel, who he had finally managed to strap into her car seat after what felt like a two-hour battle with a small, sharply clawed, and exceptionally loud badger.

'Abi, will you get here now?' Eric shouted.

'I'm helping.'

'Now.'

Sulkily, she blew Mabel a kiss and trundled over. Eric handed her the coat and she slipped her arms into the sleeves. Something flashed on her finger.

'No way,' he responded. 'What did I say about taking that ring to school?'

'But, Dad—'

'We've had this discussion. It's too precious. If you lose that—'

'But I won't—'

'No, because you will not be taking it.'

'But I—'

'Abi!'

Abi pouted. Her nostrils flared.

'Do not make me tell you again,' Eric said. Slowly she began sliding the ring off her finger.

'Thank you,' he said when the item reached the end of her finger. He held out his hand. 'Now give it here.'

Abi looked at the ring in her hand. She lifted her eyes to her father. 'I'll put it up in my room,' she said. 'That way it won't fall out of your pocket when you're at the doctor's.'

Eric hesitated.

'Fine, but run,' he said. 'We're already late.'

Abi bolted up the stairs to her bedroom before he had even finished. He sighed and turned his attention to Mabel.

'Just so you know, I'll be back early afternoon. They're not doing call backs 'til next week.' Katrina continued to hover by the door.

'Are you not staying up there? I thought you'd want to see people?'

She shook her head. 'No, I need to try to get some audition videos sent off. I need to focus myself. If I stay in London, I'll just end up seeing people and going for cocktails.'

'We don't mind.'

'No, the sooner I get myself a job, the sooner I can get out of this hell.' Her hand flew to her mouth. 'I'm sorry, Eric, I didn't mea—'

'It's fine.' Eric waved her apology away with his free hand while the other one attempted to fit a singing cow mobile to Mabel's car seat.

'Honestly ... I just ...' Her cheeks coloured as she searched for some way to backtrack on her insult. 'I'm so grateful for what you're doing. And I'll be back early enough to pick Abi up from school, if you want? I know Thursday is normally when Yvette gets her.'

Eric chewed on the thought. So far he had been doing the school runs there and back and there was no denying it caused a fracture in the day, but if Yvette wasn't going to come back, he would have to get used to it. Besides, it was quite clear Katrina had offered out of desperation.

'It's fine,' he said as he checked Mabel's nappy bag. 'Hank was going to come around and help me put away the stuff in the loft, but it's not a problem. I can tell him to come around another time.'

'Don't be silly, you've already had to cancel on him twice now. He'll probably stop offering to help soon.'

'Possibly,' Eric agreed.

'Please. It would make me feel better.'

Eric gave the thought another moment.

'You're sure you don't mind?' he said, yet again.

'It would be my pleasure,' she replied, with a smile that almost looked like she meant it.

Three seconds later and Abi thundered back into the kitchen.

'All done,' she said, then picked up her school bag, which had somehow appeared out of nowhere, and stamped over to the front door.

'Come on, Dad,' she yelled back when the door was already ajar. 'We're going to be late otherwise.'

At the school Abi bolted out of the car before Eric had even wished her goodbye. He wound down the window and called across the car park.

'Hey, what about a kiss?'

Abi stopped, wrinkled her nose, and sprinted back to the car where she promptly flung open the back door and landed a sizable kiss on Mabel's forehead.

'See you later, Dad,' she called as she darted back across the tarmac and through the school gates.

※

DOCTOR'S APPOINTMENTS were not something Eric had dealt with when Abi had been young. Prescribed office hours, not to mention late meetings and long commutes, meant it had fallen on Suzy to be the flexible one when it came to arranging for Abi's vaccinations and check-ups. He had started off interested enough, making sure he asked about current weight percentiles and that type of thing, but by the time she was six months old, it was commonly presumed that if there was anything he needed to know, Suzy would tell him. This time, however, it was all on him.

'So, this vaccine is a three in one,' the doctor told Eric as she tried to pin Mabel's arms down. 'This will be the first one. She'll need the booster in another three months.'

'Booster in three months, got it,' Eric said, making a mental note to add a reminder on his phone the moment he had a hand free.

'And don't be concerned if she has a bit of a temperature, either tonight or tomorrow. Vaccines can do that to them. Some paracetamol suspension should bring it right down if you're worried, but really, I don't think it will be an issue.'

'Temperature, paracetamol suspension,' Eric repeated.

'Okay then, if you can hold her steady for me ...'

For a split second, Mabel's squirming stopped. A heartbeat's worth of silence followed, before she scrunched up her eyes, opened her mouth, and wailed.

'Well that's all done,' the doctor said, pressing a plaster onto Mabel's bottom and pulling up her nappy, pushing the baby firmly into Eric's hands.

'I'll see you two in three months' time.'

She remained standing and tilted her body to the door, indicating that their time was up.

One more thing survived, Eric said to himself as he headed out the door, one screaming baby in his arms.

※

'THE POOR THING sounds like she's having a tough time of it,' Cynthia said as they sat on the deck chairs outside her shed.

After the doctor, he had gone back home, picked up Lulu, transferred Mabel into her pushchair, and headed down to the allotment. Eric had hoped the gentle stroll would help loosen up some of the muscles that had been tightening around his healing bones. And a gentle stroll may well have done that. What he hadn't counted on was the weight lifting involved regarding all the paraphernalia that came with going for a walk with a baby. A well-stocked nappy bag, Eric had discovered, was a considerable weight. It had started out light enough – just a couple of nappies, wet wipes, and a bottle – but then he had remembered what the doctor had said about a temperature and threw in a bottle of Calpol too. Given that, in Eric's mind, a temperature would most certainly mean some form of excess fluids, he packed two changes of clothes, plus a hat, blanket, and woollen onesie in case the weather changed, along with her favourite cuddly toy and two dummies should she start to grizzle. By the end of it, he was stuffing half of her belongings in the tiny side pockets. Twenty minutes after his arrival at the allotment and he had so far used exactly one muslin.

'Fingers crossed this audition goes well.' Cynthia continued with their conversation about Katrina and her stress levels. 'I'm sure that would help matters a lot if she could have some work to go to. It would no doubt take her mind off things.'

'I suspect you're right.'

Eric bounced Mabel on his hip as he cast an eye over his neighbouring plot. With Cynthia's help – and he suspected a few other secret squirrels – he had managed to get the allotment back into good order. In truth, it was probably the best order he had ever had it in since he taken it over a year and a half before. Somehow, the allotment fairies had managed to pull out the weeds, turn the soil, and still get more, healthy looking green shoots poking out the dirt than Eric thought possible. Now it was simply a matter of not killing them off.

'I can't imagine how tough it's been for her,' Eric continued. 'Although I think having Yvette out of the house has helped a little bit. She's not walking on egg shells quite as much.'

'I can imagine.'

'Honestly, the sooner all the paperwork is sorted and Katrina can leave, the better. I mean that as nicely as possible.'

'I understand.' Cynthia reached over and took Mabel from Eric's grasp.

'And everything's sorted for your meeting tomorrow? Nothing you need help with?'

'The solicitor thinks it should be okay. She's on the ball. She knows. We're not exactly a typical case, but there's a bit of money coming in from Yvette, assuming she comes back, we've no criminal convictions, great character references from Abi's school and so on.'

'I'm glad Lydia came through.'

'So am I.'

'That sounds good.'

'It is. Soon, fingers crossed, our strange little family will be a little bigger,' Eric commented. Beside him Lulu barked.

Eric's phone began to buzz. He tapped at the screen to see the name, *Abi's School*, flashing boldly.

'I need to get this,' he said, taking a few steps backwards. 'It's the school.'

The voice on the other end spoke at him for nearly a minute, but after the first fifteen seconds Eric had all but stopped listening. His knees had begun to wobble and on attempting to speak he found his throat hoarse and dry.

'Don't worry,' he said, clipping Lulu's lead to her collar, then whipping Mabel out of Cynthia's arms. 'We'll be straight there.'

CHAPTER 21

THE BLINDS IN Mrs Woodhouse's office were closed. Eric couldn't help but feel the shadows helped accentuate various aspects of the room; particularly, but not exclusively, the boy's bruises. Each glimpse of purple blooming on his jawline caused Eric's stomach to somersault. The boy was snivelling, wiping his snotty nose with the back of his hand, with his eyes going in sequence from the head teacher to Eric and glaringly to Abi, before turning back to the door again. Abi, by contrast, was stony faced and silent. Sitting slumped down, hands on her lap, she wasn't entirely free of scrapes. There were a few small grazes on her knuckles and she had ripped through the knees on her trousers, but there was no denying who had come off worst. Once or twice, she brushed the broken skin of her closed fist. Once or twice she reached out and took Mabel's hand. Other than that, she remained motionless. The silence was thick, intense and perforated only by occasional barks which filtered through from outside.

'I should go and see Lulu, she's upset,' Abi said, finally breaking the tension with a weak and feeble version of her ordinary voice.

'You can stay exactly where you are,' Eric said.

Mrs Woodhouse glanced at the wall clock. 'I'm sure she'll only be a moment.'

Mabel grizzled in his lap.

'I can't wait all day,' Eric said. 'She's due another feed.'

'I understand that, Mr Sibley, but I'm sure Ryan's mother will be here any moment.'

Five long and tortuous minutes ticked by before a knock at the door finally snapped them all away from their thoughts, causing them all to jolt in their seats.

'Come in,' she said.

The door opened. A pale woman, wearing running trousers, trainers, and a sports top, stepped into the room. If she had been exercising, she had managed to do so without breaking a sweat, Eric considered; either that or she was wearing some new industrial type of make-up. Her nails also didn't look made for a workout, with a multitude of gems incrusted in the top.

'Oh, Ry-Ry.' Her hand flew up to her mouth before falling back down to touch the broken skin on Ryan's jaw. 'Who did this to you? Tell me, my darling who did this to you?'

Ryan sniffed unintelligibly into his hands.

'Thank you for coming, Mrs Lakeman, if you could just sit down,' Mrs Woodhouse began.

'This is unacceptable.'

'I understand that you're—'

'I will be writing to the governors about this, you can mark my words.'

'Please, Mrs Lakeman, if—'

'And the council. Don't you think—'

'Mrs Lakeman—'

'My husband is very influen—'

'Mrs Lakeman!'

Everyone jumped. Even Mabel, who suddenly stopped sucking her dummy and looked around. Finally, Mrs Lakeman appeared lost for words.

'If you could please sit down,' the head teacher said, having now regained her composure, 'then perhaps we would be able to talk this over.'

With a huff and a totter more suitable to heels than gym shoes, Mrs Lakeman took a seat next to Ryan. All eyes in the room – bar Abi's – were fixed on Mrs Woodhouse. She lifted her glasses to the top of her head and rubbed her eyes before lowering the glasses back down to the end of her nose.

'As you can probably tell,' she said. 'This lunchtime, Abi and Ryan were involved in an altercation.'

'An altercation? My poor boy's been beaten half to death.'

The teacher inhaled and continued.

'The thing is, we are having a bit of difficulty getting to the bottom of what happened. We have a few witnesses, but what we really need is for the children to tell us in their own words. That's the only way we can ensure the punishments are fair. The last thing we want is for someone to shoulder all the blame because they won't tell us what happened. What *really* happened.' Her eyes were on Abi as she said this, although Abi's gaze was, by contrast, still down, her lips tightly sealed.

'I told you,' Ryan piped up, with a whinging voice that cut straight through Eric's ear drums. 'She attacked me for no reason. I was just playing.'

'Abi?' Eric placed a hand on Abi's shoulder. 'Is this true?'

Her eyes stayed down.

'Abi, please,' he said. 'You won't get in trouble. I just need you tell me the truth that's all. You know you won't get in trouble if you tell the truth.'

A long paused filled the cramped head teacher's office and when Abi finally looked up at her father, her eyes were watery, and her lips trembled.

'It's not true,' she said.

Eric's heart tugged. He squeezed her shoulder. 'Okay. So, what did happen?'

She was shaking. A sliver of slime dribbled from her nose, and Eric could tell that any second now she was more than likely to dissolve into a blubbering heap.

'Please, Abi,' Mrs Woodhouse interjected. 'We just want to know what happened.'

Abi eyes remained locked on Eric and her lower lip began to wobble at such a pace it shook the tears out from her eyes and down her cheeks.

'You're going to be mad,' she quivered.

'Of course I won't. Not if you tell me the truth.'

Her nostrils drew flat as she pulled in one more deep breath.

'He broke it,' she whispered. 'He broke it on purpose.'

'Broke what, Abs?'

Slowly she opened her palm and held it out to him. Eric gasped.

'You brought it to school?' he said, the air tightening in his lungs as he looked at the object in his daughter's hand. 'You brought it to school anyway, when I specifically said you weren't allowed to?'

'I'm sorry, Daddy. I'm really, really sorry.'

Abi's lips were not the only ones trembling. Eric felt his own body shaking at the sight of the twisted metal. Thirteen years Suzy had had that ring. It was the first piece of jewellery he had ever given her. Thirteen years since he slipped it onto her finger at the top of a Ferris wheel while the snow fell around them like some perfect romantic comedy final scene, and now it was nothing but a piece of scrap. Holidays abroad, moving-house. It had even been swallowed once by Lydia's old English sheep dog. That ring had survived everything thrown at it. Until now.

'I'm sorry,' Abi said. 'I just wanted to take it with me. I just wanted to keep it with me.'

Eric locked his jaw and nodded his head. His grip on Mabel tightened.

'You didn't mean for this to happen,' he said finally.

'I didn't. I didn't, Daddy. I'm sorry. I'm really, really sorry.' Abi was shaking her head. Tears tumbled down her cheeks, one after another after another.

'So,' Mrs Woodhouse said, suddenly reminding Eric that there were several more people in the room besides himself and Abi. 'If I am to understand this correctly, you brought something to school that you shouldn't have, and it ended up broken—'

'He broke it,' Abi said. 'He snatched it from my hand then he threw it across the playground and jumped on it.'

'That's not true.' Ryan's snivelling had been replaced with a far more defensive attitude. 'It was an accident.'

'It was not.'

'She let me hold it and I dropped it.'

'You stamped on it.'

'My foot slipped.'

'I'm sure it did, darling,' his mother replied.

Abi snarled. 'Your foot did not slip. And you snatched it from me.'

'You gave it to me.'

'I would never let you touch it! You don't even wash your hands after going to the toilet!'

'That's not true.'

'Yes, it is. I'd never let you touch anything of mine with your shitty hands.'

'Abi!' Eric and Mrs Woodhouse were immediate in their response. Abi's nostrils flared, her look of venom so severe Ryan slunk back behind his mother.

After a sigh, the head teacher pushed her glasses back to the top of her head and leant forward, placing both hands on the desk in front of her.

'Well,' she said. 'I feel like I have a much better idea of what happened now. And it pains me to do this, really it does, but Abi, I'm going to have to place you on a two-day suspension. Ryan, you're free to go back to class as soon as you offer Abi an apology for breaking her toy.'

'What?' Eric's outrage was so loud that outside the window Lulu began to bark. 'You're kidding, right?'

'Mr Sibley—'

'He gets off scot-free? He provoked her.'

'I understand how you feel—'

'Clearly not,' said Eric. 'Abi was reacting to him.'

'Mr Sibley, you should be aware that I am currently overlooking Abi's utterly inappropriate language. I understand that she was upset about her toy—'

'Toy? That is not some *toy* as you put it. It's her mother's engagement ring. Her *dead* mother's engagement ring, that she wanted to bring to school so that she could feel close to her. To her mother. Who is now gone.' The head teacher pursed her lips.

'I'm very sorry to hear that, Mr Sibley.'

'And you're telling me that it's fine that this little ... little ... boy, stole it from her and stamped on it for no reason other than the fact he's a bully.'

'I dropped it!'

'Oh, shut up, Ry-Ry,' Eric responded. Mrs Woodhouse balked.

'Mr Sibley, I'll ask you to watch your tone please.'

In his arms Mabel began to whimper. Eric sucked in a deep a breath. 'This is not all right. If all he has to do is apologise, it should be the same for Abi.'

'It should not,' Ryan's mother piped in. 'Look at my poor baby's face.'

'Why, so I can see what a snivelling, wet, lying little thug he is?' Eric replied.

Mrs Woodhouse hissed. 'I understand you're upset, Mr Sibley. I really do, but we have a no violence policy.'

'Yeah, well perhaps you should have a no twat policy and stop little shits like this getting away with bullying,' Eric said.

The head teacher's face blazed, but Eric didn't care. He reached down his spare hand and offered it to Abi.

'Come on, Abs,' he said. 'We're going home.'

BACK HOME HE was not so supportive.

'You can sit upstairs in your room until I know what to do with you,' he said. 'Right now, I don't want to look at you.'

'I'm sorry, Daddy. I'm really, really—'

'I don't want to hear it, Abi. I said no to you taking that to school. You disobeyed me, you *lied* to me about putting it away, and now it's ruined.'

'Please—'

'Upstairs,' he said, focusing his attention on Mabel to try to temper his rage. For a minute Abi's stifled sobs were the only sound between them, until finally came the sound of her footsteps heading upstairs.

'Not you,' he said, as Lulu immediately left to follow. 'You can stay down here.'

The setter cocked her head and looked up at him with her big, amber eyes. She whimpered once, quietly, then again, a little louder.

'Fine,' Eric said. 'It's not like anyone in this house actually listens to me.'

Wagging her tail, she scampered up the stairs in search of Abi.

At two-thirty, Hank came around to help move the boxes up into the loft. Eric had considered cancelling again, considering the state Abi was in, but given how long it took them to get any jobs done at the minute, he decided not to change his mind and kept to the arrangement.

'It's a sad state when a sixty-year-old fella with one leg is more able than you are,' he said to Eric.

'Tell me about it,' Eric replied. 'I was gonna give it a go myself, I'm feeling fairly fixed up if I'm honest, but—'

'No, you don't want to do that. Not until you're properly healed. It'll take twice as long to sort you out if you mess it up again.' He reached up and pulled the ladder to the loft down.

'You just hold me steady, I'll do the rest.'

In twenty minutes, the pair had successfully managed to relocate all the *to keep* boxes into the loft and all the *to go* boxes to the back of Hank's car. In the kitchen Eric flicked on the kettle and managed to fish out some soggy custard creams from the back of one of the cupboards.

'I know I keep badgering you,' he said placing a mug down in front of Hank, 'but are you sure you haven't heard anything from Yvette? It's been a week. I understand that she's upset, but I really thought we'd have heard *something*.'

Hank dunked his custard cream in his tea and cleared his throat a little.

'I just want to make sure she's all right,' Eric pressed. 'Almost all her things are still here. Her clothes, her books. I want her to know she can come and get them if she wants. We can arrange a time to make sure no one is in the house. Or you and Jerry can pass them onto her if she prefers?'

After sucking the tea from the biscuit, Hank finally looked up.

'I've not seen her,' he said. Eric sighed. 'But ...' Eric straightened up a little. '... Jerry went to her dance class yesterday.'

'And?'

'And it was still on. She was still there, so she can't have gone that far can she?'

'Well how did she seem? Was she all right?'

'I don't know. Ask Jerry. I was out with Scout.'

'But she was okay?'

'Good God, man, are you always like this?'

Eric nodded, proving once again that he had failed to listen to anything Hank had actually said. At least she was still doing her dance classes, he thought, dunking a biscuit into his tea. That meant she wasn't planning on leaving. Or at least not for a while.

'Hopefully, she just needs a bit more time,' he said.

'Hopefully,' Hank agreed.

The pair sipped silently at the cups of tea, both lost in their thoughts. The house was unusually quiet; no television, no crying babies, no Abi banging around as she practiced yet another dance routine. Eric was about to ask Hank if he wanted another drink, or to see if he wanted to stay for dinner, when his phone rang. He ambled over to the windowsill, looked at the screen and answered.

'Maggie? Is everything okay?' In less than ten seconds he had his answer.

CHAPTER 22

ERIC THANKED HANK profusely as he grabbed his car keys from the bowl by the door.

'Are you sure it's okay? I can take Abi with me if you want?'

'Don't you worry. You just deal with Katrina and Mabel. Abi and I will be fine.'

Eric bent down, placed his hands on Abi's shoulders, and looked her squarely in the eye.

'Remember, young lady, you are grounded. Seriously grounded. If I hear of you trying anything ...'

'You won't,' she promised.

'I hope not.'

He left the door open as he sprang into the car and sped down the road.

Burlam police station was a three-minute journey away, although until that day Eric had only ever seen the building from the outside. It was unremarkable — yellow brick and double-glazed windows — and had it not been for the eight-foot sign and lone squad car out the front, it could easily have been mistaken for a house. He swung the car into the reserved parking, cut the engine, and jumped out.

'Eric,' Maggie said, already outside the front door waiting for him. 'Thanks for coming so quickly.'

'What happened? Is Katrina okay? Who attacked her? Has she filed a report?'

Maggie rested a hand on his shoulder.

'Katrina's fine. The officer is just finishing taking her statement. He's probably already done.'

Eric nodded and made a move to pass her, although bad timing meant that Maggie side-stepped at exactly the same time and blocked his way. Eric tried a second time but the motion was repeated. On the third attempt, he realised it wasn't a coincidence.

'Maggie?' he said. 'What is it?'

A car drove past with its windows down and music blaring. Eric watched as Maggie's line of sight drifted past him and down the road.

'Maggie, what's happened?' he said again.

She turned her gaze back to Eric, whose insides shuddered. He was amazed he hadn't noticed her nervousness before. Her hands were dug deep in her pockets as she shuffled her feet in the gravel. Even beneath her hefty veneer of bronzer, she was obviously pale.

'Maggie?'

'Before you go in, there's something you should know.'

'Oh God, oh God.' Eric could feel his legs trembling. 'She's injured? They took out her knees, didn't they? She can't dance. That's what you don't want to tell me isn't it? She won't be able to work again? She's paralysed. Oh God, Maggie, is there an ambulance coming? Where's the ambulance?'

'She didn't want me to call you,' Maggie continued, ignoring Eric's far from subtle panic attack. 'So, I didn't, but then Katrina asked me to call you, so I had to.'

Eric stopped panicking long enough to frown.

'I don't understand. What do you mean she didn't want you to call me? You said she asked you to call. You're not making any sense.'

'I think you need to try to be patient. She didn't want you to know about this. Honestly, I think it was all a bit of a misunderstanding. There's been a lot for her to deal with lately.'

'Maggie, I—'

At that moment a dim light flickered on in Eric's mind.

'Maggie,' Eric said, stepping forward and pushing his shoulders back. 'I think you'd better tell me exactly what is going on, right now.'

Inside Burlam police station was a relaxed affair. Hardly the crime central of the UK, most of their callouts involved moving on people who had had one too many after a night out or standing on the entrance to the bends with a speed camera ready to catch any over-zealous drivers as soon as they dropped into the 40mph zone; even Eric's father had been caught by them in Sally a few years back and that was saying something. Occasionally the police were required for break-ins – normally the result of bored high school children seeking kicks – and now and again they were called in to deal with private family disputes and bust ups. It had to be said, however, any domestic affairs dealt with in Burlam were not normally as public as this one.

❦

'YOU ATTACKED HER?' Eric said, slamming his fist down on the table in front of his mother-in-law. 'What the hell did you think you were doing?'

Yvette scoffed. 'I think *attack* is a bit of a strong word.'

'People called the police, Yvette. You swung your hand bag at her head. Repeatedly. I'd say attack is exactly the right word.'

Yvette shimmied her shoulders in annoyance.

'And I missed, didn't I?' she huffed. 'Clearly if I'd wanted to hurt her, I could have done.'

'They put you in a police car, Yvette. Outside of Abi's school. All of her friends saw you handcuffed. If nothing else, think of Abi.'

Yvette straightened her back.

'Did Abi see?'

'No, thank God. What the hell were you thinking?'

Yvette's jaw tightened.

'What the hell was *I* thinking? *I* pick up Abi on a Thursdays. I *always* pick her up on a Thursday.'

'*You* were missing. And Abi wasn't even at school. I'd already had to pick her up.'

'Why?' Yvette eyes flashed with concern. 'What's wrong, is she okay?'

Eric sighed, massaging his forehead with his fingertips. He couldn't help but dwell on the absurdity of the whole situation.

'That's not what we're dealing with right now. The fact remains that you attacked Katrina, Yvette.' Eric said. 'She could press charges, you know that, don't you?'

Yvette snorted. 'She won't do that.'

'You don't know that.'

'She won't.'

'She might.'

※

'I won't,' Katrina said. 'I'm not going to do that.'

Eric had left Yvette in the police station and piled Katrina and Mabel into the car. After the sight of Ryan Lakeman at the school, Eric had been expecting a full display of bloody lips and a twisted nose, but in fact Katrina showed no signs of the attack at all.

'I should have known.'

'Honestly, it's fine. It was only because someone else called the police that we had to come down here. I don't even think she hit me.'

At least Yvette had been right in saying she missed, although whether the action was deliberate or accidental remained to be seen.

'So, you talked to her then?' Katrina asked, clipping in her seat belt and dropping her bag down at her feet. 'What did she say?'

'Not much.'

'Is she going to move back in?'

'She's thinking about it,' he lied.

The truth was he had begged Yvette to come home. He had used every guilt trip he could think of – Abi missed her, he missed her, no one made vegan meatloaf like her – but none of them worked. He even pulled out the whole *It's what Suzy would have wanted* line, but she saw straight through it all.

'I will not live under this same roof as that harlot,' she had said repeatedly.

'Nine weeks,' he told her. 'I'm seeing the solicitor tomorrow, it might not even be that long,' he tried.

'She pawned my grandmother's engagement ring.'

'And it was a mistake.'

'You can say that again.'

Eric clutched his head.

'So you want me to give up. Let her give Mabel away?'

It was a low blow. Mabel was bouncing on Yvette's knee as he spoke. Had it been anything else in her hands, Eric suspected she would have thrown it at him.

'You know I don't,' she snapped. 'But trust me, the last thing this little one wants is to be visiting her batty granny – or whatever the hell I am – in prison, and that's what'll happen if I have to live with that woman.'

Mabel wriggled and squirmed in her grip.

'She's needs feeding,' Eric said. 'I didn't bring anything with me.'

'Well I'm not asking you to stay.'

'No, you're not, are you.' He rose to his feet and held out his arms for Mabel. 'Come and see the girls, at least. Abi needs you. I promise I'll keep out the way.'

Yvette's chin moved in a way that may have indicated a nod, or may have gesticulated something quite the opposite. A uniformed police officer sidled up beside her.

'We just need to get a couple more details,' he said.

With one final look, Eric turned to the door, leaving his wife's seventy-year-old mother talking to a policeman with no one by her side. If Suzy had still been alive, she would have slapped him. And he would have deserved it.

Katrina gazed out of the window.

'Once again I try to help, and once again we end up worse than where we started,' she sighed.

'You are not responsible for this,' Eric assured her. 'And if you want to press charges, I'll support you all the way.'

'Nah,' she said. 'Besides, knowing my luck I'd end up stuck here for another six months while we tried to sort out the legal stuff.'

Eric laughed. 'I completely forgot. How did the audition go?'

She turned back to face him and, for what he suspected was the first time since her arrival, a genuine smile formed on her lips.

'It went well,' she said. 'I think it went well.'

'When will you hear?'

'We'll know about call backs by the end of the weekend.'

'Well good luck,' Eric said. Her smile lingered for a fraction of a second longer before her mind and gaze drifted back to the window.

At home, Abi was still in her room.

'I've said she can come down,' Hank told Eric. 'Even said we could go take the dogs for a walk down by the marina, but she won't come out. She's pretty upset. This whole thing has really got to her.'

'What happened?' Katrina asked.

Eric sighed. 'It would appear Yvette is not the only one in the family with a quick left hook. She managed to get herself suspended from school.'

'Suspended?'

'I don't think that's what is upsetting her though, is it?' Hank replied.

'No,' Eric said. 'I don't think it is.'

Eric knocked twice on the door and waited. When no answer came, he placed his hand on the handle and froze, thinking that perhaps she had used the chair trick again and that he would once more be forced to climb up a ladder, broken ribs and all. Fortunately, she had learnt from that lesson.

'Abs?' Eric said, his head peering into the room. 'Can I come in? I'm not going to get cross. I promise. I just want to talk to you. That's all.'

She grunted non-committedly. Eric took the gesture to mean yes.

'Whatcha doing?' he asked.

Lulu lay with her head on Abi's lap, while Abi lay flat on her back, staring at the ceiling as she moved something around and around in her hands. Her cheeks were streaked with tears and the skin around her eyes was puffy and red. Eric didn't need to look too closely to know what the object in her hand was.

'Abs,' he said, shifting Lulu across to make room on the edge for him to perch. 'Are you okay?'

She shrugged. He sighed.

'I know. Me too.' With his eyes moving momentarily away from his daughter, Eric reached down and rubbed the soft fur of Lulu's tummy. She had changed so much since he had first brought her home. Her feet no longer appeared too big for her body and her face had grown longer and narrower. She was barely recognisable as the same dog even. He wondered how much the same could be said for them.

'Abs, I know you're upset about school—'

'I don't care about school. School's stupid.'

'I don't believe you.'

'Well it's true. I hate it. All the teachers are stupid and the kids are mean and I didn't want to go back there anymore anyway.'

She snapped her head around to the side and sniffed. Eric held his breath. Suzy would know what to do, he thought. She'd know the exact thing to say to have her smiling and laughing again. But Suzy wasn't there. That was the whole problem.

'I know school's hard right now,' he said after a minute. 'And I know you're upset about the ring too. That's the real reason you don't want to talk to me, isn't it, because of Mummy's ring?'

Abi's eyes returned to the ceiling. A stray tear escaped and rolled down towards her ear. Eric caught it with his finger.

'That's why I came up here,' he said. 'Because I wanted to tell you something. Do you think you can sit up for me? And can you fetch your book? The one from Auntie Lydia? Can you grab that for me?'

'Why?'

'Because I want to show you something.'

Slowly, Abi pushed herself up onto her elbows before reaching under her pillow and pulling out the large, blue album.

'You sleep with it there?' Eric asked. 'Under your head?'

She nodded. 'That way I know she's in my thoughts.'

Eric swallowed the lump that had risen from his heart.

'Okay,' he said. 'So, we need to find your baby photos. Or ones when Mummy was pregnant. Do you know where they are?'

Without a moment's hesitation, she flicked the book open to the correct page.

'These ones are my favourite,' she said, pointing to the new-born images with Eric and Suzy gazing adoringly at her. 'Everyone looks so happy.'

'That's because they were. We couldn't believe our luck, getting such an amazing little baby. Even then we knew you were special.'

Abi scoffed. 'I'm not special,' she said.

'Yes, yes, you are,' he said. 'But you know that. You know how special you are.' The smallest of smiles flickered on her lips. 'Anyway.' Eric brushed his hand against her cheek. 'That's not what I wanted to show you. I wanted you to see something else. Look at your mum's hands. What do you notice?'

Abi's brow creased as she scoured one picture then the next. When every photo on the page had been suitably studied, she shook her head, confused.

'I don't get it,' she said. 'What am I meant to be looking at? There's nothing on her hands.'

'Exactly,' Eric said. 'When your mum got pregnant, her hands and feet got really big. Well, lots of her got big, but especially her hands and feet. It was pretty gross.'

'Why?'

'Why was it gross?'

'Why did they get big?'

'Oh, I'm not sure. I think the doctor said it was something to do with water retention or something, although personally I think it was all the Big Macs she was craving. Anyway, because her hands were too big, she couldn't wear her engagement ring anymore. Even the new one I'd got her.'

Abi frowned and studied the pictures again, only looking back up when she was satisfied Eric was telling the truth.

'What did she do?' Abi asked. 'What did she do with the ring?'

'Well,' he said. 'We came up with a different solution.'

For the first time since entering the room, Eric stood up. He reached inside his shorts pocket and pulled out two items; a needle-nose pair of pliers and a thin chain.

'What are those for?' Abi asked.

'I'll show you. Can you give me Mummy's ring?'

Abi's lips began to tremble again.

'It's all broken,' she said. 'I tried and tried, but I can't fix it. I tried glue and tape a—'

'Give it here,' Eric stretched out his hand. 'Let's see what I can do.'

Reluctantly Abi handed over the ring. Eric took the snapped end between the end of the pliers, and squinting in close, began to twist the metal carefully. He pushed down, pressing out the jagged edge, taking his time to ensure he was doing the best job possible. When it was finished, he had a perfect eyelet. He took the chain and slipped it through.

'See,' he said, holding it up before motioning for Abi to spin around so he could fix the chain around her neck. 'Exactly the way your mum used to wear her ring when she was expecting you. And,' he added, lifting the fabric of her T-shirt forward a little. 'You can tuck it under your shirt so none of the teachers will know that you're wearing it to school. Just don't tell anyone about it this time, will you?'

Abi nodded serval times. Her mouth was open, her eyes down at her chest.

'I won't,' she said, holding the new pendant by her heart. 'I swear. I'm going to grow up. No more locking doors, no more messing around. I'm going to be a grown up now. I'm going to be perfect.'

Eric sat back.

'You don't have to be perfect, Abs. And you don't have to grow up. You're doing just fine.'

'But the—'

'Believe me, you're doing just fine.'

Eric reached in and wrapped his arms around his daughter. A moment into the embrace, she pulled herself back and look of worry still etched across her face.

'Dad, this thing with me at school,' she said. 'It's not going to affect us getting to keep Mabel is it?' she said.

Eric lifted her hand and stroked her head. 'Of course it isn't, don't be silly,' he replied although something uncomfortable had begun to churn inside his stomach.

❦

ONCE AGAIN, Helen Eaves had arranged to use her husband's office before opening hours to see Eric. She invited him in with a professional and well-trained smile before motioning for him to sit. It didn't take long for the smile to disappear.

'I'm going to be honest. If we had had this meeting yesterday I would have said we were well on track for sorting things in record time. But you need to be honest with me, Eric, did you really call a ten-year-old boy a twat in front of his mother and the head teacher?'

Eric's eyes tried hopelessly to find somewhere to settle.

'You heard about that?'

'I did. I do pilates with Ryan's mum. She was absolutely fuming.'

He shrugged apologetically. 'Would you believe me if I said this kid really is a twat?'

'Oh, I don't dispute it for one second. Like I said, I've met his mother. The point is, you can't go around swearing at children. Not when you're trying to become a foster parent and adopt one.'

Eric fiddled with the inside of his pocket.

'And Abi's been suspended from school, as well. Is that true?'

'It's just for two days,' Eric said.

Helen nodded and typed something into her computer.

'Will it make a difference?' he said. 'I mean, could this actually stop me getting to keep Mabel?'

'This? No, I don't think so. All your references went to the judge before this, and we could claim the boy was bullying Abi—'

'Which he was. He definitely was. You see she took her mother's—'

The lawyer silenced him with her hand.

'I can't see any major issues with this; after all, she's doing pretty well considering. What about the fall off the ladder?'

'You heard about that too?'

'I assume you're still in good physical health?' she said, brushing over his surprise with expert efficiency. 'No permanent damage? Nothing that would stop you taking care of a new-born?'

'No. No I'm practically back to normal. I'm better than normal in fact. I'm—'

'Fine. That's fine.'

Eric was about to let himself relax with relief when he saw a word teetering on her lips. He prayed he had misread her, that with everything that was going on his intuition was simply a bit off kilter. After thirty seconds, when she still hadn't spoken, he was the one who said the word he so desperately didn't want to hear.

'But ...' he said. 'There's still a but?'

She nodded. Eric's insides tightened.

'Your mother-in-law,' Helen said. Eric blanched. 'This is a small town, Eric, you know that. Things travel fast. That fight, yesterday, outside of the school, it wasn't good.'

'But Katrina has said she won't press charges, she didn't even call the police.'

'But it is on the police records. You have a violent woman living under your roof, who is attacking the mother of the child you want to keep.'

'She's hardly violent.'

'That's not the way a judge would interpret her actions. You can see why this doesn't look great, can't you?'

Eric refused to answer.

'But, she's not,' he said instead.

'I know you want to defend her, Eric,' she sighed. 'But this is serious.'

'I mean she's not. Not living under our roof, that is. She moved out.'

'When?'

'About a week ago now.'

Helen Eaves began tapping away at her computer again.

'Where's she living now?' she asked.

Eric coloured.

'Well, I'm not sure, exactly.'

'But she moved out completely? Took all her belongings?'

'Well ...'

The lawyer drew her tongue along her bottom lip before withdrawing it back into her mouth where it proceeded to make a series of smacking noises. Eric's stomach swelled with increasing intensity.

'But this has got to be good?' he said, when the smacking filled silence had grown too much to bear. 'If she's not living with us anymore, then she's not a risk to Mabel. She's not linked to me. I'm still fine, right? We're still fine?'

Eaves tapped her fingers on her chin as she thought.

'The problem is, there's no consistency. If you want to foster Mabel—'

'Adopt.'

'Let's not get ahead of ourselves. If you want to foster Mabel, then you have to be able to show that you can provide a stable, loving environment for her. That means you don't have people moving in and out constantly.

That you're not swearing at children. That you aren't having to pick family members up from the police station.'

'Yesterday was a particularly bad day,' Eric tried.

'I can see that.'

She picked up a pen and jotted something down on the paper in front of her.

'What about the job front, can you show that you have a stable income yet?' she said.

Eric pursed his lips. Eaves sighed.

'I'm going to be honest, Eric, if we can't sort these things out, fast, it's going to be a lot harder to get Mabel than we first anticipated.' She rose to stand, indicating that the appointment was over. 'I wish I could carry on longer,' she said. 'But I have appointments I need to get to, and I can't afford to get caught in traffic.'

'I understand,' Eric said and stretched out his hand to shake hers. His grip was still around hers when he decided to speak one last time.

'Suppose I did sort out those things,' he said. 'The money, Yvette. Showed that I don't just scream at every child willy-nilly. Then do you think I've still got a chance? Then do you think we could still get Mabel?'

Helen pressed her lips together in a line.

'That's a great deal of things to sort out in a very short space of time, Mr Sibley.'

'But if I could...'

'Then yes, it would make life substantially easier.'

'Thank you,' he said. 'Thank you very much.'

CHAPTER 23

ERIC SAT IN the car at the marina turning the card over and over in his hands. Mabel was in her car seat next to him, batting at a mirror that hung from her in-car mobile. Lulu and Abi were at Cynthia's for the first full day of Abi's external suspension. Eric had given Yvette's number to Cynthia and asked her to call. Even now, Yvette was refusing to pick up the phone to him, and a bit of Abi and Yvette time felt like the exact thing the pair needed.

Katrina was the only one in the house, practicing for her call back audition. Since hearing about it last night, her desperation for the job had multiplied. Maybe it was the need to get away from Mabel and the house, maybe it really was a fantastic opportunity. Either way, Eric just hoped that when that time came, Mabel was with them, not with some other family.

He turned the card over again, marking it with his fingerprints. For over a year, the card had stayed tucked away in one of the slots in his wallet. He had considered throwing it away on multiple occasions – after all, he never thought there would be a day when he would use it – yet he hadn't. It had stayed in there, always in the back of Eric's mind.

He had been offered several cards that day, but this particular person had stuck in Eric's mind far more than the dozens of others that had made the same proposition. Even Norman, who could find fault with a saint, had no snide remarks to offer when she left. She was obscenely wealthy – obviously, they all were – but she had an ease about her, like she could just as easily have worked in the local florists, or been a friend of his mum's growing up. When she slipped him her card, it wasn't with the normal, *I'll give you a great price for it* or *I've got a buyer who's desperate to add one of these to his collection.* Her response was much gentler. Much more genuine.

'I know there's probably no chance whatsoever,' she had said, brushing her hand against the sea green bonnet the same way Eric so often did when he stood next to Sally. 'But just in case your circumstances change, and you want to make sure she goes to a loving home, I'd take very good care of her.'

'Circumstances would have to change quite considerably for me to give her up,' Eric had said.

'I understand completely,' she had laughed. 'But the offer will always stand.' And just like that she had disappeared into the crowds of other cars, leaving Eric alone with Sally and Norman and their bacon butties.

It was only Mabel's grizzling that spurred him into dialling the number. If he didn't ring now, he would end up waiting until this evening, when she may be out, or the next day, or the next, and the truth was that he needed the whole thing done and dusted before he lost his nerve. His lungs were already quivering at the thought of what he had to say, and each time he let his mind rest for a moment, his father's face would appear, berating him for yet another failure. Clenching and unclenching his fist one last time, he dialled the number, took a deep breath, and pressed *call*.

The phone was picked up in less than two rings.

'Josephina Vandoor,' a curt voice said down the end of the line. Eric's voice caught in his throat.

'Ms Vandoor,' he said. 'It's Eric Sibley. We met last year at the Purton car show.'

A pause hovered down the line. Eric waited to see if more explanation was needed. It wasn't.

'Eric,' the woman's voice was substantially more relaxed now that she had assessed he was not a cold caller – not entirely, at least. 'With the beautiful DB4. Sally, wasn't it?'

'It was indeed. You have an excellent memory.'

A polite chuckle made its way down the earpiece. 'You have an excellent car. I have to say,' she said. 'I wasn't expecting your call.'

'No,' Eric agreed. 'I wasn't expecting to make it, if I'm honest. But my situation has changed. Quite considerably.'

Another small pause rested between their words.

'Then perhaps we ought to meet up,' she said.

'That would be great,' he said. 'How soon are you available?'

***

SALLY HAD BEEN around since the beginning. Where other children had memories of playing with cousins or neighbouring children, for Eric, there had been Sally. She was the car in which his father drove him to boarding school on the first day, a shy and terrified eleven-year-old, with trousers that hung too long and a tie he struggled to do up without his mother's help. She was the car in which he was picked up at the end of term, each time a little bit taller until eventually he had outgrown his father. She was the car which had delivered Suzy to the church on their wedding day – although George didn't let them take her to the reception venue as initially planned due to the horrendous weather conditions. She was the car that Eric had always assumed he would drive Abi to the church in when her wedding day finally came around. She was more than just metal and wood, gears and a motor; she was his life, his memories, a symbol of everything he had worked towards, but he knew there was no other way.

'Do you want to take her for a final drive?' Ms Vandoor said. She had arrived in Burlam by train, cream trousers and a tweed jacket paired with ankle boots and a headscarf. 'I'm happy to sit and have a coffee somewhere if you need a little more time? I'm sure this can't be easy.'

Eric shook his head. 'It's fine. We've said our goodbyes.'

And they had. He had taken her out yesterday for the whole morning, not even bothering to plan a route. He had simply taken whichever turning he fancied each time they met a junction.

When he came back to Burlam, it was through the back way, arriving by the cemetery. Parking up on the gravel driveway, he cut the engine and stepped outside.

'Hey.' The headstone was still shiny and new, not yet faded by weather and time, and yet it felt like a lifetime ago since he had been forced to say goodbye. A spray of flowers had fallen onto its side.

'I'm sorry I don't come here that often.' His eyes glanced briefly at the words – *Mother, Wife, Daughter, and Sister* – before turning away and refocusing on the flowers. 'It's just not that easy, you know. I didn't know if you'd, well ... you know ...' Each sentence was punctured by silence. Seeking forgiveness wasn't something Eric was comfortable doing in any environment, but seeking forgiveness from his dead wife was even harder. 'I'll make an effort now. I'll try to come more. Bring Abi. And Mabel too. She looks just like you. I wish you could have had a chance to meet her. I wish you were doing this with me.' He blinked, trying to halt the stinging in his eyes. Eric wasn't a religious man, and had no intention of changing his views now, but on the minuscule off-chance that Suzy actually was listening, he knew there would be no point trying to hide anything. 'I know about the books,' he said. 'And Lydia's baby.' He shook his head and sighed. 'You could have told me. You could have trusted me. Why did you think you had to worry about it all on your own? That's what I was there for. We were supposed to be a team. We were always supposed to be a team.' Somewhere in the distance a car horn beeped. Eric turned his head to the road. Sally was parked up in the exact same position, just like she had been all those years ago when he had visited his mother's grave. The only real difference then was that Suzy had been there.

'I wish you were here to tell me I'm doing the right thing, because I'm terrified without you. I'm terrified I'm going to mess everything up. For Abi, for your mum, for Mabel. I just wish there was some way you could let me know that I'm doing this right. That I'm doing the right thing.'

Once more Eric lifted his eyes to the headstone. *Suzy Laurel Sibley. Adored and adoring, you will be forever in our hearts.* If ever he were in need of a sign, Eric thought as the tears tumbled down his cheeks and splashed on the ground by his feet, it would be now. He moved his eyes from the gravestone and scanned the rest of the cemetery. It didn't have to be a big sign, a small one would do, like a bird, or a flower, or a song drifting in from somewhere. He waited in silence, straining his ears and eyes for anything, before leaning over, straightening the flowers and then kissing the top of the headstone.

'I'll be back soon,' he said.

After that he had driven Sally home and shut her in the garage ready for the next morning.

'If you could take good care of her,' he said to Ms Vandoor as he handed over the keys. 'She's not just a car.' And then, because he didn't want a grown woman to see him crying like a baby at the loss of a heap of metal, he turned and walked back into the house.

<hr />

After numerous conversations with Hank, Eric decided that trying to get all the women of his house around one table at the same time was not going to be a good idea, if it were even possible at all. Jerry did agree, however, to pass Yvette a small – in size only – token at his next dance class. Everything had gone through as planned, faster than planned. Katrina had got the job and was champing at the bit to leave, Abi's suspension felt like it was over before it had even started, and Eric was in limbo, waiting to see if had all been worth the sacrifice.

The following Thursday evening he waited, pacing up and down the length of the kitchen.

Katrina had headed out into town after giving him some vital information the day before, and both Abi and Mabel had been in bed for hours leaving only Lulu for company.

'It'll be worth it, girl,' Eric said, not even stopping his pacing to reach down and stroke her. 'I know it will. It will. As long as she takes it. As long as she sees it. Just don't let her throw it away. *Please*, don't let her throw it away.'

The phone call came through at a twenty past ten. Eric fumbled with the screen as he struggled to answer it.

'Did he give it to her?' he said, the moment his thumb landed on the button. 'Did she open it? Did she see what it was?'

'He gave it to her,' Hank replied.

'And ...'

'And she opened it.'

Eric clenched his fist and thumped the air.

'So, she'll come?' he said. 'She'll meet me for breakfast tomorrow?'

'No, not exactly.'

Eric's free hand went limp at his side.

'What do you mean? She opened it, right?'

'She did.'

'And she saw what was in it?'

'Apparently so.'

'Then why won't she meet me for breakfast?'

Hank didn't respond, Eric could hear his breath, each inhalation and exhalation rattling down the line.

'I don't understand. What did Jerry say? What did she say to him? Hank? Han—'

The shrill of the doorbell cut him short.

'I'll let you get that then,' Hank said, and while Eric couldn't see, he was almost certain he had spoken with a smile.

'I COULDN'T EVEN BELIEVE it. I cried. In front of my whole class. Can you believe it? I cried. Goodness knows what they think of me now.'

'A fair few of them have seen you naked,' Eric reminded her. 'So, I can't imagine you've gone down in their esteem too much.'

She coughed as she swallowed her drink. A moment later her smile was gone. She was sitting opposite Eric, drinking her second glass of the wine she had brought with her as a peace offering. So far Eric had stuck only to juice.

'I take it this means what I think it means?' she asked, her face laced with pity. Though, Eric noticed with a peculiar sense of optimism, it was the first time in what felt like an eternity that pity was caused by some other reason than Suzy's passing.

'It was ridiculous keeping her,' Eric said. 'Cars are meant to be driven. Not locked away in a garage.'

'But I thought it was for Abi? Abi's inheritance.'

Eric laughed at his own words.

'What's she going to want more, a car, or a family? There wasn't really any choice, was there?'

Yvette reached across and took his hand.

'For what it's worth, I think you made the right decision. But you didn't have to do this. You didn't have to get me the ring back.'

Eric glanced down at Yvette's hands.

'In the spirit of honesty, I think it only fair to tell you Katrina was involved too. She's set up a payment plan. It's only a bit a month, but now she's got this job starting next month, she wants to try to pay it back. Plus the job works out perfectly, they have two months of rehearsals before they go on the road. So she can stay here until then.'

Yvette frowned, the creases on her forehead deepening at the name.

'That's all very well, Eric, but I can't come back. I can't. I meant what I said about not being able to live under the same roof as her. You've got to understand that, don't you?'

'I do.'

'Maybe when everything with the fostering is sorted, and she's moved out. Maybe I could move back in then?' she said.

It was Eric turn to frown. 'Actually, I was thinking maybe not.'

'Pardon?'

'I was thinking that maybe you wouldn't move back in here at all.'

The colour drained away from Yvette's cheeks. 'Eric, I know I caused a fuss—'

'If Mabel's moving in, we're going to need the extra room for her.'

'But you have to understand—'

'And we can't not have a spare room. Otherwise where would Tom and Lydia stay when they visit?'

'I can always sleep on—'

'And as the money from the car was a bit more than expected, and we're not exactly strapped for cash at the minute, I thought that perhaps it might be time to get that garage conversion done. Give you a bit of space of your own?'

'But I—' Yvette's chin quivered as she stopped mid-sentence. 'What?'

'And as we don't need the garage space for Sally any more, I thought you might like to turn it into a dance studio and save you spending half your money on renting.'

Her whole body trembled. Wine sloshed up the side of her glass.

'You mean it? You really mean it?'

'Of course I do,' Eric said. 'I want my bloody house back.'

She laughed. It was a good laugh, full of love and gratitude and hope for the future, and they both felt it, they had turned a corner.

In true Yvette style, she swept up to her feet in dramatic fashion and wiped away her tears with the back of her hand.

'If you don't mind, I'm just going to give Lydia a quick ring. She'll be thrilled.'

EPILOGUE

ERIC LEANED BACK into the sofa. For the first time in a long time, a feeling close to contentment stirred inside him. There was still a long way to go, but he could see it now, a future that was more than just survival. A future where he would raise his girls to be part of something great. To be something great.

Five minutes later Yvette appeared back in the room.

'Everything good?' Eric asked.

'Everything's good,' she said. 'To be honest, my relationship with Lydia is the one really good thing that's come out of this mess. And Mabel of course.'

'Of course.'

'Do you want to stay for another drink?' Eric asked. 'Mabel's due for another feed in half an hour.'

'You know what, that sounds brilliant.'

Eric rose and took her glass.

'Talking of Lydia, you know I only learnt a couple of weeks ago that Lydia's first name is really Stephanie. I'd never had a clue before.'

'Stephanie?'

'She told me when I saw her. Stephanie Lydia.'

Yvette squinted up at Eric, looking at him in a way that indicated he may have had one too many.

'*Stephanie Lydia?* She's having you on, I'm afraid.' She put the glass to her lips and took a sip. 'What a ridiculous notion. Stephanie Lydia. My girls would have ended up with the same initials then. Goodness me, what a funny idea. I wonder why she told you that?'

ALSO BY HANNAH LYNN

If you have enjoyed the adventures of Eric and his family so far then you can either dive straight into book 4, **Peas, Carrots and Lessons in Life,** or why not save some money and pre-order T**he Peas and Carrots Series - Volume 2**, which contains the three remaining novels in the series along with a bonus novella.

Peas, Carrots and Lessons in Life

The Peas and Carrots Series - Vol 2

Enjoy the up-lifting conclusion to the wonderful *Peas and Carrots* series.

Eric attempts to find a new vocation in life and a **second chance at love**, if he isn't too afraid to take it. Yvette's life takes on an interesting development with **the return of a familiar face.** And Abi undergoes her own trials as she grows into a wonderful young lady. **Plus a whole host of other adventures** along the way with lots of familiar faces and a few new ones to spice up the mix.

INCLUDES books 4, 5 and 6 in the Peas and Carrots series, plus the short novella, *A CHRISTMAS PROPOSAL*.

The Peas and Carrots Series - Vol 2

PEAS, CARROTS AND LESSONS IN LIFE

After another moment's pause, and far from confident that he knew the direction, Eric started towards the reception.

Fortunately for Eric, and the school, it did not take long to confirm that neither of the missing students had been abducted, unless said abduction involved gathering a massive group of children outside a group of lockers.

'Rosie?' Eric said, hoping that he had picked the correct scowling student with laddered tights and sarcastic look on her face. 'What are you doing? You need to get back to class.'

'Two minutes, sir. Honestly. They're going to get him out now.'

'Get who out?'

Eric peered over the mass of heads to find several teachers were also in the gathering, two crouched down by the lockers, one more standing and trying to keep control of the crowd.

'It's Billy Gordon.' A boy, Eric suspected could have been Stanley from his class, sidled up beside him. 'Jayde Willis in Year 11 bet him three ciggies that he couldn't shut himself into one of the Year 7 lockers. But he did it. He's been in there nearly twenty-five minutes.'

'What?' Eric peered again at the scene. It was apparent now that one of the crouching teachers was Roger, whose balding head was dappled with beads of sweat.

'Why haven't they got him out?'

'Mr Parker reckons it's the gum.' Another student, who Eric equally thought could be Stanley, joined in their little discussion. 'The door's jammed and they reckon it could be the gum.'

'Chewing gum?'

'Yup, like cement apparently.'

Eric turned back to the scene. He wasn't entirely sure how much he believed in the cement properties of chewing gum, but currently couldn't see anything to discredit the fact. The teachers were certainly taking the situation seriously.

'Why don't they force it open?' he asked, noticing a crowbar on the ground by Roger's feet.

Both possible Stanleys shook their heads.

'Health and Safety.' One sighed. 'They've been trying to decide if it will be worth it for the school's reputation if he suffocates in there – which they don't think will be likely due to the non-air tightness – or if they end up stabbing him with a crowbar, or toppling the whole thing over as they try to get him out causing a concussion or brain damage or something. That one could crush someone else too.'

'Probably one of the teachers,' said the other Stanley.

'Surely that wouldn't happen?' Eric was starting to feel a little concerned.

There was no denying it was compelling viewing. Every wobble of the locker caused the crowd to *ooh* and *ahh* and grab each other in response, while the teachers on the ground were joined frequently by new intrigued onlookers.

'All right, you two.' Eric pointed at the exact point in between the two possible Stanleys in the hope that the correct one would assume he was talking to him. 'We need to get back to the classroom.'

'But, sir, he's nearly—'

'Now, or my first job here will be putting you straight into detention.'

'But we won't know what happened.'

More Mayhem and mishaps

Life has finally settled down for Eric Sibley and his family; Abi and Mabel are happy, his mother-in-law is on hand for support, and life has begun to have a sense of normalcy and routine to it.

But, with cash flows running low, Eric has to acknowledge it is time to re-enter the world of employment. Unfortunately, jobs suited to former high-flying recruitment executives are of short supply in the sleepy town of Burlam.

When the opportunity to do some teaching at the local school arises, eager to inspire young minds and make a 'difference', Eric decides that this could be just the job for him. Will he pass with flying colours or end up with a 'could do better.'

Join Eric once again in the fourth instalment of the ***Peas and Carrots Series***.

To continue reading Peas, Carrots and Lessons in Life simply head over to Amazon.

ACKNOWLEDGMENTS

Massive thanks must go to both Emma, Jessica and Vector Artist. To Emma and Jessica for her amazing skill in helping me get this book edited, and to Vector Artist for taking on board all of my ideas to create yet another dynamic cover.
Thank you to all of my beta readers who take the time to read early drafts and offer valuable feedback, especially the eagle-eyed Lucy, Kath and Niove, as well as support and encouragement. Please know that every recommendation to a friend, share on social media or kind message, means so much to me.
Thank you to my husband who helps me find the time to write and tirelessly checks and double checks and keeps me on track.
Lastly, thank you to every reader who has taken the time to read my work and listen to my stories, and to the amazing bloggers who have done so much to help me along this journey.

ABOUT THE AUTHOR

Hannah Lynn is an award-winning novelist. Publishing her first book, *Amendments* – a dark, dystopian speculative fiction novel, in 2015, she has since gone on to write *The Afterlife of Walter Augustus* – a contemporary fiction novel with a supernatural twist – which won the 2018 Kindle Storyteller Award and Gold Medal for Best Adult Fiction Ebook at the IPPY Awards, as well as the delightfully funny and poignant *Peas and Carrots series*.

While she freely moves between genres, her novels are recognisable for their character driven stories and wonderfully vivid description.

She is currently working on a YA Vampire series and a reimaging of a classic Greek myth.

Born in 1984, Hannah grew up in the Cotswolds, UK. After graduating from university, she spent ten years as a teacher of physics, first in the UK, then around Asia and on to the Austrian Alps. It was during this time, inspired by the imaginations of the young people she taught, she began writing short stories for children, and later adult fiction. As a teacher, writer, wife and mother, she is currently living in Amman, Jordan.

STAY IN TOUCH

To keep up-to-date with new publications, tours and promotions, or if you are interested in being a beta reader for future novels, or having the opportunity to enjoy pre-release copies please follow me:

Website: www.hannahlynnauthor.com

REVIEW

As an independent author, I do not have the mega resources of a big publishing house, but what I do have is something even more powerful – all of you readers. Your ability to offer social proof to my books through your reviews is invaluable to me and helps me to continue writing.
So if you enjoyed reading **The Peas and Carrots Series**, please take a few moments to leave a review or rating on Amazon or Goodreads. It need only be a sentence or two, but it means so much to me.
Thank you.